HOLLYWOOD
ON THE
TIBER

A novel by

Kieran Somers

ORIGINAL WRITING

ISBNS
Parent : 978-1-78237-853-2
epub: 978-1-78237-854-9
mobi: 978-1-78237-855-6
PDF: 978-1-78237-856-3

A cip catalogue for this book is available from the National Library.

Published by Original Writing Ltd., Dublin, 2015.

Printed by Clondalkin Group, Glasnevin, Dublin 11

This novel is dedicated to my mother and first teacher, Anna Somers

CONTENTS

The dream is a lie, but the dreaming is true.

– Robert Penn Warren

CLOSING SCENE

'Max. Max. You waited too long Max. You didn't come in early enough that time.'

The jagged voice coming from the control room was slightly tetchy. The speaker was not satisfied with what he had just seen or heard. He was certain there was a problem of timing, an unusual imprecision in technique. His leading actor was off by several milliseconds, entirely out of character for him, and the consequences were obvious. Image and sound were not aligning in the seamless way they were meant to.

'Let's all have a think about this before we try it again,' di Stefano instructed.

The dubbing director, with brow-line glasses and large expressive eyes, had originally been a stage actor himself; his manner retained a distinct element of the melodramatic. On occasion he could become quite verbose, even excessively animated if a problem on the job was persisting. A botched pronunciation or a swallowed syllable was often the bane of his existence. But he knew that an element of calm was called for just at this moment. Minds after all were weary in spite of the time of the day. As director, it was important that he maintain a sense of poise in the face of the laborious process. Most important.

Beside him in the control room sat his colleague Giacomo Romano, a sound engineer with extensive experience in the dubbing industry; at a further remove from them both, ensconced at a small table with tiny lamp, was the synch editor Ilario Tessario. The pint-sized Neapolitan knitted his brow as he scanned a barely legible screenplay. The three men occupied the sound control area where an outdated mixing console dominated their foreground. Faded master controls and declining switches protruded from the analogue dashboard; smudged channel input strips and grazed audio level meters were in dire need of buffing up; the majority of dials and controls sported obvious signs of never-ending wear and tear; and there were certain sanitary imperfections also from coffee cup stains and ash residue.

The personnel in this confined space felt slightly run-down themselves. The current session had ticked past the significant three-hour mark. The final stretch of dubbing the new feature film titled The Proper Citizen into the Italian language was proving annoyingly problematic. In a separate booth, by himself, Salvatore Pez diligently obeyed di Stefano's command. The projection assistant was just starting out at Universal Recordings (this was his first full assignment) and, as he immobilised the 35 millimetre projector for the umpteenth time, perceiving the unique clatter of internal mechanisms grinding to a sudden halt, the words of caution someone had imparted to him about the tediousness of the work became just that bit more convincing and true-to-life. This was no kingdom of shadows he had passed into; rather it was a realm chock-full of tiresome retakes and only fleeting bits of performance. And Salvatore had really hoped to see a lot more this first time around. He'd been particularly eager to observe the voice actor currently standing on the studio floor. Word on the corridors of Universal Recordings was that he was very good; one of the best working in the business.

Beyond the slanted glass divide of the control room, Max Pellegrino looked at the suspended picture before him. The image on the ceiling-recessed screen was framed in low key lighting. The shadowy tones seemed appropriate. He was still tired from the previous day's efforts on the film. They'd worked up to 8 o'clock in the evening and he hadn't slept very well that night. His performance was suffering on account of this. The delivery, normally so crisp and incisive, had become sluggish as the morning rolled on. Now it was after midday and an unmistakable stupor had infected his speech. He knew he'd have to perk up quickly or else they'd be there for a good deal longer than necessary.

'Just give me a minute or two,' he called out to di Stefano.

'But leave the picture as it is for the time being,' he requested of Pez.

'Take your time Max,' di Stefano responded.

'No problem Mr. Pellegrino,' said the newest member of staff, 'take your time...ahem...just like Damiano said.'

The 39-year old actor began to rouse himself in the soft dim of the studio. It was a routine he'd used many times before: a modus operandi when things weren't panning out and he needed a second wind. He adjusted the light on the eye-level lectern directly in front of him, diluting its glare, and focused first on his breathing. A mouthful of air was sucked in, held for a moment, and then puffed out again. Breathe properly he told himself. You must breathe properly. It's support for the voice, it gives substance to emotional expression. Breathe from the diaphragm, not the chest. He inhaled a slow, deep, cleansing breath, allowing the respiratory muscle to expand, his lungs to fill with air. He then exhaled completely; careful not to let any vestige of breath get caught in his chest or throat. Placing his hands below his rib cage, he lowered his jaw, allowing two very slow preparatory breaths; blowing out completely after each one. He allowed a third deep breath to occur, holding it for a second or two, and then readjusted the light to its previous position. He began to re-read the speech, clearing his throat with a series of mild coughs as he went along. He closed his eyes, visualising what had to come next. What he had to do.

Remember who your character is he told himself. Be in the moment. Get the words off the page.

He began to hum then, gradually progressing the wordless tone into yet another mild cough. He performed the guttural sequence a second time, and then a third. Just for good measure.

In the projection booth a puzzled Salvatore scratched his head. Why is he droning like a bee he wondered. Is this part of the film?

Max placed his thumb against his chin and extended the tip of his little finger to the cardioid microphone in front. The distance from one to the other was in the region of six inches – just the way it was meant to be. Technically correct he thought. But there could be considerable gain if I were to...

He glanced at the lines on the lectern one more time. It would be necessary to rationalise the suggestion he was about to make. Not everyone would welcome it.

'I'm going to move closer to the mike,' he told the inhabitants of the control room. There was the predictable confab before a response came from behind the glass.

'I don't think that's such a good idea Max. There'll probably be significant pop if you get any closer.'

Romano's comeback as ever was logical, grounded in technical savvy. But it was also something more than that. The hard-nosed sound engineer was not in the habit of placing great value on the ideas of others. Proposals by actors most especially of all tended to bring out his more obstinate side. Max was ready for this.

'I think the scene will benefit if I get closer,' he argued, 'he's making a speech to a large crowd. Under normal circumstances I'd be all for delivering it loud and thunderously. But that isn't the approach here. It's not what this character is about. He's not one for the old-testament fire and brimstone stuff. There's an intimacy about the way he's communicated with people during the course of the film. It goes for gatherings like this as well. He's a talker rather than an orator, a conversationalist as opposed to a speechmaker.'

There was a slight lull before the control room's follow-through.

'It sounds like a speech to me Max,' Romano countered.

'Yes, it's a speech Giacomo, I'm not denying it's anything else, but what I'm trying to suggest here is that the manner of it...his style...it's as if he's addressing one or two people as opposed to one or two hundred.'

'It still sounds like a speech to me Max. And if you get closer, there'll likely be pop or some other distortion coming from the mike. There are quite a few words starting with B's and P's so you're going to have lots of plosive sounds.'

'I'd still like to try it closer and see how it goes. What's required is a more informal effect. A softer pitch. Further away and the speech sounds colder...less...'

'Friendly?'

'Yes, that's pretty much it.'

Max tried to anticipate what further piece of wisdom might be dispensed by his disinclined colleague. Romano would not simply give up his argument. He'd probably put forward the idea of...

'A pop shield so Damiano,' the sound engineer proposed, as he strategically involved the director in the discussion. 'A pop shield in front of the mike will eliminate anything we don't want on the soundtrack.'

'Yes, yes, that would appear to be the way to go,' agreed di Stefano, 'Max, how do you feel about that?'

The actor grimaced at the mere mention of a pop shield. He hated that contraption like no other. Sure it served a practical purpose, but that bent coat-hanger would put even more of a gap between him and the mike. And hadn't he just explained it was precisely that he wished to remove? How am I going to get through to that expanse of obduracy he wondered, as he visualised the fleshy Romano leaning back, self-important in his ergonomic chair. Nothing else for it but another run-through he figured. Perhaps the acoustic blimp would get it the next time. But then again, probably not.

'Could we watch the scene once more Damiano,' he requested.

'Sure Max, the whole thing?'

'Yes, through and through.'

'Salvatore, let's have it again.'

'Sure Damiano. Will I begin as the scene does or just before he starts the speech?'

'The speech! Thank you! Someone at least is on the same page as me!' Romano said dryly.

'Giacomo please.'

'I never said it wasn't a speech Giacomo. Please don't misrepresent what I said.'

'You said it was a conversation Max. You said he was a talker so I'm looking forward to hearing him talk. Yet again.'

'Giacomo please. Max, at what point do you want Salvatore to start it?'

'At the very beginning of the scene please. Just before he goes up the steps.'

'No problem Mr. Pellegrino,' Salvatore said compliantly as he prompted the opto-mechanical device back into action. The process of returning the film to the exact point the actor had requested took a few moments, but the projection assistant was well up to the task and soon arrived at it. He then set the onscreen action into regular playback. A veritable hush permeated the studio floor and control room as the closing act beamed onto the screen in diffuse shafts of contrasting light. At the lectern, Max watched the preliminary shots, mindful not to change his stance. He was much closer to the mike than six inches; quite determined to remain there.

A rally of some sort was taking place. There was a large crowd gathered in a drearily conceived town square. The architecture of the location was stark, disaffecting. A small quadrangle of expanse was framed for just a moment. It was unremarkable: brick, gravel, concrete slab, and float glass the predominant elements of the backdrop; hard landscaping, mitigated in a few places by the occasional tree or foliage, gave off a hemmed-in feeling.

A humble county courthouse in the attenuated federal style was singled out by the roving camera. Flat tablets, smooth panels, nondescript friezes were outlined. From the hard matrix of material below sprouted a few craggy steps ascending towards the local establishment of law. At the base of this gathered the apprehensive horde. Dank autumnal weather showered down on them in an unremitting way. A squally breeze agitated bits of garbage.

The participants in the assembly were barely discernible at first. Enveloping twilight fashioned a camouflage effect. Weighty slickers and collapsible umbrellas completed this veiled impression. The multitude looked as if it were nothing more than a coalition of canopies. But this was only an establishing shot. Presently the camera got in amongst them, dollying smoothly from one face to the next. A tableau of middle America was represented by this tracking shot. Young and old standing side by side: haggard elders, assiduous fathers, careworn mothers, expectant young men, doe-eyed pretty girls, callow teenagers, small children; brought together in the persistent rain. There was a reason for their wandering out in such inhospitable conditions and it was about to be revealed.

A collage of sounds arose then as whispers were exchanged, murmurs intoned. All eyes, at first glancing about here and there, became concentrated on a focal point in the square.

He's coming some of them could be heard saying. And then those utterances became more pronounced and uniform. He's here they said. He has arrived.

The shoes were the first article of his to come into view. A low camera angle followed as weighty footsteps were carefully picked in the spraying wet. Beads of moisture were tossed in the air, landing randomly on the hard surface. Smart chestnut-coloured wingtips hardly seemed to be the most sensible choice of footwear for such an inclement evening as this. And yet they were entirely appropriate for who he was and how his story had played up till now.

The trailing camera gradually panned up the entire extent of his shapely frame. The trousers of his suit wafted as the breeze continued to seethe. An azure raincoat sealed off the matching jacket worn underneath. A side profile of his pale complexion formed a mid-shot. The expression was sombre yet purposeful.

He passed through a section of the crowd, eyes fixed dead ahead, and went up to the raised area in front of the courthouse. An over-zealous supporter who offered the protection of an umbrella was motioned away. No he mouthed. Such shelter could not be accepted by him at this point. He had to receive the downpour. The rain would be cleansing, purifying, releasing. The moment was about atonement. What better way to display remorse for your shortcomings than a good drenching. He turned and faced them, a modest smile giving way to a more solemn countenance as he began to speak.

'Friends,' he said, 'I have acted improperly in these last few days and, for this, I most humbly request your forgiveness. An ordinary man may lose his way from time to time. He strays from the path, falls into bad practices, and begins to entertain savage notions which are normally abhorrent to his character. Soon, however, he realises the error of these wicked ways and he returns to the true course his life is supposed to follow. This is the ordinary man. His actions have consequences for a few. But certainly not for all. However, when a man, such as myself, entrusted by many to carry out duties and abide by values he has promised to hold sacred, drifts from his individual path, a great dereliction becomes possible. A dereliction which might in time injure more than just a few...'

Max noted the beat in the speech which followed these words. One, two, three, he counted, before Don Taylor resumed his heart-to-heart with the gathering.

Taylor was the American actor playing the lead role in The Proper Citizen. He was a major Hollywood star and Max had been dubbing his voice for the Italian market for over 12 years. He was a year younger than Max and the similarity between the two in age was no mere coincidence. A standard practice in the dubbing industry was to allocate voice actors to counterparts of a similar age as themselves. Another important tradition was that these voice actors tended to retain the same English-speaking counterparts throughout their entire careers; this for both the sake of artistic consistency and audience familiarity. And so, the ages of individual actors were close to one another in the interest of such regularity. Suspension of disbelief after all was unlikely to extend to the notion of an octogenarian providing the voice of a man half his age. Nor would it do if a dubbing actor in his early twenties replaced the voice of a Hollywood veteran in the throes of mid-life. Robert de Niro had to continue sounding like Robert de Niro; that is, the Italian version of Robert de Niro. The same was true of the Italian equivalents of stars like Redford and Newman, Al Pacino, and Don Taylor.

Max had first dubbed Don Taylor's voice in 1983. The film was a comedy-drama called Wouldn't It Be Nice and it represented a breakout role for the actor which he proceeded to take advantage of. Full blown movie stardom beckoned and by the end of 1985 the actor had starred in a further four films, all of which performed extremely well at the box office. His A-list status was cemented.

Taylor was a star for over a decade now and Max had remained his Italian voice all that time. He dubbed other actors as well, but Don was the most famous name he represented and, no holds barred, also his favourite.

The Proper Citizen was the 28th feature film for which Max had provided Don's voice and it seemed to the Italian that the Hollywood star was pursuing a noticeable change in the direction of his career. The political-drama was a far more highbrow piece than he normally did and, on screen, the actor's very appearance confirmed what Max already had a sneaking suspicion about – Don Taylor was looking to move away from the more lightweight roles which had been the bread and butter of his career to date. Don Taylor wanted much less of the light-hearted and a lot more of the serious-minded. The evidence was there in front of him as he watched The Proper Citizen's coda play out. The actor's customary well-groomed appearance had been dispensed with. In its place was a much more subdued look which at times bordered on the dishevelled. His character was a man under great strain and tumult of mind. Don evidently wanted to highlight this by way of a worn-out expression, beleaguered aspect. This was a side to him which films like All My Friends or New Haven Green had never ventured to suggest. The target audiences of the multiplexes simply would not have accepted him that way. They wanted the star and the package that came with him. They wanted the archetypal Don Taylor film with its leading man flashing those dreamy eyes of his as he negotiated his way through yet another romantic misadventure. But this time they were not going to get that formula. And they might not even get Don himself. Or at least not the Don they'd grown so accustomed to.

150 minutes of screen time had passed by and not once had any of the stock elements of a Don Taylor film appeared – there was no enduring love interest in the story; no starry-eyed sequence in which the actor swept some lovely young co-star off her feet; the plot was muted and, on occasion, downright depressing, with little cause for the star to flash the trademark grin he was so famous for. Visually, there were also some notable absences: a dearth of extreme close-ups on the actor; key lighting on his face employed sparingly; zoom-ins no longer picked out the ruddy glow of his cheeks or the wholesome lustre of his skin; the prominent bushy eyebrows were plucked and reduced to a patchy state; the normally coiffed hairstyle was scruffy and unappealing. Don the delectable had given way to Don the unglamorous. Max couldn't help but guess this was part of a strategy designed to set in train a professional makeover. What was it called? A career move?

He inspected the image of the actor more closely now, as the latter continued to deliver his 'man more sinned against than sinning' type speech. He grasped what was happening. Don was signalling a shift towards the more character-driven pieces he clearly wished to be in. He was starting to think about his legacy as an actor.

He was no longer as fresh-faced as he'd once been. Of course he wasn't. The onset of one's thirties had such an effect. Lines and wrinkles turned up in places where they'd never existed before and became more visible; skin became less elastic and wore flaws and discolorations; hair gradually became greyer or, worse still, started to recede. Imperfections were accentuated. Features of quality wilted. All things eventually shrivelled up. It was no different for anyone; no matter who you were. Even the great Don Taylor was at the mercy of time.

It had started for Max as well. The Italian was trying to be more mindful about his lifestyle, had begun taking supplements and vitamins recommended in a magazine. He jogged four times a week for exercise and occasionally went to the gym. He'd given up smoking years ago; not just because of the health risks, but also because cigarettes dried the mouth out quickly and, over a long period of time, could potentially damage the vocal chords. Not something a voice actor would want to have happen. To minimise any fine lines or crinkles appearing on his face, he used a moisturiser daily and cut down on his sugary intake. He retained a vigorous physique, which complemented an erudite air. He dressed relatively well, but by no means considered himself a bella figura. At six foot he was quite tall and had a full head of hair which, mercifully, had not yet required any hair dye. He took care of himself and looked well for a man who was just eight months shy of his 40th birthday.

40. He thought about that from time to time, the significance it held for many. Some people were petrified by the notion of getting older, but it made no great impression on him. Naturally, things were changing he knew but that was just the way of the world. He had changed and who was to say he might not change again. Lately, he'd read somewhere that the ageing process should be approached as a new enjoyable challenge. That made perfect sense as far as he was concerned. In any case, what choice did he have? What was important was that one looked after oneself. Time was not something you could fight against and hope to defeat. The things he did like jogging, the facial cream and vitamins were not an attempt to forestall what was inevitable. They were about something else. They were about a need to continue imagining that one fine day he would wake up and realise he no longer needed to come into the studio. Or any other studio like it for that matter. Keeping himself in a rude state of health, and fine appearance, was important. He would require more than just his faculties to be intact if it so happened that...

Don's right arm shot up onscreen in a show of defiance to the crowd. Max's attention came back to the closing moments of The Proper Citizen. He made a mental note of this gesture, coming as it did just before the final line was delivered. It was an important moment and he decided to copy it when the time came to record the scene. Even in the confined space of the studio physical movements enhanced authenticity. Improvisation and spontaneity had always worked well for him. He strongly believed they added another layer to the recording. Just because you couldn't see something didn't mean it wasn't there.

It was all over then. The speech came to an end and the film with it. The damp congregation broke into applause one final time as Don's character saluted them. The rain had stopped by this time. The power of his words had dismissed the storm clouds overhead. Umbrellas were lowered in unison. A brave new world was on the horizon he promised them. This was just the beginning of it. The camera zoomed in slowly for a parting close-up of Don the serious rather than Don the debonair. His smile was weary, but he appeared a resolute man. He looked as a proper citizen should. Honourable.

The screen faded to black and the credits began to roll.

'Well,' said di Stefano, 'did we all see enough that time to make it work?'

'And hear enough as well,' Max added, remembering he might yet have one or two more words with Romano.

The sound engineer rose to the bait.

'I accept that it's a softer speech, as he says, but I stick to my gut instinct that a pop shield should be used,' he said.

'It will only serve to put more distance between me and the mike Damiano. I want to get closer because that's the very essence of the speech: intimacy. He doesn't yell what he has to say to them. It's far more refined than that. He tells them a story like you'd tell your children at bedtime. In a calm manner. There's a familiarity to the scene which the director and Don Taylor clearly wanted to get across. You can imagine what they might have said to one another on the set; why they decided to do it this way. Sometimes these important decisions are made on set at the eleventh hour. It's what gives film-making its resonance.'

'Now you're the one making a speech Max.' Romano's voice had lost none of its sarcastic flavour.

Max turned around and glared at him.

In the projection booth a captivated Salvatore speculated as to what might happen next. He'd heard about disagreements that sometimes took place and it seemed he was about to witness his first full-blown one. This was real drama at last he thought. Far better than the film.

In the control room Romano leaned back in his chair. Di Stefano sat forward in his. The sound engineer had heard enough. He wanted to get shot of this film sometime this century and had no desire to entertain lectures on film-making techniques, or on-set ad-libbings. They weren't here to re-invent the wheel he thought. He said that to the actors often enough in the hope the message would get through. But some of the more obstreperous ones never listened to his advice. They were too busy... acting.

Beside him, the former actor that was Damiano di Stefano decided that an even-handed approach was required to appease the belligerent parties. The director was well aware of the time of day and even more mindful of the fact that tempers were frayed. He knew how to distinguish a mere squabble from an out-and-out confrontation. The cautionary voice in his head told him this one was shaping up to be the latter. One other thing swayed his decision to employ tactics and play tactful. Out of the corner of his eye, he spied Ilario Tessario sitting up at his table as if he'd just woken up from a deep sleep. The intimation of mounting hostilities had even caught his attention. A very ominous sign indeed.

'Take it easy both of you,' said the director, 'I'm never going to get this film finished on time if you continue taking pot shots at one another. I've listened to both sides of the argument and I can see where you are both coming from. Giacomo: yours is the technical guidance and it's much appreciated. We have to consider the quality of the recording just as much as we have to put value on the performance. The last thing any of us want to come out of the studio is a substandard piece of work which the distribution company will most definitely not thank us for. As always, your commitment to the highest standards is second-to-none. Thank you for your input.'

Romano grumbled somewhat sensing where the director was going with this. Di Stefano, taking no notice of him, continued.

'Max, as ever you pull out all the stops to get as much as you can out of your performance, and then some more. Even when it's clear you are very tired yourself.'

The actor allowed a wry smile, acknowledging he was a bit drained.

'I commend you for your observation of the scene. It is a speech of a different kind and the way you present your argument, I think, justifies you getting one chance to try it without the pop shield.'

Romano tried to interrupt, but di Stefano was quick to cut him off.

'Giacomo, I'm going to give him one chance and one chance only. If it doesn't work out, if those dreaded plosive sounds you fear so greatly are an issue, then we'll do it either with the pop shield or in the normal way. This is what I'm proposing and this is what you're both going to accept.'

The director looked directly at Max with those animated eyes of his.

'One chance only,' he emphasised, 'and if it can't be used then you agree to either of the other two ways. Ok?'

'Ok Damiano. And thank you.'

'Salvatore, we need to have it again please. This time we are going to record.'

'Certainly Damiano. From the top?'

'Yes Salvatore, though not from the top of the film please. Some of us have families.'

This provoked a good-natured laugh from both studio floor and control room. The tension was broken. Another minor war averted.

Salvatore once again returned the film to the beginning of the scene. The individuals in the control room primed the dated instruments. Max moved closer to the mike again. Four inches would do he figured. Romano would not hear a single plosive sound. He was determined about that. The piece he'd recently read on the ageing process came to mind. A new enjoyable challenge he thought. This is one.

'It's ready,' Salvatore declared from the projection booth.

The film had backtracked to the melancholy square and its microclimate.

Di Stefano sat forward in his seat and addressed the studio floor.

'Ready?' he asked Max.

'Ready.'

'Salvatore, you may...oh just one moment please...'

Di Stefano had one final piece of direction to give.

'Max, remember not to wait too long to come in this time. You missed the mark before. I know that you're tired and...'

'I'll get it spot on this time Damiano.'

'Thank you Max.'

The actor requested a few moments so he could repeat his breathing exercises. And humming. And guttural sequence.

Remember who your character is he told himself. Be in the moment. Get the words off the page.

'Ok, I'm ready,' he said.

The recording was completed from start to finish. The actor executed it with precision and textbook delivery.

When it was finished, di Stefano turned to Romano in the control room.

'Well?' he asked, 'any undesirable echoes?'

The sound engineer shook his head. He was far less imperious now.

'None,' he replied, 'it was quite flawless.'

'Good,' said the director 'Max, that was very good. Let's do it one more time for protection.'

'Sure.'

'Salvatore, if you will.'

The closing scene of The Proper Citizen was played back again from beginning to end.

For the second time that day, it was impeccable.

Di Stefano's voice came up as it concluded. He was satisfied. More or less.

'That was perfect,' he told Max. 'Do it again.'

A Man doesn't Cry in the Street

'Max, did you get it finished?'

The voice was that of Carlo del Piero, one of the younger actors at Universal Recordings. Max had worked with him a few times in the past and he knew him to be very good at his job. Carlo was bright and eager and, most importantly, he wanted to learn at all times as he'd explained to Max during their first project together. This was a commendable trait and Max admired the younger man for it. Carlo wanted to be so much better than he already was; he wanted to raise his own bar, expand his range. There was a lurking impatience in his professional demeanour which Max recognised all too well. Carlo was doing fine for himself all things being equal. He was voicing a number of the twenty-something actors who'd emerged in the early 1990's, and for that reason alone could be considered fortunate. Some of these young Hollywood stars were doing several films a year. That meant work and lots of it for a dubbing actor such as Carlo. He needed as much of it as he could get to support his girlfriend and young son.

There was a restlessness in his bones and it pronounced itself in just about everything he did. When he talked his voice sounded overwrought as if desiring a different subject matter. His lanky frame was constantly twitching in this direction and that. The long strides he took when he moved bespoke of an ambition that was far from satisfied. But in the studio he sure could get it together; and hold it together as well. There were no edgy shudders or fidgety wobbles in front of the lectern. His voice levelled out and flowed, as it was required to. Carlo was a paragon of professionalism once he hit the floor and got into his stride. It didn't matter so much that away from the mike he appeared to suffer from a perpetual state of jiggles and joggles.

'Yes, we got it finished,' Max told him as they walked towards the entrance, 'it took time but we got there in the end.'

As usual he found himself straining to keep up with his taller colleague. Carlo was always walking ahead; that was part of his make-up and you had to increase your own pace at least two-fold to match his. Sometimes Max found this to be a chore but today he didn't mind. The Proper Citizen was finally finished. He could move on to the next bit of work, whatever it might be. In the meantime there was a boring corporate gig which would occupy his time. But that didn't matter so much right now. He was done with another project. There was a suitable feeling of achievement. Or at least something close to it.

'Hidden Peril,' Carlo declared sombrely as they exited the studio building, 'now there is a cautionary tale if ever I've been involved in one. I swear Max it's going to be the end of me. I've got twenty minutes off now and then it's back to the millstone that film is becoming.'

'Problems?' asked Max.

'Problems,' said Carlo grumpily, 'it all started when our venerable director, who you're more than familiar with, decided to change the actress voicing the female lead. Now anyone could have told him she was unsuitable from the start. So the change that was eventually made meant re-recording, which I can tell you hasn't gone smoothly. It's put the rest of us under pressure to get this finished on time. That's why I'm only getting to stick my head out the door for a few minutes. Then back in there again for God knows how much longer this afternoon.'

He looked back at the building and frowned.

'Have time for a coffee?' Max asked. He definitely needed one himself. Carlo looked just the way he felt. Dog-tired. Running on empty.

'Sure,' said Carlo, 'but like I said not much time. Never much round here.'

They sat in a small café close to the Basilica di Santa Maria Maggiore. Carlo knocked back a doppio. Max sipped a latte.

'It's not the first time something like this has happened,' he told the younger man. He hoped he didn't sound too mollifying when he said that. Annoying things happened on the job every so often. It was par for the course. Sometimes the wrong actor was hired and had to be changed. Max had seen it many times before: performers at odds with the role they were playing; some sounding too gruff for comedy, others too light for drama. Not all of the miscastings got replaced though and it was frustrating when an actor out of his or her depth was kept on. There were budgetary considerations to be taken into account after all; as well as availability of suitable actors. Finding the perfect voice for every single role was not a realistic proposition. They were merely there to do the best they could. Max was told this one time by a snappy director. If the film was good enough, so what if a voice down the cast list didn't sound right? Did an audience really care about that? Who would even notice? Far more important that Max concentrate on his own performance the director said. It was the job of the technical team to measure the overall production. The actor was just an element in this. He ought to have sufficient faith in his colleagues. Besides, miscastings happened in Hollywood as well, didn't they? And then audiences got both the miscast face and voice in tow. That was a far worse thing than some off-key voice in a smaller role down the list. Wasn't it? Max had heard their arguments many times. He'd disagreed with them on more occasions than even he cared to remember.

'I know it's not the first time this has happened,' said Carlo. He'd been waiting for his more experienced colleague to continue but in some way the other man had become lost in his own thoughts.

There was no reply coming so Carlo repeated himself. 'I said I know it's not the first time Max. Not the first time,' he said.

Max snapped out of whatever arc his mind was following. He nodded in agreement. Carlo carried on.

'They simply don't understand what we have to do in there to make our performances happen,' he said, 'they don't appreciate that there are no props or scenery in the studio to help us. We don't put on make-up. We don't wear costumes. All we do is mimic and copy as far as they are concerned. God forbid that we should ever have something constructive to say. One time I remember having a discussion – if I can call it that – with a director in another recording studio. He was like an immoveable rock, would not budge this way or that. Every single thing had to be done his way right down the line. I was a younger actor back then.'

Max smiled at this. His colleague was still young. No more than 28 perhaps. He liked Carlo in spite of the latter's tendency to moan from time to time. And he wanted to tell him how important it was he continue to develop his style and vocal range. He could almost hear the words someone else had once said to him: your style will come from knowing who you are Max, and what you think about things such as human nature. The better you can give expression to attitude and emotion, the more your range will increase.

Carlo was still talking.

'...and I didn't know any better but to pick an argument with this lump of obstinacy,' he said, 'so we quarrelled over this one point and then we moved on to a more general subject. Two words were what we disagreed about. You know what they were?'

'No,' answered Max, shaking his head.

'Representation and interpretation,' said Carlo.

Max nodded, chuckling quietly.

'For him the task we perform in the studio, whether it's Universal Recordings or some place else, was one of representation. Nothing more. In other words, mimic and copy as I said. Naturally, I argued for interpretation. Naturally, I lost in the end because he was this veteran director and who was I to suggest he change such a long-held belief. After that I learnt to pick my fights more carefully. And to always weigh up the opposition in terms of age and inflexibility.'

They both laughed. Max finished his coffee.

'You know one of the best pieces of advice I've got in this job came from you Max,' Carlo said.

'Oh! And what was that?'

'We were rehearsing – our first project together – and I was having difficulties with the character I was...'

'Representing?' Max interrupted light-heartedly.

'Yes, representing,' Carlo said ironically.

'I was having difficulties with what you might call the emotional pitch of my character. I couldn't quite get into it and you were good enough, as you always are, to take me aside and pass on some words of advice.'

'What was it I said?'

'You simply told me to get the words off the page. You said, find the emotional hook in the character and already you will be 90 per cent of the way there.'

'That sounds terrible actually, and completely vague.'

'But you were right about it. And I've used that advice ever since.'

'Well I'm glad to hear it. I just wish I could write better lines than that. Then I might have a future as a dialogue writer as well.'

Max paused for a moment, collected his thoughts.

A pretty waitress scooped away their cups, asking if there was anything else they wanted. They answered no.

Carlo did a quick time check.

'They can wait the full 20 minutes,' he muttered.

He looked out onto the square. The granite obelisk in the centre had always appeared ugly to him. Without hieroglyphs it was drab, unremarkable. Nothing more than a poor imitation.

His colleague's voice brought him back inside.

'We shouldn't paint them all with the same brush,' said Max, 'I've known quite a few technicians in my fifteen years in the industry. Many of them were fine people, highly skilled in their profession. There was this director in particular, the best one I ever had the privilege to work with. I've never met anyone like him who knew his trade so well and practised it so capably. He used to sit in the smallest room, sit at his editing table and spool whatever film he was working on back and forth on the moviola. All the time mouthing the words aloud so they'd match the movements of the actors. I've never seen dedication like that anywhere before or since. He was a writer as well and he always tried to find the ideal translation for something, a word or expression, so that it would fit in and not sound limp. That didn't always happen of course and he would often have to compromise, substitute or use some equivalent. At those times he'd often remark as to how there are no literal translations for certain things. That we have to accept this. And his voice would be tired then. Sounding resigned. But every once in a while there'd be a spark of excitement in his face, and you'd know he'd made some discovery. Found some very precise translation he'd been searching for. And on those days he'd say the job was worthwhile, that it wasn't just assembly-line labour.'

He smiled as something else came to mind.

'He always said that a good line was a terrible thing to waste.'

'Sounds as if he was a hell of a professional,' said Carlo.

'Yes, he was,' said Max. 'A very rare breed.'

The afternoon sun was struggling to make any sort of impression over Piazza dell'Esquilino as the two men headed back to Universal Recordings. A few tourists were exiting the nearby Basilica, peering about as they did for a suitable-looking restaurant. Not far behind them emerged a uniformed police agent of the Vatican City State. He was finished his shift for the day and going home.

Max was returning to the studio for just a few moments to pick up a gabardine trench coat he'd left behind. He had plans to have dinner with his sister and niece that evening. He needed to get back to his apartment to have a shower and change.

'I've often wondered what finishing a film is like for the actors that we voice. Different to here no doubt.'

Carlo's remark took Max by surprise. He'd always supposed that an actor as good as Carlo had some experience in feature films. Whenever they met, they chatted about work, nothing much else besides. Max realised he'd never really had a proper conversation with the younger man. He knew Carlo had a son but not a whole lot else. He'd never asked his colleague how he decided to choose acting. Was there a particular moment in his life he could remember? Was he satisfied with his career?

'You haven't done any features yet?' he said, trying hard not to sound surprised.

'Yes, I have,' replied Carlo, 'but so far they've all been small roles. A day here, two days there. Hardly enough to claim any experience. Certainly not enough to know what it's like to be on a feature from start to finish.'

The entrance to Universal Recordings loomed just a few steps away, but Carlo no longer seemed in any great hurry to get there. His 20 minutes was up, but he didn't give the impression of one concerned about this.

'I thought you'd have known that about me,' he said to Max. 'Around the studio they say you take a great interest in who you are working with, how they'll contribute to the film you're dubbing.'

'That's true,' joked Max, 'I have been known to poke around.'

'Is it for the benefit of your performance?' asked Carlo, 'or for the rest of us as well?'

Max smiled economically. The question was direct. Carlo was not one for beating around the bush.

'It's a combination of both I suppose,' he said, 'there are always ways to better your performance. And preparation is usually the key. Did you know there's an exercise you can do which involves opening your mouth in a yawn position and...'

'Yes, yes Max, I know all about those exercises. Like the one in which you do a sweep with your voice from high pitch to low. You told me about that before. Also how important it is to breathe from the diaphragm and not the chest. But what I'm really asking you is...'

'A man doesn't cry in the street!!'

Carlo's voice was drowned out by a prickly bellow coming from the doorway of the studio. Two figures stood there.

One was a mixing engineer called Vivarelli. The other, a director by the name of Bava. The raised voice was Vivarelli's, a short stocky man; but what he lacked in height, he made up for in volume.

'A man doesn't cry in the street!!' he repeated.

This only served to infuriate his colleague more.

Bava was a tall and thin man in his mid to late forties, a ruddy glow set into his complexion. This was more pronounced than usual. He looked like a man being driven around the bend. He wasn't a bad director. Max had normally found him to be reasonably sharp and often insightful in the projects they'd worked on. Nor was the reddish hue, so characteristic of his cheeks, to suggest that he was a man easily rattled or excited. His disposition, by and large, was composed, as was his professional demeanour. But now he appeared like an outraged citizen trying to get his own back on some unruly goon. The frustrated director arched his frame all the way forward until he was eye-to-eye with the shorter man. He'd seldom looked this irritated before. In fact never thought Max.

'Again let me get this straight,' he said firmly, 'you mean to tell me you erased the entire recording for that scene without consulting anyone? Especially me?'

Vivarelli nodded his head boldly.

'Yes, I did,' he replied, 'because a man doesn't cry in the street!!'

Bava paused for a moment to take this in, but it was clear he couldn't figure out his wayward colleague.

'But it's in the film for God sake,' he said, vexed at the cavalier attitude, 'this is a 20th Century Fox release and we have a deadline to meet!'

He suddenly became alert to Max and Carlo's presence; Carlo in particular. Turning, he sought to draw him in.

'Can you believe this idiot?' he said to the actor, 'the recording you did of your character crying in the street for Hidden Peril. You had it done perfectly. I came back to it again just now. The scene is still there, but the sound of your character crying because his life has collapsed all around him is gone! So I ask this clown what has happened to it, and he tells me he has taken it out.'

'That's right I've taken it out,' Vivarelli interrupted, 'I took it out because a man doesn't cry in the street. Perhaps that sort of thing happens in America, or in other places, but in this country a man doesn't cry in the street.'

Bava looked skyward as if seeking some divine assistance. There was none at hand.

'Please let me find an escape from this madness,' he moaned.

'Carlo, I'm sorry to say you are going to have to do that scene again owing to Luciano's unwelcome sense of initiative!'

'You mean I'll have to cry all over again?' the actor enquired, a mixture of bemusement and impatience.

'I'm afraid so.'

'It should not be re-recorded! It does not happen here! It should be left out!' Vivarelli said one more time.

'I have to cry again??'

'Yes, Carlo. Luciano, the scene is going to be recorded again whether you think it happens in real life or not. We're not interested in real life here or your notion of it. The reality that exists for us is that the film has a due date. It's required of us that the sound recording be in place.

I imagine they told you we had targets to meet when you first joined us.'

Vivarelli continued to shake his head.

Bava disregarded this and went back inside, calling out the time to both Carlo and Vivarelli as he did so.

'Well I guess you're going to be crying again,' Max said to his friend.

'I guess I am. Hidden Peril indeed, it says it all in the title,' said Carlo. He glared at Vivarelli.

'You better not tamper with that recording when it's done,' he warned him, 'otherwise you will know what it's like for a man to cry in the street!'

GOLDEN PIPES

Max left his apartment at 6 o'clock and drove along the west bank of the Tiber towards the Prati area of Rome. His older sister, Antonia, had moved to the tree-lined suburb two years earlier following the break-up of her marriage. She said she'd chosen the residential district to the north of Vatican City as it seemed to her an excellent place to raise her child. There were lots of community facilities close by, as well as a good public transport system in the area, and such important details had informed her decision.

She lived in a small but tasteful bungalow not far from Viale delle Millizie with her 10-year old daughter Claudia. Max called on the two of them as regularly as he could. He felt a keen obligation about this which had not been so pronounced while his sister was married. Antonia's separation, though painful for her no doubt, had given him a reason to become more involved in their lives. He adored his small niece and understood that she had a special place in her heart for him as well. The child's innocence was positively infectious. Claudia often quizzed him about his personal life. At times he felt a genuine concern in her childlike entreaties that he ought to settle down like most people.

The last time he'd seen them was a week before and, following such a discussion, he told her not to worry so much about him. He told her some people preferred this kind of life; that, rather providentially, it meant he had more time to spend with them. The child's response was to the point. She informed him quite categorically that she would not accept this kind of life for him. In as firm a tone as she could possibly muster, she said he deserved more than to be living alone in a fourth floor apartment in Monteverde Nuovo. The semi-high rises there were impossible to tell apart she said. Monteverde Vecchio, on the other hand, would be much more suitable for him. If he got married, he could buy one of those impressive-looking villas for himself and his wife. Then he would really have a home and not a beehive she said, affecting a haughty tone for greater effect. He laughed at this, but it only served to madden her more. She told him he should not do that, just because she was a child. It wasn't fair she said; especially as all she was trying to do was lend him a hand. She was about to say something else then, but her mother intervened, telling her it was time for bed. For once, Claudia did not try to stay up with them any later; instead she went to her room without a further word. It bothered him to think he'd hurt her feelings in some way. Later, he was truly sorry he had treated her heartfelt advice so skittishly. The child cared for him after all; she was only trying to tell him that. He felt ashamed for having been so flippant towards her.

He parked across the street from the bungalow in his usual spot, right next to an immaculately maintained Uno Bianco which never seemed to move. Walking up the small drive past his sister's Alfa Romeo 155 (they had a similar taste in cars; his was an Alfa Romeo 90), he wondered if Claudia would still remember how he'd been so jokey, and possibly thoughtless, a week before. She probably would remember. How would she act he wondered. Would she pretend it had never happened?

He rang the doorbell and waited for a reply. Claudia's silhouette appeared in the frosted glass. Max pulled his jacket uncomfortably. All of a sudden, he felt on edge.

'Hello there,' Claudia said as she pulled open the door. Her brow was furrowed, the normal cheery look absent.

She does remember he thought; and she isn't letting it go.

'I'm not late, am I?' he asked. He didn't know what else to say.

'No, you're on time like always,' she replied, brusque about it.

He was not a parent himself, but he'd seen more of her over the last two years, and observed in that time how his sister dealt with the odd sulk or fit when it came along. Better to be direct with the child Antonia said.

'She has a father living in Palermo who she only sees a few times every year. From him she gets an excess of mollycoddling. That makes it all the more important, and necessary even, that I be clear-cut in my parenting. To be any other way would be a disservice to us both.'

Ok he figured, that's how I'll approach this. No softly-softly. No trite remarks or corny expressions. In any case, Claudia doesn't want that from me. The previous week was proof of this. Before going in, he'd ask her if something was wrong. Did she have something she wanted to say?

But the child was a step ahead of him in her ruse. In an instant, she dropped the charade and went back to her normal, happy self. She had taken him in successfully; a measure of revenge was exacted. It was time to enjoy this little victory of hers.

'Fooled you,' she told him, 'you see, I can act too. And I still think you should get married some day.'

His sister did not pursue any such interrogating when it came to her brother's private life. Antonia seemed to accept that Max was content with his bachelor status. She rarely, if ever, asked about girlfriends. Antonia had her own private practice as a civil law notary. She was busy a good deal of the time with this and as a single mother. Her interest in many things had waned in recent years. Her brother's associations and liaisons no longer provided the fascination they once had. Quite often, she bemoaned the fact that there were simply not enough hours in the day.

They never spoke about the break-up of her marriage. Max knew there'd been another woman, but the more specific details were never laid out to him. He thought to ask, but got the impression his sister did not want the conversation. One evening, shortly after the divorce, they were having a bottle of wine together. Antonia and Claudia were living in a rented apartment in Borgo at the time. Claudia had been put to bed and the two adults decided to imbibe a little. They chatted for a while about many things, but not the divorce. As the conversation began to ebb, Antonia decided to turn on the TV. She liked movies as well.

The late-night ones were her best chance nowadays. She flicked around for a few moments before landing on a channel showing the Marcello Mastroianni comedy Divorce, Italian Style. Uh-oh thought Max. A film about the comic misadventures of a decadent Sicilian nobleman trying to bump off his wife did not seem timely. He was not mistaken. As soon as the famous actor, sporting a slicked-down hairstyle, began to suck his lips, Antonia understood what film they were watching. The television was switched off right away. His sister remarked how she had more than enough of the subject to last her a lifetime. After that, there was silence between them; punctuated only by the draining of their glasses.

Max and Antonia were not from Rome originally. The two were born and grew up in Ariccia, in the Alban Hills to the south-east of the capital. Ariccia was one of the 13 towns known as the Castelli Romani; not quite as famous as other Castelli, like Castel Gandolfo or Grottaferrata, but significant nonetheless in Roman and pre-Roman mythology and religion. It had associations with the Goddess of the hunt Diana; also the forest God Virbius.

In more modern times, the town was renowned for its porchetta di Ariccia. Max could recall, quite painfully, a few occasions in his grandmother's house being coaxed to eat the pork with herbs and wild fennel. He detested the meat now as an adult; the faintest whiff of it in a restaurant causing him to seek out the nearest men's room.

The Italian film market during Max's formative years comprised of three tiers of movie house. New Hollywood productions and domestic releases were premiered in the first-run, or prima visione, theatres located in the larger Italian cities like Rome and Milan. After playing in the prima visiones, these films were then pedalled through the second-run theatres (seconda visione), and the third-run (terza visione) theatres, which were located in towns and smaller cities.

Ariccia had a terza visione theatre. The price of a ticket there was much cheaper than prima or seconda visione. Although he was not quite as persuasive as some of his friends, Max was competent enough in the delicate art of cajolery. Generally, he was able to wheedle the amount required for a ticket from either his father or mother. On occasion, his grandmother was resorted to as well.

The movie house in the town was of the provincial variety. The foyer inside the entrance was kitschy, decorated in a shade of maroon. The tawdry hue was covered over somewhat by an assortment of well-preserved movie posters. Recognisable faces of the classic Hollywood era looked down as patrons sauntered into the auditorium. This, in contrast to the adjoining space, was plain and unadorned.

The theatre allowed smoking. In an effort to lessen the haze which swelled during performances there was a huge sliding roof. The opening of this corresponded with the intermission during every film. Few left their seats though, preferring it seemed the clandestine darkness of the interior. Even in summertime there was no mass exodus. Performances were generally late in the evening time; after dinner normally. The predominant gender of the audience was male. As terza visione theatres regularly changed their bill, spectators came and went during shows. There was little regard usually for the disturbance that might be caused fellow viewers. Some stroppy regulars, who considered themselves cineastes, objected to these noisy exits. Now and again there was a minor fracas when one of the aficionados took exception. But, generally, a respected hush came down once the feature started. Propriety was largely observed; up to the points of intermission and conclusion.

At first, Max went to the peplums which were the most popular cinema entertainment throughout Italy from the late 1950's to mid-1960's. These flamboyant attractions set in a classical past involved stories and variations on the perennial theme of good versus evil/hero versus villain. They were mostly populated by supernaturally strong musclemen, captive princesses and mythological creatures. Max saw films such as Son of Spartacus, Samson in King Solomon's Mines, Hercules the Avenger, The Beast of Babylon against the Son of Hercules, Goliath and the Sins of Babylon, The Terror of Rome against the Son of Hercules, Son of Hercules in the Land of Darkness, Samson and His Mighty Challenge, and the memorably titled Hercules against the Sons of the Sun.

The peplums played out in luscious colours and widescreen techniques of the day. The young Max was awestruck by the splendour he saw. For him the pictures playing in the movie house offered distraction in his small town where not a whole lot happened from day to day. The movie house was a panacea for such tedium. A diversion from the familiar.

In the spring of 1965 a spaghetti western called Per un Pugno di Dollari arrived in Ariccia. The first instalment of the Dollars Trilogy had in fact been released the previous September, but its arrival at the terza visione theatre was delayed longer than normal owing to its box office success.

Max's father, who worked in the nearby town of Albano Laziale on the train service, had put a firm restriction on his son's cinema-going. He said that Max's trips to the movie house had become too frequent; that he ought to devote more time to his school work. A portion of his free time should also be given to regular everyday things boys his age got up to, whatever they were, he added. One of the restrictions decreed that Max could not attend his beloved movie house for at least six weeks, or until such time as his reports from school improved. The nine-year old quickly recognised the seriousness of the situation. He might not get to see Per un Pugno di Dollari. In spite of its popularity, the western would be gone before the time was up and, certainly, long before the surly Professore Badalamenti would see fit to write him a positive report. Action was called for. In the absence of monetary wherewithal (Max's grandmother had been warned not to give her grandson any), the boy knew a degree of resourcefulness would have to be employed. The admission fee for the movie house in 1965 was not a great amount of money, but it still

HOLLYWOOD ON THE TIBER

represented a sum Max did not have; nor was he likely to have it unless a suitable scheme could be planned. He came up with one quickly. A central feature of it involved his voice.

On the third Saturday of March 1965, Max went to the movie house early in the afternoon, long before anyone would be turning up to attend the first performance of the day. He chose this particular Saturday knowing his father had been called for manual work at Roma Termini. He would not return until much later that same night. His mother and sister were also occupied for the day. Antonia's confirmation was not far off. There was a dress to be bought, other matters to take care of.

Positioning himself in a strategic spot, just to the left of the entrance door, Max put on a discarded garment of his mother's. He'd crudely fashioned it to appear like a toga. This he wrapped around his frame by holding it under his right arm, half behind, half in front. The back part he folded over his left shoulder; the front part he folded over his left shoulder as well. Now properly turned out like an ancient Roman citizen, or as close as he could manage, the boy waited for the first patrons to arrive. As soon as they did, he began to recite some of the lines he'd heard in the peplums. For added effect his performance was reinforced by a piece of leaden pipe he'd found on the street. This doubled as a sword, though hardly the kind Hercules or Spartacus would have used. Max swung it about flamboyantly, mimicking the Italian bodybuilders who starred in the peplums.

The key weapon in his dramatic armoury though was his voice. His repertoire included impressions of Maciste, Hercules, Ursus, Samson, Spartacus, Goliath, Ulysses, and the Cyclops, whose caricature he further amplified by putting one hand over his right eye. His voice soared as he performed scenes of confrontation and combat. It plummeted as he enacted the more heartfelt, philosophical. It deepened, to the great amusement of his audience, when a more sombre, morose tone was required.

He was an instant hit. Those present clapped and cheered. Max held out his palm and they expressed their admiration in hard currency. Grateful, he told them how much he wanted to see the film playing, with this American actor called Clint Eastwood.

In a very short time, he'd put together the required sum. He disposed of the leaden pipe which had served as his first prop. He removed the improvised toga, doubling it over several times until it was nothing more than a baggy mass of fabric. Entering the movie house then, he left behind the peplum characters for ever. A new kind of hero waited inside. One who didn't care. One who did things his own way.

Word of Max's amateur dramatics got back to his parents before long. In a small town like Ariccia confidences, indiscriminate acts and, most especially, public bouts of vaudeville, were impossible to keep under wraps. Most people in the area, for example, knew about the wayward young aristocrat who'd seduced the sister of his unsuspecting fiancée. The vast majority were also aware of which unfortunate husbands were cuckolds, which were budding Lotharios. Stories were quickly spread, gossip peskily disseminated, hearsay trickled through the grapevine. Often it found its way back to family and friends. Max had not considered this in his otherwise perfect plan.

It was his mother who first got wind of it when she was congratulated in a grocery store about her son's acting abilities. Asking what this was about, she soon built up a report which was then passed on to her husband.

Giorgio Pellegrino was not a man usually inclined towards outbursts or physical displays of authority. And yet he could make exceptions on occasion when he needed to. This was certainly one. His wilful son had disregarded his wishes, had made an exhibition of himself; made an exhibition of them all begging in a public place. Giorgio could only imagine what the local tongue wags were saying about this.

'No child of mine is a scrounger,' he said angrily, as he applied a leather strap to his son's backside. 'We do not beg in this family. There is enough money for us all. No one resorts to this kind of shameful behaviour. Do you understand?'

A barely audible whimper from the recipient confirmed he had.

Having finished with the rounded portions of his son's anatomy, Giorgio told Max to hold out his hand; that same hand which had so brazenly appealed for money, undeserved as it was. The young boy took umbrage at this. He didn't like being called a scrounger. More to the point, the money had not been undeserved. Of this he was absolutely certain.

'They gave me the lire because they liked me,' he protested, 'because I was good.'

His father caught hold of him. He shook him to-and-fro until he recognised there was little value in the action.

'What do you mean they liked you?' he asked, still seething, 'Federico Agostino said that you looked ridiculous in...in...whatever it was you were wearing.'

'Federico Agostino wasn't even there,' said Max, 'Federico Agostino never goes to the cinema.'

Giorgio realised this was probably true. Agostino was a prig. Both he and his wife – the bumptious Ricadonna – were critical of everything. The movie house, they said, was an abode for depravity and vice. Clearly, the old killjoy had heard an account from someone else.

'Still though, it sounds like an appalling display, the like of which this family will be embarrassed by for many months to come,' said Giorgio, not wanting to concede too much to the naughty ragazzo.

'Think of your sister as she approaches her holy confirmation,' he said, pointing to Antonia, watching passively with her mother. 'We are not performing monkeys in this family Maximillian. When your sister goes up to be anointed, to receive the holy spirit, do you think she will be imagining herself some sort of luminary? A VIP?'

'No sir.'

'Exactly. She will be modest as she should be. Modesty is a very important thing Maximillian. It grounds us and it keeps us as who we ought to be. Not those characters you see in film. The simple life is the one which is the real world. It's the one in which your sister will be confirmed in a few weeks' time. It's the one in which your reports from Professore Badalamenti will greatly improve. And it's the one in which you will not be going to that movie house for the rest of this year. Now show me your hand.'

'But they really did like me. I earned what I got. You should have seen me...'

'Maximillian, I think the intention behind your cloak-and-dagger exercise was so that I would not see you.'

'Yes sir.'

'Now show me your hand.'

His initial flirtation with drama having ended badly, Max did not perform again for some time. He applied himself better at school, as per his father's orders; played more often with his friends; went to the movie house less so, only now to see major releases like Per Qualche Dollaro in Piu and Il Buono, Il Brutto, Il Cattivo. The swords and sandals of the peplums had been replaced by the ponchos and stand-offs of the spaghettis.

Towards the end of 1967 Antonia was chosen to lead the Festa della Signorina, a religious procession to the Santuario di Santa Maria di Galloro outside Ariccia. It took place every 8th of December. The 8th was also Max's birthday, but very little attention was paid to it that year. The build-up to the Festa dominated; his parents talking excitedly about their daughter's prominent position in it. What dress would be most suitable for Antonia on the day? Should she wear something modest or perhaps a little more eye-catching? What type of shoes would be appropriate? Leather? Canvas? Wood? What had the young woman who led the procession the year before worn? Should they allow Antonia's grandmother to design the ensemble as she'd offered? Nonna was waxing lyrical about the upcoming event just as much as they were. She was full of pride regarding her granddaughter. It would be a truly wonderful day she predicted. Antonia would lead the Festa in a graceful way, befitting her role. She would be a household name in Ariccia on the 8th. An important person, and rightly so.

Their discussions became more and more animated as the day drew closer. It was Festa this, Festa that. Max wondered if any of them recalled the advice his father had given him a few years before. On the subject of modesty and restraint. He'd spoken about his sister then using those words, referring to her as some sort of paragon. And now this change in attitude. Giorgio rubbed his weathered hands together as he looked forward to the Festa. His enthusiasm swelled to fever pitch when he saw

Antonia's outfit for the day: a combined effort between her mother and grandmother.

In the midst of this commotion, Max felt side-lined. The 8th would be his twelfth birthday. Have they completely forgotten about it he wondered. He looked on as the smallest of refinements were made to Antonia's clothes, growing ever more disgruntled.

The day itself arrived and his suspicions were confirmed. For a present he was given a Sicilian marionette; not at all what he wanted. His parents wished him a happy birthday, but then returned to the familiar subject. The weather was looking good outside they said. A beautiful day for the procession. Just perfect for Antonia. But this is meant to be my day thought Max. I don't want to share it with anyone else. Or the stupid Festa.

Dressing up, as he was told to do, he wondered if there was any way of escaping it. What if he ran off to the hills for the day? Would he be missed? At some stage perhaps. His mother or father would ask if he could see Antonia. If he was gone, there'd be hell to pay. The same thing would happen if he tracked off someplace else. Like one of the other Castelli towns. Or the movie house.

The procession got under way in the early afternoon. It followed the traditional route like all others. As far back as Max could remember. There were a few stops along the way. Certain shrines and monuments had to be venerated. The cortege slowly ambled its way towards the Santuario, in a tedious, meandering fashion.

Max felt restless as the rituals were observed. More than just restless. He'd taken part in the Festa before. It was a bore at the best of times, but he'd never quite despised it the way he did now. He was angry his birthday had been put aside. It's completely unfair he thought. I have this day just once a year and this silly caravan has to take place. Worse, they have my sister leading it. And it goes on and on, without end. If this were a film, the scene would be over already. Better still, they wouldn't allow it in the story. Lack of narrative drive. Absence of plot development.

His mood got worse when they eventually got to the sanctuary.

The crowd gathered at the last stop. Trying his best to remain hidden amongst them, he was suddenly ushered to the front by his father.

'Come and see your sister,' Giorgio told him, 'she looks wonderful.'

From this vantage point Max could see Antonia only too well. His sister looked the part, no doubt about that. Virtuous and chaste; just the right degree of piousness. But that was to the untrained eye. That was to the unsuspecting who knew nothing, as he did, about the maddening fuss which had taken place in his house. No one else knew what an annoyance it had been. No one recognised what he could see as he studied her face more closely, spotting conceit, self-importance. Antonia was just as caught up in it as the rest of them.

He caught her eye then and she winked at him, just as she'd done so many times before. When matters of upmanship were at stake between them she always flashed that twinkle which seemed invisible to everyone but him. Even his parents had never noticed it. Max was furious. He'd have to get his own back now. No two ways about it. But what could he do? How could he outdo Antonia's performance? With a performance of his own naturally. That was the answer.

Returning home before the others, he searched for the necessary props. On an antique clothes stand in the hallway he retrieved an old poncho raincoat his father used for work. It was shabby, dog-eared in places, but otherwise intact. He overcame the problem of its size by doubling up the ends with safety pins. A toy gun and cowboy hat he'd got on a previous birthday when, happily, there was no Festa lunacy were also obtained. But the final item was more difficult to come by. A Toscano cigar of all things. Now that was a real challenge. No one in his family smoked. He thought of old Maurizio living close to the Fontana delle Tre Cannelle. He smokes cigars he remembered. They might not be Toscanos, but anything will do.

Maurizio was surprised by the request; but he was a good sport, happy to help.

'A cigar you say Max,' he exclaimed, puffing out some air, 'you can certainly have one which I didn't finish. Nowadays, I'm not so inclined to smoke them all at once. That's what old age and too many cigars do to you.'

He paused, considered the boy's likely motives.

'But why would you want something like that?' he asked, 'you haven't started smoking, have you?'

He laughed cheerfully when he heard the explanation.

'Oh that's wonderful,' he said, 'the man...boy...with no name, eh? Let me get the cigar for you. An act like that is worthy of it.'

Max decided he would stage his performance in Piazza di Corte. Many of the Festa participants would pass back through the centre of the town. An ideal location to grab their attention.

He readied himself, placing the felt hat on his head, tilting it to a low position, suggesting his character's mean nature. Ensuring that the poncho was at the correct length, he put the burnt-out stogie in his mouth. In such a way it would be visible, but not impede his voice.

'There are two kinds of people in the world, those with guns and those that dig,' he announced gravely as the first few people came into the piazza.

Soon a small cluster of them looked on as famous lines by Clint Eastwood, Gian Maria Volonte, and Franco Nero were delivered. There was applause as personages were overlapped, amusement at quotations about coffins, .45 pistols and bounties. Max had really improved since his peplum turn. He knew it too. There was a greater confidence in his bearing, more resonance in his voice. His body twisted, rotated, and coiled. He was tapping into the brutish gait of the western anti-heroes; discovering this ability in himself. His gusto surged with each turn of phrase, inflection of tone. He knew he could stay there as long as he wanted. The appreciative audience would not desert him; would not leave him high and dry as...

His father! His mother! Antonia! He had not noticed them joining the crowd. His family was returning from the Festa like everyone else. Their attention was drawn to the familiar-sounding voice causing a hullabaloo in the square. Now they were here, right in front of him: his sister gawking vacantly; his mother, her head dropping; his father scowling, no doubt weighing up what action he would take.

Max faltered. A momentary silence took possession of his act.

'Carry on with the cowboys,' someone shouted.

'Don't stop the show,' said another voice.

'Do Eastwood again Max.' It was Maurizio. He'd decided to come and watch.

Max straightened himself again. A measure of audacity returned. Feeling suitably emboldened to continue, he did just that.

'My mistake,' he said, quoting from Per Un Pugno di Dollari, 'it was four coffins.'

He held four fingers up in the air. The spectators laughed heartily, commending him with renewed applause. Max looked to his father for some sign of encouragement. Back me up he appealed to Giorgio in his mind. Can't you see they're enjoying this? The expression on his father's face loosened. A smile replaced the frown. He nodded to his son. A signal he could continue. Keep acting Max. They sure do like you boy.

And acting was just what he proceeded to do. After school, he moved to Rome. It was the late 1970's; he was hopeful the capital would be awash with opportunity. Taking an apartment with his sister, he began evening classes; his days spent searching for work. This came along periodically in the early years taking the form of bit parts in movies and television, a number of minor parts in theatre. There wasn't much money, but there was enough to live on, pay the bills. At moments of uncertainty, Max told himself it was all part of a bigger picture. His hopes and dreams would come through. He just had to be patient about it.

In 1979, he took what he presumed to be a vital step towards this. He agreed a contract with his first agent, Feruccio Benedetti, a go-getting veteran who specialised in film and television work. Benedetti was very impressed with the young actor; he'd seen him in an otherwise unremarkable suspense thriller (a giallo) that same year. His confidence that Max had the profile and appeal to go far in the business sat well with the young aspirant.

At the beginning of 1980, Max was cast in the lead role of a contemporary crime film (a poliziesco) set in Rome. It was called Deadly Days in the Eternal City. He phoned Ariccia when he signed on for the part, telling his parents his big break had finally arrived. He had no idea these were ill-fated words, that he would ultimately regret saying them.

Deadly Days in the Eternal City provided Max with an annus horribilis in 1980. On paper the film seemed a reasonable entry in the crime/action sub-genre. Its subject matter extended to the proverbial themes of organised crime, corruption, and vigilantism. There were action scenes involving car chases, heists and gunfights, tough PI's and vicious hoodlums; ingredients an audience expected. The script treatment Max was given followed a linear plot typical of the poliziesco. There were evil forces in the higher echelons of government; the shifty authorities protected the very felons they publicly denounced; the upright detectives were hindered in their efforts to uphold the law. So far, so familiar it seemed. The film was hardly going to be a classic. But at least it would make for a respectable entry.

The shooting script Max received on the first day of production was nothing of the sort. The plot had been revised from top to bottom, butchered as a matter of fact. In its place was a hackneyed patchwork: a young cop from Milan (Max's character) teams up with a local wisecracking detective in Rome. The two of them wrangle with Mezzogiorno criminals, fraudulent officials, and toadying Carabinieri. The writer/director piled set piece upon set piece. The constantly changing screenplay swelled with implausible developments; character motivation was muddy; and the problematic picture slogged towards an incomprehensible ending: Max's cop somehow acquiring a 1976 Ford Mustang II Cobra with which he weeds out the remaining bad guys, his character dispatching them with blood-spattered aplomb.

It was an excruciating 48-day shoot all told. The director, Angelino Giordano, demanded physically convincing fight scenes insisting that, as far as possible, the actors stage them in the interest of authenticity. Max cracked two ribs for the sake of such realism – an awkward boot to the midriff from one of the extras. Filming continued nonetheless due to a tight budget. The actor complained about this to his agent, mentioning other grievances as well. Benedetti's counsel was to stick with it, that the end product would justify the means.

'Battle on,' he advised casually, 'better days are just ahead.'

But they weren't. Just many more deadly ones in point of fact. The poliziesco was released in the late summer of 1980. The reviews were scathing.

'*A mess, an absolute jumble of a film,*' wrote one critic.

'*Turgid and excessively episodic,*' said another.

Max did not find himself immune to such derogatory reviews either. Like the captain of a sinking ship, he was dragged down with the vessel.

'*The young actor, Max Pellegrino, fails to rise above the mediocrity around him,*' opined La Repubblica, '*he appears in a bewildered state as if saying – how did I get into this mess? And what the hell do I have to do to get out?*'

'*Deadly days for this actor's career,*' Il Messaggero's film critic suggested.

Max was devastated by the criticism. The walkouts he heard of in Rome, Bologna, Turin, Genoa, Padua and Parma made him feel even worse. What about Ariccia he wondered. Did they walk out in my home town as well? Are they now laughing in Piazza di Corte? He became introspective, cagey about being recognised as the actor associated with that film. Withdrawing into the safe confines of his apartment, he brooded over what he should do next, if anything at all. His work suffered as he began to miss auditions and screen tests.

He had his sister to thank for her timely intervention, snapping him out of it.

Offering practical advice, as always, Antonia said, 'if you are so concerned about being seen, then why not do some work in which you don't have to appear.'

She suggested such an approach for the interim. Until his confidence was back.

Max's first job after Deadly Days was doing voiceover for a fabric softener advert on TV. He quickly followed this up with radio work, sales and marketing presentations, convention and trade show productions. It was while working in studio on a marketing presentation that he met Franco Bonacossa, an agent who represented a good many actors plying their trade in the dubbing industry. Franco was full of praise for the actor. He urged Max to realise his aptitude in voiceover and dubbing. In particular, he recommended that a full-time career be pursued. Dipping in and out of the industry would not be sufficient by itself.

'There is no point in attempting to have the best of both worlds,' he said, 'you have to build up a name and reputation for yourself with the studios so they know your value and availability. Films might come along again Max. But only you can decide if it's worth risking another Deadly Days. This work on the other hand is high-quality, reliable all year round.'

It was good advice. The dubbing business, most especially of all, offered steady employment. Everything from theatrical movies to television shows and documentaries was dubbed in Italy. The practice originated in the 1930's when Il Duce's regime decreed that all foreign films released in Italy be translated prior to release. Mussolini sponsored the creation of Cinecittà studios in Rome, declaring in the process that, 'cinema is the most powerful weapon.' More significantly, from a national-fascist perspective, he insisted that only Italian be heard by the Italian people. The sound of enemy languages was to be drowned out. Even Hollywood star names were Italianised. Fred Astaire became Federico Astorio.

Bonacossa arranged a series of classes for Max with a renowned voice coach in Florence. He began to seek work for his new client (Benedetti, by this time, was a figure of the past). The work came gradually at first. Max landed smaller roles of Hollywood actors who, like himself, were attempting to scale their professional ladder. In a relatively short time, work became more plentiful.

In spite of his agent's time-honoured advice, Max still harboured quiet ambitions to return to film work, to appear again on the big screen. He had learned a hard lesson with Deadly Days, but there remained an allure to the work, an undeniable magnetism. Movies were still the pinnacle, no matter the greater chance of failure. There was the additional enticement of stardom. Dubbing would never provide that. This will not be forever Max promised himself as he settled on a five-year plan. One fine day he'd find a part that would give him another shot at the big time. A starring role that might just capture the attention of the cinema-going public.

But severe problems which came to pass in the industry militated against this, against him and many others who might have dreamed of becoming the next Marcello Mastroianni or Alberto Sordi. Despite the veneer of festival awards and Oscar nominations, the Italian film business suffered an economic crisis from the 1980's onwards. Hollywood dominated the internal market; domestic productions struggled to compete with the larger variations coming from the new world. Italian production, which in the mid-1970's had accounted for 60 per cent of total box office revenue, dropped below 20 per cent. Movie houses fell into decay and were abandoned. Less and less capital was made available for home-grown products. Even past masters like Fellini and Antonioni struggled for backing in their twilight years. There was a decline of international interest in Italian film generally. The rise of private TV stations caused further damage to an industry reeling from the other sizeable hits it had taken. To put it in basic terms, Italian cinema was earning a smaller and smaller slice of the trade pie in a market where the hegemony of American films was an inescapable, universal truth. As a consequence, less films were made, opportunities were thin on the ground, quality projects few and far between.

Max's five-year plan was pushed out further and further as he yielded to home truths and the wisdom of his agent. He allowed the work to become what Franco said it ought to be: a livelihood, a mainstay; stable and perpetual. He became highly accomplished in his profession, self-thought mostly, and was admired by those who worked with him. Technicians and studio staff had high regard for his dedication to craft and work ethic. Fellow actors too; they gave him the nickname 'golden pipes' because of the melodious quality to his voice. 15 years passed quickly and brought him to his 196th film as a professional voice actor.

The film was called The Proper Citizen.

'I saw some of The Big Knife on television last night,' Antonia said as she partook of the linguine al salmone she'd made for the three of them. She was pleased with the way it had turned out. She'd read somewhere that flatter pasta was more suitable for fish and seafood dishes. The culinary tip was on the money. It tasted delicious. Her cohorts at the table appeared to be of a like mind, tucking into it enthusiastically. Max sat to Antonia's left sipping some of the Melini Chianti he'd brought with him. To her right, Claudia was engaged with some long strings of the linguine, obstinately refusing to become twisted around her fork.

'You've seen it Max I'm sure,' Antonia continued, 'it's the one with Jack Palance. He plays a Hollywood star who doesn't want to sign a new picture deal. He wants to be free of the studio's grip on his life, the trashy films they make him do. He also wants to save his marriage. Rod Steiger plays the studio boss forcing him to sign the contract. Ida Lupino is his wife. I've always loved her in whatever she does.'

'I do remember it,' said Max, 'but how does it go again? Does he stick to his principles and get out of it? Is there a happy ending?'

'No he signs the deal and one thing leads to another,' replied Antonia, 'things go badly, he winds up taking a hot bath and...'

She hinted at the rest of it by sliding her thumb across her wrist.

'That was bleak,' said Max, 'I thought there was going to be a deus ex machina.'

Antonia shook her head.

'If it was a deus ex machina the crooked boss would die, Jack and Ida would live happily ever after.'

'What's a deus ex machina?' asked Claudia, tuning into the frequency of their conversation.

Antonia exchanged her long-standing wink with Max. He was still the only one who could spot it.

'It's something used in a story or film Claudia,' she explained, 'sometimes a character faces a problem that seems beyond solution. A deus ex machina is used to bring about that solution. But it's often contrived, artificial.'

'Does it lead to a happy ending?'

'Most of the time, yes.'

'Then I like it, only I wish it would help me with this linguine,' said Claudia as another thread of the silky pasta defied her.

The adults laughed. Max poured more wine for his sister.

'Speaking about Hollywood stars, I see Don Taylor is arriving here soon,' Antonia observed, 'he's starring in a new film about Antonio Meucci. They're making it at Cinecittà. He's grown a beard for the part just like yours Max.'

'Yes, I know,' said Max, patting the collection of hair on his chin. 'We just finished work on his new film today – The Proper Citizen. As a matter of fact, I'm going to meet him.'

'You're going to meet him?!'

Claudia popped her head up again, suspending the latest round of her pasta skirmish.

'You're going to meet him?!' she repeated.

'Yes.'

'What for? Is it to do with work?' Antonia asked.

'Pretty much. His brother got in touch with the studio a few weeks ago. He wanted to know who does Don Taylor's Italian voice. Since it's me, I was invited to meet him.'

'His brother? Why would his brother be looking for you?'

'Because he's also his manager.'

'Oh. That's convenient.'

Max stared at the bowl of his wine glass, which was of the Bordeaux variety. The Chianti rolled to the back of his mouth as he inclined it. His fascinated audience became impatient with such nonchalance.

'So?' Antonia asked first.

'Where and how?' Claudia weighed in.

'There's a publicity event of some sort being held in Piazza Santa Maria in Trastevere next Wednesday. It's to promote The Proper Citizen, which is due out shortly, and also give some exposure to the Meucci film.'

'I didn't think Don Taylor was in need of any more exposure,' said Antonia. 'So you meet him and that's it?'

'Not quite. His brother seems to think he needs some dialogue coaching for the Meucci film. He asked for me as I've been doing him now for so many years and...'

'Ah. I get it,' said Antonia, 'so you meet and greet first. Then, later on, you give him the lowdown on his voice.'

'Something like that.'

'Uncle Max, will you be excited about meeting him?' Claudia interrupted. She was brimming with curiosity.

'Well perhaps just a little excited Claudia,' replied Max, 'after all he is a very famous actor.'

'But you're an actor too,' she said, giving it an air of importance.

Max looked to Antonia for assistance. His sister simply beamed a wide grin, raising her glass. You're on your own on this one her expression said.

'He's a much bigger actor than I am Claudia,' said Max, 'more people see what he does. A lot more people.'

'But they hear you. Don't they?'

Max decided to chance getting technical on the subject. Antonia wouldn't mind. She appreciated it when he explained things to her daughter.

'The pictures are bigger than the sound,' he said, 'they always have been. Did you know that the pictures came before the sound?'

Claudia nodded her head. She knew this very well.

'Yes indeed,' he carried on, 'with stars like Charlie Chaplin and Buster Keaton.'

He knew she'd recognise Chaplin's name. Keaton though less likely.

'Then they made this film called The Jazz Singer, and picture and sound came together. Synchronised.'

'What's synchronised?'

'It's when you see the picture and hear the sound at the same time.'

'Couldn't they have you in there instead? At least for some of the films?'

'You wish,' chuckled Antonia.

33

'Well they tried that once Claudia. Many years ago Hollywood films were re-done in countries like Italy, with actors like me. But they stopped doing that.'

'Why?' asked Claudia, persevering with the interrogation as usual.

'Well for one thing it cost too much money to do it that way. And also by then the stars were the real reason people went to the movies. They didn't want to see someone they didn't know. Would you?'

Claudia thought about this for a few moments. Then she smiled, satisfied she had the perfect answer for him. One he most certainly would appreciate.

'But I'd know you,' she said.

THE A-LISTER

D on Taylor glanced at the daily edition of La Repubblica in his hotel room. It was like all the other newspapers he'd seen since his arrival in Rome. It was in Italian and he couldn't speak a word of the language. On page 2 of the broadsheet there was a picture of him arriving at Fiumicino Airport the evening before. A short article accompanied the picture. It was about the star and the reason for his visit to the Eternal City. Some of the words he could make out quite easily: attore, Americano, famoso, celebrita. No great difficulty in any of that. There was also mention of Antonio Meucci and Cinecittà. About the new film he assumed.

It wasn't his first time on a shoot in mainland Europe. Three years earlier he'd top-lined in a romantic comedy set in Spain. A Marriage made in Madrid was about an inveterate bachelor who finally meets his love match at a wedding in the Spanish capital. Don could still recall all the column space that'd been devoted to him by the local press: where he ate, what shows he went to in his downtime, which members of the royal family he was invited to have dinner with. Newspaper people he thought, shaking his head. They seldom differed from one place to the next. When they wrote about actors like him they employed the same sounding words. Famous in Italian looked similar to its Spanish equivalent. So did celebrity. Probably star as well. In French there were words like celebre and fameux. Portuguese had protagonista and celebridade. He wondered how the Italian reporters would behave towards him. Would they badger and pursue as some others were wont to do? The word paparazzi came to mind, along with some of its more unsavoury connotations. Paparazzi thought Don. Isn't that an Italian word?

The actor yawned and put the newspaper aside. The ornate sofa table in front of him had a leather-bound hotel directory and some sightseeing brochures. The majority of these were in English thankfully. They might come in handy later on. Don stretched out on the sofa. He rubbed the outline of his beard. There were a number of pretty cushions on the chesterfield. Some of these tumbled to the floor as he moved about. Heaving a sigh, he smiled weakly, considered his new surroundings.

The Via Veneto suite of the Majestic Hotel was well appointed for a star of his fame. There was exquisite handmade furniture wherever the eye roved. Here in the living room was the most delightful 1930's fireplace, enhancing the feeling of sumptuousness. Extending beyond this space, a private terrace with gazebo and open-air whirlpool overlooked the fashionable Via Veneto itself. Sounds arose from trendy establishments below. Elsewhere, the sleeping quarters were likewise opulent: a queen size bed with expensive pillows and Egyptian cotton sheets. Next door to it a decorated bathroom with Calacatta Arabesque marble.

A lively porter had given Don and his wife, Lee, a concise history of the hotel when they first arrived. Leading them to their room, the luggage-toting employee itemised an abundance of details about the Majestic's past. He spoke proudly about members of high-society and royalty who'd stayed within its four walls. With a twinkle in his eye he also touched on some of the movie stars and show business people who'd passed through. Once in the suite the dutiful member of staff brought their attention to the room's features and added extras. There were terry slippers, courtesy sets and complimentary bathrobes; a mini bar in the living room stocked with miniature bottles of alcohol, soft drinks and fruit juices, as well as candies, cookies and crackers. A pristine desk set rested on an elegant study desk; a stately-looking armoire for clothes storage. The room had facilities for making tea and coffee, two television sets, a high-fidelity radio and a 'safe safe' as he put it. This inadvertent turn-of-phrase drew a laugh from the American couple. Don insisted that their custodian accept a well-earned tip. Producing a small wad of lire, he began to leaf through it. Right away, he saw there was a problem. He had in his possession, it appeared, thousands of these lire; in fact not just thousands, but tens of thousands. There were notes which read 1000, 2000, 5000 and 10000. What the hell is it with this screwball money he thought, browsing the faces and symbols, hoping for a clue. How do I work out what these denominations are actually worth in the real world? A 50000 note popped up then. Don gave up all efforts at deduction. He handed the guy a red-violet 1000 note bearing an illustration of the Italian educator Maria Montessori. The porter smiled dryly at this, expressed his thanks, and left the room without further delay. It was over breakfast the next morning that Don's brother, Todd, enlightened him as to how this conundrum of a currency operated. His tip, generous as it seemed, was not exactly going to put the fellow's kids through college. The big shot actor had given the conscientious porter the equivalent of a paltry half dollar or so. Lee laughed when she heard this.

'That's the last we're likely to see of him,' she joked, 'and he was trying so hard.'

Don was also amused. But in the back of his mind he felt somewhat mortified. That porter will probably curse my name for all time he figured. The high-flying Hollywood star would be nothing more than a cheapskate to the indignant employee. So much for the excessiveness of Hollywood. And so much for Don Taylor's fabled sense of largesse.

The irony was that he'd known quite a few hotel porters in his time. Long before he became famous. It was on account of his mother's place of employment. Helen Taylor worked in the restaurant of the Culver Hotel in downtown Culver City, California. She raised two boys by herself in the city known as the 'Heart of Screenland'. Don's father died when he and Todd were young. The two boys spent a lot of time in and around the pie-slice-shaped hotel. Don in particular. The six-storey building at 9400 Culver Boulevard, like the small city itself, had a long and eminent connection with the film industry. This was not lost on a boy who aspired to be an actor from an early age. He listened to stories told by Helen's co-workers about some of the stars who'd come to stay there as part-time residents: Clark Gable, Douglas Fairbanks, Greta Garbo, Judy Garland, Joan Crawford, Lana Turner, Buster Keaton, Frank Sinatra. Don longed to become as famous and iconic as they were. From a retired concierge he heard tales about two of its former owners: Charlie Chaplin and John Wayne. The old man wasn't able to confirm if the story about Chaplin selling the hotel to the Duke for a dollar was true; but he was more than willing to fill the boy in on their habits and personalities. The Duke he liked well enough; Charlie less so. Flamboyant he always said when referring to the silent movie star.

'Too much to say for himself and far too cocky about how high up in the world he was, where it was gonna take him. Duke Wayne on the other hand, well he was quite a fella. A real star and gentleman to boot.'

Helen and the boys lived in a small hilly neighbourhood called Blair Hills. The family had been there since the mid-1950's. Mike Taylor read about a Venice Boulevard property developer, Stone & Stone, which had purchased the lower area of the hills from La Cienega West to build single family homes. Helen and he were hoping to have a large family. As roomy houses were in short supply at the time, he was attracted to this development offering good-sized dwellings. The location was the site of a former oil field and at first Helen had concerns about this. What if the ground in the area was unsteady she said. What if there were hazards which might only come to light after they moved in? Can't we wait a while longer before we decide? Surely something else would come up before long. Her husband though was a decisive man. Mike believed that opportunities such as this did not come along too often; he was not for passing it up. He told her other families were being drawn to the area as a place to raise children; that they could not wait for ever. As soon as he'd allayed his wife's fears, he purchased one of the first twelve houses built on Vicstone Street. It was 1955. The following Halloween weekend they moved in. A cement strike left houses with no porches in the beginning. There were no sidewalks on the street either. But it was home. In 1956 the couple's first son, Don, was born. A year later, Todd arrived. The couple were expecting a third child when Mike passed away suddenly in 1958. Shortly after his death Helen miscarried.

Blair Hills was a closely-knit community owing to its unique rural setting in the middle of an urban surrounding. Most residents were families with babies and small children. A low percentage in homeowner turnovers meant people knew each other well, socialised together. There were barbeques during the summer months; the annual Independence Day picnic took place without fail. The Blair Hills Residents' Association was set up at an early time and became instrumental in the Blair Hills Park which was located on the site of an old oil sump. The kids played softball and other games in the park; the wives gossiped. Life was good.

The Taylors had a comfortable existence thanks to a life insurance policy Mike had taken out. Helen did not need to return to the work place until the early-1960's, by which time both Don and Todd were attending the local elementary.

As it so happened the job she took was in the Culver Hotel.

Don spent much of his time at the hotel and in the downtown area of the city where he watched eagle-eyed for famous stars and up-and-coming actors. When he was not on the streets, or in the Culver lobby, he tried to get access to the lots of the city's studios: MGM, Culver Studios and Forty Acres, where films such as The Wizard of Oz, Gone with the Wind, Citizen Kane and King Kong had been made. More often than not, he was unsuccessful. Heartfelt appeals to indifferent security guards were a challenge to say the least, but occasionally he was allowed on to see the filming of shows like Lassie, Hogan's Heroes and The Andy Griffith Show. Don quickly realised this particular medium was not for him. Television simply was not Hollywood. It was not the same thing as the bright lights of the big screen; much smaller as far as he was concerned. By the time he went to high school he had an appetite for the celluloid industry only. No other career remotely interested him. School – well it was just another unwelcome distraction he would have to tolerate in the meantime. He was still in his formative years. There was enough time yet for the foray into Hollywood where he imagined a great future for himself.

He wasn't afraid of the hard work that would be required to get there, the setbacks that might come along the way. He looked across from Culver to the Los Angeles neighbourhoods which surrounded the smaller city: there was Mar Vista, West Los Angeles and Palms to the north; Westchester to the south; the Baldwin Hills and Ladera Heights to the east; and the neighbourhoods of Venice, Playa Vista and Marina Del Rey to the west. He was encouraged whenever he did this; as time went by did it more and more often. Not far to go he told himself from this vantage point. Not far to go at all. Tinseltown was just a few heartbeats away, the real centre of the motion picture industry, and Don was going to make more than a few hearts flutter.

He met Lee while attending Culver City High School. It was 1972 and they started seeing each other. She was not the movie aficionado he was so on weekends he'd take her to the Studio Drive-In on the corner of Jefferson and Sepulveda. The outdoor theatre had a capacity of one thousand cars and it was there, in front of the 80-by-100 foot screen, that he introduced her to the magic of motion pictures and making out. From time to time they brought Todd along with them, usually at his mother's insistence. The established condition was that the car be their private space during the feature presentation. Todd sometimes hid in the trunk until they were past the ticket box. The spare money was spent on popcorn and candy. Todd was a sucker for Hershey bars. His silence about fogged-up windows and similar tell-tale signs was secured by way of the great American bar. On one occasion they went to a double feature of Logan's Run and The Spy Who Loved Me. The teenager's price was doubled that evening. So too were the number of Hershey bars he asked for.

The three of them did many things together and this group dynamic of theirs got stronger as time went on. School came to an end. After graduation Don and Lee moved to the LA beachfront neighbourhood of Venice. They both obtained temporary jobs and rented a small apartment. Todd stayed with his mother in Blair Hills, came to visit on weekends. The three took a regular walk on Saturday evenings along the two-and-a-half mile promenade running parallel to Venice Beach. This weekly pursuit was availed of by Don to bring the other two up to date on developments in his fledgling career. He gave them blow-by-blow accounts of screen tests which had taken place, try-outs in the offing. There were encouraging signs to report every so often. An audition sometimes led to a walk-on role or bit part. But there were disappointments as well. Don didn't always have upbeat reports to file at the end of the week. Every so often feedback was discouraging, even downright off-putting. One time a particularly gruff casting director told him to forget about pursuing a career. Sure he had a pretty face, but no acting chops, and pretty faces were ten a penny in this town. The critique put Don in low spirits. It was not until the following Saturday that he picked up again. Strolling along the ocean front with his brother and girlfriend, as per usual, he told them he had doubts for the first time. Perhaps the casting director, jerk though he was, had something. Perhaps he didn't have what it took to go all the way. It was all very well to be eye-catching and whatever else, but scratch beneath the surface and what else was there. Was there anything more he could offer? The others rallied around him immediately. Todd reminded his older brother that knock-backs were part and parcel of the industry. No one ever said it was going to be easy he pointed out. Initial kicks in the teeth like this were not uncommon.

'Why should you be different to any of the rest of them?' he asked Don. 'Even Redford had to start small and take his fair share of shit. Does it appear to you he gave up?'

Lee backed him up.

'Use it as motivation,' she told her despondent boyfriend, 'whenever you go to screen tests from now on just remember that little prick's face and tell yourself you're going to be much better than anyone else there. You can show him how wrong he was. When you make it, when you get your break, that phoney will have to quit his job. Because he'll realise he was the one who failed to spot what you have. He was the one who passed up on Don Taylor, and there's no place in this town for oversights like that. His mistake, your motivation,' she said kissing him on the cheek as a polite Todd turned away, watching two kids pass by on trendy inline skates.

In 1982, the same year E.T. was released and Eddie Murphy made his film debut, Don was cast in an ensemble comedy called Many Fish in the Sea. The film was released December of that year and did respectable business at the box office. Reviews were generally positive and Don was singled out by a number of critics who remarked on the young actor's adroit sense of comic timing and appealing persona.

'*Don Taylor may not be the lead just yet, but he certainly has all the essential qualities to become the leading man,*' Variety's Brenda Hall suggested in her appraisal. '*He has an amiable onscreen disposition, certainly pleasing to the eye. If he is fortunate enough to obtain more generous parts in the future, then he might be someone worth watching. This critic for one will pay attention.*'

The analysis was on the money. Don was cast as the central character in Wouldn't It Be Nice that same year. The production, which wrapped the following January, was given a Memorial Day weekend release. It grossed an admirable $92,600,000 at the box office, ranking it as one of the most successful films of 1983. Playing in theatres at the same time as Return of the Jedi, the comedy-romance surpassed expectations and forecasts of analysts who had not projected such a return.

It was a turning point in the career of its lead. Almost overnight Don made the transition from supporting actor to sought-after leading man. Through his agent, Dean Rosenberg, he received numerous offers of work. His sign-on fee consequently rose with every part he took on.

1984 and 1985 were two further stellar years in this progression. Four more films were released and their performances in terms of earnings left no one in doubt as to the bankability of the rising star. Don's face became globally recognised. He appeared on chat shows, was photographed attending sporting events. He went to the Golden Globes and Oscars, waved from the red carpet to his adoring fans. He was invited to film festivals the world over and jetted to overseas premieres in Europe, Canada, South America, and Australia. Two of his films played out of competition at the Cannes Film Festival. The actor was mobbed by members of the press and public wherever he went in the Riviera city.

He married Lee in Los Angeles shortly after the 1986 festival and the couple returned to the south of France for a two-week honeymoon. In a restaurant in Nice, Don ran into Tom Steiner, a Hollywood agent with the long-established Dexter Simonoff talent agency. Steiner congratulated the actor on his recent nuptials and suggested they get together for lunch when back in LA. Don paid little heed to the conversation. He had no interest in having an informal meeting with the agent. He knew of Steiner by name, had heard a few things about his reputation in the business, as well as the impressive client list he looked after. The star was well used to being courted by prospective suitors who wore expensive suits and employed industry buzzwords as a fashion. There was a familiar routine which they went through. As a prized asset he knew he was fair game for these head-hunters and their sycophantic lingo. But in any case he was satisfied with the job Rosenberg was doing. Dean was a good agent; together they'd made some good choices along the way. Why would I want someone else apart from Dean he thought. He's more than just a representative, he's also a friend. And you don't cut friends out of the loop when it suits you; especially when it suits someone else. Steiner was not going to hear from him when he got back to LA. He decided that much on the spot. There was going to be no lunch between them in a month's time, even in a year's time. Loyalty was an important thing after all. He was no agency bed-hopper. He'd sleep easier at night that way.

Six months later he saw Tom again at Spagos in West Hollywood. The agent smiled as he approached, extended a warm greeting.

'We keep meeting in restaurants it seems,' he said jovially, 'first it was Nice and now a little closer to home. How are you?'

Don exchanged pleasantries and made a hurried enquiry as to the state of business at Dexter Simonoff.

'Oh! So you haven't heard?' said Tom, affecting a surprised tone. 'A few of us have left DS and gone out on our own. We've formed SLR, as in Steiner Lovett Reeves, and set up offices in Century City. It's very exciting. The majority of our individual clients have come with us I'm happy to say. But of course we're looking to expand our lists and our portfolio generally.'

He paused for a moment, a measured smile appearing.

'We never got around to lunch and that was my fault Don. The last few months at Dexter Simonoff were hectic as you can imagine. My partners and I were working on our exit strategy. As a consequence, I neglected certain things that I'd normally give my full attention. You know I'd like nothing more than for the two us to sit down to a good steak and salad some day and...'

'I'm happy where I am Tom,' Don said, cutting him short, 'I'm happy with Dean.'

'I realise that Don, of course I do. I've no doubt that you're happy where you are at the present time, and who with. Contentment is a very important thing in this business as you clearly understand. You earn... well I know what you earn per movie because it's my business to know these things. Your career is in a very good place, no arguments about that. You make lots of money for people in this town who in turn pay you top dollar. Everybody wins. Earnings, wherewithal: these are very important things and we hope for them to carry on in perpetuity. I was making more than enough money at Dexter Simonoff. I could have stayed where I was. I didn't have to go. No one forced me out. My partners and I didn't get fired. In the end, we simply walked out the door and not one of us ever thought to look back. You want to know why?'

Don shrugged his shoulders by way of response.

'Because we all needed the same thing in our professional lives. A shake-up. A re-vamp. Collectively we'd reached the point where an adjustment was needed. We knew it was time to go out by ourselves.

We're seeking a new direction in this organisation of ours. We feel this town needs it as well. We're building an agency that's going to energise things around here. An outfit that's going to service the careers of our clients like no other. You should give me a call sometime. Even if it's just to shoot the breeze. An actor as fine as you should at all times be...'

'Tom I appreciate the charm offensive, but like I said I'm happy with Dean. He's been my agent for a few years now and...well...I'm satisfied.'

'Yes Don, but are you absolutely, positively overjoyed with him? Are you thrilled to bits with your agent, the work he's doing for you?'

'We mostly see eye to eye on things. It's good enough for me.'

'Well that's just fine Don. Harmony is something we all aspire to. But if anything ever changes in that relationship, if you ever feel Dean isn't pulling out all the stops, you make sure to get in touch with us. SLR is the name of the firm. We're geared up to work for our clients 24/7. No exceptions. And no searching for the middle ground or compromising which is what I've heard Dean has a tendency to do sometimes. We hold firm for our clients and make the deals on their terms.'

'That's useful to know Tom. See you around.'

At the time it sounded like nothing more than agent chutzpah to him. For the most part at least. These guys were always blowing their own trumpet he thought; making gung-ho promises to work every hour of the day God saw fit to send. Nothing original about that. The conversation would have slipped out of his mind entirely had it not been for the reference Steiner made to Rosenberg's propensity for making concessions. Every so often Dean shilly-shallied when more decisive action was called for. He was not the most argumentative of individuals, unusual in his profession, and he backed off on occasion when a stronger hand was required. Five Moments from Your Life, Don's most recent vehicle, was a case in point. The whimsical fantasy had grossed over $150,000,000 at the box office in the summer of 1986. Although pleased with its success, the actor had felt a certain degree of frustration with his agent's failure to secure a better profit participation deal. It wasn't the first time this had happened. He was concerned it would not be the last bit of backpedalling by Dean.

Don didn't hear another word about SLR until two months later when he was at a birthday party in Glendale. A producer's daughter was turning 16. A number of prominent members of the film community were invited to the coming-of-age party, and to pose for photographs with the young lady. The champagne flowed as the evening went on; tongues loosened as they usually did at these gatherings. Insider chat touched on a variety of familiar themes: which director had been sleeping with his female lead during a recent film; what high-flying executive had lately checked himself into a rehab clinic; which celebrity couple were about to announce an end to their short-lived marriage.

'Have you heard about the set-up Tom Steiner and his partners have over in SLR?' a slightly inebriated executive asked his friend. Don was in touching distance of them.

'No,' the other replied, 'Tom's a smooth operator. His departure sure left a gaping hole at Dexter Simonoff.'

'Well he might want to think about filling a few gaping holes of his own,' said the other, 'I hear their offices in Century City are pretty bare due to the small loan the bank extended them. Tom and his partners are using card tables and folding chairs for furniture. Their wives meantime are taking turns on reception.'

'That's gutsy. The three of them certainly have balls.'

'They sure have. I wouldn't fancy telling my old lady she had to do some sort of half-assed roster.'

The two men laughed and moved off in the direction of the bar. Don knocked back his own drink and suggested to Lee it was time to leave. The two of them bid the host and the birthday girl goodnight. Lee fell asleep in the taxi on the way home. Don thought about what he'd overheard: card tables and folding chairs. He couldn't get it out of his head. I got the wrong impression of Steiner he thought. The guy is for real. He means business. Those are humble beginnings, he must really believe in what he's doing. He remembered the garage sale furniture he and his wife had bought when they rented their first apartment in Venice. Those were humble beginnings as well. But from such acorns.

It struck a chord with him. He was more than impressed.

The next day he called to the SLR offices in person. Tom's wife, Lydia, was on reception. She dropped her cup of coffee when she saw him come in. The actor said he wanted to see Tom if possible. He apologised for the unannounced nature of his visit; explained he'd considered a phone call in advance, but didn't want this to feel formal. He wanted to keep it low-key, at least for the present time. Lydia buzzed Tom right away. The enthusiastic agent materialised in an instant.

'Hello there,' he said greeting the star modestly, 'I'm glad you came down to see us Mr. Taylor. So?'

Eight years they were together now, the actor and agent. Eight very good years spanning the end of one decade and the first half of another, during which time their careers went from strength to strength, and they became powerful men in the industry.

SLR's client list grew quickly; its staff numbers rose to 300, and in 1991 it relocated to custom-built headquarters in Century City. The tables and chairs used by the original partners were kept for posterity. The new three-storey building, with a 75-seat screening room and gourmet kitchen, had a glossy, high-class feel to it. By the mid-1990's the company had approximately 800 of Hollywood's top talent in film and television and over $100 million accumulated in revenue. Tom sat on the board of SLR serving as talent agent to a number of Hollywood actors, including Don. True to his word, he shifted negotiating leverage from the studios to the talent, and was well-known for his attention to detail. To his own individual clients, he was as extravagant as he was assiduous. Birthdays and Christmases were used as opportunities to express the never-ending gratitude of the company to its most prestigious clients. Superior hi-fi systems, state-of-the-art gadgets and appliances were dispatched to the homes of Don and other important stars for anniversaries and as the holiday season approached. Lee Taylor arrived home one day in mid-December to the sight of two unfortunate mailroom employees attempting to unload an oversized treadmill outside her house. Feeling sorry for the two guys, she invited them in for coffee. When they politely declined, she informed them that she would only accept the machine if they had coffee. They promptly agreed to the coffee.

On Tom's watch Don turned out a number of hit movies during the period. He reprised his role in a Five Moments sequel and appeared in a few more romantic comedies besides. A fantasy crime-comedy with animated elements was the third highest grossing film of 1989; an age-changing comedy the following year similarly stormed the box office; two out-and-out action films were completed doing more than respectable business; a fantasy-drama was bookended by a dystopian science fiction film and a non-musical remake of A Connecticut Yankee in King Arthur's Court, both of which employed the recently expanded CGI technique; and two legal thrillers were delivered in consecutive years in the early 90's.

The grosses for his films continued to rise as the old decade was replaced by the new: $156,000,000 was his best in 1988; $227,000,000 in 1989; in 1990 $244,000,000 represented his top performance to date and better was yet to come. He went $272,000,000 in 1991 and then $321,000,000 in '92; $368,000,000 was taken in for the second legal thriller – The Offshoot – in 1993 and this figure was succeeded by $389,000,000 in 1994 for the much-anticipated second Five Moments sequel.

The Hollywood Reporter declared him 'The Paramount Star of his Generation' in 1991 and Daily Variety weighed in with its 'Don the Distinguished' article the following year. Premiere magazine regularly listed him as one of the 100 most powerful people in Hollywood.

In 1993 he did a candid interview with Vanity Fair in which he acknowledged that his acting in some of the earlier films had been average at best. Some of it was done on cruise control he admitted, expressing a desire to embark on a new phase in his profession.

'I've thought about some of those films,' he said, *'and I've tried to be as honest with myself as I can. A few years ago a film critic, whose name I won't mention in these lines, referred to me as the 'king of the saccharine smash.' Perhaps he was right about that. I'd like to be able to move forward and take on more serious roles, character-driven films in the future. I'm moving into the second half of my thirties now and that's the aspiration I have for this next chapter of my career. I hope my agent keeps getting the calls of course. But most especially of all, I hope some of those calls are for the kind of projects I'd like to concentrate on from now on.'*

His agent did not entirely agree with him on this point. Tom was in favour of a more balanced approach, as he saw it.

'Absolutely do the cerebral stuff if and when it comes along,' he said one day, as they discussed a potential first look deal, 'just be mindful that you do a certain amount of juggling between that sort of work and your more, how can I put this, habitual endeavours. The last thing we want is for you to churn out a spate of worthy melodramas, so-called, and in the process lose your fan base.'

When the actor said he didn't want to be a latter-day Cary Grant for ever, that he wanted to expand his repertoire, the response he got was a variation on the same theme.

'Don I'm not for a moment asking you to be some latter-day Cary Grant,' Tom said, 'all I'm advocating here is that you continue tipping your hat to the sure-fire thing. There's a template that's worked for you many times. Abandoning it entirely would be like cutting off your nose to spite your face. And apart from all of that, you're wrong about one thing.'

The actor asked him what that was. Tom slapped him playfully on the shoulder, chuckling light-heartedly.

'Even Cary Grant didn't play it goody-goody all the time,' he said. 'Did you never see Suspicion? The Talk of the Town?'

Despite this little changed as far as the actor was concerned. He signed up to a second Five Moments sequel that same year, on condition this be the very last of the series, and agreed to the optioning of a big screen adaptation of the old TV series The Man from Atlantis. Tom waxed lyrical about this latter project.

'Webbed hands, webbed feet, superhuman strength, and lots of shots of your torso; it works for me baby,' he raved.

A full year later though The Man from Atlantis had not moved anywhere fast. In a moment of amusing effrontery, Daily Variety reported that things were not exactly going 'swimmingly well' with the in-development screenplay. There were re-writes, additional scenes, and then further revisions; significant problems were encountered in relation to the final act. Not one of the four writers hired to date had managed to resolve it. Concerns were also expressed about the difficult logistics of shooting so much of the film in the water. Just think of The Abyss someone reminded. That was no picnic for Jim Cameron or any of his crew. Budgetary estimates rose when the aquatic elements of the story were factored in. The budget would likely rise further as production got underway. That was the hard lesson learnt on films like The Abyss and Waterworld, still a year away from hitting theatres. The nascent project stalled under the weight of mounting apprehension and unresolved storyline.

For Don it was an absolute godsend. Hand on heart he didn't want to do The Man from Atlantis. Playing an amnesiac aquaman who swims like Flipper he thought. Where was the challenge in that?

45

It was 1994 and he was still on the look-out for a character-driven script. The film that would usher in the second era of Don Taylor. But it wasn't turning up. Other scripts arrived on his doorstep instead. More of the same he'd read hundreds of times over. Tom forwarded them all as if nothing had been said or understood between them. Lines of communication between the actor and agent became somewhat strained. Don returned screenplays and story treatments. He declined to take a number of calls from Tom and enlisted his brother's help. Todd didn't waste any time. Within a week he unearthed a screenplay which had been kicking about in development.

The Proper Citizen surfaced a few months before the second Five Moments sequel blazed a trail at the box office. Don picked it up, decided it was the one for him right away. His agreement to sign on, for a substantially reduced fee, was more than enough to get the film the green-light. The Proper Citizen began shooting in June and wrapped in mid-August. Post-production was frantically rushed in order for the film to be released in time for Christmas; also so that it would qualify for Academy consideration.

The Oscar nominations did not come to pass though. Far from it in fact. The Proper Citizen opened to a lukewarm reception from columnists and reviewers. They found fault with its self-important tone, the preachy manner, the drawn-out running time.

'When you are preparing to roast the turkey this festive season, take especial care that it is not as overcooked as the plot of The Proper Citizen,' one critic wrote acerbically. 'Don Taylor's shift into lofty political drama is not so much overdone as it is carbonised. It is one variety of fowl that will not soar.'

The film's performance at the box office was even less exceptional. It fared poorly in monetary terms and represented a well-below par performance for Don. By the end of January 1995, the film had earned a paltry $29,900,000. Numerous theatres by then had given it the chop. The end result was underwhelming and Tom Steiner hoped it would demonstrate to his client the importance of choosing his thought-provoking pieces more carefully. The agent had felt distinctly overlooked during the course of The Proper Citizen production. He was particularly aggrieved by the position of importance Todd Taylor had assumed for himself.

God damn fraternal factotum he thought, the next time he does not get to choose what Don becomes involved in.

As it turned out he didn't. Don chose it all by himself. The project was called Echo of Passions. Before long, it had a commencement date for principal photography at Cinecittà Studios.

Tom had accompanied the three of them on the long flight from Los Angeles to Rome. The agent had booked into the Majestic Hotel as well and was in a room just down the hall from Don and Lee. His presence felt more than just a little askew.

'It's cockeyed and it's stepping way over the line,' Todd complained to his older brother. Lee for her part found it unsettling. She didn't appreciate having Tom around in such close proximity, likened this kind of scrutiny to that of an intrusive parent.

'It's like Dad checked into the hotel to keep an eye on the naughty kids,' she said, 'and there I was thinking I'd finally moved beyond my childhood years.'

And Tom had travelled all this way on such a pretext. He'd brought his 15-year old daughter, Vicki, along with him declaring it the perfect opportunity for the two of them to bond; moreover, for the teenager to benefit from an educational trip around the historic city.

'Roman Holiday,' he'd referred to the trip over dinner the night before.

'My princess looks just like Audrey Hepburn did back then,' he said, putting his arm around the fatigued-looking teen, 'tomorrow we start on the sights, and you better hope you can keep up with your old man young lady. 'Cos he's pretty good at scuttling around these old ruins when he gets going.'

Except that it was now after 11 in the morning and Tom hadn't gone anywhere. He hadn't even left the hotel with Vicki. His progeny was having a lie-in he explained to the others as he entered the room, seating himself in a vintage leather armchair. Looking out towards the terrace, he remarked as to the pleasant weather.

'Perfect conditions for sightseeing,' he said, and he was dressed appropriately in pristine white tennis shoes, nylon cargo pants and a long-sleeved travel shirt. His bearing was cordial this morning, a complement to his informal rig-out, but in spite of that there was more than just a suggestion of his business-like second-self. For one thing he had in his possession the same buckslip pieces of paper he used for taking notes. His trademark felt pen he held tightly in his fleshy hand. He was a little overweight and, at 51 years of age, needed to address this. His doctor had told him to keep an eye on his blood pressure. A vacation and general break from the office were prescribed. His skin had a sallow tone to it suggesting a recent holiday in the sun. Tom jotted down some notes as he listened to Todd Taylor go over his brother's agenda. His handwriting was practically illegible. Many a personal assistant had laboured unsuccessfully to make sense of the scrawl. His meticulous side craved detail and he insisted on a like approach amongst his underlings. An unsuspecting new recruit incurred his wrath once by remarking on the meandering style she encountered. That was following a lengthy meeting with a prestigious client of his. It was regarding a project Tom was definitely not in favour of. He'd advised a re-think to his client; specifically not to do the film. His counsel though fell on deaf ears.

The film was The Proper Citizen. Don Taylor made it clear how badly he wanted to do it. He got his way in the end of course, he was a star after all; stars could get insipid material like this under way. Tom's notes from the meeting recorded his dissatisfaction in a typically long-winded fashion. This caused the newcomer to make her ill-advised comments. Tom lost his temper with her. It had as much to do with the irritation he felt after the meeting as it did with her observations. The hapless assistant went from plain-spoken to tearful. An apologetic Tom told her to take the rest of the afternoon off. He subsequently binned his notes, decided that a sense of perspective was called for. This would be a one-off he imagined. A never-to-be-repeated glitch. He was a practical man after all. Despite his client's folly, it was important their professional relationship be sustained, not suffer any further damage.

And when the tedious piece of drivel that was The Proper Citizen lived down to his expectations, the agent was sure Don would be more amenable to his advice. Back to basics with the next one he could hear himself say. Trust the nuts and bolts Don, they've taken you this far. There were more things he could say about bouncing back, starting over, but he was certain the leading man would get the message. Don was smart. He was in this game long enough. His next cinematic endeavour would be a tonic, a pick-me-up, to get his aficionados back on side, restore his box office clout. There would be an agreeable sense of the natural order resuming. Tom wouldn't even have to use the trite told-you-so. It would be understood.

But the natural order was not resumed, and the sum total of everything said and done these past few weeks, months in fact, came to mind again causing him an intense sense of displeasure. He wondered how exactly it had come to this. What had possessed his client of late? What had brought about this radical departure of his, misguided as it was? Did he suppose it to be a mid-career indulgence he could engage in? Or was it something else? Something far more serious? Professional brinkmanship? An adieu to mainstream work for good? How long did he expect to keep it up? Did he think his name could buoy any shitty piece of work? Because it sure hadn't worked for The Proper Citizen. And why was he no longer listening to the one person who knew where his best interests lay? The one person who understood what his career was about, where it should go from here. There are other possibilities which can be explored Tom thought. Other tangents can be followed which are not as high-risk as this one. But will he listen to me any longer? Will he give a damn about what I have to say?

As he mulled it over one of the slips of paper he was writing on came loose. The small sheet of buckslip, no more the size of a US dollar bill, wafted across the room, landing under the feet of his client. Don reached down and picked it up. He took a quick look, shook his head.

'As long as I live I will never be able to read your notes Tom,' he said, 'I think there must be a reason why you make them so difficult to work out.'

'There's no reason Don,' Tom replied, extending himself to retrieve it, 'I don't believe in being secretive. What I put on paper is not intended to be some sort of code. My handwriting is what it is and, unfortunately, it seems I'm not the only one in my family who has difficulties in that regard. Why it was only a few weeks ago that a teacher of Vicki's complained about the way she writes and...'

'Yeah, where is Vicki?' Don asked, cutting him short.

'In her room. Like I said it's the jet-lag. Kids are more prone to it. We had the same thing last year when we took her to Euro Disney. Took her a full two days to snap out of it, but she was right as rain by the time we travelled on to Paris.'

'Well that's too bad Tom because I hear the lines for things here in Rome can take quite a bit of time.'

'The Vatican Museums and Sistine Chapel especially,' added Todd.

He was a shorter version of his brother, also good-looking, wore full-framed glasses. Sensing there was an argument on the cards he took them off, sat down beside Lee.

'The Vatican Museums and Sistine Chapel especially,' Don said. 'You're here for a week Tom, right? Well that doesn't give you much time, does it? You and Vicki should be on your way already. There's so much to do and see here in Rome. If you lose a day you might never catch up. You might not make it to the Colosseum or St Peter's. What a disaster that would be.'

'It's ok Don. We know what we're doing and what places we're going to see. We did out an itinerary before leaving LA.'

'Well as long as we're not holding you up,' said Don, glancing sideways at his wife and brother.

'You're not holding us up at all Don,' said Tom, fastidiously putting his papers in order, 'I'm going to give Vicki just a while longer and then it's away we go. Gotta stick to that itinerary after all. And yes we do know about those lines and waiting times. Thank you for mentioning it.'

The agent concluded what he was doing, returning his attention to the here-and-now.

'All done,' he said, smiling circumspectly, 'for my own information, you know.'

'I don't doubt that,' said Todd, 'he's been writing those notes ever since he came in.'

'That's true,' agreed Lee. She was dressed elegantly and had an urbane quality about her, consistent with a well-mannered upbringing. Having recovered from a recent bout of bacterial pneumonia, she'd decided to accompany her husband to Italy for the duration of the shoot. It wouldn't affect her recuperation the doctors had said.

'What about it?' Tom argued back, 'I'm just noting what my client is doing these next few days so that I can...'

'So that you can what?' Don asked sharply.

'So that I can do my job Don. That's all. So that I can do my job. That's not such an objectionable thing to you, is it? It's the way I operate, it's the way I've always conducted my business. You know that. It's made great careers for us both Don. You and I. And we still have lots of good things ahead of us in spite of...'

Don waved away the hackneyed speech. Rising to his feet, he caused several more of the cushions on the chesterfield to fall to the floor.

'So this itinerary of yours Tom,' he said, 'I'm hazarding a guess you're going to take Vicki to visit Cinecittà Studios as part of it?'

'For sure Don. Why wouldn't I? Vicki loves films like the rest of us. I told her about the ones that were made there. Ben Hur...Cleopatra...'

'And what about the Echo of Passions production office? Will you be visiting that as well?' inquired Don.

'I might drop in to see the sets for the film Don. No great significance in that. Just curiosity on my part. I'm sure Vicki would find it interesting too.'

Don smiled sarcastically in response to this.

'Tom you're really putting yourself out on this one, aren't you?' he said. 'First there was the wounded reaction to my decision to do this film. That was followed by all those efforts you made to talk me out of it. You told me to reconsider Man from Atlantis, which was no closer to being ready.'

'Or any good for that matter,' Todd chimed in.

'Besides that you said there was an infinite number of projects I ought to consider. But none of them were any good Tom. In fact the vast majority of them were downright bad.'

'Is that why you had your brother read all the material I sent you Don? Because you'd already made up your mind?'

'Don is pursuing a change in his career Tom,' Todd interrupted, 'he knows that you're against it, that you'd do anything to get him back doing the sort of films you think he should be doing. You jumped on a plane here to nose around for a couple of days; maybe to see if you could arrange for someone at the studio to pass on information about how things are panning out. Something for you to write more notes on those stupid pieces of paper.'

'That's absurd,' Tom remonstrated, 'you make it sound like I'm here on some sort of reconnaissance. All I'm doing is spending time with my daughter, as well as availing of the opportunity to visit the studio, appraise things for myself.'

'Well at least you're admitting that much,' said Lee, 'before it was the smoke and mirrors of the educational expedition and how we'd barely notice you. We all know why you're really here Tom. It's to poke your head around corners, rattle some cages before you head home. You've come here to flex your muscles, let certain people know you're in town. All it's going to achieve is to create difficulties for my husband.'

Tom pulled a face saying he took exception to this remark.

'I would never try to cause difficulties for Don,' he said categorically. 'Don is my client, a very special client, and I try to do what I feel is right for him, facilitate the course of his career as best as possible.'

'But that's exactly the problem Tom,' argued Todd, 'you're overstepping the mark. What you're currently doing isn't facilitating Don's career.

You're trying to impose your will over him, bit by bit. You're a control freak Tom. It's got to stop. You've got to cut Don some slack. Allow him more freedom in his choices.'

'Staying on a different floor in the hotel would be a start,' said Lee.

'Staying in a different hotel would be a helluva lot better,' said Todd.

'It's what I got allocated,' Tom protested. He stared at Don who was saying nothing.

'Don, believe me when I say that everything I do, however loathsome it might seem to you, is done with the best possible intentions. It's done to protect you and the career we've both worked so hard for.'

'Protect me from what?' asked the actor.

'To be frank about it, non-descript pieces of shit like the Proper Citizen which are doomed from the get-go.'

'I thought you didn't want to discuss that again. You're going back on what you said Tom. Next thing I know you'll be saying Ishtar was a misunderstood masterpiece.'

'Or that Hudson Hawk was every bit as good as Die Hard.'

'He mentioned Cleopatra. Wasn't that a flop as well?'

'It was, especially if you allow for inflation. Nowadays it'd cost in the region of…well a lot more than an Ishtar or Hudson Hawk.'

Tom sighed deeply as he tried to get a word in edgeways. He didn't appreciate industry jokes. They were counter-productive; quite often in bad taste as far as he was concerned. Any employee at SLR engaging in such banter was given a stern dressing down.

'What I'm trying to say here, if you'll allow me, is that in almost 100 years of film-making the fundamental things an audience expects haven't changed. They want romance, mystery, intrigue, car chase scenes, explosions, action in the bedroom, good versus bad, David versus Goliath, adventure, shoot-outs, battles beyond the stars. I could go on, but I think you get the idea. These are story concepts, narratives, which have been successful time and again. Audiences identify with them because they know what they want. They also know what things they don't want, and clearly 160 minutes of Don attempting his best Broderick Crawford impersonation they had no appetite for. The fish stunk from the head folks. We all saw how Don's usual fan base avoided that dish. Now just try telling me I'm wrong about that.'

'You are Tom,' Don answered, feigning disbelief, 'Broderick Crawford?! I'm personally hurt by that. I was trying for Henry Fonda. How could you have missed it?'

'Well God knows Don. There certainly was plenty of time for me to get it.'

'160 minutes like you said.'

'Not counting the credits. I stayed on in West Hollywood for them. There was at least another five minutes.'

'The music was good though. Enrico what's-his-name did a great job. It made it worth staying on for those five minutes.'

'Did you get a copy of the soundtrack Don?'

'Yes I did. Two in fact. I'll give you the extra one when we're back stateside.'

'Can I interrupt for just a moment again if you're done with the music?' Tom said impatiently.

'Sure Tom,' replied Don. He had cheered up quite a bit, was appreciative of how his wife and brother were rallying to his cause, as they always did. They understand why I'm here, what I want to do, he thought. They understand what the Meucci film could mean to me.

'Don I'm not the bad guy in all of this,' said Tom, putting as much sincerity into the statement as he could manage. 'I have huge regard for you – professional and personal. I value our friendship.'

'Is that a fact?'

'Of course it is. I'm not trying to rule your life or your career,' Tom said, exchanging a glance with Todd, 'but equally I don't want you doing too many of these films one after the other. I'm advocating a more sensible approach. Keeping up the sure-fire things; a think-piece here and there.'

'He'll still advise you to do more of the commercial Don,' said Todd, 'you'll end up doing more of the same old, same old.'

'Don, I'm simply encouraging some prophylactic measures here,' said Tom, ignoring Todd, 'I'm like a dermatologist, just trying to deal with a cosmetic problem before it becomes deep-rooted.'

'A dermatologist! That's a new one Tom. I've never heard that before.'

'He's certainly getting under my skin,' said Lee.

'He has that charming way about him,' added Todd.

'I can see this isn't going to get me anywhere at the present time,' Tom concluded. 'I took a crack at rationality when we were still in LA. It didn't work then and I shouldn't have expected it to work now. You're here in Rome Don. Here to do this film and there's absolutely zero I can do about that. I urged you to be cautious about agreeing to this part, as you know.'

'Quite the reverse Tom, you told me in no uncertain terms not to agree to it.'

'Be that as it may, you went ahead and accepted it in spite of my advice. So here we are.'

'Here we are indeed.'

'No doubt about that.'

'Lots of doubts Don. Too many.'

The actor thought about this for a moment, rubbed the hair on his chin and upper lip. It was dark for the most part, some tiny flecks of grey. Don smiled ironically.

'It's still the beard, isn't it?' he said.

Lee giggled when she heard this. She was familiar with this particular saga.

'The beard? What's your beard got to do with anything?' asked Todd.

'Tom is deeply troubled about my having it in this film,' Don replied. 'He thinks it's unsightly.'

'But that's preposterous. Meucci had a beard. It's just a reflection of the fact.'

'That's what I told him.'

'I think it looks good on you,' said Lee. 'You look wise.'

'I always have been,' Don said with a playful wink.

'So what's the problem then Tom?' asked Todd. 'Beards were popular back in the 1800's. Just think Abraham Lincoln, Charles Dickens.'

'I think it looks unclean. I prefer the clean-shaven look myself,' said Tom.

'You're in the wrong business Tom. You ought to work for Gillette.'

'He also disapproves of the fact that I die in the film.'

'Jesus Tom! This is too much already! Of course Meucci dies. That's tended to happen to most people born in the 19th century you know.'

'I'm simply opposed to its portrayal onscreen.'

'Why's that?'

'Because it's a downer Don. It's depressing. It will do nothing to raise the tone of this film, miserable enough as it is already.'

'What would you suggest instead? A song-and-dance routine?'

'I would suggest a good many things, but I don't have David Cousins' ear as you well know.'

'I understand you guys are less than amigos para siempre,' said Todd, 'I'm also guessing he didn't mention you in his Oscar speech last year.'

'The fucking Academy committed its worst sin ever when it gave that son-of-a-bitch the Oscar for Best Original Screenplay,' Tom exclaimed. 'He was done with directing as far as we were concerned, and more than just a few happy about that I might add. He wins an Oscar and it's as if the slate is wiped clean. It's like they said to Attila the Hun, look we know you invaded and plundered for all those years but...'

'Tom you're exaggerating this out of proportion.'

'No, I'm not. David Cousins the writer is one thing; and David Cousins the director is something else again, but David Cousins the fucking producer!! He will bring new meaning to the expression out of control.'

'He's a good director Tom.'

'He's a good writer and that's what he should stick to. There are only so many fights a man can pick with his own prose. But give him back the director's chair and all bets are off. Aggregate Pictures will have faxes and memos toing and froing about magic hour shots, multiple takes.'

'So he's a perfectionist. He believes in what he's doing.'

'He's an obsessive Don, a fixated fusspot who will have you doing 40 plus takes of a scene. You've heard those stories about him. Reducing grown men to tears, demeaning anyone who dares question his M.O. He's a bully and I don't buy into these stories about how he's become a reformed character, found peace within himself. Bullshit. There is no rehabilitation for an intransigent asshole like that.'

'Tom, you're no one to preach about that. Does coming all the way to Rome to personally cast your beady eye over my brother's film not strike you as totally obsessive? I mean there are programmes for this kind of behaviour. I, for one, think you should sign up.'

'Thanks for your two cents' worth Todd, but I'm fine just the way I am. And I will be proved right about David Cousins. As soon as that fucker gets the bit between his teeth, he'll be the insufferable prick he's always been.'

Lee stood up.

'I'm getting tired of this conversation,' she said, 'and the vulgarities are too much.'

'I'm sorry Lee,' Tom said apologetically.

'You should be,' said Don, 'and you're absolutely right dear, this discussion has gone on long enough. It's time to wrap it up. Tom, go and take your daughter around Rome for God sake. Enough already with the manoeuvrings and schemes. I'll be able to handle David Cousins.'

He took a quick look through the doors leading out onto the terrace.

'It's a beautiful Spring day out there,' he said, 'and I'm taking my wife and brother to see Rome.'

'That's the best bit of news I've heard all morning,' said Lee.

'Shall we then?' Don asked, motioning them towards the door.

'How about we all go?' suggested Tom, 'if you just give me a few minutes, I can have Vicki ready. We can check the city out together.'

Don looked at his wife and brother, gauging their reaction.

'I don't think that's such a good idea Tom,' he replied, 'and besides, didn't you say that you were here to bond with your daughter?'

'Well...yes...but we could do with the company as well. A week is a long time. The two of us will have lots of opportunities to be together.'

'Well then, isn't now as good a time as any to start?'

'You don't want us tagging along so?'

'To be perfectly honest, no Tom. Be with your daughter. Let me be with my family.'

He opened the hotel room door, ushering the others through.

'By the way Don how's your Italian?' Tom asked. 'Do you have any basic words to get by?'

'Well I know ciao,' Don replied, 'that's for hi, isn't it?'

'It's also used for bye,' Tom told him. 'I read that Italians speaking English often confuse hello and goodbye on account of it. They arrive someplace and they say bye; they go to leave and they say hi.'

'You don't say?'

'I do indeed,' Tom said, grinning smugly, 'so don't be surprised if you experience that while you're here. It's a common mistake they make.'

'I'll keep it in mind,' Don said. 'Would you pull out the door as you leave Tom. We won't be back until much later.'

'Sure Don. No problem.'

The actor paused for a moment before leaving.

'Oh and Tom,' he said.

'Yes Don?'

'Ciao. And, incidentally, that is for bye in this case.'

In a Lonely Place

In another part of the city, Max made his way on foot to the home of his long-time agent and mentor Franco Bonacossa. Franco lived in an apartment in Via Margutta, close to Piazza di Spagna and the famous Spanish Steps, and Max took his accustomed route to the street from the north by way of Piazza del Popolo and Via del Babuino. The picturesque cobblestoned street where his agent dwelled had once been the home to modest craftsmen and artisan traders, but, in more recent times, had become a popular location for modern art galleries, pricey antique shops and trendy restaurants. It had a reputation for being an exclusive neighbourhood where various performers and luminaries, such as Federico Fellini and his wife, Giulietta Masina, lived and although in extent no more than a charming narrow lane, it nonetheless retained a lush garden ambience with its leafy trees and pendulous vines.

The street had a long association with the fine arts (as well as with its exponents) and its lofty status originated in the 16th century when it was declared a tax-free zone for artistic practitioners. The area became home to painters, sculptors and antiquarians (the majority of them Italian, Flemish and German) who replaced warehouses and stables with houses, workhouses and gardens; as a succession to this, many of these former studios had been converted into flats and apartments, as was the case with Franco's pleasant domicile.

The veteran agent had resided in the district for 24 years now and, of late, had been operating his business from the confines of his apartment. At the time of this adjustment he told Max that the decision was grounded in personal reasons, as much as it was based on commercial ones. As a joke he likened his new arrangement to the circumstances of those bygone marble workers and masons who'd lived and plied their trade out of small huts in the locality.

'My conditions are far better than theirs were,' he observed light-heartedly, 'a little more elbowroom and, undoubtedly, more conveniences and luxuries than those poor souls ever had. But we share the same autonomous spirit in terms of our practice and organisation. We are independent and self-regulating, free-thinking and progressive.'

To Max's mind, however, there'd been very little evidence of any such vim and vigour lately. As he drew closer to the address, he speculated as to what state of affairs he would encounter this time around. Franco's wife, Gabriella, the principal administrator of his business, had passed away three years earlier and the woman the agent now engaged seemed to be doing very patchy work.

On the occasion of their previous get-together, Max couldn't help but notice how disordered everything was in Franco's office: several damaged ring binders, piled sloppily on the carpeted floor, bulging outwards like distended abdomens; and more than just a few of the plastic file folders, scattered here and there, were coming apart at the seams. In the far left-hand corner of the room stood two metal filing cabinets which had come from Franco's old office. The top of each unit was in dire need of polishing and some of the drawers underneath were only half-closed, as if their contents were deemed inconsequential. Franco's own desk was also symptomatic of the general malaise. The large pedestal bureau was encumbered with post-its and other bits of crumpled paper; there were faded business cards which incorrectly indicated the former address of his business; some used paper towels and dried-out wet wipes requiring overdue disposal; two or three weathered manila folders with no apparent purpose; a surplus of minute paper clips and detached staples; and, last of all, a half-spent pack of Nazionali cigarettes, in spite of doctor's orders that he abstain from that most deleterious of habits.

The conspicuous clutter and general air of disorder bore out a certain amount of what Max had been hearing through the grapevine. There was gossip flying around about the parlous state of Franco's business. Max had caught more than just a whiff of this in the course of one-to-ones with other actors and industry insiders. A week earlier, during the Proper Citizen sessions, two or three people at Universal Recordings had asked him about the agent and his present circumstances. Damiano di Steffano was one of them. Another was Carlo del Piero.

'So what is the up-to-the-minute news on Franco?' he enquired in that searching way of his, 'I understand Pietro Brazzi didn't renew his contract with him; nor did Erika Morante a few months ago.'

'Erika has left Franco?' Max said reacting in surprise. Erika had been with Franco as long as he'd been. Her departure from him had to be a bolt from the blue.

'She made a break for it indeed,' his counterpart replied, 'Franco is how old now? He must be getting on at this stage; in every sense of the word.'

'He's in his late 60's,' Max informed him.

'Well that adds up,' Carlo declared without hesitation, 'sounds as if he's on the downward slide, don't you think?'

'Don't write him off just yet.'

'I'm not, but many others are it seems. If you pay any attention to the rumour mill the outlook for him isn't very promising. Some of them are saying he's dying a slow death…professionally-speaking I mean.'

The pronouncement was to a certain extent harsh, but it wasn't without foundation. Franco was old-school and he'd progressively become a less and less effective agent these last few years. This was an inescapable fact and, try as he did to turn a blind eye to it, even make excuses, Max couldn't deny the reality and the knock-on effects it had for him. During his early years as a voice actor Franco had been a peerless representative of his. The older man knew the business inside and out. He worked hard on behalf of his new client: made the calls, did the promotion work, sent out the auditions, arranged for the recording of sessions and demos, handled the billing, and took care of the payment follow-ups.

And, in stark contrast to that, he rarely performed any of those tasks any longer. More often than not Max was the one doing the groundwork nowadays. He arranged appointments, documented sessions, and kept a schedule of bookings and recordings. He'd learnt a great deal about the inner mechanisms of the industry, on account of his close relationship with Franco, and he applied this knowledge diligently as the latter's level of interest appeared to wane.

It was not so terribly onerous in truth. The reputation of his work preceded him and he was highly regarded. But it did beg the niggling question as to why he really needed Franco anymore. The old man clearly was far from the vigorous go-getter he'd been in days gone by. Perhaps it was an age thing as his sister said. Antonia referred to it as the 'abdication of motivation' explaining she'd seen it happen to one of her own former colleagues. She also suggested it was time for him to acquire a new agent.

'High time in fact,' she said emphatically, 'why should you be doing all the menial work and paying him a fee he hasn't even earned?!'

It wasn't quite as straightforward as that though; and he certainly did not want it to be so cutthroat-like if the time ever came. Franco had been more than an agent all these years. He'd been a friend as well, and Max felt genuine affection towards him. It was Franco after all who had offered his younger self the much-needed encouragement and guidance he needed following the Deadly Days debacle. It was Franco who had stepped in to the breach at that low ebb. He'd pointed out the most practical way forward for the young man and counselled him wisely as to how he should develop his career. And Max had become stronger as a result of it. Both personally and professionally. As an actor he'd discovered his true vocation; at least that was what Franco always said. There was real quality in the work he performed. The constant stream of job offers and contracts was a testament to his abilities. Franco did not doubt this. He never allowed his client to doubt himself either. He impressed upon Max the importance of believing in everything he chose to undertake and, most especially, to believe in himself without question.

When Max's father died in 1989, Franco attended the funeral in Ariccia and offered a consoling ear later. He listened intently to the stories his client recounted about the old movie house, where he'd first discovered the joy of cinema, and the problems he'd encountered with his father on account of this. Franco laughed aloud when he heard about the peplum performance and the spaghetti western sendup. These were truly wonderful moments he said; even if they had not seemed that way at the time.

'Your father no doubt was proud of you,' he said when the amusement between them had subsided. 'He knew you wished to achieve something in your life and was fortunate to live long enough to see it come to pass. I always tell you to believe in yourself Max, to never have doubts about the skills and abilities you have because they are great and they will continue to sustain you. There's something else that I can tell you now. Something you may not have realised before. Your father believed in you just as much as I do. Why else do you think he allowed you to follow your dream after that day in December? He saw something at the moment in time, was privileged in fact to see it, just as I did nine years ago.'

The correct thing to do was to retain Franco. He decided on that much as he arrived at Via Margutta and proceeded in the direction of the agent's apartment. It was important to be steadfast about such things he told himself. In spite of what others were recommending. Antonia and Carlo were entitled to have their opinions on the subject, of course they were, and Pietro Brazzi and Erika Morante were equally at liberty to make their own individual choices. His decision was a matter for himself as well and he would stick by it regardless of what anyone might say. He could imagine his sister's reaction in particular. Antonia would conclude that his reasons for persevering with the old man were sentimental, and she would promptly encourage a re-think. But he wouldn't consider such an about-turn and he would make this very plain to her. Sentimental reasons? Of course there were sentimental reasons he would tell her in his defence. No point in denying it. Guilty as charged and so forth. But there was method in his rationale as well and he would make her understand what it was. Franco was still a seasoned pro and he knew his way around the intricacies of negotiating and brokering like few others in the business did. A different agent might not necessarily bring such a quality to the table he'd tell his sceptical sibling. Especially someone younger than Franco. All well and good to advocate the virtues of new blood, but what if there was no substance behind all of that. And this was something Franco had in spades: experience, know-how, savoir faire. Years spent working behind the scenes for actors like Max had fostered such intrinsic qualities in the old trouper. Antonia would not be able to mount any reasonable argument in the face of such obvious plus points. Even if she tried she would not sway him in his determination to stick it out with what he knew and who he knew. Loyalty was an important thing. Franco had done his bit 15 years before; and for much of the time since. Now it was his turn.

He rang the bell and waited for his friend to come to the door. It was almost one o'clock. The appointment had been set for the hour mark and Max was a few minutes early as was his customary way. Franco would not be surprised by this. He knew Max very well – like the back of his hand as he often joked – and the latter's sense of punctuality was something he frequently commended.

No answer from him yet though so Max pressed the bell a second time, took a step back. A group of American tourists he'd seen a few minutes earlier in Via del Babuino passed close to where he was standing. They were led by a guide who described the artistic associations the charming street had developed over time. Puccini and Verdi were alluded to; as were Wagner and Debussy.

'In 1917 the famous Spanish painter Pablo Picasso worked here,' the smooth-talking chaperon informed his guests. 'The world-renowned Italian director Federico Fellini also lived here – at number 110 – with his wife Giulietta. As did the Italian painter Renato Guttuso. And Truman Capote came and settled in this area when he visited Rome. He wrote his short story Lola about a raven who lived with him at his apartment, which was located at number...'

'Hello Max,' Franco said in his familiarly cheery manner as he answered the door, 'I do believe you've lost weight since I last saw you. How many months ago was that?'

The older man looked tired and timeworn. He smiled softly as he invited Max inside, gazing for just a moment at the sightseers traversing his neighbourhood.

'Tourists, eh?' he remarked to his client behind the closed door, 'I can remember when this area first started to become popular with them and let me tell you that was neither yesterday nor the day before.'

'How are you Franco?' Max enquired. 'Did you have a good Easter?'

'It was reasonably good,' Franco replied impassively, 'my son came from Turin with his wife and two daughters for three days so, as you can imagine, we spent a good deal of time out and about in the city. On Sunday my daughter-in-law cooked dinner for us all. She insisted and it turned out to be a very bland portion of lamb let me tell you. On the next such occasion I will insist, and we will dine out instead.'

The two of them shared a hearty laugh about this.

'Come into the living room,' said Franco, 'my office is in need of some spring-cleaning and Mariella is not due again for...'

He examined his wristwatch uncertain of what arrangement was in place.

'A few more days yet I think,' he said, 'lately, I always seem to lose track of when she is booked to come in. A few weeks ago she arrived and I thought that it was an impromptu thing. I said to her 'Mariella, is this a spur-of-the-moment visit? I would much prefer if you followed whatever timetable we agreed on.' Sure enough though she corrected me about this. And let me tell you she can be quite a formidable lady when challenged. Since that time I've mostly steered clear of her when she is here, sat in other rooms, gone out for coffee; that sort of thing. I suspect she thinks that I'm cowering away from her. Recoiling at the mere hint of her presence; and you know what – I am.'

He winked good-humouredly as they sat down on a three seater sofa. He looked robust enough now, a little on the gaunt side perhaps, but was tanned and well-turned-out for their engagement. Perception is reality he used to tell Max over and over. From the very beginning of their relationship, the actor had this advice drummed into him whenever he went for auditions or recording sessions.

'The way people view you, and the way you present yourself, is the impression you'll leave behind. It's vital that impression is a positive one,' the agent sagaciously instructed.

The young actor argued this point at first.

'Why should it matter how I look?' he asked. 'The work is not visual. I'm acting from behind a microphone. Who's going to pay attention to what I'm wearing or whether I'm clean-shaven?'

'It matters because you are a professional performer; and a very gifted one at that,' Franco told him in response, 'your proficiency behind that microphone, which you refer to, should be complemented by the appropriate attire and appearance. If you do not dress respectfully Max, then do not expect to be treated respectfully. And respect in this business is of the essence. It elevates your name on lists and obtains for you the sort of reputation you want to have.'

Perhaps this is why he has chosen not to hold our meeting in his office today Max thought. On the previous occasion, it had been in a mess and Franco must have only become conscious of this fact after he left. The notion that it might still be in a similar condition, possibly even worse, was not an appealing one as far as he was concerned. It spoke volumes and corroborated some of the things that he'd heard. In spite of Franco's dapper apparel it was clear his livelihood was still in a slump. This nosedive of his was continuing and there was no sign he was pulling out of it. And the idea of him hiding in his own home from some glorified maid, who only occasionally bothered to clean the place up properly; well that was bordering on the ridiculous. Max began to revisit his earlier thoughts.

'You heard about Tullio Addobbati no doubt?' Franco said.

'Yes, I did,' answered Max, 'I didn't get to the funeral because we were working on the Proper Citizen at the time. Did you go?'

'I did. It was quite moving. Lots of very fine tributes paid to him and a large turnout by his friends and many others who he worked with.'

'I was sorry that I couldn't make it, but work.'

Franco's expression became more reflective.

'Let me tell you, I would like to be sent off that way myself,' he said. 'Like Tullio was. Warm eulogies, dear friends and people who I encountered over the years.'

'That day is in the far distance Franco. You have a good many years left yet.'

Franco smiled wistfully.

'Sometimes I wonder if I do Max,' he said, 'and other times I wonder if it would really be such a good thing if I had.'

'What do you mean by that?' Max asked.

'I'm talking about solitude Max, loneliness. Quite often days go by here and I see no one. I suppose I should be grateful that Mariella comes in every now and again. But she...well as I explained.'

'You have your work Franco, don't you? That gives you purpose. And besides that, you must still have a great many connections with people who respect you and value your company. Call on them. Meet them for a coffee or drink. Go out and enjoy yourself.'

'Yes, my work,' Franco said ponderously, and Max wondered if he would mention those former clients of his who had left recently. Pietro's departure must have smarted. And Erika's? Quite another degree of hurt surely.

Franco was not going to broach the subject though. Max decided he would not either.

'Speaking of which I forgot to ask you how the Proper Individual went,' Franco said.

'The Proper Citizen,' Max corrected.

'Yes, of course, the Proper Citizen. And was what's-his-name in the studio as difficult as ever?'

'You mean Giacomo Romano?'

'Yes, that's the one.'

'No more than usual. We don't see eye to eye as you know. Creative difficulties I suppose is the correct term. But, then again, creative seldom enters the equation when he's involved.'

Franco chuckled in a thoughtful way. He began to perk up somewhat.

'Max you are one-of-a-kind,' he said. 'You've always pushed yourself to the absolute limit, and you usually manage to push everyone around you as well.'

'I have you in part to thank for that,' Max replied with a grin, 'you taught me most of what I know. The rest of it I must have picked up off the side of the street.'

'That streak of perfectionism you have for one thing.'

'I think the majority of them would refer to it as my streak of obstinacy.'

'Perfectionism, obstinacy, whatever you choose to call it. From day one I could see how talented a voice actor you were. That first demo of yours that we sent out, it was a remarkable piece of work. You remember it?'

'You gave me a lengthy pep talk beforehand about the A-B-C's of voice acting as you called it. The piece was titled The Industrious Disposition of the Honey Bee and it took me four takes to get it right.'

'Three actually. I also gave you my lecture on the core elements of a good performance. You pretended not to be too bored by it.'

'You could have been a voice coach yourself Franco. God knows you understood it well enough.'

'Ah yes, but I would never have had the same amount of fun doing that.'

'Even so.'

'And in those early days you gave us all a preview of what was to come. I remember how you always wanted to fix the script yourself; of any grammatical errors or confusing phrases you came across.'

'You knocked that much out of me at least.'

'With a degree of difficulty as well,' Franco said jovially, 'I told you that the client isn't interested in anything else you can do beyond your performance. Discover the character in the copy and you'll be most of the way there.'

'Those were words of wisdom. I've never forgotten them.'

'I know you haven't. I do still follow your work you know.'

Max shifted uneasily in his seat.

'I'm a little anxious about this biotech narrative,' he said, 'those copies are often put together by inexperienced writers and they're pretty dull at best. There can be an awful lot of technical terms as well.'

'You'll be fine,' Franco said reassuringly, 'just remember you're still a character telling a story. Passion, power and profit is usually the angle they go for.'

'Yes, I know. Is it here for me to take?'

Franco shook his head.

'I'm afraid they haven't sent it over yet Max; something about revisions the managing director is insisting upon.'

'He wants more technical terms put in I bet.'

'And even if he does, you'll fare fine as usual.'

A brief silence came between them before Franco moved on to a more important subject from his perspective.

'Max,' he said hesitatingly, 'I don't know how closely you study your calendar, but it's almost that time of the year again.'

'The renewal of our contract? It's due soon?'

'Yes, it is.'

'Well then, I'll get to it as soon as I can.'

It was now Franco's turn to shift about uneasily. He stared at his client intently hoping for a more meaningful undertaking than this. It was not coming though in spite of his fixed gaze. Max did not look at him directly. Franco decided he would have to press the matter further.

'I know that I haven't been as dutiful in my work as I should be these past few months,' he said, 'things have been in a state of flux ever since Gabriella died. Well more than a few months now that I think of it. Gabriella is dead three years.'

Max nodded, said nothing.

'I have some new strategies I'd like to show you in the not too distant future,' Franco continued, 'I've been working on them in my office and, when they're complete, we can sit down and have a proper brainstorm.'

'Sounds good Franco,' Max replied, although the level of enthusiasm in his voice was hardly sky-high.

'Perfect,' said Franco, 'I think you'll like what you see. Hopefully, it will see us both into the 21st century. And beyond.'

He paused perceptibly for a moment before going on.

'I'm not planning on retiring any time soon you know,' he said resolutely, 'Tullio Addobbati did and six months later he got bad news from his doctor. Retirement to me would be practically the same as a slow death. I think I'd feel like the character in Umberto D. All I'd need then would be a dog named Flike and I'd be living an equivalent of that particular story.'

'I'm sure that won't happen Franco. There are a great many people in this industry who hold you in the highest regard. They won't suddenly forget your worth or the wealth of experience you possess.'

'I'm very glad to hear you say that Max. It's more than encouraging to hear it coming from you. It gives this old-timer a great deal of hope for the future.'

Franco reached for a packet of Nazionali cigarettes which was close at hand.

'My doctor of course tells me that I shouldn't, but...'

'We all have our soft spots. There's nothing wrong with the occasional craving.'

'True,' Franco agreed. He took a drag of the cigarette, inhaling slowly.

'So, was there anything else?' asked Max. 'Since you don't have the biotech script yet, would you mind sending it on to me as soon as you get it?'

'Of course I will. Along with the contract. Should be no more than a few days.'

'I'll get cracking on it,' Max said rising from the sofa. 'Nothing else then?'

'Nothing pressing. Just remember about the renewal.'

Max nodded. Franco rose to his feet and escorted him to the door.

'So Don Taylor is in town,' he observed. 'Here to make a film about Antonio Meucci. I wonder if it will turn out to be any good.'

'Who's to say,' said Max, 'perhaps it will.'

'Will you perchance be running into your counterpart at any point in time while he is here? I understand his wife has come with him for the shoot as well.'

Max had not told Franco about the publicity event in Piazza Santa Maria. Or about the dialogue coaching. For a moment he considered doing so, as he had with Antonia, but then chose not to. Why should he need to know he thought. It's only a bit of coaching. Not an audition or recording. And besides, he didn't arrange this either.

'Ah no Franco, I don't expect I will,' he replied lying badly. 'Don Taylor would be moving in very different circles to a lowly actor such as me.'

'A very fine actor you mean; one of the best voice actors I've had the privilege to work with,' Franco said clapping him on the back. He opened the door and walked out a few paces onto the street.

'So you'll promise to come see me sooner the next time?' he said. 'Don't leave it so long again. A client might very well do that. But not a friend.'

'I will,' Max told him. 'I'll put a date on my calendar.'

'Along with the one for the renewal,' Franco said reminding him just one last time. He smiled warmly but there was a slight pall of doubt registered in his countenance.

'Remember Max, great things still ahead of us,' he said as vigorously as he could manage. 'Soon now I'll have my second wind and I'll be...'

Max didn't catch the rest of what he had to say. A plethora of street sounds arose, coming between them. Franco's voice tailed off as he began to walk away.

ROME, OPEN CITY

It was a most pleasant day out and about in the Eternal City, well above the average temperature for this time of the year, and providence was certainly favouring Don and his family. The actor, his wife and brother began their excursion on Via Veneto, walking along the salubrious tree-lined pavement which curved up from Piazza Barberini to the gardens of Villa Borghese. They talked about where they should go, what sights should be taken in this first day in Rome. Some famous place names were suggested. A consensual wish list began to take shape and, as they ambled along the fashionable street, they attracted the attention of several waist-coated waiters, all seeking to lure the passers-by into the environs of their high-priced restaurants and cafes. Todd took it upon himself to issue a polite decline in the native tongue.

'No niente,' he said to the first few who approached them, even adding an apologetic, 'mi dispiace,' for good measure.

At the outset he was quite proud of his efforts, and justifiably so, as he pointed out to the other two. The younger of the Taylor brothers had brought a phrase book with him and studied it diligently on the flight from Los Angeles. He'd read that the locals in Rome appreciated all attempts at communication in their language, no matter how muddled such efforts might seem. His book also advised that pronunciation was not so difficult as the sounds used in spoken Italian could all be found in its English equivalent. It's true he thought when he first perused the paperback; it's really not that difficult. He looked forward to employing the specific terms recommended between the pages. One of these was mi dispiace, and he used it now for the sake of practise as much as for the impression of good manners it conveyed.

'Mee-dees-pya-che,' he intoned conscientiously. It sounded entirely passable as far as he could tell.

'No niente, mi dispiace,' he said a few more times before deciding to switch to the far more expedient niente by itself. They'd been encouraged to have a seat in a number of establishments within a short space of time, far too many by his reckoning, and, in spite of his erstwhile intentions to embrace the lingo, the expression had already grown tiresome and most certainly repetitive. Good manners he thought, enough of that already. None of them really give a damn about it anyway, and he wished there was a more comprehensive phrase which would deflect the solicitations they were continuing to encounter. His book, practical as it was, had not advised on a situation such as this. Nor had it offered any examples of how to employ more direct means of getting one's message across.

'Is it just me?' Todd questioned aloud as yet another niente was reeled off by him, 'do I seem incredibly emaciated all of a sudden? I was sure I had a hearty breakfast back in the hotel, but my buddies here seem to think otherwise.'

Don and Lee giggled at his rising irritation.

'I'm serious,' Todd continued, grumbling, 'once or twice is fine by me, but when I'm asked ten times, then it starts to bug me just a bit.'

'I think they're trying to wind you up little brother,' Don suggested playfully, 'this just isn't your day so far, is it? First it was Tom and now these guys.'

'We're not going to talk about him again already, are we?!' Lee said sounding peeved at the mere mention of that name.

'It wasn't me who had a set-to with him,' Todd said cutting in before his brother could reply, 'I was an innocent bystander compared to the way you were getting stuck in.'

'You called him a control freak Todd! That's hardly sitting on the fence, now is it?'

'He is a control freak. I was just stating the obvious. Niente, niente,' Todd told yet another dutiful attendant. 'I wonder what the Italian for pain in the neck is.'

'Or the bane of my existence?' said Don.

'I was referring to the waiter,' his brother informed him.

'So was I,' replied Don. He put his arm around Lee's waist, pulling her closer.

'Why, what's with this?' she enquired jokingly, 'are you trying to humour me all of a sudden Mr. Taylor?'

'Not at all Mrs. Taylor,' Don replied beaming, 'but in respect of that out-of-bounds subject…'

'Here we go…'

'I always think of the immortal words of Sam Goldwyn at times such as this. Old Sam said that you've got to take the bull between your teeth.'

'By the horns you mean?'

'Nope. Sam mixed it up as he sometimes tended to do. On occasion, Sam's English was about as good as Todd's Italian. But it has a degree of substance that funny turn of phrase, don't you think?'

'There's a certain irony to it I suppose,' Lee accepted.

'That's what I was thinking,' said Don.

Todd chewed on it for a moment.

'And that's what you did back there, is it?' he said. 'Took the bull between your teeth?'

'I think so. I hope some of it sticks this time round.'

'I wouldn't be so confident about that Don,' Todd said shaking his head, 'Tom is still going to snoop around as long as he's here. A week is more than enough for him to kick sand in a few faces, stir things up just the way he likes. His sightseeing and bonding with Vicki – so-called – will come to an abrupt end before long. Then expect the Tom Steiner we all know and adore to emerge. A leopard never changes its spots.'

'Sam Goldwyn couldn't have put it any better little brother.'

'You just watch out for yourself Don,' Todd implored, 'as Mr. Goldwyn also put it – he'll give you as much trouble as Mussolini had in Utopia. If you allow him to.'

They shared a collective laugh about this.

From the corner of his eye Todd caught a glimpse of just one more ardent hand readying himself as they drew closer to a café. The angular blonde gentleman looked as if he was having a good morning on the job: numerous chatty heads protruding from amongst the budding shrubs and miniature trees on the decking outside his place of employment. From inside there was also a discernible buzz and resonance drifting onto the street. Good for business all round, but there was room for a few more of course. There was always room for a few more, and Todd could make out how keen he was to entice them in; just as he had done with so many others. He considered the meagre expanse of his Italian vocabulary one last time. Niente came to mind again, but he was fed up of using that and, as for mi dispiace, he'd long dispensed with it. No, he decided, this time I'm going to say no on my own terms and I'm going to make it memorable somehow. But what to say, what to say. The solution to his problem presented itself in the form of one more Sam Goldwynism. Todd sniggered quietly to himself as he conjured it up. Deviously, he returned the other man's wide smile as they moved onto his patch.

'Prego,' the cordial member of staff said greeting them, 'table for three, is it? May I recommend that you join us for...'

Todd cut in on the sales pitch in double quick time. He delivered his reply in a very deft manner, as well as he'd hoped to do.

'No you may not,' he told the bamboozled-looking employee, 'include us out.'

The three of them explored the Villa Borghese gardens for a time and then visited the Galleria Borghese, which accommodated a considerable part of the Borghese collection. In the twenty-room gallery they saw works such as Truth Unveiled by Time by Gian Lorenzo Bernini, David with Goliath's Head by Caravaggio, Deposition by Raphael, and Titian's Sacred and Profane Love. In the open air of the park they admired the water clock, the Tempietto di Diana, the Villa Borghese Pinciana and the Alpini monument. There were a number of fountains in the grounds which caused Todd to make inquiries as to where the more celebrated Trevi fountain was. He referred to the Baroque structure as, 'the one used in that Fellini film with what's-his-name cavorting in the water with that Swedish bombshell.'

At Don's insistence, they caught a cab to the Trevi district and walked the rest of the way to the famous water feature. The actor was mindful of his wife's spell of illness, which had only passed a short time before, and he was anxious she should not over-exert herself. Lee for her part though was more than amenable to the opportunity of rambling about on foot. As a general rule of thumb, she preferred to do her sightseeing in a non-sequential, meandering sort of way, and was most definitely not one for the safe haven of escorted tours or visitors' guides. Outings of this nature – meaning daytrips in far-off or unfamiliar places – ought to be conducted in an entirely indiscriminate manner she believed. Maps, manuals and brochures were all well and good, but they were definitely forbidden once the act of promenading got underway, and she left her travelling companions in little doubt as to the dire consequences they faced if she happened to spot a Lonely Planet or Rough Guide. She was especially captivated by what she'd seen of Rome so far. The user-friendliness and proximity of places of interest was most appreciated by her.

'Everything is so accessible,' she remarked, 'it's like the city is at your fingertips and all you have to do is reach out and take hold of it. There's something tremendously open about it. Stretch out your hand and there's a famous fountain for you to dip it in. Extend your horizon in the least bit and an impressive monument lies in your path. Or a remarkable museum or gallery to be delved into. Rome is endearing itself to me very quickly. I think the two of us are going to get along famously.'

Her famous husband was enjoying himself as well. They all were in fact. Following their saunter through Trevi, Don and his loved ones decided to turn their attention to Piazza di Spagna where they planned to ascend the monumental stairway between the Piazza and the Trinità dei Monti church. Before this venture was undertaken though a much-needed respite was agreed upon and they took a breather at a pretty café adjacent to the foot of the Spanish Steps. From their open-air position they marvelled at the distinctive combination of architectural edifices which the long triangular square presented. For Todd there was little doubt that the most attractive feature was the Trinità dei Monti church at the top of the steps. In spite of his own confirmed scepticism on spiritual matters, he liked the configuration of churches in general, and the French Gothic church with Renaissance façade, which dominated the steep slope, was pleasing to his eye. Don, on the other hand, preferred structures which were less imposing than this. Before taking his seat, he inspected the fountain of a half-sunken ship just below the steps: the Fontana della Barcaccia. He liked its decorative pieces very much: suns and bees and coats of arms inserted on the surface, but reserved the lion's share of his admiration for the centrepiece: the stricken vessel itself, from which water spilled out in a calm and graceful way. Returning to the others, he declared it his favourite thing in the square. It was a strange looking piece, a curiosity without doubt, but there was an originality to it as well, and he wondered what its background was.

'Buildings and structures mean very little to me unless there's a history behind them,' he said, 'I suppose I need something tangible to remind me someone once sat down and planned how something like that would appear. It makes it more personal when there's a story to it. Not just bricks and mortar.'

Lee gave him a peck on the cheek.

'I like that idea as well,' she said, 'it's something that this city has a lot of – history. Individual stories set against the past. Like the one I read about John Keats dying here when he was only 25. He passed away somewhere close to the Spanish Steps I think. I wonder where it was?' she added, glancing sideways.

'John Keats?'

'The English Romantic poet. He had tuberculosis and his friends thought the warmer climate might improve his health.'

'Well they got that much wrong.'

'Apparently so. It's sad to think about. I read a poem of his once. The famous one about the nightingale. There was a line in it about him being half in love with death. It's haunting.'

'And extremely miserable as well,' her husband said, 'I can't imagine why anyone would be in love with death.'

'I think it's about resignation, acceptance,' Lee offered in response.

'I think it's morbid. I don't think we'll be seeing John Keats the movie anytime soon.'

'Tom certainly won't let you do it,' said Todd, 'we've all heard his thoughts on that subject.'

'You mean the unmentionable one, don't you?' Don said with a mischievous wink.

'Yeah, sorry. He whose name we shall not dare mention.'

'It's ok you boys, I can take it,' Lee said as she continued to look about the square.

'You've never died on screen Don come to think of it, have you?' said Todd, 'even in that science fiction film a few years ago when just about everyone else bought it. It was like an intergalactic version of Hamlet so many people died at the end.'

'Except for me. They wanted to do a sequel.'

'That's right. What happened to that?'

'Development hell little brother. Too many heads got involved and between them and all the contractual mind-fucking – pardon my French – a zero-sum game was played out. At one point I remember it was pitched as Blade Runner meets Soylent Green. In any event, it didn't happen. Nor is it ever likely to.'

'Soylent Green, eh? I think of all the actors I've seen, Charlton Heston does death the best. God knows he's died in enough films to last a lifetime...'

Todd stopped up short. Both men guffawed at his verbal gaffe.

'Yeah, I know,' he said, 'now that was an authentic Sam Goldwyn moment. Nothing contrived about it at all.'

A waiter arrived at their table and took their orders. Lee asked for a large coffee and small Quattro Stagioni pizza.

'What does Quattro Stagioni mean?' Todd asked the waiter.

'It means four seasons sir. The toppings are artichokes, olives, mushrooms and prosciutto. Parma ham as you would call it.'

'Well that sounds good to me. I'll have one of those as well, only in a larger size. We'll call it the long four seasons if you catch my drift.'

The waiter smiled politely and jotted the order down.

'And for you sir?' he asked turning his attention to Don.

'Anything you can recommend?' the actor enquired, his eyes fixed on the other man.

'The pasta di primavera is especially good today sir. Primavera in Italian means spring and you might say that it's an appropriate time to have this dish.'

'You talked me into it,' Don said nodding agreeably as he passed back the menu, 'I'll have an americano with that please. Make it a large one as well.'

The waiter scribbled quickly on his notepad. In an instant he went back indoors.

'Did you see what just happened there?' Don said. 'Did either of you notice?'

Both Todd and Lee replied no.

'He didn't recognise me,' Don said, 'and in fact I don't think anyone has so far today.'

'Are you sure? I thought when we were at the Trevi Fontain that group of Japanese tourists were paying attention to you.'

'No, they weren't. They were too busy taking photos and tossing coins.'

'It's because you were wearing shades and a baseball cap.'

'But I'm not now, am I? I have a theory as to why he didn't know me.'

'Possibly because he doesn't go to the movies?'

'He speaks almost perfect English. I think he goes to the movies,' Don said confidently.

Lee threw her eyes up to heaven.

'Since when is perfect English synonymous with the movies?' she inquired, 'there's a lot of really bad English in films if you ask me.'

'And in any case, they dub everything here,' Todd added. 'Subtitles are not the thing in this part of the world. Same goes for France, Germany and Spain.'

'I know that,' Don replied, 'but I guarantee you a guy like that, obviously well-educated, knows cinema. Probably goes on a regular basis.'

'You're in a very presumptive frame of mind today, aren't you?' said Lee.

'Not at all, I'm just saying he clearly didn't recognise me in spite of the explanation about the pasta and your four seasons. He had plenty of time to figure out who I was.'

'And the point to all of this is?'

Don smiled.

'It's the beard,' he said. 'Tom may not like it, but it works for me. I'm no one special all of a sudden. And you know what – I'm enjoying it this way.'

'You don't mean that,' Lee said stroking his hand where it rested on the table, 'and if there's one thing for sure it's this: you could never become just plain ordinary. You've done too much for that to happen. Topped the bill too many times to simply become anonymous.'

Don smiled at her affectionately.

'You're probably right,' he said, 'the only thing that could change all of that would be more dead ducks like the Proper Citizen. That and...well... the great leveller itself.'

Ok he thought. That's probably a bit too bleak. Better to lighten things up again.

'Or maybe I could start a Proper Citizen franchise,' he proposed roguishly. 'That would surely usher in the twilight of my career fast enough.'

'Don stop,' Lee giggled. 'If Tom heard you he'd probably have a heart attack.'

'We could ensure the great man's demise by forcing him to sit through the advance screenings,' Todd suggested, 'the papers would call it death by test screening.'

'Or death by preview.'

Lee went into hysterics at the idea of these macabre scenarios.

'You two are going to burn in hell for this,' she exclaimed, 'Tom may be bad but he wouldn't deserve that.'

'Are you sure?' Todd asked her. 'He might be very happy to go that way, on the job so to speak.'

'Todd!!'

'I wonder where the dead man walking is now,' said Don. 'Is it possible he's already found his way to Cinecittà?'

'There's every chance of it,' said Todd, 'sparks will fly if he runs into David Cousins.'

'What's Tom's problem with David Cousins anyway?' asked Lee.

'Problems as in plural,' Todd replied, 'a few years ago Cousins had him thrown off a set...well, perhaps that's too strong. At any rate, Tom was requested to leave.'

'He was thrown off,' Don interjected, 'an unstoppable force met an immoveable object; except that the immoveable object happened to have a sufficient number of flunkies at the time to do his bidding.'

'Could he really do that?' said Lee. 'Tom is a pretty powerful man. I'd have imagined kicking him off a film set was hardly the best career move.'

'It happened, but he never did anything about it afterwards,' Don told her. 'David Cousins' career went on an unexpected hiatus.'

Todd sat forward in his chair.

'Don, what Tom said to you back in the hotel about David Cousins, about him being the producer and all of that? Is it possible he might have something when he says Cousins will sooner or later fall back into his old habits? The excessive amount of takes and everything else.'

'He also mentioned something about him making grown men cry,' added Lee.

Don chuckled at this.

'Don't worry you two,' he assured them, 'David Cousins is not going to push me around because I am who I am and he knows that. And in case you want to know who he is, I'll tell you: he's a director resuming his career after a lengthy lay-off. His approach, for that reason, will be cautious, softly-softly. He will not want to tread on anyone's toes. Least of all mine, and even if he does attempt it; if I get the faintest hint of anything heavy-handed, I'll make certain it is a never-to-be-repeated occurrence as far as Echo of Passions goes.'

'I'm glad to hear you say that Don,' Todd said visibly relaxing again.

The waiter and one of his colleagues arrived with their dishes.

'The coffees in a moment,' he promised.

'Remember to make them large ones,' Todd reminded him as he went back inside.

'No problem,' he called back.

Don plunged his fork into the pasta bowl and began to stir the bow-tie shapes around.

'As long as we're on the subject of Mr. Cousins, when am I due out at the studio?'

'Day after tomorrow,' his brother replied as he sliced his pizza into small portions. 'Meantime, as in tomorrow, you have that publicity thing to attend.'

'Is that really necessary?' asked Don. 'Is there any way I can get out of it?'

'You promised to do it Don. It's a promotion thing for the Proper Citizen; as well as pre-promotion for Echo of Passions.'

'But I'm doing pre-promotion with Jen Carrington in Cannes. Isn't that enough?'

'If there was a Cannes, Italy I might say yes; but since it's in France, it won't quite pass muster for the people here. It will be quick Don. Just an hour or so. And it'll give you an opportunity to meet Mr. Pellegrino.'

'The actor who is my voice here, right?'

'That's the one.'

'Do you know if he sounds like me?'

'I honestly don't know,' replied Todd, 'yours probably isn't the only one he does by the way. I read somewhere that these dubbing actors often do several voices. There was one guy, for example, who did John Wayne, Kirk Douglas, Richard Widmark and Lee Marvin. The same guy! And one lady did Kim Novak, Elizabeth Taylor, Audrey Hepburn, Judy Garland and Natalie Wood! It's quite a collection, isn't it?'

Don looked unimpressed, heaved a sigh.

'Well I just hope my guy doesn't have too many others on his slate,' he said, 'I'd hate to sound like Richard Widmark or Lee Marvin.'

After lunch, they planned a visit to the Colosseum, which Todd, in particular, was keen to see. But first there was the small matter of climbing the prominent steps in front of them. It was 2 o'clock and the piazza was still jam-packed with people. The steps had ramps and stairs which intersected, opened out like a fan, and were adorned with hundreds of vases of flowering azaleas for the annual Mostra delle Azalee. Colours of pink, white and red were prominent, and Lee's declaration that the Scalinata looked like, 'something out of a daydream,' didn't seem at all out of place. At the corner, to the right of the steps, she paused for a moment close to a cream-coloured building, studied a banner sign which hung on its side wall. It read: *Keats Shelley Memorial Association*.

'This must be it,' she said to the others. 'This must be the place where John Keats passed away. Let's have a look inside.'

'What about the steps?' asked Don.

'They'll still be here when we come out,' Lee replied.

Don and Todd began to go up the steps, but making headway was difficult because of the large crowds. Don stepped on a German tourist's hand by accident. The young fräulein screamed out in pain. Her shrill expression of discomfort caught the attention of a number of people close by. Some of them rose to their feet to see what had happened. The German lady herself stood up, massaging her aching digits. Her countenance of displeasure transformed however when she recognised the face before her, despite his shaggy appearance. The well-known name triggered a rapid convergence. Don's secret was out. His brief spell of anonymity at an end, the actor smiled graciously as bodies gathered around him. Pictures were snapped, brochures were thrust in his direction for signing.

His family members stood back, watched him work the crowd. For Lee it was a familiar sight. She'd seen this many times before; did not mind delaying as long as it was not too drawn-out. As if mindful of this, Don peered attentively in her direction. He shrugged his shoulders, mouthed an apology as he smiled for photos.

'Can't be helped,' his wife whispered back. She was well used to this scene and understood what it meant for the present moment in time. Their visit to Keats' house would have to wait just a while more.

Brief Encounter

Max got up early the following morning and went for a jog in the gardens of Villa Doria Pamphili close to where he lived. His exercise regime consisted of a half hour energetic blitz in the grounds of the landscaped park and, after that, a more relaxed stroll back to his apartment in Monteverde. He seldom altered the pattern of this schedule and only bowed to change or deferment on the rare occasion. Sometimes a pressing assignment intervened and he was forced to prioritise it ahead of his workout. A spell of inclement weather could also come along from time to time. The previous December he'd gone a full 11 days without exercise on account of some harsh seasonal weather. The festive period, with its associated excesses, served to accentuate a feeling of impatience regarding the dearth of activity. He felt listless and longed for a quick return to his usual routine. He was a creature of habit when it came to such day-to-day matters preferring to avoid rests or disruptions of any sort. Nor was he one to make sudden adjustments to the route he normally stuck to when out jogging in the park. The particular track he frequented took him through the two sections of the extended villa grounds, which were divided by a road running partially in a natural defile. There was a welcome atmosphere of peace and quiet in that location, far away from the din and commotion of the surrounding city, and this sense of calm engendered a feeling of security and composure. At times, it felt like being in a far-off place; the estate had an ethereal quality to it with its pictorial expanse of undulating hills, lakes and immutable pines. No cars or mopeds thankfully. Perfect peace which was seldom disturbed.

8.45 in the a.m. his wristwatch read as he completed his circuit. Lots of time yet he thought as he decided to extend his ambit to the campus of the American University of Rome. The university grounds were less than a kilometre away and it would take no more than a few minutes to get there. Time was not of the essence just yet. The appointed hour of one o'clock was still a good way off. And, in any case, he'd been reminded about the all-important rendezvous the evening before. By a most unexpected source.

The telephone in his kitchen rang at precisely 9 p.m. He'd only just finished dinner and was drying some dishes.

'Pronto?' he said throwing the towel over his shoulder.

'Could I speak to Max Pellegrino please,' the tentative voice on the other end asked. The words were enunciated carefully so as to be as intelligible as possible.

'Yes, this is he,' Max replied switching directly to the required language.

'Ah…hello Max…my name is Tom Steiner,' the accented voice said persisting with the measured delivery, 'I represent Don Taylor.'

A concise pause succeeded this announcement.

'Meaning that I'm his agent,' Tom added as clarification.

'Yes, I understand that,' Max said, 'as his agent you act on his behalf in film deals and so forth. You promote the interests of your client and defend them also, if needs be.'

'That's absolutely correct,' came the other man's response as he allowed his manner of expression to loosen up. 'You have a very good command of English I have to say.'

'Thank you.'

'I'm afraid I don't speak any Italian myself,' the agent said apologetically, 'this conversation will have to take place in your second language if you don't mind.'

'Not at all.'

'I think that getting hold of a new language is a truly admirable pursuit by the way,' Tom said matter-of-factly. 'My own daughter, Vicki, for example. I always say to her how useful Spanish would prove to be, on account of where we live, but being the wilful teenager that she is, she doesn't listen to me. I think Spanish cuisine would be of more interest to her than Spanish verbs.'

'Learning a language isn't an easy thing,' Max observed. 'It takes a lot of time. A good deal of patience too.'

'Well I respect anyone who has done it as well as you have.'

'Thank you again,' Max replied as he attempted some hasty guesswork regarding the call.

'Let's get down to brass tacks here Max,' Tom continued, 'tomorrow you're attending this photo op in...'

He rummaged for the place name but was unable to remember it.

'Trastevere,' Max prompted.

'That's it. These publicity events are effective interactions if they are used well. If not though, they're a total waste of time.'

'You don't seem to be very enthusiastic about it.'

'Well I'm not the one responsible for its scheduling. Don's brother manages his affairs and also handles PR. He agreed to it with what's-his-name?'

'I'm afraid I don't know anything about the circumstances behind it,' said Max. 'Mr. Taylor's brother contacted the studio where I do some of my work. I was invited to meet him at the Trastevere occasion.'

'As an introduction for the dialogue coaching you might be helping him out with?'

'That's my understanding Mr. Steiner, yes.'

'Call me Tom by the way. Now look Max, I don't normally go quite this far in the representation of my clients, and I wouldn't necessarily want Don to know about this call if you get my meaning.'

'I understand Mr. Steiner...Tom. I won't say anything about it when we meet.'

'I'm very glad to hear that Max. Well, it's about one of tomorrow's components. Unfortunately, as you may have heard, The Proper Citizen hasn't quite been the commercial or critical success that Don, or I, had hoped for. We both of us invested a lot of time and faith in the project, but sometimes, even with the best will in the world, these things don't pan out the way you want them to.'

'What a pity, and I thought it was very good,' said Max.

'That's very illuminating Max. But you see right there is one of the things I wanted to talk to you about in advance of tomorrow.'

'About The Proper Citizen?'

'Yes. There's no other way of saying this, so I'll just come out and say it – if the topic of conversation happens to move on to that particular subject, I would ask that you not volunteer an opinion about the film to my client.'

'I don't understand.'

'I simply don't want you to say what you thought about it,' Tom said candidly, 'good, bad or indifferent. The fact that you like it is just fine; between you and me it's not an issue. The problem though is that my client is in a sensitive place right now. I want him to put the disappointment of that film behind him once and for all. In an ideal world I wouldn't have him do any further publicity on it. But the thing, as you know, is the film hasn't opened in this country yet so...'

'It makes promotion an obligation.'

'That's exactly it Max. I'm glad we're on the same wavelength.'

'But what if he asks me what I thought of it?' Max enquired. He considered it a legitimate question and a likely scenario.

'Just try and avoid the subject Max. As best you can. You know of the phrase to beat around the bush I imagine. If Don does ask, tell him yours is a very methodical kind of work, that it's difficult to get a feel for a film. If you have to, feel absolutely free to bore him to tears with details about what it is you do in the studio. My client has never exactly savoured post-production work so that ought to switch him off very quickly.'

A telling chuckle emanated from the agent's end of the phone line.

'I'm sure I can come up with some uninteresting stories,' Max assured him, 'I've worked in the dubbing business for 15 years now and...'

'There was another thing Max,' Tom said cutting him off in mid-sentence. 'The other component to tomorrow, as you realise, is the movie Don is due to start shooting here soon.'

'The Antonio Meucci film.'

'That's it. Now about this dialogue coaching that you may be assisting with – has anyone gone into the specifics of it with you?'

'Actually, no,' said Max, 'the brother you see – Mr. Taylor's brother – expressed an interest in obtaining my services because I do his voice here in Italy. I think he said I'd be best placed to help Mr. Taylor. According to the studio.'

'So you never spoke directly to Mr. Taylor about this, the brother I mean?'

'No, as I said no particulars have been discussed yet. I assumed the

Trastevere introduction would be the first step.'

'Don't you have an agent yourself?'

Max thought of Franco, recalled the disorder in his office.

'I do,' he said, 'but he's getting old and I...'

'That's ok,' said Tom, 'I don't need to know about your personal affairs.'

The agent fell silent as he pondered matters to himself. Max speculated as to what he might ask for next. What is this man's reason for wishing to talk about something that might not happen he wondered. Is he trying to prevent it from taking place? He decided to move that particular discussion forward.

'I expect he wants to sound as accurate as he can,' he suggested, 'his voice and accent that is. Authenticity is something we also do our best to produce in the studio. It gives the film more credibility. The audience appreciates the effort even though you might not think it.'

His remarks were met by a noisy clearing-of-the-throat sound as Tom liberated a glob of mucus.

'It goes back to The Proper Citizen again Max,' he said picking up his train of thought, 'my client needs a shot in the arm in every sense of the word. You might not credit this, but even a big star like Don Taylor needs his confidence boosted from time to time. It's not an ego thing mind. He's every bit as human as you and I.'

'I didn't doubt that,' said Max, and he was immediately aware that a hint of sarcasm had crept into his response.

Tom didn't seem to pick up on it.

'He's a sensitive guy,' he continued, 'although he wouldn't admit that to anyone, least of all me. And so, as far as the dialogue coaching is concerned, what I think is important, above everything else, is that he needs to believe it's going well. And that he's going to be wonderful in this role.'

'I'm sure he will be.'

'So if he does ask for your assistance Max, whether it's on the set or on a one-to-one basis, I'd like for you to tell him that it sounds perfect. At all times. I'd greatly appreciate that. We all would.'

'So, for that, I am to offer an opinion?' Max said, and this time the sarcasm in his tone was unmistakable. The agent must have detected it now he thought.

'Once again I'm happy to note we're on the same wavelength,' Tom said, and it wasn't apparent he had. Max found this all the more annoying. He decided to express himself in a more direct way.

'So it's of no consequence if he fails to nail it, as the phrase goes,' he said.

Tom laughed tersely in response. Finally, he'd picked up on the irony.

'Like I said before Max, you have a very impressive command of English,' he said dryly, 'and the answer to your previous question is like this: it's of no consequence whether Don nails it or not. The film won't be marketed on its linguistic merits or the accent employed by its leading man. It'll be promoted as a Don Taylor movie. That'll be its main selling point. And by the way, the authenticity of an accent is not the so-very critical matter you seem to think it is. The film-going community don't pay any attention to that. I know they don't. And I've been in this business over 30 years. We've all seen Amadeus and that worked just fine. Eight Oscars could not have been that wide of the mark.'

'I've only seen it in Italian actually,' Max said.

Tom ignored this.

'Oh and Max, one more thing,' he added, 'I imagine they told you to turn up ahead of the time tomorrow.'

'They did,' said Max. 'I always do.'

'That's good. So we'll see you then. And Max – remember.'

'I know. Mr. Taylor isn't to hear a word about this.'

'Mum's the word, eh?'

'Mum's the word.'

Max left his apartment just before midday and travelled the short distance to Trastevere on foot. The neighbouring 13th district of Rome, on the right bank of the Tiber, seemed an unusual location for the holding of a publicity event as far as he was concerned. Especially for someone of Don Taylor's renown. True, the rione was part of the centro storico, but it had a different character to the rest of the city with its labyrinthine alleys and medieval houses. The area around Piazza Santa Maria was especially distinctive for these narrow winding thoroughfares; the square itself lacked the expanse of other more accessible ones on the left bank. The mix of street vendors, students and prospective artists gave the place a bohemian flavour. Cobbled streets intertwined and were remarkable for the liberal extent of ventilating laundry adorning them. The district retained its working class independence and was most certainly no Trevi or Prati. Max wondered why it had been chosen for a film star about to embark on a major production in the country's leading studio. Was it a superficial exercise for the sake of appearances he wondered. Nothing more than a hasty going-through-the-motions exercise to put Don Taylor on view for his adoring public? Or was there another reason for its selection? He couldn't get his head around it. Trastevere was fashionable, unquestionably diverse, but it was also curiously out-of-the-way. Off the beaten track as the term went.

A couple of happy-go-lucky teenagers whizzing past him on mopeds changed the pattern of his thoughts. He was still annoyed about the previous evening, about the phone call. Why had it been necessary for this self-important agent to contact him? Did agents in Hollywood micro-manage to this extent? And what about the requests he'd made regarding the Proper Citizen and dialogue coaching? Don't talk about that subject and say that the other one is just fine even if it isn't true. It smacked of arrogance and condescension. He didn't appreciate the agent's quip about being in the business 30 years. Or his prompt about showing up on time. I'm a professional as well he thought. Not some greenhorn or sloppy amateur who needs reminding about punctuality.

The customary boom from the cannon on the Janiculum Hill told him it was midday. He was already at the appointed place. Trastevere's focal square was normally a popular spot for mums with strollers, chatting locals and guidebook-toting tourists, but today the piazza had a very different feel to it. At the lower extremity, the end opposite its most prominent building, the Basilica di Santa Maria, a temporary wooden stage had been constructed for the event. From the position of the octagonal fountain (across from the age-old church) frontward, the square was divided by two horizontal lines of interlocking steel barriers. Down this narrow passage Don Taylor would make his way to the platform greeting fans and well-wishers on either side. Access to the structure could only be gained if one had the say-so of a rather dour-looking security guard who stood at the opening. The fellow would have to be approached in due course, but, as of yet, there was no need to go up so early. It would be pointless to wait backstage for that length of time so Max decided to sit down on the steps of the old Roman fountain. He pretended to people-watch.

A respectably-sized crowd began to form within the boundaries of the two allocated areas. At first the spectators trickled in leisurely, and in small groups, but after the half-hour mark an increase in their volume became more obvious. The majority of them were in the 15-55 age bracket. There was a large contingent of the 20 and 30-somethings. Members of the print media assembled in a separate section close to the front. A few of the more opportunistic ones remained at the back supposing, as they did, that Don Taylor would enter the square at this point. Single lens cameras were primed, the amount of light was measured with intricate-looking gauges. On the makeshift stage, in front of them all, a colourful master-of-ceremonies got his pre-arranged routine underway. The crowd did not require much encouragement and they responded enthusiastically to his every prod and refrain. As the time of Don's arrival drew ever closer, the tempo was upped and they were whipped into a frenzy of exhilaration.

'Who is the greatest film star in the world?' the animated emcee asked.

'What is the name of the silver screen's most celebrated actor?' he probed.

The much repeated name echoed around the piazza.

At 12.45 Max decided it was time to proceed to the behind-the-scenes area where Don and his party were due before taking to the stage. He'd waited for what he believed to be a reasonable length and had got an opportunity to see the burgeoning mass. It was palpable and it could only be caused by someone of Don Taylor's fame. Spirits were high and some good-natured trades were taking place between those who'd arrived early, acquiring optimum viewing positions in the process, and their more tardy counterparts. In a handful of cases gestures were animated and a small amount of jostling took place. But on the whole it was amiable. Nothing disagreeable in sight.

Max drew up beside the towering security guard at the entry point. He introduced himself.

'My name is Max Pellegrino,' he said, 'I'm meant to go backstage before Mr. Taylor and his group arrive.'

The square-jawed officer consulted an inventory he had to hand.

'Don't see you here,' he said after a quick examination. 'Was your name added at the last minute?'

'No, I don't think so,' said Max, 'I was invited a few weeks ago. Mr. Taylor's brother contacted the studio where I work. I'm an actor also.'

'Would I know you from anything?'

'I wouldn't think so,' Max replied. 'I mostly do voice acting.'

The hulking security man considered this for a moment.

'Not the sort of thing you can put a face to so, huh?' he said.

'I guess not,' said Max. 'Look it's important that I get up there before Mr. Taylor arrives. It's arranged for me to meet him before he goes on stage and...'

'I'll contact my boss,' the other man said reaching for a walkie-talkie fastened to the belt of his pants. He clicked a button and turned away. Max glanced about uneasily, attempting to listen in on the conversation. All he could hear from the other end was a series of crackling noises. From the corner of his eye, he noticed a small boy staring at him. He gave the youngster a smile. This was reciprocated with a friendly wave.

'All right, you're good to go,' the security guard told him.

'Thank you,' said Max. He felt mightily relieved.

'I'm sorry for the misunderstanding. It seems there is another more up-to-date list apart from the one I have. Naturally, I'm the last one to know about it.'

'It couldn't be helped,' Max said politely as he went through heading straight towards the stage. He saw the small boy pull on his father's jacket as he walked past. The parent dropped his head, listening to his son's question.

'Daddy, who is that? Is it anybody famous?' the kid enquired pointing in Max's direction.

The father looked at Max quickly, then shook his head.

'I don't think so son,' he replied. 'He might be one of the organisers. Or perhaps he's a newspaper man.'

There were additional members of security backstage and they were joined by a number of staff from a well-known public relations company in Rome which was handling the campaign for the Proper Citizen. Also in attendance were two representatives from a distribution company which had the even more onerous task of marketing the film.

'What did you think of it?' one of them asked Max after he'd been introduced by an associate from the PR firm. The actor remembered Tom Steiner's request. It seemed to him the instruction only applied to the agent's client. No one else. He felt free to respond honestly.

'I liked it,' he said in a forthright manner, 'perhaps in terms of length it could have been shortened somewhat.'

'Tell me about it,' she commented, 'if it was up to me, I'd have the fucker sent back to the editing room and it wouldn't see the light of day again until an hour minimum was gone. 3 hours is way too much to give over to that kind of hokum. Less is more as they say and life is definitely far too short.'

She looked at him more closely, measuring his reaction.

'You of all people must surely agree with that,' she said. 'Doesn't it make your work a lot easier if the film isn't a Gone with the Wind or Ben Hur?'

'The job is repetitive and it can be monotonous,' Max agreed, 'but sometimes a longer film presents fewer problems than a short one. It depends on the complexity of scenes and the amount of overlapping that takes place. A fast-moving comedy, for example, could be just as difficult as a political film like this one.'

'Well, give me the comedy any day of the week,' the distribution lady said, 'the only memorable thing about the Proper Citizen for me was the end credits. Of course, officially-speaking, and in the capacity of my work, I'll say that it's a wonderful example of contemporary cinema with a profound and important social message. I get to be quite a different person when it comes to my job. Almost schizophrenic you might say. I imagine we all do where work is concerned. Act it out a bit.'

'I guess you're right about that,' said Max. 'From time to time there's a part we have to play. Sometimes the performance is pushed on us.'

A sudden flurry of activity and burst of sound told them something was happening outside in the square. On stage, the vigorous emcee went into overdrive.

'He's arriving!' he roared at the top of his voice. 'Don Taylor will be amongst us any moment now!!'

The appearance of a white stretch limo heralded the film star's entrance into the piazza. The long vehicle was skilfully manoeuvred into position and, amidst flashing cameras and blaring music (The Beatles' version of Twist and Shout), Don emerged saluting the multitude. Dressed in a tanned leather jacket, and chic pair of khakis, he was flanked by his wife, brother, and agent.

'Let's hear it for Don!' the emcee boomed as the actor began to make his way towards the stage. Progress was deliberately unhurried as he worked the crowd expertly moving from side to side of the manufactured passageway. Outstretched hands were gratefully shaken, individual photos willingly facilitated. It was all very deft and co-ordinated, but successful in its express purpose. Don beamed broadly as he pressed flesh up close and personal. All very exciting indeed thought Max who was peering from around the corner of the stage. He recognised Don's wife from pictures he'd seen. The younger man must be his brother he supposed. And as for the other person, he could only guess this was his agent; the man he'd conversed with less than 24 hours before. Or rather, the man who'd dictated to him.

'Well, you've got to hand it to Don,' the distribution lady said, 'he certainly knows what people want. And gives it to them in spades.'

Fifteen to twenty minutes went by before Don and his entourage finally got backstage. The actor arrived in first and was offered a fruit juice which he thankfully accepted. Then came his wife, brother and agent who were also handed refreshments. Don handed his glass back to the pretty blonde attendant, glanced around quickly.

'Hello everyone,' he said, 'I'm very glad to be here. It's good to see you all.'

Introductions were the next order of business, pleasantries were passed back and forth. The actor took a keen interest in what the public relations people had to say to him about how the publicity machine operated in Italy. The distribution people he spoke to next, joking about how their work was cut out.

'I'm afraid I've given you a difficult task this time,' he said casually, 'a poisoned chalice to be more precise. What kind of miracles can you work here in Rome? Could the Pope be prevailed upon to do something for us?'

This drew some good-natured laughter all round. The distribution lady went into character as she'd promised she would.

'It's often the case, we find, that a film which hasn't performed in the States the way it deserved to do, fares much better in Europe,' she offered. 'Audiences here are much more receptive to this kind of entertainment. It's not so much that the film-going public are more high-brow but that they're…better acquainted with alternative expressions of culture and cinema. Take the French with Godard and Resnais for example. Here in Italy we have Pasolini and Bertolucci.'

'Jesus! Was it really that bad?' Don asked humorously.

'Not at all,' she replied, without missing a beat, 'I found it to be a very worthy piece. There was so much that your critics in America seemed to overlook.'

'The film itself for one thing,' said Don. He turned his attention to Max.

'And who is this? Another one of your colleagues?'

'This is Max Pellegrino. He's the actor who provides the voice for your films in Italy.'

'Aha! So you are the man!' said Don taking Max's hand and shaking it enthusiastically. 'I've heard a good deal about you, though sadly I've never caught any of our work together.'

He smiled warmly and called out to his wife.

'Hey honey this is the guy who is my voice here,' he told her. Lee nodded an acknowledgement as Max said hello. Todd was also introduced.

'Say maybe you should be the one doing the talking out there,' Don suggested to him. Max laughed at the notion.

'It's you they'll want to hear,' he said.

'Though seriously,' Don said, 'and we were talking about this earlier...' He winked at his wife.

'Am I easy to do?'

'You're not difficult,' Max answered directly.

The star looked puzzled by this.

'They say that imitation is the sincerest form of flattery,' said Tom as he moved in to their space. He shook Max's hand.

'Hi, I'm Don's agent Tom Steiner. We are always honoured to meet the home-grown talent when abroad. The Italian film industry has a very proud history. I understand the dubbing industry here is second to none.'

'Thank you,' said Max, but he had no great desire to talk to this man. He noticed Don was still looking perplexed and concluded an elaboration was necessary.

'What I mean to say Mr. Taylor is that you articulate very well,' he offered by way of an explanation. 'What you say is always clear and that helps a great deal in the studio.'

'Is that a fact?'

'Yes, it certainly is. We have some very fine people working in our studios, but no two actors are exactly the same. Some are more difficult to do than others.'

'Ah, I see. And what about those dodgy Asian monster movies I used to see as a kid? The most frightening thing about them I remember was the way the dialogue was always a few seconds behind.'

'It was the same with a lot of the martial arts movies in the 60's and 70's,' said Todd. 'They moved their mouths like they were shot full of amphetamines. All that came through in English was the least amount of words. I understand it has something to do with the fact that languages like Chinese are structurally different to our own.'

'They were poorly done in any case,' said Max. 'How ever dissimilar two languages might be, there's much that can be done in the studio to overcome such difficulties. The films you mention were probably dubbed too quickly. Without any great technical attention or experience. That doesn't happen here.'

'I'm relieved to hear it,' Don said cheerfully.

'Yes, there would be nothing worse than for the audience to hear my voice continue after your mouth had closed,' said Max, 'or to see your lips move after my voice had finished.'

'Yeah, I guess not. I would hate for that too. Of course for my next film it should be easier, shouldn't it? Meucci was Italian after all.'

Max shook his head.

'It won't be of great importance,' he said. 'What might be of more significance is your beard, which I assume you've grown for the role. That will make it easier.'

'Why would that be?' asked Don.

'Because the audience won't be able to see your lips as clearly.'

'Very good,' said Don. 'I like your beard too by the way.'

He smiled deliberately at his agent.

'You see Tom! It's already paying dividends. And as for death – that must be a real cinch to do. Right Max?'

Lee and Todd laughed at this. Tom tried hard not to frown.

'You speak English very well,' Don said to Max.

'Thank you. And do you have any Italian?'

'I'm afraid not. I know how to say hello but beyond that…you'll have to teach me a few phrases before I…'

He was interrupted by one of the public relations people hovering close by.

'Mr. Taylor sir. The emcee is about to introduce you. If we could have you over here so you'll be ready to go on stage.'

She pointed to a position where five wooden steps led up to the podium.

'No problem,' said Don. 'Are you all coming up?'

'It's not necessary Mr. Taylor. If you, your wife and brother, and Mr. Steiner go on that will be more than enough.'

'And what about my friend here?' Don said drawing attention to Max.

'He only came here to meet you Don,' Tom interrupted.

Don did not accept this.

'Well we could have done that any old place, couldn't we?' he said. 'What do you say Max? As long as you're here, you might as well come up and see the fireworks.'

Max was uncertain.

'I wasn't expecting to appear with you,' he said.

'Come on Max,' Don said insistently. 'It'll be like a slice of Hollywood on the Tiber.'

'Well ok then. If you want me to and it's not a problem.'

'That's the spirit. This is your public too. Why shouldn't they get to see you?'

Don and his group were escorted to the foot of the steps. Max waited with them as the emcee built his introduction up to a crescendo.

'He is the star of the soon-to-be-released The Proper Citizen,' he exclaimed. 'He is here to portray our own Antonio Meucci in a film to be released next year.'

'Say Max, did anyone ever tell you that you sound like me?' Don asked as he rested against a handrail.

'No. I don't think so,' replied Max.

'How many years have you been doing my voice?'

'Since 1983. Twelve.'

'Never once in all those years?'

'I don't have a recollection of anyone ever saying it to me.'

'That's extraordinary. Don't you think?'

'Why?'

'Because I think you sound like me Max. I think you're a good match for me.'

'I think he is as well,' Lee agreed.

'Not many people have ever heard your voice Mr. Taylor. Only those of us in the studio really. Apart from that, it's very probable the majority of your fans don't know what you sound like.'

Don nodded his head.

'Well personally, I don't think they're going to be too shocked out there Max. Because, like I said, I think you're an acoustic dead ringer for me.'

'Mr. Taylor! Time to go up!' a voice from behind prompted.

The emcee's words rang out clear and loud.

'Let's give a rousing welcome for...DON TAYLOR!!'

Don paused for a moment before going up the small flight of steps.

'Ready?' he asked the others.

His eyes met Max as he reached for the handrail.

'It's going to be good working with you Max,' he said. 'I look forward to the things we'll do with my voice.'

'Ladies and gentlemen, boys and girls, it gives me great pleasure to present to you the most famous film star in the world. The one and only...DON TAYLOR!!'

'Chowww!' Don said energetically as he took to the mike. His appearance on stage was met with the anticipated gusto of the multitude which continued to shout its approval in spite of the iffy pronunciation. Some responded with their own ciaos; others fired off flash photography.

'Ciao Don.'

'Benvenuti a Roma.'

'Ti amo Don!! Ti amo!!'

'Chowwwwwww!' Don repeated more ardently than before. The elongated w he employed caused some mild-mannered giggling amongst his fans. Even so, they roared their lusty appreciation.

'Ciao Don. Ciao amico.'

The star, suitably emboldened, decided to take a stab at a thank-you. His grazie, regrettably, was every bit as mangled as his ciao. A few more of these abominations followed, each one as painful as the last; but the throng persisted with their applause and acclaim. Notwithstanding the several crimes against proper pronunciation.

Max watched and listened. He heard the verbal bloopers as well. Poor guy he thought, he certainly didn't get any coaching before going on here. And why is he drawing out the words like that? Any more stretched and they'll be downright rubbery.

He clapped through the contorted ciaos and garbled grazies like everyone else, but began to wish he hadn't come on stage. It was not the enjoyable experience he'd hoped it would be. He felt awkward, out of place. He didn't belong here, in spite of what Don had said. This wasn't his public. It was Don's. It would always be this way. It didn't matter if the actor couldn't distinguish a ciao from an arrivederci. Or tell apart a prego from a per favore. All that mattered was that he was the man, the star, the here-and-now. The rapture and euphoria was his and his alone. No one else there counted or carried any weight in this moment. Not the balding emcee spewing out an infinite amount of accolades and platitudes. Not the pretty wife who almost certainly stood by her spouse's side on all such occasions. Or the deferential younger brother stroke manager. Nor the fastidious agent who seemed to have an aversion for the direction his client's career was taking. And, most definitely, not the unidentified other guy standing at the back of the platform. A spot where he now hoped he would not be seen at all. Hollywood on the Tiber Max thought. He no longer wanted to see it. He wasn't part of it. It was exactly what the father in the crowd had told his son. He wasn't anybody famous. There was only one person here who fitted that bill. The tumult was for him alone. No one else. For the star. For the star. For the star.

Another thought popped into Max's head then. And he felt absolutely ashamed about it.

THE FALLEN IDOL

Lee Taylor decided that Friday morning and afternoon were to be given over to some badly needed shopping time, a pursuit she had not had an opportunity to indulge since arriving in Rome. She'd enjoyed doing the tourist bit up to this point, nothing more certain than that, but also wished to entertain one of her pet sources of recreation. Overseas shopping sprees were especially to her liking. She'd frequented well-known addresses in other European cities in this way: Avenue Montaigne and Rue du Faubourg in Paris; Oxford and Regent Street in London; Bahnhofstrasse in Zurich; Stroget in Copenhagen; and Drottninggatan in Stockholm. She'd been reliably informed that the Italian capital was on a par with the best of these. A close friend of hers, Naomi Bancroft, had vacationed here of late and from her Lee had received some opportune pearls of wisdom on retail therapy Roman style.

Naomi advised her to begin at Piazza di Spagna and use that as a jump-off point. Between there and Via del Corso was a network of streets where there was a plentiful array of small designers selling one-off, hand-made outfits; individual shops in which one could purchase bespoke shoes; and numerous studios and boutiques housing work-of-art jewellery, ceramics and leather goods. Big name designers such as Armani, Valentino and Versace naturally were prominent in this area as well, but Lee wanted to seek out the smaller, off-centre establishments offering more specialised product. There was an element of adventure entering these artisan studios and backstreet workshops, an ambiance which the flagship outlets could not hope to emulate, and Lee was determined that this preliminary tour of the area would give her cause to return several more times during her stay. She was not disappointed. In an upstairs workroom, close to the junction of Via Condotti and Via del Corso, she made her first purchase: an elaborate leather handbag obtained at a comparatively reasonable price. The innate consumer in her appreciated the moment considerably, but of even greater import was the personal touch which the owner of the business added. The silver-haired proprietor insisted that his customers (whom he evidently did not recognise) stay on for an espresso prior to resuming their expedition. He also demonstrated some of the tricks and techniques of his profession. All his products could be made to a certain specification he told them; handbags, purses, wallets, belts, everything which they saw on display. He recommended a number of other establishments close by which Lee attempted to commit to memory. A few smaller items were duly purchased before lunchtime: a pair of stylish shoes, a box of amaretti cookies and, last but not least, a floral lace scarf which she immediately put around her neck.

They dined in a small trattoria close to Via del Babuino, a street which the old man had made reference to on account of its designer clothes shops, jewellery emporiums and book stores. He vouched for Via di Ripetta and Via del Corso as well; and suggested they pay a visit to Piazza Venezia which was at the end of the Corso.

They were by themselves for this portion of the day as Todd had decided to check out the Roman Forum and neighbouring Tarpeian Rock. The Forum, in spite of its historical prestige, had not appealed to either of them as an absolute must-do. Don, for his part, was not especially unhappy about having passed up the opportunity to see the collection of ruins. As for the Tarpeian Rock, Lee had no desire to view the steep cliff overlooking the Forum which had been employed in the past as an execution site for murderers, traitors and all manner of wrongdoers. It was much too gloomy a place to contemplate she said, let alone visit.

They conversed about other things instead. The start of the Echo of Passions shoot the following Friday was chief amongst these. The previous day the three of them had met with David Cousins at Cinecittà Studios. Lee had not encountered the director before and remarked on how well-mannered she'd found him to be.

'He isn't in the least bit the way Tom describes him,' she said, 'I was expecting some Machiavellian-type character. Instead, there was this perfectly civil and quite charming man in front of me.'

'I wonder how he'll get along with Jen Carrington,' Don mused.

'They should work well together, shouldn't they?' said Lee. 'Any reason why they shouldn't?'

'David has had a bit of a chequered past with his leading ladies,' Don told her. 'In fact, I would think that volatile is probably a more suitable word.'

'In an amorous way?' Lee asked.

'Far from it actually. David, as you've heard, had a name for being overly-assertive and loud-mouthed towards his actors and subordinates generally. Lots of chewing-out went on. His style on set by all accounts was testing and very demanding. No one was spared his wrath when it kicked off. On more than a few occasions he found himself at odds with his players.'

'Reducing grown men to tears like Tom said?'

'Once or twice I understand and if the names I've heard are true, then he's managed to affront both sides of the gender divide. There was an elderly actress he was directing one time. The scene in question required her to knock on a door and wait for a response. Straightforward you would think. The actress did the scene the first time and he asked her to do it again. After the second, he asked for a third take, then a fourth, and a fifth. It went on and on like that: her rapping on the door and him asking her to do the action over and over. After 20 takes, she complained that her knuckles were starting to become sore. But David insisted she go back over it again. He didn't offer any direction; just called for the scene to be re-done so that it would look proper and authentic as he put it. After take 35 the frustrated lady rounded on her director. 'Mr. Cousins,' she said in her best West Virginia accent, 'as you might be aware I'm 79 years of age and, being of such advanced years,

I believe I have divined a certain amount about life and its connotations. I do not claim to know everything about everything, but I have accumulated a fair amount of knowledge in my time and I consider that such understanding extends to my fellow human beings, who I've always tried to oblige as best I can. As I've been trying to oblige you here today Mr. Cousins. In spite of my aforementioned wisdom, I can honestly stand here, as I've been doing now for some time, and tell you I cannot fathom what you want out of this scene. What more can someone possibly do with the humdrum of knocking on a door? Is there some abstract meaning you're hoping to wring out of this which none of us are aware of? If this door ever does happen to open, I will go inside and refuse to come out again.' He got her to do three more takes before moving on.'

'My God Don! Is he going to be that way on your film?'

Don shook his head.

'He isn't going to have the opportunity dear,' he said, 'and quite frankly, I don't expect he'll have the inclination towards it either. Like I said, he knows who I am and, in the same way, he also realises where his own career is at. A second chance is a precious commodity not to be spurned. I can't imagine David will look that particular gift horse in the mouth. No, he'll play ball alright; as sure as the turning of the earth. It's the smart thing to do. He's no dummy as you've seen first-hand.'

'He certainly seems the bright boy,' remarked Lee, 'but why did you just wonder about him and Jenny Carrington? Might there be difficulties between them?'

'I seriously doubt it, but I suppose it would be foolhardy to rule it out as far as anyone else on the film is concerned; and Jenny falls under that particular category. But don't worry she'll have a powerful ally on the set. If David Cousins steps out of line, or even makes half an attempt to do so, he'll get a timely whisper in the ear about how he's to conduct himself. About why it's in his best interest to restrain that less savoury side of his character.'

'You'll step in and sort him out that way?'

Don smiled, winking at her assuredly.

'Yes ma'am, I most certainly will.'

'Then Jenny Carrington is a very lucky lady, and she doesn't even realise it.'

'Why is she lucky? What doesn't she realise?'

'She has a protector in you. A knight in shining armour.'

She squeezed his hand as he pulled her close for a tender kiss.

'Just you,' he said, 'you're the only one I want to protect. I don't want to be a knight or a gladiator to anyone else except you.'

'That's nice to hear,' she whispered, 'sometimes it's difficult you know.'

'Yes, I know.'

'I'm glad I came. For a while there I didn't know if I'd be able to.'

'I never doubted it,' said Don, 'I knew you'd get your strength back. I knew you'd be here.'

'We have a lot to be grateful for,' said Lee.

'A lot.'

She wiped a tear from her eye, began to laugh cheerfully.

'My God, listen to the two of us,' she said, 'we belong in one of those tacky souvenir stores where they sell Vatican ashtrays and plastic Pietas. If David Cousins' writing was as schmaltzy as this, I'd suggest you jump ship right away Don. No one would ever take it seriously. You'd end up with another Five Moments sequel. Only this time there'd be body-hugging costumes and horse-drawn carriages instead of fast cars and members only jackets.'

'It could be a bit restrictive I suppose,' Don agreed, 'but at least the time travel element would still be there.'

He asked for the bill and produced some lire notes from his pocket.

'Ever since that evening in the hotel,' he said, 'I've been doing my best to get to grips with this money. I don't think it's going to happen.'

'You should buy a wallet from the friend we made this morning,' Lee suggested, 'you heard what he said: about tailor-making all his products. I think I'll go back tomorrow and get one made for you.'

'That's exactly what he wants you to do,' said Don, 'but if he can come up with a design that helps me cope with this crazy currency, I'll take ten of them.'

A waiter came to their table and left the bill for him to decipher.

'I wonder how Todd is getting on at the Forum,' said Lee. 'He really ought to get a girlfriend for himself when he gets back home. It's been how long since he split up with Janet?'

'Eight months.'

'Perhaps he could meet someone here,' she said, 'then he wouldn't have to go looking at ruins by himself.'

'You know what he's like honey. It's got to be picture perfect or nothing at all.'

'His standards are far too high.'

Don fumbled with the legal tender. A number of dark blue notes exhibiting the image of Alessandro Volta were clumsily assembled.

'Here you go,' he said to the returning waiter, 'keep the change.'

'Grazie signor,' the waiter replied.

As they were leaving the eatery, Lee noticed an original mounted poster for the 1961 British film The Roman Spring of Mrs. Stone. The artwork, containing representations of Vivien Leigh and a youthful Warren Beatty, attracted her interest and she read aloud the blurb at the bottom left-hand corner of the picture.

'The story of an American woman and her abandonment in Rome,' she said. 'Her abandonment? That's a strange way of putting it.'

'Do you know what it's about?' asked Don.

'It's based on a novel by Tennessee Williams,' Lee replied. 'She's a famous actress on her way to Rome for a holiday with her husband. Only he dies on the plane.'

'Too bad.'

'But she decides to complete the journey anyway and stays on in Rome. Then a young Italian man played by Warren enters the arena and it all gets very complicated.'

'Warren tends to have that effect. So how does he fare with the Italian accent? Does he pull it off convincingly?'

'It's a long time since I saw it, but I don't think he does.'

'How bad was it? Nick Nolte did one for Lorenzo's Oil and a lot of critics slated that part of his performance. With any luck, Max will spare me such a fate.'

Lee did not seem to catch this.

'Her abandonment?' she said reading the same two words inside the framed picture again. 'That doesn't seem right to me. I don't think what happens to her qualifies as an abandonment.'

'What are you talking about?' Don asked. 'Who gets abandoned?'

'No one as far as I'm concerned,' said Lee, 'you only get abandoned if you're deserted, right? Otherwise, it's not something that's done to you, but that you do yourself.'

'You've lost me honey; I've never seen the movie so I don't know what Vivien Leigh does in it. What about Warren?'

'He plays a gigolo. She takes up with him.'

Don raised his eyebrows.

'Well, in that case she definitely doesn't get abandoned,' he said, 'sounds as if there is abandoning going on, but it's of a very different kind.'

They went from the trattoria directly to Via del Corso and walked the remaining extent of that street before emerging out at the northern end of Piazza Venezia, where traffic poured into the large square. The Corso had served as a racetrack during the Roman Carnival for an annual running of riderless horses and, at the speed which traffic moved through onto the square, it was hard to imagine much had changed. The street was 10 metres wide, with space only for two narrow footways on either side, and Lee decided not to stop at any of the shops here eager as she was to see the piazza. She felt a little tired, but was determined not to tell her husband. The piazza was very close now, she'd come this far and was going to see it; walk around, and only then propose they catch a cab back to the Majestic. A little more progress every day as she saw it. Her energy levels were beginning to return to normal, she hoped they would be fully restored by the time they'd travel back to the States in late summer. The doctors had told her not to expect too much at first. And they'd also cautioned against over-exertion which could in turn lead to stress and possible relapse. One of them had reminded her of this just before coming here. Rome was a good idea generally he agreed, but it was important that she pace herself accordingly. She should confine herself to appropriate activities and distances he counselled and, most importantly, rest as soon as she felt the onset of any physical weariness.

Such a sensation was upon her now, but she was confident about her reserves. A few more steps and they were almost there she told herself. A little more progress every day. She was happy about that. Her sojourn in Rome had begun well; there was every reason to believe it would continue in the same vein. Soon, she would be fully fit and one hundred per cent in the whole of her health again. The future looked rosy. It was as bright as those azaleas she'd seen on the Spanish Steps a few days before.

Her recollection of the next few minutes was distressing and, later on, she would tell the powers that be how much it upset her to talk about it. The two of them walked into the central square, where several thoroughfares intersected, and paused briefly on the western corner of the Corso and piazza, where the Palazzo Bonaparte was situated. Lee remembered how impressed they both were by the plaza.

'It felt good to be in such a wide open space,' she said, 'up to that time we'd spent our day negotiating winding lanes and cramped streets. It was practically a relief to have this big sweeping area in front of us.'

In front of them also, on the southern side of the piazza, was the shimmering white marble shrine built in honour of Vittorio Emmanuel II. Il Vittoriano, as it was known, occupied a site between the square and Capitoline Hill. It was remarkable for its grandiose stairways and Corinthian columns and, above all else, its focal point: the imposing equestrian sculpture of Victor Emmanuel himself.

Don suggested they get a closer look and tried to determine the most convenient way across the square. They crossed from the entranceway of the Palazzo to the footpath and walked as far as a pedestrian crossing situated midway. From this point on the road a traffic rotary, comprising of lawn and colourful flowers, could be accessed. The foot of the monument was no more than a stone's throw from there.

As was subsequently reported in both domestic and international media, an on-duty policeman, directing traffic at the junction of the Corso and piazza, saw a man dash from the grassy island onto one of the main arteries of the square. He appeared to be in pursuit of an item of clothing. The delicate lace scarf which Lee had acquired earlier that morning had come loose and was gusted onto one of the outside lanes of fast-moving traffic. Don didn't go after it right away. Instead, he waited for what he supposed was a break in the flow of oncoming cars, before making a bold attempt to retrieve the garment. He could certainly run fast enough the officer said but, unfortunately, it was his very speed which put him directly in the path of an approaching fourth-generation Maserati Quattroporte. The driver, Pietro Albanese, had no knowledge of Don's presence on the section of road beneath the enormous mountain of white marble until it was too late.

The four-door saloon, which was travelling at 50 miles per hour, slammed ferociously into the actor. The front bumper of the vehicle crashed against his legs; his lower appendages were rapidly accelerated up to the speed of the car, whilst his head and torso remained comparatively still. As the Maserati continued to move forward, Don's lower extremities began to wrap around the contour of its front end. His pelvis and torso twisted and his whole body was scooped up from the ground in a rotational lift. His upper body then spun towards the hood. The windscreen of the car fractured as his head smashed into it. Albanese jammed desperately on the brakes. The vehicle skidded to an eventual halt and Don was thrown forward. His body tumbled and rolled on the hard surface before coming to a rest just ahead of the now-stationary car. The activities on the busy piazza were transformed in an instant. Unassuming passers-by, who'd been going about their daily business, quickly became active participants in the unfolding drama. A sizeable crowd gathered around the stricken pedestrian who was bloodied and motionless. The traffic officer arrived at the scene and requested those present to stand back. He asked if there was a doctor at hand. A few others also yelled for assistance. An ambulance was called and the official assured the victim's wife, who had identified herself, that help was on the way.

Inside the damaged Maserati, Pietro Albanese did not stir for what seemed to him like an eternity. Two or three minutes passed before he could even feel his hands again. They were still clinging on to the steering wheel rigidly and he only separated them as someone banged on the window beside him. They inquired if he was ok. Albanese mumbled a reply, shook his head gravely. A dreaded sense of foreboding overcame him. He did not know if the victim of the collision was dead or alive. Lifelong experience suggested the former. A sense of professionalism then kicked in. He told himself he would have to help this man whatever the situation. The cause of the accident didn't matter. He had a job to do and, in spite of the circumstances, he was going to do it. He unfastened his safety belt and got out of the car. Once more there were voices in the background asking if he was injured. Some enquired as to what had happened. Albanese disregarded them and made his way to the spot where the man's body lay prostrate. Calmly, he asked some of the bystanders to step aside. He had a duty to perform. A portable leather bag with hook-and-loop openings convinced those in his path to give way. There was an inner circle formed around the body and, at the centre of this, Albanese saw the traffic officer and the victim's wife. And then he saw Don. As he suspected, it didn't look good, but he reminded himself these matters never did.

The woman looked up, alert to his presence. She saw the bag at waist-level, nodded.

Albanese straightened his posture, announced himself sombrely.

'I can help,' he said, 'I'm a doctor.'

Don was taken to the Agostino Gemelli Hospital in the north-west of the city where he was treated for the injuries he'd sustained. They were considerable. The actor had suffered a traumatic injury to the head, which was causing his brain to swell, and medical personnel in the hospital worked hard to stabilise the patient and prevent any further injury from occurring. Don was intubated and put on a ventilator. A number of intracranial hematomas he'd sustained as a result of the accident were removed by surgical suction and he was transferred to the intensive care unit on the ground floor of the hospital. A medically-induced coma was decided on due to the life-threatening nature of the inflammation which had risen so dangerously high. The star was registered as critically-ill and given the last rites by a chaplain. The hospital padre spoke with Lee and Todd outside the ICU and tried to assist as best he could. He explained he was here to offer support at this moment of anxiety. He enquired as to the injured party's religious status and, perceiving their reluctance to discuss this, went on to say that it did not matter what faith or allegiance the gentleman had, or indeed if he had any. He told them he was available at all times for counselling, spiritual care as he preferred to call it, and gave them the number of his pager.

'Where the hell is Tom?' Todd said as the well-meaning cleric left them by themselves. 'He should have been here hours ago!'

There'd been neither sight nor sound of the agent all day in spite of the numerous messages Todd had left for him at the Majestic. The younger Taylor brother had heard about his sibling's accident while returning to the hotel in a taxi. He'd struck up a conversation with the driver who asked what part of the States he was from. When Todd said California, the cabbie made a passing remark about the broadcast he'd heard on the radio just 15 minutes before concerning Don Taylor. He referred to it as a 'terribile incidente' which had taken place on a busy street. Very quickly Todd realised something serious had happened, but he was not to know the gravity of the situation until he got to the hospital and met his sister-in-law. Externally the actor had suffered several lacerations to the scalp and other soft tissue injuries, which they both noticed when they were allowed to see him. The ICU matron referred to a torn knee ligament and a fractured pelvis as well, but added that these injuries were insignificant compared to the far more critical head injury. On the matter of Don's chances for recovery, she was professionally circumspect and unwilling to offer an opinion.

'At the moment he is a very sick man,' she said, 'we watch him closely and look at the pressure inside his head. Anything very high is not good.'

'Is it high now?' asked Todd.

'Yes,' she replied, and paused before continuing, 'too high; that is why we have him sleep like this. It may take much time before he can be woken.'

'And what if it gets higher again?' Lee asked. 'What if it doesn't come down at all?'

'Signora Taylor, we are doing everything we can for your marito…I mean husband. The doctor will be here soon and will discuss with you.'

The doctor saw them just before Tom arrived and, from him, they inferred a similarly grim outlook. There were few positives at the present time he said. Mr. Taylor's condition was in the balance; the slightest of fluctuations could have serious consequences. Paralysis or brain damage were real dangers the patient faced he told them. They should also be prepared for the other scenario if matters got any worse.

'I have to say this to you because there is a strong possibility of it,' he informed them solemnly, 'right now Mr. Taylor is in a battle for his life. We cannot say if he will survive this. He may or he may not.'

Lee sobbed in Todd's arms outside the ICU as a dishevelled Tom got past some hospital security deployed there to keep the press and general public at bay.

'Where the hell have you been?' Todd shouted angrily as he saw the agent approach, 'I left messages for you Tom! I left my sister-in-law alone several times just to try and get word to you. Where were you that you didn't pick up? What took you so long to get here?'

Tom shook his head and with a tremulous voice explained.

'I've just come from another hospital myself,' he said. 'After breakfast this morning, Vicki started having pains in her lower right side. We thought it was the food at first. But she got much worse. By midday she was crying from the severity of it.'

'Jesus!'

'So I took her to a hospital close to the hotel, the Umberto First as it's called. Turns out it was appendicitis, acute at that. She had it taken out an hour ago.'

'Tom, I'm sorry. I wasn't to know.'

'That's ok,' said the visibly-shaken agent, 'of course you couldn't have known. I didn't know anything myself until I phoned my wife back home. She's an early riser, but I deliberately put off the call until after the surgery so I'd be able to tell her our daughter was recovering. That she'd be fine. I figured that bit of in-built assurance would make it easier on her. Wouldn't be quite so hard-hitting. Little was I to know she had something much worse to tell me. Then I was the one left reeling. It's all over the news there already she said. I came as soon as I could.'

'I'm really sorry Tom,' said Todd. 'She's a strong kid. She'll make a fast recovery.'

'I know she will. No doubt about that. But what about things here? How is Don? How bad is it?'

'It's bad,' said Lee as she gave him a tearful embrace. 'He was hit right in front of me and didn't regain consciousness. They've put him in a controlled coma.'

'He's been given the last rites.'

'My God! How did it happen Lee? Was it the driver's fault?'

'I gave the police a statement as to the exact details of the accident,' Lee replied as she took a seat on the corridor. Todd and Tom remained standing.

'No fault of the driver's. Would you believe he was a doctor and ended up helping Don? He might even have saved his life for all we know.

Anyway, what I told those policemen who interviewed me was this: my husband is a gallant man. He has certain old-fashioned, romantic ideals. Like some of the characters he's played in the movies. Like a knight in shining armour. Sometimes he shows this in so small a way only I can see it. And then other times, just as happened today. I bought this beautiful lace scarf you see and it was blown onto the street. Don was adamant he could get it in spite of the traffic and, although I pleaded with him not to, he went anyway. His last words to me were, 'wait right here princess. Your caballero will return presently.' I didn't mention that last part to them. I'm pretty sure they wouldn't understand it.'

'It must have been an extremely difficult thing to do Lee. You were very strong to have managed it alone.'

'I got through it. What more can I say?'

'Still though, it's admirable. I'm just so sorry I wasn't here any earlier. You must have felt...'

'Abandoned?'

'Yes.'

'It's funny,' said Lee, 'earlier on I was thinking of that word as if it had just the one meaning. Now I realise that isn't the case.'

'What happens next?' asked Tom. 'Is there any kind of medical intervention?'

'There was a procedure carried out before Don was transferred to ICU,' Todd said, 'beyond that they're saying there's no other invasive treatment that can be risked.'

'He's in far too fragile a state,' added Lee, 'that's why they're making sure he doesn't come to. Waking up right now is not what they want him to do. It's what I want him to do but...'

She lowered her head beginning to cry again. Todd sat down, put his arm around her.

'He's a fighter Lee,' he said, 'there's every chance that...'

He looked up at Tom who appeared completely rattled by the day's events.

'Tom, I know this is asking a lot of you, especially with Vicki in the hospital as well, but could you make a few calls? Talk to some people?'

'Of course I can,' said Tom, 'I'd be happy to help. Has anyone from the Cinecittà production office been in contact? David Cousins or Andrew Ford?'

'Not that I know of,' Todd replied, 'I guess you better start with them.'

In the courtyard adjoining the main entrance to the hospital members of the press assembled as they waited for updates about the actor. Outside transmission vans for Italy's national public broadcasting service RAI, and the private television network Canale 5, were in evidence, as was a five-man crew from CNN. They were joined by a number of domestic print media: journalists and photographers from newspapers such as Il Messaggero, La Stampa, Corriere della Sera and La Repubblica. There were members of the general public present as well. Concerned fans of the star who wished to make known their support. Some were interviewed for the news segments which would appear later that evening. A swiftly put-together banner two of them had created was held aloft for the benefit of snapping cameras. The message conveyed was simple: 'Forza Don' it implored.

There hadn't been this level of commotion or attention on the hospital since May 1981 following the attempted assassination of Pope John Paul II. In the same way as that previous event, speculation was rife. The only formal statement the hospital had provided had come shortly after Don's admission to the A&E department. On that occasion a rather po-faced spokesperson had delivered a concise report, but categorically declined to answer any questions directed his way. Every manner of a story and rumour was on the loose at that stage and the unfortunate representative, confronted with a profusion of such whys, wherefores and what-ifs, had been compelled to retreat indoors as quickly as he could manage. His promise that there would be additional updates as the hours passed had not been made good on either. And time was moving on. Industrious minds, cognisant of targets and deadlines, were starting to mull over how the news item would be presented to readers and viewers. What exclusive insights could be imparted that would not seem unfounded? Were there any revelations in the offing which would alter the nature of the story? Or a specific nugget of information, a disclosure perhaps, which would necessitate a shift in the pitch and tenor of a primed bulletin?

The afternoon glow was giving way to an evening sunset. With it was emerging a collective focus. Inevitably, reports would have to be filed, pieces to camera performed. Facts, so far scant, would have to be settled on; flimsy hearsays discarded for the present time. The news couldn't wait for ever. Tight-lipped officialdom would not stand in its way. There were only so many vox pops and fillers which could be used. The public would expect a certain level of detail and description. The earlier version of events, relating how the world-famous star was in a critical condition, was already an old narrative. More meat would have to be put on that proverbial bone. And soon.

Max arrived at the hospital just before Tom Steiner read a prepared statement to the media. Since learning about the accident, he'd deliberated as to whether he should come or not. He wanted to find out what was happening but had doubts as to whether proximity would bring him any closer to the hard facts. Like most people he'd heard the theories and suppositions. The actor being close to the end of his life was foremost amongst these. He didn't want to believe this, but word on the street supported the claim. A horrific collision that few people would survive was how one eye witness described it. Another gave a similar testament:

'An impact that the human body is not meant to endure and not one which I believe it can withstand. It was truly awful,' she said.

Max moved amongst the crowd endeavouring to pick out the news correspondents in its midst. If anyone here has an inkling as to the true state of affairs, it must be a reporter he figured. A member of the print media would most likely have their ear to the ground. He gave the TV crews a wide berth; too prominent for his liking.

A young man entering some notes in a soft-covered writing pad caught his eye. He looked like a journalist in spite of his fresh-faced appearance. He certainly wasn't an aficionado anyhow. Max was sure of this. There was purpose in that singular countenance of his. No ordinary person jotted down shorthand at the rate he was going. This guy might very well have his finger on the pulse Max thought. There were a good many of his profession in the courtyard, but his youthful conviction was a recommendation in itself. An older more cynical man would probably be less approachable. They might not be willing to share their understanding of the situation so readily. Max had little interest in engaging in rambling chat at this moment. A crusty hack with a jaded opinion of the world was the last thing he wanted. Give youth its chance he reasoned. Or at least give it a chance to offer up some details it might be aware of. He stood alongside the other man, allowing an interval of five minutes to pass before speaking.

'Hello,' he said, 'it's been a long day, hasn't it? Are you here as a fan?'

The pen movements stopped for a moment. The younger man smiled.

'Reporter actually,' he said 'although you wouldn't believe that if you were to talk to my boss. He calls me his referred pain. Suffers from a gallbladder problem you see and the discomfort it causes is projected to another part of his body. His right shoulder I think. In that same way he says I'm the source of an ache he feels all over. Says he tolerates me just as he does his badly-behaved organ. And so I've come to be known as his referred pain.'

Max laughed.

'Sounds as if you're good at your job,' he said.

'What makes you think that?'

'Most of the time it's the persistent ones that give the ulcers and the heart attacks. Isn't that what they say? I get the same complaint myself from time to time.'

'Are you the one giving it, or in receipt?'

'Most definitely the one giving it. I couldn't tell you the number of times that...'

He stopped short, deciding not to say anything more.

'Is there any news coming out?' he enquired tentatively.

'Nothing of any great consequence,' the reporter replied, 'I understand the first 48 hours are the most important with these sorts of things. Some of my esteemed colleagues here are preparing their articles with a number of possibilities in mind. In this line of work you have to give yourself options for what might happen. Right now I have two endings to this story. One of them I'll more than likely use today. The other may be drawn on in the fullness of time. If it's as bad as they say it is, then I imagine it will be.'

'Jesus!' exclaimed Max. He wasn't sure if he was more taken aback by the enormity of that piece of information or the impassive approach of these writers.

'We're just readying ourselves as best we can,' the reporter said. 'It's a tragic thing to happen of course, but people are going to want to read about it so someone's got to put pen to paper. Bad news sells papers as surely as night follows day. It's an ill wind and so forth.'

He noticed that the stranger beside him was no longer listening. Max was staring off into the distance as if recalling a memory or seeing something for the very first time. The younger man studied his profile. There was something about his face that looked familiar he was certain. Something about that indeterminate expression. But he couldn't quite place it.

'So what's got you out here this evening sir?' he asked. 'If you were a newspaper man, I'd recognise you. I don't think you're here with these other people either. What's your reason for being here? Did you know Mr. Taylor personally?'

His question never got an answer. Two figures emerged from the hospital and walked towards the formation of press cameras, voice recorders and handheld microphones. One of them was an ashen-faced Tom Steiner. The other, a female translator. She addressed those gathered, introduced the Hollywood agent. Tom unfolded a piece of paper and began to read from it. He paused after every few sentences allowing the translator to catch up. The content of the statement was bleak. Worst fears were confirmed. Don Taylor was fighting for his life. His chances were 50/50 at best. Perhaps even less.

It went on in that way; so on and so on with the gloomy tidings. Before it was finished, a number of people began to leave. A few were distraught, others simply jaded. Max was one of them. But he wasn't tired. Nor was he manifestly upset. He was just going home. There was nothing else to do.

COMA

Don was kept in a controlled coma as the medical team in the Agostino Gemelli maintained a close watch on him. He did not deteriorate any further. Nor did he improve in any meaningful way. His life remained in the balance as the pressure inside his head stayed at a dangerously high level. Changes from hour to hour were registered, but they brought little in the way of comfort or the prospect of imminent recovery. Sometimes the critical figure dropped a few notches, but never for very long, and not to the extent his family wished for. Fleeting glimmers of hope were quickly offset by reversals. His doctors said that such a state of flux was typical and could last for a considerable period. When asked by Lee as to how long this time might be, they shook their heads and said they did not have an answer. The language barrier added a further complication. One or two of the specialists had no English whatsoever and this made communication well-nigh impossible. Gestures and reassuring smiles would simply not do. It was Todd who made the suggestion that a translator be employed to assist Lee. The woman who'd translated Tom Steiner's statement on the first evening at the hospital came to mind. A phone call was made and she arrived promptly. Francesca became a permanent fixture by Lee's side over the following days. The two women became friendly and were constantly seen together in the vicinity of the ICU where Lee spent most of her time. She'd moved closer to the hospital now and only returned to her hotel late at night. The opulence of the Majestic Hotel was no longer attractive, nor did it seem appropriate. She confided in Francesca about this saying she could not justify it as long as Don was where he was. The Italian woman listened attentively as Mrs Taylor talked about her husband. Every anecdote and piece of information was received with good grace and kindly compassion. She smiled warmly as she heard stories about the couple's early years together; how they'd eked out an existence on a shoestring budget. Don's ensuing career and his wonderful successes were glossed over quickly. Personal details about him were of much greater importance. His fondness for jazz music and the works of Jules Verne were talked about. Also, his inclination towards seafood and Beaujolais wine. Pretentious types annoyed him as much as slow-moving morose people did. He appreciated those who were light-hearted and quick-thinking. He had a habit of clicking his fingers when in a thoughtful or agitated state. Often this indicated displeasure with something or someone. Such moments though were few and far between. Their life together had been a wonderful one and its particulars were essayed right up to the time of recent events. Don's struggles with the Italian currency were tempered by a description of what had happened that afternoon in Piazza Venezia. Francesca believed it might be better not to relive that moment too many times. When away from the anxiety of the intensive care unit, she suggested walks around the grounds of the complex which was on the verge of the Pineto Regional Park. Lee, however, preferred to stay close by. She hardly ever agreed to a walk in the open air. The non-descript corridors of the single-block building became uncomfortably familiar to them both. Lee in particular. They frequented the hospitals' cafeterias and its restaurant when the need for sustenance arose. Francesca was adamant that Lee should eat regularly in order to maintain her strength. It was important she said that Lee be prepared for what would come when her husband would regain consciousness. She forecast a long rehabilitation, but was certain Mr Taylor would be restored to the fullness of health. Lee's misgivings about the possibility of such a recuperation were dismissed by her companion who told her to set aside such pessimistic notions. It sounded too much like an order and Lee began to wonder if her personal conduit was being excessively upbeat. Was Francesca advocating sanguinity for the mere sake of it? Or had someone recommended she behave this way? Lee tried to figure it out. If the other woman was doing so of her own accord, then she was exceeding her brief. She thought it unlikely that any doctor or member of staff had encouraged such a course of action. Lee became guarded and regulated the scope of her chronicles. She reprimanded herself for having been too plain-spoken with this stranger. Those earlier reminiscences of hers had fostered an overly sympathetic response which was not the intention. Francesca treated her far too compassionately now; her expressions of support seemed contrived, maudlin. And Lee had no desire to be pitied. She was not the injured party after all. She was not attached to that automated contraption designed to move breathable air into and out of the lungs. Her husband was the one hooked up to those ghastly-looking machines and tangles of tubing. There were no intravenous lines extending from her arms. She did not want this special treatment, the same way she did not wish to be medicated with words. There was enough of that mawkish drivel being directed at her without this woman contributing to it.

One afternoon as they were passing through the main reception area, she spotted a handwritten piece of paper pinned below a four-pointed crucifix. The text of the message consisted of only a few words and read:

'*Salvami o Dio, perchè le acque mi sono penetrate fino all'anima.*'

Curious to know what this meant she turned to the translator, asking her to decipher it. Francesca studied the words carefully. She delayed for a moment after she'd figured out its meaning.

'It's very sad,' she said.

'What does it say?' asked Lee.

'I think it must have been written by someone who is in great despair,' Francesca surmised. 'Someone who has lost hope or perhaps lost someone close to them. I think it is from a psalm.'

'What does it say?' Lee pressed once again.

'It's so sad,' replied Francesca. 'So sad.'

Lee lost her patience then. This woman she'd employed to provide a service was now refusing to do her job. Who did she think she was? What right had she to hold something back? Had she forgotten what she was here to do? Sick and tired of the kid gloves treatment, she turned on her employee and spelt out what was expected of her.

'Goddamn it Francesca!' she said as they stopped in the foyer, 'I want you to tell me what that note says. I don't want to hear about how sad it is. Or why you think it's better I don't know what it means. When we come face to face with those doctors later on, I want a word-for-word translation of what they're saying. No exceptions for any of them and no hesitations coming from you either. To the letter. This past day or so I've got the feeling that what you tell me is a lot less than what they have to report. I don't want the blue-pencilled version of things Francesca. Do you understand me? Just because we've become friends doesn't mean you get to choose what you think I should and shouldn't hear. You don't cherry pick the information for me like that. You do your job the way you're supposed to do it and that obligation resumes from here on out whatever the circumstances are and how ever bad the news might get. Do I make myself clear?'

Francesca said sorry and admitted she had delivered an edited version of a recent update. She was told not to worry about it. Lee said she understood why she had done it, but did not want such an act of withholding repeated. They both agreed it was time to get some air. They walked out the doorway passing the reporter who had conversed with Max a few evenings before. The young man recognised Lee, but resisted a strong urge to enquire as to her husband's well-being. Instead, he disappeared inside.

Francesca spoke for the first time since their slight altercation.

'About the page on the wall,' she said, 'it is from a psalm and it reads – 'Save me oh God, for the waters are come in unto my soul.'

'Thank you Francesca,' said Lee.

They continued walking then in silence.

Principal photography for Echo of Passions, which had been due to commence in Cinecittà Studios on Friday the 28th of April, was postponed because of the accident which had befallen its leading man. Scuttlebutt about what might be in store for the film focused on the possibilities of its stakeholders unearthing a solution which would be fitting and amenable to all parties. It was not going to be a trouble-free process. Tough decisions lay ahead. With every passing day, viable options were becoming fewer and fewer.

The studio co-financing the film and responsible for its eventual distribution, Aggregate Pictures, was itself at something of a crossroads. The unexpected passing of its long-serving chairman, Harry Krentzman, and the appointment of a new man at the helm, Elza Wooldridge 'Cy' Younger, had taken place at about the same time as the studio experienced a perceptible dip in its fortunes.

The company, founded in 1936, following the merger of the ARO chain of motion picture theatres and Spielmann Pictures Corporation (Niklas Spielmann – an Austrian-born American businessman and pioneer of film and television), had been a dynamo for output in the 1950's and 1960's. As other mainstream studios fell into decline during that heady period, Aggregate went public and prospered to a significant degree by adding to its portfolio relationships with independent producers and production companies.

In the 1960's it diversified into television, enjoying considerable success in this medium, and astutely backed two highly-successful franchises as well as other well-admired projects. On the basis of its box office successes during this period, most especially the effervescent Tyler Pinkerton detective series, the company became an attractive property. In 1969 its existing partners sold majority control to a New York-based conglomerate, McWhirter Limited, whose other interests ranged from construction materials and fiberglass panelling to the foodservice and car rental sectors. The wave of cinematic home-runs was diminished for a time during the benchmark 1970's, but this contraction was softened towards the end of that decade by a number of critically acclaimed and award winning films.

The 1980's and early 1990's heralded the studio's most financially lucrative period. Aggregate produced a number of effects-driven blockbusters and also tapped into the burgeoning teen comedy genre. There were historical and dramatic films turned out, as well as thrillers, horrors, action films, and some hybrids, straddling several genres. In an important corporate context, Aggregate took over the sales and distribution wing of a competing studio. The bigwigs at McWhirter appreciated the magnitude of this arrangement and looked forward to increased earnings. They figured the bigger the slice of pie, the more revenue which would be brought in. It was a clear-cut optimising of market share and would surely boost takings and cause bank balances to swell. Several people would become even richer than they already were.

The head of operations at Aggregate during this fruitful period, Elza Wooldridge Younger; 'EWY' or 'Cy', as he was better known, was about as un-Hollywood an individual as one could possibly imagine. Hailing from Aberdeen in Monroe County, Mississippi, Cy had grown up uncertain of where his life would evolve outside the small city. His father, a trial lawyer with a steady practice, recommended he follow his lead into the business. His mother, on the other hand, favoured the medical profession. Cy was not so crazy about either idea. His uncle on his mother's side, a playwright, suggested a career in the entertainment business. Cy was sufficiently intrigued by this proposal and travelled to Los Angeles where his relative was residing. Uncle Larry had written a play which had been highly successful off Broadway and the movie people, as he called them, had come knocking on his door. He was signed to a three-year contract at Aggregate Pictures and, with foot in the door, managed to cajole some informal chats for his nephew with the execs. Three interviews followed on from this. At the last of these the incumbent chief of operations, Bryan Rabineau, told the young man he did not believe LA was the place for him. He was also of strong opinion that the film industry and Cy were not a match.

'I've been hearing what a nice kid you are,' he said courteously, 'and I'm glad to see my people here are still capable of delivering accurate reports. But don't you think this town is going to be too much of a culture shock for you? You're this inoffensive, gentile kid from Mississippi coming to LA to work for a predominantly Jewish company in a predominantly Jewish business. What makes you think you can fit in? How would you expect to assimilate?'

Cy told the high-ranking executive a story.

'I was brought up in a Southern Baptist Church,' he said. 'We had an outspoken preacher who, every Sunday, without fail, stood up and told us that if you don't believe Jesus Christ is the saviour, and that Jesus was born to save your sins, then you're going to hell. One evening, over dinner, I asked my Mom about this. She's religious, as is my father. Uncle Larry's the spiritual black sheep of the family as you know from his plays. I said to her, 'Mom, why is it that Mr. Johnson, who comes to service every week, but who's nasty to his kids and drinks too much is going to heaven just because he's a Christian? And Mrs. Lieberson, who gives to poor black kids, and opens her shop whenever people like us need something, is going to hell?' My mother sat upright, taken aback I suppose by the forthrightness of my question. 'You're absolutely right' she said, 'as long as we all believe in God, we all deserve to go to heaven. Mrs. Lieberson is a wonderful woman and she'll reap her reward in the next life.' The Liebersons you see were the only Jewish family in the neighbourhood. They had to travel over an hour to get to a synagogue in some other place.'

That was more than enough for Rabineau. He put Cy on the payroll at once and told him to report for work the next day.

'I'm going to give you a chance kid,' he said, 'because of your story and what it tells me about you. I wasn't going to hire you, you know. I was about to tell you to take a bus back to Aberdeen, find a nice girl, get a safe job, and settle down. Now I find I can't say that because it could be a mistake for us both. Only time will tell of course. But somehow I think I'm doing the right thing here today.'

That was 1956, about the same time as the studio embarked on its own first golden age. The years went by quickly. Cy applied himself industriously, working his way up through the various departments of the company. Promotions were achieved and take-home-pay got raised, but none of these work-related occasions were ever marked in a conspicuous way. Whereas many of his peers celebrated advancement with cocktails or lavish get-togethers, Cy preferred to keep his head down and continue the work he was doing. His rise was not meteoric. It was unspectacular. But also unbroken.

One of Cy's most admired colleagues at Aggregate was Albert Nathaniel 'Bert' Balaban. Bert had come to the studio by means of a different route to his Monroe County friend. A Californian, born and bred, Balaban had attended Beverly Hills High, followed by USC, and always professed a keen interest in the business. His father, Matthew Balaban, was a popular actor on television and was represented by the influential William Morris Agency. Bert hung out on the set of his Dad's TV show as a youngster seeing first-hand how a periodically running series was put together. The actual filming of episodes interested him greatly, but he also wanted to learn about the other stages of production. He wasn't afraid to ask questions and his inquisitive nature was remarked upon by family and friends. A few of the high-flying agents from William Morris attended his bar mitzvah. Given Bert's proclivities towards the business, they joked there was already a place set aside for him in the agency's mailroom whenever he wanted to start. Their suppositions were ball park; approximate, but not quite precise. After college and the navy reserve, Bert figured that, more than anything else, he wanted to be a producer. Television seemed like an obvious choice. But what about the movies he thought. For the sake of form, he interviewed for a job at William Morris. Of more personal significance though was the meeting he attended at Aggregate Pictures two days later. After a few weeks he was offered jobs at the talent agency and studio. The same conditions and terms were offered with both. Aggregate, however, tallied more closely with the line of business he wished to enter. Of the two, he decided to plump for that.

Cy and Bert were an unusual pairing at the top of the Aggregate food chain. Answerable only to Harry Krentzman, the contrast in style between the two men was stark, but it did not detract from the quality of work they invested in the studio. As heads, they were equally responsible for the day-to-day running of the company and were fortunate to have a good business relationship. Bert held Cy in high esteem on account of the latter's meticulous work ethic and his dogged nature when it came to budgets and costings. Always the numbers man, Cy could be relied upon to pull a figure out of thin air or spot discrepancies in a second-rate financial statement. He was more interested in contracts and bottom lines than movie people or Hollywood lore. As for Balaban, Cy valued the younger man's personable side and envied ever so slightly his affable disposition. They had little in common outside of the workplace. Bert, the socialite, was very much part of the in-crowd and believed money was there to be spent. He had an expensive home in Cheviot Hills and threw parties on a regular basis for friends and co-workers. From his father he'd learnt the importance of networking and putting oneself out there. He used social occasions as acts of endearment and was never reserved when it came to mingling with actors, directors and fellow execs. He fancied himself an intrepid explorer as well and on certain weekends was known to spirit a group of his choosing away to some little-known mountain pass or obscure wilderness. He believed that life was an adventure and had more than a streak of boldness coursing through his veins. His judgement was generally sound when it came to making choices, and backing projects, although there had been a few instances when he'd over-egged the pudding as well – an outlandish idea to film a musical based on the life of Cora Pearl, the 19th century courtesan of the French demimonde, being one, and it was his older colleague who judiciously advocated restraint, saving Aggregate a good many dollars which might otherwise have been frittered away.

The success stories the company enjoyed were credited in the main to Bert the go-getter, not Cy the run-of-the-mill. The self-effacing gent from the Magnolia State was considered an outsider in spite of his length of time in the business. His name did not conjure up profile or cachet, nor did he move in the fashionable circles as the man-about-town Balaban. There were no powwows held with high-powered lawyers, no informal getaways arranged with fellow industry supremos. Never one for the glamorous shindig or black tie affair, the Mississippian was something of a lone wolf preferring to spend his free time on the beaches of California, Hawaii and Mexico. In these places he indulged his enthusiasm for the collecting of sea glass. To the uninitiated (of whom there were many), he revelled in his detailed explanations on the hobby; how combing shorelines for the physically and chemically weathered glass was something he enjoyed more than most things in life. His office in Aggregate's Niklas Spielmann Building contained several decorative jars of the frosted pieces he'd collected over the years. The back of each receptacle was labelled with a list of where the various fragments within it had originated. There were common specimens of kelly-green, brown and clear white; as well as less widespread shades of jade, amber, forest-green and soft-blue. Pride of place was reserved for the extremely rare pieces of cobalt and cornflower-blue which he'd discovered on a beach in Nova Scotia during the first low tide after a storm. Like many of his fellow enthusiasts, Cy had observed that in recent years authentic sea glass was becoming harder and harder to come by. Factors such as increased numbers searching for it and glass items being gradually replaced by plastics were the main reasons for this. This latter-day scarcity had led to some less scrupulous individuals tumbling poorer pieces and others going so far as to create artificial shards using acid and rock tumblers. Cy declared his personal disgust every time he happened upon these mock-ups. It was such an underhanded practice and went entirely against the spirit of the activity. He approached his beloved pastime in a genuine way. He tried to apply such standards to most things in life as a matter of fact. What the hell was wrong with some people? Why couldn't they conduct themselves in a like manner?

The news that Bert Balaban was taking his leave of Aggregate in May 1993 was said to have come as a great personal let-down to Harry Krentzman. But it was not greeted with a corresponding degree of shock in other quarters of the industry. Confidants and intimate associates recalled how for many years Bert had chewed over the notion of forming his own production company. When he eventually set his mind to doing it, few deemed it a regressive step for him. Many pronounced it long overdue. Movies were part of Bert's genetic makeup after all they said. He had done a marvellous job at Aggregate, but now that he was getting older, it was time for him to become a little more mercenary and self-fulfilling in his philosophy. It was time for him to concentrate on his own legacy. His professional standing in the film community was already secure and without blemish. In areas of intellect, taste and business acumen, Bert had few peers and the upshot of his departure from the studio he'd served so well would surely be considerable. Trades such as Variety and The Hollywood Reporter certainly thought so and were not reserved about weighing in with their sentiments. Bert's leave-taking was tantamount to the heart and soul of the studio being eviscerated one of them suggested. Another surveyed the position of the company and speculated as to what path management might take from there. It concluded the immediate difficulty facing Aggregate was that there seemed to be no obvious replacement at Century Park East capable of filling Bert's shoes. Perhaps no one could take his place it said; adding that, in show-business parlance, he would indeed be a tough act to follow.

A blinkered in-house advancement policy, encouraged by the majority-holding McWhirter, had not helped either. Variety, for its part, construed a state of affairs whereby there were few candidates worthy of stepping up to the mark. Harry Krentzman had a real predicament on his hands it opined. Horse trading with the intransigents at McWhirter was no mean feat at the best of times. Final say as to who would take over Bert's portfolio was an important decision, but the degree of autonomy the present chairman enjoyed had lately been trimmed back as a result of an unanticipated $75 million pre-tax loss the previous year. The New York parent was calling for more stringent control systems and a regime of greater accountability to be ushered in. Sliding stocks and furrowed brows on Wall Street were of concern; the organisation wished to avoid further surprises and embarrassments of this nature, which went down badly with nervy shareholders and testy investment bankers. A model closer in alignment to its own was the preferable arrangement and McWhirter's board, desirous to impose such a watchful strategy, began to prescribe objectives and guidelines for its errant subsidiary. In this transformed landscape the New York outfit made it abundantly clear that it wanted to be consulted on all important decision-making matters, appointments and successions included. The message to Harry Krentzman was as stark as it was formulaic. Recommendations could still be made, but they would now be subject to more rigorous vetting. The chairman's preferred choice as regards his new head of production, whoever he or she was, might not necessarily be sanctioned by the East Coast.

The thorny issue never came to a head as it transpired. There was no showdown at the Aggregate corral because a mere two months in the wake of Bert's parting, the chairman made his own exit from this mortal existence. Aggregate was thrown into even more confusion by the untimely demise of its principal officer. The resultant decision to choose Cy as his successor was, for the most part, received unenthusiastically on the sidewalks of Tinseltown. In spite of Cy's innate ability to control costs, and his positive relationship with New York, conventional wisdom had his elevation as nothing more than an obdurate corporate gesture bereft of imagination. This was a man after all who had no showmanship or sense of style about him. In a town which so prized these qualities. He was not establishment and had no familial roots, like a Zanuck or Selznick, and, therefore, had no pedigree. Popular theories as to the real reason for his promotion abounded. It was a selection brought about by pig-headed bureaucrats who wanted a puppet rather than a player the naysayers said. He would be nothing more than a sycophantic yes-man shuttling from coast to coast with income statements and ledgers. What the McWhirter chiefs evidently wanted was an innocuous flunky and boy had they ever got one. As much seemed to be confirmed in the press release regarding their chosen man's appointment. It began:

'We are truly delighted to announce Elza as the new chairman in the context of his long-standing service at Aggregate Pictures.'

Many did not bother to read beyond that point. There it is they decided. The dye has been cast. From the south-west corner of the Spielmann Building, twelfth floor, this administrator, this lackey, would supervise and orchestrate the studio's divisions; delegating and re-organising where instructed to, whilst all the time providing an approximation of internal continuity. Stiff-necked formalities had been paid their due. Investors and managers could bask in the surety of business as usual. Business as usual my eye the cynics said. More like business in its repugnant conglomerate state. Industry analysts and community connoisseurs were uniform in their derisory mind-set. A joke doing the rounds about town was that the McWhirter president and CEO, William Davis Fischer, had made an error in appointing this glorified accountant chairman of a major film studio. He should have been sent to head up their fiberglass panelling division the jibe went. God knows he's as lightweight as plastic.

Whatever the particular circumstances behind his appointment, Cy was fully aware of the job he had to do and what matters would require his most urgent attention. The restoration of in-house morale at Aggregate was one such thing which needed to be addressed. Months of uncertainty, caused by one staff member's leave-taking, and another's natural passing, had undermined confidences and added to anxieties. Unsure of what lay ahead for the studio, and with respect to the security of their own jobs (there were constant rumours of an impending McWhirter bloodletting),

AP employees had lost a considerable amount of initiative and purpose. There was little appetite for the pursuit and development of projects which some feared they might never see to completion. Production executives, accustomed to the constant ebb and flow of the business, felt a new and more heightened degree of unease. Plan B's were considered, pre-emptive strikes devised. Gallows humour became commonplace on the corridors of the twelfth floor as fatalistic execs feigned nonchalance and joked about the inevitable cull. Some, fully expecting the hammer to fall, had already begun looking for new homes. Minds were distracted, temperaments frayed. Project development at the beleaguered studio ground to a virtual standstill as a consequence.

This period of unrest had been allowed to linger for far too long. New managers, when finally installed, had an unenviable task on their hands. Staff movements, promotions, and organisational re-configurations would not only take up more time, but would prove to be problematic as well. Not everyone was happy with their new job descriptions. A few as-you-weres also dissented. Getting passed over provoked several vociferous complaints and led to two resignations. Such changes in personnel and policy served to further impede production development. When the dust eventually settled the powers-that-be realised this downward trend needed to be reversed and quickly.

In the wider industry a recent series of lacklustre and routine projects had dimmed Aggregate's lights. It had fallen several notches in the pecking order. Agency submissions, copious just a few short years before, were now fitful at best. Remainders, seconds and scraps became the order of the day as Hollywood watched and waited for the new and unproven cast of characters to distinguish itself. Cy knew his team would be judged solely on its own merits and would not be granted the temporary respite of a honeymoon period. Excuses would not be tolerated on either east coast or west. An unforgiving town as LA would scarcely pay heed to the narrative which told how the studio's current nadir had begun well in advance of Bert Balaban's departure. Internal memos and contractual agreements might well back this story up (and demonstrate that the great one was in fact fallible after all), but it would not attract any great degree of sympathy for the fire-fighters at Century Park East. Nor would it engender any special favours. The new regime would have to earn respect and this would only come about if it achieved a turnaround in its own fortunes. And Cy was perfectly aware of this. The age-old standard that you are only as good as your last movie applied to a studio as much it did an individual actor or producer. So too with the maxim that failure is an orphan, success has many parents. In the present climate the incoming boss needed more than a few good movies. Failure was not an option. Success could have as many moms and pops as it wanted. Just as long as they were employees of Aggregate Pictures.

The 58-year old began intently and, true to form, without any great sense of occasion or fuss. His first act was to put forward a number of proposals to the taskmasters at McWhirter. Foremost amongst these was the recommendation that one Anthony Chouraqui, the existing head of European production, be raised to the position of overall head of production. Taking over Bert Balaban's old job would not be without its challenges, but Chouraqui, an amiable San Franciscan of French extract, was adept (and trade-literate) and had already begun work on putting together a remodelled production team. In spite of his best efforts, and those of his underlings, the process proved laborious and time-consuming. There was dead wood to be cleared out (McWhirter insisting on a certain amount of jettisoning), and some further decampments took place through 1994. That year was no less exacting than its predecessor and bore out intuitions that Aggregate would not simply ride out the proverbial storm overnight. The snowball effect continued apace and by the first half of 1995 the alarming scarcity of properties was an unpleasant fait accompli. A lengthy production hiatus in the second half of 1995 would lead to an equally fallow distribution gap in the corresponding period of 1996 (and perhaps extend into some of 1997). The studio had just one movie going before the cameras in the first six months of calendar year '95 and it was a period piece shooting overseas. This was not sustainable. A number of aggressive acquisitions would be required. Production execs were encouraged to land the next big thing. Best seller lists were examined, theatrical figures pored over. Projects in turnaround at other studios were analysed. Costs of development, plus interest, were verified and outlays were prepared. A societal stratagem was fixed upon whereby managers were to contact key figures in the community and invite them out for lunches or drinks. Resistances were to be lowered and friendships courted. The message to be broadcast was that the studio was open for business, amenable to all ideas and offers. Suggestions that it was facing a depleted roster of talent were not to be brooked. Chouraqui prepared his team for such innuendo.

'Tell them that we are here to stay,' he instructed, 'as the Ira Gershwin lyric goes, 'not for a year, but forever and a day.'

He had rhymed off a similar spiel about a year earlier when dining with Art Brackman, an agent friend of his. Like so many around town, Brackman had heard the gossips concerning Aggregate and enquired as to whether these were true. His question was loaded ever so slightly he admitted because he had a client who had just recently completed a new screenplay. Would Aggregate care to see it? This same client knew all about disruptions and unexpected interludes he said. He was on the comeback trail and wouldn't it be quite the thing if an upturn occurred for both parties. David Cousins' fortunes improved much sooner than the studio's. He won the Oscar for Best Original Screenplay at the 66th Academy Awards in March 1994 and embarked upon his own second coming. His script, concerning the Italian inventor Antonio Meucci, became a sought-after commodity and Chouraqui stepped up his overtures to both agent and writer/director. He briefed his boss on the progress of these negotiations.

'Slowly-slowly,' he reported, 'but I think we can land it.'

Cy nodded from behind his walnut desk and asked to be kept up to date.

In early May of that year, Brackman upped the ante on the Meucci project (which was now titled Echo of Passions). Around town he let it be known that his client was looking for a firm commitment from a studio to co-finance the film in tandem with the Italian-American investors Cousins had gathered together. A budget estimated at $40 million would be required and it was hoped that one of the majors would have the backbone and big bucks to pony up. Cousins' private backers had insisted their exposure be limited to $12 million so, in theory at least, a ballpark sum of $28 million was required. Pitching the script once again, at Aggregate's weekly story meeting, Chouraqui told his colleagues that it was original, well-executed, and, most crucially, would be snapped up by a rival studio if Aggregate did not make a play. At lunchtime that same day he ran into Brackman who reminded him of the other suitors lining up. The agent said Warners were close to making an offer; and that Fox remained firmly in the hunt. Universal had yet to declare its hand, and he acknowledged that Paramount had, with much regret, dropped out of the race.

'But, and I tell you this in confidence as a friend,' he said baiting the hook, 'David would dearly love to make the deal with AP. He's admired the studio for years now, believes it to be an organisation which protects and enhances the productions that come under its wing. David is a great director who is ready to be great again. He would appreciate an arrangement whereby his creative endeavours are respected and facilitated.'

So there was one of Cousins' prerequisites Chouraqui surmised. He'd heard the former enfant terrible was holding out for a similar agreement with the other interested parties. Relating this particular stipulation back to his superior, Chouraqui was asked if he believed David Cousins could be a great director again. More importantly though, did he think he'd be less trouble than in the past?

'Some of his previous films went significantly over budget and fell behind schedule,' Cy observed, as he brooded over this requirement, 'and then of course there were all those other things which were said to have occurred.'

He stared at his lieutenant closely; heavy-lidded eyes, just like Robert Mitchum, and hoped he'd make an argument. Anthony was fitting into his new role just fine, but he still had quite a bit to learn; an area he certainly needed to work on was his powers of persuasion. He was gratified when Chouraqui rose to the occasion accordingly.

'I believe in personal growth and change Cy,' the 36-year old said, 'and I do believe he has put those days behind him. As for the other matters, well...we can monitor those closely, rein in anything that appears excessive. Art Brackman maintains his client has a singular approach which, on previous occasions, has led to a tendency to overcompensate; shooting too much in other words. David hated to go to dailies and discover he hadn't got the footage. He assures me his client has mellowed and just wants to get back in the director's chair. I can understand that. He's an artist who feels a deep and resonant obligation towards his work. He wears it on his sleeve.'

'Now did he say that last part, or was that you?' Cy asked with a good-natured grin.

'That was me Cy,' Chouraqui replied directly. 'I want to deliver this property because it's what I'm supposed to be doing here. I've got to give you a reason to keep me around. Every time I come in here lately, it seems to be for all the wrong reasons, or because I have another piece of bad news. For once I'd like to have something constructive to say. If I continue with the downbeat stuff, you're likely to either fire me or fire something in my direction. And I'd rather live a little bit longer; and close a few deals.'

His response was met with an explosive bark of laughter. Cy swivelled in his chair almost playfully, tapping the surface of his desk. Chouraqui felt strangely honoured to witness such a rare moment of diversion. The intimacy was somehow pleasing.

'I've been with this company a long time,' the chief said, as he became more thoughtful again, 'there's a lot you see going on over the course of 38 years. Some of it you're involved in and then there are other things you only hear about at meetings and on hallways. Bert was the deal-maker here, as you know. He always said that you get the brass tacks sorted first; in other words make the deal, and torture yourself about the minutiae later on. What I'm hearing from you is enthusiasm about this story, real hunger to crack into it and that's a pleasing thing in itself.'

'I hope I didn't overplay my hand,' Chouraqui said somewhat apologetically, 'it's cost me money playing poker in the past I can tell you.'

'Not at all,' his boss replied genially. 'Bert used to do it as well. There were a few times when Harry told me to pin him down, literally.'

'I'm enjoying the rush just as he did,' said Chouraqui.

'Good. So do you think we should make the deal?'

The gangly deputy paused before giving his answer.

'What do you think Cy?' he asked tentatively.

The chairman's expression changed markedly. He was dissatisfied with the response.

'No, Anthony,' he said firmly, 'you don't get to ask that sort of question. Not any more. You have to tell me whether you think we should make this deal or not. There are no sounding boards here you'll notice and any confidants you might have in the outside world do not have right of entry.'

Chouraqui nodded his head appreciating he deserved the put-down.

'Hand on heart Cy, I think we should make the deal,' he said.

'Then let's do just that,' his superior enjoined.

'I'll make the call to Brackman,' Chouraqui said as he turned towards the door.

'By the way, who does he have in mind for the principals?' Cy asked. 'That budget will be pie in the sky if he wants big names.'

'There's provision in the budget for regularly-priced leads as well as the rest of the cast. He realises that anyone above those scales would have to agree to reduced fees.'

'That's good. We don't want him exceeding limits before things get going. But those Italian-American friends of his might help in that respect. They're not penny-pinchers, but, then again, they won't suffer too many overspends either.'

'They'll probably want to have a say on casting matters,' Chouraqui ventured. 'The ethnicity of the lead for example.'

He left the office.

Cy reflected on this. It was not inconceivable he thought. Anthony could well have a point. The Italian-Americans might want one of their own.

On Friday morning 28th of April, the scheduled first day of filming on Echo of Passions, Cy sat down with Anthony Chouraqui and Aggregate's head of business affairs and legal, Danny Rosner. The meeting was convened at Cy's request and had a sole item on its agenda. The intervening week since events in Rome had brought little in the way of elucidation or resolution. The studio's announcement that the film was on hold had not succeeded in playing down concerns or lessening hearsay on either side of the Atlantic. At Cinecittà, David Cousins and his crew were instructed to remain in-situ and carry on with preparations. Apart from some second unit work, which could proceed without main cast members, there wasn't much else they could do but wait. The assumption that Aggregate would have to replace its leading man deepened as reports from the hospital filtered through. The question soon became not one of if, but when. Another point at issue was how this onerous task could best be discharged. Never a palatable choice at the best of times, finding someone to take the place of the incapacitated star would have to be handled sensitively, as well as with commensurate alacrity. Failure to source a replacement within an appropriate time period would spell doom for the troubled project. This was a scenario Cy was mindful of and one he most definitely wished to avoid. Aggregate's market position was still far too fragile. A renaissance would only come about if it demonstrated its ability to once again deliver successful product. Losing a prestigious asset at this moment in time would only lend further weight to perceptions that the studio lacked grit and was rudderless. It would be declared another touchline fumble. And worse might follow. The film could imaginably be picked up in turnaround, or at the eleventh hour, by a competing studio. David Cousins had already mustered independent financing for the project within the Italian-American community to the tune of

12 million dollars. These investors were, by all accounts, a tenacious bunch; absolutely insistent that the film should go ahead with another actor. It was not beyond the bounds of possibility that the production company would entice another major in if Aggregate decided to back away. Warners, for example; close before, but beaten to the punch. Or Fox. And what of reputations then if a different outfit stepped into the breach, realising a critical, perhaps even a commercial hit? What would be said about an organisation which had relinquished one of its valuable commodities in such a spineless fashion. Very little Cy realised. But, also, more than enough.

There was another thorny issue to be grappled with, and the meeting he'd called with Chouraqui and Rosner was to settle this matter once and for all. Don Taylor would have to be removed from the film without further delay or prevarication. Deference and tact had been paid their due. The moment had come. As part of his contract, the star had agreed to a reduced fee in keeping with the film's budget. So too had his female co-star Jennifer Carrington, cast as his wife. Both actors had signed pay-or-play contracts. This meant that, even if the film did not come to pass, they would be entitled to full remuneration. In other words, their agreed fee in the absence of a single frame of celluloid. Major studios like Aggregate were willing to agree to contracts of this nature because they wished to attract high-profile talent. For the actor or actress, the desirability of a pay-or-play clause was understandable. If a production unexpectedly imploded, or if they were replaced for some other reason, an empty schedule and lost earnings would be the most likely outcome; especially, if other work had been turned down in the meantime. Pay-or-play's offered a safety net to the actor in the event of such circumstances. They gave protection and security in an industry where instances of change, or termination, although not frequent, were not uncommon either.

As principal financier, Aggregate had accepted the pay-or-play terms of Don and Jennifer's contracts. These were standard conditions, reasonable in the context of cut-rate salaries and marquee players. It was for the studio to decide how it would wrap up Don Taylor's association with Echo of Passions. Fully aware of the actor's medical condition, Cy knew his contract would have to be discontinued so the pursuit of his replacement could begin in earnest. He looked at the man sitting directly opposite him in the conference room on the twelfth floor; imagined what recommendations he might have to put across.

Danny Rosner's voice was casual, but his manner suggested thoughtfulness as he bent and re-bent a book of matches. Close-set eyes swivelled as he spoke. Huge spectacles gleamed in the early morning sunlight. A lawyer by profession, with some 25 years' experience in the business, Danny had recently shed 30 pounds on the express advice of his doctor. He looked a whole lot better for it too, but was adamant the diet would continue until an even 40 was discarded from his frame. That meant a strict regime and controlled daily intake, disciplines he was not accustomed to heretofore. Most of all he missed his morning coffee and Danish, which his secretary usually procured for him at this time. But Judy was in on the plan and had received strict instructions not to put such items of temptation in his way. A couple of times he peeped at the door as footsteps were heard outside. They weren't his secretary's though. She had no reason to appear. He had everything he required for the discussion at hand. An important matter needed to be resolved and this was no time for thoughts about caffeine or yeast-leavened pastries. Judy would not be coming through that door toting Styrofoam cup and paper bag for the simple reason that he'd told her not to. Time to put that syrupy image out of his mind. He concentrated in spite of an uneasy feeling he'd had since coming to the office. It was a hazy morning in Los Angeles; the oppressive yellowish smog out on the street seemed symptomatic of a far greater malaise. It was vaguely dispiriting and, try, as he did, he couldn't explain it. What was the cause of it he wondered. His own edgy mood? The recent ups-and-downs experienced by the company? He couldn't put his finger on it. Spreading his hands out on the racetrack-shaped table, he attempted to convey some good news. For a change.

'The pay-or-play deal is not the immoveable object it appears to be in this particular case,' he declared, his ample bulk rolling in behind the statement. He glanced furtively at his colleagues before continuing.

'The wording of Mr. Taylor's contract allows us an out without having to pay a cent,' he explained, 'there are the usual scenarios whereby full compensation is payable; if, for example, the film doesn't happen, or if we remove him because...say...he isn't working out in the role. Lots of other variations on the same theme. These agreements are very much on the side of the party who's disadvantaged when a studio or independent calls time on a production. I can well understand the attitude of the guy who once said that indies and pay-or-plays should never be bedfellows. There's not enough money in that area; too much of a chance they'll never make it to the nearest picture house. And besides, granting those sort of provisos to lesser lights is just plain dumb as far as I'm concerned. If you want to get paid for something you might end up never doing, then you make a name for yourself in the first place to give good reason for companies such as ourselves staking our money on you because of your rep, or the box office clout you've had in the past.'

He stopped talking realising he'd gone off on a tangent. The other two remained silent.

'I'm sorry,' he said, 'what I'm trying to say here is we're not legally bound to pay if there is a force majeure or some other kind of default. If it turned out that our leading man had an undisclosed criminal record in a country or territory we suddenly relocated the production to, then there would be a breach of contract as well. That's neither here nor there in this case of course, but it illustrates a point. Instances of sudden death or disability are also grounds for one of the parties to conclude the other cannot fulfil its obligations. Instances of disability Cy. Incapacitation. That sums up Don Taylor's current medical state from top to bottom. I've seen the reports and I've spoken to two experts in the field. Don will not be physically available for this film. He may never be available for another film from what I understand. Hence our obligation in the matter is spent. Our end of the bargain is over and done with and we can walk away.'

He sat back in his chair, waited for reaction.

Anthony Chouraqui jotted down some details. His boss spoke as he continued to write.

'That's all well and good in theory Danny,' he said, 'but don't we run the risk of being utterly vilified if we choose that course of action. This is a human being after all, not a stock or share, and if we treat him like he's nothing more than a commodity, then I see little else but scorn and derision for an awfully long time to come. We have to think of what's decent here, even if there are nuances and qualifications offering us a cut and run. Taking the financial hit would not be the act of emasculation you might think it to be. It would not say we're a pushover or soft touch. Instead, I think it would demonstrate what worth we place on individuals in our employ. Remaining loyal to them at their most vulnerable moment.'

Anthony Chouraqui voiced his agreement. Rosner, though, was not convinced. Sitting forward in his seat, he pushed some sheets of paper which he'd neatly terraced to one side.

'I respect that position Cy,' he replied, 'but I'm telling you what the whole story is and how, from a legalistic point of view, I think it should play out. Now you can preach me the sermon of what's morally correct to do in a situation such as this and I will hold you in high regard for seeing it that way. The case for playing Good Samaritan is certainly strong here, I won't argue that, and it's not because I see Don Taylor as some needy stranger. He is far from that, but the fact is he's lying critically ill in a hospital bed in Rome and that's what the rest of the world does see. There's a counter-argument to that principled stance and it goes something like this: setting a precedent such as the one you're inclined towards could be a dangerous thing to do, and the community would probably not thank you for it. If we were to decide not to pay Don his fee on the basis of his disability, then there's every chance we will be viewed a bête noire and slated in almost every quarter. But not within the industry itself. I guarantee you that. It's a pragmatic real-world decision and it ought not to be swayed by emotive factors. The community will respect that; even if they don't exactly rush out to applaud us for it. Right now it may seem like a no-win situation, but it is a way forward, and rest assured we wouldn't be committing any sort of wrongdoing or legal transgression. If you can live with that dull ache in your ear for a time, I promise you it will eventually go away.'

'Anthony, what do you think?'

Cy turned to Chouraqui who'd finished making his notes and was leaning back in his chair, hands folded in lap. Chouraqui improvised for a moment before taking a firm line. 'On the one hand,' segued methodically to, 'on the other.'

'In the final analysis, I have to side with Cy on this,' he told Rosner. 'You're perfectly aware of the parlous state of affairs that's existed at this studio for some time now Danny. We're hurting badly and our image has been largely tainted due to circumstances outside our control. But mistakes have been made internally as well. I'm just as guilty as anyone else in that respect. You remember the book we were considering back a few weeks ago and I recommended that we make an offer. But only in terms of a minimum bid.'

Rosner signalled his recognition of the subject matter.

'I suggested a lot more for the rights based on a floor price which escalated with performance of the book on best seller lists; plus a gross percentage of box office receipts to sweeten the deal,' he said.

'And I should have listened to you,' said Chouraqui. 'We all should have. If we weren't prepared to go as high as you suggested, we shouldn't have made an offer at all because the agent was insulted by the bid we put forward.'

'I didn't know that. The part about the agent's reaction I mean.'

'I confided in Cy about it at the time but didn't care to broadcast it otherwise.'

'I see.'

'The point to my story Danny is this – I think there are an awful lot of fences we need to mend in this town and we need to start that process with several reach-outs.'

'This being one of them?'

'Absolutely, and a very important one at that. For me it's the lesser of two evils. If we dispense with Don's services, as we have to do in any event, we ought to do so in such a way that there are no bitter feelings or recriminations on either side. The disadvantaged party's most especially. In this case, much more than just plain disadvantaged as we well know. Our generous act would ensure we do not incur the wrath of the press or, by the same token, the public. Quite the opposite in fact. The crucial point of the exercise is that there is no fallout. And I don't believe that a dangerous precedent is set.'

'I accept your argument that avoiding any further bad press is a good thing, but as for the matter of precedent, I think we'll have to agree to disagree on that.'

'Fair enough, but as you do that consider this – if we cut Don loose without a cent – lawful as it might be – there are certain undesirable knock-on effects it could have for future projects; most particularly this current one. We're battling against the clock here as you know. An accident happens to our leading man a week before shooting begins and where does that leave us? In a pretty precarious situation and that's being understated about it. An eleventh hour replacement is something no studio has ever been able to pull off without difficulty. Especially when it comes to sourcing someone it might have a preference for, or an actor who the director might think a reasonable fit. We've drawn up a list and I can tell you that the top five on it are currently engaged on other projects. We can't wait for someone's availability so the range of potential candidates is already narrowed down. All right, so we lumber on philosophically. We look at the ones who are free, but, upon closer examination, it turns out several of them have upcoming commitments which will not tally with our scheduled finish date. This list of ours is very short now, chances are it might contain just a few. But these individuals might not be so keen on the role or the film. It's work of course but they figure other offers will turn up if they keep their schedules free. So now we have to persuade and flatter; but isn't our position compromised because of the way we've behaved towards our previous lead? How can we anticipate what Don's fellow actors might make of it? There could be a lot of ill will in the community Danny and, as a settling of scores, the guild might direct its members not to participate in our little venture in Rome. The rest of that tale you can imagine is pretty lamentable and its ending is especially disagreeable for us. No actor means no movie and no movie has us up the shit creek without a paddle. So this is more than just about being decent. It's also about doing the prudent thing and being farsighted.'

'It's about giving ourselves a fighting chance to make the film,' Cy added. 'You talk about principled stances and real world decisions Danny. Well let me tell you about one such principled stance that took place in the real world. There was an actor a couple of years ago who had a pay-or-play contract with a studio just like ourselves. I'm sure you've probably heard the story and, if you've heard it, you know who I'm talking about. Anyway, he had his pay-or-play in place and the project never saw the light of day. It was abandoned at an early stage in pre-production because the projected budget escalated and the main stakeholders withdrew. That actor was entitled to claim complete financial restitution under the terms of his contract. He was a hot property, in serious demand at the time, and he'd probably turned down half a dozen roles just to keep his calendar open for the one that nosedived. But he didn't pursue it as he could have. He didn't look for one cent from the studio, said he didn't want to add any more to the costs of a production that wasn't going to be. Was that the right decision to make you might ask. Did it suggest he was a chump for not taking the money he had a right to? Personally, I don't think so. We're going to settle our affairs with Don Taylor in this fashion regardless of the legal arguments against it. We're going to honour our pay-or-play contract with him even if the poor son-of-a-bitch never lives to realise it. At the very least we'll be able to say we're helping out with the hospital bills. Danny, I know this goes against your better advice but this is how I believe it's got to be. If we can set things in motion this afternoon, I'm hoping his family or representative can be officially approached with our proposal.'

'His agent is Tom Steiner,' Rosner said. 'He's still in Rome. We can make contact through SLR.'

'Danny, can you make that call?'

'Of course I can Cy. And I do understand the rationale behind this decision. I might not agree with it, but I do recognise its value.'

'Thank you Danny. So, if there's nothing else, let's get this done and dusted.'

The two men rose to their feet and gathered their personal effects. Cy remained seated. Rosner cadged a cigarette from Chouraqui who looked puzzled by something. Removing one of the Pall Malls from its soft pack, he proceeded to ask the question on his mind.

'There's just one thing Cy,' he said, 'that story about the actor who so generously decided not to cash in on his pay-or-play. Was that Don Taylor?'

Cy looked at Rosner. The two of them exchanged a knowing grin.

'No, it wasn't,' Rosner said, shaking his head. 'Don would have taken the money because Tom Steiner would have told him to take it. Even if he tried to resist it, Tom would make sure he'd take the money.'

Version Originale

David Cousins' day wasn't getting any better. Since early morning he'd had a splitting headache and the phone call from San Francisco had not improved matters. It came as he was discussing some particulars with his unit production manager and first assistant director. The three men were sitting in the Talking Telegraph production office in Cinecittà, the centre of operations for the Echo of Passions shoot, and the below-the-line members of staff were bringing their director up to speed. First AD, Kirk Evans, was still hiring some crew members. A second assistant director who'd been taken on had subsequently dropped out and it was now necessary to find his replacement. He informed Cousins he had two possibilities in mind, both of whom were locals, and quickly ran through their resumes. A decision was taken to employ the more experienced one.

Andrew Ford, the unit production manager, was also busy. He reminded Cousins that a stills photographer had yet to be hired, as well as reporting on-going alterations to the production schedule. Wardrobe and props had submitted new figures which were at variance with the working budget. Ford complained about this, but said the revised amounts would have to be accepted. A period piece such as this required the highest of standards after all and these departments were vital cogs in such an enterprise.

Adjustments across the board had become commonplace since the time of Don Taylor's accident. Wholesale rescheduling had taken place and many elements of the production had been put on hold. Cast members like Jennifer Carrington had deferred their arrival which had necessitated flight cancellations and postponements of accommodation. The actress' agent expressed a serious concern about his client's timetable and subsequent commitments after the Rome shoot. A rearranged finish date would have to be determined as quickly as possible he said so that Miss Carrington could fulfil her contractual obligations. It was imperative the completion of filming not be pushed out too far or his client's position would be compromised. The inevitable question regarding Don Taylor's replacement was broached. The agent mentioned he'd heard the studio would be making a formal announcement soon. He asked Ford if he knew anything about this. Ford replied that he didn't. The caller from Los Angeles persisted nonetheless.

'You guys will have to get cracking on acquiring a new actor as quickly as possible,' he said. 'So far this lack of action on your part hasn't exactly inspired confidence. There are stories floating around and most of them don't bode well for your film. Perhaps it's time you started listening to some of them.'

Lorenzo Mastrodicasa was of a similar frame of mind when he phoned from the Bay Area. The foremost contributor amongst Cousins' Italian-

American investors was unimpressed by the inertia and delay, and was not hesitant about making his sentiments known. Was there a response yet from the studio he tersely enquired. All the dragging of feet and procrastination was making his partners nervous about the money they'd invested. Of course they realised that some of this had already been spent. They weren't idiots and understood that the pre-production process was not without its expenses. But what about efforts to ensure the project would move forward he asked. They wanted assurances about that and he, as the original backer, was their mouthpiece. It was his regular diatribe and David Cousins had listened to it every day since the accident at about the same time. 3.30 in the afternoon in Rome meant it was 6.30 in the morning in San Francisco. That wasn't good he figured. Mastrodicasa was either an early riser or else he was getting up for the especial purpose of making this same call each morning. Once or twice the Italian had even suggested coming to Rome himself or sending a representative in his stead. The investors were anxious he said sternly and he could understand why. In every other line of business plan B's were at hand and changes in personnel were made as they arose. Why was this so different he asked. Why so much tippy-toeing around the issue when a firmer approach was required?

'We understand the sensitivities which are at play here,' he said, 'but these do not justify an abandonment of responsibility. Deaths and accidents happen all the time. It's a simple fact of life. The occurrence of a tragedy does not mean we lose sight of our objectives, nor should it detract from the determination to realise personal goals and ambitions. When we first met David, you spoke about the resolve you had to make a comeback. I was greatly impressed by this. A good many of us were. It would be very remiss of you to stumble now. Wouldn't you agree? We would be most disappointed as a group and our expression of this would be collective. Make the film David. The story of Antonio Meucci deserves to be told. You are still the director who can make that happen.'

The independent backer continued to pontificate as Cousins sipped some tepid coffee from a white-glazed mug. Evans and Ford had left the office a few minutes before and he was by himself with the peevish voice. The director put his feet up on the telephone desk in front of him, his trademark leather boots, worn more to augment his 5'7 height than for the sake of style, resting on the surface, and tried to think of something more agreeable than this. He wondered what Mastrodicasa was implying when he spoke about expressions of disappointment being collective. What the hell did that mean? Was it some sort of half-assed threat? And what about the not so subtle accusation that he was in some way giving up on the film? How dare the moneyed greaseball make such a suggestion. The difficulties arising from his leading actor's mishap were exceptional, they wouldn't just disappear overnight. Did the grumbling eyetie not understand this? As director he wasn't responsible for what had happened and yet words such as remiss and abandonment were being tossed at him. Did Mastrodicasa imagine he was speaking to some johnny-come-lately or this week's hack for hire? He wasn't either of those things, and he was certain he deserved more respect than this. His track record entitled him to as much.

David Cousins was born on the 28th March, 1949 in Portland, Oregon, the first of two children of Edward Cousins and his wife Sarah, both of whom were qualified general practitioners. David's family lived in the Alameda Ridge area which was one of the oldest neighbourhoods in the Rose City and also one of the most well-to-do. Regarded as an average student in school, the young man fought against his parents' demands for more study and better grades by skipping class and consorting with troublemakers. A favourite preference of his was to take in double features at the famous Bagdad movie theatre on Hawthorne Boulevard. This was far better than attending social studies classes or maths as far as he was concerned and, in spite of his parents' best efforts, he remained an underachieving student with an only passable grade average.

For his fifteenth birthday, David's father gave him a present of a Kodak Retina IF camera. Believing that his dreamy son needed an activity to discipline his mind, Edward did not anticipate it would set in motion an enduring interest in the visual arts and filmmaking in particular. After high school, David enrolled at Portland State University where he completed an undergraduate programme in film. He directed a short horror film titled Rewarded in Death as part of the course, but did not enter the film industry directly when he first moved to Los Angeles. Instead he worked in advertising for a number of years specialising in television commercials. He made adverts for Chesterfield Cigarettes, American Airlines, Nestle, Taco Bell and KFC, among others, and gained a reputation for his employment of stylish visuals and extravagant set designs. On the prompting of a former girlfriend, he began to write scripts for television, selling mostly to popular series of the era such as Barnaby Jones, The Streets of San Francisco and The Rockford Files. Although he didn't consider himself a very literary person, he discovered to his surprise that he had a natural flair for writing dialogue. In the absence of the wherewithal to buy books or option properties, he decided his best chance to move up to film directing would be to write feature length screenplays.

He penned a spec script called Mother Road which was sent to a number of producers and executives by his then agent Ken Rosenthal. The screenplay was well received and attracted a good deal of interest. Three independent production companies put forward bids for it and one of them agreed to terms allowing the untested director to helm the shoot himself. Cousins accepted a total fee of $75,000 for writing, directing and editing the film; which itself had a budget of just over $900,000. Released in March 1979, just as its creator turned 30, Mother Road met with widespread critical acclaim, enjoying a fine box office haul of $15 million to boot. Likened by many to Bergman's Wild Strawberries, the film told the story of a widowed man in his late-seventies who decides to leave his home in Chicago and travel to Santa Monica via America's famous Route 66. Along the way there are interactions with other characters and moments of self-discovery. The elderly protagonist contemplates all that has gone before and attempts to confront previous failings in his life. He remembers his wife, who he lost to cancer, and accepts that their relationship was imperfect at the best of times.

'We had no children,' he tells one of his fleeting confidants, 'and that fuelled resentments and caused great regret in our later years together.'

There are no flashbacks employed but the tenor of the film is very much rooted in the past. The central character, Sam, is observed in searching close-ups and much of the camerawork is mounted subjectively. The individuals and occurrences he encounters serve more as reminders and reveries than the catalyst for renewed vigour. The septuagenarian willingly accepts opportunities to tell stories about his life, as if wishing to unshackle himself of these memories. At first this works, but he soon realises he can no more divest himself of those bygone days than any other person. In the film's penultimate scene, a young woman he has met harangues him for trying to purge his guilt on this journey of introspection.

'It seems to me you were the one who didn't want to have a family,' she tells him, 'why else would you feel the need to embark on a self-serving odyssey? Don't you get it? You're far too old to turn over a new leaf. You're past redemption.'

Sam's silent reaction to this charge indicates she has hit a raw nerve. The central character is alone at the end. Finally arriving at the beachfront city on Santa Monica Bay, he walks to the landmark pier at the foot of Colorado Avenue spanning the Pacific Ocean. Gazing out across the expanse of water, his eyes begin to fill with tears and he whispers his dead wife's name. The conclusion is mute and Sam's remaining days seem unpromising.

Mother Road hinted at the visual prowess and finesse which David Cousins would bring to bear in his subsequent work. The film was praised for its use of locations and the pictorial qualities assigned to each stage of Sam's journey.

'*The encouraging shades of auburn and beige through the Missouri and Plains sections give way to more subdued tones as the film reaches the Southwest and California,*' one critic wrote in relation to this.

The director's penchant for unusual camera angles and compositions gave the film a distinctive feel, but they also conspired to put it slightly over budget. Location work brought with it disagreements with guilds, unions and local authorities. In Oklahoma, a ferryboat operator refused the crew permission to shoot on board so Cousins went to the state authorities, followed by the state attorney; in the end the police were summoned in to resolve the matter. Such an incident gave an early insight as regards his tenacity when it came to productions matters. His rather overbearing manner on set was also a cause for comment. The relationship between David and Mother Road's principal actor, Daniel Willow, deteriorated as the shoot progressed. It was the older man who coined the nickname 'Little Caesar' in reference to his heavy-handed director.

Buoyed by the considerable success of Mother Road, Cousins proceeded to make a number of films in the 1980's which were highly praised and scored moderate to favourable at the box office. The stories he wrote, and adapted, were often about loners desiring to be honourable and idealistic in a world portrayed as uncaring. 1985's Pangs of Youth was such a case in point. In it a quixotic youth attempts to become a better person and contribute to the small town community in which he lives. Frustrated, however, by his early inability to advance this cause, he relapses and resorts to petty crime. At a pivotal moment, he steals a car and attempts to flee the jurisdiction. He is eventually brought to task and treated unsympathetically by local law enforcement. The defence which he provides as to the motive for his actions is dismissed out of hand and he is put away.

Critical approval, which had been bestowed so willingly in the first few years, became more qualified as the 1980's drew to a close. Although for the most part complimentary towards his work, a number of reviewers and columnists identified a recurring pattern in the director's oeuvre.

Writing for the Los Angeles Times, film critic Bill Downey implored Cousins to move on from, *'all this despair'* and voiced his opinion that it was, *'time for the director to abandon the Boo Radley types who so dominate his work.'*

Variety's Rebecca Harrison was less acerbic, but nonetheless of a similar mind:

'One would hope and pray that Mr. Cousins never makes a comedy,' she remarked, *'it would literally be laughter through tears.'*

As if heedful of such analysis, the director chose as his next project a musical fantasy set in contemporary Memphis. Bluff City came about at a time when Cousins was luxuriating in the freedom accorded him by producer Frederick 'Bear' Topolski, for whom he'd delivered a financially successful horror film titled The Waxing Moon. A veteran of the industry for over 45 years, Topolski encouraged his flavour of the month to make a personal film.

'Something that you would care to go to yourself,' he suggested. 'Something that you could imagine taking your daughter to see.'

Recalling how he'd always enjoyed the spectacle of the great musicals of the 40's and 50's, Cousins decided he would make his own contribution to that particular genre. He wrote a story treatment about several fictional characters attending the annual Memphis Carnival and, rather than shoot on location, declared his intention to make the film within the confines of a studio where he felt sure he could exercise total control. The Tennessee city was recreated on a series of sound stages, with extravagant models of three-dimensional fidelity doubling for its key landmarks. The Memphis Walk of Fame in Beale Street was constructed with pain-staking exactitude, as were structures like the Chucalissa Indian Village, the Orpheum Theatre, Sun Studio and a variety of sumptuous backdrops. The director even toyed with the notion of constructing a Graceland replica, but abandoned the idea as the budget quickly began to spiral.

The shoot itself went disastrously over time and was crippled by a tumultuous series of boo-boos and technical hitches. Cousins fell out with his first choreographer and had to replace him just prior to the start of principal photography. Rehearsals and set-pieces were complicated and the ever fastidious director ordered take after take of each song and dance routine. The cast and crew wilted under such pressure and estrangements occurred. T-shirts with the caption *'It's all a Bluff'* were secretly distributed by an unhappy set designer. 'Bear' Topolski also became riled by the excessiveness and squander which he saw. 25 days of additional shooting, plus an increase to the cost of the title sequence and special effects, meant that the jukebox musical required a further $6 million. The producer clashed with his wayward director, who he claimed had broken his contract. Cousins reacted coolly to this informing Topolski he could pull the plug any time he so desired, as long as he could live with the consequences of such an extreme action. Realising that the film was already at too advanced a stage, the agitated producer relented and secured the extra capital. As collateral, he put up a small studio facility he owned in Burbank.

Bluff City proceeded to bomb at the domestic box office. Against an eventual budget of $38 million, it grossed a miserable $2.5 million in its first 20 days of release quickly disappearing from sight. Overseas it fared somewhat better, but not nearly enough to rescue it or its director's reputation. Several critics questioned how Cousins could have got it so wrong; a select few suggested delusions of grandeur.

'A ham-fisted attempt to reinvent the great Hollywood musical of a past age,' wrote the New York Times' Gilbert Bradley who was normally an advocate of Cousins. *'This is the director's own Paint Your Wagon, and like so many of those four-wheeled vehicles that headed west, his enterprise looks destined never to reach the frontier. There will surely be no opportunity to circle the wagons for this shambolic mess. If you are a musical aficionado, take my advice and rent out a Gene Kelly or a Fred Astaire instead of going to see this drivel.'*

Cousins was stung by such broadsides and he shielded his own defeat by declaring a temporary moratorium in his career. His marriage to fashion photographer Penny Gordon had ended during the Bluff City production and he decided this was a fitting juncture for such a time-out. The couple had one daughter, Vanessa, who was in her early teens. She was an inquisitive young lady and asked her father how long he thought this career break of his might last.

Smiling at her wistfully, the director felt bloodied but unbowed.

'I'm not certain honey,' he replied, 'you know someone once said the movie business is the only business in the world where the assets go home at night. Well, I'm going to be home now for quite a bit. And when they want me back, I'm sure they'll call.'

The call took almost two years to come and, when it did, it was in relation to a spec script he'd written during the second year of his professional hiatus. The Travelling Companion won the Oscar for Best Original Screenplay at the 66th Academy Awards breathing new life into David's career. Accepting the Oscar, he thanked the Academy and paid special tribute to Vanessa.

'I'm back in the game baby,' he declared triumphantly, 'you inspired me to never say no, to always believe that I could, and I thank you from the bottom of my heart.'

His rousing speech was well received by the audience in the Dorothy Chandler Pavilion and, bearing the award in one hand, Cousins blew an air kiss to the cameras.

The evening was not entirely without its blemishes though. Later on, at a post-awards party, a plucky young journalist attempted to broach the subject of the Bluff City debacle. Did the writer have any moments of regret about that he enquired. Did he accept that many of the misjudgements had been his responsibility alone?

Cousins, predictably, did not take kindly to this at all. Ramming the 13½ inch statuette into the other man's face, he gave vent to his annoyance.

'Tonight I talk about this and nothing else!' he roared before storming away. Bystanders who witnessed the incident said the director was acting like a wild man.

Cousins first heard of Antonio Meucci prior to The Travelling Companion, and while he was still working on Bluff City. The inventor's name was mentioned in The Godfather Part III, released in December 1990, and, curious about this man he'd never heard of, the director carried out some preliminary research. Based on his initial studies he penned a story treatment and then expanded this into a first draft screenplay. The script, provisionally titled Meucci Project, was shelved just as his ill-fated musical hit movie theatres nationwide. Following that particular fiasco, the director briefly tinkered with the notion of returning to Meucci. But a gruelling production schedule on Bluff City had drained his energies and he opted instead for a much needed sabbatical. When he eventually returned to writing, it was for the smaller scale project which netted him several awards, including Oscar. Meucci did not seem like a runner at the time and he knew the director's chair was well beyond his reach. The Travelling Companion changed all of that and put his name back in the frame. By March 1994, he'd made several revisions to the working draft screenplay, and his award-winning exploits later that same month made him one of the assets again. Movie producers and studio executives began to phone once more. At the best restaurants in town, contemporaries in the business offered congratulatory handshakes. The right people were sitting up and taking notice. His agent, Art Brackman, related as much when they sat down to discuss the future, and any ideas David might have in the pipeline.

'You are most definitely back in the game as you said a few days ago,' he told his client, 'and what we now need to do is strike while the iron is hot. David, they're badgering me daily, asking me the exact same question – does David have any proposals or outlines he can send over to us? Let me ask you that myself; do you have anything in mind for your next project? It doesn't have to be precise or comprehensive; in fact, it can be as sketchy as you like. As long as you have something and as long as it's not another musical.'

His client sat forward in his seat, grinning confidently.

'As a matter of fact I do have something, and it's well past sketchy,' he said. 'What's more, I already have some investors who are interested in it.'

The story of Antonio Meucci piqued his interest because here was another one of his beloved outsiders. The Italian-American inventor, whom several academics credited as being the originator of the first telephone, was certainly an honourable and idealistic man, but, like so many, his beliefs were almost snuffed out by merciless establishment powers who cared more for profit than person.

Born in the San Frediano borough of Florence in 1808, Meucci was the youngest student at the city's Academy of Fine Arts (at the tender age of 15) and when his meagre funds ran out, he continued his studies of chemical and mechanical engineering part-time. He became employed at the Teatro della Pergola in Florence as a stage technician and, in 1834, married a costume designer by the name of Esterre Mochi, also employed at the theatre. It was during this time that Antonio was alleged to be part of a conspiracy relating to the Italian unification movement, and he was subsequently imprisoned for three months on the basis of these suspicions. In 1835, Meucci and his wife emigrated to Cuba where he accepted a job at the Great Tacon Theatre in Havana. They remained in Cuba for 15 years, during which time he developed a water purification system and a device through which one could hear inarticulate human speech. This latter apparatus he named the talking telegraph.

In 1850, the couple departed Cuba and moved to Staten Island, New York. Antonio opened a small tallow candle factory and made a point of employing a number of fellow Italian exiles outcast from their homeland owing to their involvement in the Risorgimento. Giuseppe Garibaldi was among those who were given lodgings in the Meucci home. The general even worked in Antonio's factory.

By 1854, Esterre was an invalid due to rheumatoid arthritis. In spite of his wife's debilitating condition, Antonio continued with his experiments and, between 1856 and 1870, developed over 30 different types of telephone based on his initial model. He became bankrupt during these years and experienced poverty, but nevertheless continued with his work.

In the second half of 1870, it was reported that he was able to capture a transmission of an articulated human voice from a significant distance. In late 1871, unable to afford to register a definitive patent for this, Meucci took out a patent caveat which had to be renewed on an annual basis. At the end of 1874, he could no longer afford to renew this caveat and what occurred subsequently became the subject of historical debate; especially amongst patriotic Italian-Americans.

A central matter which would have to be tackled in respect of any story about Meucci would be whether it would support the notion that he was the first person to invent the telephone. Having informed himself by way of a number of accounts and particulars on the subject, David Cousins came to his own conclusion. His first draft script left little doubt as to how he appraised the longstanding dispute between champions of Meucci and defenders of Alexander Graham Bell.

Apart from such matters of interpretation, there were a number of themes which the director recognised in the Meucci story. His screenplay depicted a life which, in its compass and scale, was both tragic and extraordinary. Antonio suffered many setbacks in his personal and professional life, but the thrust of the director's composition gave emphasis to an indomitable spirit, as well as an exceptional mind. There was, for instance, the Italian's devotion to his ailing wife. An article of information Cousins took on board at an early point related to how the inventor set up a communications device connecting her room to his own workshop.

The terrible accident which befell him also offered a great deal of dramatic potential. Travelling from Manhattan to Staten Island on the Westfield in July 1871, Meucci was nearly killed when the steam engine of the ferryboat exploded, leaving him severely burned. During his stay in hospital Esterre, desperately in need of money, sold many of his working models, including the teletrofono prototype, to a second-hand dealer for a mere six dollars. Unable to recover this, Antonio worked tirelessly to reconstruct his invention and improve its design.

His perpetual fascination with all things scientific was a constant motif and this was accented with reference to the persistent threat of deprivation. Throughout his life Antonio pursued numerous experimental lines of research and had a keen interest in physiological conditions and their electrical responses. Cousins found the inventor's desire to treat pain and cure illness especially worthy and he consciously built several references to this into his screenplay. He figured that, at the very least, his parents, the doctors, would appreciate it.

Finally, there was the tragic injustice which occurred and those final few years after he'd lost his beloved Esterre when Antonio bravely squared up against the forces of Bell and his cohorts. The case taken up by the Bell Telephone Company taxed the old man considerably. The limited evidence he had to demonstrate his priority over the electromagnetic telephone did not help his cause and he was accused of fabricating records and backdating journal entries. The judge at the trial, a notorious supporter of anti-immigration policy, did not believe Antonio's defence. He ruled in favour of Bell stating that the Italian was not able to provide adequate evidence. Antonio's declaration that he understood the key principles of the invention was rejected by the case-hardened magistrate who, adding insult to injury, described the Meucci system as nothing more than an elaborate 'string telephone.'

'It was not a string telephone. It was a great deal more than that. The use of the phrase by Wallace was an outrage suggesting as it does tin cans and paper cups. If Meucci had been able to sustain his caveat after 1874, then that Scottish interloper would never have been able to take out his own patent. He would have had nothing to steal and, therefore, nothing to show. It would have then been realised who had the string telephone and who was in possession of the genuine article!'

Lorenzo Mastrodicasa looked into the clouds over San Francisco collecting his thoughts, then twisted in his chair, facing back towards his guest, and leaned both forearms heavily on the desk in front of him. The captain of industry was rangy and white-haired with a lopsided grin, but he had sharp eyes and radiated success by way of his authoritative demeanour and cracker-barrel directness. David Cousins sat on the sofa in his 17th floor office and tried to figure out which actor might have played him in the movies. A name that crossed his mind was Randolph Scott, as he appeared in Ride the High Country. He was tall as well and, just like him, Mastrodicasa's features were burnished, almost leathery. The Italian-American wasn't the strong silent type though, and Cousins found it easy to imagine that, for more than 25 years, he'd presided over a multi-million dollar establishment, which owned several companies in the Bay Area and further afield. There was more than a hint of steel in that incisive manner of his and he was not reticent in his conversation either.

'This story of yours offers a great opportunity for historic redress,' Mastrodicasa said, 'there are a number of facts which need to be brought to light. A motion picture would indeed be a valuable way of achieving that goal.'

It was late January 1994 and the director had been summoned to meet with the entrepreneur and self-styled philanthropist. Mastrodicasa's place of business was situated on Montgomery Street, in the financial district, close to the world headquarters of Wells Fargo, and within walking distance of the Transamerica Pyramid. He politely enquired if his guest might care for a view from the top of the iconic building at number 600.

'The room has a 360-degree view of the city below,' he said, 'it's possible to stand in the centre of it and survey the horizon in every direction. It's a real spectacle.'

'My understanding was that members of the public can only access the first floor lobby,' Cousins said as if disputing this latter statement. He wondered if his host had extended the invitation as a courtesy or crude attempt to impress him. In any event the businessman certainly seemed to have great pride in his city. They'd talked about little else since his arrival, and it was already a quarter past two.

Mastrodicasa smiled graciously and corroborated his ability to make it happen.

'I know a few people in this town,' he said, 'and they know me. On a couple of occasions I've attended parties and small gatherings there. San Francisco's skyline is quite a thing when night falls. There are more than a few words to describe it of course, but if I was to choose one I think it would be this – drama. Real drama in that vista of lights and beacons. And you come from a business that specialises in drama. Don't you?'

The uneven smile was flashed. The sharp eyes focused.

'Yes, I suppose I do,' Cousins replied, and he wondered if the word drama was being employed as an indirect reference to something else. It was not such an outrageous notion to suppose this seasoned mogul had already conducted his inquiries. No doubt he'd been briefed about Bluff City and other things.

'We look for stories which have dramatic potential,' he said, 'audiences relate to situations which put the everyman to the pin of his collar. And as for tragedy, well that most definitely brings out viewer empathy.'

The conversation moved on to Antonio Meucci and his place in such a canon. Mastrodicasa voiced his fervent hopes for revisionism. Cousins talked about story arcs and internal rhythms. He explained how he'd first discovered the story and how that moment felt.

'It was like it was inside a block of white marble,' he said, 'and all I had to do was chip away at it and find him inside.'

The practicalities of getting the project off the ground were eventually discussed. Unsure of what the businessman might have to offer, and aware of his own limitations in this particular field, David decided to wing it somewhat.

'An initial investment of say...ten to fifteen million would be a huge fillip,' he said. 'I can't imagine there would be many studios that would fail to notice an outlay of that sort. If we had capital in that region, then I'm certain we'd attract lots of interest.'

'Would it not be possible to produce the film independently?' Mastrodicasa asked. 'Surely that amount of money would go a long way if used properly. I venture to presume you've never attended one of my speeches on this topic Mr. Cousins. I'm a great believer in extracting as much value from every dollar I spend.'

Cousins shook his head, dismissing the idea.

'My guess here is that you're talking about cutting corners Mr. Mastrodicasa and we can't do it with a film like this. A period piece must have an authentic look and feel to it. A limited budget will not buy you either of those things. It will get you cheap and tacky. I'm fairly certain that isn't what you want.'

'No, of course not.'

'And, in any case, we need a studio; not just for the additional financing, but also for distribution at the other end. You have your beliefs Mr. Mastrodicasa and I have my own. One of them is a preference for the one-stop-shop. I like dealing with an organisation which is there from beginning to end. It simplifies matters and homogenises the enterprise. As someone who's worked many years in the business, I can tell you it's an immeasurable resource to have on your side.'

He listed a few studios which could facilitate such an arrangement. Aggregate Pictures was amongst them.

Mastrodicasa accepted the logic, but was uneasy.

'Isn't there a danger it could take a very long time for it to reach the screen?' he said. 'My areas of expertise are utilities, construction and real estate. The film business remains a mystery, but I have heard accounts of projects stuck for years in what I believe is called development hell.'

'Which makes it all the more imperative that we present this as a firmed-up package. Financing from your end, I assume of course; myself as director.'

'Ah yes, I wanted to ask you more about that. You didn't direct your last script – The Travelling Companion – did you?'

'No, I didn't. That one I did exclusively as a writer.'

'Were there specific reasons for that?'

It was a calculated question. David appreciated the shrewdness and timing of it.

'I think you know what those specific reasons were Mr. Mastrodicasa,' he replied. 'You make a mistake in this industry and memories are very long. I'm looking to start over here. The Travelling Companion was the first step in that process. Now I'm trying to move up to the next rung.'

'I respect the candour Mr. Cousins. So long as there won't be any legacy issues that might impair our prospects.'

'There won't be. I will work flat out to get this movie produced. As I said, a firmed-up package would strengthen our hand. We want to fast-track the production and avoid the risk of any unnecessary delays. They lead to turnarounds and re-writes which can significantly alter a script such as this.'

'I assume you mean in a negative sense?'

'Most definitely in a negative sense. David Brown, whom I'm sure you've heard of, once said the problem with almost all screenplays is that there's a first draft by the tenth writer, instead of a tenth draft by the first writer.'

'He was speaking about the importance of continuity I take it.'

'Precisely. My agent, Art Brackman, is a very canny operator. With him I can present this as a property that a reputable studio ought to row in behind. As director of a piece that I've written, I'd deliver the vision we're both looking for. A studio gives this to a director for hire, and he's only going to want to develop it further. In other words, change it.'

The idea was a repugnant one for Mastrodicasa. He shook his head disapprovingly.

'My associates would not want that. Nor would I.'

'Who are these other people by the way?' Cousins asked. 'When we spoke on the phone you described them as being more than acquaintances, but less than partners.'

'And so they are.'

Mastrodicasa came from around his desk and joined Cousins on the two-seater kubus.

'Have you ever heard of the Order Sons of Italy in America?' he asked.

'I can't say that I have. I imagine it's a fraternity of some sort. Connecting members to the old country. That kind of deal?'

'That amongst other things. It's the largest organisation of its kind in the United States. A central objective is the promotion of Italian culture and the preservation of heritage and traditions.'

'Sounds very worthwhile.'

'The Grand Lodge of California is based here in San Francisco, Mission Street to be exact. As one of its delegates, I have many connections in the wider community.'

'Some of the associates you mentioned?'

'Indeed. I took the liberty of passing your screenplay on to a number of them. Like me, they were highly impressed by it.'

'And they're interested in making an investment, like you?'

'We would provide a certain level of funding for the Meucci project. The sum accumulated would be deposited in an escrow account here in San Francisco. Most likely, it will be substantial. Or at least considerable enough so that you'd be able to get your foot in the door with one of those studios you referred to.'

'And in return?'

'In return you address the misrepresentation. You already have in your screenplay, but the message won't reach a wider audience until it comes to the big screen. My associates and I aren't chasing plaudits Mr. Cousins. Nor do we expect kudos when the film is released. Naturally, a few production credits would not be frowned upon.'

'I'm sure I could swing two or three additional credits in the fullness of time. Yours would be one of them.'

'Very good. In the meantime, I'd very much like for you to meet the others.'

'Sure, we can arrange a time and place...'

'Let us state a time and place now – Saturday the 19th of February next. My weekend residence in Marin County. Unless you have a prior engagement?'

'No, I don't. Jesus! You have this planned out, don't you?'

'I'm always prepared Mr. Cousins. I like to be in control.'

'So I see. It makes me wonder as to whether I came here today for an appointment or interview.'

'I wanted to be sure that the man who wrote this wonderful screenplay is the same man who can translate it into a wonderful film.'

'And am I?'

'Yes, I believe you are David. A little on the defensive side perhaps, but on the whole I'm convinced. And I liked The Travelling Companion by the way. My wife and I went to see it before Christmas. I understand there's talk of Oscar nominations.'

Cousins smiled as he loosened up for the first time all day. The pressure was off. His mission to Montgomery was a success.

'There's speculation alright,' he said, 'it would be very flattering.'

'Tell me, was your original work changed to a great extent for it?'

'No, fortunately not. There was some tinkering but it didn't get mucked around. As I said, that's the value of getting a story from page to screen in a short period of time.'

'Good. And it certainly shows.'

Matrodicasa slapped the director's knee as he stood up again. He buzzed his secretary to inform her Mr. Cousins was ready for his limo ride back to the airport.

'So, we'll be in touch,' he said as they shook hands.

'I expect I'll hear from you first Mr. Mastrodicasa.'

'You will.'

His secretary knocked and advised that the driver was waiting downstairs. Cousins followed her to the door, but turned back as something came to mind.

'There's one other thing I wanted to ask,' he said.

'Oh yes?' said Mastrodicasa who'd returned to his desk.

'It's about your name. Am I correct in thinking that it means...?'

The businessman looked up for an instant and nodded. He'd been asked the same question before. Probably countless times.

'Yes,' he answered, 'literally it means master of the house.'

A few weeks later they met for the second time. On this occasion it was at Mastrodicasa's plush villa in Marin County, which was not far from George Lucas' Skywalker Ranch in neighbouring Nicasio. The Italian-American played master of ceremonies for the evening as he introduced his director 'friend' to the other potential investors. There were formal introductions, followed by some puns and anecdotes. The host joked about how he'd first heard of Cousins' activities on the Meucci project, and the delight this information had caused him.

'I had a ringing sensation in my ears for days after I learnt about it,' he quipped, provoking an amused response from his stylish guests.

In the company of such designer outfits and sparkling jewellery, David Cousins looked practically unkempt. He'd bought a new pair of Frye cavalry boots a few days before, but otherwise his attire was entirely casual. Dressed in a flannel-lined denim shirt and pair of Levi 501's, the director's style differed from the Yves Saint-Laurent's and Armani's around him. A mild rebuke aside from his host, Cousins performed with great aplomb fielding questions from would-be financiers. Over the course of the evening, and subsequent dinner, he observed how little the majority of them understood about the industry. They knew about films of course, and could name their favourite ones, but a grasp of the internal workings stumped them. A few were genuinely astonished at how long the process could take. Others asked about the various stages involved. Were development and pre-production the same thing? What percentage of budget was normally spent on set designs? Was this figure significantly higher for movies set in the past? What processes took place at post-production stage? Was there a marked difference between the directors' cut and final cut? The questions kept on coming.

Seated beside an older lady from Napa Valley, David knew he had his work cut out when she asked if he knew who a certain director was. She'd seen a film on cable recently and one credit had especially caught her eye.

'It read directed by Alan Smithee,' she said, 'I'm sure I've never heard of him. Are you by chance familiar with his work?'

Cousins smiled politely, attempted a reasonable explanation.

'He's not a real person,' he said, 'Alan Smithee is actually a pseudonym.'

'Not a real person?' she repeated.

'It's a name that's used by a director when he decides to disown his own work.'

'Why would someone do that?'

'Many reasons, but chiefly because he's unhappy with the finished film. It's often on account of the fact that the studio has taken away creative control.'

'Like the final cut that you mentioned before?'

'That's one way they can do it.'

The woman shook her head solemnly. Her expensive Cartier earrings dangled freely.

'That seems like such a shame,' she said, 'and a waste of time and effort. It's like a composer finishing an important opera, only to discover that someone's changing it to a silly pantomime.'

'That's a good way of putting it.'

'Have you ever had problems of that kind Mr. Cousins?'

'I came close to it once or twice, but nothing as serious as that.'

'Oh.'

David decided it was time to change the subject.

'So, you enjoyed the script I take it?'

'Absolutely wonderful Mr. Cousins. Tears came to my eyes.'

The director bowed to the praise. Silently, he hoped a more material expression of her admiration would follow.

'Who do you see playing Antonio Meucci?' she enquired.

'I really don't know,' David replied, the question catching him slightly off balance, 'normally I write parts with actors in mind, but I didn't for this one. I guess I still regard him as something of a mystery. Just like I do our Mr. Mastrodicasa.'

They both looked at the man seated at the top of the table who was regaling two of his guests with stories about Frisco real estate.

'Lorenzo's a very great man,' the woman said, 'you're lucky to have him on board.'

'He came on board very much of his own volition.'

'Yes, that would be more like his style,' she said, with a meaningful smile.

It was the moment to raise the stakes.

'It's our mission this evening to get people on board I suppose,' Cousins said deliberately, 'personally, I'd like to know what people here are thinking.'

His table companion smiled once more and pressed his arm.

'Don't worry about that Mr. Cousins,' she said encouragingly, 'where Lorenzo goes, many have a tendency to follow. He's a leader of men. You'll see. Your coffers will fill up now that he's here.'

They did fill up. To the tune of $12 million dollars. With the acquired funds Cousins established a production company devoted exclusively to the project, named Talking Telegraph Productions. He also drew up a preliminary budget with the assistance of an eminent production accountant. Locations proposed at this juncture included Staten Island, Florence and Santo Domingo. The director was especially keen to shoot in the capital city of the Dominican Republic. It had doubled as Havana before, for The Godfather Part II, and he was reliably informed that the incumbent administration was very conducive towards foreign enterprise. He remembered how Charlie Bluhdorn of Gulf and Western had been so passionate about the island. It was easy to see why. The country had great natural beauty and, during his lifetime, the Austrian-American industrialist had constantly invited producers, directors and movie stars to his Casa de Campo resort. Cousins himself had visited the enclave four years before. He'd played golf on the famous Diente de Perro course whilst there and swore to return some day to capture the spectacular rocky coastline and ocean views on film. Echo of Passions could accommodate a filler scene with such a magnificent backdrop he figured. If it was good enough for him, and Charlie Bluhdorn, then it would surely be good enough for others as well. The Italian-Americans included.

To help bring his screenplay to life, he engaged a concept artist to storyboard and create illustrative drawings. He brought some initial examples of this artwork to a meeting with a producer friend of his in mid-March 1994. The other man reacted positively to the pitch he heard, observing that the story was quite powerful with some terrific visual ideas, but passed on the opportunity of becoming involved due to existing commitments; also because he had doubts regarding the film's marketability.

'Frankly, I don't know who your target audience might be David,' he said, 'a historical piece like this would need several components to reinforce it. I think for starters you need a few names in there. At least one of them should be a headliner.'

Ditto Aggregate Pictures' Danny Rosner in respect of such an opinion. A 28th June 1994 memo from the head of business affairs, consequent upon the formal deal between studio and production company, referred to the express desirability, as he saw it, to attach a marquee name to the project. Although generally supportive and admiring of its distinctive merits and themes, Rosner feared the little-known story would otherwise be difficult to put across.

'The presence of a bankable star is an absolute must in my estimation,' he wrote. *'Without this important element I foresee an onerous task for publicity in territories where the character has never been heard of. And there are many of those I imagine.'*

The memo went on to indicate that the services of an A-list actor could be obtained if the terms of his contract were made attractive enough. A reduced fee with share in profits, for example. This would represent the most desirable outcome for the relevant parties. The scenario in which the prospective actor might not be willing to forego his customary salary was also envisaged.

'The notion cannot be dismissed out of hand,' the memo stated quite categorically. *'In spite of budgetary considerations, it might be prudent to acquiesce in such a set of circumstances. Costly as it might be at the outset, our leading man's asking price would be justified if his name can guarantee the sort of opening this film will require. On West Coast, East Coast and all those places in between.'*

David Cousins' favoured locations for principal photography were identified as an, *'area where a more expedient and, surely, cost-effective solution exists.'*

Rosner's proposed solution was Cinecittà Studios in Rome which, although quickly catching up on its American counterparts, was nonetheless a cheaper venue.

As a professional courtesy, the late June '94 memo was passed on to David Cousins. The director studied it; reflected on its contents; and then did something few, including Danny Rosner, could have predicted. He flew to the Italian capital and agreed to Cinecittà as the centre of operations. Florence and Staten Island were duly abandoned. As was Santo Domingo, most notably. A personal letter addressed to Rosner, and copied to Cy Younger and Anthony Chouraqui, was laudatory in respect of his, *'insights and ideas for the Meucci project.'*

'In particular, I welcome your valuable advice regarding the wonderful facilities in Rome,' the director wrote. *'Standing there, as I did, on the expansive backlot known as The Ranch, I realised how much sense it made. And not just for financial reasons alone. But for aesthetic and cultural ones also. How appropriate it will be that we make this film of*

ours in the country where its protagonist came from. It's very meaningful and I've no doubt my Italian-American friends will be just as enthused as I am. Once more my thanks, and I look forward to many more such instances of progress on our film. Yours etc. David C.'

Chatting about it in Cy's office soon after, Rosner made known his own impression.

'It's an opening gambit pure and simple,' he said. 'An experienced chess player couldn't have done it any better. He's giving us something now, as a gesture of goodwill, and expecting to cash in on it further down the line. I don't know what he'll look for in return. But the demand will come.'

His considered opinion was spot-on. In August of that same year, Cousins objected to a number of revisions to his screenplay as put forward by Aggregate's story department. Above all else, he took exception to an internal memo which urged a, *'more upbeat ending.'* Complaining about the member of staff responsible for the document, who he described as, *'an interferer,'* and, *'talentless scribe,'* he penned an obdurate response to Anthony Chouraqui.

'The screenplay is cast-iron,' he stated tersely. *'It does not require any additional modifications or fine-tuning. My understanding was that we were of a like mind regarding this. To be informed to the contrary is extremely jarring at this point in time. I do not propose to undertake any of the recommendations made by this individual. Or anyone else in that division of your organisation.'*

He was not greatly surprised when Aggregate refused to climb down on the matter. But this did not weaken his resolve. Further memos and communications sailed back and forth. The stalemate lasted for a number of weeks and impacted on other aspects of pre-production. For their part, the Italian-Americans grew impatient with the squabbling and lack of headway. Their kingpin contacted the headstrong director who assured him the end would justify the means.

'A compromise will be hammered out,' Cousins promised, 'and I expect they will more than meet me half way.'

An agreement was eventually reached in early October. The much-discussed ending received a perfunctory re-write. Apart from that, little else was changed. David Cousins had his minor victory and Danny Rosner bore an I-told-you-so look.

But it was time to move on. Already well into the fall and still there was no actor for the central role. Rosner's June 28th memo was as relevant as it had ever been.

David Cousins noted as much in an interview given to Variety at about this time:

'It's a critical piece of casting,' he acknowledged. *'Perhaps the most important one I've ever been involved in. We want to find a suitable fit, but there is the element of time which must also be factored in. Both myself and the studio are in favour of an early summer '95 start.*

Unfortunately, the four or five actors we've approached to date have other commitments during this period. Jennifer Carrington, whom we hope to secure as Meucci's wife, also has a very full schedule. Her involvement is dependent on us finding a lead who will be good to go during the specific time frame. That puts us in April or May as far as I understand. So between now and then, here's hoping.'

Questioned about his reputation for being demanding of cast members and crew, the director maintained that this was born out of his insistence on perfectionism:

'I'm only really interested in the work,' he replied. *'People should not find that a difficult thing to understand. I'm certainly not always easy to work with. I hold my hands up to that, but if the film is better as a result, then my being a pain-in-the-ass is worth it. I've never stepped on to a film set looking to win a popularity contest. Directing isn't about that. My job is to do the very best that I can and encourage those around me to do likewise. Orson Welles once said that a writer needs a pen, an artist needs a brush, but a filmmaker needs an army. If that's the case, then I accept I'm a tough commander-in-chief. And I do my best work when the actors and technicians understand this, understand me. They can trash me as much as they like in private, but, on set, I expect them to appreciate what it is that I do.'*

Don Taylor had no first-hand experience of what it was the director did, but all that would soon change once he accepted the lead role in Echo of Passions. The actor had been forwarded a copy of the script previously, but had declined on the basis of scheduling conflicts. When his diary freed up in early December 1994, just as The Proper Citizen was debuting in theatres, he contacted Anthony Chouraqui and enquired as to the film's state of play. The informal nature of the communication took Chouraqui slightly by surprise, but he did not miss a beat. Yes, the part was still up for grabs he confirmed. Yes, the intention remained it would begin principal photography circa April/May 1995. Somewhat boldly he asked if the present call amounted to an expression of renewed interest. The answer he got was music to his ears. He immediately telephoned David Cousins and, a few days before Christmas, preliminary discussions were entered into with the star. The following month, the deal was finalised. A press release to this effect was quickly circulated. For an agreed fee, lower than he would normally command, plus a 10 per cent share of profits, Don Taylor would play the part of Antonio Meucci.

David Cousins though was not fully convinced. He had reservations about the casting, in spite of the excited noises it was generating in other quarters. The Italian-Americans included. Mastrodicasa and his cronies were waxing lyrical about it. As were Aggregate Pictures and Anthony Chouraqui, now figuratively sporting a feather in his cap.

The director's reaction was guarded. It was too much of a fait accompli for his liking. Notwithstanding the tenor of his response to

Danny Rosner's June memo, he'd privately hoped for an actor with less of an A-list status than was proposed in that document. To this end, he'd suggested alternative names to the studio; but these B and C trial balloons of his were rejected. Aggregate had held out for a major name, at a cut-rate price, and had pulled off something of a coup. This was not the best outcome as far as David was concerned.

His gut feeling was that a star of Don Taylor's repute would not be amenable to the particular style of direction he favoured. There would be every chance of opposition on set if the commander-in-chief was getting tough, or perceived as doing so. Disagreements would probably arise and, in the event of an impasse, it seemed unlikely the studio would weigh in behind him when it would be far easier to err on the side of caution, and on that of the influential leading man. He recalled what Alfred Hitchcock, one of his idols, had once said regarding this whole delicate area. Speaking candidly, as he always did, the iconic director declared that as soon as you cast a major star in a film, you immediately compromised your vision. This creeping anxiety of his found no cause to dissipate; especially when, at a sensitive moment during pre-contract negotiations, the star requested a significant alteration to be made to the script.

A recurring motif in the screen story related to the fact that Antonio Meucci, throughout his entire life, had possessed a very limited command of the English language. During the course of his research David had seen frequent reference to this. He considered it a theme worth presenting, and incorporated a number of scenes dramatising the immigrant's frustrations with the language barrier during his 39-year tenure in Staten Island. Later, in the screenplay, this was given heightened effect as the encumbered inventor tried in vain to demonstrate the authenticity of his teletrofono prototype. Don Taylor made it abundantly clear he wanted this element of the story to be taken out. The actor saw no justifiable reason for the theme's inclusion. The movie would be in the English language after all he pointed out. This impractical and unnecessary plot device would only serve to confuse audiences.

'Just think of how it would go down in Appleton, Wisconsin or Kearney, Nebraska,' he said in his measured way. 'Like a lead balloon I think. No, please, get rid of it. This is one thing I ask for before I sign on the dotted line.'

He signed in due course and the offending scenes were scrubbed. As requested. Demanded more like, as far as David Cousins was concerned. The understanding he had worked out with Aggregate's story department the previous October had protected this part of the story, as well as several others. Now it was history and at the behest of the film's leading light. In one fell swoop, Don Taylor had wrought a substantial change and, in the process, demonstrated the measure of his power. A dreadful premonition began to take shape in Cousins' mind. He wondered if this was just the opening salvo. What further revisions would be foisted upon him in the time to come? Was there anything inviolable in his precious script? Was everything fair game? Apparently so he concluded. To his own surprise, and dismay, Mastrodicasa and his cohorts did not express the antipathy he expected. Their reaction, more precisely, was low-key; almost serene. Of course it was regrettable that this facet of the story was being lost their principal said. But sometimes compromise was necessary. Years in business had taught him as much he declared, all matter-of-factly. The implication germane to the message was as blatant as its speaker intended. Now get on with the task in hand he was saying. Go and make the movie.

And he was not being understated at the present time either. 3.45p.m. the sun-shaped clock in the production office read as its sweep hand completed another rotation. The businessman was still on the line and David's migraine was persisting. He reached for a container of paracetamol on the desk, knocked two of them back. His head was heavy and the throbbing sensation was not helped by a deluge of indiscriminate thoughts. He wondered if the sun had come up yet in Marin County. It was early Friday morning in California. Mastrodicasa stayed there on Thursday nights and at weekends. He'd explained this to the director as he gave him a guided tour of his villa before the dinner party in February '94.

They lingered in his study for a few minutes as he showed off some artefacts which he said were close to his heart. There was a 19th century partners' desk he'd obtained in Vermont; a landscape by Cézanne from his impressionist period; a Ford typewriter from the 1890's; a rare Chinese Cloisonne clock; a Florentine Renaissance-period credenzia; a set of French boiserie panels; and a civil war non-commissioned officers' sword dated 1861.

Facing out onto a sizeable veranda, a comb-back Windsor armchair received a particular mention. Mastrodicasa spoke about how he often watched the sun rising from this vantage point. He did some of his reading here he said and proceeded to show his guest an impressive collection of first editions he'd gathered over the years. Amongst others, there were rare copies of The Conformist by Alberto Moravia; The Will to Believe and Pragmatism, both by William James; Room at the Top by John Braine; The Leopard by Giuseppe Tomasi di Lampedusa; If This is a Man by Primo Levi; and Christ Stopped at Eboli by Carlo Levi.

The head of the household also took the opportunity of displaying a number of business periodicals, to which he'd contributed articles. Two of these titles Cousins could recall: *"As My Father did Before Me"* was one. The other was *"Level-headedness and Nous: A Vision for 21st Century Enterprise."*

And Mastrodicasa was still talking about vision now. His thoughts about where their film should go from here. The time for advancement had come he said; enough with all this inaction and uncertainty.

'I've always been able to see a way forward no matter how discouraging the circumstances are,' he said, 'I have a technique for that purpose. I create a vision in my head. One of what the end-product should be. And most of the time it comes to pass. What I see in my mind's eye becomes a reality. You are a director David. A creative thinker. As soon as we finish this call, I want you to try this technique. Think of it as a practical tool. A catalytic agent. Picture the end-product in this case. The outcome which puts our film into movie theatres. Form that vision in your mind. Determine to bring it to the one and only conclusion it should have.'

Cousins hung up and, instead, toyed with the notion of taking two more pills. His head was splitting. His eyes felt tender. Techniques he thought. Visions! He could barely see past the end of today. There would be more meetings convened. More discussions with Evans, Ford and others. He had also asked his driver to take him to the hospital later on. A courtesy call to see how Don Taylor was. It wouldn't serve any purpose, but out of respect.

Don Taylor was unconscious. Oblivious to the problems his accident had created. Aggregate Pictures would soon be announcing his removal from the film. Then the search to find his replacement would begin. The major star is gone Cousins thought. Who would be coming in his stead? All of a sudden it dawned on him. Don Taylor the major star is gone he said to himself. The actor replacing him could be one of those B or C names he had a preference for. Aggregate would probably have no choice in that regard now. Certainly time was not on their side. He suddenly felt much better. This was a catalytic agent indeed. A Hitchcockian twist with a difference. One the master of suspense himself would no doubt appreciate. The director sat back and smiled. His body relaxed for the first time all day. He could see more clearly now. An end-product indeed. In the absence of a major star, he might not have to compromise his vision as much.

The Italian Job

In San Francisco, Lorenzo Mastrodicasa received his late-evening appointment at the scheduled time of 8 o'clock. Vincente Ravenna was punctual as always and the two men engaged in some small talk before coming to the purpose of their meeting. The 48-year old former arm wrestler had flown in from Cleveland Hopkins earlier that afternoon. Sipping a herbal tea, he talked about airport lobbies, in-flight entertainment and the particular benefits of flying United Airlines as opposed to Continental. He was especially appreciative of the opportunity to travel business class and thanked his host for picking up the tab. It was extremely considerate he said and added to the good working relationship which the two of them enjoyed. Most of his clients weren't this generous. One or two even had the audacity to dispute some of the expenses he ran up whilst in their employ. But he'd sorted them out. Made them see things his way.

'I had this job in St Louis six months ago; it came about from a contact in Detroit,' he said, pushing back his dark mess of hair. He wasn't a very tall man, no more than 5'7, but was rugged and more than packed a punch. As a pro he'd won over 40 international titles, across three different weight divisions, and earned a reputation for his ability to defeat much larger opponents. But a fateful match-up against a 350-pounder in Las Vegas five years before had put paid to that. His arm wrestling career at an end, and money quickly running short, the Murray Hill native recognised he needed to get himself into a new line of work. One that paid well, but was not 9 to 5. He liked being on the road and knew that an office-bound job was not for him. In spite of a college education, it was too late for this old dog to learn new tricks he told himself. Much more practical to seek out a living doing what he knew best. Something that was hands-on and put to use the skills he'd mastered in the bras de fer arena: strength and an array of techniques to overcome any resistance encountered.

'The assignment was relatively straightforward. I was there and back inside four days so there were very few incidentals,' his story continued, 'one of them though was my hotel bill and the client decided he wasn't going to ante up for the place where I'd decided to rest my head. Seems he had a flat rate in mind as regards my accommodation needs. Problem was he only communicated this to me when it was too late. I always enjoy my trips to the Bay Area Mr. Mastrodicasa and, no doubt, you're aware of the fine hotels I've stayed in during my sojourns here. I eat simple, I don't drink, and my car rentals are nothing fancy. I don't go looking to create unnecessary extras. But when it comes to the roof over my head, even the temporary one as it is, I do insist on a particular standard. It's the one and only thing I won't do shoestring style. And I expect my employer to understand this. You know my father dabbled in a bit of arm wrestling when he was a younger man as well. Some of my forearm size I'm sure I got on account of genetics. When I first started on the road, he gave me a piece of advice. He said you can eat in as many second-rate diners or lowlife roadhouses as you like, but never go on the cheap when it comes to the lodgings you pick out. Away from competition you'll need an environment which is restful and clean. Something that befits who you think you are and what you hope to achieve. Now of course, this advice of his didn't tell me in plain words to stay in the MGM Grands of this world. That part of it evolved over the years. I admit I got accustomed to a certain lifestyle on the road. Upscale and decorative is what I incline towards. And I make no apologies for that. I'm a better operator as a result. The high-class surroundings enhance my work which, if I may say, is not lacking in its own quality. But the jerk in Detroit didn't get this. That hotel wasn't on my list he said. Seems he had a special index of establishments and if you went beyond it, you were paying your own way. The Renaissance St Louis was one he did not approve of. Excessive he called it and disproportionate to the job I'd done for him. So now he's questioning the nature of my work as well, and I'm not having that. The next day I took a flight to Detroit and booked myself in at the Atheneum Suite in Greektown. I was in the city for just one night and we settled the account on my terms, which included his reimbursing me for both the Renaissance and Atheneum. The flight to Detroit as well. I travelled coach knowing he'd definitely resist the idea of business class. Needless to say that cheapskate will not be availing of my services again, nor do I want his business. As I said, the place where I sleep is an important feature of what I do. It's one of the things I require and having it as part of the package enables this hired hand to get the job done to everyone's satisfaction.'

He smiled assuredly and took another swig of his non-caffeinated beverage. Lorenzo Mastrodicasa sat forward and downed the remainder of a gin and tonic his secretary had fixed him. Susie had thrown him a quizzical look as soon as Ravenna had arrived. She'd been asked to remain behind on one or two previous occasions for such an end-of-day engagement and had gathered its late scheduling was far from accidental. Vincente Ravenna was not the kind of individual who called during normal working hours. To the PA, he looked like an enforcer, a veritable bulldog of a man. Quite what her boss had in mind for him, she could not say. Nor did she wish to know. Every time he dropped in, she simply provided him access, and made the same herbal tea he requested – Kava. He once joked that he took it because it promoted chattiness and relaxation. Well he seemed perfectly comfortable in his own skin as far as she could tell; and he was not exactly wanting in his verbal skills either. That much was borne out by the prominence of his voice as she heard it through the door, unintelligible though it was.

'Well, I can guarantee you that the location I have in mind has plenty of fine hotels,' Mastrodicasa told his visitor. 'Your destination on this occasion will be Rome. The hospitality industry there is not a phenomenon of yesterday or the day before as I'm sure you know.'

'Rome, che bella!' Ravenna exclaimed, 'but why Rome Mr. Mastrodicasa? Has it got something to do with this film I understand you're involved in?'

'Indeed it does Vincente. More than enough to do with it.'

'Well I'm intrigued. Like every other man on the street I've heard about the accident that happened to the actor over there.'

'Don Taylor.'

'Yes, Don Taylor. But he's in a coma, isn't he? What influence could I possibly bring to a situation like that?'

'It's got nothing to do with Don Taylor Vincente. He's out of the picture, if you'll pardon the expression. The director of the film is the reason I'm asking you to go there. A man by the name of David Cousins.'

'David Cousins? I'm not certain I've seen anything he's done.'

'He's been in the movie business a number of years now. I've only seen one or two of his films I have to admit. Last year he won an Oscar for writing. This will be the first film he's directed in quite a bit of time.'

'I see. He's making a return to the game.'

'Exactly. But the element of distance means that I don't have a precise impression of what's happening on the other side of the Atlantic. What I need is a pair of eyes and ears at ground level. Filming was supposed to have begun today, but Mr. Taylor's accident has impeded that. It's a week now and the matter hasn't been progressed the way I think it should be. In either Rome or Los Angeles.'

'You mean in terms of finding a replacement for Don Taylor?'

'Yes. I have a good friend in Los Angeles, an entertainment lawyer. He's been keeping me up to date on developments as they occur. The studio is about to remove Don Taylor from the film. Not an earth-shattering revelation but...'

'It's progress.'

'Yes and no. Undoubtedly, the studio will now move to find another actor as quickly as it can; however...'

'You're not absolutely convinced Mr. Cousins will play ball?'

'It's a possibility; although in the interest of self-preservation he may accept who they propose. My friend in Los Angeles tells me eleventh-hour replacements of this nature can be difficult. Mr. Cousins might have very little choice in the matter.'

'Well then, problem solved, right?'

'Perhaps, but there remains a lingering doubt in my mind which I cannot seem to shake. The misgiving refuses to go away.'

He produced a copy of Variety containing the interview with David Cousins.

'I had occasion to read this interview again,' he said opening up the specific page, 'Mr. Cousins gave it last year, shortly after there'd been some difficulties between him and the studio. Issues about the story as

I understand. My lawyer friend brought it to my attention at the time, suggesting I have a look at it. I paid it very little heed at first. I knew a little about David Cousins' past reputation. Not everything of course, but enough I supposed. More importantly, I believed him to be in earnest when he told me how he was longing for a second chance. The word appetite was used if I'm not mistaken. He spoke of a deep-seated desire to return to the director's chair. I felt he merited the chance. He'd written this wonderful screenplay and who better than the author to bring the story to the screen I thought.'

'That sounds a reasonable assumption to come to Mr. Mastrodicasa. Hollywood has lots of guys who write and direct their own stuff nowadays. Sly Stallone has done both a number of times. Acted as well in those films. I take my hat off to such guys.'

This aside of his though went unnoticed. Instead, Mastrodicasa passed the trade magazine across to him.

'This article in Variety bothers me a great deal at the present moment,' he said, 'the voice I hear in it is not some individual talking about how he's drifted from the path. There are no regrets stated that I can make out. He practically takes pride in his own obstinacy. He admits that he's difficult, wears it like a badge of honour.'

Ravenna studied the picture of Cousins for a moment.

'Have you been in contact with him since Don Taylor's accident?' he asked.

'Every single day.'

'And what's his attitude?'

'It's shifty, defensive. This morning's conversation was no different from the others. I've been pushing him naturally, perhaps a little on the excessive side; but it's the only way I know to provoke a response. He ended the call by reassuring me the film will go ahead in the fullness of time. What that means, I have no idea. Again I suggested the possibility of going to Rome, or sending someone on my behalf. Needless to say, the reaction to this was less than enthusiastic.'

Ravenna leaned forward in his chair and looked for somewhere to put his emptied mug. Spotting no obvious place, he decided against putting it on his host's desk, and, instead, gripped it tightly in his oversized hands.

'No, I don't think it's a good idea you going to Rome personally,' he said, 'but someone else absolutely. That someone being me? The idea is I go there and be the eyes and ears you require?'

'That's the idea. Right now it's the only move I can think of, and I've given it serious thought. My associates obviously don't need to know about your presence there. I wouldn't even know how to begin describing what your role is.'

An ironic smile appeared on Ravenna's face.

'That's quite alright Mr. Mastrodicasa,' he said, 'they won't know I'm there. If extreme measures are required then...'

Mastrodicasa shook his head and gestured for restraint.

'Only if it becomes absolutely necessary Vincente, and not any time before I decide there are no viable alternatives. I want discretion. Use your own good judgement in that regard. But nothing explicit you understand. Your personal methods are only to be employed as a last resort.'

Ravenna indicated his understanding of the instruction.

'It will make for a change,' he remarked. 'Last year when I went to see Gutierrez on your behalf, the directive was unlike this one.'

'If I remember correctly, I told you to do whatever you thought the situation necessitated.'

'That's what I meant.'

'I've never asked you what it is you do or say to these people, but in Gutierrez's case I have to admit a certain curiosity. Can you tell me what happened?'

'No, I'm afraid I can't Mr. Mastrodicasa. I don't disclose the particulars back to my clients. It's sort of a professional code I have. Most of the time it's better you don't know. Let's just say that Mr. Gutierrez came around to your way of thinking.'

'He came around alright, after you called around.'

'I made certain self-evident things self-evident to him. It got done.'

'Well I appreciate results Vincente. It's all about getting the correct outcome. I want this film made the way it was intended and planned. It's very important to me. A subject that's been close to my heart for many years.'

Ravenna nodded intently.

'Yes, I wanted to ask you about that. A man as powerful as you could have involved himself in this business years ago. Why now Mr. Mastrodicasa? Why this particular film?'

The businessman clasped his hands and picked out a spot in the room over Ravenna's left shoulder. He directed his narrative to this.

'My parents came from Florence,' he said, 'my mother's family lived close to the historic centre; my father's from a suburb called Galluzzo. They came to this country in between the wars; two years before I was born. From my mother, I first heard stories about Antonio Meucci. He'd passed away in Staten Island in 1889, but she was more than determined her children would know who this man was. She claimed that her grandfather was an acquaintance of Meucci's, before he left Florence for Cuba. Now I don't know how true that is, or how well my great-grandfather knew Meucci, if indeed such a relationship existed. But the story got passed down. The connection was set out to us and we accepted it for what it was. It was part of our history, part of our collective story. My mother taught us a great many things about the old country. Tradition. Heritage. Values. I grew up learning about my past from her. The future, that was my father's domain. He was the one who introduced me to business. I learnt much of what I know about commerce and trade from him.'

'He was obviously a very good teacher,' Ravenna commented. 'Your mother as well.'

'So you can imagine my feeling when I was first told about this man from Hollywood. He'd come to do research for a film he was writing.'

'Cousins?'

'Yes, David Cousins. I was made aware of his visit by the museum director.'

'What museum is this?'

'The Garibaldi-Meucci museum on Staten Island. In life the two men knew each other you see. Garibaldi resided with Meucci and his wife for a period of time.'

'I didn't know that.'

'Not many people do. The same way they don't know of Meucci himself. For years I attempted to come up with ways of getting his name into wider circulation. Finding a mass audience so to speak. But the answer eluded me. Try as I did with publications and donations, there didn't seem to be an effective method. Several times I was on the verge of giving up. Antonio Meucci was destined to remain a historical footnote. A page that gets skipped over in the annals of time. Then came this man Cousins and the screenplay he was putting together. All of a sudden it became clear to me. The answer had been there all along, but I'd overlooked it. Cinema, this was it. A film could reach out in ways books and journals can never hope to do. And in the process it would provoke discussion. Stir up arguments. At the very least, ordinary people would be made aware, have an opportunity to decide for themselves. Instead of this one-dimensional version of events. You know it's often said that history is written by the victors. In this case the loser was never given a proper hearing. But now there exists the chance of tipping the scale. And from that who can say. Maps and borders are redrawn all the time. The past is also adjustable. It too can be revised.'

The man sitting opposite him looked very impressed with this. Ravenna clenched his left hand and rapped it against the shoulder of his chair in a show of admiration.

'Those are wonderful sentiments Mr. Mastrodicasa,' he said, 'I feel just the same way about the old country myself. Did you know my family has the distinction of sharing our surname with the city from where we came?'

'Ravenna?'

'That's correct sir. Ravenna. Like you, I was born and grew up in the States but feel a strong connection to my roots. I think of it as home and make an effort to go there at least once every two years. It's like a pilgrimage to me and the places I visit there are my shrines. The Mausoleum of Galla Placidia. The Rocca Brancaleone. The Basilica of San Vitale. The Church of Santa Eufemia...'

'Vincente.'

'The Basilica of Santa Maria in Porto. The Church of San Giovanni Battista. Dante's Tomb which is near the Basilica of St Francis...'

He considered this last reference. It was perhaps a tad misplaced.

147

'I'm sorry for bringing up that last one Mr. Mastrodicasa. I know the leaders in Florence have been trying to get his remains back for years. I guess the authorities in Ravenna are even more stubborn than some of the characters I encounter.'

'Thank you for that Vincente. It's an education.'

Mastrodicasa leaned forward in his seat, returning the conversation to the relevant.

'In two days' time I want you to board a flight which will take you close to home,' he said. 'Do you have any other assignments in the short term requiring your attention?'

'No, Mr. Mastrodicasa. As a matter of fact I was thinking about a vacation when your call came through.'

'Good. Because I don't know how long I'll require your services on this occasion. It could be several weeks. Even for the duration of the film when it begins.'

'I won't pack lightly. I know these things can take time.'

'Oh yes, the film you worked on while you were an arm wrestler. What was it called again?'

'Over the Top.'

'Sylvester Stallone was the star?'

'That's absolutely correct sir. Sly is a heck of a guy. A real professional. I worked with him and some of the other actors. Even appeared in a scene myself.'

'Well then I think you're a good choice for the job Vincente. As I said, eyes and ears at first. Low key. Trips to the studio will be required naturally. I want to know as much as possible about what's happening over there. David Cousins informs me the downtime is being put to good use. Set construction and such things. Talk to the workers if you can. Get the lowdown from them.'

'No problem. There's just one thing Mr. Mastrodicasa. The real action will be taking place in the production office. Every film has one. Without access to that I might not get as comprehensive a picture as you want.'

'I realise that. From this end, I'll keep you updated on news from LA as it reaches me. This information you can use as you assess the situation. Check that David Cousins is doing what he's being told. You won't need to enter the production office for this purpose.'

'I'll improvise. I'm real good at that. Like an arm wrestling bout, a specific technique can be brought into play.'

'Good. And if Mr. Cousins or anyone should ask who you are, I think the answer is you're one of my business consultants. Ok?'

Ravenna laughed when he heard this.

'Mr. Mastrodicasa, I am a business consultant,' he said. 'My card even says so.'

'Yes, of course. It's a nice touch. So business class to Rome then. My secretary will look after your flights. The hotel you would like to pick yourself I assume?'

'That would be much appreciated sir. But it will cost you.'

'As long as the film gets started Vincente.'

'And finished Lorenzo.'

Mastrodicasa extended his hand and the two men shook.

'Mr. Cousins I think will provide us all with a few moments of drama before the end of this,' he said. 'He seems to have an aptitude for it. A notion that he must play the prima donna. It's not a performance I wish to hear about Vincente. Your particular skill set might then be required. If it comes to pass, I suppose I will never learn of what it was you did. Just like those other jobs you've done for me.'

'That's right Mr. Mastrodicasa. Not a chance of me telling you. The code I have.'

'Better I don't know, eh?'

'Let's put it this way – if I have to show him which one of you is the more powerful, then I will. It will be clearly explained to him and he'll accept it.'

He paused for a moment.

'I don't think you've ever watched the sport I was engaged in, have you?'

'No.'

'The object of it is simple really. The winner is the man who succeeds in pinning his opponent's arm to the surface. Victory comes about because his strength and endurance is greater than the others' resistance. I won a lot of matches during my time on the road, but there were defeats as well. The one I remember most also happened to be my last. 31 seconds it lasted and at no point of the contest did I think I could possibly win. And for a spell of time afterwards I had problems dealing with it. Couldn't come to terms no matter how much I tried. My career was over, but it was the going out on a loss that really got me. It was my father who made me see sense in the end. He talked me out of it the way no flashy psychologist could have done. 'Son,' he said, 'what you got that day in Vegas was the sweetest kind of defeat. The one where you don't get a glimmer of hope. The one that rules out those what-ifs later on. I was there, I saw it. So don't let it get you down. Be content in the knowledge. You were nowhere close to winning.' He was right about it. That snapped me out of it straight away. And nowadays, when I'm on a job, I think about my father's advice. I try to provide that sweetest kind of defeat. To the individuals you and other important men ask me to deal with. Never give them the vaguest notion it's going any other way. Winner's arm over loser's arm – bang. Not a chance of reprieve or turnaround. Mr. Cousins will be no different Lorenzo. If it comes to it, he will get the sweetest kind of defeat as well. Not a whiff of anything else. I will make certain of that. And he will make your movie.'

Corporate Copy

" *Biotechnology is the use of living systems and organisms to develop or make useful products, or any technological application that uses biological systems, living organisms, or derivatives thereof, to make or modify products or processes for specific use. For hundreds of years, mankind has used biotechnology in agriculture, food production and medicine. In our present age, the final quarter of the 20th century, biotechnology has expanded to include new and diverse sciences such as genomics, recombinant gene technologies, applied immunology, and the development of pharmaceutical therapies and diagnostic tests. An exciting time for the industry as a whole, and here at HQD Pharmaceuticals, we are committed to setting standards of development which will be acclaimed not just in Europe, but the world over.*"

Max did his best to stick with the text, but couldn't go on any further. The corporate script made for dreary reading. Unexciting was not even the appropriate word. The document was convoluted and interminable. It was everything he'd been dreading, and precisely what he'd expected: poorly written copy with a glut of information in the shape of facts and figures; complex names and phrases; industry-specific terminology. A script written to be read, not spoken. It would sound more like a lecture than a performance. The biotech industry Max thought. It was never going to be a barrel of laughs, but this was something else again. The amount of preparatory work he'd have to do would be barely covered by the scanty fee. And all that jargon would add up. He could foresee three recording sessions which would take a lot longer than planned. Could even push into a fourth he imagined. Skimming through the dense language, he realised this was more than a distinct possibility.

Bioinformatics; antigenic determinants; glycoproteins; complementary nucleotides; electrophoresis; homologous chromosomes; pharmacogenomics; monoclonal antibodies; pre-symptomatic testing; and restriction fragment length polymorphism.

It was unrelenting and mind-numbing. Max sighed noisily to himself, put the script face down on his coffee table. Not much chance of making any of that sound natural he figured. The manuscript contained no references to music, no indications of any sound effects, and no directorial cues whatsoever. It was soulless, non-descript. There was no mood or rhythm he could distinguish. But then again, what to do with somatic cells? How could palindromic sequences be made to sound remarkable?

Max sat back and considered what options he had. None came to mind. Instead, he remembered the first time he'd done a narrative script like this. It was for a cosmetics firm based in Rome. His agent had got him the work just like now. It was 1981 perhaps, no later than 1982. Make-up products were on the rise. There were a large number of substances and processes referred to in the copy script. The young actor was apprehensive about the materials and components he saw mentioned in it. What could he do with long sections of inventories he asked. How could he possibly describe chemical exfoliants and witch hazel solutions with feeling?

'You're a storyteller,' Franco told him, 'and stories are about relationships. Find the relationship in the story you're telling. Use the dramatic principle of having a conversation with another person. That's what a solo performance should be about – speaking conversationally, while always having the expectation of a response.'

There was certainly a story about a relationship he could think of at the present time. It concerned a voice actor and his long-standing agent. The one entrusted with the business of the other was no longer giving effective support. And more critically, his influence in the wider business, once upon a time his strongest suit, appeared to be a thing of the past. The present contract he'd agreed on behalf of his client illustrated this point. As part of the deal, Franco had assented to a buyout clause. This meant his client would receive a one-time-only flat fee for his efforts. There would be no time limits applicable to the use of his work; no residual fee payable; even if the marketing video were used for evermore. This irritated Max more than anything else. No residual fee was the same as no residual value on his work. And God knows this particular job was going to make him work. To accept a buyout was like leaving money on the table. What's more, it was professionally degrading. His time was valuable. He could be working on other things. Why the hell hadn't Franco got him a timeframe? At least that would justify his commission. He was in the industry long enough to know better. Had he bothered to request one? Was he thinking straight?

So much for new strategies and brainstorms thought Max. The renewal of their contract was no longer a foregone conclusion as far as he was concerned. Franco would have to be told this. That only seemed right. Fifteen years was a long time. No one deserved to be cut loose without fair warning. And the older man might respond to the ultimatum in a positive way. Because that's what this is Max thought. An ultimatum. A declaration by him that things couldn't go on the way they were.

Reaching for the portable telephone, he could hear the conversation forming in his head. It would go something like this: the time had come for them both to reflect on where they were he'd say. Fifteen years Franco. Ever since that piece for Bialetti. A lot of water under the bridge. Good times and bad. You sent me a steady line of work through it all and I'm forever in your debt. But the last few years have been different. I'm sure you know that as much as I do. You've lost your focus, your drive. It started after Gabriella died. And I wasn't the first to notice. Others saw it before me. But it became clear to me as time went on. I was doing more of the legwork. You were booking me in for jobs I didn't want. This latest one pretty much tore it for me. You've always told me to put a premium on the abilities I have as a voice actor Franco. You gave me that piece of advice the first time we met. You said never sell yourself short Max. Because you need to command respect in this business. You need the guys in the control booth to know who you are and what you can deliver. It's like the film industry itself you said, you're only as good as the last thing you do. So where does this kind of job have me in all that? What does it say about my value? And if I keep on taking work like it? Without the conditions that I should be getting. It makes me look like a non-union greenhorn who just came out of acting class. It doesn't make me look like an actor who developed under your wing. I got better at my profession over the course of time and a lot of that is down to you. You helped me make inroads when I might just as easily have backed away. And I still want to be associated with you Franco. But only as long as you want to stay associated with this business. So let me ask you – is that what you want?

He repeated this last part as he looked up Franco's number.

'Is that what you want?' he said.

The phone rang before he had a chance to dial.

'Hello, Franco?' he said automatically.

'No, it's Antonia,' his sister replied on the other end.

'Sorry, I thought it was my agent. I just got a package from him.'

'Work-related?'

'Of course.'

'I hope you're not doing all the donkey work still. He'd better be earning his fee.'

'He is as a matter of fact,' Max replied cagily, 'just sent me over some voiceover work.'

'Well that's good,' said Antonia. 'Anything interesting?'

'It's for a pharmaceutical company; research and development, so lots of scientific stuff going on.'

'Claudia would like that,' said Antonia, 'she's not reached middle school yet and already she's talking about going to the liceo scientifico.'

'She's like her mother. She wants to get ahead.'

His sister laughed at this.

'Well compared to her I'm a layabout,' she remarked, 'ever since she saw Jurassic Park she's been hooked on science. Keeps talking about cloned dinosaurs and DNA. I swear to you, I think I've got the next Marie Curie for a daughter.'

'There's nothing wrong with that. Just think of all the awards and Nobel prizes.'

'I'll be satisfied with the plain old school competitions thank you very much. Success is a good thing, but it can have its drawbacks as well. You remember what dad used to say about money, don't you?'

'That rich people don't know who their friends are?'

'That was it. I think it also applies to success. When you have it, you don't know if people are friendly with you because they like you, or because they like what you have. Famous people must have that problem a lot of the time. Working out who is friend and who is freeloader. I guess like the rest of us, it's only when the chips are down they learn who their real friends are.'

'I suppose so.'

Antonia paused for a moment.

'Don Taylor's wife must be going through that,' she said, 'finding out who is there for her. It's of comfort I expect when someone calls or visits. But she's a long way from home.'

'I imagine that's the least of her worries right now.'

'It's how many days since the accident?'

'Three.'

'God! It feels longer than that. Maybe it's because of the way the newspapers and television have been covering it. They make these stories feel as if they've been around for eons.'

'That's their business. They keep it in the public eye for as long as they can.'

'At least they're not camped outside the hospital like they were a couple of days ago.'

'There's little point in that now. The hospital is providing updates. There's not much change from day to day.'

'And what about Mrs. Taylor?' Antonia enquired.

'She's made it clear she's not talking to the media. No interviews or questions. On the whole I think most journalists would respect that wish.'

'Most would.'

Antonia allowed another gap in the conversation.

'You could visit,' she suggested, 'you wouldn't be going there with questions.'

'I don't think that would be such a good idea,' Max replied rubbing his forehead pensively.

'Why not?' asked Antonia.

'Because I'm neither family nor friend. There's no reason for me to go there.'

'To see Mrs. Taylor.'

'I doubt she'd remember me all that well. And even if she did...'

'I think she'd appreciate it,' said Antonia, 'like I said she's far from home. There can't be many people she knows here.'

'I guess not. But what would I say? Don Taylor is still in a critical condition according to the papers. I can't just show up and ask his wife how he is. The whole thing would seem contrived. Not natural.'

'Max, a terrible accident which leaves a man fighting for his life is hardly a natural thing either, now is it?'

'You have a point sis.'

'And besides, you don't have to ask how he is when you go to the hospital. There are other things you can say apart from that.'

'Such as?'

'You could talk to her about that day in Trastevere. About how much you enjoyed meeting her husband.'

'And how much I'd looked forward to working with him.'

'There you go. Just be careful the way you say it. Keep it in the present tense as much as you can. Don't talk about him in the past.'

'I'll be careful sis. I'll go in the next few days.'

'No! Go either today or tomorrow!' Antonia said insistently. 'Don't leave it any later. You do that and it's likely you won't go at all. The pharmaceutical thing can wait, can't it?'

Max glanced at the offending script. It was still there. It certainly wasn't going away. The thought of having to work on it remained a disagreeable prospect. Fucking buyout clause he thought one more time. Why should I sweat blood and tears on this? I'll get down to it the day after tomorrow.

His sister was on the same wavelength.

'Come on,' she said, 'you work far too hard outside the studio. Give yourself a break. The stats will still be there for you in a few days' time. I guarantee it.'

That's true thought Max. Antonia was right. The facts and figures could wait. They weren't going to vanish into thin air. All the polyvalent vaccines in the world couldn't make that happen.

THE HOSPITAL

Fabio Paparazzo felt certain he could get the story. It was there, literally waiting for him. At the Agostino Gemelli. Don Taylor's wife was at the hospital every waking hour of the day. He'd heard as much from the members of staff he'd spoken to. Some of them practically knew Mrs Taylor on a first-name basis. They remarked as to how natural she was. Unaffected without doubt. No airs and graces about her at all. And truly dignified as well. Dealing with a situation that no one would want to have thrust upon them. Admiration was voiced for the way she conducted herself. Few could imagine themselves coping as well as she appeared to be. Grace under fire one of the senior porters commented as he spoke about her to the 29 year-old reporter.

'A quality this lady has in abundance,' he said, 'you only have to observe her for a short time to make it out. When you next see her, I think you'll know what I mean. There's a calm there. It's not a look of resignation mind. But something else. I can't quite put it into words. Perhaps a writer like you would be able to.'

Paparazzo hadn't noticed any such expression yet. But he certainly knew Mrs. Taylor by sight. Twice already he'd encountered her as he came seeking news about her husband. The most recent occasion had been the day before. He was entering the hospital building. She was on her way out. Her translator was by her side. Her name was Francesca and his understanding was she was from Milan, just like himself. The Barona district someone said. That was close enough to where he'd grown up.

At the time he'd entertained the idea of addressing his compatriot directly. Enquiring as to where she was from perhaps. Or better still he thought a slight deception. Why not pretend he recognised her from somewhere. His old alma mater, the University of Milan for instance. She looked to be about his age and quite possibly had studied there. A degree in languages seemed a reasonable assumption. And if he was right about this, if the ploy worked, then an opportunity would present itself as regards Mrs. Taylor. He could tell the unfortunate woman he was aware of her request for privacy, and respected it as well. But so many people wanted to know about the events in Piazza Venezia that day. There was still a good deal of conjecture surrounding her husband's accident. Too much in fact. At least by giving her version of events, she could put some of that to rest. Set the record straight as one might say. Just a few minutes of her time was all he needed. He'd write an article that would be faithful to her words. Francesca could translate it for her afterwards he'd suggest. The newspaper he worked for was called Il Quarto Stato and perhaps his fellow Milanese had read some of his work. At the present time, he specialised in show business, lifestyle and leisure, but hoped to move into current affairs, the area in which he really wanted to make his mark. But that piece of information was beside the point right now. What's more, it might be damaging to his prospects of getting the all-important interview. The last thing he wanted was for Mrs. Taylor to think him nothing more than an overly-ambitious hack. Personally, he favoured the term single-minded when it came to describing himself. He'd been working at the daily since February '94 and was still considered one of the new kids on the block. The never-ending coaching and lecturing that came with the territory was not a source of enjoyment for him. Mostly it came from the old hands in the office; those self-satisfied ones who talked and acted as if they were prime movers in the paper industry as a whole.

Guido Schiavone was one of them. A thirty-year veteran of the business, the silver-haired features editor from Orvieto had taken it upon himself to act as informal mentor to the younger man. Fabio had much to learn about his chosen profession he was forever saying. The kid from the north was not exactly an apt pupil. Sure he had potential, and a way with words, but these were not enough. He needed to work on his everyday manner. Particularly when it came to interacting with sources and leads. There was a certain equilibrium one had to maintain, and the would-be future Ischia International award winner had not yet learnt how to keep himself in check.

'You have a streak of brashness in you which is a double-edged sword,' Schiavone said as he pored over this topic, 'in this line of work it is a valuable asset to have at your disposal. You're persistent Fabio and that will get you so far. It will take you through doors that might otherwise remain closed, past all manner of security personnel and individual minders. But take care you don't employ it to the nth degree. Know when it should be cast-off. The subjects of your stories, the people you interview, will respond in the fashion you want provided you give them good reason. Be cordial Fabio. Don't always go on the offensive. Pull back when necessary. The direct question may be the expedient one, but it isn't always the most appropriate. Tease matters out as you go along. Keep your patience and hold your tongue. People will open up if you allow them. Every person wants to talk, including those in the spotlight and public eye. Never make them feel your sole purpose is to force them to talk.'

As he arrived at the hospital, Paparazzo again considered how he might best introduce himself. The idea of using the translator as a medium was still an appealing one. It would be a beginning at any rate. A few words exchanged between them and some idle banter about Milan perhaps. And then the focus of his attention shifting to Mrs. Taylor. This would be the tricky part he knew. How to make that progression as natural as possible. Without her recognising the crude mechanism behind it. Followed then by the obligatory moment when he'd have to identify himself. And tell her why he was here. She might very well protest at his forwardness. Ask if he wasn't aware of what she'd requested. It was a simple enough instruction really. Did he not understand it? Why then was he choosing to overlook it? No others from his line of work had been this brazen. Why wasn't he mindful as they were? Did he expect she'd grant him an interview just because he'd spoken to Francesca? Just because he happened to be from the same city as her interpreter?

If there was to be such a scene of remonstration, he hoped it would lead to this moment. He was prepared for it, had a response at the ready which, with any luck, would appease Mrs. Taylor. More than that hopefully; give her the good reason to talk which Schiavone referred to. Yes, he'd come to ask questions; about that day in Piazza Venezia. But more besides. The forensic details of the collision were well known. What he wished to establish was all that had gone before it. What the couple had done before the fateful incident. How they'd spent their time since arriving in Rome. This is the angle I want to pursue he could hear himself say. The interpretation I want to present my readers with is the human one. The one that goes beyond impassive metaphors and cold representations. Those matters have been gone over enough. By those other men in my line of work who you commend for not being as brazen as I am. I've approached you today because the tragedy surrounding your husband deserves a different brand of journalism. Your own anguish too is worthy of something more than remote coverage. That last bit sounds good he thought. Honest without being too maudlin. The subject of his article would surely open up when she'd hear that. The exclusive would be his then. Back at the office the scoffers would be tongue-tied. Even old Schiavone would be properly bowled over.

The main wing of the Agostino Gemelli, the Polyclinic, was quieter this afternoon. At the front desk the receptionist was directing an elderly couple to a particular ward by means of an intricate floor layout. Managing a quick smile for the well-turned-out reporter, she continued in her efforts to explain the route the pair needed to take.

'There are a set of elevators further down this way,' she said, indicating the passageway ahead, 'the ward you're looking for is on the fifth floor. As soon as you come out of the elevator, just follow the directions I gave you.'

'Good afternoon sir,' she said turning to Paparazzo.

'Good afternoon,' he replied.

'Don't you look dapper in that lovely suit,' she said, 'you must be visiting someone?'

'I'm here to meet someone,' he answered. 'Have you by chance seen Mrs. Taylor today? Don Taylor's wife.'

'A few times,' she nodded, 'there's no change as regards her husband if that's what you want to know. Mrs. Taylor has been here since early this morning, as she has been every day so far.'

'I'm aware of that. Would it be ok if I waited here?' he asked pointing to a seating area opposite the desk.

'Of course sir. You can stay as long as you wish. If there's any further news on Mr. Taylor, I'll let you know. Is there anything else I can help you with?'

'No, thank you. I'll be fine just here.'

A small notebook he had stuffed in his trousers' pocket bulged as he took a chair, obliging him to remove it. Glancing this way and that, he wondered how long it might be before Mrs. Taylor would appear. It was 2.25 according to his watch and it was at about this time the day before he'd passed them at the entrance door.

The minutes went by and no sighting of either woman. The intrepid reporter checked the time again and again.

2.51.

3.07.

3.24.

3.48.

Still no sign. Noticing a wall clock hung behind the receptionist's work area, he compared the reading on his own timepiece with this. A minute, more or less, separated the two. He had 3.49 now. It was moving on to 3.50.

4 o'clock came and went but it did not occasion the appearance of the Hollywood wife or her companion. Fabio examined an old concert ticket he'd discovered amongst the clutter in his wallet. It was for a 1991 performance by Bryan Adams at the Palatrussardi in Milan. He was puzzled by this. What the hell was I doing at a Bryan Adams concert he wondered. Was I dating at the time or trying to pick someone up? He couldn't make head or tail of it. A song by the Canadian rocker came to mind. It was called "Cuts like a Knife." By coincidence, he'd heard it on the car radio a few times recently.

'It cuts like a knife,
But it feels so right.'

He began to hum it to himself without knowing why. It was stuck in his head. Bad tunes had a tendency to do that. His ex-girlfriend used to laugh when he'd serenade her with songs both of them found unbearable. They'd broken up in January and, although he'd got over it, there was still a forlorn sensation which raised its head from time to time. Giulia had moved down with him to Rome and was still living in the city. Only he didn't know where. Mail arrived in her name but he had no forwarding address. She hadn't given him one reasoning that the break-up should be as complete as possible for both their sakes. That was silly he thought; and rather impractical as well. As a consequence, he now had an accumulation of correspondence in her name with which he could do nothing. His post box in the apartment building had become a small-scale dead letter office. Despite the fact that she was no longer living there, Giulia continued to receive more letters than he did. It was an odd state of affairs to say the least. He wondered if Bryan Adams or anyone else had written a song about that. His mind drifted further. He thought about Mrs. Taylor's interpreter, Francesca. She was quite pretty actually. He wondered if she was single. How long might she be living in Rome? Did she also refuse to leave forwarding addresses after splitting up with ex-boyfriends? Probably not he decided. She appeared quite level-headed from what he could make out. People who wore glasses had always given him that impression. They looked so cerebral and balanced. And quite sexy as well. Francesca was vaguely reminiscent of a young Ornella Muti. She was graceful and pleasing to the eye; did not look at all out of place beside the other woman.

The interpreter and Mrs. Taylor emerged from one of the elevators down the hall and came walking towards the entranceway. Paparazzo began to raise himself out of his seat as they drew nearer. He caught the eye of the receptionist who smiled again, as if divining his strategy. She said hello to the two ladies as they ambled by, and watched on as a relatively tall gentleman, dressed almost as well as the young reporter, interposed on them. Paparazzo saw this happen as well. He'd been ready to approach Mrs. Taylor before she went outdoors. And now this interloper had got in his way. Where did he come out of he wondered. Had he been waiting all this time as well?

The other man addressed Mrs. Taylor and sought to introduce himself.

'Mrs. Taylor,' he said, 'I'm Max Pellegrino. You may not remember me, but we met a few days ago.'

She did remember him and they spoke for a few minutes. Francesca stood to one side. Fabio attempted to eavesdrop, but could only pick up on snippets of their conversation. Mrs. Taylor thanked the visitor a number of times. The stranger accepted her gratitude in coherent, near-perfect, English. He was glad to have come he said. Only sorry it hadn't been earlier. The hope that her husband would soon recover was also conveyed. She thanked him once more and then a warm embrace was exchanged. The brief meeting came to an end. Mrs. Taylor and Francesca decided against going outdoors; instead, they returned to ICU. The stranger for his part did not leave until they were out of sight. He watched them disappear and only then proceeded towards the entranceway. He looked contented in himself; as if an obligation had been fulfilled. A matter settled conceivably. Or a promise honoured. Paparazzo did not know either way. But he was certain of one thing. He needed to find out. No two ways about it. His job demanded as much.

'Excuse me,' he called out to the other man as he emerged from the Polyclinic.

A strong glare from the late-afternoon sun required Max to position his hand over his eyes as he turned.

The reporter moved closer.

'Max, isn't it?' he said, 'I saw you inside just now. I thought it was you.'

'Do I know you?' Max enquired.

There was something vaguely familiar about the younger man, but he couldn't quite put his finger on it.

'We've met once before,' Paparazzo told him, 'you don't know me in the strictest sense. Introductions weren't made when we last spoke. I guess they weren't such a priority a few days ago.'

He paused and regarded the spot where they were now standing.

'In fact, I think it was just about here,' he said, 'last Friday evening if you recall. It was after Don Taylor's accident. I was here and so were lots of other people. You turned up as well.'

Max ruminated over this for a moment.

'Yes, I do remember,' he said, 'you were telling me some things about the story. I left before Mr. Taylor's agent finished his statement. I didn't see any point in remaining on past that.'

'You were upset I'm sure. A good many of his fans were when they heard the news. People crying and friends hugging. A teenage girl even told me she was going to hold a vigil for him at her school. Unfortunately, I didn't have the presence of mind to ask her which one. It would have made for a good story, don't you think? A short article perhaps. Don Taylor's grief-stricken fans unite in their sorrow. A display of solidarity for the Hollywood hero.'

'I'm sure you have plenty of material already,' said Max. 'You said something about bad news selling papers. I can well believe that. It's your business I suppose.'

Paparazzo nodded his agreement.

'It certainly is my business,' he said. 'But don't make the mistake of thinking that stories like this are the be all and end all of my profession. I cover a lot of show business stuff. Most of it is actually quite upbeat. It's not all about doomed relationships and misguided artists. There are lots of good things happening also. Which reminds me,' he said, smiling deliberately, 'I was covering this particular item last week which I think we would both categorise as...well...being the converse of bad news. It was about a famous American actor who'd come here to start shooting his new film. He was doing some publicity for that and there was also mention of his latest film due to be released shortly. Whatever the purpose behind the event, a lot of people turned up to see him: fans, admirers, cinema enthusiasts. They all came out to catch a glimpse. Hear a few words. There was lots of smiling and posturing. It's part and parcel of these things. The star waves and gives the public what it expects to see. He's in the foreground as only he should be. Everyone else makes up the backdrop. They're the supporting players, if that doesn't sound too theatrical. They understand how they're meant to perform and they never come between the star and his audience. Blending in I guess is the way you'd describe it. Wives, girlfriends, family members; sometimes the agents and publicists appear as well. They know what their function is. It's to bestow emphasis on the leading man. Make him seem even more important than he already is. Showing their appreciation and applauding his every word. Wide smiles when he makes a crack. Noisy cheering when he wraps it up. But this promotion was a little bit different. Not everyone on the stage was playing their part. You see I noticed this one individual who didn't seem to fit in. He looked apart from it all, at a remove, and the longer it went on, the more obvious it became. For me at least. I don't know if anyone else saw it.'

He paused before continuing.

'That was you Max, wasn't it?' he said, 'you were that person I saw up on the stage.'

'Yes, it was me,' the actor replied.

'Why were you there?'

'It was a meeting arranged with Mr. Taylor. We were to do some work together.'

'What sort of work?'

'Does that really matter? It won't be taking place now.'

'Yet here you are.'

'I don't follow?' said Max.

'Meeting with Mrs. Taylor. Passing on your best wishes, no doubt.'

'It seemed the right thing to do. I think she appreciated it.'

'I'm sure she did. But it doesn't answer my previous question. What work were you taking on with Don Taylor? Why did it necessitate your being in Trastevere?'

'I don't see how that's any of your business Mr....'

'Paparazzo. Fabio Paparazzo is my name.'

'It wasn't of any great consequence. Mr. Taylor required a service. I was going to provide it. Once we were finished, he'd get on with his work and I'd get on with mine.'

'Which is acting, isn't it?'

Max nodded.

'I'm an actor, yes,' he said.

'And a very restrained one at that,' the reporter observed. 'Why are you so guarded in your response? I thought someone in your position would be only too willing to...'

'What do you mean someone in my position?' snapped Max, 'you don't know anything about me.'

'I know enough Max,' Paparazzo replied with intent in his voice, 'I saw the look on your face that day and it told me plenty. You didn't want to be there no more than Mrs. Taylor wants her husband in that hospital bed. We both know that. You were brought on stage to be one of the supporting cast members. That's the purpose you were to serve. One of the subordinates. Nothing more than a minor character.'

The tactic worked. His quarry was suitably provoked.

'Let's be very clear about something Mr. Paparazzo,' Max said sternly, 'I'm not a subordinate. I never have been and I didn't consider myself to be one that day either.'

'Max, it doesn't matter what you thought you were. For all I know you may have been lured out there for some other reason. Maybe you were charmed into it, I can't say. But to the crowd you were just another nonentity. And you realised it as soon as you got out there in front of them. I know you did. I saw you. It was written all over your face. You were pigeonholed and you didn't like it one bit. Just tell me I'm wrong and I'll leave you alone.'

The actor looked daggers at him.

'There's no need to tell you anything,' he said angrily, 'I'm leaving now. If you want a story, I suggest you look somewhere else for it.'

He glanced back at the hospital.

'And don't think about looking for it in there either,' he said, 'Mrs. Taylor asked for privacy as you well know. The last thing she needs right now is a loud-mouthed ass like you prying into her affairs.'

He turned his back and began to walk away.

Paparazzo called after him as he went.

'I'll look for it wherever I have to Max,' he said. 'In this place or that. I'm not afraid of putting myself out there. Unlike you, I don't play second fiddle. And I will get the story by the way, in case you're interested. Mark my words, I will get it.'

An hour later, the reporter was politely refused an interview by Mrs. Taylor who informed him she had not changed her mind about doing interviews.

THE MAJESTIC

It was a wet Thursday evening in Rome and Tom Steiner was braving the inclement conditions as he returned to the Majestic from a short walk. The 51-year old had borrowed a large umbrella from the hotel, and ventured as far as Porta Pinciana, close to the entrance of the Villa Borghese gardens. On his way back along Via Veneto, he peered in at the assorted café-bars and restaurants lining the fashionable street. They were busy in spite of the rainfall. Stopping at the well-known Café de Paris, he briefly considered going inside for a drink. It had been a long week. He felt the need for a pick-me-up. So much had been going on over the last few days. It was difficult to take it all in. On a personal level, the agent had been spending the greater part of his time between the Agostino Gemelli and Umberto First hospitals. Vicki had been discharged the day before. She was doing much better now, but was still weak following her appendectomy. The fact that her appendix had ruptured had obliged a longer than expected hospital stay. It had also prompted her mother to fly in from Los Angeles. Lydia was staying at the Majestic now as well. She was there with their daughter. The two of them would be wondering where he was gone. He'd said he was only going to stretch his legs, but then decided on something more extended. Outdoors had looked inviting despite the unpleasant weather. A quick drink in the café was an appealing idea, but it seemed more practical to have one back in the hotel bar. Chances were it wouldn't be as full as this.

Tom didn't fancy sitting in a crowd right now. He wanted to clear his head. This was the reason for his walk. Take a little time out he figured. Escape the madness for a few minutes. It had worked for a time, but his mind kept returning to the here-and-now. The unavoidable facts. His client and friend was not going to recover from the injuries he'd suffered. Almost a week since the accident and the reality of the situation was as clear as day. Don Taylor would not be emerging from his coma. At least not the Don Taylor Tom had known personally for so many years. And certainly not the Don Taylor the entire film world had grown to love and admire so much. It was all too depressing. Tom felt a tear swell in his eye and tried to wipe it away. Foolishly he used his other hand which had been swinging freely in the downpour. The moisture only made the matter worse, forcing him to come to a standstill. He pulled out a tissue, mopped his wet face.

His mind wandered back to the early days at SLR. Don was one of their first major-league clients. An unexpected poach and an absolute coup. Securing the already famous actor had sent out an important message to the rest of the community. SLR had arrived and was here to stay. Tom owed so much to the star. Don's decision to switch to the gestating talent agency had come at an opportune moment. It gave it a much-needed impetus at a time when some were dismissing it as just another ephemeral organisation which would not survive. The stories about the makeshift furniture Tom and his partners, Ernest Lovett and Larry Reeves, had been using were true. With fond memories, Tom recalled how he'd brought Don through to their offices that first day, when he'd dropped in, and how the actor had laughed when he saw their arrangements.

'Seriously fellas,' he joked, 'you've got to get yourselves some real desks and chairs or I'm out of here. You can't have me worrying that one of you is going to take a tumble from those shitty seats. An injury in this office could hurt me more than it hurts you.'

As a good will gesture and, more importantly, a display of confidence, he sent them over a batch of furniture the following week. Desks, tables, chairs, shelves and filing cabinets were all provided; more than enough to get them up and running properly. A note accompanying the delivery read:

'To Tom, Ernest and Larry – three stand-up guys, who can now safely sit down.'

Don had been a real stand-up guy himself as well. Their collective fortunes had prospered hand-in-hand and the two men built up a strong rapport over the passing years. True it was that their relationship had hit a rocky patch in more recent times. Don was hell-bent on pursuing a new direction; one he felt his career was crying out for. Tom did not entirely agree with this. If it ain't broke, don't fix it was his philosophy. He tried telling his client this, but Don was not for turning. The Proper Citizen was accepted in spite of the agent's better advice, and even that shambolic flop had not discouraged the actor. Another challenging piece – so-called – was decided upon. The new film triggered more friction between the two. Tom tried everything to change Don's mind. He talked about the need to alternate certain types of projects. Interchanges and trade-offs were encouraged. He pleaded for an approach based on rotation as opposed to revolution. But to no avail. The star was bound for Rome in April. He was going to play Antonio Meucci no matter what happened, regardless of any consequences, come what may.

What came of course was something that everyone was now trying to deal with as best as they could. Lee; Todd; Tom; Aggregate Pictures; even David Cousins. Notwithstanding his aversion to it, the agent knew full well that Don would have to be removed from the film. The studio had no choice in that regard. The production could not be delayed for an open-ended period. Word had it that Aggregate would soon be tabling the termination of contract. It would surely be in the next few days. By that time Tom would most likely be back in LA. Lydia, Vicki and he were leaving on Saturday. There was nothing else to be done in Rome. He wasn't going to accomplish anything by hanging around. Don was in the hands of the doctors now. No one else could help him. The sort of assistance Tom specialised in was of no use here. It was time to turn the page. Simply time to go home.

Entering the lobby of the hotel, he headed straight to the front desk to return the brolly which he'd folded down.

'Thanks for the loan of this,' he said to the receptionist, 'it certainly isn't an evening for the faint-hearted out there. Rome changes in the rain like so many other cities do. I hope it passes soon. My family and I are going back to the States on Saturday.'

The receptionist said she was aware of this and took the dripping umbrella from him.

'Oh signor,' she said, 'there is a man waiting to see you. He has been upstairs in the bar for the past twenty minutes I think. I explained you were out and wasn't sure when you'd be returning, but he said he would wait.'

'Did he now?' Tom said puzzled as to who this might be. He wondered if it was Andrew Ford, the Echo of Passions production manager, who he'd met a few times since coming to Rome. Or one of the other Americans working at Cinecittà Studios. It couldn't be David Cousins he was certain. Their paths had crossed once or twice at the hospital, and they'd been civil to one another for Lee Taylor's sake, but surely he wasn't calling. There was far too much bad history between them for that.

'I need to phone my wife upstairs to let her know I'm in. Can I use your phone?' he asked.

'Of course signor.'

The phone rang twice before Lydia picked it up.

'Hello hon,' Tom said, 'I'm just back in and have to meet someone at the bar. I should be up in half an hour or so.'

'No problem dear,' she replied, 'Vicki and me are watching an Italian TV host called Mike Bongiorno. He's an amusing guy. We've no idea what he's saying, but it's very entertaining.'

Tom took the stairs up to the first floor and looked about the chic bar. There were one or two couples sitting at the smaller tables, European-sounding from their conversations, and a small group of lively English tourists towards the back.

At the bar sat a young man nursing a bottle of Peroni. He was by himself and appeared to be waiting on someone. Presuming this to be the caller, Tom sat down beside him.

'My name is Tom Steiner,' he said by way of introduction, 'I was told you wanted to see me.'

'I'm very pleased to meet you,' the stranger replied, 'my name is Fabio Paparazzo. I write for Il Quarto Stato, a newspaper based here in Rome. I've heard about you in the past Mr. Steiner. Head of one of the most powerful talent agencies in Hollywood. Your name is closely associated with so many famous people. I could probably mention any number of individuals who you know very well.'

'You could,' Tom replied, 'but I didn't quite catch your name.'

'Fabio Paparazzo.'

'Paparazzi?!'

The reporter shook his head.

'Paparazzo,' he repeated.

'That's your surname?' the incredulous agent said.

'That is my surname Mr. Steiner. The term paparazzi actually comes from a Fellini film, La Dolce Vita. The character of the news photographer was named Paparazzo and I guess it took on a life of its own from that. You can imagine the number of jokes made at my expense.'

'I bet,' said Tom, 'I think I've heard it all now! I'm talking to a newshound called Paparazzi!'

'Paparazz-o,' the other man emphasised again. 'Paparazzi is the plural. I'm by myself as you can see. I came here hoping you might have a few words to say about the events of recent days. A great deal has happened, but the story is far from a conclusion. Who better than a man like you to offer an opinion on what might follow in the time to come.'

Tom sighed, rolled his eyes.

'I'm not talking to the press about this Mr. Paparazzi,' he said, 'what I said outside the hospital last Friday represents all I have to say. Quite frankly you're wasting your time if you expect me to do otherwise. I know this game too well and I've had first-hand experience of how reporters like you blow these things out of proportion. I understand there are no tabloid-type newspapers in Italy, but that doesn't mean you guys don't know how to sensationalise. No is my answer and that's how it's going to stay. Now, if you'll excuse me.'

He slid down off the bar stool.

Paparazzo remained sitting on his.

'Mr. Steiner, there's no need for me to sensationalise this story any more than it is,' he said, 'or to blow it out of proportion. It already is that way. It's a news item that's taken off like a juggernaut. The moment your client, Mr. Taylor, stepped out in front of that car, it became this thing. I think you're frustrated because there was no way you could control it. Not here in Italy. Back in Hollywood you have measures of dealing with situations like this. A publicity machine that suppresses just as effectively as it promotes. Drug addictions, marital break-ups, accidents which require a cover-up. The information is either streamlined or it's not made available at all. You refuse to talk to journalists like me because of the different culture you know exists here. Rome is not Los Angeles. The journalistic style is different as well. We write it as it is. Not how someone thinks it ought to be.'

He was interrupted as the English tourists began to pass out by them. They were leaving for another venue. Discussions were loud and animated. The next location was the matter under consideration. A few said hello to them both in merry voices. One lady told Tom to cheer up. He looked far too vexed.

'Always look on the bright side of life,' she told him.

A verse of the famous song broke out amongst her group. It continued as they went down the stairs and out of sight.

'Life's a piece of shit, when you look at it,
Life's a laugh and death's a joke, it's true,
You see it's all a show, keep laughing as you go,
Just remember that the last laugh is on you.'
Paparazzo smiled.

Tom, however, was not amused.

'Well Mr. Paparazzi, perhaps you can fabricate a story out of that,' he said in a voice loaded with sarcasm, 'famous Hollywood agent in drunken singsong with English revellers. You could say it was brought on because his client had been in an accident. He was feeling low and looking for answers in the bottom of a bottle. Dress it up whatever way you want. Personally I don't fucking care. In less than 48 hours I'm out of here. I'll leave all the ballyhoo to yellow journalists like you. I'm sure I don't need to explain that word to you – ballyhoo. No doubt you get the context.'

'I get the context Mr. Steiner, but there's one other thing. You attended an event in Trastevere two days before Mr. Taylor's accident. It was to publicise your client's presence here in Rome as well as the film he was about to begin. You remember that I assume?'

'I remember it. What's it got to do with anything?'

'There was another actor in attendance that day.'

'Another actor? Who was that?'

'His name is Max Pellegrino.'

Tom thought about this for a moment.

'Oh the mimic, the dubbing guy. Yes, he was there at someone else's invitation.'

'He was going to work with Mr. Taylor on the film I understand.'

'In a limited capacity. Some dialogue coaching or other. You've got the wrong end of the stick if you think it was anything more than that. An hour or two would have been more than enough for Mr. Taylor. He's a very fine actor.'

'So is Mr. Pellegrino. One of our best in fact. I paid a visit yesterday to the recording studio where he does a lot of his work, dubbing films of Mr. Taylor and other stars. Many of the actors who work there have training for stage and screen. Our national film industry unfortunately doesn't offer a lot in the way of career opportunities nowadays, so they move into dubbing and voiceover work because it provides them with employment and income. For instance, there's a well-known Italian actor named Giancarlo Giannini who has dubbed both Jack Nicholson and Al Pacino. In the 1970's he got an Oscar nomination for best actor. But how many people do you think know about that? Not a lot I can tell you. The industry is undervalued by members of the public. Most of these actors are nameless to them.'

'Well, that's the price of anonymity I guess,' the agent said derisively. 'So what's it got to do with me?'

'It's got nothing to do with you Mr. Steiner. But in Mr. Taylor's absence the producers of the film in Cinecittà will be seeking to replace him as quickly as possible. Isn't that so?'

'That would be a fair assessment; but bear in mind that comment is off the record.'

'I understand that finding a replacement actor at such short notice is not always such an easy thing. A twelfth hour replacement.'

'The expression is eleventh hour actually.'

'No, Mr. Steiner. In this case it is twelfth hour. The film was supposed to begin tomorrow, wasn't it?'

'It was supposed to begin tomorrow, yes.'

'So what do they do? Or should I rephrase, what have they been doing?'

'Most likely, and again off the record Mr. Paparazzi, they'll have put together a list of first preferences and from there checked schedules and availabilities. Representations will be made to establish if there are suitable gaps for those actors who are not currently working. The end date for principal photography will be tossed around to see if there's an individual who's a fit. Of course he'll be subject to approval of the creative and monetary forces behind the film. The process is a difficult one, but it's not without a possible resolution. A few years ago one of my clients had a production cancelled and was available to step in to such a breach. Only for him, who knows.'

Paparazzo motioned his understanding of the situation.

'It sounds every bit as complex as I thought,' he said, 'few potential actors at the ready, and even the ones who are might not be appropriate for the role. Then it's on to a second and third list I suppose?'

'If such a need arises,' said Tom.

'This client of yours who replaced another actor at the last moment, do you think he saved the production? I mean, do you think they would have found someone else?'

'They might have, but not as good as he is, and was in that film. He also got an Oscar nomination; same as your Mr....'

'Giannini.'

'If you say so. I honestly don't remember that name.'

Paparazzo stared at the other man more intently.

'Mr. Steiner,' he said, 'there is an actor currently available who would be a fit for the role, as you put it. He has talent and experience and is approximately the same age as Don Taylor. He would be ideal for the part I think.'

'Really?' Tom replied sceptically. 'What's this heavyweight's name?'

'Max Pellegrino.'

The agent cracked up at the suggestion, patted the journalist on the shoulder.

'Well, Mr. Paparazzi, you truly have revealed yourself. When we first spoke I mistook you for a common hack. Then I called you a yellow journalist. On both counts, I was wrong. You're neither a common hack nor a yellow journalist. You're a gimmick merchant, a wannabe showman in the mould of Phineas Barnum. This Max Pellegrino is your Jumbo the

Elephant. Except he's Mumbo Jumbo. Do you honestly think you could peddle a suggestion like that? Spread the word and people would buy into such a preposterous idea? There are no overnight sensations Mr. Paparazzi. Not in the literal sense. It takes a lot more time and I can tell you an Italian nobody mimic will never fit the bill. You're backing the wrong elephant in this case. I suggest you return to the circus and find an act that's been turning better tricks. Goodnight and good luck to you. You'll certainly need it.'

He turned to leave.

'You seem to know a great deal about the subject Mr. Steiner,' said Paparazzo, 'I thought you Hollywood men believed anything is possible. What about the dream factory? To hear you put down the idea surely flies in the face of what Hollywood is about, no? My impression was you'd risen quickly in your own career. I must have been mistaken about that. Perhaps it's that which informs the opinion you hold.'

Tom swung around.

'Let me tell you about where I started Mr. Paparazzi, and how it informs the opinion I hold,' he said.

'Paparazz-o,' the reporter corrected one last time.

'My first job was for a talent agency called Dexter Simonoff,' Tom continued, 'I was with them for many years. I started out in the mailroom there, same way everyone else does. The work was tedious and tough. Long days and even some weekend errands were not uncommon. Often I had to change the toilet paper in the bathrooms and replenish the soap dispensers. Mixing chemicals for the Photostat machine was another job I regularly got. Watering plants and filling fountain pens; hardly glamorous, not things you'd associate with Hollywood. But I was willing to play my part. I knew it was what I had to do to get to the next level. I would have done anything back then for advancement. I was hungry for it. The mailroom in a talent agency is the perfect training ground. You learn that if you haven't got the patience to put up with the shitty stuff, then you're not going to become one of the elite. It's a series of tests. A wholesale exercise in humility. Everyone needs a stretch down there. A couple of times I got impatient about it. And there were a few false dawns as well. One day I was sorting mail with another trainee when a phone call came through. He answered it. 'Tom,' he said, 'it's for you. It's Mr. Simonoff's secretary.' I couldn't believe it. Milton Simonoff, the chairman and owner of the agency, calling me, a kid working in his mailroom. The secretary told me Mr. Simonoff wanted to have lunch. I couldn't believe my ears. I thought what a great place to work. The head of the company inviting one of the minions to lunch. Could it get any better than this? Yes, it could. Fifteen minutes later another call came from Simonoff's secretary. 'I'm sorry,' she said, 'I made a mistake. I thought I was calling Tony Steiner. I didn't realise there were two Steiners in the building. I'm afraid there's no lunch invitation for you. But keep up the good work. Mr. Simonoff said he's never remembered the mailroom run so efficiently.' A while after that I bumped into Simonoff himself. It was in the elevator. I got on at the 24ᵗʰ floor and pushed 25. When we got to the 25ᵗʰ floor, Simonoff looked at me and said, 'go back down to 24 and walk up the flight of stairs. Employees in the mailroom don't take the elevator one floor.' It was one of the few times he'd spoken to me and it frightened the hell out of me. But it taught me a lesson as well. There are very few shortcuts or lucky breaks; and even those that exist do not confer instant fame and fortune. I'm thinking you need to walk up several flights yourself Mr. Paparazz-o. I'm thinking you need to go all the way back down to the ground floor.'

The reporter smiled dismissively.

'Thank you for the advice Mr. Steiner,' he said, 'in spite of what you say, I intend to stay on the floor I'm on. And I also intend to write my story.'

'About this Max Pellegrino?'

'About Max Pellegrino and other actors like him. The ones who are unknown. The ones who are deserving of more exposure. Bringing them into the light so to speak.'

'By proposing that one of them could replace Don Taylor?'

'Why not? If that's what it takes.'

Tom laughed once more, indicated he was done with their conversation.

'Have it your way Mr. Paparazz-o,' he said, as he walked away, 'go and create your own Jumbo the Elephant if that's what you want. It might even get you some attention. Who knows. There's a sucker born every minute as they say. Max Pellegrino could turn out to be your General Tom Thumb for all I know. Stranger things have happened. But he will never be a Don Taylor. Mark my words. Never.'

Disappearing around the corner, he could be heard whistling the Monty Python tune. Then he was gone.

BACKSTORY

'What the hell are you doing here?' Max asked when he saw Fabio Paparazzo standing in the hallway of his apartment building. He'd just had a shower after a jog around Villa Doria Pamphili. His hair was still wet; the beads of moisture on his body were only beginning to dry off. Dressed in nothing more than a dark cotton bathrobe, he'd been obliged to answer the doorbell. It was a nuisance having someone call this early in the day. Probably one of the neighbours in need of something he supposed. Vallelunga down the hall was constantly dropping by for milk or other such items. Making a hurried apology, he would promise not to trouble his nearby resident again. But he always managed to; could always be relied upon for his absent-mindedness. The most recent visit had been occasioned due to a lack of sugar in his household as he put it. But there was just him living in the apartment Max thought. What was it with the term household and its connotations of more than one? He made it seem as if he was feeding hordes in there or something. God forbid if he ever had to provide for more than himself. That would be the day to start looking for a new apartment.

'I'm sorry to disturb you at home Mr. Pellegrino...Max,' Paparazzo said sounding almost demure about it, 'I got your address from the studio you work in, Universal Recordings. They said you'd most likely be working from home at the moment. I understand you do a lot of voiceover work as well as dubbing.'

'That's correct,' Max replied tersely.

There was no invitation to enter forthcoming. Paparazzo smiled awkwardly.

'I was speaking to one of the dubbing directors at the studio,' he said, 'a man by the name of Damiano di Stefano. He tells me you're quite an actor. Said that you've worked there for many years.'

'That's correct,' was the same distrustful response.

Paparazzo adjusted his stance.

'Look Max I'm sorry for what happened the other day outside the hospital,' he said, 'especially for what I said. I came on far too strong and I shouldn't have suggested you were a...'

'Another nonentity?'

'Yes, that was it.'

'That evening outside the Agostino Gemelli; you said something about what your boss calls you.'

'His referred pain?'

'Actually you're more a direct pain as far as I'm concerned. You certainly were a few days ago.'

'And for that I'm truly sorry Max. I can be loud-mouthed just like you say. It's a tendency of mine to charge in all guns blazing. It's been my Achilles' heel on a few occasions. Mrs. Taylor for example. With her though I tried to keep myself in check. I thought I had a means of approach that would get her to open up. But she saw me coming a mile away.'

'I'm glad she did,' said Max, 'you know when people say they're not talking to the media, they usually mean it. No interviews or questions means just that. You might think about listening more carefully.'

'As I'm doing now Max. I'm listening to you and not one bad word has passed between us.'

The youthful smile reappeared. It was more assured now.

Max relaxed somewhat but was still on his guard. From the corner of his eye, he spied Andrea Vallelunga coming out his door.

'Well I guess I'm going to find out why you came to see me at some point in time,' he said, anxious to retreat back inside, 'you'd better come in I suppose. I have a pot of coffee on if you want some.'

'Thank you Max,' an appreciative Paparazzo replied.

Max's apartment was a modestly-furnished dwelling with a regular-sized living room and kitchen unit combined. In the living space, there was an L-shaped leather sofa and a rustic oak coffee table. Some books and magazines were scattered on the table top and there was a formal-looking document propped up against a tall floor lamp. It was titled HQD Pharmaceuticals. Paparazzo looked at it for a few moments before returning his attention to the rest of the space. The wall opposite the seating area was concealed in the main by some functional cube shelving and two large film canvases. In the right-hand corner was a television set, perched on a slim glass stand; underneath it a dated VCR set into its own wooden cabinet. There were a few films close to the machine, but Fabio couldn't distinguish what they were. He wondered if the actor liked the same types of films he did. It was quite likely he thought. The prints on the wall certainly suggested they shared the same taste.

'Hey! The Good, The Bad and The Ugly,' he said eyeing one of them, 'I love that film. I must have seen it a dozen times or more. Sad Hill Cemetery and the grave of Arch Stanton. What an ending!'

His focus moved on to the other wooden frame.

'And Fellini's Amarcord. What a great comedy that is. I can never forget the scene when the mad uncle climbs up the tree and starts yelling 'I want a woman!' No one is able to get him down except the dwarf nun. I'm sure she wasn't what he had in mind as regards a female companion, eh?'

'I guess not,' replied Max who was surprised and somewhat impressed by his visitor's cinematic knowledge. 'Please have a seat,' he said pointing to the sofa.

They both sat down.

'I guess like most people I never appreciated the work that's done in the studio, converting a film into Italian,' said the journalist. 'The first film I can remember seeing in the cinema was Kelly's Heroes. I was convinced

Clint Eastwood and Telly Savalas spoke Italian just like the rest of us. It was only later on my father told me they didn't. I asked him how it was they sounded so real. Being a chartered accountant, he was only able to give me a limited explanation. Your colleague Mr. di Stefano on the other hand gave me a full-length account. I hadn't realised how intricate the process is. It opened my eyes. So many skilled technicians. And as for the actors, like you, I didn't know how accomplished so many of them are.'

Max concurred with this.

'Yes, there are many talented professionals working in the industry,' he said, 'no doubt Damiano provided you with an extensive history. He was once an actor himself. He takes a lot of pride in our work.'

'As well he should.'

'So your father used to take you to the cinema?'

'Yes, fairly regularly. The early 1970's was a good time to go. There were lots of spaghetti westerns and poliziescos; the Trinity films with Terence Hill and Bud Spencer, and Giú la testa of course. One time I sneaked in to see a giallo called The Bloodstained Shadow. I couldn't sleep for a week after it. I decided then to return to my more familiar diet of Disney's and Pink Panther movies.'

The two men shared a laugh about this.

'My father didn't take me to the cinema,' said Max, 'he didn't have a lot of time for such things. Now he wasn't one of those people who considered the movie house a den of iniquity or something. We had a few of those in our town. He thought it important that my sister and I grow up with a sense of level-headedness. The cinema didn't teach you anything practical he always said. Make-believe stories wouldn't stand to you in the everyday world.'

'He sounds like he was a harsh man,' Paparazzo remarked.

'He wasn't that harsh really,' Max replied, 'it was just who he was. No-nonsense was his style. He was plain speaking and wasn't one for the fanciful. Modesty was his mantra. He had some very definite ideas on the subject. Used to tell us it was far more important to conform to the norms rather than go against the grain. Better to be like everyone else as opposed to standing out on your own he'd say. That was the way to happiness and self-fulfillment. It was grounding your expectations in reality. Not pinning them on impossible dreams. He knew I had other ideas. Probably realised it at an early stage of my life. I wanted to do something different. Something that would set me apart. I grew up in a small town just like that one in Amarcord. It was easy to be prominent there. All you had to do was turn handstands in the main square. My father didn't like that one bit. He said it was shameful behaviour and nothing would come of it. Maintained there was no place for it in the real world. His world though wasn't mine. One time I did impersonations outside the local cinema, characters from the peplums. I needed money to see the film which was playing that week. Word got back to him and he flew into a rage. I was punished and warned off a repeat performance.'

'An order you didn't obey I take it?' said Paparazzo.

'I disobeyed him eventually,' said Max, 'try as I did, I couldn't restrain myself forever. Something happened and I just had to have another crack at it.'

'Leading to another performance?'

'Yes. Only this time he didn't stop me. He allowed me to persevere with it. I don't know what changed his mind. Perhaps he decided there was only so much he could say or do. Perhaps he believed I needed to learn my lesson the hard way.'

He shook his head and smiled ironically.

'If he'd seen me on that stage with Don Taylor a few days back, in the presence of Don Taylor more accurately, well I'm sure he'd have something to say about it. Reality, dreams; those would be his cue words. It'd be my turn to stand and listen. People tend to make speeches when they consider they have the high ground on you. If he was still alive, my father would be standing on the Esquiline Hill right now. I can't say I'd blame him for being there.'

'So I was right about that? You didn't feel comfortable up there?' Paparazzo nudged.

'It's true,' Max admitted, 'I didn't feel pleased to be there. Mr. Taylor invited me to go on. I suppose he thought I'd enjoy it. But I didn't. After it was over, I couldn't get off quickly enough.'

'Why do you think that was?'

'I knew I didn't belong up there,' Max explained, 'it was like you said: the feeling hit me as soon as we went on. I probably should have listened to Don Taylor's agent. He wasn't so eager that I appear. He phoned me the evening before Trastevere just to make sure I understood. Told me not to discuss the film with his client, not to draw out the work we were to do together any longer than was necessary.'

Paparazzo signed his familiarity with the individual in question.

'I had a chat with that very person yesterday evening,' he said.

'Tom Steiner?'

'Yes,' Fabio confirmed. 'I managed to track him down to the Majestic Hotel where he's been staying. He's going back to America in the next day or two. He said as much about you and Don Taylor working together. Told me your assignment would have only taken a few hours.'

'It's quite possible,' Max agreed, 'Mr. Taylor had asked for my assistance with some dialogue coaching for the Meucci film. Well, it was actually his brother who'd contacted Universal Recordings.'

'Not the agent so?'

'Most definitely not the agent. I think his attitude about it suggests that much.'

'It certainly does. He doesn't seem to have a great deal of respect for the work that's done in the studios here either,' said Fabio.

'I'm not surprised by that.'

'He referred to individuals in your profession as...well...I'm sorry to repeat this.'

'Go on,' Max urged.

'He called you a mimic Max.'

'A mimic?'

'That was the exact word he used. Uncomplimentary, don't you think?'

'Yes, it is. But again, no great surprise. A man like that can be as derogatory as he wants. It goes with the territory I suppose.'

'Doesn't that anger you though?' Paparazzo asked, attempting to fan the flames. 'This man takes a pot shot at your livelihood and all you can say is you're not surprised! Don't you have more to say than just that?!'

'What do you expect me to say Mr. Paparazzo? I know how the system works. I know what the pecking order is. I'm a voice actor who didn't make it the way he hoped he would. It's a fact of life I've had to accept. We don't all get to do the things we want in this business, to be the next star or make films with the big directors. So we settle. We make do. But that doesn't mean I accept what this man Steiner thinks. I know my work has value. I know what I do is worthwhile. I don't need endorsements from him or anyone else.'

'So you're perfectly content with where you are then? Is that it?' said Paparazzo. 'What happened to the boy who wanted to do something different? Did his spirit get broken this badly? Or was it that handstands and impersonations were enough in the end? The kind of cheap tricks that are more befitting a fantozziano comedy.'

'Mr. Paparazzo, I'm not saying my life has worked out without some blemishes. In an ideal world, I wouldn't be spending as much time behind the mike as I do. Of course I've thought about the alternatives. It's hard not to. But I'm almost 40 years old. My options have pretty much dried up. Perhaps I did remain in the darkness of the studio for too long. Perhaps it's been to my detriment. 15 years ago I made a film which I thought would jump-start my career. As it turned out, it almost provided the kiss of death. It practically broke my spirit as well. I came close to giving up. I wasn't able to handle the failure you see. The let-down was almost too much for me. Becoming a voice actor gave me a safety net. It ensured I wouldn't have to face such disappointments again.'

Paparazzo shook his head in disagreement.

'It also guaranteed you'd never have any success Max. At least not the sort regular people know about. You may get the principal parts in those movies you dub, you may very well be one of the best actors in the business, like that dubbing director friend of yours says, but what does all of that amount to if there's no recognition? Not a lot if you ask me. And I think not a lot to you either, truth being told. You see what I'm saying Max? You may be the big fish in the small pond, but you're also the actor who could have been a great deal more. Problem was you weren't brave enough to have another shot at it.'

Max was irritated by this.

'I think you've said enough Mr. Paparazzo,' he said, 'I think some of those bad words have passed between us again.'

The journalist remained adamant.

'You want to hear a bad word Max? Well I have one for you – nobody. That's something else Mr. Steiner called you when we spoke last night. An Italian nobody mimic. Now tell me you can put up with that. Tell me it doesn't enrage you in the least bit. If you can, then I'll leave at once.'

'Mr. Paparazzo, being a journalist as you are, I wouldn't put it past you to exaggerate those words. Knowing you, as I already do, I'd more than suspect you of putting a certain spin on them.'

The reporter's response was to produce an audio recorder from his jacket pocket.

'What's that?' asked Max.

'What does it look like Max. You make recordings, so do I,' said Paparazzo.

He pressed the playback button.

Tom Steiner's voice came up, unmistakeably him.

'This Max Pellegrino is your Jumbo the Elephant. Except he's Mumbo Jumbo. Do you honestly think you could peddle a suggestion like that? Spread the word and people would buy into such a preposterous idea? There are no overnight sensations Mr. Paparazzi. Not in the literal sense. It takes a lot more time and I can tell you an Italian nobody mimic will never fit the bill. You're backing the wrong elephant in this case. I suggest you return to the circus and find an act that's been turning better tricks.'

Paparazzo switched off the recorder.

'A nobody! An elephant! Mumbo Jumbo!!' Max repeated.

'Straight from the horse's mouth Max. How does it make you feel?'

'How do you think it makes me feel?' said Max. 'I'm back on that stage in Trastevere again. I'm frustrated. The same way I was in Ariccia.'

'Where you come from?'

'My hometown, yes.'

'So the flame hasn't quite gone out, has it? The ambition isn't completely buried.'

'Is it ever?'

Paparazzo smiled.

'I hope not Max. You see I've had a few disappointments in my own career to date. Some things that didn't go how I hoped they would. You pick yourself up afterwards and you believe the next story might be the breakthrough piece you're looking for. The one that will capture people's attention. It brought me here today.'

'Only after you'd failed with Mrs. Taylor and the agent,' Max reminded him.

'With Mrs. Taylor, yes,' the reporter acknowledged. 'From Mr. Steiner, however, I got exactly what I was looking for.'

'What was that?'

'A reaction, to a suggestion I made to him. You may have picked up on it from the recording. We spoke about the Meucci film. The considerable problem that has existed for it since Don Taylor's accident. Do you know how difficult it can be to replace an actor when time is not on your side?'

Max shrugged his shoulders.

'I've no personal experience of the situation,' he said, 'they could get lucky. Another actor might become free. One man's misfortune could be another's opportunity.'

'That's what I said to Mr. Steiner. I proposed to him that such an actor is already available. I suggested it was you Max.'

This latter statement was met with a look of disbelief.

'Now I think you are mad, as well as being a pain,' Max said, 'it's little wonder he told you to join the circus. Perhaps it's where you belong.'

He paused for a moment deliberating something else.

'What did you mean just then when you said you got what you were looking for?' he asked. 'He obviously scoffed at your idea, as most people would. What purpose did it serve you listening to his disparaging it?'

Paparazzo smiled cunningly.

'It wasn't for me Max,' he said. 'It was for you. It was so that you'd hear it.'

'So that I'd hear it?'

'It got your blood up, didn't it? Reminded you of who you are. Not some nobody or another nonentity. You went back to that kid performing in the main square of your hometown. You showed me that look again. The one I saw in Trastevere. Mr. Steiner was something of a blunt instrument I'll admit. But a highly effective one.'

'And your suggestion about the film? Was that a trick as well?'

'Oh my proposition still stands Max. I'd like to write about you. An article about your career, its ups and downs, the good, the bad and the ugly so to speak. At the heart of it will be that very proposal. In Hollywood they'd call it a pitch.'

His hands became lively as he outlined an imaginary excerpt.

'Why shouldn't an actor as gifted as Max Pellegrino be considered for the role of Antonio Meucci? He has all the essential qualities for the part: experience and versatility. He has an excellent reputation in the profession he makes a living. There's no reason why his flair can't be reproduced on a bigger stage. Out of the shadows. Into the limelight. The only impediment is he has no fame, no celebrity status.'

'You've got that much right,' said Max 'absolutely no fame or celebrity status. No one is interested if those things are absent.'

'But they would be interested if they believed someone was worthy of fame,' Paparazzo offered, 'more importantly, if they thought such celebrity status was imminent. Just a whisper away. People become excited when they think such prospects are on the horizon. Especially for one of their own. A big Hollywood production in town. A local actor vying for the lead role. It's a wonderful story.'

'It's a lot of other things as well; and besides all that, I'm not vying for the lead role. You'd never pull it off.'

'I'm a very good writer Max,' Paparazzo said confidently, 'you'd be amazed at what I can do with words. My article would say you're deserving of this kind of break. At the very minimum, I promise it will raise your profile. And then, who knows what. There could be offers here at home. Maybe from other places as well. You'd get more than your 15 minutes of fame. I guarantee it. Think of the opportunity. When will it come again? Will it ever come again?'

He eyed the corporate document which still rested against the floor lamp.

'The HQD Pharmaceuticals of this world are ten-a-penny,' he said, 'chances like this are not. It's up to you now Max. Do you want to continue as you are? Or shall we continue with this conversation?'

He waited for the other man's reply. It did not come right away. An important decision had to be made. A leap of faith taken. The answer would either be a yes or a no. There was no place for maybes or half-ways.

Max weighed things up in his mind. So many ifs and buts. A lot of good reasons as to why he should decline. Simply say no and send this man on his way he thought. Tell him such an uncertain enterprise is not for me.

That draft response was finally scrapped. His mind inclined the other way.

'Ok,' he said quietly, 'what do you need from me?'

The young reporter commended the decision, immediately got down to brass tacks.

'The article will be mainly about you,' he said, 'you'll be its central character. Naturally people will want to know some things about you. Your background. Ariccia, for example. What brought you to this moment in time. Those ups and downs we touched on. What do they call it in a plot? Ah yes, that's it, the backstory. We're going to give them some of your backstory. And then, let the ballyhoo begin.'

'Bally what?' said Max.

Paparazzo laughed heartily at this. Placing his hands behind his neck, he rotated it from side to side.

'Ballyhoo,' he repeated, 'the word is ballyhoo Max. I only heard it recently. I had to look it up. It's in the dictionary. It's something you and I can look forward to.'

THE FRONT PAGE

'Claptrap!' said Simone Vastano, 'pure unadulterated claptrap, and that's being generous about it! As journalism goes, it's an unmitigated piece of shit and I can't believe anyone here would consider publishing it!'

The Il Quarto Stato copy editor flung his palms outward toward one of the glass panels, separating meeting room and open plan area, as if the evidence of this was there for all to observe. The head office of the daily newspaper was a small ocean of systems furniture and low-panelled cubicles save for this centrally-positioned island where senior management regularly met. Vastano's booming voice spread well beyond its confines and could be heard at every work station.

'A piece of shit journalism that has no place in this newspaper!' he said, imploring his colleagues in attendance to agree. He glanced at them separately before continuing.

There was Patrizia Adriani, the paper's news editor – 37 years old, intelligent, pretty and charming enough to have moved up swiftly in the industry. She was talented, industrious and had an impressive array of contacts in political circles. Her ability to unearth allies and draw people into her confidence was not without its detractors though. Some referred to her as the 'red-headed vixen' or simply as 'red who rules the roost.' Patrizia was aware of these names and laughed them off casually. She was more than just a pretty face. It was gratifying other people realised this as well.

Beside her sat Guido Schiavone, the features editor, whose broad-based agility was second only to his clarity of mind. Schiavone had moved from advertising to sports two decades before, but it was in features he'd discovered his true calling. He had background and brains, a keen sense of humour and innate decency. He was essential to the newspaper and had, on more than one occasion, brokered deals and concessions for staff members in the wake of internal restructurings. Pitting employees against each other in corporate combat was not his style. It achieved nothing as far as he was concerned and was a discordant element in the work-place. Solutions were always at hand he maintained; there was no problem that did not have an answer, no uncooperative type that could not be straightened out. New-fangled procedures did not impress him greatly; all too often they failed to make sufficient allowance for the human factor. This was when he got involved; advising, supporting, helping to iron out issues. Giving matters that human touch in his inimitable way. Staff appraisals, performance assessments – they were for the next generation.

The techniques Guido had evolved in the orchestration of people were simple, yet highly effective, and no one valued his contributions more than the editor-in-chief, Manfredo Canzonetta, who was presiding at the top of the table. The 62-year old sat back, shoulders squared, and listened as patiently as he could to his disgruntled copy editor. He was a workaholic who slept less than five hours a night and was one of those newspaper men who believed in overseeing every aspect of production from major to marginal. His section editors were well used to his ways and understood his expectations. In addition to Vastano, Schiavone and Adriani, there was Melania Bertucci, the opinion editor (currently out of town on official business), and the sports editor, Roberto DeMarco (vacationing in the Lake District with his family).

Canzonetta sat forward all of a sudden and began to tap his ballpoint pen flat against an opened notepad. He reminded himself that, in the absence of two of his section chiefs, there would be extra work required of him in the finalising of layouts and assigning of upcoming stories. Add another duty to that list he thought as his irked colleague persisted with the diatribe. Simone Vastano was a fine copy editor, no doubt about that, but his proclivity for histrionics was occasionally to the detriment of his proof-reading. A rant such as this one was not going to help matters the boss knew. The distraction could cause an oversight or verbal gaffe to slip in. He'd have to give the copy a second pair of eyes later on. Just to err on the side of caution. Dinner would be later than usual this Saturday evening. He'd phone his wife Antonietta as soon as the present meeting was finished.

'Hold it over again dear,' he'd say as per his recurring instruction. 'A few things have come up at this end. The troops need their general.'

A few things had come up indeed. The lean voluble man to his immediate left, the individual Antonietta referred to as the 'chirper' on account of his peculiar laugh, was harping on about one of them. Vastano was not going to let this go. He wanted it knocked on the head without further ado. Except that there was further ado, and most of it was coming from his corner of the room.

'Can we please give due consideration to a subject which has real weight and importance,' the stressed-out copy editor begged. 'The 11th June referendum. This paper's analysis of it has been superficial so far. I, for one, think it merits far more attention. There are important matters to be considered: union representation, local council elections, collective contracts for public sector workers...'

'As well as shop opening hours,' Patrizia Adriani added light-heartedly.

'And don't forget advertising breaks during films,' Guido Schiavone tacked on. 'Personally speaking, I'd like to see a lot less of those. They take away from the whole experience; remind you that the ebb and flow of everyday life is still lingering in the outside world.'

The two of them exchanged a playful grin.

The unimpressed Vastano shook his head and sighed.

'Thank you both very much for your input,' he said, 'you've actually hit the nail on the head in many ways. My point is that there's any number of significant news items which are far more deserving of column space than an obscure actor who's fallen on hard times.'

'Where does it say he's fallen on hard times exactly?' interrupted Adriani.

Vastano paused to consider this.

'Ok, it may not say he's fallen on hard times,' he acknowledged, 'but it's still one of those hard luck stories which are...'

He rummaged for the appropriate words.

'I think it's well written,' Adriani volunteered, 'there's good background information which sets the overall tone. It's a good decision to focus on just one actor the way Fabio presents it. It personalises the piece. Gives it that human dimension which Guido here is always advocating.'

'But it's where he goes with it then,' Vastano offered as a counter-argument, 'he's not willing to leave well enough alone. This proposal of his at the end, it's absurd. Who's going to take him seriously?! Who for that matter is going to take us seriously for printing the damn thing in the first place?!'

He affected the most exasperated look he could manage and zoned in on the head.

'Manfredo, surely we're not going to start putting such lunacy into print?! What would our parent company have to say about that? The stockholders as well? And this kid has form let me remind you, a reputation. The wrong kind I might add.'

His beady eyes swivelled quickly and came to rest on Schiavone.

'What do you have to say about it Guido?' he asked. 'I thought you were watching over this idiot? You're usually able to whip them into shape better than this. He's been working here how long now?'

'Since February 1994,' Schiavone replied.

'That's fourteen months. What's been happening with this guy? Doesn't he have any respect? As far as I can see, he's the same arrogant prick he was the first day he walked in. Even more so perhaps.'

Canzonetta indicated partial agreement with this. He was a tall man with an austere countenance who weighed his words carefully and seldom raised his voice.

'The kid seems to think himself a maverick or some such thing,' he said, 'more than once I've had to call him into my office and read him the riot act. Lately though I thought he'd been doing ok. There were fewer incidents that I was aware of. No further Maria Luisa Giordano scenarios at least,' he added, raising his eyebrows in Schiavone's direction.

'Maria Luisa Giordano?' Adriani repeated. 'The young starlet from that film...?

'Figlia del Barone,' Schiavone said helping her out.

'That's the one. What does she have to do with our disobedient colleague?' she asked. 'He didn't sleep with her, did he?'

'Over Faustino Brunetti's dead body,' Schiavone chimed in.

'Faustino Brunetti? As in the cosmetics Brunetti?'

'The very same one,' the features editor confirmed. 'Last September I assigned Fabio to the Venice Film Festival. He was only with us seven months at the time, but I thought the experience would serve him well. I figured all that glitz and glamour, the kid will love it. He'll soak it up like a sponge. No danger of him stepping on any toes there.'

'Famous last words I assume?' said Vastano.

'Giordano was...still is...a rising young star as you say Patrizia,' Schiavone continued, 'Figlia del Barone was her first major film. It was having its premiere at the festival. Fabio did an interview with her the day after the screening. He made some less than complimentary remarks about it.'

'Can't say I blame him in that regard,' said Adriani. 'It was a load of hokum. She was totally out of her depth as an actress.'

'The problem was Fabio felt the same way as you do. He didn't say it in so many words but...'

'His opinion was nonetheless communicated?'

'I'm afraid so. And even less tactfully than you might imagine. You see Brunetti had insisted on sitting in with his protégé as she met the fair gentlemen of the press. Each of them was given a window of ten minutes to converse with Miss Giordano. Fabio's slot lasted no more than seven. After a number of warnings, Brunetti had him thrown out. There the story should have ended, but one final act in the drama played itself out that same evening.'

Schiavone entrusted the remainder of the tale to his chief.

'Paparazzo filed the interview with us sometime before six,' Canzonetta said, picking up the narrative thread, 'he didn't mention anything about the termination of his encounter with the actress so, naturally, we assumed it was good to go for the next day. But there were a number of things about it which concerned Guido. He spoke to me and we agreed it was lop-sided at best; potentially defamatory at worst.'

'Just because he didn't like the film?' said Adriani.

'It was meant to be a routine interview. Nothing more. No frills in other words. Fabio, however, turned it into an opinion piece.'

'More a judgement piece if you ask me.'

'There were several references to the film. He described it as a costume drama in which the wardrobe and sets are more animated than the actors.'

'And as for Miss Giordano?'

'What was it he said about her Guido?'

'An actress in need of her own restoration period. If I'm not mistaken.'

Adriani tittered when she heard this. Vastano remained sombre.

'The coup de grace though was delivered as regards her association with Brunetti.'

'He started her out, didn't he? Billboards and television commercials?'

'She was christened the Brunetti Girl.'

'Faustino Brunetti financed Figlia del Barone out of his own pocket. That's how devoted he is to the Brunetti Girl.'

'An older man with a fortune and business contacts all over the world. He is her own personal baron.'

'Her sugar daddy you mean.'

'Quite the captain of industry. He's admirably active for a man his age.'

'It certainly explains why he took exception to whatever Paparazzo said to her in Venice. The doting sugar daddy got protective. Did he know what newspaper our treasured colleague was representing?'

'Absolutely,' replied Canzonetta. 'That same evening I received a phone call from him. He'd got wind of the content of Fabio's article somehow. Particularly the part in which our reporter suggested he was buying Miss Giordano's career as opposed to just backing it.'

'Jesus!' exclaimed Vastano. 'I'm glad you pulled it in that case. A man like Faustino Brunetti wouldn't have taken that slight lying down. He'd have come after us without a shadow of a doubt.'

'Oh he made that very clear to me throughout our conversation, short though it was,' said Canzonetta. 'Apart from all the legal jargon, there were some veiled threats made against our colleague as well. If we'd printed it, I very much doubt Fabio would be writing for any broadsheet in this country. He'd probably have to change his name or find another occupation.'

'Perhaps for that reason, you should have put it in,' Vastano suggested.

'I'd decided to kill it long before Faustino Brunetti phoned me up,' said Canzonetta. 'On his arrival back from Venice, Guido and I had a confab with him. We told him what standards this paper has, what kind of journalism our owners expect. No place for trashy invectives in this establishment we said. Your job is to report what's topical and newsworthy, leave the second-rate and offensive to the gutter press.'

'He sure took that advice on board,' Vastano remarked sarcastically. 'What is it with this guy? Why doesn't he listen? What's he trying to prove?'

'That he's an arrogant prick like you said,' Adriani offered. 'He's spirited and strong-willed. We were all like that once upon a time.'

'Speak for yourself,' Vastano told her. 'I wasn't like that.'

'That's true, you were just you,' said Adriani.

'I mean in the way he is!' Vastano gave back. 'Spirited and strong-willed is all well and good, but he's a different proposition altogether. Belligerent and trigger-happy I'd say. In another life, he'd be a pit bull or black mamba.'

'Metaphors aside, what are we going to do with this?' asked Schiavone. 'We've got a glaring shortfall as to features tomorrow. I was under the impression Fabio was compiling a piece on the new Zucchero album. Instead, he foisted this on me.'

Vastano shook his head again.

'As I said Guido, he's supposed to be under your wing. I think it's time this guy got a proper comeuppance.'

'I agree,' said Canzonetta, 'but, meantime, tomorrow still looms large.'

'We could ditch either the feature on Giuseppe Ferrara or Take That, as well as Paparazzo's. Come back to one of them in the next few days.'

'I suggest Ferrara is the one you should push back,' Canzonetta recommended, 'his film's been on release a few weeks now. Take That on the other hand, their new album is going to be huge.'

'Agreed,' said Schiavone, 'tomorrow's edition will be slightly lighter, but we can live with that. Ok by you Simone?'

The two men looked at Vastano.

'Of course it's ok by me,' replied Vastano, 'as long as that asshole Paparazzo is disciplined for this. He should be docked pay or something.'

'We'll deal with him in the appropriate fashion,' Canzonetta promised.

Patrizia Adriani spoke up.

'There is an alternative that none of you have considered,' she said. 'I probably will be a lone voice on this and some of you won't like the idea.'

'What is it?' asked Canzonetta.

'Print his article as is,' said Adriani.

'What?!' exclaimed Vastano. 'Have you not been sitting here for the last few minutes Patrizia? Were you not listening? This article is not going in. It's ridiculous and it's also dangerous.'

'How is it dangerous?' asked Adriani. 'I don't see anything libellous in it. Unlike the Maria Luisa Giordano situation, he has the full consent of the subject.'

'We can't be sure of that,' said Vastano.

'I am,' Schiavone told him. 'I spoke to this Max Pellegrino not less than an hour ago. I was checking up on Fabio as much as I was checking on the story.'

'Fine,' Canzonetta accepted.

'I think Max Pellegrino is an interesting guy,' Adriani continued, 'and Fabio has written him up well. I like the references to his childhood and why he wanted to become an actor.'

'It's nostalgia Patrizia, tugging on the heartstrings and nothing more besides,' opined Vastano, 'Paparazzo has sugar-coated every single paragraph. He's a manipulative writer, but he doesn't fool me. The man on the street would see through it as well.'

'I'm not so sure about that Simone,' Adriani begged to differ, 'you base your opinion on the fact that you know him. And you dislike him intensely which is obvious. But this is a good article. He may be a manipulative writer, but he's also a damned good one. I can imagine people reading this, many of them believing what he has to say.'

'Including the grand finale?!' said Vastano. 'The American producers considering this Pellegrino character to star in their film?!'

'It does seem far-fetched Patrizia,' said Canzonetta.

'Fairy-tale endings are not what we tend to speculate about,' Schiavone concurred.

'I'm not talking about fairy-tale endings here,' Adriani countered, 'I realise it's castles in the air territory and I've no doubt Mr. Paparazzo is of a similar mind. He might not admit that but...look guys...clearly what he wants to cause here is a stir. He wants to rouse people, get them excited and talking about Max Pellegrino; what he might do and what that could lead to, however unlikely a scenario it is. The notion of the small fry coming through against all the odds. We've seen plenty of it in the political arena. And ninety per cent of the time there is no happy ending. We all know that. But who really cares by then? Not the general public I can tell you. They've enjoyed being along for the ride, being part of the journey. People embrace these kinds of stories Manfredo because it reminds them of their own impossible dreams. They know they're pie-in-the-sky, in most cases unobtainable, but that doesn't stop them from entertaining the idea. It's as natural as breathing in fresh air and there's always a demand for it.'

'It's still claptrap no matter how you dress it up,' said Vastano.

His two other colleagues remained silent for a moment.

'And I thought you were an out-and-out pragmatist Patrizia,' said Canzonetta. 'This idealistic side to you is a surprise, one we rarely get to see.'

Adriani smiled graciously.

'I have my moments, and my surprises,' she replied.

Canzonetta turned to Schiavone.

'Guido, is Fabio Paparazzo still in the building?'

'Yes, he is Manfredo. He was aware this would be under discussion. Like I said, I had no idea he'd written it. I chewed him out for it good and proper. Told him you'd most likely do the same. He said he was hanging about in any case. Possibly anticipated he'd be summoned. Is that what you want me to do?'

'Yes Guido. Call him in here. Tell him to drop whatever he's doing.'

'Oh don't worry about that, he'll be here in the blink of an eye,' said the features editor as he dialled Paparazzo's extension.

'I don't understand this,' said Vastano, 'I thought we'd just made a decision. He stepped way out of line and what? Now we're going to hear him out?!'

'Most definitely he stepped out of line Simone,' said Canzonetta, 'and for that he'll earn whatever rebuke we think he's deserving of. But Patrizia may have a point in what she says.'

'I certainly hope so,' said Adriani, 'otherwise I wouldn't have said it.'

'But our reputation, our standing in the industry.'

'Oh for God sake Simone, get a grip,' said Adriani, 'this isn't going to offend any race or religion. Nor will it encroach upon any ethical standards I'm aware of. This is freedom of the press. You are familiar with that concept, aren't you? It's to do with communication and expression; some of those things we try to do around here. And what real harm can come of it? Not all our precious shareholders and patrons are holier-than-thou types. They won't suddenly rise up or defect en masse. They'll get what the idea behind this is. Every once in a while you have to toss in a grenade and provoke some discussion. If it troubles you this much, then join a cloistered order or something. The Carthusians and Hieronymites are always in the market for new recruits.'

She was interrupted by the appearance of Fabio Paparazzo at the meeting room door, loose-leaf folder in hand. He knocked on the glass pane, waited to be beckoned in.

'Please sit down Fabio,' Canzonetta instructed, 'we've been talking about your extracurricular activities. Zucchero Fornaciari is not to your taste apparently. Guido has shown us your alternative piece. My understanding Fabio was that you were told to move on from the Don Taylor story a few days ago. Was there a difficulty with that communication? Does Guido need to brush up on his interpersonal skills?'

'There was no miscommunication,' said Paparazzo, 'I understood what Guido told me. I did move on. Max Pellegrino is a different story to all intents and purposes. He's an individual I came across while I was working on the other piece. A follow-on from that if you will. I think it was serendipity that I found him.'

Vastano threw his eyes up to the ceiling and grumbled.

'I think it was scheming on your part Paparazzo,' he said, 'you're always scavenging for this sort of thing. An easy fix is what you want. Something you think will help you make a name for yourself. It's bad journalism and it's also poor individual behaviour if you ask me. You cheapen us all with this drivel.'

'I'm sorry you feel that way,' Paparazzo replied, although his tone was far from contrite.

He looked at his immediate boss for a clue. Schiavone had nothing to say.

'You should thank Patrizia here for having got this far,' Canzonetta resumed, 'you wouldn't be in this room at all if it wasn't for her. She backed you up when others were baying for your blood, myself included.'

Paparazzo turned to Adriani and nodded gratefully.

'I've admired Miss Adriani from the first day I joined this paper,' he said. 'Il Quarto Stato has moderated to a more centre-left political stance in recent years, but it doesn't shy away from criticising politicians and political parties when such need arises. I think Miss Adriani deserves much praise for that. She's a very open-minded and objective person.'

'You could learn something from her,' Vastano suggested, 'a bit of humility on your part, less of the arrogance. You can't take on all the Brunettis of this world you know. Magnates like that would squash you underfoot just for fun. And there'd be serious repercussions for this paper as well.'

'I think what Simone is trying to say is that you will only become an asset when you cease to be a liability,' Canzonetta added softly, 'this individualist streak of yours benefits no one. Least of all our copy chief when he's staring at a deadline.'

'Too damn right!' said Vastano, 'and today is no different in that regard let me remind you all. Can we make the right decision here please; the one that is level-headed and consistent and, most importantly, tells this joker where he can get off.'

'Well that's clearly one against,' said Adriani. 'As for myself, I remain in favour of having it printed. You've done well getting this guy to open up to you the way he does Fabio.'

'Thank you.'

'That's just the thing I'm curious about. Your article mentions how he's spent the greater part of his career in the...'

She examined the text again searching for the reference.

'...shadows of the dubbing studio; behind the reading desk and microphone.'

'Yes?'

'He's very forthcoming about it, isn't he? The frustrations and disappointments. Why so? What does he hope to gain from it? That carrot you dangled in front of him must have been very appealing.'

'It wasn't anything he didn't already know,' said Paparazzo. 'I told him the article might be his opportunity.'

Vastano mumbled impatiently.

'He's obviously an opportunist, just like our friend here,' he said.

'There's nothing wrong with taking advantage of circumstances when they present themselves,' argued Adriani, 'Mr. Paparazzo I think we all agree is an individual who has self-interested motives. He wants to further himself, sometimes with little regard for principles or what the consequences of his actions might be.'

'Agreed,' said Vastano, 'time and again he's shown how untrustworthy he is. As things stand, I wouldn't let him near the sports section right now. He'd write up a football match and probably manage to antagonise all 22 players.'

'You're forgetting to include the subs in that figure,' Paparazzo offered as a comeback.

'Fabio, this is not helping your cause!' Canzonetta admonished, 'Patrizia, please continue.'

'Fabio actively seeks out his opportunities,' said Adriani, 'he's what you would call a proactive type. He looks for the pay-off in a situation and believes this outweighs any difficulties. Mr. Pellegrino, on the other hand, is merely responding to the opportunity he's been presented. His motives are less devious. Of course there's an element of self-interest here as well. But it's different in his case; in many ways it's a legitimate choice and all the more understandable for that reason. He's at last-chance saloon. It's now or never. Why shouldn't he reach out and grab it. Most of us would. The rationale behind it is reasonable.'

'The social science lesson is very enlightening Patrizia,' said Canzonetta, 'but what's your point in all this? Do you suggest we publish an article comparing the Paparazzos and Pellegrinos of this world?'

'God forbid!' said Vastano.

'Not at all, much as I'd enjoy such an analysis, I doubt very much our

187

readers would feel the same way. But what they might just be partial to, what could catch their attention is this story about the everyman actor. The type of guy you could root for. What does he look like by the way? Do we have a picture?'

'I have one which he gave me,' said Paparazzo, 'it was taken in the last 12 months.'

He produced a black-and-white snapshot of a neutral-faced Max preparing for a performance in the sound studio.

'That's perfect,' declared Adriani. 'He's quite good-looking actually.'

'It's an alliance between the two of them now,' Vastano remarked.

'Well?' said Adriani. 'One or two fine-tunes apart, I think the article would be good to go. The decision is yours to make Manfredo.'

Canzonetta first sought the advice of his features editor.

'You've had very little to say about this Guido. What's your opinion? That keen intuition of yours would be appreciated at this moment.'

Schiavone leaned forward, as if with some effort, delivered his thoughts.

'I don't think my opinion should count in this instance,' he said, 'because I'd be basing it on a personal frame of mind which our colleague here has put me in ever since he showed me the article earlier this afternoon.'

He directed his speech towards Paparazzo.

'I try to approach my work as objectively as possible; you know this I'm sure Fabio?'

The reporter nodded in the affirmative.

'You don't make my task easy when you deliberately pursue something else while giving me the impression your assigned work is in hand. It's too calculating for my taste. And it sets a bad precedent. If every reporter here was like you, God knows what sort of paper we'd have. There are standards Fabio, procedures which need to be followed. I don't always agree with Simone, but he's correct when he says you look for the easy fix, the short cut. A good journalist is not defined by how quickly his work makes it to the front page. There's toil and effort that ought to come in between. If this story of yours does play out…well I'm not as convinced as Patrizia that it will be such an affair. A sideshow of a sideshow perhaps, but like most of these things it will have a limited spell. And where to from there? What next from your bag of tricks?'

He turned back to Canzonetta.

'Well I've probably said more than enough Manfredo. It's a matter for you as to what you want to do with it. If we're going to include it, I suggest we be not too overt. Low-key would be the sensible way to go.'

'We could put it well inside the edition if that's what you want,' said Vastano. 'Also I'd suggest that it not be listed in the front-page index. I don't how we'd describe it in any case. A special feature? I don't think so.'

'I agree with that Simone,' said Canzonetta. 'Sorry Fabio, but if it's going to be discovered, then people will have to find it for themselves.'

In his typically understated way, the editor-in-chief had notified those present as to his decision.

'Simone, how soon can you have it ready?' he asked.

Vastano shook his head, momentarily abandoning the commentary.

'An hour or so I'd say,' he said, glancing once more at the article. 'This picture is to be included as well I take it?'

He was handed the photo by Paparazzo.

'Plus the one or two fine-tunes,' Adriani reminded.

'It would take more than one or two as far as this is concerned,' Vastano said, 'but at any rate it will have vanished the day after tomorrow. That I'm sure of.'

'A week's salary says you're wrong,' Paparazzo piped up.

'A week's salary!' Vastano repeated disbelievingly. 'Are you going to add stupidity to that worthless repertoire of yours?'

'It's not stupidity. It's confidence. Put your money where your mouth is,' said Paparazzo. 'You've placed more than one wager on the Derby della Capitale in your time I'd imagine.'

'I'm not betting a week's salary on this thing Fabio, and that's only because I earn a lot more than you do. But I will give you three days in exchange for your week. I'll give you three days for three days.'

'Meaning?'

'Three days of my salary says this charade of yours will not have caused any noise within three days of its appearing in print. That's what I believe. That's how confident I am about it.'

Paparazzo considered this for a moment.

'Ok, I accept those terms,' he said. 'Three days it is.'

The two of them shook on it.

'The easiest winnings I will ever make,' said Vastano, 'I always enjoy taking money from an Inter fan.'

'That's rich coming from a Roma supporter.'

'If you two are quite finished, can we get on with this please,' Canzonetta requested. 'Gambling over the outcome of an article,' he said with mild contempt, 'I'm absolutely certain our stakeholders wouldn't appreciate that!'

'Thankfully, they will never know about it,' sighed Schiavone.

Vastano smirked tauntingly at his younger colleague.

'Within three days,' he repeated to Paparazzo. 'Three days. More chance of Inter winning the Scudetto than for that to happen.'

THE TALK OF THE TOWN

The article about Max appeared on page 13 in the 30th April, 1995 edition of Il Quarto Stato. It featured the same picture of the actor which Paparazzo had given Vastano the evening before. Over it ran the headline:

Max Pellegrino – Italian Actor, Quo Vadis?

Word for word, the report was as follows:

At the end of Via Urbana, close to the Basilica di Santa Maria Maggiore, lies a dreary concrete building which looks faded and passé. The structural edifice housing the studios of Universal Recordings is not a pleasing sight on the outside. It's an ugly building, if truth be told, and one can't help but feel that the best architectural makeover in the world would do little to improve its appearance. Inside, this sense of the anachronistic is no less palpable. A departed era comes to mind; the 1970's perhaps. Upon entering the building, the moulded plastic furniture is the first thing you notice. The reception area is a dark colour palette and there are a number of funky-kitsch prints along the teak-panelled corridors. The control rooms are poorly ventilated, the sound studios absolutely cheerless. The technical equipment has clearly seen better days; there are a number of isolation booths, here and there, which are more reminiscent of solitary confinement than artistic endeavour.

This is not the glitz and glamour one associates with the filmmaking industry, far from it. The studios of Universal Recordings are a great distance from the hills of Hollywood. They are, literally, worlds apart.

But although the bright lights of Tinseltown are nowhere to be seen at Via Urbana, the very finest efforts of the silver screen are. For it is here that Hollywood productions regularly come in advance of their Italian cinematic release. Why is this you may ask? What can such a humble setting as this offer the Lion Kings or Forrest Gumps? A great deal as a matter of fact. More than most would imagine.

Here in Italy we dub everything: feature films, television shows, documentaries and cartoons, which come to us from other countries; the United States, most notably. Think about some of the most famous movies in history: Gone with the Wind; Casablanca; Jaws; Star Wars; E.T.; The Silence of the Lambs. They have all been subject to the same process of translation. As a cinema-going nation, we are accustomed to hearing only our native tongue. The practice of dubbing here is a longstanding one. It began well before the outbreak of the Second World War.

The first Italian film to incorporate the spoken word was screened in Rome on the 7th of October, 1930. It was called La canzone dell'amore and starred Dria Paola, Isa Pola, Elio Steiner and Mercedes Brignone. Preceded by the world's first 'talkie' – The Jazz Singer – just three years before, La canzone was shot in three different versions: Italian, French and German, and used different casts and directors for each. It was one of the exceptions in this regard. The advent of sound in film led to a stricter regime of censorship by the fascist government of the day. Foreign language films were disapproved of for political reasons. The tradition of converting these invasive species into the indigenous tongue was not simply encouraged by the champions of totalitarianism. In the name of cultural protection, it was unequivocally demanded.

'Mussolini was adamant he did not want to hear foreign languages. And with regard to the Italian public en masse, he was unrelenting in his belief they should not be exposed to outside influences of any sort. That in a nutshell is why dubbing began. It was a response to the aural menace which sound films represented. The dictator wanted to control the minds of his people. There was no place for Clark Gable or Errol Flynn in such a state.'

The words of Damiano di Stefano, a highly respected dubbing director, who has been working at Universal Recordings since the mid-1980's. A former actor himself, di Stefano does an average twelve films per year and has just completed work on Don Taylor's latest offering, The Proper Citizen, due to be released in this country before long. The current project, needless to say, has been tinged with a certain sadness.

'Bittersweet,' di Stefano describes it.

'The accident which happened in Piazza Venezia overshadows it to a great extent,' he says. 'I expect it will open to a huge level of public interest. Hopefully, it will not have been our last time dubbing a Don Taylor movie.'

Without trying to be presumptuous on the subject of the unfortunate Hollywood star, I ask di Stefano about the actors who provide Don Taylor's Italian voice.

'There is only one,' he replies. 'His name is Max Pellegrino. He's done Don Taylor's voice for over twelve years now.'

Intrigued, I ask more questions about this actor whom I've never heard of.

'Max is one of the finest working in this business,' di Stefano says, as he gives me a whistle-stop tour of the studios. 'I can think of few who are better than him and that's high praise seeing as how I'm more than a little bigoted when talking about the quality of the work we do here.'

High praise indeed and I immediately decide to seek out the actor for myself.

Max Pellegrino is 39 years old and lives in an apartment in Monteverde. He's a tall man, handsome, articulate and thoughtful. In many ways he reminds me of one of our most famous actors: Alberto Sordi. When I tell him this, he laughs self-deprecatingly.

'It's funny you should mention that,' he says, 'early in his career, Sordi worked as a dubbing actor. He was the Italian voice for Oliver Hardy. Nino Manfredi was also involved in the industry at one time. The experience of studio work served them well I think. They both had great range and could switch between comedy and drama. The dubbing actor you see has very little to assist him with his performance. There's no scenery to inspire, no extravagant set to be in awe of. I once saw a picture of Charlton Heston and Stephen Boyd in between takes on Ben Hur. They're standing in the arena for the chariot race sequence; it was the largest film set built up to that time. There's an energised look on both their faces, Heston's in particular. That's what on-set inspiration is all about. Understanding what it is you're involved in. Being part of a great spectacle. As an actor, there's surely no better motivation.'

I determine this as an opportune moment to ask him about his own background and interest in cinema. Mr. Pellegrino does not require much enticement.

'I could talk about films all day,' he says. 'My love of them began when I was very young. There was a movie house in my town and I'd go as often as I could. I grew up at a time when peplums and spaghetti westerns were in vogue. The neorealist period of Visconti, Rossellini and De Sica had passed by then. Boys my age would not have understood films such as Paisan or Germany Year Zero. We wanted larger-than-life heroes to fill the screen with action and excitement. Hercules; Maciste; Django; the man with no name. It didn't matter to us how implausible these stories were. They were fantastic and other-worldly. That was exactly what we wanted. The movie house never disappointed. It never let us down.'

Max grew up in Ariccia, one of the Castelli Romani towns to the south of our capital. His childhood was not an unhappy one. He had loving parents and came from a good family. There was a roof over his head and food on the table at all times. He and his sister wanted for very little. They went to school together every day and to church at least once a week. They were content and there is nothing remarkable about that. Max's sister set her heart on the legal profession from an early time. Today, she is a prominent civil law notary. Max, on the other hand, his mind was inclined in a very different direction.

'Of the two of us, she's always been the more sensible,' he tells me. 'Not that I regret pursuing the career I chose. It's been good to me. Dubbing and voiceover work has given me a sustainable livelihood, a level of stability which is not available in theatre, movies, or television.'

At this juncture I interrupt pointing out that, consistent and reliable though it may be, the one thing this job does not provide is recognition and celebrity. Max, after all, is one of these dubbing actors who routinely voices a number of Hollywood stars (not just Don Taylor), and to the average moviegoer there is no obvious distinction from one set of vocal cords to the next. Only the faces on screen matter I argue. The persona *is what the public is wholly interested in, whether it's Bruce Willis, Meryl Streep or Tom Cruise. The point I'm making to Max is along these lines: high regard amongst your peers is certainly a commendable thing but, in a wider sense, and, to the man on the street, you remain effectively unknown. Who knows of you beyond a couple of fellow professionals and collaborators?*

The actor considers this for a moment. His response is honest and concise:

'That's true, my name means very little,' he openly admits.

Max has had some professional disappointments over the years. There was, for example, a starring role in a poliziesco once upon a time. The name of the film I won't mention in this article. In any case, it's likely most people won't remember it. The actor himself would certainly prefer not to. Like many, he was a casualty of the malaise which infected Italian cinema during the 1980's. The national film industry was between a rock and a hard place. A crisis of confidence would be an understated way to describe it. Resident producers laboured in their attempts to keep pace with the wunderkinds of Hollywood. The halcyon days of the 1950's and 60's were a distant memory. There were no more Miracles in Milan or 8½'s. Instead, a paucity of capital overshadowed the industry. Home-grown creations strained to raise their head. Quality films became introverted and, as a consequence, more isolated. The American blockbusters put the indigenous equivalents in the shade. Who wanted to see The Mystery of Oberwald or Ginger and Fred when we had Indiana Jones and Luke Skywalker?

What remained of mainstream cinema became swamped with the commedia sexy all'italiana. This low-brow variety consisted, in the main, of slapstick elements and liberal doses of titillation. Storylines were repetitive and formulaic. Taboo subjects were broached regularly, various states of undress commonplace.

The bawdy comedies eventually became fewer in number, but the chasm in quality remained. Money was still in short supply. The Fellinis and Viscontis were either dead or entering their dotage. A second golden era for Italian cinema seemed further and further away. The critical and box-office successes of Cinema Paradiso and Mediterraneo apart, there were still deficiencies and shortcomings which could not be denied. Especially for the native actor at ground level. He understood them only too well. There were few options as regards his career, and slim pickings in terms of quality roles. Even bit parts and minor roles were not exactly in copious supply. Practicality dictated that a viable alternative be sought out. For Max, expediency became a watchword; dubbing assignments and voiceover contracts were the new footings on which his livelihood was based.

'The first job I got after the poliziesco was an advert for a Moretti fabric softener,' he tells me. 'It was a 30-second spot and required

numerous takes before they were satisfied with it. I was unsure as to what was expected of me. Commentary, as I saw it, was not my area of expertise. I had never done that sort of work before and wondered if I'd be any good at it. Fortunately, I came in contact with a very fine agent – Franco Bonacossa is his name. It was Franco who gave me a steer in the right direction. He taught me the importance of preparation and groundwork.'

My earlier conversation with Damiano di Stefano comes to mind and I ask Max about what such preparation entails. The amount of read-throughs and physical exercises he employs is more than impressive. I'm particularly enamoured by the anecdotes he relates. There are disagreements which occur in the studio from time to time and Max does not hold anything back during such creative clashes. It might be one of the finer points of a scene which causes the difference of opinion: a matter of timing for example; or the nuance in a line of dialogue. Anyone out there who assumes dubbing is simply an exercise in reading off the page should promptly revise such an opinion.

'It's about a lot more than just the substitution of one language for another,' Max says. 'There are often a multitude of technical issues which the sound experts have to resolve. And as for us actors.'

He pauses for a moment in thought.

'For me, the single most important thing is to find the character in the copy. That's the foundation on which you build your performance. Everything else stems from it. If you don't have a handle on the character you're playing, it undermines your entire performance. Even the narrator of a fabric softener ad is a somebody. That's the way I approach it. You have to think like this: who am I and why do I believe in this product I'm trying to sell?'

This brings me back to my former thoughts on recognition and celebrity. It must have been apparent at an early stage that detergents and dubbing were never going to hit the mark. Does Max ever think about the what-ifs or might-have-beens? Does he have any regrets?

'Naturally, there are a few regrets,' he acknowledges, 'but then most people have them, don't they? Not many of us get to a state of complete self-fulfillment. I would have loved one real shot at fame. Something that would have been released overseas. A breakthrough role as it's called. Like Mastroianni in I Solti Ignoti.'

Is it possible I ask that the constant voiceover and dubbing work, steadfast as it has been, is something of a double-edged sword for actors such as him?

Max again takes a time-out before responding:

'The work was a support mechanism in the beginning,' he concedes, 'I was a young actor in need of employment and it threw me a lifeline. Part of me hoped dubbing would open up other avenues. In more recent times, it's fair to say that I've operated in a comfort zone. There's no risk involved because the jobs come up regularly, no anxiety or fear as

a consequence. Pride I guess plays its part as well. I don't have to test for work. I'm hired on the basis of my experience. I don't have to face knock-backs. Audition rejection never happens to me because there are no auditions any longer. I'm good at what I do. A lot of people don't know that of course. But the ones that matter do.'

Max is referring to his employers at studios such as Universal Recordings who frequently call on his services. It's a standard practice in the dubbing industry that actors are allotted someone who is a corresponding age as themselves. Max started out in the industry at approximately the same time a certain Don Taylor was embarking on stardom. The two were matched up and Max has provided Don's Italian voice ever since. The Proper Citizen was the 28th feature in which Max dubbed Don's voice. The actor has great respect for the Hollywood star. He knows his work better than most, has closely studied his mannerisms and onscreen deportment.

'You get to know every facial gesture, recognise specific methods from previous performances,' he says. 'The Proper Citizen was something of a sea change for him. I think it represented a point of departure. He wanted to channel himself in a new direction.'

You mean stepping out of his comfort zone Max I remark somewhat boldly.

The actor smiles cordially.

'Touché,' he replies, 'it's a brave thing for anyone to undertake. Don was doing it in the full glare of the spotlight. That made his decision all the more courageous.'

Max had completed his own duties on The Proper Citizen prior to the events of Piazza Venezia. He'd met Don Taylor a few days before the accident and was to assist him during the filming of Echo of Passions. Our conversation turns to the biopic about the Italian inventor Antonio Meucci, which the Hollywood star was due to headline. The future of the production in Cinecittà continues to remain in a state of limbo. No replacement has yet been named. Gossips and suggestions are put forward by all and sundry, but they bear little relation to facts and feasibilities. Obtaining a last-minute substitute is much easier said than done. It's not like in a soccer match where the manager can simply spring a new player from the bench. There are plans which have long since been made; schedules which are by this time full up. Many actors can not be considered because they are presently working elsewhere. Others will not be in a position to accept because of future commitments. Start dates on one project will conflict with end dates on another. The list of prospective candidates becomes greatly diminished when calendars are more thoroughly studied. Yesterday's potential acceptance turns out to be today's negative response. There have been one or two of these already as far as this writer understands. Time is not an ally to the Cinecittà production. The big clock is ticking at a rate of knots; the purse strings will not remain open forever. Very soon decisiveness will have to rise above uncertainty. Will Echo of Passions unearth its source of salvation? Or will it go to ground permanently?

A brainwave occurs and my subject is the first to be informed. Max laughs to himself upon hearing it. He calls it an impossibility.

Not so I respond. Think of it as a horse race in which many of the favourites can't take to the track. It's a wonderful opportunity for the dark horse, the unknown actor with oodles of talent. One who has spent the greater part of his career in the shadows of the dubbing studio; behind the reading desk and microphone. Sound familiar to you Max?

The actor smiles and continues to voice his reservations. But there's a faint glimmer in those hazel-coloured eyes of his. The 39-year old veteran still dares to dream. One of those what-ifs has come flooding back.

What I've suggested to Max is the idea of him being a fitting replacement for Don Taylor. An outrageous notion you think? This writer begs to differ. Why should Max not be considered for the role I ask. He is a fine actor with all the qualities for such a part: talent, experience, versatility. He ticks all those boxes. First-hand testimony has been given to this effect. There is no reason why such flair can't be reproduced on a larger stage. Max is seasoned and practised and, moreover, – take note Hollywood – he is available. That is both fact and feasibility. I put him forward for your consideration. The top dogs, currently in residence at Cinecittà, I advise you to listen. I challenge you to be brave, adventurous even. This could be the source of your salvation. Max Pellegrino may not be a household name, but he would more than make up for this with his ability. The Hollywood dream factory can enable such possibilities. Max has what it takes. Put him centre stage and he will thrive in the limelight. Reveal the face behind the voice. Bring Italy's best kept acting secret from out of the shadows. Nothing is impossible. Hollywood sells us its amazing stories all the time. Let this be such a tale – one which it adapts all the way to reality.

Max Pellegrino – Italian actor, quo vadis? To the entrance gates of Cinecittà studios this writer hopes; the 'temple of dreams' as Federico Fellini called it. Hollywood is the vocal instrument in this design. It will have final say. Project your voice Hollywood. Give a free rein to your sense of daring. Give Max Pellegrino a chance, his one real shot at fame. The words of Mr. Jolson were indeed prophetic: 'You ain't heard nothing yet' he told cinemagoers in the world's first talkie. This writer expresses a similar sentiment about Max: you ain't seen nothing yet ladies and gentlemen. But you heard it here first.

The edicola around the corner from Max's building had only just opened by the time he got to it that Sunday morning. Gino, the elderly proprietor, was busily arranging a stack of sports magazines. He did not notice the appearance of one of his regulars and was clearly surprised when he lifted his head.

'Oh! It's you Max! I didn't hear you come up on me. You know you could be a very effective assassin sneaking up like that. Are you out for a jog or something else?'

Max was sporting a pair of grey tracksuit bottoms and a stonewashed sweater. The latter he'd put on in a hurry, eager as he was to get downstairs. Smiling affably, he pointed to a daily which was not his usual choice.

'Good morning Gino,' he said, 'just happen to be up early. Can I have a copy of Il Quarto Stato please.'

The edicola vendor nodded and picked out a pristine edition for his customer.

'Not La Repubblica today?' he said.

'Not today,' said Max. 'There's something in this I'm very interested to see.'

For a moment he was tempted to let slip the reason for wanting this particular newspaper on this particular day. He was glad he didn't when he saw where Paparazzo's article was. Page 13! Only page 13! He'd hoped it would be more prominent than this. It was a let-down and no mistake. More of the bottom rung he thought. Another false dawn.

Disappointed, he walked away from the kiosk and returned to his apartment. The Il Quarto Stato was left on the kitchen table for almost an hour before he opened it again.

A phone call came through in the meantime. It was Antonia.

'I just read it,' she said. 'You must be very pleased.'

'I haven't yet,' he told her. 'I was hoping it would be closer to the front.'

'How close did you suppose it would be?' she asked. 'It's not about politics or the economy. You're not Berlusconi or Bill Clinton. They have to feature those other stories before they come to you.'

'I guess you're right,' he said, 'it's just that...'

'What?'

'Well the readers have to wade through an awful lot before they come to it.'

'It's only twelve pages. I'm sure they can bear the wait. And just think of the page number – 13! How significant is that? It will bring you good luck for sure. Circle the number with a pen. I've already done it.'

'There was no mention of it on the front-page index either,' Max said, ignoring this.

A loud sigh was clear on the other end.

'Snap out of it would you!' Antonia told him. 'It's a great article and you should be happy about it. That journalist friend of yours has captured who you are and you should be proud. I'm proud of you and I know Mom and Dad would be too. You have a niece who idolises you and her esteem will hit the roof when she sees this. Read the article you fool. Let the moment happen. Enjoy it for God sake.'

Max promised he would, but managed to put it off for a short time more. Other matters were allowed to come between him and Il Quarto

Stato. He drank another cup of coffee and browsed through some mail. A bill he'd been meaning to pay for days suddenly became a task of great importance. He got hold of his credit card and made a call to the number provided. An automated message informed him the phone lines were closed. The Banca Nazionale del Lavoro Mastercard was put back inside his wallet. It was spared the expenditure for the time being.

Max could no longer drag his heels. He picked up the newspaper, leafed through it slowly. The first twelve pages were surveyed, but barely registered. His mind was in a different place. Supposing I don't like it he thought, supposing it's not faithful to what I said; despite Antonia's opinion. What if she's wrong about it? What if she's just being polite? But then she was not one for false praise either. As a rule she did not hem and haw, but instead called a spade a spade.

Finally he arrived at page 13.

It was not how he'd imagined it would be. It was much better than he expected. There was a candour to it which was refreshing. It spoke in an honest way without attempting to be kind or cloying. His own shortcomings were not tiptoed around. That was good he thought. It was time he faced up to these. The comfort zone of the studio work; the complacent mind-set he'd allowed. It had stifled his ambition and made him lethargic. It was time to stop hiding in the dark. Once and for all, it was imperative he do something else, be someone else. He'd acknowledged how dubbing and voiceover work had thrown him a lifeline. Now his lifeblood needed a new course. Paparazzo had forced him to realise this. The young journalist had rekindled a fire inside him; one he'd mistakenly thought was long gone out.

But would the article by itself be enough he wondered. Would it provide the forward motion? And how many people might actually read it? Would they be interested enough to see more of the face behind the voice? Of greater significance, those Hollywood powers at Cinecittà. Would they pay it any heed? Would they even hear about it? Still tentative at best he imagined. If the story was to come into public view, and gain traction, it would have to be sustained in some way. At least for a sufficient period of time so that those with clout might set eyes on it.

Max scanned back over the article and re-read one of his own quotations.

'That's true, my name means very little.'

A lot of things would have to fall into place he realised. Certain elements would have to fit together. If his name was to mean more than very little, then many other names would have to read about him first. It was still a long shot. The odds were what? 100-1? Maybe more. He thought about Antonia's lucky number 13. He didn't much believe in that sort of thing, certainly not the way she did. But he drew a circle around the number anyway; just as she'd suggested. It can't do any harm he figured. He could tell his sister he'd done it if things worked out. And if they didn't, well no damage done. He'd put himself out there. It remained to be seen whether his foray into the public domain would take off.

Paparazzo's article received a moderate amount of attention at the outset, but it was nothing out of the ordinary, and far from the singular reception its author and subject had hoped for. A smattering of discussion came in the wake of the story's publication. Ordinary people talked about it casually, but there was nothing in the way of a nationwide dialogue. For the most part the item was limited to individual conversations and exchanges of the water cooler variety. Some found it an appealing piece of work and were drawn to its central character. Max's picture was admired and remarks were made about his striking good looks. What a pity a few of them said that he had not become famous at an earlier age. He seemed to have all the hallmarks required for such a status.

Other more cynical parties lampooned such thinking. This is the real world they argued. There is no place in it for the has-beens or could-have-beens. Newspapers had a duty to report more pressing matters they told their whimsical counterparts. Another unsuccessful actor counted for very little in this; especially if one considered the problems besetting the Italian nation as a whole.

There was little energy expended by either side of the argument at any rate. Office parleys and street-level murmurings dropped off quickly. Talks and thoughts soon returned to the mundane and everyday. This did not bode well for the story. The Il Quarto Stato piece, though praised for the quality of its writing, had no obvious staying power; for many it smacked more of postscript than of prelude. Yes, it was a shame a talented actor had not realised his full potential, but what could be done about that? End of story. This was the here-and-now after all. Not the make-believe of some fictional utopia where dreams of fortune and glory were realised.

Two days in circulation and no remarkable maelstrom of public interest had come about. The story was disappearing out of sight. In print media there was scant attention paid to it. A few rival papers made mention, but largely in an indifferent way.

There were two exceptions though. The first was a short analysis by Luisa Laurito, a fashionable journalist who wrote for the Rome-based newspaper Il Messaggero. Referring to Paparazzo's proposition generally, she had this to say:

It was a flutter at best, if you will pardon the allusion to the equestrian set. In spite of this criticism, Mr. Paparazzo is to be commended for his effort. He learnt of this journeyman actor, Max Pellegrino, and sought to bring him to our attention. The design was fundamentally sound. Its execution was carried out in a most proficient manner. Personally, I found myself warming to the subject himself. Mr. Pellegrino was eloquent in what he had to say. My colleague of the fourth estate chose his sound bites very well. He gave the actor a voice and pitched it to us at a suitable frequency. This writer was especially impressed by the way he prodded and coaxed his unlikely hero. Mr. Pellegrino would have done better to have encountered his interviewer some years before now. No fault of his that he didn't of course. And no great shame that he opted for a particular path, the narrative of which has been outlined in this fine piece of writing. That it is destined to fail in its express purpose, that Mr. Pellegrino will not ultimately find a wider audience, is no great surprise. But it is a pity nonetheless. This writer admits to a sense of disappointment. I like Max Pellegrino as he's presented. He's someone I could imagine on the silver screen. Just think of the time-honoured everyman plot and you might be able to visualise him the way I do. Exceptional circumstances set the exceptional man apart so they say. Max Pellegrino could have been that common hero. He would have measured up to the part. But it's just not meant to be. Sorry about that Max. And commiserations to you as well Mr. Paparazzo. It was a gutsy effort all round. This business of profile-raising is an unpredictable creature. Sometimes it happens, and sometimes it doesn't. Your central idea in this case has not taken hold. Your story has not acquired the key ingredient it needed to get going. That ingredient is reaction, broad public reaction. It's something every story needs. Without it, any news item will dwindle and eventually waste away. That's simply what happened here fellows. Lady luck was not on your side. Perhaps too few people read it; perhaps it didn't click with those that did. Either way, the spotlight did not shine. The public eye can be a fickle thing.

The second commentary was certainly less kind than the former. It was penned by the notoriously outspoken Gianluca Della Pasqua, a senior columnist with the Gazzetta di Roma. Della Pasqua, who was from the small town of Rocca di Papa in the Castelli Romani, had a long and colourful career behind him. His daily opinion piece ranged widely from local carryings-on and insider gossip to social and political happenings and, over the course of 35 years, he'd managed to vex just about every class and interest group in the land. Della Pasqua was known as the 'impartial detractor.' His trademark invective style, whilst merciless, was all-embracing and did not single out any particular individual or circle. He lingered instead on certain subject matters for a time before moving on to the next object of his ridicule. Everything and everyone was fair game.

In recent times, the columnist's bête noire had been the third-level students of Italy. He labelled them, *'lazy and disrespectful, forever demanding helps and hand-outs which amount to sizeable windfalls.'*

The three public universities in Rome, in particular, had fallen foul of his ire. As usual, nothing was sacred and no reproach spared. Pronouncing on the inferior class of student, as he saw it, Della Pasqua alluded to the Sapienza, the oldest of Rome's three state-funded universities. His remarks, as always, had an unmistakable sting in the tail:

'The general intent of this establishment is contained in its motto

which, one presumes, is as old as its original structures. 'The future has passed here' it reads. How obsolete a catchphrase that is in our present time. How truly lamentable that it no longer has any substance. Not to the majority of those indolent freeloaders who pass by it each day. They have no regard for it. They care not for its principles. The past means nothing to them. Nor does tradition. And as for the future, it truly is passing; right before our eyes. The outlook for this nation is a wretched one. The next generation is a clique of opportunists and dependents. In their hands, the future will soon be on its knees.'

This was one of a series of rants which the cantankerous writer had launched against the students. Like his other endeavours, it had not gone unnoticed and had led to some minor protests outside the offices of the Gazzetta. The next generation did not appreciate what this hoary member of the press was saying about them. They passed out leaflets on the street and chanted slogans.

'Go home to Rocca di Papa' they noisily advised Gianluca. 'Pack your opinions in a suitcase and don't return.'

Della Pasqua did not pay them any heed. He remained on the staff of the Gazzetta. Naturally he did. Management wanted him there. His daily musings boosted the newspaper's sales. People bought the Gazzetta to see who he'd offend next.

His daily column rarely had a specific heading. It was enough to see that well-known name in bold capitals. When engaged in a particular line of attack, he saw little requirement for a description or blurb. Besides, most of his contributions were an extension of the previous day's sentiments. Gianluca had a tendency to pick up where he'd left off. A change of theme was, however, deemed sufficient reason to insert a formal title. This once-in-a-while caption was put to use for his caustic reaction to Fabio Paparazzo's article. The seven words between name and text summed up the mood of the piece. Gianluca was no romantic thinker. His steadfast mind was not moved by the fanciful notions of the young upstart. This was perfectly clear from start to finish:

Max Pellegrino – Italian Actor, Hokum Say I

A few days ago an article appeared in one of our neighbouring competitors here in Rome – Il Quarto Stato. It's a paper my readers will be familiar with. Familiar in the sense that I've referenced it on several occasions in the past; that and its many deficiencies. There is, for example, its rather hazy brand of journalism which is never for or against; neither left nor right. The reporters there are paragons of diffidence and moderation. Editorials are phrased inoffensively, political expositions non-aligned. All is boringly middle-of-the-road. Even the weekly cookery section is unexciting. There is no appetite for the unusual or exotic. Far-reaching to them is a piece of soy-poached salmon or some leftover rice pudding. The staple diet of the correspondents appears to be a hybrid dish. One can imagine them devouring copious amounts of pasta all'uovo so wishy-washy are their tame opinions and halfway ideologies.

Amongst their fold is a young up-and-coming (self-styled) reporter by the name of Fabio Paparazzo. He's the one who put pen to paper recently and related to us the episodic adventures (yawn) of Max Pellegrino. Mr. Pellegrino is an actor who performs every sort of voiceover, narration and commentary. If a story needs telling, or a speech has to be delivered, then Max is the man for all seasons. According to Paparazzo's backslapping language he's the best in his business. An acoustic double who is first rate, peerless, and beyond compare. Quite an endorsement that. The author was so confident of this he had the temerity to liken his subject to the great Alberto Sordi, a bona fide actor I will remind my readers in the most emphatic way.

The eager young man gave us an insight into Pellegrino's background. We were told of an enduring love affair with cinema. A movie house in Ariccia was spoken about in glowing terms. The nostalgia practically oozed from the page. Pellegrino became an adult and decided to forge a career for himself in the motion picture industry. He imagined he could become those heroes he watched in the darkness. But, alas, external forces conspired against him. Isn't that always the way with these sob stories? A twist of fate comes along. The harsh world crushes the noble hero's aspirations. In this particular case, the reporter described his actor friend as a 'casualty of the malaise which infected Italian cinema in the 1980's.' That's a very convenient excuse Fabio. It certainly tugs on the heart strings, and portrays your subject as a victim of circumstance. But let's delve deeper, shall we. An early film of the poliziesco genre was mentioned in passing. We were told the actor would rather not recall it, the implication being it was a lesser work. The title of this cinematic effort was not supplied to us. It was a deliberate omission, and I have discovered why.

Deadly Days in the Eternal City is a film I confess I've never seen. My good fortune not to have by all accounts. Sources of mine in the entertainment field inform me it is not just a dog of a film. They go much further than that:

'A flea-riddled mongrel which should never have seen the light of day' is one such description. Another is slightly more sanitised:

'A risible plot, a cornucopia of farcical occurrences, topped only by performances which are straight from the bottom-drawer.'

Max Pellegrino's on-screen work was not spared this general damning. But I will be kind at this point and not divulge what my sources had to say about him. God knows I don't want to set back such an illustrious career. Undoubtedly, Mr. Pellegrino has no great desire to return to the high-pressured environment of fabric softener ads. But let's cut to the chase dear readers. Like a big screen story, this article must conclude with a final act. Mr. Pellegrino makes several excuses for not seeking *work outside of the recording booth. He talks about the security of employment, the regularity of jobs which continually fall into his lap. He allows Paparazzo to depict him as a sleeping giant, a great talent who has been unused for so much time. If only I had the breaks he laments. If only the second golden era in Italian cinema had occurred. Things could be so different now. My name would resonate. I could be a somebody. And the Il Quarto Stato reporter falls for it hook, line and sinker. By the end he has effectively become Pellegrino's flack.*

'A fitting replacement for Don Taylor' he tells us. The producers at Cinecittà are instructed to take note as well. Max is offered as their 'source of salvation.'

This is sheer hokum. Max Pellegrino is no more a source of salvation than I'm a King of Sardinia. He does not have what it takes to be an actor of renown, a serious artiste as one might say. The direction of his career has not been impeded by outside influences or erratic conditions. It has been stymied by the limits of his own ability, pure and simple. He is a commonplace of an actor. The moviemakers at Cinecittà will find themselves a real one in time. The natural order of things will prevail. There is no place for play-actors such as Max seeking their 15 minutes of fame. For myself, I have to express immense gratitude for this. I am a cinema aficionado as my most dedicated readers will know. I adore this great art form. Anything that debases it pains me deeply. Any attempts to lessen its aesthetic repute causes me even further offence. The article in Il Quarto Stato was such an enterprise. It was a beast, a two-headed creature, masquerading as a showbiz attraction. But in spite of the calculated veneer, we are happy to say the disguise has fallen off. The pretender has failed miserably. No matter. He still has his career, doesn't he? He still has the precious darkness of the studio. It is his finest ally and there he shall remain. End of story. Or as they say in the movies:

FINE

The Della Pasqua broadside was a game-changer. Its impact was unintended yet enormous. The tirade of disapproval served out by Rome's most notorious malcontent triggered a groundswell of response proportionate to the scorn he'd authored. It began with the group he'd been most disparaging towards in recent times – the students.

At the Sapienza University the student body president, Luciano Maggiarra, who kept a close eye on Della Pasqua's column, was spoiling for a renewal of hostilities. Poring over the latest slice of carnage in the Gazzetta, he decided to whip up support for Paparazzo's article and its main character. Maggiarra's design was simple. He gathered together his usual team, the ones who went on regular expeditions to the offices of the Gazzetta, and shared with them his plan. Della Pasqua had really outdone himself this time he told them. Purporting to be a cinema aficionado (this, Maggiarra emphasised, was news to him) Della Pasqua was now representing himself as an, 'authority on matters cinematic, artistic, who knows what else. The old bastard thinks he's an intellectual fountainhead; that he knows best about the aesthetic repute of cinema as he calls it. Does he now believe he has say-so over such things as well? That he can pronounce on whose career should advance and whose should not. We can't allow him to have the last word on this. We'll take the fight to the cinemas, perhaps the old bastard will be at one of them since he's such a devotee.'

Movie theatres all over Rome were targeted by Maggiarra and his motley crew. The students produced a snappy flyer and handed out copies at cinemas such as the Lux, Odeon, Tibur, Empire, Royal, Broadway, Adriano and Atlantic. Patrons of each establishment were urged to read Paparazzo's article and to tell their friends about it. Word of mouth would be an important component in the story's development they knew. Some of their earlier campaigns against Della Pasqua had fizzled out because of a distinct lack of viva voce. They were not about to make that same mistake again.

As part of general operations, and to drum up coverage, Luciano Maggiarra contacted three journalists in Rome: Luisa Laurito of Il Messaggero; Umberto Spada of La Repubblica; and Fabio Paparazzo of Il Quarto Stato. He tipped them off as to his fellow students' activities and invited them to give it some exposure.

Umberto Spada, who had read both Della Pasqua and Paparazzo, fancied the idea and promised to consider it. Luisa Laurito hemmed and hawed. Fabio Paparazzo, of the three, was the most reluctant.

'I have an editor who gave me one chance and one chance only,' he explained. 'If I even whispered the name at this moment in time, he'd take my head off. So I'll have to say no I'm afraid. I have to fall back in line. And besides, it's already costing me three days wages.'

Maggiarra did not understand this last remark, but thanked him just the same.

'Why are you doing this?' Paparazzo asked. 'I mean don't get me wrong, I'm all for it, but what's in it for you guys? What do you get out of it?'

The answer he got was to the point.

'Anything as a counteraction to Gianluca,' Maggiarra replied, 'the stale old bastard is not someone we hold in the highest regard.'

Nor did Umberto Spada for that matter. The La Repubblica journalist wrote a reply piece to Della Pasqua's in which he applauded the students for their, '*educated stand.*' With regard to Max Pellegrino, Spada said he did not consider Paparazzo's idea to be, '*so outlandish.*'

'*It would be weird,*' he acknowledged, '*but wonderful as well.*'

Mostly though he went after the Gazzetta old-timer, with whom he'd traded blows in the past.

'*The assertion that he is a cinema aficionado surprised me greatly,*' he wrote, '*I do recall seeing him at Fellini's memorial service in Cinecittà, but then there were thousands of people there in any case. I wonder how film-literate he really is. For example, would he be able to tell me which works of the master he considers to be the best. Does he prefer the earlier period or the later? Which is the superior in his estimation, La Strada or Nights of Cabiria?*'

Della Pasqua rose to the bait. He came back with an answer to each of Spada's questions (I Vitelloni, earlier period and Nights of Cabiria in that order) and then went on to offer justification aplenty for his arguments. Responding to the charge that he'd speciously depicted himself as an authority, he pointed out that Fabio Paparazzo had used a similar tactic in proposing Max as a fitting replacement for Don Taylor.

'*How could the young dogsbody possibly know that?*' he asked. '*Has he seen any of Pellegrino's performances? Did he sit through Deadly Days? I seriously doubt it.*'

But many others did not. Largely unresponsive just a few days before, the general public was paying attention now, its mind-set no longer casual. Spurred on by the students' campaign and the heated exchanges between Spada and Della Pasqua, Max's story made the transition from minor footnote to popular theme. Opinions were formed and positions made known. In Rome analysis of the topic was substantial; discussion arising from it reached far and wide. The principal city in the land would not be the sole repository for the debate either. Media outlets in other cities and territories quickly jumped on the bandwagon. At its second coming, the story did not just circulate, but became all the rage.

In Campania, the daily newspaper Il Mattino carried a piece on it, as did La Gazzetta del Mezzogiorno in Bari. Next it was the turn of Bologna's Il Resto del Carlino and, on the same day, the northeast's Il Gazzettino.

Two Milan-based papers: Il Giornale and Corriere della Sera allocated it what was not inconsiderable space. Il Giornale's Cesare Farina called it, '*the hippest news item in print this week.*' Corriere della Sera's Marietta Assante described it as, '*an uncommon marvel, but one which demonstrates there is an appetite for such a rousing yarn.*'

In Cagliari, L'Unione Sarda ran a feature in both the margins of its long-established broadsheet and on its trailblazing website. The Giornale di Sicilia in Palermo, on the other hand, employed more conventional means; as did Florence's La Nazione.

Prominent journalists such as Orlando Ventura, Gina Ferrara and Sylvana Lamberti all sought (and got) a piece of the action. On Italian television, the story received mentions on RAI's TG1 and TG2, as well as Canale 5's TG5 Giorno and Sera.

Daytime shows were even more generous in terms of their airtime. Tuesday's L'Italia in Questo Giorno had a studio-based discussion on the matter and this line was repeated by Wednesday's Ventiquattro Sette and Thursday's Giovedì Pomeriggio. On all three chat shows, participating audiences were invited to have their say. Mostly they were wholehearted in their views. Agreement was far from uniform about Max's prospects, but there was a general consensus on the reasons why his story had struck such a chord with his fellow countrymen.

'There is a hunger for some good news for a change,' said a female contributor on Ventiquattro Sette. Hers was not an isolated point of view.

'This country needs more of the positive and pleasing, as opposed to the gloom and despair,' voiced a young man on L'Italia in Questo Giorno, 'it's good to be hopeful even if it's for someone you don't know. It's like a second-hand optimism, it's not your own, but you feel it almost the same.'

Another put it in the following terms as he spoke into the roving mike on Giovedi Pomeriggio.

'We've had over three years of Tangentopoli and Mani Pulite. People are sick and tired of hearing reports about the sordid details and episodes of corruption. Anything that's a break from the usual fare is most welcome. Last summer the nation enjoyed such a respite during the world cup. That ended of course when Baggio blasted his penalty over the crossbar. I'm hoping that, unlike The Divine Ponytail, Max Pellegrino hits the target and puts the ball in the back of the net. Forza Max.'

Italy at this particular juncture in her history was suffering from an acute sense of national disenchantment. The domestic malaise was due to a number of factors such as on-going political inertia and massive government debt, but the overriding matter which weighed upon peoples' minds was that of Tangentopoli, or Bribesville, and the subsequent Mani Pulite investigations. Kickbacks given for public service contracts led to the arrests of many industrial figures and politicians; especially those from the main political parties. Investigations, which commenced in Milan, spread from town to town as more and more prominent figures owned up to their transgressions. In Watergate parlance, it went all the way to the top. Former prime ministers Arnaldo Forlani and Bettino Craxi were amongst those implicated. The latter's defence that, 'everyone was doing this anyway,' gave an inkling of the extent of collusion across-the-board. Public demonstrations and national rallies took place in all parts of the country. The climate of opinion became more enflamed with each new accusation and incarceration. In one particular instance, a politician broke down and admitted to his misdemeanours when two Carabinieri paid an unexpected visit to his house. Afterwards, he discovered they had only come to issue him a fine for a traffic violation. Tortuously slow legal proceedings added to the general sense of frustration, as did delaying tactics by crafty lawyers and expirations of statutory terms. It was little wonder then that sentiment and fervour with respect to national institutions was at such low ebb and, although some hoped that political, economic and ethical reforms would emanate from the judicial inquiries, many had their doubts when they considered previous restructurings and their inadequacies. Was Mani Pulite the beginning of the end or merely the end of the beginning they wondered. Was there an end in sight at all? Grave misgivings prevailed. Scandal fatigue was endemic, morale at rock bottom.

Luciano Maggiarra, who'd been invited to attend the live broadcast of Wednesday evening's Ventiquattro Sette, was asked why he thought there was such buzz on the subject of Max. Why the favourable reception for this man questioned the show's host Bernardo Gadaleta. Could he identify an exact reason for the phenomenon.

Beside the freethinking student sat Umberto Spada; he'd also been enticed to appear.

Maggiarra began by outlining how he and his companions had involved themselves in the narrative. Over and over again he used that same word – narrative.

'There is an eagerness in the air which cannot be denied,' he reasoned, 'an impatience with the old order of unanimity, of accepting the same old narrative for what it is and leaving so-called well enough alone. Far too often we're told to have patience. Be patient about the economic state of this country – it will get better. Be patient about those disreputable leaders of ours – the next group will have clean hands. Be patient about your own personal future – you will advance in the time to come, sooner or later. That's the crux of the matter though, isn't it? When will these ground-breaking events occur? Will they ever happen? I doubt it. We have to be more proactive as a nation. Clean hands have got to become hands-on. That's what our new narrative should be about – the honest and direct approach, not the clandestine one of old.'

Gadaleta attempted to move the undergraduate along as quickly as he could. Maggiarra, however, was having none of it. He continued to speak about the new agenda which he fervently believed the nation should embrace. The word narrative was used several more times. Various political thinkers were cited. The kid was on a roll. He just couldn't stop talking. And still he had not answered Gadaleta's original question.

The normally unflappable compere looked edgy. Through his earpiece, he was told to call a halt to the pontificating.

'Shut this kid up already!' his director screamed from the production-control room. 'Do anything! Go to a commercial break if you have to!'

There was a pause as an assistant whispered something in his ear. His tone changed immediately.

'Bingo!' he shouted gleefully, 'you'll never guess who we have on the phone Bernardo! He wants to address the panel directly. That stuck-up student especially. Let's roll with it.'

Gadaleta finally managed an interruption.

'Ladies and gentlemen, we have Gianluca Della Pasqua on the line,' he announced. 'Mr. Della Pasqua, as you'll know, has been involved in this discussion from an early stage. He joins us now. Mr. Della Pasqua, can you hear me?'

'I can hear you very well Bernardo,' a raspy voice answered, 'you're coming through loud and clear. Unfortunately, I've heard some other things this evening, loud and clear also. There are lots of hackneyed expressions being tossed about. Words such as proactive and narrative. I also heard patience being mentioned. At that point, I lost mine. Mr. Maggiarra is a young man and, like most people his age, he has much to learn. An impressive vocabulary and array of thoughts may seem sufficient for his enterprise, but he is in no position to offer us instruction or guidance. He should not presume to lecture. Television is a medium I have very little time for Bernardo. I rarely watch it, and with good reason. This evening I turned it on in the hope of catching a good film. Instead, Mr. Maggiarra's callow visage was the first image I saw. Beside him sits Mr. Spada I notice. Even he looks bored; which is really saying something. A piece of advice to my young friend if I may be so bold. The eloquent digressions and skilled appeals are, on the face of it, impressive Mr. Maggiarra. On a common soapbox you'd come across as educated, knowledgeable even. Many, no doubt, are taken in by you. But this listener is not one of them. The aimless rhetoric is only too familiar to him. He has heard it all before. Do yourself a favour and continue your studies Mr. Maggiarra. Aristotle tells us that education serves as a rattle for young people when older. Just ask Mr. Spada about that. He's well versed in such an occupation. Perhaps the two of you are soul mates.'

The tossed grenade had the desired effect.

Maggiarra flew into a rage and responded with a string of counter-insults. He was accompanied by the man sitting next to him. Umberto Spada pitched in with his own brand of invective. He pronounced Della Pasqua, 'an offence to liberal thinkers everywhere, an already small man who just shrank a bit further.'

On the side-line, Bernardo Gadaleta tried in vain to calm proceedings.

Gianluca Della Pasqua resumed his rant. His voice was more vigorous now, taking pleasure in the furore he'd caused. Spada and Maggiarra retorted in unison.

The interchange of slights persisted, in spite of Gadaleta's best efforts to appease. On his earpiece, his director sounded over the moon.

'This is chronic,' he said, 'but fantastic TV! Don't stop them yet. Let them tear strips off one another for a while more!'

Max was watching the show that evening as the hullabaloo and name-calling took place. Since the time of Della Pasqua's initial contribution, he'd remained tight-lipped as regards the press. A number of journalists and other media outlets had contacted him, but, to all, his response was the same.

'I don't have anything further to add,' he told them, 'nothing to say, thank-you.'

Once or twice he offered the judicious remark that the story spoke for itself. But that was as far as he would go. Better to be reserved in this way he told himself. Let others talk and thrash it out. For once less was more. Further explanations on his part were to be categorically declined.

He applied this to one and all, Fabio Paparazzo included. The Il Quarto Stato reporter had been conspicuous by his silence at first. There was no phone call; nary a word in the wake of his article. In point of fact, he only attempted a renewal of communications as the Della Pasqua/Spada wrangle was going on. Then he left a number of messages on Max's answering machine.

'Return my call,' he said, 'we should discuss a follow-up. Strike while the iron is hot.'

Max was not of the same mind. It could wait he decided. Paparazzo could wait as well. The timing ought to be exact. And it wasn't just yet.

He spoke to his sister about it. Antonia phoned several times to ask if he'd read the latest thing in this newspaper or that magazine. She was the first to tell him about the Della Pasqua volley which she disapproved of greatly. When he appeared to have little to say about it, she enquired as to why he was not more annoyed; why not rage on his part. His response was composed. He didn't mind arguments about who he was or what he could do. The important thing he told her was that it kept the story alive, held the public interest. If others wished to disagree, then that was just fine by him. They might even be doing him a favour.

Andrea Vallelunga appeared at his apartment door one morning.

'I'm not here to ask for something, for a change,' he said cheerfully, 'just to say congratulations. Well done.'

'For what?' asked Max.

'Well you're famous now, aren't you? The sky's the limit.'

He changed tack then.

'You know we've been neighbours now how many years Max? Seven or eight perhaps? And in all that time, I never knew what you did. I used to wonder about it, but you seem like such a private person, I didn't want to ask. Anyway, that's what I wanted to say. Good for you Max. I hope lots of success comes your way.'

He turned back towards his own apartment.

'And what about you Andrea?' Max asked. 'What do you do to make ends meet?'

Vallelunga smiled.

'You didn't know either?' he said. 'I'm an ocularist. I specialise in the making and fitting of optical prostheses for people who've lost an eye. It just goes to show Max, you can never tell with some people. You an actor and I never would have guessed.'

At the edicola, Gino also offered his best wishes. Light-heartedly, he asked how soon Max would be going to Hollywood. The two men kidded about it. Max told Gino he was expecting a call from Steven Spielberg any day now.

'He's doing a sequel to Jurassic Park and I've told him I'm available. I'm looking forward to working with the cloned dinosaurs. Hopefully, the tyrannosaurus won't get me until I've spoken a few lines.'

The older man, for his part, reminded Max not to forget his friends.

'If there's ever a role for a newspaper vendor, I'm your man,' he said.

Outside the Tibur on Via degli Etruschi, Max was handed a flyer by a female student. The cinema was close to the Sapienza University and was one of those the students had selected as part of their blitz.

'Please read this,' she told him, evidently unaware of who he was, 'if you can also spare the time, tell your friends about it. We want to help this man. Give his career the spark it needs.'

Max nodded politely, assured her he would do so.

'Do you think he will get far?' he asked. 'Do you think any of it is possible?'

The student thought this over for a moment or two. She delivered her answer with a confident beat.

'I think he just might,' she said. 'Anything is possible. If they give him an opportunity, I'm sure he won't disappoint. He's a very great actor you know. My sixth sense tells me we'll see him outside this cinema some day. And I'm hardly ever wrong about those things.'

Max drove to Ariccia on Wednesday. He walked around the town and visited some of the old haunts. Ariccia had changed. Some of its older buildings were revamped and no longer familiar to him. He knew the old movie house was no longer there, but had not seen its replacement until now. The new cinema was modern-looking and comprised three screens. The advertising on its front elevation boasted state-of-the-art technology. Posters of current films 'now playing' were affixed inside glass surrounds.

Max paid a visit to his childhood home. The house where he'd grown up belonged to another family now. After his mother's death in 1991 there seemed little point in holding on to it. Neither he nor Antonia had the time, or money, to keep it going. Ever the pragmatist, his sister was the one who'd advocated the sale. It was the prudent thing to do she said. Sentiment would not maintain the building or keep mother-nature at bay. Better for the house that it have permanent dwellers rather than passing visitors.

Max felt just that way about Ariccia. He was little more than a passing visitor now; virtually a stranger in the place of his birth. And even with all the recent news and brouhaha. No one recognised him. No one said hello Max.

He stopped off in Piazza di Corte for a while and, at the Palazzo Savelli Chigi, took in an exhibition of artwork dating back to the 1600's. The collection had, amongst other artefacts, the keys to the Vatican used during conclaves, the skullcap and bowl of Pope Pius IX, and trunks with toilet items from the 17th century. Max liked the stencilled leather wall coverings especially. He remembered being fond of them as a boy.

In the early evening he took a stroll on the Ponte di Ariccia. The two-storey, semi-circular arch bridge, constructed to facilitate the route of the Appian Way, had been destroyed in February 1944 and, then in 1967, had collapsed once again of its own accord. Max walked out to the centre and looked back towards the town. From his position, he could see the domed church of the Assunta, designed by Bernini, and the Porta Romana, also by the famous Baroque sculptor. Below, in the valley, lay the wooded landscape that was Chigi Park, a treasure trove of archaeological finds, fountains, and assorted verdure.

Max fixed his eyes on the other side of the bridge. He was more or less half-ways across. Somewhere in the region of 150 metres he reckoned. Another 150 or so and he'd be at the furthest point. He felt good. A summertime euphoria was kicking in. The sky was bright, nightfall an hour or two away. A lot of light left yet he figured. No hurry back. Plenty of time to complete the crossing. And after that, well, something else he thought. Something not too far-off. Meantime, get to the other side of the bridge. Go the distance. Go all the way.

AND ALL THAT JAZZ

At long last Fabio Paparazzo heard a click on the other end of the phone. It was about time he thought. It had taken long enough. Too much in his opinion.

'Pronto,' said Max.

His voice sounded different as he answered. It seemed more intense than before. Something about it which Fabio had not noticed previously.

His tone loosened up as soon as he realised who it was. Slipping back into his more familiar self, he politely asked Fabio how he was and congratulated him on the article.

'Pat yourself on the back while you're at it,' Paparazzo said, 'it would never have happened without your participation. You're the name on everyone's lips right now.'

The easy flow of his speech was abandoned as he launched into a pointed remark.

'I have a bone to pick with you though Max. Why has it taken me forever and a day to get a hold of you? I left message after message on your machine! Why didn't you return any of my calls?'

'My apologies for that,' said Max, 'I just thought it better to stay out of it for a time. I didn't give interviews to anyone else. I'm sure you realise that. I got offers, but I turned them all down.'

'I know that Max, but you could have told me as much. Straight up would have been better than nothing. Consider my position for a second. I have an editor who's been badgering me about this for the past few days. It made me look bad when I wasn't able to reach you. He had my head in a spin with questions – 'Where is Max?', 'Why the hell aren't the two of you talking?!' This morning he practically ordered me to stake out your apartment building.'

'I'm surprised you didn't.'

'I called there twice actually. Got into your building one of those times. You weren't home it seems. Or maybe you just weren't answering your door.'

'What day was that?'

'Yesterday. Wednesday.'

'I was away Wednesday afternoon,' Max explained, 'I took a drive to Ariccia.'

'Well that sounds very pleasant Max, but the fact is I'm under pressure here to get a follow-up interview with you. The newspaper which first printed your story wants to get back out in front of the others. My editor wants a reaction piece and he wants it straight from the original source. He's not inclined to take no for an answer. He's a bit like me that way.'

'It sounds as if his attitude has changed,' observed Max, 'the last time we spoke was the day before it went into the paper. You didn't seem as sure about it then.'

'I wasn't,' Paparazzo admitted, 'I'd just been bawled out by my own manager. Truth be told, it was something of a narrow margin in the end. I mean in terms of getting it published at all. We were lucky and then some. The story's gone across in a way even I didn't expect it would. I never imagined such a nationwide response. I thought the bigger cities would be the extent of it. Rome. Milan. Naples. Turin. A few more in an ideal world, but that would be its limit I told myself. I didn't count on so many others. I didn't see it reaching places like Potenza or Trieste.'

'I hadn't heard about Trieste,' said Max, 'my friend at the edicola was keeping me up to date with everything he was hearing. He never mentioned Trieste.'

'I only learnt of it myself because one of my colleagues is from there,' Paparazzo told him. 'She said it made page 3 of Il Piccolo. She's promised to show me a copy which her Mom is sending. Trieste of all places! It's remarkable, isn't it? If I was of a more charitable disposition, I'd probably offer to buy Gianluca Della Pasqua a drink. The old bellyacher almost deserves it. If it hadn't been for him...'

He mulled over his next sentence before delivering it.

'Truthfully speaking, just between the two of us,' he said.

'Of course,' replied Max.

'Well, I really thought the whole thing was dead in the water to be honest with you Max. I'd pretty much given up on it. There wasn't the response I'd been hoping for. Not enough people were talking about it. No ballyhoo. And as for my esteemed colleagues and peers in the newspaper trade, no doubt you were aware of the lukewarm reception it was getting from them. Actually lukewarm is an overstatement.'

'I had the impression it wasn't exactly the hottest thing in print,' said Max. 'I guess Gianluca Della Pasqua becoming involved was the turning point.'

'It was the saving of the story,' said Paparazzo. 'The curmudgeon didn't intend it, but that was the effect he had. His vitriol breathed life back into it in a way no amount of praise could have done.'

'And I see he's not done with it yet,' said Max. 'There was another bout in yesterday's Gazzetta. He was panning Umberto Spada and the students again.'

'He's like a Gila monster, once he takes a bite of something, he doesn't let go easily. Calling me your flack, huh? He went pretty hard on you too Max. You must have been upset when you heard about it.'

'I was disappointed for sure, but then I began to think to myself...'

'What?'

'Well I became strangely optimistic. I figured there isn't anything else of harm that can happen here, nothing less favourable. You understand?'

'I can't say I do. You'll have to explain that to me.'

The other man did not wish to apparently.

'How did it make you feel?' Max asked instead.

Paparazzo spotted the evasion. Unmistakable he thought. What's that about?

'I felt bad about it,' he said, 'I felt it was rock bottom, the coup de grace for the story. My hat off to you for your positivity, but what made you think it would turn the situation around?'

There was a momentary silence on the other end. Max's response, when it came, was not quite the essence of clarity.

'I didn't anticipate the turnaround that happened,' he said cagily, 'definitely not the scale of it. I just thought it can only get better from here, can't it? The first day you came to my apartment, you said it would raise my profile, that it would get me my 15 minutes of fame. I went on believing that. I had to believe that.'

His train of thought quickly moved on to the next subject.

'The students played their part as well, didn't they?' he said. 'The ones from the Sapienza University especially.'

'They certainly did,' Paparazzo agreed, 'one of them contacted me in the beginning. Maggiarra – the guy who was on Ventiquattro Sette. You saw it I assume?'

'I did. I'd just got back from Ariccia.'

'It was quite a riot. I thought Bernardo Gadaleta was going to have a heart attack. But then he always looks like that, even during his moments of calm. What doesn't kill you makes you stronger, huh?'

There was no reply from Max, just the sound of his breathing.

'So Max, how are we going to do this?' Paparazzo asked. 'A few days ago the paper reprinted my article about you. I put in a short introduction before it. An update on how your story has taken off. It was lazy journalism. What I had to say was news to no one. It was formulaic. I could have written it in my sleep. But I wasn't getting a hold of you so what alternatives did I have? But now we're talking again, which is good. I'd like to think you're ready to move this on in a way that's beneficial to yourself, and to my paper. Take it to the next level if you know what I mean. Cash in those chips you're holding, get yourself some added exposure.'

'My 15 minutes of fame, right?'

'It's a great deal more than that now Max. I'd say something in the order of...'

'What about Echo of Passions Fabio? What have you been hearing about that?'

'Just the same gossips as everyone else. Don Taylor hasn't been replaced. There was some incident on a US TV show. An old-time producer flew off the handle about the director.'

'Mr. Cousins?'

'That's the one; he was the object of this other guy's ridicule. A Gianluca Della Pasqua verbal offensive by all accounts. And they're saying the fallout is substantial; very damaging to what was already a fragile situation. My understanding is that few in Hollywood want to touch it now. But you know this already, don't you?'

'I do Fabio. I was just checking we're on the same page.'

'What one would that be Max?'

'Their source of salvation, as you put it,' said Max. 'You know that was the only part of Della Pasqua's article I got a laugh out of. Do you remember it? He said, 'Max Pellegrino is no more a source of salvation than I'm a King of Sardinia.'

'So you did read it Max?'

'I never said I didn't Fabio. You talk about the next level and added exposure. Well this is it. This is what you need to go after, your angle as a newspaper man.'

Paparazzo took a few seconds before coming back.

'That's what I'm trying to get at Max. The angle is you. You're the one people want to read about. They want to hear directly from you again. Not more opinions and second-hand rehashes.'

'No,' Max said vehemently, 'that's just more repetition and by-the-numbers journalism. The story isn't just about me Fabio. It's also about that production in Cinecittà. You haven't forgotten about that, have you?'

'Of course I haven't Max.'

'I'm glad to hear it. Because some other people have. The Ventiquattro show last night made that very clear to me. Only once during the entire broadcast was the film even mentioned. People were talking off the point. And as for the panel discussion, you saw what that descended into.'

'I know. The verbosity took over.'

'Exactly, as did the egos. The arguments were no longer about you or me Fabio. It couldn't have had less to do with the story. Those people were only interested in thrashing one other. And guess what, they were enjoying it. They were in a place they wanted to be. Self-glorification and all that jazz; they were lapping it up. So was the studio audience. So was everyone watching.'

'I see what you're getting at.'

'You said your paper wants to get back out in front of the others. Well I'll tell you how it can. By doing something no one else has. Take the story to Cinecittà Fabio. Your colleagues in the press have overlooked it. No one has given it any real attention. No one has asked them if they're aware of your article and everything that has followed on from it.'

'It may have been a difficulty with translation,' Paparazzo suggested, 'perhaps there's been no crossover.'

'Then someone should ensure it takes place,' said Max, 'a reporter who's been at the heart of the story for example. In the process, I'm sure that reporter would be able to get reaction from the American producers. You know how those Hollywood people are – they love to give statements and pronounce on this and that. Even when they say it's hush-hush, they expect it to be made public.'

This drew a laugh from Paparazzo.

'My God Max, you're out in front of us all it seems,' he said. 'I think it's a terrific idea. I will do it on one condition.'

'What's that?'

'If I'm successful, and get their thoughts, I want that follow-up with you afterwards. That's what I ask for in return.'

'It's a deal.'

'Wonderful. I'll contact their production office, look for an interview with this Mr. Cousins. The one who got the Gianluca-type treatment.'

A thought occurred to him.

'Max, one thing which puzzled me about our friend – how did he know the name of your poliziesco film? You told me it was obscure to the point of…as if it'd never been made you said. In fact, you never told me its name. I wonder how Della Pasqua managed to find out.'

'I don't know,' said Max, 'perhaps…perhaps his sources are as good as he claims.'

'I have my doubts about that,' replied an incredulous Paparazzo, 'Umberto Spada was correct in what he said. Gianluca is no aficionado. He just likes to think he is. It's the one thing I don't get. I've no idea how he discovered the name of your film. That part of it is a mystery to me.'

A few hours later, Franco Bonacossa called.

'Max, I've been trying to reach you as a matter of urgency,' he began. 'Why did you postpone that first session with HQD Pharmaceuticals? I got a call from their managing director. He was less than impressed.'

'I'm sorry about that Franco,' said Max, 'I put it off at the last minute. He probably has every reason to be annoyed.'

'He most certainly was annoyed Max. What was your reason? Were you not prepared? Did you not have enough time?'

'I had lots of time Franco. Perhaps too much. I just didn't feel up to it that day.'

'What?' said Franco, his voice aghast. There was a momentary fit of wheezing, a tell-tale sign of the smoker. Once it had passed, Franco pushed on grimly.

'Max, this is not like you at all!' he said sternly. 'In all the years we've worked together, I've never known you to do something like this. How can you make such an unprofessional decision? To withdraw from an arranged recording! Don't you realise you have a contract with these people? They're paying for a service! Yours!'

Max thought about that word – service. He disliked it being used to describe his work, always had. The offending contract from HQD came to mind again; the buyout clause especially. It was still an affront to him. Even more so now. And as for that tedious script which accompanied it; mind-numbing was an understatement.

He was barely listening to Franco. The older man was still going on about professionalism and reputations; both his and his client's. He sounded like a school teacher dressing-down an errant pupil, like a master chastising an apprentice.

At last he reached a conclusion.

'Have I said too much?' he asked, 'I thought it best to be plain-spoken about this. As your agent Max, I only ask that you fulfil your commitments and do your work well. You've never let me down in the past. Getting that call from HQD was something I didn't expect. It was like a bolt from the blue.'

'I'm sorry Franco. If you want I'll phone the MD and straighten things out with him.'

'No, there's no need Max. Just be there the next time. Don't stall on them again.'

The instruction doled out, he could be heard lighting a cigarette.

'There's nothing on your mind?' he asked. 'No problems I should know about?'

Max considered that an odd question to ask. He had no problems; nothing out of the ordinary. As for things on his mind – well there was one outstanding matter. Circumstances as they were, he didn't think it out of place to bring it up.

'You've seen the papers recently?' he asked as a leading question. Like himself, Franco was generally a La Repubblica reader.

'Yes, I've seen them Max. Il Quarto Stato and Gazzetta di Roma included. Your name has certainly been bandied about.'

'I'm glad to hear you read Il Quarto Stato,' Max continued, 'I made a point of telling that journalist to mention you by name.'

'Why did you do that Max?'

'Well I thought, it wouldn't hurt; in terms of your business.'

'What do you know about my business?'

Franco's tone, apathetic on the subject up to now, was markedly defensive.

'I know it hasn't been going so well in recent times,' Max replied tentatively, 'I heard about Pietro and Erika leaving you. I thought you could do with a shot in the arm.'

The self-respecting agent took exception to these words.

'I do not need any such thing,' he snapped back, 'nor do I require promotional work to be done on my behalf. I'm more than satisfied as I am Max – thank you – and I'm also confident as to the state of my business. The individuals you mention left me of their own volition. They made a professional decision, which I can accept, even respect. I don't require help-outs or come-by-chance exposure just because two people decided not to renew their contracts with me. I can survive without them and that's what I intend to do. I've always made my own way, on my terms. I've never depended on external factors, nor have I hung my hopes on unlikely situations. You strike me as being a realistic person Max; not one given over to whims or flights of the imagination. I can't imagine you're humouring any of these media people, the ones who are writing about you day after day. But on the off chance that you are, let me say this to you – don't allow yourself to be deluded by any of it. It's nothing more than the press blowing things out of proportion. They needed something to sensationalise. They always do. Your story just happened to present itself at this moment. If it wasn't you, it would be somebody else. By next month this will all be forgotten about. It's in the nature of fads that they are cast off quickly. I'm sure you realise this. Getting back to work will be the best thing for you. It will remind you of what's important, what's real. Wouldn't you agree?'

There was no reply.

'Wouldn't you agree Max? I'm not wrong, am I?'

'No Franco, you're not wrong. You go ahead and contact that MD. Tell him I'll record the first session for them whenever they want. They can nominate the day.'

'Good man. This will be good for you. Get you back on track.'

Franco began to call out his assistant's name.

'Mariella. Mariella!' he yelled. 'Where is my diary? Mariella! Where has she gone?'

Max held the earpiece of the phone to one side.

He'd considered asking Franco something, but it had become unnecessary. The answer to his question was in the conversation. It had come as soon as the agent started in on his sermon about HQD Pharmaceuticals.

Max eyed the document which was still lying against his floor lamp. Piece of shit copy he thought, all that biotech spiel, but I better do it for Franco's sake. It wouldn't be right to say no. Much as I'd be tempted to.

Finally, Franco returned to him. He had his diary in hand now. Mariella had found it in a stack of his clothes.

'My dirty laundry,' Franco joked. 'As they say you should never air it in public.'

Max managed a feeble laugh. He didn't much feel like humour. Already he was having second thoughts again.

'So, let's get you back to the studio,' said Franco, his mood more sanguine than ever. 'Terra firma to you Max. Your home away from home, eh?'

For good measure, he added in another Latin phrase.

'Always towards better things,' he said unaffectedly.

Once again, there was a quiet riposte, followed by a lungful of air being exhaled.

'Always the same Franco,' said Max. 'Always the same. And all that jazz.'

THE REPLACEMENT KILLERS

On Sunday evening, 30th April, 1995, ABC's leading talk show, Night-Time with Howard Holden, devoted its 62-minute running time exclusively to the career of the much-respected and popular film producer Frederick 'Bear' Topolski. The tribute programme, recorded at the network's west coast headquarters in Los Feliz, Los Angeles, was taking place for two reasons. First of all, there was the not-so insignificant matter of the special guest's recent birthday. Bear had turned seventy-five five days before, on the 25th of April; it was the same date of birth he pointed out to his tickled host as Al Pacino, Paul Mazursky and Edward R. Murrow.

'They are in august company to be sure,' he joked, 'or perhaps I've got that the wrong way around. At any rate, I'm delighted to be here with you Howard, and to see so many friends and peers among your studio audience.'

The second reason for the special broadcast was to commemorate Bear's 50 years, give or take, in the motion picture business. He'd started out as an assistant at Columbia Pictures, during Harry Cohn's tenure, and had forged a career of distinction from those humble beginnings. Asked if he'd known 'King Cohn' on a personal level, Bear's response was forthright and droll.

'I never spoke to Mr. Cohn,' he answered, 'I was too young and far too intimidated to have the nerve.'

Turned out in a forest-green jacket, dark-blue shirt, and gold leaf bow tie, it was difficult to imagine a time when Bear was overawed by anyone. Certainly no member of the audience present could conceive of such a situation.

Still physically-imposing, even in his mid-seventies, he had huge granite-like shoulders and a rock-solid frame, for which he'd understandably earned his pet name, and possessed a quick-witted sense of humour which glowed just like his rubicund features. On the whole, he looked and sounded every inch the elder statesman of the industry. Revelling in the role of emeritus professor for the evening (several contributors acknowledged how much they'd learnt from him), Bear was in an infectious mood and was not in the least bit stingy, or given to obfuscation, when it came to imparting personal anecdotes and wider-industry musings.

Asked by the former writer-comedian Holden if he would ever contemplate retirement and the subsequent quiet life, Bear was unequivocal in his response.

'Absolutely not,' he declared, to a vigorous round of applause, 'I'm still working and that's the way I intend to carry on. Now as most people here will know, the nature of that work has become smaller in scale, if that's the correct term to use. These days I mostly produce for TV. ABC, I'm glad to say, has been a welcome benefactor and beneficiary in that regard.

You see Howard my personal life has been slightly chequered. I've had a total of four marriages and that's a figure which one cannot turn a blind eye to. My matrimonial misadventures, well three of them anyway, are incentive enough for me to remain at work. There are immediate family members to provide for, alimonies to pay, and also the satellite houses to take care of. In many ways, the requirement to support my former spouses is the best thing that ever happened to me. It's a driving force which gets me up every day, obliges me to stay in this game. I've lots of good things to say about the subject as a matter of fact,' he said, with a knowing wink to the audience, 'the break-up part of it I would not generally recommend, but as for the alimony, as for my responsibilities to those I have been previously hitched, it works for me. I've kept several irons in the fire on account of it. But don't take my advice on this whatever you do. I'm by no means an authority figure when it comes to such matters. I'm an old dog that barks backwards Howard, like the one Robert Frost wrote about in his poem. The only difference is I keep on getting up. I'm stubborn to the last, even in these advanced years of mine.'

The witticism provoked another warm reaction from those in attendance.

'But seriously and all joking aside,' Bear resumed, 'I love the work. I love this business. Who wouldn't? I'm proud to be part of it and I'm happy to say that the duration of my involvement is still an open-ended thing. So don't write off the Bear just yet. He has more than a few roars left in him. Watch out.'

One such roar was closer at hand than anyone, including Howard Holden, expected. It was triggered when the genial host asked his guest if there were any regrets he had in his professional or private life; anything he might have done differently.

'Lots of things I would have done differently Howard, and certainly some regrets in my private world. As to my line of work...well...let me see.'

Bear furrowed his brow and thought hard.

'Any problem situations you were involved in?' prompted Holden, 'difficult circumstances such as a production going over time or budget? Perhaps there were some thorny issues you had to sort out? Or thornier individuals?'

The mnemonic cue was more than enough. Bear's countenance shifted appreciably. The bantering, avuncular gentleman of a few moments before disappeared from sight. In his place was a very different person indeed.

'There was one director who maddened me like no other,' he said, his voice unsteady for the first time all evening, 'in point of fact he almost caused me to lose my mind. His name is David Cousins and for a while there I supposed, as many did, that we'd heard the last of him. I produced two films which he directed. The first was a horror film; the second, a musical. The real horror for me though occurred during the making of the musical. It was called Bluff City. It went both over time and over budget Howard, double whammy in effect. The director you see was hell-bent on setting a new record for number of takes. He smothered every song-and-dance routine with his excessive approach; with his disproportionate sense of self. He thought he was creating a masterpiece, that he was some latter-day Vincente Minnelli. The end-product is no such thing I can promise you. I begged and pleaded for him to move it along; but my efforts only got indifferent results. The man would not listen to reason, nor would he acknowledge the shambles unfolding around him. He was forever babbling on about art being a necessary toil; that out of the hard labour and misery would come a work of merit. That distorted vision was his solely. The agony, on the other hand, was all mine. Eventually, I had to obtain additional capital, just to get the damn thing finished. I was forced to put up some property to satisfy the banks, my studio facility in Burbank. It broke my heart when I lost it. That's where my career really began. It was part of who I was. I blame David Cousins for its loss. I hold him and his arrogance responsible. Some people believe forgiveness comes with the passage of time. I don't. If I live another twenty-five years, I can't imagine myself excusing that twisted little man for what happened, and for his complete lack of sensitivity afterwards.'

'He's making a film in Rome at the moment,' interrupted Holden, as he tried to change the focus of their conversation, 'we are all aware of the tragic accident which happened to Don Taylor. How did you feel when you heard the news Fred? I believe the two of you worked together a couple of years ago?'

'I was greatly saddened by it,' Bear replied, 'Don Taylor is a gentleman and an absolute pro. He's poles apart from that other person I just mentioned.'

A light flashed in his eyes as something occurred.

'That was something I could not, for the life of me, figure out,' he said, adjusting in his seat. 'Why was Don Taylor – great star that he is – drawn towards working with this pariah? Had he not heard the critical evidence? Did he think those stories were just urban myths? It truly baffles me.'

'Anyway we appreciate that...'

'Come to think of it, how did this man get back in the director's chair at all?' Bear reflected noisily as he disregarded Holden's attempt to move off the subject, 'my understanding is he acquired backing through private investors and then used this as leverage to hook a major. The studio that got lured in is now entangled. For them, I feel a certain degree of sympathy, not much though mind you. Like a few others in this town, they looked only at the product and not the person behind it. The devil is in the detail. Which for me begs a more significant question – is there a collective amnesia surrounding David Cousins? Am I the only one who has recall? How and why has he been accepted back into the fold? Is that what an Oscar win does to people? Convinces them a fucking lowlife has made amends somehow.'

'Frederick, I think we ought to...'

'Well I for one will never be persuaded; no matter what Mr. David Cousins might choose to turn his hand to. He could put on a white outfit for all I care, carry a trumpet around, even grow himself a pair of wings, but that wouldn't make him an angel of the lord in my book!'

'We're moving on Fred,' Holden butted in firmly, 'I think this is a discussion for another time and another place.'

'Just one more thing Howard, if you will,' Bear insisted.

'One more thing Fred, and for God sake, please keep it civil!'

Bear promised he would.

Composing himself, he took a moment out, and then gazed towards the audience.

'I apologise for getting carried away just now,' he said, 'it sometimes happens when I get riled up about a subject. The one I've just spoken about is something that aggrieves me to a great extent. It would do the same to you if you were in my position. And I know what the perception of my outburst will most likely be. No doubt, people will say the old man has finally lost it. He's for the funny farm is Bear. They certainly would have lots of justification in thinking that.'

He shook his head, smiled dryly.

'An angel of the lord,' he said, 'even I'm not sure where that came from. But as for the rest of it, let me state for the record it is what I honestly believe. I would not for a second consider putting it any other way. Creative expression is a wonderful thing. I've fought many a battle in the past to support it. My friends and colleagues who are here this evening know that about me. We all need a certain amount of room for manoeuvre, writers and directors most especially. As far as artistic autonomy goes, I'm all for it. I can safely say I allow more than many others. And it was to my detriment that I gave someone too much rope on one occasion. He ended up hanging himself and me into the bargain. Now some of the fault for that rests squarely on my shoulders. I won't deny that. I saw the warning signs early on and failed to take the necessary action. I mixed things up. I failed to identify what was in front of me – rampant megalomania. And when I did, it was much too late. The director in question had a gun to my head by then. I had no choice but to persevere with him, right to the bitter end. And it sure was bitter in the end Howard.'

'I think we all get a sense of that Fred.'

'A short time after I lost the studio in Burbank, I encountered Mr. Cousins for what I hoped would be the last time. Thankfully, I've never seen him since. He was utterly unashamed over what had happened. Even more than that. So I had it out with him one last time. Just for old times' sake, though rest assured it was not done in order to remember a happier period between us. At the end of our chat I brought up Burbank. I gave him a chance to say something about it. I hoped against hope he might express some bit of fellow feeling on the subject. I wasn't asking for an outright apology. Just something to show me he appreciated the situation. The tiniest hint. I got no such thing in return. The words he threw back at me, I will never forget; or forgive. 'Fuck you and your shitty studio,' he said. He then told me to stick it…I think you can guess where Howard.'

There was an all-over hush in the studio. Not a person spoke. The audience, carefree and in high spirits just a few minutes earlier, was now a collection of dumbfounded looks. All the more so the normally effusive Howard Holden who was, similarly, flabbergasted.

Bear looked about and regarded the general discomfiture he'd caused. He'd finally done it he figured, exacted a measure of revenge. And on national television. Perfect he thought. But just one parting shot to add, twist the knife in just that bit more.

'That angel of the lord reference I made before,' he said, 'it was totally misplaced. David Cousins could never be such a thing. I'll tell you why, because David Cousins is the fucking prince of darkness!!'

In Rome, the object of Bear's very public condemnation awoke to a call from his agent. On the phone, Art Brackman sounded concerned.

'What time is it there?' he asked.

'6.30 in the a.m.,' replied a testy David Cousins. 'Can I ask that you don't make a habit of this Art. The 3.30 call I get from Mastrodicasa every day is one thing; this though is a horse of a different colour.'

'David I wouldn't be worrying about horses right now if I were you. And I wouldn't have called if this wasn't important. I thought you should hear it from me first.'

'Hear what?'

'Well the show has just ended here, but this is probably just the beginning of it.'

'Beginning of what?'

'A character from your past David. He was on tonight's Howard Holden show.'

'Enough with the mystery Art,' said an exasperated Cousins. 'Who was it? Who is this character from my past?'

Through a contact of his agent's, Cousins managed to get hold of a copy of the show later that day. He watched it by himself in the Talking Telegraph office. It was evening time; everyone else had gone home or to their hotels. Art had recommended him the seclusion.

As soon as Bear's interview was finished, the director was on the phone to his rep.

'I want to file a lawsuit against the old fuck,' he quickly declared, 'what he said about me amounts to slander, pure and simple.'

'I don't think that would be such a good idea David,' Brackman replied.

'Why not?!'

'Well for one thing the timing couldn't be any worse. Right now, you don't want to be drawing any more unfavourable attention to yourself. My advice would be to stay well clear of it. Dignity through your silence. Don't fan the flames.'

'Dignity Art?! What dignity do I have after that?! Did you hear those things he said about me? He called me a lowlife for chrissake! He said I was the fucking prince of darkness!!'

'I heard every word of it David, and none of it was good. But slapping the old boy with a lawsuit is not going to help matters. Quite the opposite I think. Your lawyer by the way agrees with me. Bear is a well-liked man around town. People in the industry respect him. They see a veneer of gravitas when he enters a room. I guess it's the kind of high regard that comes if you live long enough.'

'What are you giving me with fucking veneers Art?! What do you think my fucking veneer looks like right now? A long way from gravitas you can imagine. The fucking Bear had all the subtlety of a man brandishing an axe while standing up in a speeding convertible.'

'David I know that. It happened. But he can't be gagged after the fact. Unfortunately, it's out there now. Damage control is our only recourse.'

'I could file a civil action anyway,' the director suggested, 'and offer to withdraw if Topolski publishes a retraction in, say, four publications of my choosing.'

'No, David, that still gets you bad press. And besides, he won't retract any of it. You know he won't. He's a headstrong man. You'd never get him to do a U-turn.'

'I know,' said Cousins, 'that's another thing which comes if you live long enough – obstinacy.'

'David, one question I have to ask. The story about him running into you after Bluff City, is that true?'

'I have a recollection of it, yes.'

'Did you say what he claims you said?'

'Which part?'

'You know which part David. The one involving several expletives and you telling him to stick his studio where the sun don't shine.'

'I may have said something along those lines. It's a blur in my memory now to be honest. He was playing the poor man with me Art. As if he'd lost everything in the world and I was the cause of it.'

'Well he plays the part convincingly David. You saw Howard Holden's face after he dropped that bombshell. The whole studio was the same. It's yet another reason not to pursue the old boy through the courts.'

'How bad is the fallout likely to be?'

'Most of the trades are going to run the story from what I hear. It's turned up on CBS and NBC already.'

'Jesus Christ,' Cousins reacted flatly.

'What can I tell you? There are few things people enjoy more than watching an old-timer lose his rag on national television. That's what Network was about.'

'And as for damage control?'

'I'm making calls to the appropriate people, lionising you as best I can. I spoke to Anthony Chouraqui at Aggregate just an hour ago. 'We have every confidence in David and will continue to back him,' were his exact words. Many of the individuals I've spoken to were supportive.'

'But not all of them?'

'No, David, not all of them.'

'Oh fuck,' the director sighed, 'Mastrodicasa and his disciples. What the fuck am I going to say to him?'

'Were you not talking to him yesterday?'

'I missed the call as luck would have it. Maybe I should go on missing it.'

'No, David, don't do that. Playing dodge with your backers would be very unwise. They got you out there in the first place. Don't forget that.'

'I'm reminded about it every day,' Cousins growled. 'Usually on the dot of 3.30.'

'They've given this a name already,' Brackman submitted awkwardly, 'an amusing epithet if you will.'

'What is it?' Cousins said, heaving yet another sigh. 'Hit me with it.'

'The Bear's mauling,' replied Brackman.

There was silence for a second.

'I'm sorry, but you'd have heard about that as well no doubt,' the agent added. 'David? David? Are you still there?'

A muffled reply finally came. Cousins' voice was faint and subdued; as if he was feeling very sorry for himself.

'Big joke,' he said, 'personally, I'd have called it Bear's battering. For me that sounds better. At least it's alliterative.'

David Cousins didn't remain in low spirits for very long. Instead, he got angry. Very angry. With the whole thing. With everyone. All around him he saw problems and their perpetrators. Nothing was excused. No one was blameless. The production; the investors; the recurrent migraines; the constant phone calls; the non-stop questions and blames; Lorenzo Mastrodicasa; Aggregate Pictures.

Where would it all end he wondered. Why was it happening to him? Was it a twisted form of kismet? Was it indeed the Bear's mauling?

With respect to such criticism ('slurs cast against my character,' as he described it to others), he took note that management at Aggregate Pictures hadn't exactly fallen over themselves to stick up for him, nor to dispute Topolski's onscreen harangue. There was no full-page ad taken out in Variety or The Hollywood Reporter; no formal statements of support to the press; no personal phone calls from the likes of Danny Rosner or Anthony Chouraqui.

Art Brackman, meanwhile, was ploughing a lonely furrow. He maintained he was getting help from Century Park East, but David seriously doubted it. He didn't get the impression Aggregate had a public relations department which was that dedicated, and certainly not dedicated to his cause. It was part of a soulless multinational after all. Those dour corporate faces were all the same. So was their attitude when problems like this cropped up.

'It's the same variation on a theme,' he complained to Brackman late one afternoon, 'the very ones who talk tough, and feign support, check out of a situation when it becomes difficult, for fear they be proven not as tough as they want others to believe.'

'English here David, what are you trying to say?' Brackman replied.

'I'm saying that I'm pissed Art! Not with you by the way; you've been manfully fighting my corner from the beginning. But as for the rest of them – Aggregate Pictures – gone AWOL! Mastrodicasa: the permanent fucking voice in my head. It's the same thing with him every day – 'Where is the replacement?' 'Where is the replacement?' Yesterday, he reminded me about my 'legacy issues' as he calls them. I'm supposed to put my house in order; this coming from a guy who's got house in his fucking name. And these migraine pills I'm getting here aren't working for me. I've got severe fucking headaches Art, actual and figurative.'

'Go easy on the meds David, you know what too many of those do to you,' the agent advised.

'Art, can I confide in you about something?'

'Of course you can David. I'm here for you night and day.'

'I think there's someone following me. I mean literally. I mean I keep seeing this same guy all over the place. Wherever I am, he seems to be there. On the street, near the hotel, even here around the studios. He's not much taller than me, but he's got a stocky build. He looks like some sort of hood. I'm being stalked Art! Someone is watching my every fucking move!'

'David! David! You're unhinged! This is paranoia! You're talking like a madman! You've got to calm down. Apply yourself. Focus on the task at hand.'

'The task at hand?! The task at hand Art is getting more and more difficult to work through! Malcolm Archer told me they were having preliminary discussions with Richard Campbell about the part. I don't remember anyone consulting with me over that! If there was a memo, I sure as hell didn't get it!'

'It's not happening in any case David. Campbell's agent informed them he's no longer interested.'

'But it wasn't first checked with me! When were they going to make me privy to the discussions?'

'David, did you not hear what I said? It was preliminary! As in initial! As in no deal done without your involvement!'

'No doubt Campbell made a break for it after the Howard Holden show. Well I guess it proves every cloud has a silver lining.'

'Not in this case David. The part of Meucci has to be cast and soon. This situation cannot go on indefinitely.'

'And that explains the list Archer sent me?'

'That's the reason for the list David.'

'Which, by the way, is a piece of shit! They're throwing me nearly men. Actors who would not in a million years be fit to carry this film.'

Brackman was puzzled by this.

'I thought you wanted someone who isn't on the A-list?' he said. 'Aren't you the same guy who once said the lesser the name, the better for the film?'

'Yes, and I still believe that,' replied Cousins, 'but as for this piece of crap! You ought to see it! Names like Dan Fisher and Charlie Bennett. It reads as a who's who of who's not!'

'I've seen it David. A few are run-of-the-mill, I won't deny that, but Ben Sanders is there. He's a decent actor. I liked him in Little Big Venture.'

'I didn't see it,' Cousins said dismissively, 'I've seen two films of his and I don't see an actor who has what it takes.'

'But David he has what it takes in the sense of being available. And that's the critical thing here. Unless the part is cast soon...'

'And I heard you the first time Art. I know what it means. It means I get someone foisted on me. The next thing you know I'm Orson Welles making The Magnificent Ambersons. I lose control and I'm shut out of the editing room!'

'The paranoia is not going to help David. It's a shit state of affairs, I grant you that, but it was always going to be this way after Don Taylor's accident, who, I'll remind you, was also foisted on you, more or less.'

'That was then Art. This is now. I'm not going to accept just anyone. I want them to know that. I want an actor. And a really fine one at that.'

'Well then you're going to have to find him yourself David. Conjure one up if you have to. But if and when Aggregate settles on their man, who could well be Ben Sanders, you'll have little choice but to roll with the punches.'

With this his client became even more obstreperous.

'I'm not a yes man Art. I don't accept a situation just because it's expedient or the politic thing to do. If they try and force my hand, I'll go talk to another studio. Warners were paying attention before. So were Fox.'

'That is something you should not even think about David; and please don't repeat it to anyone else! Even if you pulled off such a deal...well you wouldn't is the simple truth. Listen to me. You could get yourself fired if you continue in this vein. You'd lose the film and your comeback all in one fell swoop.'

'How could they fire me Art? I was the one who made this thing happen! I wrote the script! I conceived this from fucking day one!'

'They might be able to do it David. They have the power and the lawyers to find those sort of loopholes; especially if they're confronted by a director making half-assed threats to talk to other studios, and refusing point-blank to consider actors who are obtainable. And you're giving them all the ammunition they need. They could justify your sacking as a necessary evil; something that had to be done to rescue the production. They're in the business of self-preservation David, even if you're not.'

'I won't let that happen,' Cousins responded defiantly, 'I'm the producer goddamit! I'd take the investors with me.'

'David, the Italian-Americans would not take your side if it came to such a thing. There would be no great act of loyalty on their part. They want to get this film made as much as AP does. You said it yourself how quickly they accepted Don Taylor's casting, and the script changes he insisted on. These are hard-nosed business people. They're not sentimentalists. There'd be no decamping with you if you were to walk or get thrown off. Forget it. It just wouldn't happen.'

Brackman paused to clear his throat.

'David, I'm going to be as frank as I can about this. Am I still your agent?'

'Of course you're still my agent Art! Jesus! What kind of a question is that?!'

'It's a very serious one David. Listen to what I'm telling you – don't start in with the mind-fuck games. They're obvious and, worst of all, they're counter-productive. You're not in the place where you were after Bluff City, true, but, then again, you're not quite flavour of the month either. The Bear's TV appearance saw to that. Tantrums and threats are not going to work. You need to do what's right here. Shape up and see this thing through. It's the smart play this time around. Trust me on this. Keep your head down and it will be to your benefit in the long-term.'

But the aggravated director was not thinking long-term. Try as he might, he could not look past the present time. No more than he could keep in check his own disposition; his own tendency towards hostility, especially when problems were mounting up. He couldn't help himself. It was a knee-jerk reaction. He felt he'd been left holding the can on this one. There was no one else standing with him, apart from Art; and his agent was six thousand miles away in Los Angeles.

It wasn't going to take much and, in the end, the breaking point came when he received a call from Anthony Chouraqui. The Aggregate head of production's timing couldn't have been worse. Cousins was having another one of his wretched days. Lorenzo Mastrodicasa was pushing hard. Faithful Art had not yet returned his call. The knife-like migraines were as bad as ever. And, out of the corner of his eye, he could swear he was seeing that mysterious hood again. The one who was loitering wherever he went. Like a cheap gumshoe in an old film noir.

The exchange which took place between the two didn't last long (Chouraqui later described it as, 'a one-way conversation in which he shouted and I plugged my ears') and the message relayed was as clear as it was belligerent. Cousins had had his fill of them all. Aggregate Pictures in particular. His was not a voice of contentment.

'He called us a spineless bunch for not rushing to his defence over the Topolski episode,' Chouraqui told Cy Younger and Danny Rosner, 'and then he started in on these serious doubts he's having about our continued involvement in the production; claims there's another studio ready to enter the fray.'

'How credible a story might that be?' Cy asked from behind his desk.

'I'm not hearing anything through the grapevine that supports what he's saying,' replied Chouraqui, 'there could be interest in time since both Warners and Fox were in the frame before we acquired it. But as to any direct lines of communication between them and David Cousins right now, none that I'm aware of.'

'Your sources at Warners and Fox are reliable?'

'As reliable as they can be. Oh there are the usual questions about the film itself. My contact at Fox turned the interrogation back on me. But he was emphatic there are no talks or overtures. It strikes me as a put-on at this moment in time Cy. David Cousins isn't talking to anyone else. The histrionics give the lie to the tale he's trying to spin.'

'But you're not writing off the possibility of him engaging one of those third parties? In the fullness of time?'

Chouraqui shook his head.

'No, I'm not,' he said, 'anything is possible. They were keen last time out, we know this. We shouldn't imagine that earlier enthusiasm has faded away.'

'I agree,' said Danny Rosner, 'this production may have already accumulated several million dollars of negative costs against it, but that would be offset by the carrot potential profits would dangle. We've done it ourselves in the past. Paying up front is not so difficult if you think you're getting a box office or awards contender. You want your Oscars I assume Cy? Or Palme d'Or in this case?'

Cy smiled acknowledging as much.

'The schedule the director had agreed to works back from a release date at Cannes 96,' he said, 'a final cut by then would be our absolute insistence, which we would seek to have entered into competition. Gordon Sawyer wants his moment of glory in the Palais. He's promised to tone down his language if the occasion ever arises.'

Rosner and Chouraqui shared a joke about this.

'How does that time frame appear now that we've lost a significant number of days?' Cy enquired on the same theme.

'It won't be adversely affected provided he starts sometime this year,' Chouraqui answered.

His response drew a look of mild rebuke from his boss.

'I'm not trying to be flippant about it Cy,' he defended, 'but there are more pressing matters than Gordon Sawyer's annual soiree on the Côte d'Azur. Jennifer Carrington's involvement in this film for one thing. If we don't establish a new start date, and soon, she will justifiably walk.'

'Contractually can she do that?' Cy asked Rosner.

'I think professionally she would have reasonable cause,' Danny replied, 'but as for the terms of her contract, we could take legal action were she to quit.'

Cy visibly winced at the notion.

'The last thing we need is more wrangling and fat lawyers getting rich in the next room,' he said.

He turned towards Chouraqui.

'What do you think?' he asked.

'I think the best solution all round, the one that does not involve courtrooms or departing actresses, is we get this director to do the job he was originally hired to do.'

'And what happens if he gets a sniff of another studio in the interim?' asked Rosner. 'What sort of measures would you be prepared to take?'

'Losing this production is a circumstance we don't want to envisage,' said Cy. ''95 is looking windswept one way or the other. I don't want that situation to get any worse.'

'We have the buy-ins to plug some of the distribution gap at least,' said Chouraqui. 'Add one or two more to the slate and it starts to look respectable.'

'What's the up-to-date position on Fire Water by the way?' Cy asked.

'Gleason's company are still intent on a quick sale to television. They want to recover the budget; there's talk of cutting it down to 90 minutes. Absolute butchery if you ask me.'

Cy shook his head glumly.

'A film that's been in the can for over a year and the backer won't put it out. Has the whole world gone crazy?'

'Why won't he put it out?' asked a perplexed-looking Rosner.

'He objected to what he saw as possible parallels to Waco. He's afraid the finished film is too hot. The gun battle and tear gas scenes most especially.'

'Doesn't he know we'd be taking all of that on if we acquire the rights?'

'He's a bit unconventional,' Chouraqui said, fielding the question, 'but I think he'll listen if the offer is good enough. This film could do 50 plus domestically if the ad campaigns are rolled out properly.'

'We seem to attracting all the mavericks and eccentrics at the present time, don't we?' Cy remarked, tongue firmly planted in cheek.

'Ever so slightly,' Chouraqui agreed.

'What's the word on high from McWhirter?' Rosner queried. 'Are they asking questions?'

'Not specifically about this project, but Davis Fischer is watching the overall. That's his prerogative of course.'

'I wish someone like David Cousins would get that for once,' said Chouraqui disparagingly, 'that we are answerable to our own masters as well. He spoke to me as if I had it in my power to flick a switch and...I mean is it my fault he got thrashed on television? Did I put Don Taylor in the way of that car?'

'Was he willing to discuss our list?'

'Not one bit. He said none of the actors on it are suitable for the character he's so methodically written. In return for our continued participation in the film – his words verbatim, I kid you not – he now wants final say on who will play Meucci.'

'Does he have any suggestions of his own to put on the table?'

'Not one Cy.'

'Well what kind of position is that to take? Someone has to be decided on. The central character is not an inanimate object, right? What did he say to Ben Sanders?'

'He called him an inanimate object.'

'Jesus! He puts it on us to find someone to his specs just as he rejects any available actor in this town. How does that play out? Where does he expect to go with it?'

'Have the trades got wind of it?' asked Rosner. 'If they detect a story in Rome, you can be certain of reports and prognoses.'

'Speculations as to the production's imminent demise at Aggregate,' said Chouraqui. 'I can just see the headlines – 'Parting of the ways for AP and Meucci.' 'Cousins and Aggregate no longer strange bedfellows.'

'Strange bedfellows or not, this man has to get things clear in his knotty little mind,' Cy pronounced adamantly. 'He's not a law unto himself. He's expendable just like the rest of us.'

Chouraqui arched his eyebrows picking out the thread.

'Would we take such an extreme step?' he asked. 'Replacing the director as well, before a frame of film is shot?'

'Currently he's driving us to such a last resort,' replied Cy, 'Danny, if the director will not accept our even-handed approach, as he's done so far; if he continues to oppose our candidates for the part, can we dismiss him? Would we have good reason as the relevant guild laws apply?'

Rosner pondered, hemmed and hawed, before responding.

'My initial thought is that we'd be on very shaky ground were we to pursue such a course,' he began. 'In a way, it's almost akin to the position Jennifer Carrington might find herself in if she tried to get out of her contract. Of the two, she would have the better chance in my estimation.'

He sat forward in his seat and delivered the balance of it.

'David Cousins is not in breach of anything as the situation stands,' he pointed out. 'He is, of course, being obstinate and employing every sort of blocking device because he he's frustrated and volatile. He's reacting at this moment in time as any individual might, being defensive because he's stung by all that's happened: Don's accident, Bear's appearance on TV. This isn't how his comeback was supposed to work out. He's clearly hurting, but I think he's using that hurt as a shield. I also happen to think he's biding his time. Waiting for the next turning of the world. I've sat here for the last few minutes and I've listened to what Anthony has said. It seems to me our Mr. Cousins could indeed be holding out for a Warners or a Fox. That's the conclusion I come to based on how he's behaving. But can we sack him for this? Can we discharge of his services as director? We can't prove that he might be delaying on purpose. That's purely conjecture and the law, as you know, has no great affinity with conjecture. So definitely no to that avenue of approach. We come back then to the issue of his obstinacy. This is very evident. Anthony here has just been on the receiving end of it. We don't doubt a single word he's told us. No one would. You couldn't make it up. Plus, this man has a reputation. He has a history for the...how did you phrase it Anthony? Histrionics. Bluff and bluster. He's gone to that particular well before. He's laying it out once more and carrying it a long way. Quite the performance you'd have to say. And quite the performer as well. But he's a director first and foremost and, as such, he's a member of the DGA. You mentioned it a few minutes ago Cy and it's of real significance here. The guild, you'll be aware, has a particular role in protecting the creative rights of the director. Those protections include the principle of one director, one picture; as well as the right to director's cut. It's all in the interest of preserving continuity of vision as they like to put it. Avoiding lobbying for credits or any other types of irregularities. Multiple directors on a film they do not like. Nor do they take kindly to one of their members being released without good cause. As would occur here if we gave Mr. Cousins his marching orders. The justification for our action would be understandable to the man on the street. He's being uncooperative. Potentially, he's dragging this production down by dragging his heels. But the DGA would care little for our side of the story, or the justification for it. Sacking this director at this point in time would be like raising the red rag to the bull. And you worried before Cy about how the actors' guild might react if we didn't honour Don Taylor's pay-or-play. Well I can assure you that would be a mere trifle compared to this. Under DGA rules you couldn't even talk to another director until such time as the present one is gone; and by then, well good luck with getting into those meetings. They're a tight bunch and they will close ranks if they are instructed to. Remember that we're signatories to the guild ourselves. It's not a choice open to us right now I'm afraid. In theory David Cousins has done nothing wrong up to this time. Firing him would most likely whip up sympathy in the community, which he'd play to the hilt. And then comes that wrongful dismissal suit. A safe bet against us there. Those fat lawyers you find so endearing Cy. And the DGA with elephant's memory and daggers drawn.'

He reached a conclusion to his evaluation and gauged its reception. Staring back at him were two affected faces. Recognising concern, Danny decided to tag on a P.S.

'But hey, I could be wrong about all of this,' he said, endeavouring to infuse some optimism, 'I garble things every so often. I misread. This is just guesswork on my part. Maybe I'm way off base. I hope I am. Maybe David Cousins will snap out of his enmity. He's in the most beautiful city in the world. All that art and history and splendour touches people. And

Rome is truly wonderful this time of year. The azaleas on the Spanish Steps are something else. Maybe our director will think differently in due course; maybe he'll be sufficiently moved, appreciate what's all around him, realise he has a film to make. Tomorrow morning could bring change. Who knows. Maybe he'll wake up and smell the…azaleas?'

'Well that line certainly wouldn't do,' said Cy, gripping his pen vice-like, 'we can't depend on some unexpected conversion in his outlook. His position, as expressed, is clearly inflexible. It won't be altered by a visit to an art gallery or by his engaging with the flowers in Rome. If engage is what one does with flowers,' he added, looking distinctly puzzled about this himself.

'You could put the casting issue back on him,' suggested Rosner, 'but that's only a tit-for-tat exercise; especially if, as Anthony says, he has no one in mind for the role.'

'No, I don't propose to do that,' agreed Cy, 'but the no-action alternative won't do either. Anthony, I think the time has come for the more direct approach. I think someone needs to get on a plane to Rome. Can you suggest a name?'

'I'd like it to be me Cy,' Chouraqui said, recognising the subtle fiat, 'during our phone call just now, David Cousins called me an incompetent; also said that we're nothing more than corporate lackeys. I've never been much one for labels, and definitely not those of the pejorative kind.'

'He got your blood up, did he?' said Cy.

'I'm not spoiling for a fight,' replied Chouraqui, 'but I feel I owe him nonetheless. I'd like to disabuse him of some of the notions he obviously has about us. In the process, and with a bit of luck, I also hope to convince him to do the job we expect.'

'You might need a good deal of that,' said Rosner.

In spite of this assertion, he nodded encouragingly.

'But I say give the kid a chance,' he advised Cy. 'He's ready for it. He has a head on his shoulders and knows a thing or two about negotiating. Plus, he's got the motivation. Both business and personal.'

'I've worked hard to set this up,' Chouraqui said. 'I want David Cousins to understand that. I want him to understand this is not just his vision alone. It's other people's as well. People who have a genuine interest in the film and want to see it carried through to completion. There are no corporate lackeys in this company, only bona fide film people. I'm going to tell him that. Allow him the opportunity to respond. But I won't accept the sort of diatribe he threw at me today. Not ever again. Face to face he'll realise that. Motivation? Sure, I've got plenty of it, like Danny says. I want to make this film. I'm head of production and it's my job to see it gets done. By us and no one else. That's preserving continuity of vision as far as I'm concerned. That's my raison d'etre to David Cousins.'

His eyes closed for a fraction behind his titanium-rimmed glasses.

'As for the incompetent remark, well I'll let that go. It was a low blow but it was said in the heat of the moment. Moving away from it, I'll behave like a prince and a friend. Tell him to be brilliant. We all know he can be. And we have complete faith he will be again. All heart and just a bit of passion. Not bad for a stiff studio official, eh? David Cousins might just get the impression he's talking to somebody else. Somebody who happens to love the movies same way he does.'

FAR FROM THE MADDING CROWD

Fabio Paparazzo got off the orange metro line at the Cinecittà station and, from there, walked the short distance to the famous film studio. It was 2.30 in the afternoon. A sun-kissed day all over the city and quite warm. Cars and mopeds roared past him along Via Tuscolana. A number of horns were exchanged as he approached the signature entrance. Out on the road, a frustrated Lancia Kappa driver was attempting to bully his way past some other road-users. The upshot was more than a few screams and angry gesticulations in response. An obscenity or two from rolled-down windows was heard.

But Fabio did not pay attention to any of this. Proceeding inside, shiny red folder tucked under his left arm, he approached the front desk, brimming with purpose. He was here for the second part of a story he'd begun almost two weeks before. A man in pursuit of a follow-up; in movie-speak, a sequel.

'Can I help you?' the receptionist asked him.

Directly above her head, clips from Cleopatra, Ben Hur and Zeffirelli's Romeo and Juliet flickered on a video monitor.

'Yes, I'm here to see David Cousins,' Paparazzo replied, adding, 'the director of the Antonio Meucci film.'

'Is Mr. Cousins expecting you?'

'We made an arrangement for me to call after lunchtime today. He's expecting me.'

'And your name please?'

'Paparazzo. Fabio Paparazzo.'

The woman dialled an internal number and spoke to someone in English.

'You can go on through,' she told the reporter. 'If you wait in the main square, someone will be with you shortly.'

'Thank you,' said Paparazzo glancing one more time at the display. A scene from Cleopatra was playing. Dick and Liz were busily smooching onscreen. Not for the first or last time he thought.

The main square inside was a sedate green lawn shadowed here and there by umbrella pines. Small bungalows, coated in Italian terracotta, dotted the nearby terrain. The studio itself was a heady mix of the past and present; a mysterious amalgam of structural grandiosity and artistic grace. On his first ever visit here, Fabio observed the warm architectural designs interspersed with large standing sets, some of them discoloured and in need of restoration. In the distance was the model of the statue of Christ from the opening sequence of La Dolce Vita. Not far from it stood a huge metal horse, originating, no doubt, from a tale of ancient lore. The Trojan Horse, Fabio imagined. It was certainly large enough and to an appropriate scale; a bit like the 1930's campus itself, both imposing and seemly.

A 40-hectare site said to consist of 280 production offices and dressing rooms, 22 stages, 82 prop stores, warehouses and workshops, the studio also boasted a 7,000 square-metre outdoor tank and the largest soundstage on the continent. Founded by Benito Mussolini and his head of cinema, Luigi Freddi, it had been designed with the ostensible purpose of functioning as a complete centre of production, with services covering everything from training through to pre-production, production and post-production. A veritable one-stop shop on an enormous scale befitting its name – Cinema City. Such lofty principles apart, there was a strong ideological rationale which underlay the studio's establishment for the fascist dictator – this was his answer to the cultural interlopers of Hollywood and elsewhere; a kind of armoury of the national imagination. The slogan, *'cinema is the most powerful weapon,'* expressed purpose and a traditionalist bent of mind.

Early Cinecittà offerings, such as 1937's Scipio Africanus: The Defeat of Hannibal, were faithful to such a philosophy. The film, bankrolled by Il Duce himself, served as propaganda for his ambitions to invade North Africa. As part of the gargantuan production, live elephants were brought in to re-enact the battle of Zama between ancient Carthage and the Roman Republic. Seven thousand people were also involved in the filming of this pivotal set-piece, amongst them a division of the Italian army, itself transported shortly afterwards for duty in the Spanish Civil War.

Following the end of another conflict, the global one which ensued, the studio was used as a displaced peoples' camp between 1945 and 1947. It only returned to a normal roster of production a few years after World War II.

In the 1950's it began to play host to a number of American productions which were in search of inexpensive production costs. Films like Roman Holiday and Three Coins in a Fountain availed of Cinecittà's considerable resources. Next came several epics ushering in a highly lucrative era in the studio's history, the Hollywood on the Tiber phenomenon. Blockbusters such as Quo Vadis, Ben Hur, Cleopatra and The Agony and the Ecstasy took up residence in south-east Rome. Cinecittà also became prominently associated with the films of one of its own – Federico Fellini. The Italian auteur fondly referred to it as his, 'temple of dreams.' His most famous work, La Dolce Vita, made extensive use of the studio with over eighty locations being created, including fashionable Via Veneto and the dome of St Peter's. In more recent times, however, the studio had experienced the same reversal in fortune as the national film industry. In spite of films like Once Upon a Time in America, The Last Emperor and The Name of the Rose, the 1980's and early-1990's had not been kind as a whole. Inflation and higher labour wages combined to limit the studio's role in the local and international film industries. And so Cinecittà increasingly became yet another Italian landmark in crisis. Without an incentive programme of the variety other establishments had to attract foreign moviemakers, it fell on hard times and lay on the verge of bankruptcy by the mid-1990's. The possibility of privatisation was looming large for the once great institution. A radical shake-up was on the cards, but progress was proving sluggish and difficult. Arguments continued to rage and in-fighting was endemic. Consensus was not such a ready thing. The saving of Cinecittà, if it indeed was to come, would not be a painless affair. In typically Italian fashion, it would be long-drawn-out and not lacking in a few dramatic twists along the way.

And 1995 certainly did not feel like the year for such recovery. In spite of Echo of Passions and one or two visiting mini-series, the outlook was anything but good. Looking around him, Fabio divined this as he regarded the landscape of conifer trees and ochre buildings; the Christ statue and Trojan Horse. Remnants of a different age he thought. More simple times. Long before there was any Tangentopoli or Mani Pulite.

In his mind the reporter began to pen an altogether different article. What has happened to the spirit of those early free-thinking cineastes he questioned; the Rossellini's and De Sica's of this cinematic world? Men who were fearless and would not be denied their vision, pioneers and dreamers as they were. And on the subject of the imaginative, what of their most prominent member? Where now is the stage for Fellini's sweet life? Has the cavalcade of independent films and personal visions departed from the grounds of the studio forevermore? Replaced by the harsh truths of faded sceneries and mounting debts? There is little pity, and surely no romanticism, in the hearts of insisting creditors and merciless bankers. And as for nostalgia, as for the amarcord of Fellini's coming-of-age story, the message to be conveyed from this corner of Rome is one which...

'Hello there. What do you think of our facilities?'

The advancing voice caught the reporter unawares. Walking towards him was a middle-aged man in uniform; a security guard he supposed. He was dressed in a navy-blue shirt and dark pants. Close to the point of his right shoulder was a clip-on leather badge. Fabio was unable to make out what its insignia stood for.

'Good afternoon,' he replied. 'Very impressive from what I've seen so far.'

The other man agreed and remarked on the pleasant day.

'I have to ask this,' Paparazzo said, as he studied both attire and posture, 'are you an actor?'

'Good God no!' the amused individual replied tapping his identification. 'I'm the genuine article, if there is such a thing. Been working here for over 10 years.'

'I'm sorry for asking,' Fabio smiled, 'being at a film studio, I couldn't be sure.'

'That's quite alright. You're not the first. One or two others have asked. I tell them it's flattering. It's nice to have a moment when a person thinks you're someone else. Don't you think? A flash of celebrity, if you know what I mean.'

Paparazzo said that he did.

'No doubt, you've seen more than a few of those in your time here,' he said.

'Every so often,' said the other man. 'The directors are the ones I remember the best. Leone, Bertolucci, Fellini of course. As for actors, De Niro I suppose is the most famous one. I'd just started working here when they were making Once Upon a Time in America. A very gracious man. It's good when we get big films here,' he said, contemplating something far off in the distance, 'they bring money and employment. Those are commodities we all need at the present time.'

'Well you must be happy then to have Echo of Passions,' Paparazzo said, guiding the conversation. 'Did you meet Don Taylor?'

'I saw him here one day,' the guard nodded, 'a very fine-looking man indeed. He seemed every inch a star. What happened to him – it's a real tragedy. And much as I don't like to put them side by side, profits and people I mean, well there's a knock-on effect, isn't there? The film might not go ahead. There's a risk at least, as far as I understand.'

'Is there much talk about it?' Fabio asked. 'Anything to suggest such a possibility?'

This elicited a questioning smile.

'Are you involved in it somehow?'

'No, I'm a journalist,' Paparazzo explained, 'I'm meeting the director, Mr. Cousins. That's who I'm waiting to see.'

The information was absorbed with a leery expression.

'You're not one of those fellows writing about...what's-his-name?'

'Max Pellegrino?'

'That's the one.'

'Yes I am,' said Fabio, though he decided not to own up as the story's originator. Something told him the man opposite did not exactly approve. This impression was promptly confirmed.

'A load of nonsense,' the guard said, 'what some people won't do for...'

He remembered who he was talking to and broke off mid-sentence.

'A lot of people seem to get it,' argued Paparazzo, 'I suppose that's why the story is doing as well as it is. There's no harm in it, and who knows some good might...'

'I don't agree,' said the guard. 'It strikes me as nothing more than shameless opportunism. Personally, I hope nothing comes of it. I'd much prefer that there be...'

He was interrupted by the appearance of Andrew Ford. The Echo of Passions production manager was workaday casual in denim jeans and open shirt. He was friendly and apologised for being late.

'I got caught up on one of those million small problems that arise,' he explained smiling, his copper-tanned skin glowing as if renewed by a recent top-up, 'but now I can give you my undivided attention. For the next 20 minutes or so.'

'And Mr. Cousins?' Paparazzo inquired as they moved off the lawn, leaving the rather sombre-looking guard behind. 'Will I have a chance to meet him? He agreed to a few minutes on the phone.'

'Yes, of course,' Ford replied genially, 'Mr. Cousins expected to have more time on his hands, but there are points of detail he's having to attend to. Mr. Cousins is very thorough in his work. He likes to oversee every aspect of production, regardless of how insignificant it might seem.'

Ford suggested they first visit sound stage 5, which was being used for a number of interior sets, including the Meucci households in Florence, Havana and Staten Island, the inventor's workshops and, most impressively, the Teatro della Pergola. The historic opera house, including its main auditorium, the Sala Grande, was meticulously recreated with its superposed tiers of boxes rather than the more traditional raked semi-circular seating. Enquiring as to why the production wasn't simply filming in the actual opera house itself, Paparazzo was informed that a number of remodellings of this had taken place over time and that the director wanted to be as faithful to the original 1661 version as possible.

'I told you Mr. Cousins was thorough,' Ford added.

They viewed two more sets relating to the theatre: the backstage area, where a scene of Meucci meeting his future wife would take place; and the control room where the imaginative hero sets up a type of acoustic telephone to enable communication.

'I love the moment when they first meet,' said Ford. 'It's very well written. And there are several cuts between them and what's happening onstage. It's a wonderful juxtaposition, should look great when it's up on the screen.'

'Is that how it actually happened? Was that how they met?' his guest asked.

The question seemed to puzzle Ford for just a moment.

'Well I don't know about that...I'm not much one for the history books...but it works really well as David has it visualised,' he said, the easy cadence slipping back into his speech, 'now let's go see Florence and Staten Island, shall we?'

In the open air, the reporter and production manager surveyed the early-19th century Florentine set. This consisted of a long flagstone-paved street with three-dimensional buildings on either side. The facades of these buildings were of the Renaissance variety with traces of baroque and neoclassical influences sprinkled liberally. Commercial fronts bore legends of the activities and trades they housed. There were old-fashioned placards announcing popular entertainments and theatrical performances which might have been in vogue. Amongst these, Fabio noticed an advert for the Carlo Goldoni comedy Il Servitore di due Padroni. A nice touch he thought, and he wondered if the director had conjured this up in a moment of self-deprecation. With private investors and a major studio breathing down his neck, Mr. Cousins was in many ways a servant of two masters; just like Goldoni's central character.

'It's all in pursuit of the historical accuracy we're aiming for,' Ford said, as they walked off the Florence street and headed towards the Staten Island set. 'Our production designer, Jack Reed, has done a tremendous job,' he pronounced, his voice full of admiration, 'we're fortunate to have some of the very best people working on this film. Ruth Benchley, our costume designer, is another one. Ruth must have trawled through countless volumes of research and history, not to mention all the fabric samples, to get the level of detail she's achieved. It's going to be an extraordinary effect. The cast members will look as if they belong in the past.'

'What about the other main actors?' Paparazzo asked. 'Have all the parts been cast? Do they all remain on standby?'

'More or less,' confirmed Ford. 'The delay I'm happy to say has been put to good use. The secondary cast has been mostly filled out. We have one or two parts which have yet to be…well…everyone knows about the leading role.'

He smiled awkwardly.

'Aside from Jennifer Carrington, the principal cast is made up of actors like Toby Devereux and Lamar Calley who play Garibaldi and William J. Wallace. Mr. Cousins has written a few composite characters, particularly for the Havana and Staten Island sections. He did it to make the film more…'

'Simple?' Paparazzo suggested cheekily.

Ford laughed politely without a trace of a sneer.

'More accessible I would think is the word,' he said.

They reached the Staten Island locale which was the most active of the sets in terms of clipboard-bearing technicians and scenic artists.

'This is a recreation of Peterstown in the north-east part of Staten Island,' Ford explained with outreached hand and trailing finger. 'Actually, it changed its name to Rosebank around 1880. Some of us have named it Rose-Peter on account of that. It's a joke, like a place that doesn't exist. Sometimes when I'm back at my hotel in the evening, and far too tired to go out or take calls, I tell the other guys I'm going to Rose-Peter. Meaning that I don't want to be disturbed. I usually am though.'

The brief digression done with, he resumed his commentary.

'This street section represents Tompkins Avenue which ran east-west through a number of the New York City neighbourhoods in the borough,' he said, 'and over there – the small house which is slightly apart from the others: that's Meucci's slice of the American dream. That's where we have the great man living.'

Paparazzo looked at the replica façade of a Gothic Revival cottage. It was simple. Unadorned. Attractive in a very modest way; and yet it captured the eye somehow. The word that came to his mind and would not leave was charming. Yes, it is charming he thought. All of this is a charming construct. If the film they make is worthy of the settings they've prepared so accurately, then it could be good. It might even emerge as a really fine film.

Right at that moment, on that thought, an emergence of a very different kind occurred. David Cousins appeared in full view. He came from around the back of the three-sided Meucci dwelling. At first Paparazzo did not know him, but he had Ford in his ear.

'That's him. That's Mr. Cousins,' he said, as he beckoned the director over to them. 'I knew he was working here this afternoon. He's not quite convinced by some of the front elevations.'

Paparazzo looked around. He saw nothing wrong with any of the structures. They all looked impressive to him. Mr. Cousins is living up to his reputation he thought. A man who pursues his vision down to the last feature and coat of paint. But what a great image that was seeing him come from the Meucci cottage. He made a mental note. I must use it in my article he told himself, but have him emerging from the front door rather than the side. That would read better.

'Hello,' Cousins said politely as Ford made the introductions. He had an intelligent face with eyes that inclined downwards, giving his smile a certain solemnity.

'That's certainly quite a name you have Mr. Paparazzo,' he observed, getting it right first time. 'You must get jokes made at your expense I imagine.'

'Only every second day,' the journalist replied good-humouredly.

The director received this with another gracious smile. He had a thickset build and seemed generally agreeable, if somewhat uneasy. He seemed generally agreeable, if somewhat uneasy. The recent problems with the film Fabio presumed. Maybe that's why he's taking such an interest in uncompleted buildings; to take his mind off other things.

They chatted easily for a few minutes about the production and the reorganising which had taken place following Don Taylor's accident. Andrew Ford took the lead here. Wearing confidence-inspiring smiles, he stated and re-stated his firm conviction that the additional time would be advantageous for the shoot in the long term.

'We're ready as ready can be,' he said, careful not to mention the one element which was still clearly missing, and Paparazzo wondered if this was for his benefit or for the man standing beside him.

David Cousins listened intently, nodding as the production manager offered some further points of detail. It was clear he was tired and anxious to be somewhere else. But he'd agreed to the interview and so suggested they adjourn to the Talking Telegraph office for the privacy it would allow. Ford returned to sound stage 5.

Cousins took his usual seat in the tasteful production office and invited Paparazzo to make himself comfortable. Behind him, on a large bulletin board, were pinned pictures of the leading actors, as well as general lists and contact details for cast and crew members. A later portrait of

Antonio Meucci was amongst these: white-bearded so in all probability taken during his time in Staten Island. Beside him was Don Taylor – the actor radiant and projecting that world-famous beam of his. Fabio wondered why he was still up there. Perhaps someone thinks it would be bad luck to remove him he speculated. Perhaps that someone is Mr. Cousins.

The director, for his part, was more at ease with the one-to-one and his delivery, hesitant and lethargic a few minutes before, was now more attentive and crisp.

He spoke about how glad he was to be in Rome, in spite of all that had happened. There was a distance from the usual Hollywood razzmatazz he said, his eyes appearing to collect light; his face, which had been pale, starting to flush as some energy sparked inside.

'Distractions are not as immediate,' he said, 'or of such a constant nature,' and added, as a joke, 'far from the madding crowd.'

'There must be pressure points nonetheless,' Fabio remarked. 'Are the money men not concerned when a film such as this is so far behind schedule? And some of the budget already spent without a single shot?'

Cousins deflected the question, and was instead laudatory of his backers.

'I owe the private investors a great deal,' he said, 'Aggregate Pictures as well. They are all being extremely patient. Of course, it hasn't been easy. As a director you arrive to put your vision on film, and you desperately want to maintain that momentum from first to last. There's always a shakedown period with a production. A time when problems are many and seem insurmountable. Normally it occurs early on in a shoot. In our case, it just so happened to arrive before the cameras started to turn. An unfortunate event. Something that was beyond anyone's control.'

Paparazzo decided to change the theme for a moment.

'I've seen a number of your films Mr. Cousins,' he volunteered casually. 'Oh?'

'Yes, Mother Road and The Frontrunners' Club.'

'Two of my early efforts,' Cousins smiled wistfully, 'I'm glad to hear that. They bring back lots of good memories.'

'Also Bluff City.'

The reference to this latter picture elicited a mournful groan.

'Well you must be one of the unhappy few in this part of the world Mr. Paparazzo,' Cousins said, 'every time I think of that film, a song comes to mind. On Broadway. We used it as one of the big numbers. The whole thing was meant to be…so much better. No one sets out to make a bad movie you know. Somehow though we arrived at just that: a bad movie.'

'There were stories that matters got out of hand,' Paparazzo said, 'you didn't exactly come out of it unscathed either. You had a quiet period for a few years, didn't you Mr. Cousins?'

'I did,' the director acknowledged. 'This is my first film back in the chair since then.'

'Does that not concern you? In light of the unfortunate event that happened to your leading man?'

'I don't exactly follow you Mr. Paparazzo.'

'Forgive me for putting it this way Mr. Cousins,' Paparazzo said in advance, 'but a director such as yourself, who's returning after a lengthy break...'

'Four years. And it was self-imposed by the way.'

'Four years, given that it's your comeback, if that's the correct word. Are you not worried this opportunity might slip away? Other men in your position would feel vulnerable. I know I would.'

'I feel just fine Mr. Paparazzo,' Cousins replied defensively, 'as Andrew told you we've been keeping very busy here...so that when the time comes...'

'Do you have a replacement lined up for Don Taylor?' the reporter interrupted.

'Not yet,' Cousins said, rubbing his brow as he looked around. 'Can I ask you something? This is not to form part of your article.'

'Of course.'

'Is there any chance you know of a good painkiller, for migraine? I forgot to bring my regular pills with me from the States and nothing I've got here has worked.'

Paparazzo flashed a sympathetic smile.

'I know how you feel,' he said. 'I also suffer from it. What have you been taking?'

The director laid a number of containers on the desk in front of him. Paparazzo mumbled to himself as he examined these. One or two of the brands caused a knowing shake of the head.

'All of these are useless,' he said, 'in my experience at least, and I've had this since I was a teenager.'

He produced a brown-tinted container from his jacket pocket.

'Try these,' he recommended. 'They usually work for me.'

The director gratefully accepted.

'Do you mind if I?' he asked out of courtesy.

'Not at all.'

Cousins swallowed two pills and downed some water.

'Thanks,' he said offering back the container.

'You can hang on to the rest of them,' Paparazzo said, 'today's one of my better days. Besides, I think you need them more than I do.'

'That's much appreciated. It'll be a great relief if they work. I might even give you a walk-on part in the film if they do.'

The reporter expressed amusement on this, but said he would have to respectfully decline. Sensing that a wall had come down, that he had gained the other man's trust to a certain extent, he determined to press the casting matter again.

'About the other headache that's not going away,' he prompted.

'You don't give up easily, do you Mr. Paparazzo?'

'No sir, I don't.'

'What is it you want to know?' Cousins inquired, his voice a model of whispery control.

'Just as I asked before, do you have a replacement actor? You can answer off the record if that makes you more comfortable.'

'Really?' said the director, raising his eyebrows. It struck him as unusual. Why would this young reporter be accepting it off the record so easily?

'Ok,' he said, 'off the record, strictly between you and me, there is no replacement actor on the horizon. Not as far as I'm concerned.'

'What does that mean for the film?'

'I don't know Mr. Paparazzo. The present studio might pull the plug. If that were to happen I'd try and sell it to someone else. I haven't tested the waters yet though.'

'So it's true then.'

'What's true?'

'There are no other actors.'

'There are other actors Mr. Paparazzo. I just don't happen to like any of them. All nonentities, all horribly drab. Before Don Taylor came on board, I was hoping to get someone less...Don Taylor, if you know what I mean.'

The smile was no longer tilted downwards. It was direct, almost confidential.

'You didn't want Don Taylor?' said a visibly surprised Paparazzo.

'I didn't actively seek him out, let's put it that way,' Cousins replied shaking his head. 'If we were still talking on a formal basis here – you the reporter and me the...so-called comeback kid – I would play the part of the distraught director, as I'd be expected to. Tell you what a loss Don is to this production, how suitable he would have been for the role, the superb performance he would have delivered. Golden globes, screen actors guild, academy awards and so on.'

'That sounds about right. I might even use some of it for my article.'

'Which you most certainly can. Print the legend as they say.'

'Was he forced upon you then?'

'Forced is perhaps too strong a word. A fait accompli would be more appropriate.'

Paparazzo grinned artfully.

'And I get the impression you don't care very much for fait accomplis, do you Mr. Cousins?'

'How can I put this subtly Mr. Paparazzo? I hate the fucking things.'

His spread fingers raked through his hair as he emitted a chuckle.

'My head is feeling a whole lot better though I must say.'

'I'm glad to hear it.'

Cousins sipped some more water and held up the glass to his face, looking through it as if it were a viewfinder.

'You make me curious Mr. Paparazzo,' he said.

'Oh? In what way?'

'You seem unconventional in your approach. You contact me for an interview to which I reluctantly agree. You arrive and we exchange pleasantries in the presence of someone else. Inevitably, the time comes when we must talk face-to-face; something I was not looking forward to I might add. And you start to ask the questions I don't want to answer. Especially the one about the main role. That same one I'm now hearing in my sleep. I try and get away from it, but you bring us back. Only now you're willing to accept my response off the record. Why so? Why the sudden climb-down?'

'It wasn't a climb-down at all Mr. Cousins. It was deliberate. I wanted you to talk off the record. I would have made that clear first time around only you began to discuss migraines and painkillers.'

Paparazzo smiled and reached for his shiny folder.

Cousins remained puzzled.

'I'm still missing something here,' he said. 'This is an interview, right? You are going to write an article for your newspaper?'

'Oh yes,' Paparazzo replied, 'by all means there will be an article. It'll be largely based on the information Mr. Ford gave me earlier. We visited some of the sets before I met you. He was very helpful. I'll include some of the things you had to say as well of course, the for the record quotes. But I don't require anything else in that regard. I needed a way in you see, something to get you on my side.'

Cousins' eyes widened and then narrowed as he studied the reporter.

'How might we be on the same side Mr. Paparazzo?' he asked inquisitively. 'Are you offering me something in return? A deal with the devil so I can get this film of mine made. That won't necessarily work. I've been called the devil myself recently on national television.'

'No nothing like that,' Paparazzo laughed, 'the colour of this folder may be red, but, rest assured, it doesn't contain some diabolical scheme. There are no favours of wealth or power in here, no guarantees that you'll get your film made if you sign on the dotted line.'

'That's quite ok. I've signed such agreements in the past,' Cousins said impishly. 'So what's in it? What do you have to show me?'

Paparazzo removed some clippings from the folder; first and foremost, he showed the director his original piece on Max.

'Max Pellegrino – Italian Actor, Quo Vadis? Your name is in the by-line I see. You wrote this?'

'I wrote it. Does that name mean anything to you?'

'Max Pellegrino,' said Cousins thinking it over. 'It seems familiar somehow. I have seen this name on some newspapers I think. The concierge in my hotel keeps on stocking my room with dailies I can't read. My guess is he's encouraging me to take up the language.'

He examined Max's photo.

'This guy has been in the headlines quite a bit, hasn't he? Is he a household name?'

'He is and he isn't,' Paparazzo replied. 'I suppose you might call him a new kid on the block. Well, actually, more a late arrival.'

'He's an actor then? As in attore?' Cousins said pronouncing the word reasonably well.

'He's an actor; was or, rather still is, Don Taylor's Italian voice. He was going to assist Mr. Taylor with dialogue coaching.'

'I wasn't aware of that,' said Cousins. 'Is he in films? Television?'

'Works exclusively in dubbing and voiceover,' said Paparazzo. 'That's the fate of many actors in this part of the world. They work in those sectors because there are precious few opportunities elsewhere. Even for bit players.'

'How long was he dubbing Don Taylor?' asked Cousins.

'Twelve years.'

'His age?'

'Thirty-nine.'

'And he's good at what he does?'

'They call him 'Golden Pipes,' at the studio where he most often works. You can take that to mean he's one of the best.'

'And why all this fuss about him?' Cousins asked, leafing through some of the other articles, 'I can't read any of these, but it's obvious there's more than a passing interest. Lots it would appear.'

'I was the one who started it,' Paparazzo revealed. 'I wrote this think-piece for my paper – an analysis of actors like Max generally, with background information about him. It concluded with a personal opinion. That's what set off everything else you have before you.'

He decided against going into the finer details concerning Della Pasqua, Spada and the students. Better to keep it clear-cut for the present time he figured. No need for the nitty-gritty.

'And what was this personal opinion of yours?'

'I made the argument that a fine actor such as Max should be considered for your film. For the part of Meucci that is.'

'I see,' the director said, without betraying any reaction. 'We have other Italian actors in this film you know – Filipo de Marco is playing Enrico Bandelari for example; and Sergio Berceto is cast as Nestore Corradi. Why shouldn't I consider either of them? Age-wise they both fit.'

'Yes, but do they appear in any of these newspapers Mr. Cousins? Would they be anything more than a passing interest if you were to cast them? Max Pellegrino on the other hand, you cast him and there's an air of originality about it. A novelty factor poles apart from the drab choices you so obviously want to resist. There would be a touch of individuality to it as well – the comeback kid making a distinctive statement to the film community. Your private investors I'm sure would go in for the notion of an Italian in the role. And the studio – a major headache removed for them. Every bit as effective as those pills I just gave you. An all-round tonic, yes?'

'There is something abstract and invigorating about it, I'll give you that much,' Cousins admitted. 'However...'

Paparazzo interrupted by gesturing at the bulletin board behind him.

'I couldn't help but notice that picture of Don Taylor when I came in,' he said. 'It suggests to me the limbo this film of yours appears to be in. You resigning yourself to a shutdown despite front elevations and paintwork. The studio putting forward actors even as they probably contemplate a termination scenario. Meanwhile, your production manager is out there busily assuring and setting minds at rest. He's talking about places that don't even exist Mr. Cousins. And if none of you are careful, if the illusion continues, this production office will soon be one of those. Give Max Pellegrino a chance. Roll the dice as the expression goes. What's the worst thing that can happen? You won't lose face by allowing someone a screen test, will you? And if he works out, if he is your Meucci, then you have a real actor and not some compromised fait accompli. You get to make your film on your terms plus,' he added conspiratorially, 'the money men would appreciate it no doubt. Max's salary would not be the equivalent of a Don Taylor. Correct?'

David Cousins smiled and swivelled in his chair. He looked amused. He looked impressed. But most of all, he looked intrigued. He sat forward and clasped his hands, bringing them to rest on the desk. Paparazzo's article was still in front of him there; appropriately positioned on top of the others. Cousins regarded it again.

'That's quite a speech Mr. Paparazzo,' he said, 'you certainly have a way with words, even for a journalist. You might want to consider a different line of business – the representative kind. You could be an agent you know. Max Pellegrino's. You sure make a hell of a case for an actor I've never seen.'

Once more, he looked at the article. And the picture accompanying it.

'Golden Pipes, huh?' he said.

A Simple Plan

'Who the fuck is this Max Pellegrino?' asked Gordon Sawyer, Aggregate Pictures' head of foreign distribution. He was seated on one of the new leather chairs recently installed in Cy Younger's office, a coffee cup finely balanced on one knee, a yellow legal pad tipping forward on the other. He looked around the office which he'd not been in for over two weeks on account of a recent vacation in the Bahamas. The decorators had been busy in the meantime. Gone was the cheerless carpeting which had been a feature of the space since Harry Krentzman's time there. Instead there was a stylish border of herring-bone parquet, enclosing a thick wool rug of some fawny colour with an interior deep-brown edging of its own. It all looked very well. Sawyer approved. His gaze moved on to the freshly painted walls which were hung with a number of contemporary paintings, each by a mid-western artist he'd never heard of before, each selected by the man sitting directly opposite him. The choices made were pretty good he thought. A series of visual motifs, distinguished by explosions of colour; the artwork was modern, but not harsh; sumptuous, but not without personality. There was nothing folksy about the taste here. Cy could pick out fine art just as well as the next man. Those heavy-lidded eyes of his were calmly and alertly open.

The scarred walnut desk at which the chairman sat was not gone the warehouse way though. There it still stood in front of the wide venetian blinds, which swung freely in the air conditioning. From behind it, Cy's face was an expression of mild displeasure as he swivelled glances between Sawyer and Anthony Chouraqui, who was also present. He didn't like questions being put back at him quite frankly and he wondered why Gordon Sawyer was doing this. It was very unlike him.

Sawyer was a tough, highly experienced man who did not suffer fools gladly, and it was not his custom to answer a question with a question. If truth be told, he was probably the most direct, often incendiary, individual Cy had ever known and that was saying something in a town where no holds were commonly barred and punches seldom pulled. He thought back to the day of his appointment to the present position. Several departmental heads and employees dropped in to his office to pass on their congratulations and best wishes. A shy man by nature, Cy found this ritual uncomfortable and not a little bit stilted. In spite of his own good news, he knew that future battles lay ahead, not least in terms of media reaction to his appointment and wider perceptions within the community. There was also the not-so-insignificant matter of adjustments which would have to take place in the organisation. Many of the compliments and hats-off were made by sheepish executives unsure of their own futures at AP. A few of them would be gone through the revolving doors within a matter of weeks he knew. As chairman it would be his responsibility, and burden, to implement the changes McWhirter was requiring. The process would be a difficult one for all concerned, but at least it would be above board and genuine, which this present charade was certainly not.

The day went by interminably; the praises and good-lucks mounted up. By 4 'o clock Cy felt he'd shaken enough hands and decided it was time to get away. Informing his secretary he was leaving early, he sidled off towards the elevators glad to have formalities done with.

'Where the fuck do you think you're going?' came a loud voice from behind as he pressed the button on the wall. It was Gordon Sawyer, unsurprisingly, a Cheshire-like grin on his face, a nonchalant air about him which was most refreshing after all the deference that had gone before.

'Don't you know you have to be here from dawn 'til dusk now that you're boss?' he continued in his typically off-handed manner.

'Well it's all yours now,' he said as they shook hands cordially, 'so don't fuck it up.' He barked in a half-laugh, before becoming more serious. 'And don't fuck me around in terms of whether my head is on the block or not. With all due respect, I'd prefer not to play those mind games at my age. That's a saddle for those younger people who aren't here as long as we are.'

He paused as the elevator doors opened and the other man stepped in.

'Oh, and by the way,' he said, 'if I didn't already say it, well done. It will take some time, but we'll get there with a bit of luck and just a little knowhow.'

The name Max Pellegrino, however, was causing Gordon to scratch his head and puff out his cheeks. There was no film he could call to mind in which he'd ever seen such an actor; no credit or supporting role which suggested itself; no listing or trade directory he had in his possession which contained a resume of previous work. It was a source of frustration for him. He didn't appreciate it when others were short of answers and was quick to let them know just that. But now he was the one found wanting in the information stakes, now the shoe was on the other foot. Or off both feet as they were in this case – Gordon's pair of Berluti handmades, he'd slipped out of them on entering Cy's office. It was for the sake of the new carpeting he said, he didn't want to risk marking it. There was also the comfort factor. His feet were tired, his mind slightly thrown like the other two men.

'I don't understand,' he said changing the focus of their discussion, 'I don't understand what the rationale behind this is. Is David Cousins trying to test us in some way? Is it a challenge?'

'A challenge?' Cy repeated, as he exchanged a quick look with Anthony Chouraqui, 'what do you mean by that?'

'A challenge, as in a fuck-you-come-get-me-sorta-deal,' Sawyer laid out in one heavily-accented New York phrase. 'This guy has a history of it. There was that musical which flopped a couple of years ago – Bluff

City, and, before that, one or two other productions. He clearly enjoys brinkmanship or whatever the fuck the correct term for it is. Fucking around with other people's time and money. Making out as if he's the big fucking man. I say we tell him to go fly a fucking kite. See him make a film about that. He likes control, doesn't he? Put him one hundred per cent in control of nothing and he controls nothing.'

'It's not as simple as that Gordon,' Cy interjected, 'you know better than anyone how distribution is lining up at the present time, and for the medium-term. Domestic and overseas can't just rely on turnarounds and buy-ins alone. That's not a staple diet for you guys. It's not sustainable for the company going forward. We need to generate in-house production. We need to get those figures up and keep them at that level. Distribution has more than a vested interest in this. You understand this only too well. If there's no product, then there's nothing to sell at the other end. And if there's nothing to sell then...look we can both retire right now, you and me, but our young friend here on the other hand,' he said, gesturing towards Chouraqui, ' he has a long way to go yet. Plus, he's got an awful lot to learn.'

Anthony Chouraqui smiled, appreciating the playful dig.

'Let's stick around for a bit longer, this company included. We still have a lot of work to do here, right? Let's leave something of use to the next generation.'

Sawyer nodded tentatively.

'What do you need from me?' he grumbled.

'Your knowledge of the overseas markets. European cinema especially,' Cy explained. 'How clued-in are our associates in Italy? Rome to be precise.'

'They're well-informed,' Sawyer replied, 'we no longer have a physical office there of course – owing to the edicts of McWhirter – but Gabriella and Roberto do a bang-up job each and every time. Cutbacks, thankfully, have not stymied their efforts.'

'How well versed are they in terms of resident actors?'

'Pretty good I would imagine,' answered Sawyer, 'but if this guy, Pellegrino, has been off the grid for as long as you say Anthony, then I have my doubts as to them knowing a whole lot about him. Of the two, Gabriella's the one I would talk to first. How many years did you say he's been in the game? As a voice actor?'

'15 as I understand,' Chouraqui replied. 'He's been Don Taylor's voice over there ever since he came on the scene. The information I have is pretty scant.'

'Who did you get the call from?' Sawyer asked.

'Art Brackman, Cousins' agent.'

'What does he have to say about this cock-eyed idea?'

'He didn't express a personal opinion.'

'I'm not fucking surprised. He has a client who's beyond the pale of fuck-knows-what.'

'He said the actor is highly regarded in his country,' Chouraqui said, disregarding the remark, 'apparently there's been a lot of media attention. Some of it's been drumming up support for him to get the part.'

'They want to see the homeboy do well, huh?' said Cy.

'I guess so.'

'More than do well,' Sawyer offered, 'it would be the most out-of-nowhere move since Charlie Bluhdorn put Bob Evans in charge of Paramount. Aside from that I don't know what the fuck else. Norma Shearer getting Bob Evans cast in Man of a Thousand Faces maybe. Does this guy even speak English though? Has anyone thought to ask that question?'

'I did,' replied Chouraqui, 'Art Brackman says his English is very good. And not too strong an accent either.'

'How the fuck does Art Brackman know this?' Sawyer enquired.

'He was quoting from David Cousins. They've already spoken.'

'What the fuck?!' said Sawyer, 'what do you mean they've already spoken? On who's authority? In what capacity?'

'Cousins made the contact. He's still the producer Gordon.'

'In fucking name only!' Sawyer shot back. 'How much finance has he sunk into this production? Not a fucking cent. Meanwhile us boys holding the purse strings have to listen to this sort of shit. It's degrading I tell you. If we want to get this movie made, we tell him who the fuck we think should be in the part Cy. We impose our will on him. Not the other way round.'

'I would be careful as to how we might go about doing that,' Cy replied evenly, 'we should appear to be giving him a fair hearing at the very least. Do you know what the nature of this conversation was Anthony? What was discussed? Did Brackman say?'

'He said the context was pretty general. Cousins wanted to hear how he sounds. He set up a meeting for today, at which time he intended to offer him a screen test.'

'Jesus Christ!' Sawyer uttered volubly, 'where does he get off with this shit? What about the actors you were proposing? Why isn't he testing any of them?'

'He refuses to, said our list was uninspired, that none of the actors were suitable. This would have an air of originality to it if it worked out. A far-reaching bit of casting that would knock the industry for six. His words, according to Brackman.'

'It has an air alright,' opined Sawyer, 'and all of it is hot. Since when are we in the business of indulging such preposterousness? Does David Cousins think us some screwball outfit?'

'I don't think he figures us for that Gordon,' Chouraqui said, directing himself towards Cy, 'but what the particular manoeuvre is here, I just can't say. Is he trying to force our hand? Hoping that we'll actually pull the plug?'

'I could live with that scenario,' said Sawyer. 'You want a plausible reason to get out, well he's providing us with one. An on-going irreconcilable difference is what we call it. And this latest slice of bizarro is the match in the powder keg. We cut our losses and we walk away. Not ideal I realise but under the circumstances. Needs must when the devil drives and so forth.'

Cy Younger shook his head disagreeably.

'First of all,' he said, 'I'm sick to death of the jokes on the subject. These past few days, I've been hearing the same wisecracks on the corridors outside. I want it to stop. Right now. Anthony. Gordon. Both of you tell your staffs to knock off the one-liners. This should not be a source of entertainment to anyone in this organisation. You overhear one more quip, and I want you to take that person to task. Remind them where they are and what it is we do. We develop projects. We make movies. That involves getting hold of properties and watching over them from start to finish. It does not entail bringing said properties to a half-done state and then watching ineffectually as they're relinquished away to competitors. We're not in the casting-off trade. We don't discard without good reason.'

'I realise that Cy,' said Sawyer, 'but how far out do you intend to go on this? What's the maximum value we extend ourselves to? And what sort of concessions do we allow in getting there? There's ineffectual expressed if we don't have sufficient end-product, or a glut of projects in turnaround. I fully agree with that. But, equally so, weakness will be perceived if you give up too much to one individual. It's a dangerous fucking strategy given this director's form up to now. He won't recognise a line in the sand unless it's drawn for him in a very clear-cut fucking fashion. And even then, it's a monitoring exercise which I don't envy anyone the task. Times like this I'm glad I work in distribution. I wouldn't have the patience for a David Cousins to be absolutely frank. I'd probably kill the son-of-a-bitch or have a heart attack myself in the process. Either way, someone would be put out of their misery. AP most likely. You as well.'

'Thank you Gordon. It won't have to come to such eventualities I hope.'

Cy nodded casually before turning to the other member of staff.

'How would you describe your relationship with the agent?' he asked Chouraqui.

'Art Brackman?'

'Art Brackman.'

'It's pretty good. I've known him several years. A very capable man. He has street smarts and the ability to deal with a situation on his feet. He learnt to read memos and correspondence upside-down when he first started out in the business, when he was still working in the agency mailroom. He wanted to get ahead as quickly as possible, figured information was the key. His colleagues gave him the nickname 'Snoopy' on account of it. He used to linger in offices and conference rooms just long enough to understand what was going on; to see what type of deals were on the table. Always reading upside-down, so the bosses would be less likely to know what he was doing.'

'Is he still adept at doing that?'

'Reading upside-down?'

'Grasping matters from an unusual standpoint. Understanding problematic individuals. Fractious ones for instance.'

'Such as clients like David Cousins?'

'Especially clients like David Cousins.'

Chouraqui mulled this over for a moment and nodded.

'I think he has a good working relationship with his client,' he said, 'if that's what you're asking. Some of it has amounted to damage limitation over the years. I heard he had to broker several truces between David and Bear Topolski during the Bluff City shoot. The two men weren't talking. Art was the go-between. He has a reputation for above and beyond the call of duty. And Cousins is quite often that.'

'You fucking said it Anthony,' murmured Sawyer in a peevish tone.

Cy for his part leant back in his chair, folding his hands in his lap, and focused intently on something he'd written at the beginning of the meeting.

'You think he could be prevailed upon for such an enterprise again?' he asked without looking up. 'The above and beyond sort?'

'It depends on what you have in mind Cy.'

Younger looked up and stared at Chouraqui's bronzed forehead, as if the answer were written there.

'What I have in mind is your trip to Rome. We discussed the desirability of such an excursion,' he clarified for Sawyer's sake. 'Well I think you have more than good reason to go now, don't you? If we agree to this screen test he wants to put on, he can hardly object to the idea of us attending it. Right?'

'I guess not,' said Chouraqui, 'and who else do you see there?'

'Along with you, Malcolm Archer on the casting side of the equation. And Mr. Brackman perhaps, if he can travel at such short notice.'

'For the David Cousins side of the equation?' asked Sawyer casting a dubious look.

'For the steadying effect his presence would have, we hope,' said Cy.

'And someone his client would listen to,' added Chouraqui.

'Exactly. A familiar face; and a voice of reason as well. You'll probably need it if and when...'

'When I think,' said Sawyer. 'So the intent being following the academic exercise that is this screen test, Anthony lobbies for one of our preferences.'

'As a matter of upmost importance,' said Cy, as he turned to Chouraqui, 'it won't be the easiest bit of negotiating you'll ever do Anthony, but my thinking is that with Archer and Brackman on your side, your job might be somewhat less laborious.'

'Do we know for a fact the agent will play ball?' asked Sawyer.

'He'll play ball alright,' Chouraqui informed him, 'Art's a pragmatist. He knows what's in his client's best interest.'

'It's a fucking shame his client doesn't know what's in his best interest,' said Sawyer. 'You could have put this thing to bed a long time ago. But hey, a stopover in Rome is always a good thing. You might even get to see some of the famous buildings there, from the seat of your taxi.'

'Thanks,' said Chouraqui dryly, 'when in Rome as they say. Ben Sanders is the one I'm pushing for I suppose?'

Cy nodded.

'Ben Sanders,' he said.

'One of our nominees he doesn't particularly care for?' asked Sawyer.

'One of those,' replied Chouraqui, 'he's available, but for how much longer I can't say.'

'That's what makes the Rome trip all the more imperative,' said Cy, 'the window of opportunity will not remain open forever. He has to appreciate it as the most expedient solution all-round.'

'Good luck with that,' voiced an unconvinced Sawyer, 'Ben Sanders is competent enough, but he's pretty unremarkable. Not the kind of actor who will exactly set the screen on fire.'

'He will do well enough,' returned Cy, 'and besides we still have Jennifer Carrington for the marquee. What are the alternatives? What? If we don't cast an actor soon, we won't have her, a marquee, or a film.'

'Point taken Cy,' answered Sawyer, 'I'm just thinking aloud here. Mollifying is one thing, but converting someone to a diametrically-opposed position is quite another. I just hope you boys can make it fly over there Anthony.'

'They'll make it fly Gordon,' Cy chipped in, putting emphasis on his belief in the undertaking, 'and I appreciate the difficulty you have with this. It's not hugely appealing to me either, but it must serve as a means to an end. If Mr. Cousins is given the impression we've considered his idea seriously, that we've indulged him appropriately, then reciprocation may be easier to come by.'

'And if not?' asked Chouraqui. 'If he continues to resist Sanders and the others?'

'Then expect the agent to lead him away into private consultation. If he's as good as you say, he'll outline the options available to him. I'm thinking he'll recommend a show of good faith under the circumstances. A do-the-right-thing entreaty. He's street-smart you said? Prides himself as someone who can do the difficult?'

'Very much so. And Art remembers how we agreed to several concessions on the script last October after Cousins' rant against our story department. Would a Fox or Warners' cavalry simply ride in and not insist on changes to certain aspects of the production? Would he expect no fresh vetting from one of their story departments? Art will have considered all the permutations. And he'll point out those known unknowns. Like I said, he's a pragmatist.'

'Good. Then he's an invaluable ally to us in more ways than one. Get him on that plane to Rome.'

'Will do Cy.'

'Gordon,' Cy said, turning to Sawyer, 'I'd like for you to contact that associate of ours in Rome. The one you said would be able to get us information.'

'Gabriella?'

'Yes. I'd like for Anthony to be equipped with some details regarding this Italian actor Pellegrino. If only for the sake of appearances, I want him to be able to display enough knowledge about his career. And make absolutely certain David Cousins is within earshot when you drop those interesting facts,' he added, raising his eyebrows in Chouraqui's direction.

'All part of the sleight of hand?' said Chouraqui.

'We're taking his idea seriously,' Cy reminded him, 'making him feel we're giving something, even as we expect something in return. You've always impressed me with your encyclopaedic knowledge of the industry Anthony. It's time to add a few more facts to that database mind of yours.'

'Well I've always liked Italian cinema,' Chouraqui remarked, 'plus, it's a long flight to Rome. No problem.'

'Good.'

'On that very subject, it's getting late over there,' said Sawyer, eyeing his watch, 'I should be able to catch Gabriella just before she goes to bed.'

He rose from his seat, catching the legal pad before it tumbled to the floor, and slipped back into his Berluti loafers.

'I'll get those details for you as soon as I can,' he told Chouraqui, 'might not be until later though. I imagine Gabriella will have to dig up stuff. Literally.'

'Fine. Thanks.'

'When was Cousins meeting the actor again?' he asked as he drifted towards the door.

'It was this afternoon, their time.'

'And this much-vaunted screen test?'

'If he's in earnest about it, or wants to appear that way, it should follow on quickly.'

'Well get him to stall on it so you can be there. No point in missing the show or exhibition or whatever-the-fuck you might call it.'

Cy rolled his eyes quickly.

'Let's just get it done,' he said, 'what we choose to call it is of no consequence. The jig has gone on for far too long. It's time to get this production back on track. No further disruptions if we can manage that please.'

'I agree,' weighed in Sawyer, 'turn this fucking whim of his around as fast as possible.'

This triggered a thought in Anthony Chouraqui's head. He felt duty-bound to put it into words.

'There's one thing we haven't considered,' he said, 'and I hesitate to bring it up.'

'What is it Anthony?' asked Cy. 'Tell us what's on your mind by all means. You're amongst friends here.'

'This actor, Pellegrino,' Chouraqui said, 'what if he isn't the second-rate we're expecting him to be?'

'How do you mean?'

'What if he isn't so lousy? What if he's actually good?'

Gordon Sawyer scoffed at the notion immediately. Wheeling around in the doorway, he rejected it all.

'I would have no worries as far as that's concerned,' he declared stoutly. 'He won't be. Not a chance of it. Why else do you think he's been a voice actor for 15 years? Because he's good? Because he's a fucking Olivier?'

Mumbling something else to himself, he took off.

Cy for his part exhaled noisily.

Chouraqui managed a weak smile.

'Well I guess that settles that,' he said, 'all we have to do now is...'

He'd thought of something amusing to say, just to lighten things up, but, observing his boss's appearance, decided to set it aside.

'I'll get on the phone to Art Brackman so,' he volunteered directly, 'see how he feels about Rome in May.'

Cy nodded.

'Thank you,' he said.

He went back to work.

Transatlantic

Anthony Chouraqui sat on the Alitalia flight bound from LAX to Rome Fiumicino and skimmed through the pages of Daily Variety. There was nothing remarkable in the trade paper for that day. A short piece written by Todd Rosenfelt was the only thing of note he could pick out. It related to the film in Rome. The caption read: *'Cousins' Echo Still in Casting Limbo: No Start in Sight.'*

Chouraqui read the article carefully. It was innocuous enough he decided. The same names mentioned as potential replacements for Don Taylor. Ben Sanders and a couple of others. No mention of anyone else. Just a rehash of the several days-old story, pepped up with a few opinions of the writer's own.

Well Mr. Rosenfelt is perfectly entitled to those Chouraqui thought as he doubled over the magazine. Sitting back in his cradle seat, he tried to relax. It wasn't easy though. He'd never been a good passenger and was prone to recurring bouts of travel sickness.

A flight attendant came through and asked if he needed anything. She offered a choice of blanket or duvet for his comfort. He wondered what could possibly be the difference between the two, especially on a long-haul flight such as this.

Promising her he was fine, that he required neither, he returned to his browsing of Variety. Todd Rosenfelt's by-line reappeared in due course, as did his article concerning the, *'open-ended affair in Rome'* described by him. Chouraqui felt obliged to read over it again. Just to be absolutely certain. So that there's no doubt in my mind he thought. And then have a rest. Although that seemed unlikely. He quickly toyed with the notion of asking for another soft drink. Carbonated beverages helped apparently. But how many was this so far he wondered. Seven? Possibly eight? And the flight over 13 hours all told. He'd be running to the lavatory every ten minutes at this rate. Putting the idea out of mind, he tried to re-engage with the musings of Mr. Rosenfelt. More figures cited in this. All of them having to do with the Echo production. Approximate expenditure so far. Estimated cost if there was a shutdown. His head began to spin again. Outside, the plane went into a momentary pitch. Chouraqui tugged on the elevated armrests.

Next to him, a reassuring voice came up.

'I wouldn't worry too much about that,' said Art Brackman, 'par for the course on these journeys. Nothing more than a slight dip.'

The single-aisle cabin of the Boeing 767 facilitated a three-plus-three layout in business class. The two men were seated together. Across the way from them, in the opposite row, Malcolm Archer, the prominent casting director, was sound asleep. There was some light snoring coming from his direction. He hadn't noticed a thing.

'You don't care very much for flying, do you?' Brackman continued.

'Orson Welles said there are only two emotions in a plane: boredom and terror. I'm thinking yours is the latter.'

'It's not terror,' Chouraqui corrected, 'I just don't travel very well. Have had it since I was a kid. It doesn't help when the plane banks suddenly.'

'I didn't know that Anthony.' Brackman sounded sympathetic. 'And with all the flying you have to do. It can't be easy.'

'It's a spatial disorientation thing,' Chouraqui explained, 'so this doctor in San Francisco told me. Motion felt but not seen. Domestic flights are normally ok. I request a window seat. A view of the ground or lower clouds means you can see your progress. That makes a big difference. To the body and mind.'

He tapped the side of his head.

'Jesus Christ! Why didn't you say so? We can swop seats,' suggested Brackman, who was indeed next to a window.

He moved forward to stand up.

A hand came across stopping him. It was Chouraqui's.

'Art, would you look outside and tell me what you see,' he said.

Brackman obeyed, peered out the window.

Nothing out there. Pitch black. No light or clouds and, most certainly, no ground visible. He saw his companion's point.

'I get it,' he said, 'we're in the dark up here. No reference points. A lot of good it would do sitting at a window that doesn't give you a view.'

'No view, no cure,' Chouraqui said, with a shake of his head, 'and they call it a natural response in healthy individuals; the doctors and so-called experts.'

'What do they know, eh?' said Brackman looking around.

His eyes came to rest on Archer.

'Well at least Malcolm should be wide-awake in Rome,' he observed, 'but as for you and me.'

'Coffee will be my crutch,' said Chouraqui. 'I stayed up in meetings in Paris for 36 hours straight once. I don't know how much coffee I consumed in that time. A lot I think. Maybe a cup for every hour, if that's possible.'

'And that was after a flight like this? With no clouds or view either?'

'Very much the same,' replied Chouraqui, 'but I'm better prepared for it now. I know how hard I can push myself. I intend to push myself very hard this time out, as is necessary.'

He allowed it to sink in gently.

Brackman smiled intuitively.

'I understand what you're saying,' he replied softly.

'What was your guy's reaction on the phone?' Chouraqui asked. 'When you told him we were coming to pay a visit.'

'It was composed,' Brackman said, without having to think. 'All he said was – oh?'

'All he said was oh?' Chouraqui repeated incredulously. 'He had a hell of a lot more to say to me when I spoke to him. Many words were used and I don't remember oh being amongst them.'

Art Brackman moved around in his seat.

'What can I tell you Anthony?' he said, 'David is a complicated man. He has many sides. Even I'm not sure I've seen them all.'

'He's full of twists and turns alright,' said Chouraqui, 'and you told me he'd mellowed.'

'Because that's what I believed,' Brackman said in his defence. 'He tried a few things after Bluff City; took up meditation for one. I used to get calls from him telling me how he was building up his internal energy and life force. He said he was working towards an indestructible sense of well-being.'

'Evidently he got there,' Chouraqui muttered sarcastically.

'My client is an extremely talented individual,' Brackman said, 'but he does not always see the wood for the trees. He gets himself too heavily involved, loses his sense of proportion. Part of my job, as I see it, is to try and knock that back into him. I will warn you now in advance, I don't always succeed.'

Chouraqui signalled his awareness of this.

'No one is expected to bat a thousand all the time Art,' he said, 'but on this particular occasion we need to get damn close.'

'The Howard Holden show did no one any favours,' Brackman said, 'David took it personally that AP didn't do more. It's much of the reason why he bawled you out over the phone.'

'What more did he expect us to do?' Chouraqui asked. 'We conveyed our expressions of support through you Art.'

'Which I duly passed on.'

'Well what then? Did he anticipate holding of hands? Soothing words of comfort? Excuse us blockheads at AP, but we never figured David Cousins for the kind who needed mollycoddling.'

'He's a proud man is all I'm saying,' replied Brackman, 'understand that, as his rep, I have to play the part of apologist from time to time.'

'But that doesn't involve you endorsing this threat of his, does it?'

'Of course not Anthony. And ever since he started making waves about that, I've been overstating certain things. Like I said, I try to knock some sense back into him.'

'Certain things? Such as?'

'Such as the possibility of AP firing him off the film. Now there's no need to be cagey with me about it. We've known each other long enough. You guys have discussed it, haven't you? Between you and me, I can appreciate why you would examine such an option.'

Chouraqui shrugged and gave up the acknowledgement.

'We examined the possibility for a very short time,' he said. 'Danny Rosner's advice was fully against it. Muddying of the waters he is doing, but there's no just cause otherwise. Not at this particular juncture.'

'That's how I would have read it as well,' Brackman corresponded. 'David would go after you. And the DGA would back him up.'

'We have little doubt about that,' replied Chouraqui, 'but thanks for your efforts all the same. It looks as if he saw through your trumped-up representation.'

'I'm afraid so,' said Brackman.

He called over a passing flight attendant and ordered a scotch whisky.

'I could do with it,' he said half-seriously, 'conversations about David sometimes have this effect on me. I'm good, but I need my coping mechanism just like the next man.'

Chouraqui nodded, smiling.

'I would join you,' he said, 'but it wouldn't be the most fantastic idea. It's bad enough I won't be sleeping. Toss a hangover into that mix and I'd be an ogre in Rome.'

'One is enough to deal with,' Brackman said casually.

The flight attendant came back with a Dewar as requested.

The agent took a sip and set it down.

'In Scotland it's called a wee dram,' he said, 'but I prefer to give it a different name: a necessary nip.'

He laughed, relishing the description.

Anthony Chouraqui made no comment. Instead he returned to the subject of their discussion.

'Since we're being so upfront about matters, can you answer me something?' he said.

'I'll try,' said Brackman.

'This threat of your client's: to move the production to another studio, if such a suitor were to come along. Is it genuine in your opinion? Is he hoping for such an eventuality?'

'I think so,' said Brackman, 'he seems...in earnest...if that's the appropriate phrase.'

'And only because he feels disrespected? He's in a huff over things that didn't come to pass? After Bear, was there some template we were supposed to have followed?'

'It's not the only reason he gave me,' Brackman volunteered, 'David also believes a different studio would have more traction in terms of getting a suitable replacement for Don Taylor. He doesn't think you guys are at the races in that regard. He knows you're in a bit of a slump.'

He sounded uncomfortable saying this.

Anthony Chouraqui's response was one of creeping exasperation.

'Oh I see,' he said, 'so another studio is going to come in and resolve everything for him. Are they? Wave a magic wand and, hey presto, here's your actor. Not a Ben Sanders, or a Richard Campbell; not even a Fisher or Bennett, but someone none of us have thought of up 'til now. That's quite a miracle he's expecting, isn't it? Has he never heard of schedules or calendars? They have a sort of bearing.'

'That's fully appreciated by your fellow traveller Anthony, but David doesn't think like we do. He demands and expects. Everything else is a technicality.'

'Was it a technicality last October as well Art? We gave the man just about everything he wanted. Would another crowd give free rein like that? All over again?'

'I know the answers to those questions Anthony. They're self-evident.'

'And as for this suitable replacement for Don Taylor, how does he define suitable exactly? He wouldn't or couldn't explain it to me a couple of days ago. Would he suddenly have the answer for Warners or Fox?'

'I seriously doubt it,' said Brackman, as he knocked back the rest of his Dewar, 'I think a good deal of his frustration comes from the fact he hasn't found his actor. He's never been able to relate anyone to the part you know. It's eluded him all this time and, for someone who hankers after control the way he does, it's a source of genuine irritation.'

'Of course it is,' said Chouraqui, 'he's a control freak. No one would ever be good enough. At AP we knew how he felt about Don Taylor. The passive-aggressive reaction was not lost on any of us. He probably thinks Don's accident was some kind of providential act. The search for Meucci began again. Finding this mythical actor of his. Except that he doesn't exist. He's strictly a fabrication in his head. And his character will stay on paper until he accepts that; if such acceptance ever occurs.'

Art Brackman voiced his agreement. Understanding his client better than most, he said he knew the intricacies of his mind, and how these were often contrary to one another; especially when it came to facts and realities. The desire to create and foster a perfect piece of work was nothing unique in the David Cousins narrative he said. The director had a reputation for pushing himself around-the-clock, and insisting others do the same.

'When you asked me to join you on this mission to Rome,' he said, 'it reminded me of a previous film of David's from a couple of years ago. My client is as fastidious in the promotion of his films as he is in their making. Every contingency has to be covered. He thinks about how many trailers and prints should be made; what type of stills and explanatory text newspapers and press releases require; who should be invited to preliminary screenings and marketing previews. That level of analysis he brings to both domestic and overseas. For the Italian release of the film in question, the studio had retained the services of a young publicist in Rome. I can't remember his name, but I've no doubt David would. God knows he called the poor son-of-a-bitch enough times. That's a gross understatement in fact. There was a torrent of nit-picking calls from him. Plus a flood of contradictory instructions which I can tell you wore down enthusiasm and resolve pretty fast. The guy, as I understand it, was an admirer of David's work. That too was finally eroded. In the end, he wired David care of the studio. The cable read: 'I quit. STOP. As a filmmaker you are a genius. STOP. But as an employer you are an idiot. STOP.' I have a copy of it in my office. Nicole Sands gave it to me. She has one framed on her wall. The kid was spot-on. David is a pain-in-the-ass. But he's also a genius.'

'I wish I could be as blunt as that,' said Chouraqui. 'I'd outstrip candour.'

'Of course you would,' said Brackman, 'but then you wouldn't need me for this finessing exercise. Would you?'

'Good point,' said Chouraqui, yielding to the quick rejoinder. 'How long were you holding fire on that one?'

Brackman grinned almost roguishly.

'Well I figured it was going to be a long flight,' he said, 'and seeing as how you weren't falling asleep.'

'No chance of that,' said Chouraqui, 'and not just on account of my motion sickness.'

'Concerns?' asked Brackman.

'Yes, concerns,' replied Chouraqui.

'And there you were a few minutes ago,' said Brackman, 'stretching for those baseball metaphors. Any minute and I thought you were going to start talking about extra innings. Or swinging for the fences.'

'Both would be fitting,' said Chouraqui. 'David Cousins is right about one thing. AP is in a slump. This company needs to get back to the business of making movies. And it's my job to see that happens. You know what Echo of Passions represents to us Art. Most people about town do. It's not just simply another movie. It's a defining moment, potentially a way back for us. If we can push this production forward in spite of everything that's happened, in spite of your client's…best efforts… vivifying the malaise so to speak, it's a demonstration to the community that AP is a viable operation again. That it no longer sits on the bottom rung. Getting the patent back on the commercial and high-quality. Echo we see very much in that latter group, as you well know.'

Brackman said he did.

'I do want to help,' he said emphatically. 'I've had high regard for Aggregate over the years; and, personally speaking, I think your boss has been unfairly portrayed and spoken of in certain quarters. Bert Balaban was a force of nature, no doubt about that, but a company's fortunes are not down to just one man. Too many of our associates overlook that. Including my client. For all his highbrow intent and artistic-speak, David too had his 'if Bert Balaban was still there' moment. Just the other day in fact. I'm sure that comes as no great surprise to you.'

'I can't say that it does,' said Chouraqui. 'It's become a familiar refrain.'

'I'm going to do everything I can in Rome,' Brackman told him, 'and for my client as well. I want him back at work. I want him doing what he does best. All this talk of moving the production to another studio I find just as objectionable as you do. AP has stuck with this project in an admirable way. You guys ought to have the credit when it comes due, when the film opens; when, hopefully, it gets recognition; wins some awards on the circuit.'

'Thank you,' said Chouraqui, 'right now I'm willing to settle for a lot less than that. Just some recognition of another kind. A little compromise.

That will do for a start. Or restart as in this case.'

Again Brackman promised his support. He would do everything he could. In Rome. At Cinecittà. Wherever they'd sit down to face his client.

'We might just turn this thing around,' he said on a positive note. 'Reagan ended the cold war after all. But even if we do get David to acquiesce, knowing his style as I do, there's one thing we can absolutely count on before that.'

'What?'

'A performance,' said Brackman, 'and rest assured it will be dramatic. Highly.'

The flight roared on.

THE GREAT MOMENT

Max still wasn't ready. He wasn't there yet.

It was the morning of the screen test and his preparations had hit a stumbling block. There was not long to go now. In a little while he'd have to be leaving in order to get to the studio on time. 11 o'clock was the designated hour at Cinecittà; sound stage 8 the venue. He would have to sort out these problems he'd been having all morning. And fast.

This was not the day to be making mistakes or tripping over lines he told himself. This was the day to be word-perfect, to be inspired. Nothing less would do. But what he was hearing on the playback was just that – less. Well below par in fact.

He'd recorded himself a number of times as he read through the script pages. It wasn't sounding good. Not like him at all. For one thing there was the dropping of ends of words: the d's, b's, t's, p's, and g's were especially troublesome. He was losing a good many of them; like an amateur, sloppy and untested. Not thinking through to the end of phrases. The brain rushing from one word to the next. It was an unusual lack of focus, a dearth of concentration, and he was puzzled by it. The content wasn't the problem. The evening before he'd been just fine. The playbacks had been seamless, his technique unhindered. Best of all he was starting to get a feel for the character. Of who this individual was as he related to the scene.

So why this patchiness all of a sudden he wondered. Why am I so wide of the mark? He listened again and again before finally getting it. The answer lay in another part of his performance. It was in his voice. In those lungful's of air. He was breathing out too quickly as he spoke. There were too many breaks in his delivery, and he was picking the wrong moments for these.

Going over it in his mind, he soon realised why. The tell-tale signs were all there: the quiver in his speech; the tremor in his hands; the rise in his heartbeat. Instantly recognisable now that he was alert to them. He was anxious, energised, restless, itching. He hadn't felt this way in how many years? How much time was it?

He needed to slow down, to work on his breathing. Acquiring a wine bottle cork, one he kept aside for such situations, he placed it flat in his mouth, as if it were a stubby cigar. For a moment he thought of that evening in Piazza di Corte, of Maurizio, the Toscano, and the spaghetti westerns. He bit hard on the stopper and began to read the dialogue out loud. From the top, he emphasized every vowel, consonant, and syllable. After a number of dummy runs, his jaw and tongue were becoming suitably tired. Removing the cork from his mouth, he switched the portable recorder back on. He went through the scene once more. Unhurried. With purpose.

He listened back to it quickly and then jumped in all over again. Only this time with greater gusto and emotion. This time as an actor giving it socks. Wrapping it up yet again, he wound back and hit the play button. The post-cork version was a big improvement. Max was relieved. Back in the game he thought as he drank some grapefruit juice, swishing it about in his mouth. Closing his eyes, he breathed in deeply and released gradually. Remember who your character is he told himself. Be in the moment. Get the words off the page.

As a reflex, he put his thumb against his chin and stretched out the tip of his little finger. But there was nothing there to touch. No microphone or lectern. For a change. Not even the dreaded pop shield, so valued by Giacomo Romano. Just good clear empty space.

Max laughed at the redundancy of his action. He would not be needing any of that paraphernalia today. The only thing now required was a little good fortune. The rest of it would be up to him. He was pepped up. Jesus it feels good to be doing this again he thought. How did I stay away? Fetching his jacket and car keys, he went to leave. But he'd forgotten something and it caused him to do a quick turn on his feet. Those precious pages of script he remembered. He couldn't leave them behind. He'd worked on them now for the last two days. They had his handwritten notes. Self-directions which only he understood. Cues as to when to raise the tempo, and when to level-off. Pointers that could make a world of difference. A world of difference to his world.

Taking hold of them, he was determined to come back having given it his all. When next I pass through here he thought as he left. Perhaps a momentous occasion will be that bit closer. It might be no further away than my own doorstep.

'This is a pivotal scene in the film, one which reinforces Meucci's love for his wife; just as that very devotion seems to be most in question.'

David Cousins was sitting outside the Bar della Pace two days earlier; ivy-clad walls to his rear, sunlit terrace directly facing him. He'd elected to sit in this spot as he liked to watch people go by, especially on a fine day like this. The 19th century bar in Rome's historic centre lent itself to such an activity. A short distance from nearby Piazza Navona, it had a steady flow of people coming and going from that famous square. Some entered its hallowed space on their travels, just to admire the interior of gilded baroque and Venetian-plastered walls. Others stayed on longer to sample what was reputedly the finest espresso in the city. When Max met Cousins outside the bar, the director professed no desire to drink coffee or admire structural designs. He was intent on his purpose.

A storyteller, first and foremost, he wished to relay some of the more noteworthy aspects of his 145-page script. Four of these sheets were passed to Max in due course. This was the scene currently under discussion. Cousins was laying it out in detail; breaking off at times as his eyes roved and isolated certain forms and figures. He apologised, courteously, explaining that the drawn-out period in the production office was the main reason for this. And besides, he was keeping a look out for someone in particular. He didn't say who it was and Max did not think to ask.

The director pressed on with his description:

'It's following an accident which happened to him when he was travelling on a ferry between Manhattan and Staten Island,' he explained. 'While he was recovering in hospital, his wife sold some of his working models, including the all-important teletrofono prototype, to a second-hand dealer. Naturally, it comes as a huge blow. He's been burnt in the accident; they're scarcely above the breadline, and now this.'

He studied the other man closely as he read the dialogue. Max did not look up.

'As you can see it's a potential breaking point for them both,' Cousins continued, 'he's crestfallen at the thought that so much of his work has been surrendered for a mere pittance. She's equally distraught believing he values that same body of work more than her.'

He stopped again, allowing the commentary to sink in. Still there was no response. Instead, just total focus.

Cousins decided to wait before going on. He sipped his Campari and watched as a young family rambled along with their personal guide. The children looked bored stiff. Probably too early to bring them to this virtual museum of a city he thought. What a waste.

'Finished,' said Max, who had now returned to their conversation. 'It's very well written Mr. Cousins.'

'David, please...and thank you.'

'David.'

'So do you think you can get a handle on the character from this?' Cousins asked. He wondered if the Italian would understand the expression and decided to put it another way.

'Is there enough there for you to...'

Suddenly, and to his own bemusement, he was struggling for the words himself.

'Enough of a handle?' Max said pitching in, 'yes, more than enough. I like how it concludes – with him telling her she is his life force, that which sustains him. Well you're the writer, so I need hardly go on.'

He smiled agreeably and David Cousins had a thought.

'It's one of the themes of his story as I see it,' he said. 'Meucci was an outsider for much of his life. Poverty, suspicion and treachery, those were just some of the things he struggled against. It just occurred to me that, if you do this screen test, you'll be the first actor to portray him. Albeit for four pages of script.'

'No one else?' asked Max, a look of pleasure shooting across his face. 'Did Don Taylor not read through the screenplay?'

'He read it, but in a private capacity,' said Cousins. 'You don't ask a man like Don Taylor to audition for a part, not without great insult being imparted. His agent you can be sure would have objected.'

'Tom Steiner?' Max said.

'Tom Steiner indeed. I take it you've had the pleasure?' Cousins said, his voice loaded with sarcasm.

'I met him in Trastevere when Don Taylor was doing publicity,' said Max, 'and there was a phone call before that. He doesn't have very much regard for the work we do here in the studios.'

'He wouldn't get any of that,' said Cousins. 'There's no profile to it and, therefore, no angle. Agents like Tom Steiner are only interested in you when you grace the cover of Vanity Fair. Or if your latest film is tracking well. Then they go after you like the shameless parasites that they are. It resembles a cheap brand of science fiction – Invasion of the Talent Snatchers.'

'It sounds as if you have your next idea,' Max said grinning.

He liked the director based on what he could observe. David Cousins did not appear so difficult. No more than say a Giacomo Romano. There were no protruding spikes on display up to now. True, he'd been somewhat insistent on where they ought to be seated at first.

'We're either outside, or we're outside,' he wisecracked, but the tone was such that he seemed to be expecting an argument about it. Max, for his part, had no cause to oppose this. He certainly had no desire to ruffle the director's feathers at so early a stage, and on so moot a point. David Cousins, he decided, had a brilliant mind. He was insightful, analytical, and single-minded in his opinions. And clearly he was used to getting his own way. But they'd found common ground on a subject, namely Tom Steiner, and that was something at least. For the time being it would do.

They chatted randomly for a couple of minutes. Movies, music, and the theatre were kicked around. Cousins voiced his admiration for the works of Pirandello. A play called Right You Are (If You Think So) he talked about in particular. It was about conflicting versions of the truth as told by the main characters he explained.

'I like that kind of approach,' he said, 'presenting the contradictory and self-serving accounts in the same way. It's comparable to Kurosawa's Rashomon. The unreliable narrator. The plot twist at the very end.'

He then brought them back to the more immediate.

'They call you 'Golden Pipes' I understand,' he said. 'That journalist Paparazzo who visited me at Cinecittà told me about the moniker. It's quite complimentary. Do you think it's well-earned?'

It was a direct question, concise and to the point. Max framed his response shrewdly.

'What's the point of a name, if there's no basis for it,' he quipped.

Switching to a more modest tack, he elaborated, 'it started out as a joke when I was doing one of my early feature films. I was voicing a character who was dashing and highly cultured. He was a hypnotist who took his clients in and made them do things against their will, always to their detriment and his general advantage. During one of the recording sessions, I had to be especially flamboyant. It was a scene involving a private investigator who just so happened to be the love interest. The engineer in the control room turned to the director and said – apparently – 'he sounds just like the silver-tongued bastard he's playing. Gold-plated. Like he has the yellow stuff lodged in his windpipe.' From that came 'Golden Pipes.' To the best of my knowledge.'

'That's a good story,' said Cousins. 'Do you remember all your films that well? The characters too?'

'A good few,' said Max, 'I'm closing in on my 200th film as a voiceover actor; not all of those were leading roles though.'

'Impressive,' remarked Cousins, 'and how do you feel about the leading role in this case? Is it worth my time testing you? Mr. Paparazzo thinks so. You have a real confederate in him by the way, or ally I should perhaps say.'

Max's answer on this occasion was at the ready. He'd been expecting this.

'I try to find the emotional hook in the character I'm playing,' he said, taking a quick look at the pages again, 'and, subject to what you would want, I think I'd be able to deliver. I consider myself something of an outsider as well here. I've come this far in a roundabout way, as you know. I'd like to go further.'

As a wrap-up he offered, 'I'm very proud to be the first actor to portray your Meucci Mr. Cousins…David. I'd also like to be the only one.'

That final part was a little bit deliberate he knew, but at least it showed genuine intent. He wouldn't be auditioning simply for the good of his health. Provided, of course, David Cousins would still be offering him that opportunity.

The director didn't say anything more about this until it was time for him to leave.

'Hang on to those,' he told Max, who was giving him back the pages of script, 'you'll need them for the studio. Cinecittà that is.'

Max nodded, understanding what this meant.

'I'll have the production office phone you later with the arrangements,' Cousins said. 'The studio bosses knew we were meeting today. They're pressing for this to be run off quickly. Get it done with is their attitude. I'm sure you don't want to be regarded like that Max; as someone to be brushed aside. Passed off as just another actor on the pile.'

'No, I don't,' said Max, 'I've waited for this chance a long time.'

'And it's plain to see,' said Cousins. 'You can use that. As well as the emotional hook. Remember what I told you about the scene,' he continued, as he rose from his seat, 'it's about love, frustration, affection, guilt. On the day, I'll give you direction as best I can. The balance of it then will be on you.'

They shook hands and the director stepped out onto the walkway.

'I'll work hard on it,' Max told him, as he moved off, 'I'm grateful for the opportunity. I'm going to put myself in your hands.'

The director smiled and waved a see-you.

'Be careful what you wish for,' he called back, 'you might just get it.'

David Cousins sat in the dining room of the St. Regis Hotel and took his breakfast at the same time as every other morning – French toast with bacon and barley coffee, or caffè d'orzo, as he'd learned to call it. It was seldom he deviated from this. He was an early riser and his gastronomic preferences were well known to the staff, as was his inclination towards room service in the evening-time when he returned from the studio. The set of choices then was narrowed down to either a pasta dish or pizza. By and large, the director went for something close to the top of the menu. He seemed pressed for time, as a rule, and munched noisily on his food as he made phone calls and pored over notes.

Neither a carefree tourist, nor an impassive businessman, he was here for a lengthier stay than the majority of the guests. The employees knew why of course, why his sojourn was drawn-out like so. This was the director of the new Don Taylor film they murmured in the kitchens, and over folded bed sheets. The one which would be shooting at Cinecittà before long. Behave with upmost respect towards him they were instructed. He's one of Hollywood's elite. One of their top directors.

Then things changed completely. Don Taylor's accident cast its pall. If deference had been the standard hitherto, the director was now a figure to be enabled and assisted no matter what the need. In this regard, the maître d instructed his waiting staff to fill any order taken; the brigade de cuisine were in on the act and similarly prepared. At the front of the house, the receptionists were told to prioritise incoming calls and faxes for the American. The head concierge also promised to up his game. For one thing, he began to leave more dailies in his large suite, including the Italian editions. He thought it unlikely Mr. Cousins understood the language, but figured why not. It was all in the performance of service. Keep this very special customer happy. And don't ask about the film. Too sensitive a topic by far. An enquiry, however innocuously meant, could potentially be misconstrued.

'I'd like egg in the basket please,' Cousins told the waitress who was attending his table. She was pretty, with dark hair and a pleasant smile, but his order drew a puzzled look and he thought he knew why.

'No French toast this morning,' he explained, 'I feel like something different. Egg in the basket would be good, if it's not too much trouble for your chef. Bacon on the side to go with that.'

'Egg in the basket?' she repeated. It was obvious she didn't recognise the culinary delight.

'Sure,' Cousins said patiently, 'it's very easy to do. It's an egg fried in bread with a hole in the middle. Simple. No more than five minutes.'

The blank expression did not go away. David sighed under his breath. It was going to be one of those days he figured. Well I won't be ordering Wesley Dogs here any time soon. It would definitely take too long to explain that.

'Shall I get our chef for you?' the girl offered, bearing in mind how this particular guest was to be treated.

'No need for that,' said Cousins, as he reached for a slice of bread to demonstrate. Cutting a hole in the centre of it, he simulated the breaking of an egg. She smiled as he did so; this progressed to a laugh when he hissed the sizzle of the frying pan.

'This is why I'm a director,' he told her, enjoying the moment of fun, 'it's what they pay me the big bucks for.'

'I understand now,' she told him. She disappeared away into the kitchen.

His instructions were productive. Ten minutes later the egg in the basket landed on his table. It looked perfect, tasted even better.

'Wonderful,' he complimented, 'I couldn't have made it better myself. Thank the chef for me, will you.'

The girl said she would and, feeling suitably emboldened, asked him about his face.

'I had two accidents in my bathroom this morning,' he told her, employing broad sweeps and lively motions. 'First of all I was shaving and cut my bottom lip. It opens every time I move it now. A damn nuisance. And if that wasn't enough, I slipped on the floor a few minutes later. Banged my jaw on the edge of the bathtub. It's sore, but, fortunately, I have pills for migraine. Do I look all beat up?'

'Beat up? What does it mean?'

Cousins searched for an analogy.

'Like I was fighting Mike Tyson,' he said. 'Beat up by Mike Tyson. Only then I'd have a lot more than a cut lip and busted jaw.'

'Ah Mike Tyson,' she said, 'yes you look like an opposite of him. Not so good. Your day I hope will get better. But first expect a third.'

'I'm sorry?' said Cousins. 'A third?' Now it was his turn to be confused.

'In Italian we have a saying,' she told him, 'non c'è due senza tre. It means there are never two without three. So expect a third thing to happen. I hope it is nothing bad.'

That got him to thinking about the three men who were in town for Max Pellegrino's screen test. Anthony Chouraqui most especially. Pretty obvious why he'd come he thought. Aggregate Pictures had enough of this standstill. They wanted the cameras turning at Cinecittà. But what might they offer up in exchange for going forward? How desperate were they really?

He was aware of the reports and commentaries which were still knocking around. Only two months previously, The Hollywood Reporter had run a story titled: *'Aggro at Aggregate: Not So Cohesive a Bunch Any Longer.'*

The article, penned by Jeff Forman, was not just another submission on the post-Harry Krentzman/Bert Balaban organisation. It delved deeper. Forman conceived of a situation whereby the financiers in New York now held the upper hand in the company, *'in the wake of one prominent death, several departures and a succession of box office let-downs.'*

He wrote, *'under the hegemony of McWhirter Limited, as confirmed by recent white papers and commercial reports, expect more of the economising and a good deal less of the imaginative. Regrettably, there is a shortfall on the creative side of the studio. The money men are not just coming, they are already in place. Moderation will abound.'*

The reporter noted the lack of upcoming productions on the Aggregate slate and declared it, *'symptomatic of the overall frailties in a company grappling within, even as it tries to persuade and win around a sceptical community.'*

Echo of Passions was mentioned incidentally (this was March and prior to its own troubles) as a project of *'some interest.'* Don Taylor was attached Forman noted. A rejuvenated David Cousins would be at the helm. But one project alone would not paper over the cracks. More would be needed the reporter opined. But he did not quantify or ballpark a figure. That task, he said, *'might be an exercise becoming the suits and their adding machines.'*

Tallying it all up, David Cousins figured he had an edge of sorts. One way or another, Aggregate Pictures needed to get this film made. That was what the anecdotal evidence was saying; it also seemed the raison d'être for Chouraqui's jumping on a plane with Art Brackman in tow. He didn't need to ask his agent for confirmation of this. Reading between the lines, it was as clear as a precious stone. Echo of Passions was valued by management at AP, in spite of everything to date. They did not want to give it up. Brackman had hinted at as much during their last phone conversation. Rushing to get to Los Angeles International on time, he termed it, 'an indication as to how serious they are about your film. They want to keep it and will wage war if needs be.'

The director was thinking more along the lines of a truce now. But peace would have its price he decided. Any agreement would have to be tipped in his favour. And with regard to the casting issue, exploratory would simply not do. He wanted the actor that he wanted. That could be Max Pellegrino he believed, provided he tested favourably. He liked the way the Italian had come into view. It reminded him of finding Meucci, of how he'd explained it to Mastrodicasa – inside a block of white marble of a different kind. An outline. A rough draft perhaps, but one which he could develop. Fashion and shape his performance the way he wanted it. What the actor had said to him at the Bar della Pace still resonated.

'Subject to what you would want,' he'd said. That was good. Likewise about putting himself in the director's hands. Better still.

There was one final thought and it gave him even greater pleasure. He smiled as he tucked in to the last of his prima colazione.

Fabio Paparazzo had put his finger on it. On the subject of Max; what casting this unknown would mean, what it would signal. An air of individuality according to the reporter. The director had every reason to agree with this. Such a far-reaching thing would bear all the hallmarks of a David Cousins coup. The community would be talking about it for months on end. It would be his moment. Permanently ingrained.

A big fucking I AM BACK he thought.

Anthony Chouraqui, Art Brackman and Malcolm Archer arrived at Cinecittà and were ushered directly to the Talking Telegraph production office. There they were received by David Cousins who, surprisingly, was full of chat and good-will. Most conspicuous of all was the director's enthusiasm about the screen test that morning. He was very hopeful he said; had been greatly encouraged by his meeting with Max Pellegrino two days before.

Anthony Chouraqui nodded, but did not say anything. The atmosphere between the two was civil, respectful, but hardly warm.

As if aware of this, Cousins fixed his attention on Malcolm Archer.

'We've missed you at the St. Regis,' he said, 'how did it go in Pasadena?'

Archer, who was in his early 50's, and had the kind of irresistible poise that is integral to Hollywood, pumped a fist and replied, 'nailed it.'

'Good for you,' said Cousins approvingly, 'you're still the man.'

'Well they won't be shipping me off to La Brea Tar Pits just yet,' Archer quipped.

Neither Brackman nor Chouraqui knew what they were discussing and did not take the trouble to ask. There was more pressing business at hand.

Cousins and the three met Max on sound stage 8.

The introductions were quick-fire. Chouraqui and the others took their seats to the left and right of a camcorder mounted on a tripod. The footage would be reviewed later on Max was told.

Taking the part of his wife for the audition was Oriana D'Ambrosio – an established actress from Verona who would have a small role in the film as Meucci's mother. She mouthed a good luck to Max while David Cousins issued his final instructions.

'Now remember what we talked about the other day Max,' he said. 'You can only take it so far. You have to portray something that is not quite anger, but rather dictated by a sense of misfortune. You've just returned from the hospital, you're badly burnt, and she's sold many of your most valuable articles. How ever deplorable an act this may seem, you have to keep in mind why she's done it. It's born out of self-preservation. What else did she have to live on while you were recuperating? What choice did she have? She is incapacitated and, therefore, extremely vulnerable. Your performance must arrive at a sense of forgiveness. You have to hold her in your arms just as you embrace this understanding.'

He added drolly, 'but there's no need to cosy up too much. The guys over there have had a long flight and I doubt they're in the mood for public displays of affection.'

Oriana D'Ambrosio laughed at this. Max's response in contrast was subdued. He was just eager to get on with it.

They performed the scene once from beginning to end. It seemed to go well.

Max homed in on the forbearing aspect. He delivered the line, 'you are my life, my endeavour, my love; without you my work would be deprived of its reason,' trusting that it was as it should be. This is surely the way the director wants it he thought. He told me as much today and when we first met.

David Cousins, however, wasn't saying anything. No tips or pearls of wisdom came from him. Instead, he called for another run-through.

The actors duly obliged.

When they were finished, Cousins stepped forward again.

'Once more from the top,' he politely requested. Max wondered if he was looking for something else from the scene. Or, more to the point, from him.

He was about to ask this, but decided against it. Play it just like before he thought. It's too late to make changes now. And besides, the director hadn't told him to do anything different. Why should he then? Fiddling with it might be the worst thing to do. It could take from the impression he was creating; if, in fact, he was creating an impression at all.

Oriana D'Ambrosio was stirred anyhow.

'That was fantastic Max, very moving,' she said, as Cousins finally called a halt to proceedings. The two of them exchanged kisses and he offered to walk her to her car.

A number of thank-yous came from the men seated – Chouraqui, Brackman and Archer. They shook hands with Max, but gave absolutely nothing away.

Nor did David Cousins for that matter. The director's tone smacked of the commonplace and was impossible to read. His poker face too as he bid him a ciao.

'Very nice Max,' was all he said. 'Very nice.'

Less than an hour later in the Talking Telegraph office the screen test was replayed on video. David Cousins asked that the last of the three readings be viewed. This was the one in which the acting was truly remarkable he enthused. And not just Max Pellegrino. Oriana D'Ambrosio likewise.

'It's enough to make me wonder if I should give her Jennifer Carrington's part,' he joked casually. 'She's marvellous also. So much acting talent in this country,' he remarked, as a wily insert, 'needless to say it's too often out of sight; hidden, unless you know where to go looking for it.'

Malcolm Archer professed himself of a like mind. But he had a question nonetheless.

'How did you find him?' he asked. 'By accident or design?'

'More like good fortune,' Cousins replied vigorously, 'something we needed badly on this film. Wouldn't you say?'

This last bit appeared to be directed towards Anthony Chouraqui, so the AP representative spoke to it.

'There is a lot to be taken into account here,' he said. 'Yes, the actor is good. I won't deny that. Much better than any of us expected I think. But there are other considerations David.'

'Such as?' questioned Cousins.

'Such as the sheer eccentricity of it all,' said Chouraqui. 'How would we begin to rationalise a decision of this magnitude? Where's the good reason in it?'

His mind wandered back to the conversation he'd had with Cy Younger and Gordon Sawyer two days before. The AP boss had regarded this as no more than an academic exercise, a means to an end he'd called it. Gordon Sawyer being Gordon Sawyer had dropped in one of his typically acerbic comments, 'fucking Olivier,' was the extent of his contribution. And what Anthony had seen on the sound stage, and now again on video, was not Olivier. But it was pretty damn good. Too much so perhaps. He tried hard to shut out that feeling. He hadn't wanted Max Pellegrino to be exceptional, and he wasn't, but things would be a lot easier if the actor hadn't been any good at all.

'It's right there,' Cousins answered him, pointing at the TV screen, 'the justification is in the performance you've just watched. Do you need to be reminded of it again?'

'No, I don't David,' said Chouraqui. 'No need for another replay. I get it. He's good. Acting chops certainly and he looks the part as well. But I worry even so. It's my job to do that. My thinking on this has to be across-the-board. There are other people in this playpen aside from you and me. The stakeholders, the studio, your independent investors too.'

'Who by the way do not think this an eccentricity,' said Cousins. 'They love the idea. The Bay Area gives it the thumbs up.'

This gave Chouraqui pause for thought.

'David, I wish you hadn't discussed this with anyone else,' he said, 'especially before this morning. It's precipitous and not just a little disrespectful towards us.'

Cousins received this censure balefully. The laid-back approach was done with. The atmosphere turned rather ugly.

'I felt disrespected as well Anthony,' the director shot back, 'but maybe one thing Bear Topolski said is true – maybe you guys do feel yourselves entangled. Well fine, if you want out, you can have out! This is your big fat chance!'

He slammed the video remote down on the desk. His round face was now a deep crimson.

Here it was at last then. The ultimatum. The face-off.

The other participants stayed quiet for the time being. Malcolm Archer's eyes did a roam of the ceiling. Art Brackman, meanwhile, was formulating, carefully formulating. But before he could weigh in, Chouraqui was there ahead of him.

'David, you misinterpret and you misrepresent, often wilfully I think,' he said. 'Aggregate Pictures want to move forward on this. We very much want to make the film. Why? Because we believe in it. Fully. We have confidence in the vision you've put on paper, and storyboarded, and everything else to this point. And we want to stick around for the final part of it. The transition to screen. I ask you to keep that in mind. Also this if you will – we are all movie people here David. No exceptions to that. And none at Century Park East either. In spite of what some sections of the press would have you believe. We want the picture with art written all over it. Which we know you, more than most, are capable of delivering.'

He motioned to his left where Brackman was sitting.

'Before we did this deal, you told Art how you respected us as a studio that protects and enhances its productions. Well that's what we're seeking to do. Look past the flimflam and hyperbole and you'll see that.'

Cousins stood his ground. His arms folded, he was still in defensive mode.

'You're applying yourself to the protecting side of things as I see,' he said, 'but as for the enhancing bit. Not so good. You asked me if I had an actor, which I didn't at the time, but now I do. And he's a perfect fit. You said so yourself.'

'David, I said he can act and has the look of the part. But he's not a name. Therein lies the difficulty for us. And for distribution, the exhibitors, and half a dozen other groups. He's no more a star than I'm the president of France.'

'He will be a name if you guys have the sufficient backbone for it,' responded Cousins, 'that news item alone will push him to the fore. By the time the film goes on release, everyone will have heard of him. Interest levels will be sky-high. And in case I'm not being absolutely clear about this, my proviso is that he be cast as the lead. That's how we move forward on this Anthony. That's how you get your picture with art. So think imaginative. Think ground-breaking. This morning we've had the privilege to witness a great moment. Speaking for myself, I found my Meucci in it. Of this, I'm absolutely certain. And I won't be budged on it, Anthony, Malcolm, Art,' he said, looking at them one at a time, 'Max Pellegrino is my choice. Make that happen and we all get to make this film. Aggregate Pictures included.'

Chouraqui remained unemotional. A sharp nod of the head signified that, for him at least, an impasse had been reached. He'd been expecting resistance naturally, but in a different place. The plan had been that Max Pellegrino would be off the agenda by now. But here he still was. They had not moved away from him. His screen test had added another layer of complexity to a tricky situation.

Chouraqui saw no point in mentioning the other actors now. Where would that conversation go? Nowhere at the present time. The director would just keep bringing it back to the other man. What about Max? What about that great moment of his? Any other names would be rejected out of hand. Simple as that.

He crumpled up a piece of paper in his pocket. It was a list he'd jotted down before leaving LA. Some interesting facts about Max Pellegrino as provided by Gordon Sawyer's contact in Rome. Chief amongst these was an entry about his high-standing in the dubbing industry. The AP head had taken note of it, but little else. It was a side issue, a nothing, he decided. In a career that was likely brimming with such trifles. He chided himself for this. Fuck, 'fucking Olivier,' he thought. He'd listened too well to Gordon Sawyer and his two cents' worth. Moreover, he'd underestimated the Italian. Plainly, he was not just some cockamamie voice actor. The guesswork had been way off base. The fact of the matter was now biting him on the ass.

Chouraqui was feeling tired. But there was no rest for the weary. Particularly with this conundrum on his hands. He had to get on with it. Sort it out come hell or high water. He heard the sound of rising liquid. Then a spurt. A pot of fresh coffee was brewing. The aroma was an agreeable one. It smelt of caramelising sugar. I could go for some of that right now he thought. God knows I could use the kick. He flagged his empty cup and asked for more joe.

'Can I get some of that please,' he said, 'I didn't get any sleep on the flight over, and I have a hunch it's gonna escape me for a time to come.'

ACE IN THE HOLE

The weekly review meeting at Aggregate was held on Friday as usual. Cy Younger presided at the head of the conference table, his notes impeccably arranged and at the ready, if and when he needed them. Spread out before him, in a facing semi-circle, were seven others in the AP hierarchy. They were: Anthony Chouraqui, head of overall production; Danny Rosner, head of business and legal affairs; Gordon Sawyer, head of foreign distribution; Natalie Fleischer, head of ancillary markets and sales; James Plessner, executive vice-president for European production; Elizabeth Margules, executive vice-president for domestic production; and Roscoe Eisenberger, head of domestic distribution.

The purpose of this once-a-week sit-down was clear enough in theory. Information was to be exchanged by way of status reports on every project, no matter what stage of development or production. Problems and red flag issues were broached, solutions put forward and chewed over. Hour of the day permitting, other decisions were also taken in this committee environment. From time to time, casting and director selections were tendered for assessment.

For the most part Cy encouraged the free articulation of ideas and opinions. He felt it important, constructive even, that production and distribution bounce ideas off one another. This was a holistic approach, an all-in concept, upon which he personally set great store. He called for the streamlining of attitudes and objectives. For far too long now, the branches of AP had operated as disparate entities. The company's recent woes had drawn sharp attention to this. Cy wanted to foster discipline and enforce a structure on matters of mutual significance. No longer would there be a tolerable framework by which one division could hold the other responsible for poor decision-making.

Distribution, particularly, had been culpable in this regard. All too often he'd heard the likes of Sawyer and Eisenberger fall back on that old reliable. Such-and-such picture had fallen flat because the earlier stage of the assembly line had not done its job properly. Or perhaps it had done it too well in some cases. Got behind a project which frankly didn't deserve such support. This was a constant gripe of Roscoe Eisenberger. Why the hell did production bankroll this tripe he invariably asked following on from the latest disappointment. And how could his department be expected to perform miracles? If the merchandise reeked, then no amount of perfuming would have an effect. He recommended the hammer should fall in the appropriate place. And on those who were to blame for the Kathy and Harley's of this world. Or the shambles that was No Corsage for Miss Thompson. The time for remedial action was now he said.

But Cy was determined to be even-handed. A state of balance was his natural inclination. Yes, production should submit its ideas to distribution as well as to him. The marketing people could have a direct influence over commodity, but, as an upshot, they could no longer blame production for making mediocre movies they weren't able to peddle. If they participated at foundation stage, then they should also be liable at foundering, were it to occur. As a management technique, it seemed straightforward enough, and even made a degree of sense, but in practice it more often resulted in a state of disorder. Distribution personnel found the abundance of story ideas, treatments, synopses – effectively the nuts and bolts of production – wearisome in the extreme. They were not, by background or experience, a fit for such purpose. And worse still bulky scripts (there always seemed to be one when least desired) and best-selling novels took up valuable time diverting attentions away from other important matters. The guys working at the latter end of the chain were expected to deliver in terms of pickups. Their numbers of late though were not so hot. They were not reaching target. And with the current lack of home-grown material, the pressure was mounting. Workloads of several were overburdened, hours in the day too few.

Production staff were not a bunch of happy campers either. They felt devalued by this new arrangement in which they were obliged to submit every idea and treatment to individuals whose artistic taste they considered negligible at best. Who were these people to have a say they muttered between themselves. How could an exec in distribution, junior or long-serving, have insight on setups and payoffs all of a sudden? They couldn't was the unequivocal answer. And yet here they were.

Well-intentioned as it was, the arrangement was serving to fuel resentments and hostilities. Jeff Forman's Aggro at Aggregate report was more perceptive than perhaps its author knew. AP was indeed a company grappling within. It badly needed some hits and barnburners. Whatever it would take to kick-start morale.

Elizabeth Margules believed she had one of these.

The 41-year old vice-president from Riverside was generally unhurried in her style, but this morning she had the lungs of a longshoreman and a machine-gun ratatata to boot. Was it because she was keenly aware of having to pitch to her colleagues on the other side of the house? Most likely. In any event, it was turning out to be quite a presentation. All in attendance were suitably enthralled. Even the nonbelievers from distribution had stopped picking at their Danish's as they listened. Margules was in a good place and, adding weight to her argument, was the fact that she could claim affinity for the target audience. She had production know-how to vouch for this.

Age of Majority she described as a latter-day Stand by Me. With an edge. It involved older characters than the 1986 film. The gang in this case was on the cusp of adulthood. Hence the title. Queried about its significance, she explained it was to do with having greater years and being of full age. The progression from being a minor to a grown-up was one often fraught with torments and hitches she said. This was the script's strong suit. The themes were long-established, but it was their dramatisation here which was so effective. And affecting she observed with emphasis. A brief debate arose as to what exactly in terms of age separated a minor from an adult. Margules quickly sought to explain this in the context of the story. She said it was 18 generally; for this reason there was no one of Gordie Lachance's vintage in the story. Cy Younger pointed out that in Mississippi the legal age was actually 21.

'Same as in Puerto Rico and Bahrain,' he added, as if this might be enlightening.

Elizabeth Margules pushed forward. She remarked on the matters of sexual awakening and alcoholic consumption which informed some of the more thoughtful moments of the script. And then there was the subplot linking in the character who was hankering after freedom before his 18th birthday. This guy was in a hurry and had, as part of his reasoning, evidence of financial self-sufficiency. The petition scene in the family court was particularly amusing and well-liked by all. Margules continued at breakneck speed and did not let up until she was finished. In conclusion, she said that Age of Majority ought to be acquired by AP. The right price and usual conditions would probably do it. 1.5 million with a gross percentage was agreed as the ceiling Aggregate would go to for this slice of evolving life.

Other matters and issues followed: the script progress, or lack of, on Slamming the Doors, a novel still gracing the bestseller list which the studio had acquired; legal uncertainty as to whether they had the right to remake a certain 1940's screwball comedy; what to do about a financing commitment that had been given to Harry Krentzman three years previously – the other party's legal advisor was screaming renege renege in his client's ear, oral contracts and so on.

Natalie Fleischer gave the lowdown on a difficulty which had arisen in relation to a film Aggregate had obtained as a pickup, and agreed to screen out of competition at the Cannes Film Festival. Losing it for Love was a breezy comedy, with a scheduled mid-summer release, and Fleischer recounted how some menial had only just advised her that the slot at the festival was no longer available. This decision she said was based on rumours surrounding the film; but worse than that was the impertinence of the French staff not to communicate their decision to the studio.

Losing it for Love had neither been easy nor smooth and, instead of affection, had engendered quite opposite feelings for those concerned. The film had gone way over budget for the original investor. Aggregate had stepped into the breach and taken on a completion bond. The fee for this was set at three per cent.

Fleischer complained sullenly about the complete lack of courtesy displayed by those involved. Evidently, they'd been listening a little too well to the grapevine and had assumed the film would not be in the can by the allotted screening date of 24th May. She enquired around the room as to whether any late overtures could be made to have it put back in:

'I don't want it to appear as if we're begging them to show it,' the magna cum laude graduate from Salt Lake City said, 'it's just that the exposure wouldn't hurt.'

Gordon Sawyer piped up telling her he knew someone close to one of the festival's board of directors. He said it might yet be possible to have the film restored to the schedule; adding that if he got a result, Natalie would owe him a bottle of Dom Pérignon. Fleischer replied she had no problem with this deal.

James Plessner had received an overlong script from a first-time writer living in Montreal. It was rank amateurish and sloppy, but there was a quality to Cathedral Silence which was undeniable. Plessner, a self-effacing Bostonian, apologised seeing as how the European market was his more proper remit.

'This is clearly something for domestic, Elizabeth or Anthony,' he said, before being told by Cy that it was quite alright to dip into other territories every so often.

'As long as it's cleared in advance with myself and the colleague in question,' he instructed good-naturedly. 'We don't want treading on toes or accusations of self-aggrandisement. But I like it when there's a crossover such as this. We all learn from one another. Just make sure I hear about it at the earliest possible moment. I won't always agree. But on this occasion – go.'

Plessner was told to negotiate a minimum deal with the writer and then sit on it.

Anthony Chouraqui said he had an idea as to what director might be interested.

The morning was pushing into afternoon and it was time to talk about another director and the ever-changing terms – demands – of his deal.

As a preamble, Cy traced the history of the situation. He said he was aware those present already had a wealth of knowledge vis-à-vis the troubled production. This was to recap for himself as much as anyone else. It was still difficult to fathom all that had happened he said. A major star cut down in his prime. Don Taylor fighting for his life, although indications now were that he would pull through.

He then fast-forwarded to more recent events. The replacement casting matter and how that had gone. And how it hadn't.

For the final piece of the saga, the chief handed over to Anthony Chouraqui. He asked his colleagues to keep an open mind on what they would hear.

'I want a frank exchange of views on this,' he said, 'opinions, how ever diverse, are to be put on the table. No one is to leave this room griping about how they didn't have a say. Anthony, in your own time please.'

Chouraqui got down to it right away. He brought his fellow players up to speed, guiding them through the Rome mission with appropriate detail. The main object of this had been to get the production back on track he said. And, in an out-of-the-ordinary way, this could yet be accomplished.

'Or at the very least, there may be a solution on the cards,' he said, adding, 'I use that word – solution – with a certain frame of reference in mind. The director you have to understand is fixed in the stance he's taking. He won't move or give in on this. We talked it over for hours with him, went through every imaginable option, but it came back each time to his same express position.'

'Which is what?' asked Gordon Sawyer, who suspected he knew the answer.

'To cut a long story short, it's that the Italian actor, who was auditioned, be signed up to play the central character,' Chouraqui responded.

This revelation was met by a number of 'I beg your pardons' and 'come agains' from around the table.

Sawyer waited for the cacophony to die down before starting again. He addressed himself to both Younger and Chouraqui.

'What happened to the giving-in-return you were both counting on?' he enquired. 'The way I remember our conversation, David Cousins was supposed to be the one capitulating and yielding to common good fucking sense. What the fuck transpired to impede that from coming to pass?'

'A very fine screen test,' Chouraqui told him brusquely, 'perhaps not quite Olivier, but not third-rate either.'

This did not appear to strike a chord with Sawyer. Holding a pen between the tips of two extended fingers, he continued without apparent recall.

'I warned you the act of conversion would be extremely difficult in this instant,' he said, 'you knew who you were dealing with. You knew where the points of resistance would be. Effective fucking manoeuvring is supposed to be about achieving an advantageous outcome Anthony. I doubt very much you're going to be inducted into the John Foster Dulles hall of fame any fucking time soon. Your partners in crime too – Archer and…what was the agent's name?'

'Art Brackman,' said Chouraqui, 'and they were both of great value to me in Rome. Not one of us went there with our eyes closed. We knew it would be uphill. We were expecting difficult and then some. The mistake we made, that I made personally, was that I took something for granted. I presumed it to be a token exercise. To be got out of the way quickly and then we could move on. It was the first item of business we had. We never got away from it. The director saw an actor he wants for the lead. He refuses to consider anyone else. He won't test anyone else.'

'And Ben Sanders?' Elizabeth Margules asked.

'No one else,' Chouraqui said definitely. He looked edgy, coiled.

'Sanders is gone in any event,' Natalie Fleischer informed them in her matter-of-factly way, 'I heard it over lunch at Ca'Brea yesterday just as the problem with Losing it for Love was raising its head. Ben Sanders is going to Cannes as well. Trouble is he's staying in Europe for an extended period. He's got himself a mini-series set during the Seven Years' War.

It'll be shooting through to fall.'

'I'm not surprised by that,' Sawyer pooh-poohed. 'There's a lot of history to water down. Mr. Sanders may live to regret it wasn't a much shorter affair.'

'That's neither here nor there,' Margules complained. 'He was a candidate, an option, someone we could have lived with.'

'Not us in distribution,' Sawyer cut in. 'Roscoe and I discussed it before. We don't see anything of substance. He's nondescript, about as exciting as a one-trick pony. Blink and you won't miss what isn't there.'

This got under Elizabeth Margules' skin. She had a gentle voice, and a normally tolerant disposition, but when occasion called for it was not afraid to express herself bluntly.

'Are these impromptu analyses standard in distribution now?' she asked. 'Casting is something we in production kind of take an interest in as well. You know? I thought these meetings were held to appraise in tandem. Not be told one department has already delivered its verdict. Where's the parity in that?'

'It was an exchange of opinions, nothing more,' Sawyer gave back. 'For my part I'm glad Ben Sanders is unavailable. A period piece with him would bore anyone with half a brain to fucking tears.'

'That's not the point I'm making and you know it Gordon,' said Margules. 'Distribution gets to strong-arm enough around here. If you're going to ride roughshod over us, at least have the decency to do it in our presence. I'd much rather have my ideas shot down by crowd than by clique.'

'Did we not just agree to your Age of Majority?' said Sawyer.

'That made for a change,' said Margules, and the acrimony was evident in her tone, 'but it may be that you and Roscoe chewed the fat over that one as well. It seems distribution think themselves the kingmakers.'

Cy decided to step in.

'I think this is better dealt with at another time,' he said. 'For now let's concentrate on immediate matters. Interactions and collaborations I propose we address in isolation. Separately and when there isn't an urgent item such as this.'

Faint murmurs of agreement hovered redundantly about the room.

'Can we backtrack to something Gordon said a moment ago,' Roscoe Eisenberger requested in his California-by-way-of-Delaware accent. He was two years older than Sawyer, with AP three years longer, and could be every bit as obdurate as his associate in distribution.

Cy nodded his consent.

'I, for one, am puzzled by this reference to manoeuvring,' Eisenberger said. 'Was there a deliberate tactic with respect to Italy?'

'There was,' Sawyer told him, 'but it didn't exactly bear fucking fruit.'

'The audition was meant to be an artifice, to function as a doorway in,' Cy said.

'And now that door is very much fucking bolted,' remarked Sawyer.

'We had to make a play of some sort,' Cy continued, ignoring this, 'the intention all along has been to get this production moving again. In the absence of a leading actor, how else would that be possible? Were we to abandon? Just walk away?'

'I said that would be the preferable thing to do,' Sawyer reminded him.

'I know you did,' said Cy, 'and where do you suppose that would put us? How do you see the present configuration lining up Gordon? Our stock in this town has fallen off enough. Reputationally there is no more we can afford to give away.'

'Reputationally, it's the attempt at duplicity that bothers me,' said Eisenberger.

'Which backfired spectacularly,' added Sawyer.

'In one sense it did,' Cy conceded, 'and I'm to blame for that more than anyone else. I underestimated someone's resolve and ability.'

'We both did that,' said Chouraqui.

'David Cousins has resolve alright, I'll give him that much,' said Eisenberger, 'but as for this fabled ability of his. He doesn't always turn it on guys. He doesn't have a perfect score card.'

'Far from it,' said a like-minded Sawyer. 'We all know the havoc that fucking musical of his wreaked. There were more follies in it than Ziegfeld ever had.'

Chouraqui offered a clarification to them both.

'I wasn't referring to David Cousins just then,' he said. 'I meant Max Pellegrino. His resolve and ability.'

'The Italian?' said Sawyer, his eyebrows elevating almost to the tip of his hairline.

'Yes, the Italian,' Cy said quietly. 'I think by now Anthony has conveyed the impression he made. Four men saw the audition in Rome. One of whom was Malcolm Archer.'

'And what's his recommendation?' asked Eisenberger.

'That the decision is ultimately ours to make.'

'Meaning?'

'Meaning he recommends the actor who tested.'

'That's ridiculous,' said Eisenberger, 'and thankfully it is just that – a recommendation. Malcolm is a fine casting director. But he has the luxury of his profession. He's insulated. Set for life. He can afford to throw the occasional curveball.'

'Which he's done once or twice before,' Elizabeth Margules chimed in. 'They weren't accepted, but what did he care.'

'Thank you,' said Eisenberger, 'production and distribution on the same wavelength at long last. There's hope for us yet.'

Margules held back a rueful smile.

'The point being he has absolutely nothing to lose,' Eisenberger continued, 'he won't be doing the heavy lifting here. And no one would associate this with him. Not in the fullness of time anyway. Us ladies and gents at AP on the other hand, well do I need to go into it? A faux pas of this kind would stick like shit to a heel. What then of reputations and stock?'

'Too fucking right,' said Sawyer, 'and even if we need the film this badly, we shouldn't be tipping our hat to that fact so fucking overtly.'

'How were things left in Rome?' asked Natalie Fleischer.

'They were left as open-ended as we could manage,' answered Chouraqui, 'but he doesn't want to hang about.'

'He was more than happy to do that just a few days ago,' James Plessner commented. 'Can we not take another pass at it sooner than...?'

'Absolutely no point,' Chouraqui told him. 'Art Brackman, his agent, was not able to coax or urge him.'

'And he's another of the mesmerised, right?'

'That would be a slight overstatement, but generally speaking, yes.'

'That puts the Italian's fan base at what three? Four?'

'Four including Cousins. What's more, he's the guy's benefactor,' said Sawyer.

'We'll all be that if he gets the part,' sighed Eisenberger.

Cy forced his way back in. He shrugged hugely.

'Witticisms aside, let's be honest about this,' he said. 'We have no other actor. And even if we did, it's clear the director will not agree to anyone else. He has told Anthony he will not proceed with the film unless the Italian is given approval.'

'So proceed without him then,' said Eisenberger. 'Fire his ass.'

Danny Rosner's voice finally came to life.

'Not an option we can contemplate,' he advised, shaking his head. 'Far too many things stacked in his favour. Plus he's the producer, how ever elastic a term that may be to some people here. Others, I can assure you, would see it differently; argue it very successfully as well. Especially those with a legalistic bent of mind. And besides all that, if we were to sack him, who directs the thing? We wouldn't come within a hair's breadth of another director. Certainly no time soon.'

'Are there no extenuating circumstances?' asked Eisenberger.

'Of course there are, but he hasn't given us any,' said Rosner. 'Before he didn't have an actor, now he does. He can justifiably say problem solved. Let's make the movie.'

'That's exactly what he's saying,' said Chouraqui.

Rosner dropped his hands between his knees, leaned forward in his chair.

'You can not fire a man who wants to go to work,' he said, 'well actually you can fire him, but how is it possible to defend that act. It isn't. In the absence of our director committing a crime, or suddenly losing his mind, or something else totally outrageous, he remains with us. Gordon, I realise it's not what you wanted to hear. Any latent homicidal tendencies you might have, I would suggest be controlled. Short of you killing him, there's no other way at the moment. My apologies for the not-so-glad tidings.'

'You don't seem so terribly cut up about it yourself Danny,' Sawyer observed. 'What's your opinion on this fucking mess? Do you want to compound it too? Right now you sound like you have the appetite for it.'

'I can promise you I do not, nor will I ever have, an inclination to compound difficulties for this company,' Rosner answered back squarely.

'But you're not exactly ill-disposed to the concept from what I'm hearing, are you?'

'I think it represents the best way forward. The only way forward most likely.'

'The lesser of two evils?'

'I didn't say that,' Rosner replied, parsing Eisenberger's words, 'if there's another course of action you can suggest then please – by all means.'

Eisenberger remained stony silent.

'Case in point,' Rosner went on, 'our beloved Tyler Pinkerton. The next one up for him is what? One? Two years away?'

'Two years,' answered James Plessner, who was sitting next to him. 'It won't be going into pre-production until next year at the earliest.'

'That puts it in 1997 so,' Rosner worked out, 'and that would mean a break in the series of how many years?'

'Five in effect,' Plessner advised, 'subject, of course, to the back catalogue dispute being cleared up once and for all.'

'That will make it the longest break in the series if I'm not mistaken. Right?'

'Yes, but it did almost get up to three-and-a-half once. Back in the 70's.'

'Still though,' Rosner said insistently, 'can the significance of that be grasped by everyone? That's five years at this remove. And it could change again.'

'Your argument being?' Eisenberger queried.

'Tyler Pinkerton is illustrative of our central problem,' said Rosner. 'It's the whole thing in microcosm. Cy is quite correct in what he says – our stock in this town has fallen off enough. Lack of ventures into the market place is killing us.'

'The script submissions are getting better Danny,' said Margules, 'today's meeting for example.'

'Yes, but the only way for that figure was up Elizabeth. And it's nothing remotely like a couple of years ago. It's fine to be acquiring properties again, but none of them will be in theatres anytime soon. In fact, chances are Tyler Pinkerton might get there ahead of them. Meantime, there is a deficiency and it needs to be worked on.'

'And what we have we must hold,' Cy included, 'that's of critical importance. If not, then we are regarded as just a piecemeal outfit. There's not much esteem in the occasional or the up-and-down. Even less so in the way of business.'

'I agree,' said Rosner. 'The key right now is to exhibit those more durable qualities.'

Roscoe Eisenberger contorted at this.

'Danny, let me jog your memory here,' he said. 'Do you happen to recall a memo from June of last year? Written by our respected head of business and legal. In it, he talked about the desirability of attaching a marquee name to this film. What's happened to that? Why the contradiction all of a sudden?'

'Yeah,' Sawyer corresponded. 'Un-fucking-qualified as it is.'

Rosner answered them both.

'Obviously a lot has happened since then,' he said, 'and besides, I think we could make it work to our advantage.'

'We could?!' Eisenberger boomed. 'That's quite a sweeping statement. I don't know how production would feel about it, but as for distribution, and marketing. How do you sell someone no one's ever heard of?!'

'You do it with intent,' said Rosner. 'You draw attention to the fact and you do it as unashamedly as you can. This is the point of difference which separates our film from all the others. This is its unique selling point. The guy no one heard of up until now. The newcomer, who is actually an old hand, and getting his big opportunity. Right there are the ingredients for a publicity campaign.'

'For the johnny-come-lately it's aces to be sure,' Sawyer disparaged.

'In terms of the marquee though, Jennifer Carrington would have to get top billing,' James Plessner submitted.

'As only she should,' agreed Elizabeth Margules. 'Vivien Leigh was ahead of Marlon Brando in the credits for A Streetcar.'

Sawyer performed an exaggerated double take.

'Can you hear yourselves for chrissake?' he said. 'You're talking about a classic film and two Oscar-winning actors as if they were one and the same with this.'

'Brando was also an unknown back then,' Chouraqui reasoned.

'Not on Broadway he wasn't,' Fleischer corrected. 'The play came before the film.'

'Yes, but Liz's point is that Vivien Leigh was chosen because she was Scarlett O'Hara. The others were not anywhere close to her level of fame.'

'But we're talking about Brando here! And he turned out to be a sensation.'

'So could Max Pellegrino.'

'It's not that kind of role Anthony. Antonio Meucci is more like a boy scout compared to Stanley Kowalski.'

'Yeah, there's nothing in it to equal the Napoleonic Code scene.'

'Well now you're just being totally unfair,' said Chouraqui. 'You're arguing there's not enough dramatic meat in the role. Which there is by the way. How long is it since either of you read the script by the way? Did you read it in its entirety?'

'Last year sometime,' answered Eisenberger.

Gordon Sawyer's response was shiftier.

'I read most of it,' he said, his voice leaden, 'didn't care very much for it. A spinach movie if you ask me. Good for you perhaps, but hardly mouth-watering fare.'

'What about this screen test?' asked a curious Rosner. 'Is there dramatic meat in that as you say?'

'Yes, very.'

'And he manages to pull it off?'

'More than.'

'Well in that case, would it not make sense for us to see it? At the very least we can decide if the Italian should go forward for the next Streetcar revival.'

Cy went along with this. Without further formalities, he suggested they descend the one storey to the eleventh floor screening room.

On their way down, there were slivers of conversation, and one or two bellyaches.

Anthony Chouraqui talked to his fellow cinephile, James Plessner, about an old King Vidor film called The Crowd.

'The director wanted a fresh face for it,' he said. 'He picked out an extra he saw on the MGM lot and cast him in the lead role. So there is a precedent for this kind of thing. It would not be the first time.'

Gordon Sawyer meantime had concerns closer to home. And away.

'What do I say to the guys in Cannes if we go ahead with this fucking madness?' he speculated noisily to Roscoe Eisenberger. 'How do I explain it in French or any other fucking language?'

Natalie Fleischer too had questions of her own. These were more internally prompted.

'Has this been vetted by New York already?' she whispered to Elizabeth Margules. 'Was what we just sat through a done deal?'

'Do you think it was?' asked her colleague. 'Has Cy already seen the audition?'

'Of course he has,' replied Fleischer. 'He had to be familiar with it ahead of the meeting. It's not his style to go into something unrehearsed. Besides, when all is said and done, the final decision is his. If McWhirter have no great problem with that, then it becomes reality. In all probability, he was testing it out on us as much as anything else. Clever guy.'

They arrived in the screening room and picked out individual seats.

Discarded coffee cups and ashtrays were moved out of the way. A redolent whiff of cigarette smoke hung about from a previous day's viewing.

Cy asked for their fullest attention, promising it would not take long.

'As I said from the get-go, opinions are to be voiced without reservation,' he said.

He signalled to Freddy, the projectionist, to begin.

They watched the scene three times; in the order it had been recorded. The third, again, was clearly the best.

Absolute silence during this last one.

Even Gordon Sawyer managed to keep his heavy breathing in check.

The lights went up when it was finished.

Cy thanked Freddy and told him to take a break.

He then stood up in front of the others, avoiding the temptation to divine immediate reaction by appearance.

The direct approach was the preferred one.

'Well?' he asked.

Sweet Smell of Success

The announcement that Max Pellegrino, obscure Italian actor, who just so happened to be Don Taylor's screen voice in that corner of the world, would take the leading role in David Cousins' delayed production, Echo of Passions, was met with extensive kinds of reaction. At a domestic level, most of these were favourable.

In Rome, La Repubblica kicked up its heels pronouncing the decision, *'a wonderful finale to this most popular of stories.'*

Writing in his column, Umberto Spada hailed it as, *'something those of us with open minds and generous hearts can feel glad about.* He continued, *'most people are in possession of these attributes, and thankfully so. The news is a victory for optimism – something those more cynical elements rubbish as naivety. Today the dreamers have their riposte to such belittlement. It's Forza Max. Give it everything you've got.'*

La Repubblica was one of many to weigh in on the news.

Il Messaggero's Luisa Laurito penned her hopes that, *'this is the beginning of great things for the actor. There were very few of us who knew anything about him a short time ago. And when he first appeared in black-and-white, hardly any could have cared less. But what a change in his fortunes, a veritable deus ex machina. Films are normally the sole domain of such unexpected triumphs. Now we have one in the real world. It has brought Max Pellegrino to prominence. Let's hope what he does with it will make for a fitting next chapter. A worthy successor to the excitement and coverage up to now. What a great sequel that would make.'*

In other cities and regions, the acclaim was similarly bestowed.

'Max emerges on the biggest stage of all,' swooned Corriere della Sera's Marietta Assante. The journalist went on to extol the actor for his modest deportment throughout the preceding frenzy, *'but now he must arm himself for the tumult and upheaval which will come his way. His name will adorn column inches in the time ahead. Expect the rummaging Max. It goes with the territory.'*

Florence's La Nazione put its two cents' forward describing it as, *'a truly avant-garde moment, the sort of thing mainstream cinema so rarely attempts.'* It commended especially the Hollywood studio behind the decision, identifying it mistakenly as, *'Accumulated Pictures, based in Los Angeles.'*

And from Il Gazzettino, the inevitable, perhaps, *'La Dolce Vita for Max,'* which continued, *'the name of the little-known voice actor is on everyone's lips. He will now be seen as well as heard. Sound and image come together opportunely.'*

Il Quarto Stato's response was surprisingly low-key. Fabio Paparazzo welcomed the news, but looked forward deliberately to an exclusive with the man of the hour.

'*The story originated in these pages,*' he reminded his readers, '*and we intend to follow it every step of the way. Max's breakthrough has been hard-earned. He's waited a long time for it. But there won't be much in the way of respite. The cameras will be rolling very soon. We hope to get his thoughts before then.*'

Gianluca Della Pasqua had a final word to say on the matter. Then he would be done with it he swore. Despite the turn of events, he was remaining firm in his convictions. He would hold out and be proven correct in the long run.

'*The tawdry vignette will be brief, the dazzling kitsch will soon fade,*' he predicted. Elsewhere, Max was referred to as, '*that pretender who has backed into the limelight. The charade however will unravel. This affectation of his will be laid bare.*'

Stateside, response to the casting was less effusive and more industry-specific. The Los Angeles Times' Bill Downey wondered if it represented, '*a plumbing of the depths for Aggregate Pictures; an indication as to how low the studio would go to keep hold of the Rome production.*'

The Daily News in New York suggested there was occasionally a, '*gossamer divide between fact and fiction. In this case a Hollywood studio has presented us with a scenario few writers could have concocted. The rest of this narrative is anyone's guess. How it ends will be the basis for many an anxiety and jagged nerve.*'

The Chicago Sun-Times put it in more basic terms: '*Hollywood lays a wager on Italian John Doe,*' it stated.

The Denver Post was more forthright, referring to what it called, '*the intangibles surrounding the choice.*' Regarding Aggregate Pictures, it concluded, '*in effect they are taking a shot in the dark. On a big X.*'

USA Today, on the other hand, was jauntier in tone. It broke the news with the eye-catching, and less judgemental: '*It Could Only Happen at the Movies.*'

Tom Steiner read the headline in the national daily, but no further than that did he care to go. Instead he consulted Daily Variety. Todd Rosenfelt was his unambiguous self. '*Aggregate takes major chance on unknown actor,*' he reported in a prominent caption on the front page. Rosenfelt gave an account of the events which had led to this, '*extraordinary selection*' as he labelled it. He also touched on the problems Aggregate Pictures had been having on the production to date, writing, '*the studio, under the watch of Cy Younger, has been afflicted by more than its fair share of troubles in recent times. It's difficult to understand a decision of this nature, no matter what light one puts it in. Was AP really so bereft of choices? Had every other option been explored? Or does the explanation lie elsewhere? Is there another agenda? A subterfuge at play? A reasonable person might well argue gimmick here. Something that's done to grab attention. If so, they've succeeded in that much. But the outcome of their decision-making will not be apparent for some time yet. The film's premiere is at least a year away. Reckless choice or inspired pick? We will just have to wait and see. Including the powers-that-be at Aggregate Pictures.'*

Tom closed the trade, stood up, and walked around to the front of his desk. Leaning against it, he stared out through the transparent doors. The layout of the floor was roughly a square. He had one corner of it. Another belonged to Ernest Lovett. Another was the domain of Larry Reeves. The fourth was the literary department, and whoever was in the hot seat there. Right next to his office was one of the small kitchens in which the trainees were responsible for keeping the fridge stocked and the coffee hot. Failure in either of these areas would incur much finger-pointing and the ensuing wrath of Ernest Lovett.

The philosophy of SLR was simple, and it was impressed on new recruits from an early time. Tom took personal charge of this. The first few years of the company, he and his partners had spent a lot of time with the trainees. They wanted people they liked. People they thought would fit in. They were looking for a certain type – individuals who could communicate. Tom knew how important this was. He still included it as part of the induction he gave when a newbie walked through his door. He instructed them as to how this business was about sales, and the first thing you sold was yourself. If you couldn't do that, then it was time for a career rethink. No point in kicking around here for a few months. Later on, for those who were sticking it out in the mailroom, or other menial station, he'd offer a variation on this advice.

'Working hard and getting the notice you deserve is all well and good,' he told an underling one day, 'but most of us here – your bosses I mean – couldn't care less about that. It's the fuckups we recall. You'll be judged on those much more than the wonderful job you're doing. It's not complicated. Do what you're told and avoid the half-assed or nearly-complete. We may not always appreciate it when you do, but you can be damn sure we'll remember it if you don't.'

In all his years in the business he was certain he'd never seen anything like this. Off the wall to be sure he thought. Aggregate Pictures wasn't taking a leap of faith as gentler voices suggested. It was potentially fucking up on a monumental scale.

He told this to Susie, his personal assistant of two years. Every now and then they shot the industry breeze together. Unlike other assistants in the organisation, Susie was not required to answer the phones. Tom already had a secretary for this.

The 27-year old often grumbled about his holding her back.

'I want off this desk, I want to be an agent,' was a familiar chant of hers. Mostly they kidded about it, but there were some serious exchanges as well.

'I've become much too invaluable to you, it's my own undoing,' Susie pronounced on one occasion, as she canvassed yet again for her future. 'You have to give me my break Tom. I joined SLR for more than this. I can't be your schlepper forever.'

He agreed with this, but quickly found excuses to defer her promotion. She was indispensable to him after all. Susie never fucked up. Occasionally, he felt guilty for slowing down her advancement, for not giving her what she deserved. And today more than ever. She was all over the announcement from AP. Saying what a great thing it was. Passing comments as to how some people had all the luck.

'Me, I'll be on this desk for another two years,' he overheard her say to Jean, his secretary. 'Kids starting in the mailroom this morning will get ahead before I do.'

By mid-afternoon, he didn't want to hear any more about it. So he called her in, invited her to take a seat. Susie perched herself on his couch. Tom's office was catching the heavy sun. Sitting directly in front of her, he appeared like a shadow.

'What's up?' he asked.

Without missing a beat, she went straight into it.

'Just the usual,' she answered. 'I'm still outside. In more ways than one.'

Tom was in no mood for the cryptic metaphors.

'So you keep mentioning,' he said. 'All day you've been on it. Ever since you came in this morning, absolute overdrive.'

'No doubt you'll say you've heard it all before,' she replied.

'Yes, I have,' he said, 'but never as annoying as this. We get on well together Susie, but don't forget your position here. I'm your boss. I'll decide when it's time.'

'Of course,' she said, folding her arms.

'And what is it with this AP story?' he resumed. 'Why the hell are you comparing your situation to that? There is no comparison young lady. It's a fly-by-night thing. Nothing else. Do you honestly think that guy is ready for it? He isn't. I saw him in Rome. I saw the rank amateur that he is. David Cousins will walk all over him. The experience for him will be like taking direction from a cape buffalo.'

Susie tittered faintly. She knew Cousins wasn't on Tom's Christmas gift list.

'That's better,' he said. 'Remember what you're getting here is an education. A foundation. I want you to understand the business inside out. You think you've been moving too slow and you're probably right. You're overqualified. You have been for the past two years. I needed to be sure you had the endurance for it. I don't want to waste time and money training someone and then have them go off to another company or different career. I want someone who loves what they do.'

'You know I love it,' said Susie. 'I just get impatient. When I started on your desk, I knew it was a plum job.'

'And still is,' Tom joked.

'It's made me hungry for more, going to the weekly meeting for one thing,' she said.

'I'm very glad to hear it,' he said. 'I told you I'll decide when it's time. And it's time. There's an opening coming up in lit. I know it's a department close to your heart, what with all those books you recommend me. You interested?'

As soon as her excitement and heartfelt thanks were done, he had words of advice.

'Ron Kramer is not the easiest person to work for,' he reminded her, 'but your attention to detail is so good, even he should be impressed. Expect the job to take every hour of the day God sends you. Ron won't let you have it any other way.'

Susie said she knew this. She gave him a hug. He told her to go celebrate.

'Have some fun in the meantime,' he said, 'because your life is going to change again. You'll be living on the telephone. Your office will be a second home. Forget having a personal life; there won't be time. But love every second of it. We want you to succeed. Sell yourself, as you always do, and there's no way you can miss kid.'

Susie went out leaving him alone. Tom beamed as he watched her tell Jean the good news. He felt pride in her. A little pleased with himself as well. He'd done the right thing. Backed a winner. Good judgement had prevailed in this part of town at least. And as for that other farce. He was going to put it out of his mind. It wasn't worth any more thought. He doubled his copy of USA Today and binned it. Daily Variety he placed in his out-tray. Susie could have it. She took the editions he was finished with. It would be a memento of the occasion. The day she got promoted in SLR. Something worth remembering.

In another office, down the broad corridor from Tom's, a young agent named Jonny Lewysohn was trying to put a call through to Rome. It was taking time. Jonny was anxious. He needed a boost. Things had not been going so well recently. He'd been partying too much for one thing. And taking his eye off the ball as a consequence. A few nights before, he'd got very drunk after a premiere in Westwood. The next day in the office played out like a comedy. Only without the canned laughter. One boneheaded thing led to another. An argument with one of his clients prompted a summons from Tom Steiner. He berated Lewysohn for being an idiot. Told him to cut out the booze and get himself back on track. Or else.

'I'm gonna kick your ass all over town before I let you blow this,' he said, all at the top of his lungs, 'start impressing the hell out of me again, like you did in the beginning. Get your fucking mojo back. Get your head out of the fucking bottle.'

It was a wake-up call. That was how Jonny chose to regard it. He was determined to get back the fine rep he'd worked so hard to earn. The same resolve which had brought him out here in the first place. The son of a banker, who'd dropped out of Harvard, he airbrushed his defunct college education. He did have a degree he maintained. The references could be provided at the drop of a hat. The fake stationery was at the ready.

In spite of his eastern credentials background, Jonny was brash and hyper. He'd shown as much, set himself apart from the rest, with a curiosity combined with fearlessness that allowed him to get involved with those in positions of authority. It had served him well so far, but it wasn't going to take him all the way. He still had a lot to learn. His focus was too scattershot. He tried to juggle too many balls. No one thing got enough of his attention. He was not like Tom Steiner's PA, Susie Shukat. And this chink in his armour had become more pronounced recently. Too much of the high life as he had to acknowledge to himself. It was time to take a step back from all that. And take a few towards solidity.

'Pronto,' came up a male voice on the phone.

Lewysohn was temporarily lost in thought and did not hear it.

The man on the other end followed up with a question.

'Chi è?' he asked.

Jonny sprang into life.

'Mi chiamo Jonny Lewysohn,' he said, and then switched, 'I'm looking for Max Pellegrino. Is this he?'

'This is Max,' the voice replied. 'Can I help you?'

'Yes you can Mr. Pellegrino,' said Lewysohn, as he twisted a Blackhawk pencil between his fingers, 'let me introduce myself. I'm an agent with one of the top entertainment agencies here in Los Angeles, California. Your name is appearing everywhere today, coast-to-coast in this part of the world. It's quite something.'

'Thank you,' said Max, unsure as to whether this was a compliment.

'Mr. Pellegrino, forgive the time of day. I realise it's night there, but I'm calling you because of the unique position you find yourself in. You have a great opportunity to capitalise on it.'

'You mean the film here in Rome?'

'Not just this film Mr. Pellegrino, future films, future roles. You're hot property right now. Not just on the historic streets of Rome. Here in the hills of Hollywood as well. Let me cut to the chase Max. May I call you Max?'

'Of course.'

'And you can call me Jonny. That's Jonny without the h incidentally. In case you want to write it down.'

Max asked him to spell his surname and Lewysohn obliged. The agent then resumed. Employing a catchy tempo as he went along, he did not mince his words.

'First of all, do you have representation at the moment?' he asked.

Max replied yes. He told Lewysohn about Franco and the many years of their professional relationship. The agent listened intently. There were a number of uh-huhs as he processed the information. Then some more questions.

'And are you happy going forward with Mr. Bonacossa?' he asked. 'Given your changed, and much-improved circumstances, do you intend staying with him?'

'I haven't discussed that yet...in fact we haven't spoken,' Max said flatly. He deliberately let his answer hover there to see what the other man would say.

'You haven't spoken to him?' Lewysohn repeated, exaggerating the incredulous tone. 'I find that very strange Max. If he's your agent, why isn't he talking to you? You're his client and you just struck gold! He should be paying you more attention. Don't you think? Like the Cannes Film Festival, for example. Was that mentioned to you?'

'Yes, something about an existing arrangement involving Don Taylor and Jennifer Carrington. They were due to appear there?'

'That's correct,' said Lewysohn, 'pre-publicity for Echo of Passions. Believe me, it begins this early nowadays. The plan was they'd attend the last weekend of the festival. Give interviews, take promotional pictures, beat the drum generally. They still want to go ahead with all that, with you and Jennifer. Again, it's a great opening for you. Cannes is a mecca for publicity man. You'll get to raise your profile even more. The timing couldn't be any better. As a matter of fact, I'll be there myself.'

'Perhaps we could meet then?' Max suggested.

Lewysohn's response to this was to up the ante.

'That would be good Max,' he said, 'but I didn't call you today to organise a get-together. I think you can appreciate that. I'd like our relationship to be on a more formal footing before then. In short, I'd like to represent you Max. I know I'm just a voice on the phone right now. No different from any of the...perhaps you've had offers already?'

'No,' replied Max. 'You're the first one. My sister and friends have called. Some people I know through work as well.'

'But not your agent?'

'No,' said Max, as he spied the HQD Pharmaceuticals copy which was beginning to gather dust. 'The day of the audition at Cinecittà, I withdrew from a job he'd set up for me. It wasn't because I thought I had the film. I didn't know. It was for other reasons.'

'What was the job?' asked Lewysohn.

'It was voiceover work. The kind of thing I've done many times.'

Jonny cleared his throat and pushed on further. To Max his logic combined common sense and rhapsody.

'Well then, can I suggest you were already making a break with him that day,' he said, 'you probably had no idea just how well the audition had gone. Maybe I didn't get it you thought. Maybe I didn't nail it the way I ought to have. I know lots of actors think like that. And yet, in spite of those doubts, you turned down perfectly good work. That in itself tells me a lot Max. It speaks of someone who wants change. And now you're most definitely going to get it. Only question is, who do you want in your corner? Mr. Bonacossa? Or someone else? It's up to you.'

'You'll have to let me think about it,' said Max. 'Can I get your number please? I will call you back as soon as I can.'

'Sure,' said Lewysohn. He included the international code as he gave it out.

'And what's the name of your company?' Max enquired as a by-the-way. 'Is it well-known in Hollywood?'

'It is Max,' said Lewysohn, chuckling, 'but I'd be misleading you if I called it mine. The name is SLR. But the L in that doesn't stand for Lewysohn. I'm just one of the foot soldiers trying to ply his trade.'

'What does SLR stand for?'

'Steiner, Lovett, Reeves,' said Lewysohn.

'Steiner?' repeated Max. It was the only name that registered with him.

'Yes, Tom Steiner,' said Lewysohn. 'Do you know of him?'

Before Max could answer, he put it together.

'What am I saying? You probably met him when he was in Rome with Don Taylor. Right? I heard you met Don. Which means you most likely met Tom. The two of them were best friends. Tom has taken Don's accident real badly. He doesn't show it, but it's there nonetheless. We care about our clients at SLR Max. What more can I say? I hope you'll bear that in mind when you think it over.'

He decided to throw in one extra inducement. Just for good measure.

'I also hope you'll get back to me soon. Like I said, Cannes is very much on the horizon. It'd make good sense for you to have new representation by then, if you so decide. You know I was at the Venice Film Festival last September. Wonderful occasion. And the city, out of this world. I learnt a few phrases in Italian before travelling. I'm one of those people who believe in making the effort. Too many of us go and just expect the locals to speak English. Well not me. I think it's disrespectful, even an imposition. Anyway, going back to what I said about this opportunity you have – raramente Max. You know what I'm saying? The kind of thing that comes along very seldom. If at all.'

'Thank you,' said Max.

He was still thinking about the name which had come up. He wondered if Tom Steiner had okayed this approach to him. In all likelihood no he imagined. God knows he'd been condescending enough before. And then there was that Italian nobody mimic remark of his. How could that be forgotten? No chance. This guy Lewysohn was acting of his own accord he figured. Had to be. Well there was nothing wrong with that. Certainly not from his point of view. What's more, he could visualise what Tom Steiner's reaction might be.

Smiling he said, 'thank you for the call. I will get back to you quickly. I promise that. Cut to the chase as you say.'

Tom almost blew a gasket on hearing the news.

'When I told you to get your mojo back, I meant concentrate on the fucking essentials,' he bellowed irately.

Jonny Lewysohn stood at the back of his office. Po-faced, but defiant. He tried to answer back, but was waved down.

'I'm far from finished,' Tom said. 'For once, listen! What the fuck has got into you? What made you think a short-term fluke like this was worth chasing? And without telling anyone! Without having regard to the fucking guidance myself, Larry, or Ernest would be able to give! We've over 90 years' experience between the three of us! Does that count for nothing with you? Or is it something else? Do you have some kind of professional prescience all of a fucking sudden? Because if you do, you better give it up here in double quick time. Well?'

Lewysohn raked through his hair before he answered. He was not one to retreat behind a wall of wounded silence. Not afraid either to stand his ground when he thought he was right. But it wasn't worth screaming back. Especially at the boss. His voice was quiet. It was calculated to force Tom leaning forward to hear.

'You've always told us to empower ourselves,' he said.

'What?'

'Obsequious servility; that's something you mentioned from day one. How you don't believe in it as a concept. How you want us to think on our feet. Go with our instinct from time to time. Well that's what I'm doing here. I'm listening to my gut.'

'Which may be full of booze still! Did you dry out like I told you to? If you made that call under the influence, that's it for you! Done! Outta here!'

'I didn't make the call under the influence Tom,' Lewysohn replied, 'I did it sober as a judge. The way I intend to do everything from now on. I've turned over a new leaf.'

'I'm not sure that's such a good thing,' said Tom. 'It's demeaning to this agency far as I'm concerned. Bad enough one company in this town goes and makes an exhibition of itself. But two! And us, the ones who handle Don Taylor. They'll cast us as fucking lowlifes. Parasites who have no thought or feeling beyond the deal. Always the fucking deal with them they'll say. It's a debasement quite frankly.'

This caused Lewysohn to reconsider.

'I didn't think of it like that,' he said, a more diffident tone creeping into his voice.

'Of course you didn't!'

'Do you want me to call him back?' the agent offered, 'say that we're having second thoughts on account of...'

He was unable to conjure up a plausible excuse.

'No,' said Tom. 'You've already put it out there. Backpedalling would make us look even worse. Just leave it with him as is. With a little bit of luck he might say no. Or maybe some other jerk will make him an offer. What did you say about commission and scale?'

'Nothing,' replied Lewysohn. 'I figured it too early for that conversation.'

'Well you did one thing right at least,' said Tom.

'And if he accepts? If he says yes?'

'In that case, you have to stick to what you offered him – representation. By you. Note I lay emphasis on the by you part. As for myself, I don't want anything to do with it. Nor do I want to hear about it if and when...'

He formulated the thought crossing his mind.

'Are you acquainted with David Cousins?' he asked.

Lewysohn nodded.

'I met him at a post-Oscar party last year,' he said.

'And how did he strike you?'

'Seemed like a nice enough guy. A bit high-strung perhaps. I guess it was the buzz he was getting off winning the Academy Award.'

'You got him on a good day,' said Tom. 'I just hope you're ready for the bad. And all the bullshit that goes with it.'

Lewysohn's posture inclined.

'I saw Fred Topolski on the Howard Holden show like everyone else,' he said. 'I know he had an ill repute back a few years ago. He's done with that by all accounts.'

Tom shook his head firmly.

'Don't count your chickens on that score kemosabe,' he said, 'the David Cousins I know is loitering with intent. And look at the way things have panned out for him! A two-bit actor he can push around. A studio that caves in more than a dodgy mineshaft. Jesus! The fucker must feel absolutely stoked. He must think all his Christmases have come at once. I hope you're equipped for his festive season pal. You have your work cut out for you if your Italian friend says yes!'

Fabio Paparazzo found Max in the gardens of Villa Doria Pamphili. The actor was out for a late morning jog. He saw the journalist approaching and wondered how he'd known where to look. The two men shook hands. Paparazzo offered his congratulations.

'You're still a difficult man to get hold of,' he remarked, his face a half-smile, 'I stopped at that edicola close to your building. The owner said he saw you leaving in your tracksuit, told me here would be my best bet.'

'You got me,' said Max, raising his arms aloft.

'I'm not so sure I have,' replied Paparazzo. 'There's still the outstanding matter of the follow-up interview. You remember that? You agreed to it before I went to. Cinecittà.'

'Yes, of course,' said Max, 'a lot has happened since then.'

'It certainly has Max. A virtual whirlwind. More than ever before, people want to hear your reaction to it all. How does it feel to be a celebrity? Are you excited or nervous about what lies ahead?'

'A bit of both,' said Max, and he stopped in mid-sentence. 'I don't want to give an interview at the moment though Fabio. The timing might not be so good.'

'I disagree,' said Paparazzo. 'I don't think it could be any better.'

'Yes, it could,' said Max, 'at a further point in time – when filming has begun. I could invite you to Cinecittà for an exclusive from the set. By then I'd be more comfortable with this new situation of mine. Hopefully, I'd be doing well in the role also. Proving myself worthy of it. That's very important to me.'

'I can see it is,' said Paparazzo, 'but how about giving me the best of both worlds. A few words now. Your initial thoughts at the very least. And later on, sure, I'll visit you at Cinecittà. Just try and keep me away.'

'No,' said Max, remaining adamant, 'I'd prefer to do it like this. No airs and graces before it starts. Strictly low-key.'

'And Cannes? Do you imagine that will be low-key?'

Paparazzo nodded.

'Yes I know about that,' he continued, 'you're to do publicity for the film with Jennifer Carrington. They have you booked in at the Carlton Hotel I understand. Very chic indeed. There'll be lots of photos and interviews. Shaking of hands and rubbing of shoulders. All that is part and parcel of the festival. But hardly low-key Max. Wouldn't you say? Not the kind of to-do that goes unnoticed.'

'That's different,' said Max, 'I have no choice. It's something I'm obliged to do.'

'And I'm obliged to do my job Max. Help me out here. A few words is all I ask. I want to be ahead of the Cannes crowd. Over there I'm only another scribe. Just one more hand plying his trade.'

'Are you also going to France?' asked Max.

'Yes, I am,' Paparazzo told him. 'Il Quarto Stato wants to track your every move. I have instructions from my editor to stay hot on your heels. Go where you go. Report what you have to say. He's usually a subtle man, but on this occasion. Not that I mind by the way. Jennifer Carrington will be there too. Now she is a very good reason to follow you around.'

'Sounds as if you like her.'

'Who doesn't Max? She's a peach. A face like hers was meant to be in the movies. A star of the...'

The journalist's mind changed course.

'Incidentally,' he said, 'have you heard the latest about Don Taylor? His condition has become more stable. He's been moved to a high dependency unit. Then it's a Solventi ward. And, after that, back to the States.'

'That's good to hear,' said Max.

'He'll never act again though,' said Paparazzo. 'I understand he may have difficulty communicating. Plus the likelihood of a wheelchair is being mentioned. For the rest of his life. What a terrible thing to happen to anyone.'

'Terrible indeed,' Max agreed, shaking his head.

'You haven't been back to the hospital since?'

'No.'

'Will you go again?' Paparazzo asked, eyeing him more closely.

'I don't think that would be such a good idea,' replied Max.

He was interrupted by two ladies who clearly had recognised him. They were not shy about it either. Bright and breezy twenty-somethings, they spoke to him, offering their good wishes. One was blonde with shoulder-length hair. The other was darker; attractive in an open, easy way. On the inside of her left wrist was a nautical star tattoo. Paparazzo noticed it as he surveyed this flash of adulation.

'So how does that feel? Must be good?' he said when they were gone.

Max was self-conscious in his reply.

'I'm not sure,' he said. 'It's a new experience for me. I'm a greenhorn when it comes to that kind of thing.'

He smiled to himself.

'What is it?' Paparazzo asked.

'I was just thinking about Gianluca Della Pasqua,' Max explained. 'What he might say if he were here. Something unfavourable no doubt.'

'Always,' said Paparazzo.

Max affected the columnist's raspy voice.

'Can't even handle the attention he's getting now!' he said. 'What an undeserving interloper! What a travesty to film-making the world over!'

'That's an uncanny impression,' said Paparazzo. 'You really capture the old boy. Words and attitude. But give praise where praise is due.'

'What do you mean?'

'I mean that without Gianluca's contribution – vitriolic though it was – none of this might have happened. It came together real well when you think about it. The more he frothed, the more he whipped up support for you.'

'I guess so,' said Max. He seemed eager then to change the subject.

Paparazzo, however, was not letting it go.

'How do you think he knew the name of your poliziesco Max?' he asked again. 'Any ideas? Personally, I haven't been able to figure it out.'

'Is it so important that you know?' Max said.

'Not important, but I'm curious,' said the journalist. 'It's my business to be that way.'

'Off the record?'

'Yes. You actually know?'

'I do,' said Max. 'I told him the name. I was the one who tipped him off about it.'

'You did?'

'Knock it off Fabio,' said Max, a conspiratorial lift to his eyebrows. 'You had an idea. That's why you kept asking me.'

'Ok, I had my suspicions,' Paparazzo admitted. 'The last time we spoke you raised them. Plus I knew Gianluca's sources weren't as good as he claimed. Those quotes about your film he probably made up. Unless?'

'No,' said Max. 'I didn't feed him those word for word. Just put some ideas forward.'

'Negative ones?'

'What else? He doesn't incline towards the positive.'

HOLLYWOOD ON THE TIBER

'But why? I don't get it. And, more to the point, how? Did you ask him to write that article? Did you make some kind of deal with him?'

'No,' said Max. 'I never told him who I was. I made an anonymous call to his office. Decried your article saying what a contemptible thing it was. What an offence to cinema and all its traditions. I didn't know if he'd listen. But he did. And he wrote his counter piece. The rest of it you know.'

Paparazzo still looked baffled.

'Your article was fading fast,' Max continued. 'You said so yourself. Something more was needed. Or else it would have disappeared without a trace. I read a lot about films Fabio. Publicity too – the old Hollywood press agents and industry insiders. One of the most famous of them was a guy called Harry Reichenbach. He started out in New York City. Eventually made it to Los Angeles where he was retained by the studios for a thousand dollars a week. This was the early 1900's so a thousand dollars was a lot of money. It said a lot about Harry's ability and reputation. He knew how to turn just about anything into an event. And how to draw people in. I read this one story about him that stuck in my mind. He was working in a small art shop early in his career. They'd printed a lithograph of a nude girl standing in a pool. Copies were selling for ten cents apiece, but no one was buying it. Harry came up with an idea of how to move it. He figured get an authority figure to condemn it; that will get people's attention. So he phoned up the head of the Anti-Vice Society. Complained about the picture which he'd installed in the shop window. It took time, but he got the reaction. The society expressed its moral outrage. It demanded the picture be removed and, when the shop refused, it appealed this to the courts. Result – the picture became an overnight sensation. It got into the newspapers everywhere and was a bestseller. Seven million copies were sold. And all by this flurry of negativity. The attack made it a success. It aroused interest levels which was exactly the intention. September Morn even had songs written about it, jokes told on the vaudeville stage.'

Paparazzo mulled this over. His brows were knitted. Silent seconds passed. The journalist's chin tilted before he spoke. Then it tilted further.

'You mean you set all of this up?' he said. 'By playing Della Pasqua?'

'I took a chance,' Max replied, 'I didn't know for sure how it would turn out. First I had to depend on his writing the article. After that, I had to hope for a response.'

'Which most certainly came,' said Paparazzo. 'The students and the newspapers. Umberto Spada and the others. That's fucking brilliant Max. What a stroke of genius. And what a wily bastard you are. Almost as much as I am.'

Max's face remained set, unsmiling, but not defensive.

'It worked out,' he said, 'but these things don't always. I got lucky. A whirlwind as you put it.'

'Let's hope for your sake you don't reap it,' said Paparazzo, his tone slightly indignant. 'You played me too Max. Take the story to Cinecittà you said. And I did just that. Now maybe you didn't know how that would turn out either. But the fact is it helped you get that screen test. One more step along the way.'

'We helped each other,' said Max. 'You got a story. I got a break.'

Paparazzo was not swayed by this. Visibly chafed, he kept on at it.

'With all due respect, I think you benefited the most from this,' he said. 'And I don't like being stage-managed Max. I prefer to leave that to actors like you.'

Max ignored the jibe.

'You'll get your follow-up Fabio,' he said, 'just not today. I look forward to seeing you in Cannes. A familiar face is always a good thing.'

The journalist's response to this was barbed.

'You'll be seeing me alright Max,' he said. 'I have to follow you, keep tabs on what you're doing. I'll be the first one you look for in the crowd. Because you know me Max. And I'm beginning to know you too. Just a little.'

Without saying anything else, he walked away. Max watched him leave. Going the other way then, he returned to a light jog, picked up the pace as he left the park.

He had to be in another place soon. There was something else he had to do.

THE LONG GOODBYE

An hour later, Max was on Via Margutta standing outside Franco Bonacossa's apartment. He rang the doorbell and waited. It was getting close to lunchtime. There was an agreeable aroma coming from one of the neighbouring apartments. The clinking of silverware told him a family was already dining. Elsewhere, he heard two neighbours squabbling over a noisy dog. The pet's name was Rocco and, depending on one's side of the argument, he was either man's best friend or just a plain mutt.

Max was glad Franco had agreed to see him at this time. He hadn't told him why he was dropping by, but he knew the agent might well guess the reason. He felt on edge about the meeting. It was no small thing quitting Franco after all these years. A big departure and he wondered how the other man would take it. Badly? Philosophically? Or in some other way he could not foresee. He took a deep breath and got ready. In the background, and out of sight, the canine quarrel went on. Accusations of hypersensitivity were refuted with claims of sleep deprivation.

Franco smiled politely when he answered the door. They exchanged a double-cheek kiss. He suggested they talk in the living room. A movie was playing on the TV. It seemed to be Visconti's La Terra Trema. There were grainy shots of hollow-cheeked fishermen and turbulent waves. Franco turned down the volume. The black-and-white images continued to flicker as he took a seat.

Straight-faced, he offered Max his congratulations.

'No doubt you've heard it many times by now, my own best wishes are hardly required,' he said in a rather flat voice.

'It's much appreciated anyway,' said Max, who had not missed the colourless tone. There was silence for a few moments. Franco toyed with the idea of a cigarette, resisted the temptation, and put it back in its packet.

'You never came back to me about our contract,' he said, broaching the subject. 'I sent it over shortly after the HQD script if you remember.'

His posture was taut, voice subdued. He was putting it out there deliberately. Fully aware of what the likely answer would be.

'Yes, about that HQD job,' said Max, going around it the long way, 'I spoke to the managing director, Vitale; explained to him I wouldn't be available owing to...well you know. He was fine about it all things considered; even wished me luck. He said he'd return to you for another name.'

'He hasn't done that yet,' said Franco, folding his arms and looking out the window absently. 'Nor do I expect him to.'

'My fault?' said Max.

Franco turned back.

'No, no Max,' he answered, 'the responsibility for this lies with me.

I don't allow others to take on my mea culpas. Never have done. I'll contact Vitale and see what can be worked out. Maybe we'll do business together again. Maybe not.'

He looked out the window once more, and then returned to the scene.

'There is something you need to tell me?' he asked forthright. 'I think it best we be direct about this or otherwise we talk in circles. You've been offered a deal somewhere else I take it?'

'Yes,' replied Max, a quick nod of his head. 'An outline of one at least.'

'From where?'

'Los Angeles.'

'Hollywood?' said Franco.

'Yes, Hollywood.'

'I'm very happy for you Max. I didn't want for us to go on pretending just now. I know what a strain that can be.'

'I was going to tell you as quickly as I could,' said Max. 'I just didn't want to be too blunt about it.'

Franco laughed quietly.

'Didn't think I could take it, eh?' he said plainly. Another laugh followed and Max was unsure as to what it meant. He decided to proceed cautiously.

'I owe you so much Franco,' he began, 'I've learnt a great deal from you, about voice acting, about the business as a whole.'

'But that isn't enough for you any longer, is it?' said Franco. 'You wish to spread your wings. Do new and different things.'

'I need to Franco,' Max replied firmly. 'This is my opportunity. It won't ever happen for me again. I have to grasp it and not let go. Hold on for dear life if necessary.'

This prompted a concerned look from Franco.

'I've never seen you this way before Max,' he said. 'Be careful about what you want. Every man is the artisan of his own fortune. Just don't become a hostage to it. It can be a fickle thing you know. One moment you're up, the next you're down. Remember who you are. Keep a hold of that.'

'I will,' said Max, but he was somewhat bristled by the advice. 'Do you not think I can make a success of this?'

Franco tried to steer clear of a response.

'It doesn't matter what I think,' he said. 'That's not the issue. I'm simply telling you there are possible downsides and disappointments. You know this very well.'

'Yes, I do,' said Max, 'but you didn't answer my question. It's important that I know. Do you think I can make it a success? Yes or no?'

Franco remained silent for a few seconds. His fingers gripped his kneecaps. When he eventually spoke, his voice was leaden.

'You want a vote of confidence Max? Is that it?' A resounding endorsement?'

'Your support is important to me Franco. But your honesty is more.'

The agent nodded and delivered his opinion.

'I don't think it will work out for you Max,' he said, his eyes dropping to study his hands, 'because you weren't meant for this. And I don't think it was meant for you.'

He focused more raptly on the actor and continued.

'The papers make you out to be a big name now. A star in the making some of them say. Well I think they're wrong about that. And I think you're deluding yourself. You're not a star. You're not any of those things they print. The reporters have hyped you without foundation; for the reason that you represent column inches and circulation to them. I feel sorry for you Max. They're profiting from you and you can't see it. You're so caught up in the moment, you're not thinking of what might happen next.'

He broke off and reached for the packet of Nazionali again.

Max's eyes followed his movements as he pulled out a cigarette and lingered, as if in two minds about what to do with it.

Franco glanced sideways at him, alert to his gaze.

'My apologies if I've said too much,' he whispered. 'You asked me. You pressed for something as you always do.'

He made an effort to lighten the tone.

'In the studio, I know of those things you do to coax and bring others around to your point of view,' he said. 'Giacomo Romano above all. You're very good at it. A pro.'

The tenor of his speech did a rotation back.

'But that's the studio Max. Out at Cinecittà on the other hand, a very different thing. I fear for you. I fear you'll be out of your depth.'

'Why?' Max asked tetchily.

'Because you don't have the experience to handle it,' said Franco.

Max lurched forward in his chair.

'Is that all?' he said. 'Nothing else?'

'Max, you haven't been in front of a camera in how long?' said Franco. 'You're not seasoned for this kind of thing.'

'But that's not what you're getting at. Is it Franco? You don't think I'm good enough, do you? That I don't have the capability.'

'No, I don't think you do,' said Franco, giving it up. 'There's a huge gulf between acting in front of a mike and acting in front of a camera. I don't think you appreciate that because you've been away for so long. And quite honestly, you don't have the time or the faculty to make it up either.'

This rankled Max greatly. He gave vent to long-standing frustrations.

'I've been away so long because you encouraged it,' he said. 'All these years you've regarded me as a voice actor and nothing more. It's why you book me in for shitty jobs like HQD. The pharmaceutical industry, health care, semiconductors, leisure, textiles. You've delivered them all Franco. Put them on a plate and I always turned up. The exaggerated compliments you laid on thick – 'Well done Max.' 'Great job Max.' 'The bosses at Alitalia love that voice of yours.' 'The guys at Telespazio head office owe you one.'

He drew breath and came down a notch or two.

'You told me to believe in everything I do,' he said, 'well I believe in this. I believe in me in this. HQD Pharmaceuticals is not as far as I can reach. Nor is the dubbing work. I can handle bigger things. With this film, I can accomplish something people can see and hear. Don't you understand that Franco?'

He was already regretting some of the things he'd just said.

Franco cobbled together a response. There was a mournful tranquility to his voice.

'I hope you can accomplish something Max,' he said. 'I really do. If you've had those aspirations all this time, then I'm only sorry I didn't know. I served you badly.'

'I'm sorry too Franco,' Max replied. 'It was unfair of me. I have to take responsibility for much of it myself. What I said in the newspaper is the truth. I was operating in my own comfort zone. I didn't stretch myself at all, didn't put myself out there. It became too easy to blame you. As I did just now.'

'Water under the bridge,' said Franco. 'I hope we can remain friends.'

'Of course. It's not something I want to lose,' said Max.

This gave him pause for thought.

'What about your business though Franco?' he asked. 'My leaving isn't going to help matters. Is it?'

'Probably not Max, but I'll battle on. I was aware you were obtaining most of the work yourself these last few years. Pietro and Erika the same. Eventually, it became too much for them. But you...I think you might have stayed with me if this hadn't come along.'

Max had nothing to say to this.

Franco continued.

'Your loyalty has meant a great deal to me,' he said. 'It didn't escape my notice how you always referred those clients back to me. So I'd get my commission.'

Max shook his head modestly.

'Don't give me too much credit,' he said. 'It was because I knew you were better at negotiating a higher fee than me.'

The agent smiled wistfully.

'If I was twenty years younger who knows. A Hollywood production such as this one – I'd relish the chance to haggle with those fellows.'

'I bet you would,' said Max, 'but I'm going to do pretty well as it is. I've never seen a pay day like this one before Franco.'

'That's good Max,' said Franco, 'but remember it's not everything. You'll make lots of new friends no doubt. Some of them may gravitate towards you for reasons less than friendship.'

'I know,' said Max. 'I'll watch out. My father had a saying about that. It sort of fits.'

'Keep it in mind so.'

'Franco, about the film at Cinecittà; what you said about me not having the ability to pull it off.'

'Max, let's forget about that,' said Franco. 'I was out of line. It was unprofessional and I had no business saying it.'

'Is that really what you think?' asked Max. 'That I'm out of my depth? That I won't be up to scratch?'

'Max, I may have overstated somewhat,' replied Franco. 'I guess I was a little envious when you first came in today. Plus, I had an idea as to the reason for your visit. It was small-minded of me. My apologies.'

Max accepted this calmly.

'I thought I noticed something when I got here,' he said, 'but then I wasn't exactly bringing you good news. No cause to meet me with open arms. I'd probably have acted the same way.'

He crossed his arms on his chest and moved on intently.

'I got the screen test though, didn't I?' he said. 'I mean they wouldn't have given me the part if I'd been no good.'

'No, they wouldn't have,' Franco agreed. 'It shows I have even less of a right to venture a judgement on it. I wasn't there. So what could I possibly know?'

Max nodded. He became more animated, more insistent.

'It was a wonderful scene,' he said, his upper body angling forward again. 'The kind you want at such a moment. Packed with dramatic force. The rest of the script too. It's an actor's jackpot. I won't mess it up. I will make the grade on this.'

'Well like I said, I'm very happy for you Max,' Franco said casually. He glanced in the direction of the TV. On the screen a man was offering Lucky Strike cigarettes to a couple of teenagers.

Franco grunted his recollection of this.

Turning back to Max he said, 'do you know how this story goes? The main character tries for a better way of life. Starts a business by himself. It doesn't work out. A storm comes and destroys his boat. Many other things go against him as well. In the end, he has no choice but to return to work as a day labourer.'

'I remember it,' said Max. 'The wholesalers win, the fishermen lose. It's resigned defeat in the final scene. Far from a happy ending.'

The older man agreed with this. He talked about his own future then, and that of his business; mapped out how he intended to have one more shot at it all before retiring. He hoped it would last a long time. A long goodbye he called it.

Max listened courteously, although he doubted it would turn out so well. It seemed to him Franco's day was already done. Why postpone the inevitable he thought. Why drag this out any longer?

Franco engaged in some vague chat about them working together again one day. Max wasn't much interested in this, but didn't have the heart to say so. Instead, he wished him all the best in the time ahead. Franco thanked him.

Throwing in an afterthought, he said, 'you know, there will always be work for you in this industry. If the American production doesn't...'

He stopped short deliberately, allowing his visitor to intuit the rest.

'I know that Franco. Thank you once more. For everything,' said Max.

He wanted to leave immediately. This was not a discussion he wished to have.

Standing up, he made ready to go.

'Let's say farewell, but not goodbye then,' said Franco as they shook hands.

Max understood what he meant by this. His old agent did not believe the Hollywood film would be a winner for him. So much for the talk about being the artisan of my own fortune he thought. In his eyes, I'm still a regular voice actor. Always will be.

'Goodbye Franco,' he said.

'Until the next time my friend,' said Franco.

With what he hoped looked like a smile, Max said, 'I hope the long goodbye goes well for you. I'm sorry I probably won't be part of it.'

LEADING LADY

At the Hotel Negresco in Nice, Jennifer Carrington was wide awake. It was half past eight in the evening. She'd arrived in the French city earlier that day after a nonstop flight from Los Angeles. By the time she checked into the hotel, it was already mid-afternoon, and the 32-year old actress was suffering through her first bout of jet lag. She tried to get comfortable in her fifth floor room. Lay on the bed for a time and, when that didn't work, resorted to a magazine. It was one of those complimentaries provided by hotels, geared especially for the business traveller. There was the latest news on airlines, airports and car rental companies. Other features of note as well – Hotel Room Cardio gave tips on how to, 'burn fat on the go.' Several of the recommended exercises required nothing more than a medium-sized pillow; one involved use of an imaginary jump rope. Hoping against hope that something might cause her to nod off, Jennifer sifted through it. Anything to get over this infernal insomnia she thought. But she knew from previous experience it would take a couple of days to adjust to the new time zone. And then there were the headaches and irritability that went with it. Feeling suitably glum at this prospect, she decided to go downstairs. A nightcap probably wouldn't help she knew, but, then again, how much harm could it really do?

Entering the beautifully textured bar with walnut woodwork and tapestry, she immediately spotted her agent, Barry Falk, at the counter. Barry had his tie removed and shirt collar open. His sleeve cuffs were folded back twice. He was holding a drink in a contemplative way; gazing at it as if this were the elixir he too needed, something to shut those keen, birdlike eyes of his, something to decelerate that nimble mind he possessed. His pink round face was always cheerful. He grinned amiably when he saw the actress.

'You as well?' he said jokingly, as she pulled up a seat beside him. 'Hey where's Lily?' he asked, looking around. 'What the hell is her trick?'

'No trick,' answered Jennifer, in reference to her personal assistant. 'She's out and about as far as I know, wanted to see something called the Bay of the Angels.'

'Sounds fitting,' Barry remarked playfully, 'Lily's always come across as the virtuous kind; strong principles I think. What she makes of us movie folk, I can only hazard to guess.'

'Speak for yourself,' Jennifer told him, as she attempted to discern the contents of his glass. 'So is it working?' she asked.

'This?' he said, balancing the glass as best he could. 'Hard to say. It's my third one and I don't feel anything. Not tired. Not awake either. Something in between I guess. Like it's all up in the air for me. I may not sleep for hours yet,' he added flippantly. 'Neither might you. We could sit here and see who passes out first. At least Lily would get you to your

309

room. The bar staff could mop me up off the floor.'

Jennifer rolled her eyes quickly, pretending to be indifferent to this.

'Now I think you are drunk, or getting there,' she said.

A moustached bartender appeared to take her order.

'I'll have a chardonnay please,' she requested in a velvety whisper.

She was alluring and graceful with well-defined features; the most admired of which were her ripe lower lip and electric blue eyes. Swishing back her fair hair in the low-lighting, she looked dazzling, in spite of her weariness. It was true what Ned Hollander of People Magazine had written about her – those glamorous looks made her performances all the more captivating.

'There is something remarkable about Jennifer Carrington,' he opined after her excellent turn in Aria, *'by herself, she lights up the silver screen in a unique way. An actress who is imbued with both talent and elegance.'*

Barry Falk naturally knew her better than most. Her agent now for over seven years, he could remember the first time he'd seen her perform. It was a television movie version of Cat on a Hot Tin Roof. Jennifer was playing the part of Maggie the Cat Pollitt.

She followed this up with another Tennessee Williams re-imagining – Night of the Iguana (this time in the role of Maxine Faulk). Again it was for the small screen. By then, Barry had her firmly on his roster. And he knew she could go well beyond the confines of TV and stage. The only thing which stood in her way were her insecurities. Jennifer was deeply afraid of failure. She was the classic combination of angst and doubt. Majoring in acting at Illinois State University, she'd hoped to be accepted into the rigorous Masters of Fine Arts in Acting offered by that same institution. When she was turned down, it was like a hammer blow. The fierce disappointment eventually abating, she decided to move on, and move away. By-passing the obvious avenues of regional theatre and commercials, she headed to Los Angeles. She acted in several student films and obtained small roles in a few independents. Bartending and waitressing represented periodic income. It took time, almost four years in total, before Cat on a Hot Tin Roof got her the type of notice she'd been craving. A phone call one day brought Barry Falk into her professional life. The ebullient William Morris agent could hardly believe how she'd remained without representation for so long.

'Do you not consider it detrimental to your progress?' he asked when they first met. Jennifer was sitting on the ottoman in his office. Barry normally used it as a footrest and he wondered why she'd chosen to sit there. She looked uneasy, nervous. He soon figured out the ploy.

'You in a hurry to get to your next appointment Jennifer?' he asked directly, but with a gentle lilt.

She admitted she was free for the rest of the day.

'There you go,' he said tactfully, 'how about I buy you some lunch? I know a good place for…say what kind of food do you like?'

Jennifer expressed a fondness for Pink's on North La Brea Avenue. Over Chicago Polish hotdogs and fries, she opened up more about herself.

'I was in two minds about coming to see you today,' she admitted.

'I know you were,' said Barry, as he wiped a smidgen of ketchup from his chin. 'Why the hesitancy about meeting? Us agents don't always bite you know. There are at least a few clients I haven't sunk my teeth into recently.'

The drollness put Jennifer more at ease. Barry had an unaffected manner about him which she found refreshing. He seemed dependable, the kind of person one could talk to in confidence.

'Things have started to happen very fast all of a sudden,' she said. 'I'm afraid of crashing down to earth if it gets to be too much.'

Barry encouraged her to amplify.

'I had a let-down a few years ago, I don't want to go through all that again,' she said, and she told him about Illinois State and the MFA. The rejection had intensified uncertainties which still lingered; that much was crystal clear.

The agent put in his two cents' worth.

'Seems to me you're much better off without that,' he pronounced, 'it made you come out here, didn't it? This is where a flair like yours belongs. Your Cat Pollitt was wonderful. It deserved to be seen by a wider audience. That's one advantage TV has over theatre. A greater distribution. But let's talk about an even bigger picture, shall we?'

Which they did.

Barry learnt more about Jennifer's background. An only child, the actress came from Aurora, Illinois. She grew up in Exposition View, a residential area to the west of the Fox River. Exposition was largely a middle-income community; established places of residence, but not old. The family house, close to Sullivan Road, was built sometime in the late 1940's. Jennifer's mother, Judy, taught elementary in Beaupre school on the east side. Her father, Leonard, worked in the control tower at the municipal airport in Sugar Grove. Jennifer was a student at her mother's place of employment to the age of 12. She was mindful at all times of Judy's stern proviso that she be a model amongst the other schoolchildren. She found it difficult to make friends and felt scrutinised more than just a little.

'The other kids were practically baiting me to fuck up for those six years,' she confided to Barry, as they finished their hotdogs. 'It was like being under a giant microscope with them and my mom.'

The fear of being a disappointment, of failing herself and those around her, carried into adult life. Her parents had never exactly enthused about the line of work she inclined towards. The MFA rebuff they cited as proof that it was not meant to be. Jennifer herself bowed to this common sense for a time. She thought about her options long and hard. Office manager perhaps? Administrator? Bank teller? Elementary school teacher?

That was that.

'In the end I caught the Greyhound to LA,' she told Barry. 'I was playing the part of the loser too well; brooding over this programme I'd never get on in a million years. I figured if it goes pear-shaped for me out here, at least it won't be as conspicuous. I'll be one in a vast number. Just another girl who got off the bus and didn't make it.'

The girl in this case became more than that. She signed up with William Morris, with Falk as her agent, and began to obtain more auditions and screen tests. Having representation at last, and getting her proverbial foot in the door, was the key. She landed some minor roles (This Party's Over, Tales of NYC, and It Looks like the Sky to Me) before advancing to more substantial parts (Blink of an Eye, Garden by the Sea, and The Uncommon Life of Nathan Edwards). The Funny Thing about Friendship and While You Were in the Other Room provided a two-fold breakthrough in 1991. Both were romantic comedies, a genre she was not very keen on, but they were necessary rungs on the ladder as Barry said. The box office numbers bore him out in this regard. Friendship did $195,000,000 domestically; Room fared even better posting $212,000,000.

The William Morris crackerjack aimed to enhance the star's rising profile. He encouraged Jennifer to hire a publicist, suggesting Cindi Reynolds of Meredith PRC. Reluctantly, the actress agreed to this. Barry and Cindi worked hard on her behalf, but it wasn't easy. Her insecurities apart, Jennifer was an unapologetic cynic when it came to matters PR and image management. She disliked photo calls, was unwilling to indulge the stock-in-trade razzmatazz of the industry, and even in one-to-one interviews found it hard to dissemble when required.

'It was as if she wanted to be there and not there,' Reynolds complained to Falk after a press junket in the early autumn of 1993. The film being touted was a remake of The Bad and the Beautiful (Jennifer was in the Lana Turner role) and, by this time, the actress was firmly established in the public eye. She had done Two Hours in Paradise and I Forgot to Remember to Forget – both considerable successes – but there remained for Reynolds a few uneven edges which needed to be smoothed out.

'This half-hearted approach, the one that practically hollers I have no interest in being here, has to be done away with,' she told Falk. 'She is far too mechanical and does absolutely nothing to disguise it. A bit of energy would go a long way, instead of just flopping out there and waiting for them to pass through.'

Writing in Entertainment Weekly, Glenn Nadler inclined towards such an opinion:

'Miss Carrington has an unmistakable quality on the big screen,' he observed, 'but in the flesh she is rather taciturn. There is an aloofness which is difficult to disarm.'

And Cineaste's Edgar Meyers had much the same view: 'There is in the actress's gaze a sort of questioning, the look of an existential doubt,' he wrote that same fall.

In 1994, Jennifer bought a house high up on Miller Drive with views of both the Valley and La Cienega. She had it outfitted mostly with white furniture and invested in some art, although very little of it went on the walls. That same year saw the end of her relationship with the experimental musician and producer Dennis Louiso. The two had been an item since 1991.

Asked about her feelings regarding the break-up, Jennifer was typically circumspect.

'It's tough, yes, but sometimes people grow apart,' she said at the premiere of Round the Table. For once she was happy to talk about the new film, and even let slip what her next cinematic outing would be.

After The Ruby came First Lady of Virginia, which was vigorously encouraged by Barry Falk. Jennifer was unsure about the biopic of Martha Skelton Jefferson (Thomas Jefferson's wife who died at the age of 33 before the latter became president) and demurred saying she felt like a short hiatus. Her agent asked why.

'A break is not in your vocabulary, never has been,' he said, 'so I have to insist on the real reason for this. It's a wonderfully written part Jennifer. Why wouldn't you want to do it? Is it the subject matter? Something else I'm missing here?'

His client said she liked the part very much, but had doubts as to her own suitability.

'I may not be ready,' she said. 'It's come perhaps five years too soon. I need to learn more things about the trade first. Then...'

'Then the part will be gone to someone else,' Falk pointed out.

Jennifer sat down on his sofa and gave up the truth of her thoughts.

'The Ruby isn't doing well,' she said. 'I finally have a flop on my hands.'

Falk disagreed with this.

'Jennifer, The Ruby is not going to be a flop,' he said. 'It will break even, possibly show a small profit at the end of its run. There's overseas yet to come. Don't despair. And for God sake, don't allow it to be the cause for missing out on this film. A year from now you'll regret it. Trust me.'

'I do Barry, but it's difficult,' the actress replied. 'I'm afraid of not being good enough. It's a phobia I have and there's no way around it. Every time I start work on a film, I have this same dread. What if I don't measure up? What happens then? The Ruby was no different. I lay awake the night before it began. I think it was worse than ever. And look how it turned out.'

'Jennifer, the reviews were fine,' said Falk, 'it just didn't quite get across, that's all. It's a tiny glitch on an otherwise impeccable track record. So we move on. Gottfried wants you for this film. I can hear it in the guy's voice. You should be flattered. Anyone would be. It's a great opportunity. You've been working towards this.'

Half-jokingly, he added, 'and by the way, if you don't do this film, I can no longer represent you. Now there's a sound basis for taking it if ever there was one. Whaddya have to say?'

First Lady of Virginia wrapped just three weeks before Echo of Passions was due to start shooting. By all accounts Jennifer had delivered the performance of her career to date. Executives at Fox waxed lyrical about the rushes and there was already talk of a possible Oscar nomination. Awards season though was months away yet and, in the meantime, there was the not insignificant matter of her tight schedule for the remainder of the year. Kith and Kin, a family drama set in Chesapeake, Virginia, was lined up a few weeks after Echo of Passions, but this window became greatly reduced following Don Taylor's accident. Like many, Jennifer wondered if the Rome shoot would go ahead. She asked for regular updates and waited. There was little else she could do. The worst case scenario from her point of view was a revised start date on Echo which might cause her to be replaced in the lead role of Kith and Kin. Barry Falk advised calm, telling his client not to fret. But even he could not be sure.

The telephone rang in his office one day. Jeff Forman was calling from The Hollywood Reporter. He was aware of Miss Carrington's timetable for 1995 as a whole and remarked as to its now tentative nature.

'Becoming more uncertain with every passing day,' he said.

Would Falk care to comment he enquired.

'No,' was the agent's reply.

Forman, however, was not done.

'Kith and Kin is most at risk in terms of your client's availability,' he said. 'Do you imagine it would be pushed back for Jennifer's sake? Or might the producers be obliged to find themselves another leading lady?'

'Jeff, you know what my answer to that kind of question is,' Falk sighed deeply. 'No comment. We are waiting to see how the situation plays out like so many others. But let me say this much – Jennifer remains committed to Echo of Passions. One hundred per cent. She is ready for this film and, indeed, hopeful it will get going very soon.'

Forman attempted to cut in.

'But please don't ask me for an opinion about who they will cast,' said Falk. 'There are lots of good actors in this town and elsewhere. And I don't know who's free right now. I haven't done the math on that. No doubt you have a list compiled. Send it over to me. I'd be very interested as to who's on it. So too would my client.'

One name that did not appear on Forman's list was that of Max Pellegrino. The Italian had begun to cause a stir in his own country, but was not yet known by the international press. This quickly changed.

On the day Aggregate Pictures made its announcement, Jennifer was back home in Aurora visiting her parents. Her father answered the phone and called her.

'It's your agent, unless I'm greatly mistaken,' he said, 'always reminds me of my cousin Lester – breathy when he has news for you.'

Barry was indeed the bearer of good tidings. He was slightly out of breath also.

'We are a go for Cannes,' he told Jennifer. 'They finally have an actor for Echo of Passions, a local, an Italian. The plan is that you do the pre-publicity before you head for Rome. First stop Côte d'Azur kiddo. Fantastic news, right?'

'Who's the actor?' Jennifer asked, plain-speaking.

'He's from Rome I understand,' said Barry, 'but that's as much as I know. Funny thing is no one's ever heard of him. Literally plucked from obscurity. Did a screen test and it was so impressive the big fish at Aggregate Pictures settled on him right away.'

'What's his name?'

Falk rummaged for a moment.

'Max, Max Pellegrino,' he answered. 'You don't have a problem with this, do you? I know it's sudden, but they had to move quickly.'

'Why should I have a problem with it?' said Jennifer, 'this way we get the film done on time, right? I was worried about how it wasn't getting fixed. Any longer and Kith and Kin might have...when do they expect it will finish?'

Barry told her what he knew based on the guesstimations he was hearing.

'It should be approximately by then, give or take one or two days,' he said, 'but no need for concern. You're set to finish before it wraps, aren't you?'

'Just before,' said Jennifer, 'the shooting schedule is a bit odd given that they're filming the courtroom stuff prior to my own character's death scene. That part of it I don't understand. Do you think they'd juggle it around if we asked?'

'There's no need to ask,' Barry told her, 'you'll be done with time to kill.'

'The time I wish I could kill is Cannes,' Jennifer said tepidly. 'Is that really necessary? Couldn't they just leave it out?'

'It's pre-publicity Jen,' said Falk, 'no ducking it. Besides, it's about time you did Cannes. Didn't you say your father has family there?'

'Not Cannes Barry, Carentan,' replied Jennifer. 'Our surname comes from there, but there's no relatives left that we know of. And, by the way, it's in Normandy, which is nowhere close to Cannes.'

'Get back here to LA Jen. Pack your bags.'

'Aye aye sir.'

Jennifer ordered a second glass of wine at the Negresco bar.

'Do you want another one of your concoctions?' she asked Falk.

The agent grinned mischievously.

'What the hell!' he said, 'one for the road, eh?'

'Tell me what's in it then,' she implored.

Falk winked at their dutiful bartender.

'He knows,' he said, nodding at the other man, 'but I'm afraid I can't tell you. There are things known and things unknown my dear, and in between are...mixtures such as this.'

'You are drunk,' Jennifer said conclusively.

'Maybe,' answered Falk, 'but it's gonna be my last one. Don't forget, we've an early start tomorrow. And then there's the small issue of traffic. Nice to Cannes may be just over 30 kilometres, but it's the gridlock that's the problem. Matches your own Circle Interchange on the I-290 I believe.'

He gazed at his client.

'Why didn't you want to stay in Cannes Jen?' he asked. 'It would have been a lot easier. We wouldn't be here by ourselves – you, me, Lily, and all those angels in the bay.'

'There are others here,' said Jennifer. 'I saw them earlier.'

'Who?'

The bartender returned with their drinks.

'You tell me what's in that thing, I'll tell you who I saw,' she said.

'Not a chance,' replied the laughing agent, waving it aside.

'Then we have an impasse on our hands,' said Jennifer.

'I guess so,' agreed Falk.

The actress became more thoughtful at this.

'I still wonder why David Cousins insists on the courtoom scenes being shot before I'm done,' she pondered. 'I mean on First Lady of Virginia I could understand the rationale. Gottfried wanted to shoot it mostly in sequence. He felt it would help my performance, and I think he got that right. Plus, I was in just about every scene. But with this, it doesn't make any sense to me.'

She turned back to Falk.

'Does it to you?' she asked him.

'I wouldn't think about it too much Jen,' said Falk. 'It may be a logistics thing, something to do with the sets, or who knows. Don't concern yourself with it. Not your job.'

Jennifer accepted this.

'Carl Gottfried took me aside at the end of First Lady,' she revealed, 'he said to me – you should be very happy about how things have worked out; to do one period piece after another, it's ideal. You carry off that part as well as you've done this one and you'll have another hit.'

'And he's bang on the money,' said Falk. 'You're on to a winning streak kiddo.'

'I'll have a sleepless night before it nonetheless,' said Jennifer. 'That doesn't go away. It's a ritual I've come to expect.'

She tipped the wide glass to her mouth and sipped leisurely. Barry threw back some of his own drink. He paused then, looking at his client. Despite everything, all that had come about, Jennifer was not much different to the young woman in frayed jeans he'd shared Pink hot dogs with a few years before. Still fiercely protective of herself, she often gave the impression of nigh-on hostility to those who did not know her better. Members of the trade press in particular did not seem to get Jennifer. A few described her as frosty; one or two others as stuck-up. Barry felt for her when he read these. They were completely wrong. Jennifer was no ice princess. She did not consider herself above everyone else, her riff was much more down-to-earth. For instance, her aversion towards Cannes he thought. And her firmness about staying in Nice. Away from the limelight where possible. Most definitely Jen all over. The sleepless nights before a film as well. But no one would hear about that part. Not even Cindi Reynolds. Her secret was safe with him.

'Lily's back,' Jennifer said, as her personal assistant waved a good-night from the door of the bar. 'I guess I should turn in myself.'

'Sounds like a plan,' said Barry, 'lots to do tomorrow. Cindi will be expecting us. I think she's staying at the Barrière Hotel.'

'Wagging her finger if we're late,' said Jennifer. 'Cindi reminds me of my Mom – I love her to bits really, but I'm also filled with fear when her wrath kicks in. And just like my Mom, I've given her the openings.'

'She'll be glad to see you Jen. But she won't be with us all day. They're taking us out to an island for a photo op. Cindi will hang about the Croisette.'

'I wish I could do that too,' said Jennifer, draining the remainder of her glass. 'The media circus is for me and Max Pellegrino I assume?'

'That's right kiddo. The two of you and a cluster of photojournalists.'

'Paparazzi in other words. I can't bear them.'

'You better get used to them. Lots in Rome too.'

'Sometimes I wish there wasn't a first amendment,' Jennifer groaned, 'as long as they don't get wind of my visit to Don Taylor. I'm not looking forward to that Barry. I want to see him, but there's also a part of me that...well...would rather avoid it.'

'That's entirely understandable Jennifer. I'll go with you if you want.'

'Thanks. That would be good. I'd feel calmer with you there.'

'No problem,' said Barry cheerfully, 'all part of the service.'

'You're the best Barry.'

'Not quite,' he kidded, 'but I'm close.'

'How many nights are you in Rome for?'

'Just the two,' he replied. 'I have to meet De Vitis. He's having problems with the Bombaata sequel.'

'And then back to LA?'

'And then back home.'

Jennifer rose from her seat.

'Well that's me done,' she said. 'Time for some shut-eye, if I can manage it.'

'Goodnight Jen.'

'Bonne nuit Barry. I'm practising my French. That's as good as it gets.'

The agent smiled, shaking his head.

'You'll have to trade that in before long,' he said. 'It's buonanotte in Italian.'

'Buonanotte,' repeated Jennifer. 'Buonanotte. Yeah, I can do that. With a bit of luck, get to sleep as well.'

Un Certain Regard

Max checked in at the famous Intercontinental Carlton on the Croisette Boulevard in Cannes. The hotel, dating from 1911, was the last of the grand hotels in Cannes which had not yet undergone a comprehensive programme of restoration, but, in spite of this, remained the most impressive place to stay during the festival. Moving through the lobby of white pillars and light marble, he could hardly believe where he was. This was Cannes man. The most prestigious and publicised festival in the world. A mecca as Jonny Lewysohn put it. But there was no sign of the Hollywood agent; notwithstanding his suggestion that they meet on Max's arrival.

Max registered and was escorted to his room by a uniformed bellboy. The jeune homme had a roly-poly figure and chinstrap beard, and he chatted eagerly as they made their way to the deluxe suite on the seventh floor. He talked about this year's festival and how it compared with previous incarnations. You saw all types coming and going he said, with apparent satisfaction. You saw actors and actresses and other celebrities you recognised, some you didn't. You saw guys in expensive suits, bags dangling from their shoulders, who wanted it to be known they were directors in town looking to make a deal; hoping their film would create enough buzz in the sidebars and find itself a distributor. You saw starlets and wannabes, many of them in skimpy outfits or tiny skirts. Some later appeared with those very same directors asking questions like – 'Why are you here?'; 'What's the name of your film?'; 'Will you make another one if you sell it at the Marché?'; 'Could there be a part in it for me?'

But nothing was quite like the tumult when a bona fide star came into view. He mentioned the scene outside the Belle Époque building a few days before when hordes of screaming fans had tried to catch a glimpse of Johnny Depp. This was an aspect of the festival which was very familiar he said, as if he had a great wealth of knowledge on Cannes lore. It was a like response to the one Madonna received when she'd come to promote her film in 1991. Also Uma, Bruce and Quentin just a year earlier. Another actor of comparable status, who'd generated his fair share of hullabaloo in the past, was recalled then. The animated voice became more elegiac. The fond memories were paired with a line of enquiry.

'Mr. Taylor is still in Rome?' he said.

'Yes,' answered Max, 'out of danger so I understand.'

'It was indeed a tragic accident which happened,' the bellboy said, 'we have welcomed him here many times over the years. He is a regular visitor with his films and always stays with us at the Carlton. Our Belle Otero restaurant is his favourite. I hope we see him again soon.'

'Yes, we all do,' said Max, and he decided not to say how unlikely this seemed given reports. 'I witnessed first-hand the kind of reaction his appearance causes. In Rome a few weeks ago. It must be incredible to see that every day.'

'Oh yes monsieur. But soon I think you will experience it yourself. No?'

'I'm not so certain about that,' replied Max, smiling, 'first I have to do something worth mentioning. Make this film to begin with.'

'What is it called monsieur?'

'Echo of Passions,' said Max, 'it's a biopic about an Italian inventor – Antonio Meucci. He's supposed to have invented the first telephone.'

'I thought it was Alexander Graham Bell,' the other man said in response to this, trying not to sound like he was challenging the guest.

This didn't bother Max.

'There's a lot of debate about the history,' he said. 'The film will come out in favour of Meucci. Not everyone will agree with that. But perhaps some will reconsider.'

The bellboy nodded thoughtfully.

'That is good,' he said. 'Anything which provokes the exchanging of views is a very good thing. To be honoured I think. Perhaps the film will play here when it is complete?'

'I think that's the idea,' said Max. 'The studio wants it to open in Cannes. This time next year. The director has agreed to deliver it by then.'

'And who is the director monsieur?' the bellboy asked. They were now on the seventh floor walking down a plush corridor.

'His name is David Cousins,' Max replied. 'An American director. He's made a number of films. You've probably seen a few of them.'

He searched his mind for examples.

The bellboy muttered a few words to himself in French. Something had clicked.

'This director I think I recognise,' he said. 'There was a man by such a name at a previous festival. He had a film in competition, but it was not well received. A question-and-answer session followed with the press. It became unpleasant. The director did not appreciate what the journalists thought of his work. In the end he stood up and said he was leaving. But before doing that, he gave them le bras d'honneur. How do you say it? A fuck-you sign.'

'That was Mr. Cousins?' said Max. 'Are you sure?'

'I think so monsieur,' said the bellboy, 'certainly a name resembling that one, if not the same. The provocateur was declared persona non grata by the board of directors. I don't believe he has returned since then.'

They arrived at Max's suite and he opened the door.

Inside, the room was ready for occupancy. The king-size bed was turned down with a candy wrapped in gold on the pillow. Low instrumental music came from a hidden speaker, the kind you heard in an elevator or department store. A fresh basket of fruit was positioned on a central table; so impeccably arranged that it looked like the Caravaggio painting.

A bottle of champagne was next to it; an envelope attached, but Max did not appear to notice this.

The bellboy rested his luggage on the floor – a small flat suitcase and two garment bags. He watched as the actor looked around. Max drew back honey-coloured curtains revealing a large terrace with a partial view of the Mediterranean. But he did not venture outside just yet. It was all so impressive. For a moment he felt he didn't belong here.

The bellboy smiled warmly and pointed to the bottle of bubbly.

'An American gentleman who is staying in the hotel requested this be delivered to your room,' he said. 'It seems you have friends here already monsieur.'

'Must be,' said Max, as he opened the envelope. A card bearing the hotel's logo was inside. The handwriting was scrawly, but decipherable. It read – 'Bienvenue à Cannes', and bore the initials JL. Max put the card down on the table and returned his attention to the hotel employee.

'Thank you for your help,' he said, offering a tip.

'Thank you monsieur,' said the bellboy, 'and if you require anything else during your stay with us, please do not hesitate to call.'

'There is one thing,' said Max. 'Perhaps you could tell me where would be good for an evening stroll.'

He followed this up quickly with an elaboration.

'Actually, what I'd like to see is the festival in action. The excitement. The goings-on. Where would be best for that?'

The bellboy thought about this and then offered his recommendation. Opening the door out onto the terrace, he invited Max to step out with him.

In the open air, he motioned towards the promenade below, which stretched as far as the eye could see. It was lined with palm trees, high-end shops and expensive-looking restaurants, but its most noteworthy feature on this balmy Friday evening was the throngs of people on the seafront; some of them descending on the public places; some wandering randomly; others moving intently towards the Palais des Festivals further up the way.

The bellboy nodded and with extended hand traced up and down the length of it.

'La Croisette,' he said. 'Monsieur could not possibly find a more exciting location in Europe right now. And as for the people who are down there – he could not have a more interesting walk anywhere in the world.'

Max was unpacking his chalk-striped suit when a knock came to the door. Quickly he hung it up in one of the closets and answered.

A tall young man with an exaggerated grin was standing in the hallway. It was Jonny Lewysohn. With an air of urbanity he introduced himself and asked if he could come in.

'I hope I'm not intruding,' he said, as they shook hands, 'I know you've only just got here. My apologies for not meeting you downstairs. There was an urgent bit of business to take care of. I really should stay away from my room during the daytime. That way I could remain blissfully ignorant as to what's happening back home.'

He spotted the untouched basket and bottle on the table where they'd been placed.

'Oh good,' he said, 'I asked they be delivered before you arrived. One thing you can absolutely depend on around here is the service, and I'm not just talking about the hotel. Everything in this town operates to the pulse of the festival and there's no messing about with details. Just keep everyone who comes here happy so they can see the films and make the deals. That's the beat that goes and it's what makes this place what it is.'

He was full of self-confidence, but appeared a little wired too. Max wondered if all Hollywood agents were cut from the same cloth. In your face with this hyper-energetic quality. But get-up-and-go is a welcome thing he figured. Another shot in the arm that wouldn't go amiss.

'It's good to have you in town,' said Lewysohn, his voice infused with gusto for the task at hand, 'and I don't just mean with regard to Echo of Passions. This is our first opportunity to get your face out there. Like I said, cashing in on this opportunity of yours – it's a no-brainer. Undoubtedly, you know that already. Right?'

'Yes, I do,' said Max, who was relieved to finally get a word in edgeways, 'and I don't intend to let it pass me by. For the next two days I'm happy to go wherever they want me to go and speak to whoever they say I should. If they want me to do interviews with large numbers of journalists, then I'll be glad to do so. If they want me to attend all-night parties, then I'll go without the sleep.'

Jonny Lewysohn voiced his appreciation at hearing this.

'Well that's excellent Max,' he said, winking. 'Personally I don't object to the all-night parties myself. They're a labour of love if you catch my drift. And as for the media – any publicity agent worth their salt will tell you it helps no end when you have four thousand journalists from all over the world in the one location. It's quite a saving of time and the coverage you get is immeasurable. Did you know that your film isn't the only one here doing a spate of pre-publicity?'

'No, I didn't realise,' said Max. 'Is it of benefit?'

'The studios certainly think so,' replied Lewysohn. 'It's about creating an awareness up front so that a favourable mind-set is in place when it comes time to the opening. Down the line, people will remember what they heard and saw. It acts as a kind of reinforcement. The idea is to get more bums on seats, sell more tickets, you understand?'

'By building up anticipation?'

'Exactly, there you go. So it's not just you and Jennifer Carrington at le festival. Pamela Anderson's been active here too. You have heard of our Pamela?'

'Of course,' said Max. 'Who hasn't?'

'Very true,' said Lewysohn. 'Baywatch travels same as Columbo. Pamela was in town promoting her own upcoming flick. It's called Barb Wire, and from what I can understand, it's a science fiction remake of Casablanca with Pamela in the Humphrey Bogart role. Needless to say, the plot is a little different to Echo of Passions.'

'No doubt,' said Max laughing, 'a lot more special effects for one thing.'

Lewysohn moved adroitly, and smiling, to other things of import.

'Tomorrow's a big day for you,' he said. 'The advice I would give is make lots of eye contact. Put yourself out there. Let them see you. Don't go hiding. Jennifer Carrington may be the star but you, you'll be the person of interest.'

'Because of how I came to be here?' said Max.

Lewysohn addressed this smoothly.

'There's no avoiding the questions that will come your way regarding that,' he said. 'Keep it on the level. Use words like grateful, appreciative, overwhelmed even. No, perhaps not overwhelmed. Stick with the other two. They sound less contrived.'

He shrugged nonchalantly then.

'All in all, just be yourself and take it in your stride,' he counselled. 'The best performance is the one that doesn't look like a performance. Ever hear that? So be natural. Yourself Max. You met Don Taylor, right? He was...is...a real pro in that field.'

'We were onstage together in Rome a few days before his accident,' said Max.

'I heard about that,' said Lewysohn. 'Tom was telling me.'

Max's eyebrows lifted at this.

'Tom Steiner?' he said.

'The one and only,' said Lewysohn, his quicksilver charm beginning to flow again, 'he was very happy you decided to sign with us. SLR is eager to acquire more clients in Europe. Getting talent like you on our books is an important objective for Tom.'

Max guessed that Lewysohn was being economical with the truth. But he saw no reason to call the agent's version into question. Trumped-up story or not, it sure was working in his favour.

'I was intending to go out for a walk,' he said. 'The porter suggested the Croisette. Would you like to join me? Unless of course, there are more phone messages in your room.'

Jonny Lewysohn's mouth stretched wide again, a Cheshire cat.

'That's a wonderful idea Max,' he said. 'I'm not going back there so why don't we hit the trail...or boulevard in this case.'

Max agreed and got a reefer-type jacket from the closet.

'Hey I like the style,' said Lewysohn approvingly. 'It's the sorta thing Edith Head might have designed. She did the costumes for To Catch a Thief which was shot here on the Riviera. They used this hotel as well. I could tell you a few stories about it. Hitchcock, Grant and Kelly.'

Max pinned back his ears as they left. His new agent – a very sharp guy it seemed – was talking about Hollywood royalty. Outside he hoped he might see some.

Max and Jonny sauntered down the gently-winding promenade with its art deco facades and overcrowded bars and restaurants. The wealthy and beautiful were out in their red-carpet fashion against the backdrop of turquoise waters and Esterel mountains. In the harbour luxurious yachts bobbed up and down. All along the Croisette glossy ads for fashion houses and cosmetic companies vied for billboard space with those of forthcoming Hollywood blockbusters. A French TV crew was recording a festival special at the Z Plage private beach club. The hostess performed her own variety of the montée des marches as she walked towards the camera delivering colourful adjectives and flashing pearly-white teeth.

After a short time, the two men found themselves at the western end of the Croisette, in the vicinity of the Palais des Festivals. An evening screening was taking place and the crowds here were especially heavy as keen stargazers of the day waited with baited breath for their idols to arrive. There were bursts of excitement and agitation here and there; mounting hysteria all over.

'There's no ceremony without an audience,' said Lewysohn as they got nearer to it.

In a little while, a small convoy of white limos arrived at the front of the building. With this, the fans went into total overdrive, cheering and screaming. The noise from behind the cordon ropes was deafening and fluctuated according to the emergence of each man and woman from the glitzy vehicles. The celebrities then sashayed in their festival attire. Hemmed in by the voracious multitudes, they flaunted their charms to great effect. It seemed to Max they floated rather than walked. This montée des marches was indeed impressive he thought. The only way to attend an event like this – as a star.

The euphoria rose to fever pitch when one actress made her appearance. She was the last to go, but undeniably the main attraction. Moving up the famous series of steps to the entrance of the Palais, she was jubilant, confident, relishing the moment, expertly greeting her well-wishers; and, as would be expected, the shutterbugs in closer proximity. Jonny Lewysohn nodded in appreciation.

'That's Laura Shepard,' he told Max. 'She's having a very good year. What a star and to think that only a few years ago she was appearing in crap like It Happened to Nancy and Vacationland. Then along came a little movie called First Evidence and just look at her now. She's the queen of Cannes and could get just about any production green-lit.'

'She's very glamorous,' agreed Max, studying Shepard's every wave and motion. 'Have you ever met her?'

'Once or twice,' said Lewysohn, 'she's represented by another agency. SLR has tried to poach her, but she won't budge. Jennifer Carrington the same. Her answer is always no too. Declines whatever attractive terms we offer. With regrets. Hers and ours.'

'What's she like?' asked Max, eyes still fixed on the red carpet pageantry.

'Very beautiful as well,' said Lewysohn, 'but different to Laura Shepard. She's not one for the razzle-dazzle such as this. Withdrawn isn't quite the word. Just less forthcoming if you know what I mean. You won't see her doing a Bardot on the beach.'

Jennifer Carrington and her group were late the following morning and it was decided that they all meet at the old harbour. From there a chartered boat took them to the Île Sainte-Marguerite half a mile off shore. Introductions were hurriedly made as they got on board. The American actress looked frazzled and for the duration of the 15-minute journey to the island sat apart with her personal assistant. She did not converse with anyone, including her own agent.

Barry Falk though was happy to shoot the breeze with Jonny Lewysohn. The pair swopped industry gossip and the latest deals done at the Marché du Film, the business complement to the festival. They also speculated as to what might win the Palme d'Or at the awards ceremony the next day. Barry's money was on The Madness of King George. Jonny's sources were telling him it would be La Haine.

Max, for the most part, was left to his own devices. He watched some water sports taking place on the landward side of the small island. It was parasailing from what he could make out. A high-speed boat was involved. Behind it a line attached to a canopy wing. A solitary figure moved to and fro in the sky. To Max he was reminiscent of a puppet on a string. But guided in reverse. Bottom-to-top. He found it odd how people enjoyed such types of recreation. Absolutely no control over what they're doing he thought. What pleasure was in that? Certainly no great skill at any rate.

For the first time since he'd arrived on the Riviera, he was feeling uneasy. It was all about to become very real. This was no longer the stuff of his wildest dreams. The new day was going to bring a lot of change with it. Both personal and professional. After this he wouldn't be able to move anonymously as he'd done the previous day. Unlike that guy up there in the parasail. Not a dot on the landscape anymore. No longer out of focus. He was coming into view now. In a very short time, they'd be zooming in on his face. He remembered what Jonny Lewysohn had said in the Carlton – four thousand journalists in the one location. What a number! How many papers, magazines, TV stations, did that represent? This was not Il Quarto Stato or Ventiquattro Sette anymore. This was truly global. A world he'd never set foot in.

He glanced across at Jennifer Carrington. She was still aloof-looking. Chatting to her assistant in a matter-of-fact way. No public persona on display so far. He wondered how she would turn it on for the cameras.

Adopt that Cannes body language he'd seen at the Palais. The one Laura Shepard had in spades. The one he didn't have. Because he was that parasailer up there in the sky. No rhythm yet for this kind of thing; no great skill. Maybe never. Bottom-to-top. Had he come here the wrong way round? Would they pick up on some lingering doubt in his voice? Catch sight of it in his eyes?

The photo-op was held on a cliff-top of the island. It was the same spot where Robert Mitchum and Simone Silva had once posed together. In contrast to that infamous episode, there was no scandal in the air; no vulgar calls by the gentlemen of the press for the lady to remove her top. Everything passed off according to plan. 20 minutes, and a few hundred shutter sounds later, and it was done. Better still, there were no questions up till now. Max was relieved.

On the return trip to the city, feeling at ease again, he tried to be more sociable. He talked to Jonny Lewysohn, who was complimentary about the photographs.

'First-rate out there Max,' he said praising. 'You're taking to this like a duck to water. And you kept eye contact with them like I told you. Real good buddy.'

Max asked if there was anything else he needed to do.

Lewysohn had one word of advice.

'You might think about getting closer to Jennifer,' he said. 'There was a tiny bit of distance between the two of you. I'm not suggesting that you cosy up or anything. Just a little more familiarity perhaps. Think of her as an old friend.'

Max observed there'd been very little time for them to talk up to now; even less so to become old friends. Lewysohn encouraged him to change that.

'Why don't you speak with her now?' he proposed. 'You have a few more minutes before we get back onshore. Rub shoulders. Chew the fat.'

This seemed like a good idea. Max agreed with it right away. He wandered over to where the actress was sitting. Jennifer and her PA occupied the same seats as earlier. Barry Falk had installed himself nearby, within earshot of them.

Max approached cordially. He smiled warmly, employing the Jonny Lewysohn technique. Jennifer raised her head.

'Would you mind if I joined you?' he asked. 'We have a long day ahead of us and I guess it would be good to...'

He was cut short immediately. Jennifer did not growl, but she did pull a grimace.

'Not just now,' she replied bluntly, 'and let's save the smiles for the cameras, ok? Like you said, it's going to be a long day.'

Barry Falk came up to him before the boat docked.

'I'm sorry about what happened back there,' he said. 'Jennifer is badly jet-lagged. We both are as a matter of fact. Just got in yesterday. She suffers from it worse than I do. Makes her irritable. As you found out first-hand.'

'That's alright,' replied Max. He was still a little thrown off balance by it. Falk seemed to sense this.

'There's background to this,' he elaborated. 'My client has been under some strain recently. She has a very full programme for this year. The uncertainty about Echo of Passions wasn't helping the situation as you can imagine. For a while there it looked as if her next role was in jeopardy.'

'Will she be available for it now?' asked Max.

'Oh, yes,' said Falk, 'she won't have much free time between the two shoots but the window is adequate. David Cousins just needs to keep to the schedule. He hasn't always done in the past, but this time...I'm fairly confident. After all, it's his comeback film. He's at reset.'

'Have you ever worked with him?' said Max.

'Me? No. But he's a heck of a good director. Just a shame he took a wrong turn along the way. That musical of his – what you would call a misadventure.'

A thought occurred to Max.

'Is this your first time in Cannes?' he asked the agent.

'Fourth or fifth if I'm not mistaken,' replied Falk. 'The last time I was here the Cohn brothers swept the board. That was early 90's.'

'I heard a story yesterday about David Cousins,' said Max, 'at least the person who told me believed it was him.'

'Oh?'

'He brought a film to the festival, but the critics didn't like it. There was a press conference afterwards and relations between him and the journalists turned sour. Is that the correct use of the word? Sour?'

'As opposed to sweet, yes,' said Falk, his eyes twinkling with curiosity.

'He made a gesture at the end of it, directed towards them,' explained Max. 'It wasn't the kind of gesture you make in friendship.'

'I think I get the picture,' said Falk, grinning.

'Did you ever hear about that?'

'I can't say I did Max,' Falk replied. 'I haven't been here for a couple of years so it's possible I missed of it. David Cousins is known to be impulsive; but then, aren't we all from time to time?'

He regarded his client as he said this.

'Take Jennifer there for instance,' he said. 'I must have explained to her a hundred times why it would be preferable to stay in Cannes and not Nice. But do you think she listened to the logic of my argument? Absolutely not. That's another reason why she's ornery right now. We got caught in traffic on the way here this morning. As I predicted we would. So that and the jetlag combined. Not a good mix on this otherwise glorious day.'

The boat drew up beside a marina berth. All aboard got ready to disembark. Jennifer, Lily, Jonny, and two members of the crew. Max and Barry as well.

The latter had one final thing to say before they got off. He spoke it in a whisper so only Max could hear.

'Jennifer's the best,' he told him. 'You can take my word for that. She just struggles with these kinda formalities. It's not her thing. Never has been. Would sooner take up an alternative lifestyle if she had the choice. But this is the job, and publicity's a part of it. No cut and run.'

He patted Max on the back.

'Don't worry,' he said, 'she'll get through the day. You both will. Enjoy it. And if you can't either, just tolerate.'

They had another photo call at midday – on a terrace in the old quarter of the city fronting onto the bay. Max and Jennifer went through the motions once again. A different group of accredited photographers captured the images. The actress was better disposed now, easy-going and accommodating throughout. Hers was a performance of duty and she was wearing the appropriate mask. Max noticed how the sun played on her mouth, how the light seemed made for her eyes, and her complexion – even in the shade – glowed. She had a cool, sophisticated manner. An unmistakable quality as she threw her head back, or brushed the hair away from her eyes. He was very impressed. Jet-lagged or not, Jennifer Carrington was radiant. Irritated or not, she was alluring. She belonged in this town, at this festival. Even if, according to her agent, it was the last place she wanted to be.

The press conference which followed that afternoon took place in the low-lying west wing of the Carlton. It was not the most exciting of affairs. There were few probing questions from the international media, and what little analysis transpired was intermittent owing to the amount of translation required. Topics ranged from Max and Jennifer's attendance at the festival to the state of cinema generally. The film being pre-promoted was discussed also. Aggregate Pictures' Gordon Sawyer was at hand for this. The head of foreign distribution was staying in a regal two-bedroom corner suite and gave off a relaxed air. The Meucci movie was going to be 'terrific,' 'wonderful,' and 'important,' he said, his hands locked together at the top table. He weaved metaphors around the story like strands of linguine around a fork.

Responding to a query about the film's likely demographic, Sawyer expressed his belief that it would have universal appeal.

'This is a classic tale with themes such as love, honour, fidelity, and desire running through it,' he said. 'If I was to narrow it down to one word, it would be this – passion. Passion as in fervour. Passion as in love. Passion as in obsession. These are concepts we can all relate to. They're the overriding motifs of what is a fantastic screenplay.'

Asked if he'd read the script, he replied, 'why yes, of course. This is a methodology we employ at Aggregate Pictures. We take great pride in the collaborative approach. As our very name suggests.'

Turning to the actors on his right – Max and Jennifer – he embraced a tone bordering on the audacious.

'The foundations for something truly remarkable are in place,' he said. 'Our two leads sitting next to me for instance. Many other elements too. You ask me how I see the film in twelve months' time? I see us in this same room. Post premiere. I see a good deal of consent, of admiration. Plaudits I imagine. That's the echo which will sound then. Mark my words. A great success to come.'

His colleagues said the same, but in a less overt way.

Jennifer talked about her own role and how it was instrumental in terms of the plot. Inevitably, another narrative was brought up and she dealt with it admirably.

'Our thoughts and prayers are with Don Taylor and his family,' she said. 'Our efforts, I hope, will be worthy of him. If it wasn't for the tragedy that occurred, I would have been his onscreen wife and that makes me think of his own wife – Lee. Everything she's gone through up to now. All the troubles she didn't ask for. The agitation of mind. The round-the-clock ordeal.'

The mood lightened to some extent when she was quizzed about the comings-and-goings of Tinseltown.

Making light of her own star status, as she was wont to do, she told them, 'you're asking the wrong person. I don't consider myself part of that world. Well that's not entirely true. I live in Los Angeles. And I make my living in the film industry. It's hard to explain. Hollywood and I have a wry take on each other. I appreciate what it represents and I'm very grateful for what it's done for me. I don't go in for the paraphernalia surrounding it, that's all. Understand that I'm not biting the hand that feeds me. I'm just saying my daily life is fairly regular. You might even call it boring. Certainly not worth writing about.'

Jokingly, she added, 'so don't.'

Max did quite well too. As expected, there was a handful of questions regarding his fast-track to the limelight. A Spanish journalist writing for El País asked how he was feeling generally. Her German counterpart from Bild enquired as to whether there were any nerves as the first day of filming loomed.

'A small amount,' said Max, 'but happily they aren't making too loud a noise just yet.'

Only one or two were vaguely tricky. The English Guardian's correspondent asked the actor if he believed himself, 'properly equipped for such a significant bounce?'

His opposite number from the Los Angeles Times vocalised in a similar fashion.

'You're taking the place of a very famous actor,' he said. 'That can't be easy in itself. Have there been any moments of doubt? Daily Variety referred to you as the 'Italian pinch-hitter.' How does that make you feel?'

'Pinch what?' said Max. 'I'm afraid I don't understand that expression.'

Gordon Sawyer judged it appropriate to intervene.

'My actor friend has earned his place at this table, and in our film, on merit,' he said resolutely. 'It goes without saying that his casting was a little out of the ordinary. But hey! Folks! That's the movie business for you. Never a dull moment. Just when you think you've seen it all.'

Slapping his 'actor friend' playfully on the back, he launched into a relevant anecdote. At least it sounded relevant. Max didn't pay attention. He got distracted. In the audience he caught sight of that familiar face – Fabio Paparazzo. The reporter had not asked any questions, but he was here nevertheless. Jotting down notes as usual. He gave a nod as his eyes met Max's. Then returned directly to his work. 15 minutes later – when the press conference ended – he left without a word.

The Palme d'Or for 1995 was awarded to Emir Kusturica's Underground, a story of two friends set against the history of Yugoslavia from World War II to the ethnic conflicts of the early 1990's. The Prix d'interprétation masculine went to Jonathan Pryce for Carrington. Helen Mirren won the female equivalent for The Madness of King George. The festival closed with a screening of Sam Raimi's The Quick and the Dead.

On the final evening, Max and Jonny Lewysohn were invited to a post-awards party at a beach-front pavilion. Gordon Sawyer, Barry Falk and Jennifer Carrington were also there. The actress, wearing an elegant black slink of a gown, departed early for Nice.

The guests partook of complimentary glasses of champagne and expensive-looking finger food, and chewed over the festival just gone by. Some of them huddled in groups on the glass block floor, analysing winners and also-rans. Others, in twos or threes, lounged on spoke-back sofas, making an effort at topics less cinematic. The architecture of the building, for example, as one resourceful lady of indeterminate age ventured.

'Mid-century modern no doubt,' she insisted, between sips of champagne. 'I just adore these barrel-vaulted ceilings, and as for the artichoke light fixtures – sublime. Don't you think dear?'

Her partner or companion, a tall trim man with blandly even features, did not answer. This conversation was not tickling his fancy. Architecture and artichokes – what next he wondered. His lady friend persevered just the same. She highlighted other features around them: the fountain and landscaped area; the paved plaza; the shaped canvases; the egg chairs.

Her eyebrows arched precipitously, but the wide smile on her face was soon reduced to an ironic smirk.

'Egg chairs,' said her intimate, grateful for the opening, 'wasn't that the kind of furniture they used for the house scenes in A Clockwork Orange?'

A like-minded individual confirmed this. Movie-speak reinstated, the connoisseurs went at it one more time. One for the road. Cannes '95, though wavering, was not quite over yet.

Jonny Lewysohn leaned against a thin pillar enclosed in stuccoed brick. He was having another drink. One of several. Tomorrow he'd be returning to LA. Back to the machinery of Hollywood and everything that attended it. The Tinseltown treadmill as he said cheerfully. But in the meantime, the night was still young. He felt like kicking back. Loosening the collar of his dress shirt, he gave the impression of one who intended to whoop it up until the early hours. Talked that way too.

'We should hit a few other places later on,' he suggested to Max, as he flagged down a passing waitress. 'Le Baoli is a great spot, and Charly's in the old town has the best cocktails. Otherwise – if you fancied it – the Palm Beach Casino. The gaming terrace there looks out over the Med.'

'Thank you, but I don't think I will,' said Max. 'I'm a little tired and...'

'Big week ahead, right? I'm very impressed Max. You're going to nail this. I have every confidence. I mean look at you,' the agent said, giving an exaggerated a-ok sign, 'you already have the poise of a movie star. Un bon debut as they say in this neck of the woods. Half the battle buddy.'

'I'm glad you think so,' said Max, who couldn't help but observe that Jonny's glass was empty again. 'I'll stay here a while longer. Mingle if I can.'

'That's the spirit,' said Lewysohn, turning on his heels, 'speaking of which – you want another one?'

'No, I'm fine Jonny. Thank you.'

'It's like a cab,' Lewysohn mumbled, as he went looking for a tray, 'there's never one when you need it.'

Gordon Sawyer was also tipsy. And just a little belligerent. Moving towards Max, he wore a disagreeable look. Not nearly the polished operative of the day before.

'Well Max,' he said caustically, 'this is quite the trip you're on, isn't it? A modern-day fantasy or the fucking equivalent of it. But just remember, a lot of good people have stuck their necks out for you. I stuck out my own yesterday. So whatever you do, don't fuck this up! Failure is not a fucking option! Bomb and you get bombed.'

He walked off abruptly. A visibly stunned Max was given no chance to respond.

Jonny Lewysohn reappeared, fresh drink in hand. He began talking about the Cannes nightlife again. But stopped up when noticing his client's face.

'I miss something?' he asked.

HOLLYWOOD ON THE TIBER

David Cousins had mixed emotions about the first day of shooting. He never enjoyed the beginning of any of his films, felt restive as principal photography approached, and likened the experience to crawling into a deep pit, one from which there would be no emerging for some time to come. The pit in this case seemed deeper than ever before. It wasn't just the delay brought about by Don Taylor's accident, but other things as well. The wrangles with Aggregate Pictures over casting reminded him in many ways why he'd been glad to be away from the director's chair. The studio had tried hard to push on him an actor he did not want, but he'd come out on top in the end through some good luck and not a little persuasion. This round had gone his way, but there'd be more to come. The little-bitty minds of those execs would not remain quiet for very long he was certain. As soon as filming would get underway, there'd be the daily progress reports, and queries if these differed in any way to the production schedule. Justifications would be expected for every bit of overage, any oversight that might come to pass. David sighed as he thought about what lay ahead. He hated this part of the process and occasionally wondered why he'd bothered getting back into it. And yet, here he was. Letting himself in for it again. Déjà vu he figured. This pit of his was no accidental thing. He'd stepped into it of his own accord, with his eyes wide open. No one had told him to do this, no one had even asked. It was in his bones. Something he could not pull himself away from.

He knew the studio executives had a job to do, but it was the way they went about it that bugged him. The frequent interrogations and calls for accountability were tiresome and he'd heard them many times before. They all amounted to the same thing – are you, the director, keeping this production on time and within budget? Are we getting bang for our buck here? Will it all be up there on the screen when it hits the multiplexes?

And then there was Lorenzo Mastrodicasa, who'd be just as clamorous on these points. The aspiring impresario would appreciate the back-breaking endeavour even less so than the studio. He knew nothing of the innumerable decisions that would have to be taken on the set each day. With a cast and crew of dozens, sometimes hundreds, looking on. Looking to the director for the answers. But also watching for him to make a mistake. David imagined how each and every one of them might anticipate a chink in the armour. The returning director out of practise and getting his cues muddled for example. Or calling print for an unusable take.

The last thing he wanted was to show any of them a sign of weakness. He was still a potent force despite his time away. That was in his bones too. It was important they'd understand it from day one.

Cousins favoured working with people he'd shot movies with in the past. He didn't like new faces on his sets and tried to get regular collaborators if at all possible.

The Echo crew was a case of mixed blessings in this regard. There were a few individuals who'd laboured for the director before, and chief amongst these was Kirk Evans, the first assistant director. Originally from Fort Wayne in Indiana, Evans had started out in the business as a production assistant between junior and senior years of high school. Graduating then to second assistant director, his duties included copious amounts of paperwork and chasing; also getting actors out of their trailers, and extras onto the set. His likeability and dedication led to his quick promotion to first assistant director at the tender age of 28. He was smart and assured; wanted to move up the ladder, although he realised it was more commonplace nowadays for AD's to transition to production management jobs as opposed to directing. Most of all, he loved location work and wished there was just a bit more of this on the Echo shoot.

'But Rome will do just fine,' he joked to a colleague. 'It's a helluva location all by itself.' He was a natural organiser and mediator, indispensable qualities on any movie set. A David Cousins one most especially.

Jack Reed, Echo's production designer, was the first crew member Cousins had hired. The two men had worked together on several occasions previously, though not on the ill-fated Bluff City. Reed from Chula Vista, California, was in his mid-fifties, a tall man with steely grey hair. He was one of the best in the business, but described his work in minimalist terms.

'The production designer is responsible for the space in which the film takes place,' he once told an interviewer. 'The best professional relationships I have are with directors who know what they want 'cos I know how to get it done.'

For Echo, Reed had answered his design brief and then some. David Cousins wanted a muted, autumnal quality; a diffuse amber colour as he referred to it – 'nostalgic, ethereal, momentary.'

Reed's preliminary sketches, of gentle sepia and pink tones, went some way towards this vision, but the director was truly bowled over when he saw the conceptual sets.

'These are wonderful Jack, just what I was looking for,' Cousins said effusively.

Such high praise from him was unusual, and he seldom gave it out. In almost the same breath, he bemoaned the production designer's absence from Bluff City saying, 'at least we could have made the blasted thing look prettier. In retrospect we did it too kitschy.'

Reed laughed this off and they promptly moved on to the next item.

The costume designer, Ruth Benchley, had worked on three previous films of Cousins. Born in Rochester, New Hampshire, the 56-year old was a Hopkins Centre graduate who'd begun her career as a scenery painter for the Rochester Opera House. She'd moved west in the late 1960's and first worked in movies as a costume sketch artist at Universal Studios. Highly regarded by actors and actresses, who valued her understated approach, she had more than 70 screen credits to her name, the most recent of which was First Lady of Virginia starring Jennifer Carrington. For the Echo production, Benchley had been her usual industrious self, but she'd also availed of the Rome-based Sartoria Tirelli, one of the most notable providers of costumes for film and theatre in the world.

'Why not?' she said candidly to David Cousins, 'to have such a facility on your doorstep – it'd be incredibly egotistical of me not to use it.'

She was a great admirer of its founding father, the Italian designer/historian Umberto Tirelli, and regretted never having met him.

'I liked his self-moniker,' she told a colleague, as they began to dip into his extensive collection, 'a fashion archaeologist – now that's making a statement with style.'

Benchley loved period pieces above all else. There was an added challenge to them which present-day settings did not provide. And she just loved what the Sartoria Tirelli had to offer with its collection of 20,000 pieces; felt just like a kid in a candy store.

Andrew Ford, the production manager, was the sole veteran from the Bluff City shoot, apart from David Cousins. The genial 41-year old from Grand Rapids, Michigan, had survived that ordeal in a typically philosophical way.

'I kept saying to myself, things will get better, the darkest hour is just before dawn,' he later told a friend. The production had been nightmarish in more ways than one, but Ford did not get demoralised easily.

'My hours are long – sometimes over a hundred per week,' he said, 'but that's a standard with the job. I accept it. I'm the guy who looks after the day-to-day stuff – locations, budget schedule, personnel. I don't have anything to do with the creative direction of the film. That's the director's turf. I'm there to support the artistic vision. Make sure the cast and crew have everything they need – cars, food, drivers, plane tickets, accommodation. Someone doesn't like their hotel, or takes exception to the manner of their driver, I'm the one who finds alternative accommodation, fires the driver.'

Ford had had to move fast after Max Pellegrino's casting. He and his assistants worked the phones, making arrangements to bring over remaining members of cast and crew, and finalising hotel rooms and apartments around the city. The stack of messages on his desk grew. Pepto-Bismol tablets were liberally consumed.

The director of photography, Miroslav Dobrovsky, had insisted that his room at the St. Regis be south-facing. He wanted the Rome sun every morning as he got up he said. It helped him begin the day, got him into the right frame of mind. Ford had to charm and inveigle in order to meet this eleventh hour request. He assured the St. Regis rooms' co-ordinator that this was of paramount importance.

'Mr. Dobrovsky is a much sought-after cinematographer in Hollywood,' he breathed down the phone, 'it would be greatly appreciated by us if you could make this exception...yes, yes, I know...it's pretty much last minute.'

Across the desk from him, one of the production assistants, Hailey Hicks, gave him a sour look. After another bout of wheedling, Ford hung up, victorious.

'Boom-cha!' he said. 'How good is that?'

Hicks threw up her eyes.

'An unsuspecting tourist just got bumped,' she said acerbically.

Ford dismissed the attempt at sanctimony.

'Them's the breaks kid,' he replied, trying to sound worldly, 'some people lose their room with a view, others are much sought-after cinematographers.'

Miroslav Dobrovsky was indeed a much sought-after cinematographer. The Czech-American was the recipient of five Academy Award nominations and had won the American Society of Cinematographers Award three years previously. The son of a film projectionist, Dobrovsky was born in Prague in 1940 and grew up in the Vinohrady quarter of the city. He studied at the Academy of the Performing Arts and worked for a number of years in the famous Barrandov Studios. Following the Prague Spring of 1968, Dobrovsky relocated to America where he became a naturalised citizen in 1970. Settling in Los Angeles, he first took employment in photo labs, as a technician and photographer, before working on low-budget features and documentaries. He came to prominence in 1976 on a futuristic film called Project: Alpha and, from then on, was high up the list of preferred DoP's. An advocate of photographic aesthetics, Dobrovsky had never worked with David Cousins. The same was true for many of the rest of the crew.

The second assistant director was Corrado La Russa and he was joined by fellow countrymen Tommaso Juliano (gaffer), Rinaldo Agosti (lighting technician), Dino Musante (boom operator), and Luigi Morena (focus puller). On the American side were personnel such as Jason Snyder (second unit director), Andy Fuller (camera operator), Nelson Decker (key grip), Penny Herrera (key make-up artist), and Judy Torres (continuity supervisor). Further down the pecking order were the production assistants. Mostly they were a combination of Italians and Americans, all of them Cousins first-timers as well.

The cast list featured several American names. There was the Baltimore native Toby Devereux who would portray Giuseppe Garibaldi. According to Screen International Devereux was an actor who specialised in, *'quietly charismatic, reliably solid performances.'* He had received Emmy and Screen Actors Guild Nominations for his work in the television series Family Corporate. In reference to the Echo shoot, he'd told a reporter he was looking forward to a, *'vacation from B'more and the boob tube.'*

The character actor Lamar Calley was cast as federal judge William J. Wallace. From Fresno in California, Calley had a reputation for playing hard-nosed types. A leading critic dubbed him the, *'master of the merciless stare.'* Off-camera Calley was gracious with his fellow actors, always willing to lend advice where needed.

'I play against type on the big screen,' he frequently said,' I'm a nice guy and not one bit like those sons-of-bitches.'

For the role of William E. Ryder, Meucci friend in the US and occasional investor, the filmmakers had secured the services of Ruben Pollard. Pollard, from Albany, New York, had over 60 films on his resume, five of which he'd directed himself. His directorial debut, No Wave Goodbye, had earned him the Caméra d'Or at Cannes.

A personal friend of Pollard's, Daniel Joyner, was added to the dramatis personae as Joe Melli, Meucci's lawyer. Joyner, from St Louis, Missouri, was best known for his work in the comedy-drama series The Ties that Bind. He'd acted on stage with Pollard in a revival of Arthur Miller's A View from the Bridge.

Joining them was Miguel Serrano, a well-established actor from Zaragoza, Spain. A vigorous campaigner on the issue of war diamonds, the 45-year old divided his time and career between European and US productions. In recent times the number of offers coming in from Hollywood had increased significantly; Serrano was at last receiving the cachet he deserved. Echo of Passions would be his 24th English-speaking part; he was playing Meucci confidant Angelo Bertolino. For research the meticulous actor read up on everyday life in late 1800's Staten Island. He observed that the borough had a high percentage of Italian-Americans traditionally. A Spanish colony was also established, but at a later time. Serrano leafed through descriptions of tan canvas tents and open-air kitchens. It wasn't in the least bit relevant to his present study, but he found the idea of this enclosed community intriguing. So many dynamics he thought – factions, oppositions – I wonder if there was exploitation, abuses of power?

The remainder of the principal cast was mostly comprised of Americans and Italians. Lesser but reputable names such as Filipo de Marco, Bryan Medina, Nino Canale, Joel Meadows and Silvano Melato.

The real-life husband and wife team of Roberto Beccari and Oriana D'Ambrosio as Meucci's father and mother seemed a particularly nice touch. Their appearance in the film was thanks to a casting associate in Rome. Malcolm Archer, in consultation with the director, signed off on this as with all other casting decisions.

David Cousins was not a Sidney Lumet type director. He seldom held rehearsals before a shoot preferring instead that actors, *'find their way on the set, as they interact with fellow players, wear the costumes, see the locations.'*

'My personal opinion is that rehearsals wear down instinct,' he once

told a writer, *'and I think instinct is important to have when the camera starts rolling. It's at that point my actors discover the emotional triggers they need. As the writer/director, I come to discover them as well. Any changes or bits of improvisation we need are employed as part of this aesthetic process.'*

One major change Cousins had made to his script was to re-introduce the language barrier theme. The scenes depicting Antonio Meucci's problems with this had been excised at Don Taylor's request, but, now that he was gone, the director saw his opportunity. He figured – why not, this is my script and I want those scenes. I compromised them before for the big name, but I don't have to do that now.

To this end, he sent a final draft of the script to Aggregate Pictures two days after Max's casting had been confirmed. The Meucci 'lost in translation' sections were restored, including the longer version of the courtroom scene. As he anticipated, the studio approved it with no comment. A handwritten fax from Anthony Chouraqui simply read: 'Fine – now go for it!' Probably no one examined it cover to cover Cousins figured. Which was just fine by him. No objections to the shooting script meant that he could proceed as wrote. Happy days. This much was set in stone. No one could dispute it later on. At least not without a hell of a fight.

Andrew Ford based the shooting schedule on this final draft script. The production manager worked it out scene by scene and, collaborating with Kirk Evans, planned each of the sixty-five shooting days. This schedule set out where each scene would be filmed – on location or on set (with just a few exceptions Echo would shoot at Cinecittà); how much time should be allocated for every scene; how many set-ups per day; how many extras, vehicles, props; what kind of electrical equipment, lighting; and how many meals. For camera movements, would cranes be required or dolly tracks? How early in the afternoon should call sheets be distributed for the following day? Was weather information in Rome reliable? At what point would they decide to move it indoors if the forecast was for rain? There were thousands of details and all of them required a decision. And money of course. The schedule told Ford what was needed and how much time would be expended. He knew that, in filmmaking terms, time amounted to money.

Principal photography for Echo of Passions began on Thursday, 1st June, with a call time of 7.30a.m. Cameras were due to start rolling at 9.30 on the first take of the first scene – an exterior shot of a Florentine street as Antonio Meucci approaches his place of employment, the Teatro della Pergola. There was no dialogue involved. Max was to make his way down the street, past a number of extras, and then enter the building.

After all the anticipation and delay, it seemed strangely anticlimactic. There was no great feeling of excitement in the air. All very business-like. Everything going at an efficient clip. The manual labourers got ready the hand-operated Titan crane on which Miroslav Dobrovsky would perch. The focus puller worked on his marks. Elsewhere, Kirk Evans rehearsed the extras who'd reported earlier to make-up and wardrobe.

'The director is looking for a sweeping view of the street,' he told them, pointing towards Dobrovsky, who was setting up the shot, 'that's the reason for the camera position. Swoopp! Swoopp!' he said gesturing with his hands.

One or two of them giggled as he spoke into his walkie-talkie.

'I need to know when David is getting here,' he said, oblivious to their mirth.

Cousins walked to the set from the production office. On his arrival, preparations for the 9.30 start were stepped up. Groundwork and equipment to his satisfaction, he showed Kirk Evans how he wanted the extras to move for this first scene. Then he went into discussions with Dobrovsky. The director and cinematographer paced around, talked about the shot. Cousins had a loose-leaf notebook containing storyboards and script. The two men walked to the end of the imitation street, clapboard buildings either side.

They were shadowed by the camera operator, Andy Fuller, and gaffer, Tommaso Juliano. Both technicians had similar hairstyles – dark tresses pulled back in a ponytail.

Looking back, Cousins saw a profusion of lights, people and equipment.

'The challenge here is to make this establishing shot different,' he said to no one in particular, 'an original touch...of interest.'

Miroslav Dobrovsky agreed with this.

'Something different,' he said, 'a view with balletic movement I think.'

Andrew Ford wandered around, shooting off the occasional pep talk to crew members and extras. The image being captured this morning would add about 40,000 dollars to the 110,000 dollars for the day. The Titan crane and 55 costumed extras accounted for this surplus. Very soon he'd go back to the Talking Telegraph office. There was more work waiting for him there; calls to be returned to the press. For the Echo shoot, David Cousins wanted a closed set generally. Staggered was the word he used now as he'd done when working with Ford on Bluff City. Interviews with him or members of the cast only allowed sporadically; on-set photographs a definite no-no. The director even wanted the behind-the-scenes footage kept to an absolute minimum. It was distracting he said. He could do without the intrusion of public relations and press kits.

Ford had a balancing act to perform. He knew well that a production such as Echo would generate more interest than usual. There was the fact of Don Taylor's accident for one thing, an unknown lead in his place another. Any difficulties with the shoot would be magnified, hitches represented out of proportion. The fun was just beginning. The production manager had to keep many factions happy – the cast; the crew; the studio monitoring the daily progress reports; the unit publicist from Rome.

Guido Morena found it all most irregular. The tall lean man with dark-rimmed glasses had a gloomy expression even at the best of times. Now it was virtually hangdog. He had a job to do after all. Mr. Cousins was not making this easy he complained. Why this neurotic attitude towards reporters? Did he not understand that media outlets expected to be catered for? And rightly so.

'My colleagues here in the press will not understand this mentality,' he said. 'They will interpret it as something other than reasonable. Hostile even I think.'

Ford tried to explain it as best he could.

'He's a confidential sort of guy,' he said, referring to Cousins, 'prefers to work in a tight environment. But don't worry so much Guido – we'll get your buddies in gradually, just let the director breathe a little first. Let him find his feet.'

Morena maintained his grievances nonetheless. As a joke Ford began to sing the opening lyrics of Three Little Birds whenever he dropped by the office.

'Every little thing gonna be alright,' he warbled in his silvery voice.

It worked and it didn't. Morena allowed a temporary grin to cross his face. But his concerns did not fade away. He wondered if or when this intransigent position would change.

Max's stand-in for the film, Livio Bacciucchi, was wearing the same colours the actor would wear for this first scene. Around him, the extras were being blocked in by Kirk Evans, who was working as quietly as possible. Miroslav Dobrovsky continued to instruct the electricians and grips on camera position and lighting.

Bacciucchi, himself a part-time actor from Milan, was just glad to have made it this far. After Don Taylor's accident, the 37-year old figured the job was gone. Either they'd pull the plug on the film itself or hire someone who was physically different to the Hollywood star. As a rule-of-thumb, stand-ins were generally the same height as their counterparts on the first team. It made sense in terms of lighting, aspect, camera set-ups. That being the case, Bacciucchi was mightily relieved when he learnt of Max Pellegrino's casting. The surprise replacement was approximately the same height as Don Taylor and himself.

As an out-of-towner, Bacciucchi would also get per diem expenses for the Echo shoot. He liked working away from home. The perks were good and he could spend his evenings reading, doing whatever, instead of having to catch up with family and friends.

'Fifteen minutes,' Miroslav Dobrovsky instructed the third assistant director close to him.

Manuela Cinquini threw him a puzzled look in response.

'But Mr. Pellegrino is on the set already Mr. Dobrovsky,' she said pointing to Max.

Dobrovsky nodded quickly and returned to what he was doing.

He had a gruff manner about him, but was clearly accomplished in his field. Max had been watching him now for over half an hour. Sitting on a plain canvas chair, with no name, he was watching all of them get ready. He wanted to be on the set as much as possible. Soak up the atmosphere; get to know the crew; take in every last detail of preparation. It was so long since he'd observed this work; an honour to be here and see this level of industry. A far cry from the hit-and-miss – mostly miss – of Deadly Days.

One thing he was uneasy about though was the lack of preparation for the actors. Especially for himself. Two days before, the main cast members had done a quick read-through of the script. David Cousins had joined them in the production office for this.

'It's good to be here at last,' he said smiling weakly, his eyes serious. There was little in the way of direction from his corner of the table however. He simply identified the characters and asked them to begin. Judy Torres sat next to him. The continuity supervisor had a large notebook propped up on her lap. She was thirty-something, had long blonde hair, and cool blue eyes. Occasionally, she shifted in her chair and that was the only noise Max could remember hearing from either of them. When it was over handshakes were exchanged. Cousins doled out some generic words of encouragement. Torres fixed her rumpled linen suit.

'It's all going to be ok,' Max heard her say as the actors were leaving.

'Sure,' grunted Cousins. 'Sure.'

And that was it as regards groundwork. Nothing else was offered or proposed. Straight into it then and here's hoping thought Max. It was the one part of this methodical structure left hanging as far as he was concerned. Watching these technicians and specialists work he thought, it's easy for them, they begin early, have the time to get things right, exact. But what if I don't get it right at first? How much time might it take me? Will I be given time? Space? Will they understand how long it's been since I was here? For an instant, Franco Bonacossa came to mind.

'Don't look so down in the mouth on the first day,' Judy Torres called out to him. 'I have to take your picture now,' she explained, waving a Polaroid camera, 'it's for continuity for the scene after this one. If your collar button mysteriously becomes undone, that's a problem.'

She faltered suddenly and then reddened.

'But what's my thinking here,' she said, 'you know all of this obviously.'

After a few Polaroid snaps of Max and assorted extras, she took her place beside the video camera operator.

Ruth Benchley and one of her assistants came on to the set to view the fruits of their labour. Benchley wore a pair of orange-tinted glasses and a jolly beam. The costume designer was taking lessons in basic Italian from her subordinate.

'Meraviglioso,' the other woman whispered in her ear. 'Eccellente.'

Spotting her, Kirk Evans added his voice of approval.

'Great job Ruth,' he said motioning towards the extras, 'they belong in the past.'

David Cousins though was having one final look-see. He wanted to make certain of sufficient variation in hair, make-up and costumes. There was nothing worse than a bunch of extras that appeared like carbon copies.

Climbing back into his tall canvas chair (which did have his name on the back of it), he nodded then to Evans.

'Clear for rehearsal! Clear for rehearsal!' Evans boomed into his megaphone. He offered one final tip to the background players.

'Now remember when Max...Antonio...walks past you, pay him no attention,' he told them. 'He is just another person like you. Average. Everyday.'

Three rehearsals of the scene, which was to be filmed in one unbroken stretch, took place. Max hit all of his marks correctly. So too did the extras. By and large.

By 9.30a.m. – the appointed time – the filmmakers were satisfied that all was ready for the first take.

The camera came up to speed.

The second assistant cameraman lifted a clapperboard in front of it. Printed on it were the names of David Cousins and Miroslav Dobrovsky, the title of the film, the scene number and take number.

'Scene one, take one,' he said slapping the hinged stick onto the slate.

The camera operator, Andy Fuller, nodded to his director.

'Action!' roared David Cousins.

The first scene of Echo of Passions took 17 takes in all. A few times David Cousins saw something he didn't like and ordered that they go again. A couple were messed up by the extras. One woman dropped her handbag, another man turned the wrong way. One or two were deemed unusable due to general crowd action. Four were discarded because of problems with lighting and sound.

'Camera transport was uneven,' grumbled Dobrovsky on one.

The next time he judged it, 'plain bumpy.'

The crane went up too late on another.

They went back to first position over and over again. Until it was just right. Two takes of the 17 were printed. Mechanical perfection achieved, they eventually moved on.

That afternoon, the first interior scene was put in the can. It was also the first involving dialogue. David Cousins tucked himself directly behind Andy Fuller's shoulder. Out of eyeline, he watched closely as Max exchanged a few lines with Gabriele Del Prete, a ski-nosed man with distinct, arresting eyes. Del Prete had a minor role as Artemio Canovetti, Meucci's boss at the Teatro della Pergola. On screen he was a fine understated actor, but had difficulty remembering his lines. The traditional but inconvenient device of painting these on giant white cardboard cue-cards was eventually decided upon. This took up extra time then as Del Prete's movements had to be carefully rehearsed so he would not appear to be reading. The off-camera assistance worked in the end. The resulting performance from the actor was just fine.

'Ladies and gentlemen. Finished on the movie – Gabriele Del Prete,' Kirk Evans announced at the end of the day. 'He wasn't with us for very long, but we thank him nonetheless.'

A smattering of applause followed. The crew members still present were tired after this lengthy first day. There were many more to come they knew. It went with the territory. Draining work quite often. And dreary more than occasionally.

As if conscious of this, Del Prete made light of the plaudits.

'No, no, please...not necessary,' he said in his theatrically pitched voice. 'I simply pass through. Nothing difficult.'

He wished them well then for the remainder of the shoot. All 64 days as was projected.

OVER THE TOP

The Echo team was back outdoors on the Cinecittà lot for days two and three of production. Filming took place under an azure-blue sky, but inched along at only a snail's pace. The secondary cast and extras found themselves with a good deal of downtime and not much to show for it. But they were getting well paid – the 'special business' ones particularly – so had no reason to complain. The longer this film took, the more money they'd earn. Livio Bacciucchi, for one, hoped it would last the whole summer. He felt like an extended break from Milan; had made a list of books to read, things to do in Rome.

The stand-in was having an easy time of it so far. The same wasn't true for his fellow countryman on the first team. David Cousins was taxing his lead actors and then some.

A scene involving Max, Jennifer Carrington and Nino Canale took up the entire afternoon of the second day. The number on the clapperboard went into double digits a few times. For one of Max's lines, it got past 20. By then the actor was tired, wondering what exactly the director was looking for. But he'd made a conscious decision not to argue or speak out as he'd done so often in the studio. No quarrels here he told himself. Stick with it and give the director what he wants. Only problem was that David Cousins wasn't telling him what he wanted at all. His direction was vague, mechanical.

'We're going again,' he kept saying over and over. 'Give it more Max. Back to opening position. Show us what you're thinking. Back to the top. Put it out there for us to see.'

'Action!' he barked, sounding like a drill sergeant.

Finally, he seemed satisfied with the emotional pitch. But this wasn't the end of it.

'Don't cut the camera!' he said firmly, 'everybody back to their opening positions and we're going again. Ok from the top. And action!'

Max performed his line once again. Cousins told him to repeat it.

'End sticks,' he instructed the second assistant cameraman, 'actually, take it away altogether. I'll cue you Max. Action!'

The second AC withdrew for the remainder of the afternoon. The clapperboard went with him. The take number on it at that stage read 28. But Max did the scene many more times. He lost count after 35. Figured it might have been in the region of 45, perhaps 50.

To Max, David Cousins was like a conductor without a baton. The director clearly knew his craft, but was not putting it across to those around him. The actors in particular were flummoxed. Nino Canale, who was playing Francesco Domenico Guerrazzi, spoke to Max after their ordeal.

'I don't know what this man requires,' he said, exasperated, 'he hints that it's something specific, but then says nothing more. Is it a riddle we're expected to solve? What kind of director is this?'

Max didn't have an answer for him. All he knew was that David Cousins' style of direction was not smoothing his return to the world of film. When he wasn't ordering multiple takes, the helmsman was absorbed with technical details. Every set-up, every bit of nitty-gritty, was pored over. The director gave the lion's share of his time to Miroslav Dobrovsky and Andy Fuller. They were his inner circle on the set. He listened to them. He talked to them. But everything else seemed to be white noise. Meaningless. Distracting. He had far more important things to do.

And when he wasn't in this huddle, Cousins was usually on a crane, looking through a viewfinder. 30 feet up there was even less occasion for discussion with his actors. Certainly none for any lengthy analyses. Which appeared to suit him down to the ground.

Before long, Max had an idea of what other crew members were thinking. On the fourth day of the shoot, they were back indoors. The elaborate set for the Teatro della Pergola was being prepared. It was taking forever. Lighting and electrical teams climbed over one another as they tried to follow the director's vision. The gaffer, Tommaso Juliano, looked hard-pressed. So too did many of his co-workers.

Max took his chair outside the set and sat alone. He'd seen enough assembly for one day. Enough tearing down as well. He read over his lines. Then did a crossword. Finally, he was called back onto the set.

'His majesty awaits,' Corrado La Russa said, as they walked towards the giant plywood structure, looming in the dim light of the sound stage. Ropes and cables flowed from the entrance. The second AD apologised, insisted he was joking. Max though detected an edge.

Tension on the Echo set grew with the long days, the constant put-downs, and the lack of progress. Everyone heard about what happened on the fifth day. A terrible thing, or a source of amusement, depending on your point of view.

One of the Italian production assistants, Rafaele Graziani, did the unthinkable. She interrupted the director during his lunchtime break. David Cousins was extremely regimented about his breaks when making a movie. He needed them to keep his energy levels up. If he didn't get a rest during the afternoon, he suffered as a result. Directing was a tough business after all. His work wasn't just confined to the set.

Cousins's face was a bright-red when he answered the door. The small room he had was adjoining the production office. It was sparsely furnished, but had a bed. He was dozing when he heard the knock. He didn't shout at Graziani, a twenty-three year old graduate from the Sapienza University; the look on his face spoke volumes. The PA tried to explain why she was there. The director's regular assistant, Evelyn Tucker, was somewhere else. A phone call from Los Angeles had come through for Cousins. Assuming it was important Graziani had not thought to take a message. Nor was she aware of the strict regulation concerning Cousins and his private room. The instant he appeared, she knew she'd done wrong. He was not best pleased.

Later that evening, a few of the production assistants went out for drinks. They felt they needed it; to blow off some steam, and went to the Bar San Calisto in Trastevere. Graziani was prevailed upon to join them. She was hard-working and popular with the others. Still mortified, and fearful for her job, she went over the encounter time and again.

'I should have thought before I began pounding,' she said. 'I never think carefully enough. I just do. That's what gets me in the hot water.'

'Don't worry about it so much,' Olivia Butler told her, 'any of us could have made the same mistake. You hear Los Angeles on the phone and you think – studio, they want to talk to the director, this is a call he needs to take.'

'Was it the studio?' asked Adam Perez, a graduate from the University of the Arts in Philadelphia.

'Nobody knows,' replied Butler, 'it's top-secret like so many other things on this production. Besides, we'd be the last ones to hear.'

'I'm betting it was the studio,' said Perez. 'They must be getting very pissed off with the daily reports. Look how far behind we are already. And less than a week in.'

'Evelyn, you hearing anything through the grapevine?' Butler asked Tucker.

'No more than the rest of you,' said Tucker. The 25-year old from Oklahoma City was leggy and easy on the eye. Already she'd been asked out on two dates.

'Sorry, I didn't tell you guys about his lunchtime thing,' she said, looking at Graziani in particular, 'there's an awful lot to keep up with here. I'm having to fire-fight more than usual.'

'We're all having to do that,' said Nestore Rosetti, who was from Genoa. 'This is no ordinary production I think.'

'It certainly isn't,' agreed Hailey Hicks. 'Extraordinary, and not in a good way.'

'Is it the most demanding film you've ever been on?' Filippo Scarlatti asked her.

'One of them,' sighed Hicks. 'I'd heard about David Cousins's fastidious side. Now I can well believe it.'

'So too can the extras,' said Perez, 'toasting under the lights while he looks for the perfect angle. I suppose they'll shed a few pounds and can thank him for that much.'

'Dobrovsky as well,' Butler added. 'The way they circle the camera. They're like two carp in a goldfish bowl.'

This drew a laugh. Scarlatti explained what a carp was to Graziani.

'He is not just fastidious,' said Lissandra Bianchi, from Novara in Piedmont, 'the man is a dictator, a bully. I wish someone would stand up to him. Tell him to behave properly. It wasn't Rafaele's fault what happened today.'

'Do you think if we spoke to someone higher than ourselves…maybe Andrew Ford or Kirk Evans?' suggested Rosetti.

'I don't think it would get you very far,' replied Perez. 'They've more than enough on their plate as it is. Let's face it folks – we're dogsbodies. At the bottom of the pecking order. The social stratification is how it is. The only ones who can take action are the execs. And I think they will if this situation continues. They don't tend to appreciate the long-drawn-out.'

Rafaele Graziani though was still in self-blame mode.

'Mr. Cousins must be under great pressure…to make so many decisions can't be easy.'

'Are you kidding me?' Olivia Butler said to her. 'Decisions he is making, yes. But are any of them in the interest of moving this thing along? Are they practical? It's the complicated on every single thing – camera angles, set-ups, marks the actors have to hit. He doesn't give a shit about the schedule. We're going to be stuck on the theatre scenes for another week at this rate. Maybe longer.'

'That's true,' said Rosetti, 'everyone is sick and tired of his, how do you say it? Antics?'

'The expression I think you're looking for is, he won't be on my Christmas card list,' said Lissandra Bianchi.

'No, not this year,' said Rosetti. 'Not this century even.'

The others laughed again. They decided to have one more round of drinks.

Adam Perez put in the order. He handed the waiter his empty glass and then sat back in his chair. Smiling to himself, he thought of a line from a book he'd once read.

'David Cousins,' he said to his friends, 'it's like how Hemingway put it – some wanted to shit on his father, some wanted to shit on his mother.'

The next day was back to interiors of the Teatro della Pergola. Max and Jennifer acted out a scene backstage in which their characters first meet – she a costume designer, he a stage technician. The script juxtaposed this encounter with the operatic drama unfolding onstage. Antonio playfully asks Esterre if she ever wears any of the beautiful outfits she creates. She replies she doesn't, adding that she's not one of those glamorous actresses. He tells her that she is as beautiful as any actress he has seen in the theatre. Smiling demurely she says, 'you're much too kind, are all technicians so charming?'

'I hope to be more than just a technician,' he answers, in a rare moment of self-promotion. 'Would you like me to show you what I've made downstairs. You see I'm an inventor. I make things to help people. This one is for communication.'

Once again the perfectionist in David Cousins raised his head. He demanded multiple takes from his actors, pushing and pushing them.

'Come on Max, work it up,' he urged. 'Show us what you're thinking. You fancy her like hell and you're not putting it out there. Is this what you call desire? Having the hots for someone? You're playing it like a frigid schoolboy for chrissake! Take off the shackles. Give us some longing, some libido!'

Jennifer Carrington smiled sympathetically as this went on. She did not go without punishment either.

Her line, 'you're much too kind, are all technicians so charming?' had Cousins insisting on 48 takes.

After each one the director said, 'that's great Jennifer, just terrific,' but asked her to do it again, and again, and again.

Finally, the actress seemed to have found what he was looking for. She gave an exceptional delivery. Everyone thought so. Max, for one, was blown away.

Cousins said, 'terrific,' yet again.

Everyone relaxed; not least of all Jennifer.

Then, inevitably, came, 'once more, please.'

Max felt sure the actress would explode. But she didn't. Somehow she held it together. Takes 24, 36 and 45 were printed. To everyone else 45 was the best of all. But Cousins called for three more after it. None of which he subsequently had printed.

Going home after another long day, Max bumped into Jennifer and her driver.

'Not going to the dailies?' she asked.

'No,' he replied. 'I'm a little tired. I'll see them tomorrow.'

'Can we give you a lift somewhere?' she offered, and then followed with a joke, 'but only as far as where you live mind. I'm not gonna help you skip town.'

'Is it that obvious?' he said with a half-smile. She was much more friendly now. What her agent had said about her in Cannes was true.

'It's practically written on your face,' she replied, 'probably mine too. I've never experienced anything like this before. I guess it's what some people in the business call protection, coverage.'

'And what do you call it?' asked Max.

Jennifer smiled at him wryly.

'Lots of things,' she said, 'none of them complimentary. You know the meaning of the word overbearing?'

'Sure,' Max nodded.

'Well that's me being ladylike about it,' she said. 'How dare he say some of those things he said to you today! A frigid schoolboy?! Who does he think he is? He wouldn't talk to Don Taylor that way. Not in a million years. And your acting was great Max. You nail it after a few takes. But still he keeps prodding. He's relentless. Insensitive. 48 takes and I wanted to scream, are you fucking crazy?!'

She forced herself to calm down.

'But how about that lift?' she said, and winked mischievously, 'only not out of town. Otherwise, we'd probably keep going.'

Max declined politely.

'Another time perhaps?' said Jennifer.

Max tried to get hold of Jonny Lewysohn that evening. He'd tried before, but the message at his office was that the agent was out sick. Max was given a home number by the switchboard.

'He might not pick up,' the lady at SLR told him. 'He's been...unwell.'

Lewysohn's voice was gravelly when he finally answered. It sounded like his throat had been dredged.

'Hello Max,' he said tentatively. 'How goes it? The film going well? Everything...good there?'

Max told him everything wasn't good. The film wasn't going well. More seriously, he was having big problems with the director.

'I wouldn't worry about it so much Max,' Lewysohn said, glossing over, 'it's early days buddy. Most of the people have never worked together before. It takes time to gel. That's why you're behind right now. Real soon it'll crank up. Before you know it, you'll be drinking cocktails at the wrap party.'

He giggled inanely, then spluttered down the phone.

Is he in a daze wondered Max. Does he understand what I'm saying?

He tried to be clearer about it. More exact.

'The problems come from the director,' he said, 'it's how he operates and how he acts.'

'I thought you were the one acting Max,' Lewysohn joked. It was another feeble attempt at humour. Max ignored it.

'It's a work practice issue,' he continued, 'his preparation and set-ups take an eternity. I know this film is more than just behind Jonny. I've heard the crew members talk. The reports going back to Los Angeles are not good.'

'Idle gossip Max. Give it time buddy. Storm clouds will blow over.'

His scratchy cough did another number.

Max grew impatient at this. One last try he thought. I'll either get through or God knows what. He waited for the rasping bout to stop, then began again.

'Jonny, how can I make you understand this? The film is in trouble. Things are not going to improve. In fact, they might get worse. Yesterday he was shooting an opera scene. It was from Mozart's The Magic Flute. 60 takes on one shot. 75 on another. Not so magical for those involved. There were concerns the soprano would collapse. She was shaking.'

'Max, buddy, relax. That kinda dedication means it'll look terrific. It will be terrific Max. The director knows what he wants. He knows you can't tell a soprano or an actor what to do. He has to lead them to that place. He's leading you to that place each time as well. Helping you discover it as he guides you. I know it might feel like you're taking a battering right now; but soon buddy, soon.'

Max held the mouthpiece away from himself. He sighed in exasperation.

Nothing doing here he decided. He doubted Lewysohn would even remember this conversation. What was the polite term for it? Tired and emotional?

'Thanks Jonny,' he said. 'I'll think about what you said. And talk to you again. Let you know what place he leads me to.'

'That's the spirit Max,' chuckled Lewysohn, 'all in a day's work. Ciao buddy.'

David Cousins sat in front of an editing machine, mounted with three modular screens, watching footage with Jerry Itzkoff, one of the assistant editors. The footage was looking good. Perfectly composed shots of the Teatro della Pergola set; intricate camera movements accomplished with fluent precision; costumes, artwork, production design, ancillary elements, all to a standard expected. Itzkoff complimented the backstage scenes, the burnished quality of the lighting employed.

'Jesus! Dobrovsky knows his fucking craft,' he said. 'I haven't seen raw material this good in a long time. He's earning his bread that gifted Czech. Another Oscar nomination on the way and he might win it for this one.'

Removing the dailies they'd been viewing, he popped new spools of film onto the horizontal mechanical bed; threaded the film through the drive mechanism, and sat back. The frames danced rapidly to speed. They were now looking at Max and Jennifer. The 'you're much too kind' scene from earlier; before he shows her the apparatus he has made downstairs. The screen was no larger than an average television set. Nothing close to what the projected image in a multiplex theatre would look like. Even so, Itzkoff continued to heap praise. Jennifer Carrington looked amazing he said; her performance nuanced, delicate.

'Max Pellegrino is the real revelation though,' he submitted. 'Everything I've seen of him so far, I like. Has a gentle weariness about him. Vulnerable too. You must be very happy David. You got yourself a fine actor all things considered.'

Cousins muttered something in response. Itzkoff strained to hear, but couldn't make it out. The director's gaze didn't shift from the screen. He kept looking dead ahead, had other things on his mind right about now. Like the phone call he'd taken from Los Angeles beforehand. Evelyn Tucker had given him the receiver without as much as a clue. Damn her he thought when he heard Anthony Chouraqui's voice on the other end. Why didn't she warn me? Doesn't she know how to give a heads-up? He was tempted to have her replaced.

Not surprisingly, Chouraqui was in a dogmatic frame of mind. He was venting the studio's concerns about overruns and delays. So far the production reports and shooting schedule were worlds apart he said. When was the director going to conform to the timetable? Did he imagine this an open-ended thing? Or that financing was unlimited?

'We're asking for a show of good faith here David,' he said, 'start living up to your end of the agreement. Stick to the daily sheets. The time that's been lost so far you'll reconcile later. Or as you go along. No more holdups please. Show us you're mindful about such things and I won't have to make this call again. And David, open up a line of communication with Tim Woodward. The way you've been shutting him out to date is not impressing anyone. Tim is there to lend a hand. Everything he does is in the best interests of the film.'

Tim Woodward was the Aggregate Pictures' location executive assigned to the film. His job was to keep tabs on progress for the studio. A cautious presence in Rome. Each day he inspected the daily camera reports, production reports, average footage, page counts and amount of screen time shot; also cash flow charts and accounts. He called in his reports every evening to Chouraqui. The overages and glacial pace of production were recurring themes. Woodward registered deep concern at what he was seeing. The deluge of film feeding into and pouring out of cameras was ominous. The stony vibe he was getting from the director hinted at tough brokering ahead.

To Cousins, Woodward was little more than a spy. Another example of those bureaucratic execs who had no appreciation for the creative process. The suits in Hollywood were all the same as far as he was concerned. They somehow believed themselves dynamic, pioneers in the industry. What a load of rubbish he thought. Not one of them had an imaginative bone in their body. Not one of them understood what it was to have a vision, and to make every effort possible in the pursuit of that vision. He couldn't tolerate these guys any longer; didn't want to deal with them, or their interminable questions. Why had they to be so invasive he wondered. And what was with the subterfuge on this occasion? No one at Aggregate Pictures had told him about Woodward before shooting began. He had to find out about it for himself on the first day. The director, the one pulling it all together, and he was the last to know. It was obvious why. The studio didn't trust him. Because he was David Cousins. They were on their guard, watching beady-eyed, through this lackey. He felt treated like a kid. It made his blood boil. Times like this the job really felt like a dry heave. Like working for a bunch of incompetents.

Woodward wasn't the only unwelcome figure on the set. The stockily-built character David had told Art Brackman about was at Cinecittà too. At first he was there on and off. But now his attendance was virtually round-the-clock. Almost as much as Tim Woodward's. Cousins restrained himself as long as he could. He tried to pay no attention to this individual, not to catch his eye. But then he saw him hanging around the Teatro della Pergola set. Particularly when they were shooting the backstage scene between Max and Jennifer. That was too much for him. He had to find out who the hell this guy was. How was he getting access to his film so easily?

Vincente Ravenna sat down beside Max on the orange metro from Cinecittà station.

'Hello Max,' he said. 'I'm glad I caught up with you. I heard you come by way of public transport every day. That's very unassuming of you. I like it.'

Max stared at him blankly. Ravenna's face was vaguely familiar, but he couldn't place it.

'Do I know you?' he asked. 'Do you work at the studio?'

'In a sense I do,' said Ravenna, offering his hand. 'My name is Vincente Ravenna. I'm from Cleveland, Ohio, in the States. My employer is a gentleman by the name of Lorenzo Mastrodicasa. I don't suppose you've heard of him?'

Max shook his head.

Ravenna pressed on.

'Mr. Mastrodicasa is an independent financier who's given money to this film,' he said. 'There's a group from the San Francisco area who've been very generous in that regard. It would be fair to say Mr. Mastrodicasa is the most distinguished one of them. A major-league player, if you know what I mean.'

'Very important?' said Max.

'Yes,' replied Ravenna, 'an American equal of someone like Enzo Ferrari. He's what they would call a mensch in Hollywood. Much admired. Very courageous with his money.'

'And what is it you do for him?' asked Max.

'I'm a business consultant,' said Ravenna, passing Max one of his cards. 'Mr. Mastrodicasa brings me in when he has a difficult situation on his hands. Or if there's an individual problem. In other words, a problem with an individual.'

Max regarded the man beside him more closely now. Ravenna was powerfully built. He had a fighter's battered nose and huge hands. He was sharply dressed in what appeared to be an Armani; exuded self-confidence, had a predatory bearing despite his soft voice.

Max decided to proceed with care.

'Is there a problem of some kind with the film?' he asked as coolly as possible. 'Everything's been going well so far. The dailies, for example, look terrific.'

'Is that a fact?' said Ravenna, an incredulous tone.

'Yes,' replied Max. 'Even I'm made to look good.'

The infusion of humour didn't alter Ravenna's course.

'Then why aren't you back there looking at the dailies Max?' he asked.

'I'm a little tired,' said Max. 'It's been a long day. I need some rest. Tomorrow we shoot the scene downstairs in the theatre. You know this I imagine?'

'I certainly do,' said Ravenna. 'I pay a guy for a copy of the call sheet. Not that it's really relevant in this case. The film is foundering Max, and badly. My client is very unhappy. I have to come up with a solution.

Justify what he's paying me.'

Max paused before asking his next question.

'What can I do about it?' he asked, 'unless there's a problem with my performance?'

Ravenna gave a friendly smile, patted Max on the shoulder.

'There's no problem with your performance Max,' he said, 'nor with any of the other actors. Even that guy on the first day. The one who needed the cue-cards.'

'Gabriele Del Prete?'

'Yes. He was just fine too. No, the problem, as I think you know, lies elsewhere. With Mr. Cousins to be specific. I'm talking to you here and now because you have a vested interest in this. I read about you and how this opportunity came along. This film could mean a lot to you if it succeeds, right? A flop on the other hand and...well I think you know how the rest of it would likely play out.'

'Do you think that's where it's headed?' said Max.

Ravenna's eyes drifted around the carriage.

'Well the omens are not good so far,' he said, 'and I know a little about movie-making. Say, have you ever seen a Sylvester Stallone film called Over The Top? He plays an arm wrestler in it.'

Max replied no.

'Well I worked on that film as a technical advisor,' Ravenna said proudly. 'As a matter of fact, did some acting in it as well. I know first-hand the amount of work and effort that goes into these babies. A helluva lot of sweat and dedication to get it right. But easy for the whole thing to come undone as well. That, I'm afraid to say, is what's happening to this film at Cinecittà. My client, reasonable man though he is, does not appreciate another man who goes back on his word. Mr. Cousins promised Mr. Mastrodicasa he would deliver the film. He isn't doing that so far. He's fiddling, gratifying himself, and worst of all being the asshole about it. Look at what went on with your scene today Max. The way he was treating you, and that lovely actress. Messing with lenses and effects and then he wants you actors like putty in his hands. It's all calculated to intimidate and subdue. A tough guy, so-called. But he doesn't know what strong-arm really means.'

The train pulled into a station. People got on and off. Max had a moment to think.

'What would your employer wish to see happen?' he asked. 'Mr. Cousins replaced? A new director?'

'No,' said Ravenna. 'That isn't the answer. They fire him and who do they get? A journeyman, probably a lesser director I think. The dilemma here is that the asshole is actually a very good director. Mr. Mastrodicasa certainly thinks so. And I agree with him. I've watched some of his movies, part of my research for the job. There was one called Bluff City. A musical. I'm a sucker for musicals Max and I sure loved it. Lots of great songs and some terrific dance routines.'

'Sounds like you're a fan,' Max remarked mildly amused.

'I am,' said Ravenna, 'and the point is he clearly understands how to make movies. Good ones too. Anyway, Mr. Mastrodicasa doesn't want him fired. He's afraid the studio would pull the plug then. Cut its losses. Or, as I said, get someone who isn't up to scratch. My client wants the best possible film made. He has a thing about Meucci; is into the boning up of history. Sees this as the perfect vehicle.'

'But if they don't fire him, what else can they do?' said Max. 'Apply pressure? I don't think he would appreciate that. Give and take doesn't seem his way.'

'It depends on where the pressure is coming from,' Ravenna suggested, a glint appearing in his eye, 'and from who. My line of work often necessitates a certain kind of pressure being brought to bear. I administer it. You follow?'

'I'm not sure I do,' Max answered hesitantly. 'Do you use influence or something? Your client's?'

'No, Max, I use my own,' Ravenna said matter-of-factly. 'I've been keeping a close eye on Mr. Cousins. Especially this past week. The situation as is cannot go on. He needs a reality check and pronto. Before he derails the whole show. I intend to give him that. But I need to do it properly. By such means that are discreet and persuasive. You get the picture?'

Max moved uncomfortably in his seat.

'I don't think this is a subject I should be discussing,' he said.

'Why not?' asked Ravenna.

'Because I think you're a uomo ascia. Aren't you? What they call a hatchet man.'

Ravenna shook his head, dismissing it casually.

'I'm a retired sportsman,' he said. 'The field I now work in happens to be a specialist one. And yes, I bring a particular intensity to it. That's true. But a hatchet man Max? I'm above that sort of thing. I'm a consultant. I mentor. And some people need lots of mentoring, believe you me.'

Max saw a stop coming up. He decided to get off, even though it wasn't his. He'd walk the rest of the way home he figured. Better than be seen talking with this heavy, or whatever he was.

'I'm afraid I can't help you,' he said, starting to rise, 'the agreement your client and Mr. Cousins have is a matter between them. I hope whatever it is you have in mind doesn't affect the film.'

'That's just the thing Max,' said Ravenna. 'I don't want to do that. God knows the film's been affected enough as it is. But I have to get a result. I need someone else on board for this. Someone who's from Rome. Someone who has a beneficial interest. For my money, that's you. You stand to gain if I sort this mess out.'

'It will sort itself out I'm sure,' said Max, even though he had serious doubts about that. 'A few more days and...'

'That ain't gonna happen Max, and you know it,' said Ravenna. 'After filming today your eminent director confronted me. I guess he knows my face now. Asked me who I was, why I'm around the set every day. I had nothing to hide so I told him; told him who my client is.'

'What did he say to that?' asked Max.

'He went ballistic to put it mildly. Started yelling, went red in the face, veins in his neck popping out like ropes. Told me to leave and not come back. Now does it seem to you that situation will sort itself out? I don't think you really believe that.'

'This is my station,' said Max, moving towards the door. 'So you will be coming back to the set Mr. Ravenna?'

The broad-shouldered man nodded.

'Most definitely,' he replied. 'I don't go away. Not until my work is done. My cell number is on that card I gave you Max. Think about what I said. A reality check is the only way. Nobody gives it as good as I do.'

THAT'S ENTERTAINMENT

The brass at Aggregate Pictures had every reason to be worried about Echo of Passions. After six days of shooting the production was already five days behind. David Cousins had less than seven minutes of useable footage in the can. A shooting schedule which had envisaged an average two pages of script per day was barely registering two-thirds of a page.

The Teatro della Pergola segment was of particular concern. So far it had consumed the greatest amount of time and money. For all their application and ingenuity, David Cousins and Miroslav Dobrovsky had only a short opera scene and the backstage scene committed to celluloid. Two minutes of screen time roughly. The elaborately staged Magic Flute portion accounted for a mere 30 seconds of this. And it had taken up two days by itself.

There remained a number of theatre scenes to film and Cousins was still having parts of the plywood structure built, torn down, and rebuilt, as well as assembling extras by the dozen. On top of that the director wanted to shoot additional opera material and was planning to recall secondary cast members for an extra day. He was adamant he needed more coverage for post-production; hadn't quite got all the angles earlier to make the scene suitably dynamic, fluid. Anthony Chouraqui got wind of this from Tim Woodward and was apoplectic.

'How much footage does he need?' he asked, 'I thought the opera was just for a series of cuts, back and forth. Not important in the overall. Visual sure, but nothing else.'

'He told Andy Ford he wants it to look spectacular,' said Woodward. 'A nod to Georges Méliès I believe he said. Like a daydream.'

'How much would this daydream likely cost Tim?' Chouraqui groaned down the phone.

'The same figure as today Anthony. Give or take. The soprano and other performers would have to be rehired. They were originally contracted for just one. He was lucky to get them for a second. Prior commitments mean they won't be available for a week or so. Cost-wise the outlay would be identical. Which, as you know, was not for a song.'

'It's not going to happen,' said Chouraqui. 'He's fallen behind enough already. A rate of almost one day lost for every day shot. He can't rip up the schedule and then put on extra days. This is make-it-up-as-you-go-along territory. Not how the business works.'

He put a call through to the production office the following day and managed to get a hold of Cousins. The Magic Flute did not come up during their conversation. Chouraqui presumed the message – AP's line – was abundantly clear.

'I told him he has a responsibility to make up the time lost so far,' he informed Woodward as they spoke on the phone that evening. 'We didn't get down to specifics, but he can read between the lines. There are to be no further dalliances with Mozart Tim. And no Georges Méliès homage. If he tries to squeeze any of it in, you're to let me know immediately. Day or night. From now on we head him off at the pass. To that effect I'm writing a memo addressed to him, you, and Andrew Ford. It'll be faxed to Rome tomorrow. We want a new schedule put together. One that takes account of the overages so far. One that proposes a feasible way to cancel them out.'

'Sure Anthony, but I don't know if he'll agree to that. And even if he does, there's every chance he'll fall behind again. Then what?'

'Then we expand on the number of options we look at Tim. And we tell him as much. If he won't do contain and control, we have to examine them all. The unpalatable ones included.'

'Jesus! Would we really go that far Anthony?'

'I hope it doesn't come to it,' said Chouraqui, 'but he has to remember what the original priorities of this thing were...still are. This sturm und drang shit he's creating benefits no one on the picture. Speaking of which, talk me through tomorrow.'

Day seven and the scene directly following Antonio and Esterre's first meeting was top of the call sheet. In it the inventor shows his future wife a kind of acoustic telephone he has made to communicate between stage and control room. Esterre compliments Antonio's creativity, then asks him about himself. Antonio tells her a little about his background – the oldest of nine children, his father, an officer of the local police, his mother, a homemaker. He also mentions how four of his brothers and sisters have passed away in infancy. Esterre is touched when she hears this.

'Childhood is an age where no one should die,' she says in a low voice as she moves around the room, describing her own background to Antonio.

A much smaller structure had been constructed for this intimate exchange and Miroslav Dobrovsky was not in raptures about it. The space was tight enough under normal circumstances; diminished to an even greater extent when packed with camera, lights and equipment. And to complicate matters further, Cousins wanted a 360-degree pan as Jennifer Carrington walked around. This involved all four walls of the room appearing in the same shot, making the lighting of it more difficult and time-consuming.

Dobrovsky bellyached to Tommaso Juliano.

'This is no fuckking picnic,' he said. 'We spend days lighting a colossus and then must adapt ourselves down to this. I blame fuckking Jack Reed mostly. His sets are always extremes – too large or too small. But this one is microscopic even by his standards. The lights will scald the actors if you ask me. A virtual oven Tommaso.'

Jennifer Carrington too had misgivings when she saw the set. But professional as she was, she got on with it. So did Max. The first couple of set-ups were focused on his character mainly. Antonio's personal history, his family. The siblings he can no longer remember.

Cousins was bearing down hard yet again, getting Max to do take after take. As usual there was a paucity of explanation or instruction. Just lots of, 'do it again. Do it again. One more. One more.'

Later in the day it was Jennifer's turn to be under the cosh – the 360-degree pan which had taken Dobrovsky and Juliano over two hours to prepare. The DoP was tracking Jennifer in his viewfinder. The important thing for him was to keep the actress in the same position of the frame.

The director watched on a monitor nearby. The heat from the lights was intense now, but even so he was insisting on, 'from the top,' over and over. 30 takes. 40. 50.

It was him going, 'one more. One more,' and the increasingly frazzled actress asking, 'What do you want David? What do I need to change? What else is there?'

It got to the stage where she was visibly distraught, telling him her Achilles tendons were beginning to hurt. 70-plus takes by then. But Cousins wasn't satisfied. For whatever reason. There was no justification supplied, no help on offer.

'One more. One more,' he kept demanding until finally – to absolutely no one's surprise – Jennifer snapped.

Leaving the set in tears, she could be heard saying, 'I can't take this kind of treatment. It's offensive.'

A little while later her personal assistant, Lily, arrived on the set.

'Miss Carrington won't be able to return today,' she said in her clipped English accent. 'She's going home...I mean back to her hotel.'

'That's quite alright,' Cousins told her in a derisive tone. 'We got what we needed here. But make sure she has tomorrow's call sheet.'

The day's work was not yet over because Max's reaction shot, all through the 360 pan, had to be filmed. There was no dialogue involved, but Cousins had him do it 45 times nonetheless. Then, at last, he called a halt to the day.

'See you all back here tomorrow morning,' he said.

Andrew Ford whispered something in his ear as they headed back towards the production office. Max caught part of it.

'No, I'm not going to have a clear-the-air meeting with her,' said Cousins. 'This is my picture! We do things my way! End of!'

Max went to the Hotel Quirinale near Piazza della Repubblica where Jennifer was staying. He'd got the name from one of the production assistants, Filippo Scarlatti.

Jennifer appeared happy to see him when she answered the door.

'Come in,' she said, 'I could use the company after what happened today. That's why you're here, isn't it? Because of the way I left the set?'

'I just wanted to make sure you were ok,' said Max.

He sat down on the sofa opposite her. Jennifer's room had period furniture and oil paintings. The walls were emerald green.

'I don't think I am,' she replied. 'I honestly don't know what to do. Tomorrow I have to face that man again and it's…I dread to think what's coming next Max. Don't you? My God we've only a week done! How much more of this is ahead?!'

'I think a lot based on what's gone so far,' said Max. 'I never imagined it would be so difficult. In my mind's eye, I was returning to film. It was all going to work out for me this time. Nothing could stand in the way. Now I have doubts. It's up in the air again.'

'I'm sorry,' Jennifer said sympathetically. 'I heard you acted earlier in your career, but it didn't work out. This isn't much of a way to come back to it. Nine times out of ten you'd get someone on the level, someone reasonable. David Cousins isn't either of those things. You got a raw deal. I think we both did.'

'You've no choice but to continue either?' said Max.

'None whatsoever,' answered Jennifer, 'and there lies another problem for me. This film is already behind schedule. Way behind. If it goes on like this, it's going to conflict with my next film. I could be replaced. I've never lost a job before. Even if it isn't my fault, I don't want that to happen.'

'Of course not,' said Max. 'You shouldn't have to. No one should allow it.'

Jennifer smiled softly.

'Unfortunately, there doesn't seem a lot that can be done,' she said. 'Barry's been sounding off about it to the studio, but there's only so much noise he can make. He's been there before. Says their attitude most of the time is just get to the end of the tunnel; live with the delays and swollen budget. They do that – sit on the fence – and I can pretty much forget about Kith and Kin. Take my word for it Max, don't ever agree to a crowded calendar. Not if you can help it. Only thing it's giving me right now is a royal pain in the ass.'

'I'll keep that in mind, if I ever have a crowded calendar,' laughed Max.

Jennifer changed tack.

'I'm sorry about how I spoke to you that day in Cannes,' she said. 'It was rude of me. I was tired from the flight, but that's no excuse. I'm not the diva type. Not in the least bit Hollywood actually. I'm from the Midwest. Illinois. Chicago hotdogs and chocolate brownies are more my style. Not a room like this. Not any of the extras. And when I see behaviour like David Cousins' it makes me mad. Today, it got to me in another way. I guess that's why I…'

Without warning, she became tearful again.

'Jesus! I don't know what's with me,' she said. 'You must think me over-the-top. Crying like my dog just got run over or something.'

'Not at all,' said Max.

He wanted to reach out to her, but was uncertain. Jennifer's right hand was nearest him so he gently took hold of it. The rest followed

357

automatically. A tender kiss on the cheek. A more passionate kiss on the mouth. They embraced warmly. She stopped crying. No words between them for what felt like several minutes.

Then Jennifer said, 'well this is a topsy-turvy day if ever there was one. And it's not even seven yet. You fancy getting some dinner. I could order room service, or we could go out? It goes without saying you know restaurants in Rome better than I do.'

'It goes without saying...because I'm from here,' said Max. He turned this over in his mind.

Jennifer threw him a quizzical look.

'What's with the deliberation all of a sudden?' she asked. 'You don't have to rack your brains over a restaurant. Do you? Anywhere that's got good pizza is fine by me.'

Squeezing tightly, she gave him another peck on the cheek.

He didn't react.

'What's up? Why so serious?' she asked.

'Sorry. I just remembered something,' Max told her. 'He said he needed someone who was from Rome. Someone who has a beneficial interest.'

'Who?' said Jennifer.

Max returned his attention to her.

'A friend,' he said, making it sound as trivial as he could, 'a friend of mine who's in town. Needs a room for the night. I'd forgotten about him until you mentioned restaurants. I have to meet him for a coffee and...'

'Then play the Good Samaritan?' Jennifer concluded, smiling.

'Yes. Do you mind? I don't mean to rush away.'

'That's exactly what you're doing,' she said, giving him a playful dig in the ribs. 'No, of course I don't mind. Go see your friend. I'll get a hold of Lily. She likes pizza too.'

'Thanks,' he said, getting up to go.

She pulled him back for a moment.

'Just promise me one thing,' she said.

'What's that?' he asked.

'Promise me next time you'll hang around for dinner. No friend. No plans.'

Max nodded, gave her a kiss.

'I promise I'll stay for dinner,' he said. 'Enjoy your evening. And don't worry about that other thing. It'll work out.'

'One way or the other?' said Jennifer.

'One way or the other,' said Max.

He kissed her again.

'Ok,' she said. 'I hope that's a promise too.'

Vincente Ravenna was waiting for him in Piazza Barberini.

'Hello Max,' he said. 'I didn't expect to hear from you so soon. There was more unpleasantness on the set today? Adam Perez told me about it. He's the one who's been passing me the call sheets.'

'Yes, more of the same,' said Max.

They began to walk around the large noisy square, no one likely to hear their conversation.

'I didn't bother getting too close today,' said Ravenna. 'I've seen enough already. I know what needs to be done.'

'You talked yesterday about your line of work,' said Max, glancing at him quickly. 'How it sometimes demands...pressure?'

'That's a faithful representation of what I told you,' said Ravenna.

'Also that it's discreet.'

'And persuasive?'

'Yes.'

'Given the correct location Max,' Ravenna elaborated. 'You see I need a particular environment – a set – the same way you actors do. Once I have that, I can get to the job in hand. There's no script for what I do, but it's a well-rehearsed routine. I don't fluff my lines, if you know what I mean.'

'No, no, I don't suppose you do,' said Max.

'You have an apartment in Monteverde, don't you?' said Ravenna. 'In a semi high-rise? Not far from the American University?'

'How did you know that?' asked Max, taken aback.

'I make it my business to know these things,' said Ravenna, smiling confidently. 'I also know the hotels where cast and crew members are staying; who drives who to Cinecittà every day; what time so-and-so goes for his morning jog. I do my research Max. The groundwork is every bit as important as the performance. I'm sure you can appreciate that being an actor.'

'Is that why you need someone from Rome?' asked Max. 'For the performance part of your job?'

'I need an empty house or apartment,' said Ravenna. 'An apartment preferably. There's less chance of interference. Closed doors. Occupants tend to mind their own business. Incidentally, is yours sound-proofed?'

'Yes, it is,' replied Max. 'I had it done a few years ago. I practise my lines there. Often I have to be loud so it made sense.'

He did a double take.

'Why do you ask me about sound-proofing? What relevance does that have?'

'Let's just say that sometimes I have to be loud in my work as well,' answered Ravenna. 'Born out of necessity you understand. It's important my target audience gets the message. They don't all respond to the soft-spoken approach.'

'And what about them?' said Max. 'Do they also contribute to this... sound?'

'What is it you're asking me Max?'

'There's no harm done to them. Is there? Physical I mean.'

They stopped walking. Ravenna turned and faced him.

'There's never any harm done Max. It never comes to that. My methods are persuasive enough. I bring individuals around to the point of view they need to acquire. In Mr. Cousins' case it's for him to start doing what's expected of him. He may be talented, Oscar tucked under his arm and all that, but he has to toe the line. This film has to get made. On time. Within budget. And it has to be brilliant. Not asking too much, am I?'

Ravenna smiled again, closed lip.

'You're sure you can do that?' said Max. 'Persuade him? He's not a submissive man as you know.'

'He's a hard-charging bully with paper-thin skin,' said Ravenna, 'I've encountered the type before. All I need is to get him in a room. Take it from there. So? Can you give me that room Max? Your apartment?'

'How does it work?' asked Max. 'Would I be there too?'

Ravenna shook his head, started walking again.

'Absolutely not,' he said, 'what I do is strictly one-on-one. No third parties. I'd need your apartment exclusively. And you wouldn't come back 'til I'm done Max. Let's be very clear about that.'

'Where would I go then?'

'You can have my hotel room. I'm staying at the Hassler, near the Spanish Steps.'

'Expensive,' remarked Max.

'My client is picking up the bill,' said Ravenna. 'I like good hotels. Mr. Mastrodicasa understands this.'

They came up to the Fontana delle Api where Via Veneto entered the piazza.

'Well then,' said Ravenna, 'are we in agreement on this? How we proceed from here. Our living arrangements for the next day or so.'

'Is that how long it will take?' asked Max.

'More or less,' said Ravenna. 'Depends on how obstinate he really is. Some guys can be broken down faster than others. You'd be amazed. Hard-core as he may think himself, Mr. Cousins has a breaking point. I give him 36 hours tops.'

'36 hours?' Max repeated. 'Won't that slow the film even more? Put it further behind?'

'Don't worry Max,' Ravenna said assuredly. 'He'll make it up. The delays will be wiped out. Efficiency will be his watchword. No more pussyfooting around.'

He looked at the marble bi-valve shell with three bees of the same material fixed on it.

'I've always liked bees,' he said. 'They're well-organised creatures. Work hard, very industrious. And mostly they don't trouble anyone. But there are circumstances when a bee is liable to attack. If it's been disturbed or has to protect itself. The bee will sting then because it has a provocation, a justifiable cause. I deliver a service for my clients when they have such justification. When their interests need to be protected. Often it's a stepping-over-the-line by another person. Or an inflexibility.

360

It's forceful, but fair. The sting in this case doesn't inflict a wound. It brings about change. Shifts attitudes. That's the assistance I give my clients and friends. I offer them my strong arm.'

Unbuttoning his shirt sleeve, he flexed his muscle.

Max eyed it, nodded.

'Forte,' he said. 'Forte.'

One of Our Directors is Missing

David Cousins did not appear for his pick-up the following morning. He was staying at the St. Regis Hotel, same as Miroslav Dobrovsky and Kirk Evans, but neither of them had seen him over breakfast. The first AD had reception phone his room, but there was no answer. Concerned about the director's well-being, he got the porter to let him in. They found the room empty. It had been slept in the night before.

'Mr. Cousins often goes out for an early jog,' Evans said, as he questioned the on-duty receptionist, 'did you happen to see him leave this morning?'

'No sir,' she replied.

'Are you absolutely certain?'

'I never saw Mr. Cousins leaving,' she said. 'I was away from the desk for a minute so it's possible he passed then. I hope he's ok Mr. Evans. I hope he isn't in trouble.'

'We're all in trouble if he doesn't show up soon,' Dobrovsky grumbled as the two men were driven to Cinecittà. 'We ran into problems when we were roughing in the lighting last night. I'm going to need at least another half hour because of it. He won't be happy when he arrives. Maybe he went on before us?'

But David Cousins hadn't, and by 9 o'clock there was a growing sense of disquiet in the production office. Andrew Ford attempted to establish a timeline.

'When did you last see him in the hotel?' he asked Evans and Dobrovsky.

'Just before I turned in,' replied Evans.

'I was working late,' said Dobrovsky. 'Last I saw him was here yesterday. The lighting for this morning's set-up is a fuckking nightmare Andy.'

'I appreciate that Miroslav, but we're kind of missing our director at the present moment. We need to make a decision on the day's work. Contact the studio.'

'Contact the local authorities as well,' Evans submitted.

The Italian state police were alerted and an officer took a preliminary report. He surmised that, in all likelihood, David Cousins had left his hotel sometime that morning and not come back. The reason why though he could only guess at.

'People often go missing because they are worried or depressed. Was Mr. Cousins in such a frame of mind?' he asked Ford.

'Not that I'm aware of,' said Ford. 'He's under pressure I guess, but he's experienced all that before. As for depression, I don't think so.'

The officer took a short description of the director; asked if there was a history of drug or alcohol abuse.

'He drinks beer, but not excessively,' said Ford. 'Drugs – definitely not. What do you think has happened officer? Is it possible he's been abducted?'

'I think it's unlikely sir. When an individual goes missing it's normally a sign of a personal problem. Not an occurrence. This is perhaps a deliberate disappearance. Most of them return after a short time. We will of course make enquiries with hospitals, emergency rooms.'

'We've tried some of them already,' Ford said, pointing to Lissandra Bianchi and Nestore Rosetti on the phones. 'Is there anything else you can do besides that?'

'Unfortunately not yet sir. This can only be given low priority. But you did the right thing to report it. Please inform us when he returns.'

Andrew Ford was not so confident about this. He changed his stance uneasily.

'I don't like this one bit officer,' he said. 'It's entirely out of character for him. I think there's something fishy going on here. And it's not 'cos I've seen too many movies.'

Ford addressed those present on the set a little while later. It had been decided to proceed with work for the day, mostly inserts and pick-ups, close-ups and short segments. Kirk Evans took charge of this. Despite the late start, he got through fifteen in total. The majority were completed in three takes or less.

'This is a very unusual situation we find ourselves in,' Ford said to the cast and crew gathered. 'We don't know what's happened to David. He hasn't been seen since late last night. We know nothing of his present whereabouts. We hope he is alright and will be back with us soon. I'm sure he will be. In the interest of the film, and with respect to David himself, I ask that you don't discuss this with anyone. Family or friends included. Kirk and Miroslav have been doing sterling work here today. They'll continue with this while waiting David's return. The studio is determined to press on and that's what we intend doing. Thank you all for your patience and efforts.'

There were theories as to what had befallen David Cousins and they ranged from the imaginable to the absurd. One version had him jumping into the Tiber at night in a fit of madness; another one abandoning the project entirely and departing Rome incognito. The most popular speculation, certainly amongst the tight-knit group of production assistants, was that Aggregate Pictures was seeking to replace Cousins and – being aware of this – the director was protesting in absentia.

'It's typical of him to be melodramatic if that's the explanation,' said Adam Perez.

'Where might he be holing up?' Olivia Butler wondered.

'God knows,' said Perez, an impish grin crossing his face. 'Somewhere underground? The catacombs maybe?'

Jennifer asked Max his opinion on the mystery.

'What do you think has happened him?' she said. 'You think he had an accident?'

'I don't know,' he replied. 'I guess it's a possibility. If he was out jogging, like they say, perhaps he became ill.'

'A heart attack or something?'

'It's been known to happen.'

'But I wonder why he hasn't turned up in a hospital.'

'They may not have contacted them all yet,' said Max. 'Official procedure can be very slow in this country.'

'It's the only reason I can imagine,' said Jennifer. 'I mean what else could there be. After yesterday, I probably seemed the more likely not to show my face again. I have to admit there's a part of me glad he's not here. That's horrible, isn't it?'

'No, it isn't,' said Max, 'he wasn't exactly being Mr. nice guy to you. And look at the way Kirk handled things today. He was polite and professional. Got the shots done and moved on.'

'Yes, but he's not a director Max. If David Cousins is sick or worse, then the future of this film is in serious doubt. Maybe they'd get someone to replace him. Maybe not. Either scenario means a lot of time and money wasted. The one good thing is I'd be free for Kith and Kin I guess.'

'Don't worry,' Max told her. 'It'll work out.'

She gave him a curious look.

'You said that yesterday evening as well. Are you always so upbeat?'

Max smiled tentatively, began to respond, but was interrupted by the appearance of Rafaele Graziani.

'Excuse me,' the production assistant said, 'Mr. Pellegrino, there's a phone call for you in the office. Somebody from Los Angeles. SLR was the name I think he mentioned.'

'Thank you,' said Max. 'I better take this Jennifer. It's probably my agent.'

It was an agent to be sure, just not the one Max was expecting. Tom Steiner's voice was tender and raw. He apologised for not being at his most lucid, said he had inflamed membranes in his nasal passages and was on a course of anti-inflammatories.

'I'll get right to the point,' he said, 'Jonny Lewysohn – your agent – I'm afraid to say we had to let him go. There were personal issues. We couldn't work through them.'

'I understand,' said Max.

Indeed he could. During their last conversation, Lewysohn had sounded every bit as bad as Steiner now did. And it wasn't owing to inflamed membranes.

'The clients he was representing will remain with us,' Steiner continued. 'For the time being, I'll be looking after them.'

He paused perceptibly, then added, 'including you Max.'

'Ok,' said Max.

'It doesn't come as a surprise?'

'What? Jonny? Or the fact of you representing me?'

'Both,' answered Tom.

'I liked Jonny,' replied Max, 'he was a nice guy. We got on well together in Cannes.'

He was disinclined to say anything else about Lewysohn. As regards Steiner's attempt to sound him out, he decided two could play that game.

'When you say you'll represent me for the time being, how long do you mean?' he asked.

'Hard to put an exact period on it,' Tom croaked in response. 'It's always a delicate thing changing agents. Or when there's an enforced adjustment such as this. That's why I'm handling it personally. Let's see how it turns out, shall we?'

'Depending on how Echo of Passions turns out?' said Max.

Tom didn't answer this. Instead he directed his attention to the more immediate.

'How is the film going anyway?' he enquired, his voice becoming grainier with every word. 'We've been hearing not so good on this end. Anything I need to be aware of?'

'No,' said Max. He wondered if Steiner somehow knew about David Cousins' disappearance. It seemed unlikely. He chose not to raise it.

'It was slow to begin with, but it's moving along now. Gathering pace.'

'Hmmmm,' Tom said contemplatively, 'well keep in touch. By the way, is there a problem with your phone? My secretary tried leaving messages for you. All she was getting was a disconnected tone. That's why I'm calling you here.'

'Must be,' said Max. 'I'll have it repaired.'

The phone in the hotel room rang later that evening. Figuring that in all probability it was Ravenna, Max picked it up, said hello.

'Is that you Vincente?' the voice on the other end asked.

'I'm afraid he's not here at the moment,' said Max. 'Can I take a message?'

The speaker identified himself.

'This is Lorenzo Mastrodicasa,' he said.

Max recognised the name from his conversations with Ravenna.

'He's in another place right now Mr. Mastrodicasa,' he said. 'I expect to hear from him sometime tomorrow.'

'Who is this?' the businessman snapped impatiently.

'This is Max Pellegrino.'

There was an unmistakable pause.

'The actor Max Pellegrino?'

'Yes sir.'

'What the hell are you doing in Ravenna's hotel room?'

'I'm staying here temporarily. Vincente is…'

'Jesus!' exclaimed Mastrodicasa. 'What's he doing involving you? I've been trying to reach him on his cell phone. There's no answer.'

'He probably has it turned off,' said Max. 'He told me he prefers no distractions.'

'Jesus!' Mastrodicasa said again, more loudly. 'I got word about this from Chouraqui at Aggregate Pictures. They're climbing the walls in Los Angeles. What kind of plan is this? I'm assuming it's Vincente behind this vanishing act.'

'It's Vincente,' Max confirmed.

'Well he's got to let him go right away!' Mastrodicasa said categorically. 'This is not like any previous job he's done for me. I never gave him the go-ahead for this action. He's playing the loose cannon. It's not appropriate. There's a schedule to this film and it's already beat-up. That's what the studio is preoccupied with. Chouraqui kept saying it to me during his call. They're at the end of their rope. Cousins stays missing and they will abandon. He has to resurface pronto or that's it. Not the kind of ending my associates or I want. Ravenna has to be told this. If you're in his hotel room, answering his phone, then you clearly have an idea where he is. Get to him Mr. Pellegrino. Fast! Have him release Cousins. Now!'

'I can't do that,' said Max. 'He told me under no circumstances to...'

'Max I don't give a damn what he said!' Mastrodicasa retorted. 'These particular circumstances go on much longer, there won't be a film! Do you understand that? No film and I think we'll both be very disappointed men. Is that the kind of ending you want?'

'No,' said Max, 'I'll see what I can do.'

'That's more like it,' said Mastrodicasa, 'and when you talk to him be sure he keeps my name out of it. David Cousins will have some amount of explaining to do. Whatever story he hatches better not have me in it.'

'I'll give him the message.'

'Good,' said Mastrodicasa, his voice loosening up somewhat, 'apart from all that, it was real nice talking to you Max.'

There was an abrupt click on the other end and he was gone.

The second day of filming without the director consisted of yet more fringe work. There were remaining bits and pieces to be completed from the evening before. Kirk Evans was at the helm once again. He appeared to be settling into the unexpected role quite well. Joked about this pop-up vocation of his; said he was mulling over the direction of his career now that his stock was on the rise.

'My resume is getting better by the hour,' he said poking fun at himself, 'I expect the agents and head-hunters to start pouncing before long. But I'm not gonna sell out. I want my work to have artistic value. No director-for-hire here.'

In spite of Evans's good spirits, an uneasy feeling hung over the day's shoot. There was the veneer of business-as-usual, but an undercurrent of resignation. Although prepared to help the AD in whatever way they could, many of the crew were thinking endgame in the back of their minds. The talk in some cases was of future projects, a topic normally set aside for the final week of filming. This atmosphere cast a shadow as morning passed into afternoon. The Italian members of the work force were especially disheartened, fearing the worst. There was a scheduled break the next day. They were not expecting to return after that.

'I was counting on this job for the whole summer,' Rinaldo Agosti, one of the lighting technicians, moaned to Corrado La Russa. 'Now what do I do? I have nothing to fall back on. There is no plan B.'

The second assistant director tossed his head, voiced his own sense of frustration.

'Kirk can afford to make jokes about himself and his career,' he said, referring to their American colleague, 'but it was of greater importance to me. I wanted this film on my CV. I was hoping to move up to first AD soon.'

Livio Bacciucchi was more accepting about the state of affairs.

'It's a great pity if this is the end, but it's not life and death,' he said to Max as the two men conversed between set-ups. 'The director has a teenage daughter I understand. It must be a nightmare for her; her father missing without a trace.'

This got Max thinking all over again and he wondered what he might do. He hadn't paid a visit to Ravenna as Mastrodicasa had demanded; had decided there was time yet. Ravenna had said it could take 36 hours. What's more, he'd told him to stay away until the job was done. There was nothing vague about that. A social call would not be appreciated. Max followed the instruction.

But as the hours passed, he was becoming more and more concerned. By 6 o'clock that evening, after filming had wrapped, he was jumpy, restless to find out what was going on. So he didn't return to the Hassler; went instead to Monteverde.

The car Ravenna was hiring was parked in his usual space. Max used his spare keys to get into the building, walked up the four flights of stairs to the apartment as he always did. He rang the doorbell and waited. There was no response. No sound he could hear through the door. He rang again. And again. Still no answer. His heart was beating faster now. He began to imagine all kinds of scenarios within. Putting his key in the lock, he turned it gently, hesitantly. Click it went. Then there was a harsh snap. Before he could push it in, the door was jerked open from the other side.

Ravenna stood there in front of him. He looked a little jaded. Most definitely annoyed.

'Max! What the hell are you doing here?' he said. 'I told you not to show up like this. What's the deal?'

He maintained his position in the doorway. Clearly didn't want Max to go any further.

'I'm sorry Vincente,' Max replied. 'There's a problem. I spoke to your client – Mr. Mastrodicasa. He wants you to let him go.'

'How were you talking to Mastrodicasa?' Ravenna asked, his eyes narrowing.

'He got me at your hotel. On the phone. He said you're not answering your cell.'

'That's true because it's switched off,' said Ravenna.

'The studio is on the verge of abandoning. Your client told me so. He also said he didn't give you licence for this.'

'Licence?' Ravenna repeated.

'The go-ahead as he put it,' said Max. 'Everybody's convinced the film is finished. If you don't release him – if he doesn't turn up – they will pull the plug.'

He tried looking over Ravenna's shoulder, but it was of little use. All he could catch a glimpse of was the prints in his hallway.

'You said it would be faster than this Vincente,' he resumed, 'no more than 36 hours. Why is it taking so long? Are there complications?'

'Relax,' said Ravenna, 'it's nothing major. He's just proving to be a tougher nut to crack than I expected. But I almost have his arm pinned to the surface. Real soon now he'll have the sweetest kind of defeat.'

This made no sense to Max. Again he began to speculate as to what was happening inside. Had Ravenna gone back on his word? Were his methods physical after all?

'Can I see him?' he asked.

'By no means!' Ravenna said forcefully. He put his hand on the frame of the door.

'You could try it Max, but there's no way you're getting past me. I think you know that. I don't think it's a scene you want to play. I've great admiration for Mr. Mastrodicasa, but he's wrong on this occasion. He never saw what was going down on that set. He doesn't understand it like you and me. There was a lot of disrespect Max. Towards you and others. Miss Carrington fell foul of it just before you phoned me. Coincidence I wonder. Or was that the tipping point for you? You could hack it, but when it came to the lady. That's the version I imagine. It sure as hell makes for a better story.'

'How's the story going to end Vincente?' Max asked. 'That's what I need to know. Will he be back on set? Will he finish the film?'

'Yes, he will,' Ravenna answered unequivocally. 'I have him in a top roll. That's a figure of speech so no need to worry. Mr. Cousins will return in one piece. Just not quite as robust as before. In other words, less the asshole. Trust me.'

'Ok,' said Max. 'Just make it soon Vincente. No later than tomorrow.'

'No later than tomorrow,' Ravenna promised. He eased up a bit, removed his hand from the frame of the door.

'So how's it going at the Hassler?' he asked. 'Has anyone noticed my sudden change of appearance?'

'I don't think so,' said Max. 'I'm keeping my head down like you recommended.'

Ravenna smiled approvingly.

'That's good Max,' he said. 'Stay in character. Keep it real.'

Going back down the stairs afterwards, Max bumped into his neighbour, Andrea Vallelunga.

'Hey there Max,' he said genially. 'How's the film going?'

'It's going well,' Max replied hurriedly. He wasn't eager to chat.

'Good to hear,' said Vallelunga. 'I must say you're remaining very modest about all this. But I knew you would. None of that Hollywood drama about you Max.'

THE RULES OF THE GAME

David Cousins arrived back at the St. Regis at 6.30 the following morning, Sunday. He was unshaven, slightly dishevelled, but generally okay. In his tracksuit pocket he still had the key to his room and insisted on going up there alone. Within minutes, there was a knock on his door. The night manager of the hotel stood before him, a concerned look fixed on his face. He asked if the director needed medical attention, a doctor or a hospital. Cousins respectfully declined both.

'Just a shower and change of clothes to begin with,' he said, his voice low and breathy. 'I have some phone calls to make. A few people are probably worried.'

He called his daughter in California first, getting hold of her just as she was going to bed. Next, there was Art Brackman.

The agent expressed his relief initially. But quickly his manner turned to annoyance.

'You've pulled some stupid shit in your time David, but this is hands-down the biggest screw-up yet,' he chided. 'Where did you vanish to? More to the point, why the hell?!'

After listening to a brief explanation, Brackman agreed to contact Aggregate Pictures and mollify them as best he could.

'This is an extremely tough one David,' he warned before hanging up. 'They may well fire you. You've given them every reason. If not, they will press for specific undertakings. You'll be obliged to pick up the pace in a way you've never done before. Bring it in on time. You'll have to do what they tell you David, irrespective of how much it will encroach on your style. And as for any opinions you might have, I'd lose them period if I were you.'

Last of all, Cousins telephoned Max, saying he wanted to see him urgently. Max got to the hotel inside half an hour, met the director in his room.

'How are you?' he asked as he entered. Cousins had taken a shower by now, looked a lot better than earlier.

'I honestly don't know,' he replied, sitting down in an armchair opposite Max. 'There are no words that come to mind. I'm a writer and I can't think of any. Quite a strange experience as you might appreciate. Not the only time lately.'

'There was great concern for you at the studio,' said Max. 'We were told to keep quiet about the situation. For the sake of the film, and with respect to you.'

'With respect to me,' Cousins said ironically. 'Thanks indeed for the consideration Max. But wasn't that wasted coming from you? Why would you need to concern yourself knowing what you did?'

His voice grew louder.

'Knowing what you facilitated! That's right Max – I know about your involvement in this whole thing. My temporary abduction as it was. The particulars of which I'm not to divulge to anyone else. Your friend Ravenna was pretty explicit about that. You saw him just a short time ago, didn't you? Got the keys back to your apartment?'

'Yes, I did,' said Max.

'Yesterday evening someone paid us a visit, or at least tried to,' Cousins went on. 'At first I thought it was help coming. You know, like a rescue. So naturally I was tempted to call out. But then I heard a voice in the hallway which I recognised. You wouldn't have answered me Max, would you? You weren't there for me. You were there for a different reason. Your motivation was self-serving.'

'My motivation was the film,' Max countered. 'It remains the film.'

'No doubt about that,' said Cousins, 'you're thinking about the time ahead. Your own future. You really don't want to go back to what you did before, do you? And there were people who thought you'd be satisfied with this one thing. The fifteen minutes of fame they wrote about you. They got you all wrong. You're not just some lucky son-of-a-bitch who caught himself a break. You're that voice I heard in the hallway yesterday. The guy who wants a helluva lot more.'

'As do you David,' Max said, taking a seat opposite him. 'I can't imagine a director of your reputation would want it to end like this. An unfinished film as part of your career? Or worse, completed by someone else. Where would you go from there?'

'I'd get back in the game one way or another,' Cousins said defiantly. 'There'd be other projects. I'm an Oscar winner Max. They gave me the Academy Award. That keeps me in cachet. I'm still good for the work.'

'But what kind I wonder,' said Max. 'Writing assignments? For-hire efforts? Just a link in the chain? That isn't the one thing you'd be satisfied with. Is it David? What you want is to be overseer. From beginning to end. What's the expression for it? Head honcho?'

'You want to talk about expressions Max?' Cousins shot back, 'I'll give you one – kidnapping. Holding a person against his will. You gave your home over to him as part of the deal. That right there is conspiracy. I could flush both of you out for it.'

Max shook his head, held firm.

'It would be your word against mine. And Ravenna's.'

'I saw the inside of your apartment. Specific details I can list. The movie canvases for instance. Clint Eastwood and Amarcord.'

Max was not fazed.

'I told you about those when we first met,' he said. 'At the Bar della Pace. You seemed a little distracted at the time. Said you were looking out for someone.'

'I was looking out for Ravenna,' said Cousins. 'He appeared a while after Don Taylor's accident. Began following me everywhere. I guess that's something you don't know about either.'

'Not at all,' said Max, 'but I'll tell you what it sounds like. A delusion

of some kind. Paranoia most likely. Did you have a breakdown David?
Is that why you went missing?'

'Son-of-a-bitch!' Cousins exclaimed. 'You're on the same page as he is.
By way of an explanation, I'm to say I had a personal episode that night.
A breakdown as you put it. The fact that I was wearing my tracksuit at
the time is beside the point according to our friend. No one will ask why
I was dressed like that. Fashion doesn't enter the equation when you're
cracking up. Those were his words. But I still have a few of my own
Max. I can try telling them the truth.'

'You can try David, but do you really think they'll believe you? You
remember at the Bar della Pace how we spoke about films and theatre?
The Pirandello play – Right You Are...'

'If You Think So?'

'Yes. You mentioned the unreliable narrator. The storyteller who can't
be trusted. A good many of our colleagues would say your behaviour at
Cinecittà up to now has been impulsive, erratic. You pursue this and I'm
thinking your credibility will be questioned all the more. Enough so you
won't be back on the set.'

'My credibility is going to suffer no matter what happens,' Cousins
said irately. 'A director who falls to pieces during the shoot. Then goes
AWOL like Agatha Christie. How does that look? It's not something
they'll forget quickly.'

'Maybe not,' said Max, 'but you ride out the storm, turn adversity
into opportunity, and you'll be highly thought of again. People like
redemption stories as you know David. One or two of your films have
been about that. Right?'

Cousins groaned loudly at this.

'He had a video copy of Bluff City,' he said, 'played it over and over in
your machine. I must have watched it more times than in editing.'

Max smiled.

'He said he liked it.'

'He's one of the few.'

'I know how that feels,' said Max. 'I once had to watch a film in my
hometown. I wasn't proud of it either. During the show I heard people
laughing. It bothered me a little, but not so much. They were right to.
It was terrible. I was leaving the cinema with my parents afterwards.
Friends of theirs, neighbours, came up to congratulate me. But it wasn't
real. They were just being polite about it. That was far worse.'

'You could handle the ridicule but not the pretence?' said Cousins.

'I hated the act,' said Max, 'all of us putting on a show, my mother and
father included. I felt like giving up.'

'What stopped you?'

'What made you come back after Bluff City?'

Cousins looked away for a moment, his fingers gripping his kneecaps.
He turned back, lurched forward in his chair, as if returning from a
distant place.

'Fine, we get each other,' he said bluntly. 'I understand what you want. I can even appreciate it. But it doesn't mean I have to like what was done to me. I guess we're going to talk about the way forward now. Provided I keep my job. Ravenna said you had ideas.'

'I'm sure he gave you a few himself,' said Max.

'More like rules coming from him,' said Cousins. 'How I'm to behave towards the actors from now on. He was very clear about that.'

'Direct us as well as directing the camera,' said Max. 'When you have to call for a number of takes, describe what it is you want. Spell it out if necessary. And when you get it, move on. No more 'do it again' David. Whether it's one take or five. Print it. On to the next set-up.'

'You mention five in particular,' Cousins observed. 'Is that my upper limit now? Anything beyond and Ravenna hauls me over the coals?'

'Ravenna will only intervene if he thinks there's an impediment to progress,' said Max. 'He has a job to do. A client to keep happy.'

'I'm well acquainted with his client,' said Cousins. 'No doubt this isn't the first time he's worked for Mastrodicasa. And what about you Max? Is it kid-glove treatment you want too? I'm not sure that will work to your advantage. I think you need to be elbowed. You coast through this and it'll hurt your performance. Then you'll be forgotten fast.'

'I don't intend to coast,' Max said emphatically. 'I'm going to work hard, closely with you David. Listen to every piece of advice from you, every clear instruction. You'll bring out the best in me. You're a great director. That's what great directors do.'

Cousins was about to say something, but the phone beside him rang. He answered it.

'Ok...ok...I'm ok,' he mumbled. 'Come down in five minutes...no... make it five.'

He put the receiver back in its cradle.

'That was Dobrovsky,' he said, 'wants to see me right away. You better leave now. I'll have to give him the official version of things. Hope he buys it. Hope they all buy it. Anyhow, I think we've said all we needed to say here. If you see me on the set tomorrow, you can assume I pulled it off. Which will make me a great actor as well.'

They both rose to their feet.

'There's one other thing,' said Max.

'Really? Just the one?' said Cousins. He sounded almost world-weary.

'We haven't come to them yet, but the scenes in America, about his difficulties with the language. I think they should be taken out. I can't see the point of them since he's speaking English all the time. An audience would only be confused. It's of no benefit.'

'It's based on fact,' Cousins asserted.

'Yes, but it's out of place here, it doesn't fit,' replied Max. 'Perhaps you can have a think about it. Make a decision.'

Cousins blinked. He heard it. Understood it. He disagreed, but his voice was nothing more than an ebbing whine.

'Don Taylor insisted on me getting rid of them before,' he said. 'Did you know that?'

'Not at all,' answered Max.

'I had little choice then either,' Cousins continued. 'He was a star, a big name. Had influence in spades. The kind people in this industry are aware of. The kind that's practically broadcast. Yours is a different sort. It's hidden, shadowy. Thanks to your guardian angel. I don't know which I despise more. I hate them both. I hate you Max. Every bit as much as I hated Don Taylor.'

This did not unsettle Max. He remained perfectly tranquil.

'No harm in that,' he said. 'We're both professionals. We'll get on with it. But take out those scenes David. The film will be better this way. I'll see you at Cinecittà tomorrow. Meanwhile, get some rest. You look as if you need it. Remember, we have a lot of work ahead of us.'

CLOSING SCENE PART II

D avid Cousins kept his job as director of Echo of Passions and quickened the production pace to the satisfaction of all concerned, Vincente Ravenna included. The daily reports called in by Tim Woodward to Anthony Chouraqui pointed to a very much improved situation. Woodward recorded his praise for Cousins, approval of the kind which had not seemed imaginable to him a few weeks before. The director's attitude had changed radically since the time of his 'personal incident.' He was co-operative now, flexible in a way he'd never been previously. More importantly, he had moved the production forward to be, at a stage in mid-July, exactly where the original schedule had intended it. This in spite of the early delays and his own temporary absence. He would eventually finish filming on the 63rd day of principal photography. Two whole days ahead of target.

His relationship with the actors got better as he allowed more discussion and analysis on the set. Jennifer Carrington, for one, was grateful and her performance benefited appreciably for all to see. With Max, there remained a slight tautness at first, but this lessened as time went by. The actor pushed himself hard and was responsive to the direction offered him. Cousins and he did not agree on everything, but a guarded sense of deference emerged. Max's work in front of the camera, like Jennifer's, was generating positive comment at the dailies. He was also having a constructive influence on the other side. When the curators of the Palazzo Baronale in Colonna unexpectedly revoked the permission they'd given the filmmakers to shoot there, Max suggested the Palazzo Savelli Chigi in Ariccia as an alternative. The relevant consents obtained, the Echo production journeyed the short distance for the day's shoot. It turned out just fine; the nine set-ups were captured in the now-familiar efficient manner. A last-minute excerpt was added and it was filmed in Piazza di Corte. Max was full of pride as he and Jennifer walked across the square together, the camera tracking nearby. There was no dialogue to be recorded and David Cousins asked them to improvise.

'Your characters are getting to know each other,' he said. 'It's like a first date, romantic music swelling on the soundtrack. Think of something amusing to say Max. Something that will bring a smile to her face.'

Max did as was requested. He told Jennifer about the spaghetti western impressions he'd done in this square many years before. About his cobbled-together outfit. About the burnt-out stogie in his mouth. It had the desired effect. Jennifer laughed out loud. So much so in fact that her reaction looked exaggerated, overplayed. The director got them to do it again.

'Not so heavy on the hilarity this time,' Cousins said. 'We have to remember where we are and when. Decorum would have been the order of the day I think. But do smile by all means. They were known to do that in the 1830's as well.'

Antonia and Claudia were all smiles when they visited the set at Cinecittà. It was the second last Thursday of production. Max introduced them around to cast and crew members. Antonia was particularly keen to see Miguel Serrano. She liked him for his films and activism off-screen. Beside her, Claudia was just happy to be there. She kept reminding Max of the word he'd told her about – synchronised.

'That's you now too Uncle Max,' she said. 'Synchronised. Picture and sound all together, all together.'

The following day Fabio Paparazzo arrived for his long-promised interview. His questions to Max were concise, routine. Nothing out of the ordinary or in the least bit provocative. He got sound bites from other cast members as well, Jennifer Carrington, Joel Meadows, Miguel Serrano, and Erik Schroeder. Later on, he observed a quick set-up, but left before it was filmed.

'Best of luck,' he said to everyone, shaking hands with David Cousins. Then with Max, to one side.

'It looks good,' he said quietly to the actor. 'I guess maybe it was worth it.'

The Echo shoot drew to its inevitable conclusion. As the days grew fewer, Kirk Evans's 'finished on the movie' announcement became more regular. One by one, the actors completed their parts and were acknowledged accordingly.

'Ladies and gentlemen. Finished on the movie, Toby Devereux.'

'Ladies and gentlemen. Finished on the movie, Filipo de Marco.'

'Ladies and gentlemen. Finished on the movie, Roberto Beccari and Oriana D'Ambrosio.'

'Ladies and gentlemen. Finished on the movie, Miguel Serrano.'

'Ladies and gentlemen. Finished on the movie, Lamar Calley.'

There was no more than a skeleton crew on hand the afternoon Jennifer Carrington's involvement came to an end. Some of them were just milling around, shooting the breeze.

'Ladies and gentlemen. Finished on the movie, Jennifer Carrington,' Evans yelled in his familiar manner. The actress, whose character by now was bedridden, got to her feet lithely and received the send-off.

'Thank-you, thank-you,' she said cheerfully, exchanging handshakes and hugs. She nodded politely at David Cousins. It was well known the director preferred to hang back during this ritual.

Max was the last to say goodbye. They embraced as two friends would. Their relationship off-screen was still under wraps. Neither one was eager for cast and crew to know.

'It's been wonderful working with you,' he said.

'You too,' she replied, and then whispered, 'I'll see you soon.'

She disappeared out the side door of the stage. Going back to her hotel. Where they'd meet later.

It got to the second last day of production and Meucci's death scene was the focus of attention. The action was taking place in the Staten Island workshop, a moderately-sized set tucked away in a corner of sound stage 5. The remaining crew members watched on as Max went through the preliminaries of the scene. He was directed by David Cousins to enter the area wearily, as if done in; his head lowered, faltering a little as he picked his steps. In between set-ups, he sat off to the side as the camera and other pieces of equipment were repositioned. He was heavily made-up and the temperature was necessitating constant interventions by the make-up artist, Penny Herrera, who was fussing with Kleenex, brushes, and combs. Max tried waving her away politely. But she kept coming at him, unrelenting. Eventually, Cousins instructed her to back off.

The atmosphere was slightly tense. The end in sight and everyone was aware of it. So near and yet so far. Thoughts and considerations moving towards the future. Reflections back on what had been a demanding shoot.

There were two guests in attendance today and few, if any, of the crew knew who they were. Lorenzo Mastrodicasa had arrived in Rome the night before. Officially, he was here on business, but the true purpose of his visit was to see first-hand how this project – so close to his heart – was being realised. To catch a glimpse of the magic of the movies. He was accompanied by an associate from San Francisco. Next to them stood Vincente Ravenna, providing a detailed commentary.

'They started with a wide shot against wall A and now they're moving in for tighter and tighter shots,' he explained. 'Next, they'll move on to wall B. The idea is to lay out the shooting order so the camera is moved as little as possible between each set-up. That way lighting and all the rest of it takes less time.'

He glanced furtively at his audience.

'I hope it's not too boring for you Mr. Mastrodicasa,' he said apologetically, 'many people find it unexciting compared to what they expect. Dullsville one or two have called it.'

Mastrodicasa shook his head in reply.

'Not at all Vincente,' he said, 'I think it's fascinating. The planning behind it is exemplary. So much orchestration. Like a well-oiled machine. I have one question though. Perhaps you can answer it?'

'What's that?'

'This third wall,' Mastrodicasa said pointing. 'I'm assuming it's wall C. When is it used? Won't it take them longer to make that changeover?'

A broad grin extended across Ravenna's face.

'You sure do catch on fast Mr. Mastrodicasa,' he said. 'It is a bigger turnaround like you say. Most likely it'll be timed for the lunch hour. Some of the construction crew take it earlier and do the work while the others are eating. They'll put in wall C and take out wall A. Very smart people these filmmakers. Everything is factored in.'

Mastrodicasa nodded approvingly.

'Very smart indeed,' he said. 'I like it. I could stay here all day and watch. As a matter of fact, that's what I intend to do.'

After lunch, with the walls moved, Cousins walked Max through the remainder of the scene. It was to continue with Meucci picking up some of his inventions, thinking on his lifetime's work, and smiling nostalgically. Then, with tears welling in his eyes, he collapses to the floor having, presumably, suffered a heart attack. *A broken heart,'* the text of Cousins' script suggested, *'and yet a look of serenity is frozen on his face.'*

The camera positions were marked with tape on the floor. There were to be 12 camera moves within the sequence and each move was numbered. Livio Bacciucchi stepped in so that Miroslav Dobrovsky and Tommaso Juliano could begin lighting. Max returned to the dressing room to get ready. Penny Herrera was waiting there for him.

He arrived back on the set at 2.20. They had a quick rehearsal and completed the first few moves with little bother. Two takes. Three takes. Two takes again. On to the next part. It was all going like clockwork. Perfect rhythm. No jarring notes. The camera was moved to the next position and lights rearranged. The tape on the floor read number 6 now. It was fast approaching the moment when Max was to simulate his character's demise. A simple keeling-over motion was all David Cousins wanted.

'Nothing too theatrical,' he'd said. 'Make it look as natural as you can. And try not to hurt yourself doing it.'

At approximately 4 o'clock, in between positions 7 and 8, and as the camera was being reloaded, a group of three people came onto the set. A space opened up quickly between them and the crew members waiting around for the next take. Some of them kept looking at these visitors, one in particular, even though they knew it was rude. Vincente Ravenna and Lorenzo Mastrodicasa included.

Don Taylor had been discharged from the Agostino Gemelli and was returning to the States the following day. Seated in a transport wheelchair – the kind with push handles at the back – he'd come with his wife and brother to see a little of the filming.

'He's communicating mostly with notes,' Lee Taylor explained to David Cousins, who'd stopped what he was doing to say hello. 'Occasionally, there are words but they're jumbled, difficult to understand. He gets annoyed when that happens. Starts clicking his fingers as he's always done.'

Cousins tactfully enquired as to Don's long-term prospects.

'We're keeping hopeful about that,' replied Lee. 'So far we've got through ICU, high dependency and the Solventi. Back home, there'll be recuperation and yet more physiotherapy. It's a long road, but we have to take it. No other choice. Isn't that right darling?' she said, rubbing Don's head.

Don mumbled something in response, but it was incoherent. He looked shrunken and had clearly lost a good deal of weight. When Max offered him his hand, he drew back, as if opposed to it.

'Don't worry about that,' said Lee. 'It's not intentional. He pulls away quite a bit. Was doing it with me at first as well.'

Under her breath, she added, 'he's uncomfortable about how he appears. Conscious about the wheelchair and everything else. I've told him he shouldn't be. He doesn't listen though. Has still got his ego intact.'

She spoke directly to Max.

'The one thing he wanted to do was come see you in the part. He's written notes about it almost every day, hasn't he Todd? After the coma we told him what had happened. The accident and its effects. True to form, all he wanted to know about was the movie. Was it going ahead? Who was taking his place? He remembered your name when we said it was you. That was a very good sign. We live for such moments nowadays.'

Don watched on as two more takes of position 7 were done, a blank expression on his face. The camera and lights were then moved for the next part of the scene. The crew got it ready. Cousins gave some last-minute direction to Max.

'Keep it simple,' he said. 'I don't want it long-winded so no crashing into things or staggering about. All you've got to do here is die. Just hit the deck, hit your mark. We'll add the heartstrings later.'

He remembered one more thing.

'And make sure you're lying face-up for the zoom. That's the final image. Apart from the flashback of course.'

'Face-up, okay, got it,' said Max. His mind was elsewhere though. He was glancing over at Don.

Don's eyes were fixed on him now. As if there was no one else on the set but him. Max got a queasy feeling. He wondered why Don had really come here. To see him in the part as Lee said? To see how he was faring? Maybe thought Max, but another explanation was presenting itself. Don wasn't just staring at him anymore. He was glowering, practically throwing daggers his direction. There was nothing blank, nothing unfocused, about this kind of look. Max could feel it burning on him as he stepped in front of the camera.

The first take was lousy.

The second, not much better.

The third, just as bad again.

Max was messing up the rhythm, making a hash of it generally. He fell too quickly. Then he lingered on it too long. He kept missing the mark. Landing everywhere else, but where he was supposed to. It was humiliating. Of the toe-curling variety.

Take four.

Take five.

Take six.

Take seven.

On and on it went. Max was hurting badly. Not just his body, but also his pride. Each time he picked himself up, he saw those same cringing faces. Every person in his eyeline. Cousins. Dobrovsky. Kirk Evans. Andy Fuller. Penny Herrera. Todd Taylor. Lee Taylor. And Don as well. The former leading man seemed amused by it all. A smug smile in full view. Max imagined he could hear the words in his eyes, in those burning chunks of coal. You aren't worthy of this. You didn't earn it. You're a fraud. Nothing more than a pinch-hitter as they called you in Cannes.

Finally, David Cousins intervened. He asked Max to step off the set with him for a minute or two. They took a little walk around the sound stage, the director pursing his lips.

'What the hell's going on?' he asked. 'You're absolutely killing it in there!'

'I'm sorry,' said Max. 'I'm a bit anxious. I guess because it's so close to the end.'

'Well pull yourself together fast,' Cousins said. 'We're up to take 12 already and your friends are watching. What's happening is not my fault. I hope Ravenna and Mastrodicasa understand that.'

'They understand it,' replied Max. 'Don't worry. I'll be better next time. It's just a small hiccup.'

'Then hold your breath good and long,' Cousins said impatiently, 'because we have to move it on. The last thing I want is Ravenna in my ear again.'

They returned to the set.

Take 13 was a huge improvement. At last Max was getting up to the tempo required. But still he didn't quite hit the mark.

David Cousins offered words of encouragement. For the benefit of those nearby.

'That was much better Max,' he said, 'unfortunately, we have to go again. Try and make the fall work too. You're doing a great job.'

Max nodded, stared straight ahead. He was determined to eliminate faces from his sight line. Don's in particular. He concentrated on not thinking about Don watching, although it was impossible not to think about him. He wasn't going to fall flat in front of the actor he'd replaced. He was going to succeed. Prove his worth.

Take 14 topped the previous one. David Cousins was satisfied.

'That's good enough,' he said. 'One good one is all we need. We can move on.'

Max did not agree.

'I'd like to do it again,' he said. 'I can get it even better. Give you a perfect one to print.'

'That's not necessary Max,' Cousins said, an edgy note in his voice, 'we got a good one in the can. It's ample, more than.'

'Please David,' Max said insistently.

Cousins sighed noisily.

'We're going again people,' he said, 'the collaborative process such as it is.'

Take 15. Max did his reflective look again. He waited a number of beats and then slid to the floor. It was on the money like before. But still he wanted to do it another time. Reluctantly, Cousins acquiesced.

Take 16 followed. Then take 17. After that, take 18. A few eyebrows were being raised. Members of the crew wondered how long this would go on for. The director clearly had what he needed. Why wasn't he calling a halt? And what was Max trying to achieve? It wasn't as if he had any lines to say. He was just falling over. How many times before he'd be happy with it? Wasn't he aching already?

Lorenzo Mastrodicasa wasn't flabbergasted by the goings-on though. Quite the opposite, he was highly impressed.

'This level of commitment is wonderful,' he whispered to his associate and Ravenna. 'Simply outstanding.'

'One hundred per cent,' Ravenna concurred.

The associate piped up.

'But is this how Antonio Meucci really died?' he queried. 'Is it accurate?'

'It doesn't matter,' Mastrodicasa replied brusquely. 'This is great cinema. Powerful.'

Close by, Lee Taylor overheard them. She glanced down to see if her husband had too. By all appearances Don hadn't. He was preoccupied with the action on set. And, oddly enough, he was clicking his fingers. Lee couldn't figure out why.

Take 19. This would absolutely, without question, be the final one. Max promised he wouldn't ask for another. Cousins was greatly relieved.

'Action,' he said quietly.

Max faced the camera, put on the wistful smile once more. In his head he began counting to five. Then drop he told himself. Be in the moment. Get the words off the page.

Looking past the director and camera crew, he caught Don's eye by accident. The burning chunks of coal were still trained on him. The bitter expression had not gone away. Without warning, the incapacitated man rose to his feet, teetering a little as he did so. Holding his balance for a few moments, he pointed right at Max.

'NO...STAR!' he roared as loudly as he could manage. 'NO...STAR!'

He slumped back into his chair then, no more words passing his lips. A hush descended over the set. Everything came to a standstill. People turned and looked, and turned back just as quickly. Lee Taylor put her hand over her mouth. Miroslav Dobrovsky grunted under his breath. Ravenna whispered something to Mastrodicasa. Max stopped and waited, peeked at the director. David Cousins was taking it in with a mild sense of shock, not knowing what Don had meant. The only thing he was sure of was that they needed to move on from this. As if it hadn't happened. He made a fast calculation.

'Well I definitely don't think we can use that one,' he said. 'It's fine though. We've got it already. Next position please.'

BEING THERE

The 49th edition of the Cannes Film Festival kicked off on the 9th of May the following year. Francis Ford Coppola was president of the jury. Films in competition included Breaking the Waves, Fargo, Secrets and Lies, Stealing Beauty, and Echo of Passions. The world premiere of David Cousins' new film was scheduled to take place at the Palais des Festivals on Wednesday the 15th of May. It had a general release date of June 6th in the United States.

Max arrived in Cannes on the evening of the 14th. He was staying at the Carlton Hotel once again. So too were Tom Steiner and festival regular Gordon Sawyer. Also in town for the Echo opening were David Cousins, Anthony Chouraqui and Lorenzo Mastrodicasa. Jennifer Carrington, who was shooting her new movie on the Warner Brothers lot in Burbank, was unable to attend. Vincente Ravenna was likewise absent; on a job somewhere in New Mexico according to Mastrodicasa.

Max had co-starred in another film since the completion of his duties on Echo. In early November he'd come over to the recording studio in West Hollywood to loop some of his dialogue. He stayed with Jennifer at her house on Miller Drive. Together they put up the rest of her paintings on the walls. Max landed a part in a drama titled When We First Saw Dawn. It was already in post-production and slated for a fall release. Next up for him was a remake of The Agony and The Ecstasy which was due to start shooting at Cinecittà in July. Carl Gottfried was in the director's chair. Bert Balaban, formerly of Aggregate Pictures, was producing. Echo contributors Corrado La Russa, Andy Fuller, Ruth Benchley and Penny Herrera were also employed on the project.

Tom Steiner talked excitedly about the new film over drinks in the Carlton Bar.

'I'm not usually one for the historical stuff,' he acknowledged, 'but I just love the kick-ass role you have in this.'

He raised his glass in a toast.

'Here's to Pope Julius the Second – the Warrior Pope! That's what I'm talking about baby! Action and combat. Should make for some great visuals. And Gottfried sure knows how to tell a story. He did a heck of a job with First Lady of Virginia. Right? Jennifer sang his praises. Didn't she?'

Tom noticed his client was pensive.

'A penny for your thoughts Max,' he said. 'You worn out from the flight? Anxious about tomorrow night?'

Max nodded.

'A little bit,' he confessed.

'That's perfectly understandable,' said Tom.

'How many reporters and journalists will be at the press conference?'

'In the Palais? Probably two or three hundred,' replied Tom, 'but no need to worry. You'll blitz it Max. All you got to do is turn on the charm and sweet-talk them. Mention Dawn and The Agony and the Ecstasy as well. Tell them what you're doing next. Take advantage of the publicity. It's offered on a plate here.'

Max considered this for a moment, smiled to himself.

'Jonny Lewysohn told me something like that last year,' he said. 'He told me to put myself out there. Not to hide from it.'

'Good advice,' remarked Tom, 'and good news about Jonny too. He's back in the game if you didn't know – working at William Morris now.'

'That's good to hear,' said Max.

'Yeah, got his act together, and I think some of that is down to me,' said Tom, a self-congratulatory tone creeping into his voice. 'I fired him and it was probably the best favour he ever got. At least that's what people have told me since. You dished out some tough love there Tom, but it was exactly what the kid needed. Half-measures or trade-offs and God knows where he'd be now. I guess I'm a good guy when all's said and done. I took a flyer on you Max. I'm sure glad I did. Tomorrow night will prove how right I was.'

'Thanks Tom, I'm very grateful to you,' said Max, even though he didn't entirely agree. He thought about what Tom had once called him – a nobody mimic. You were wrong about that he thought. You just said as much. He smiled to himself ironically.

'What's going on in that head of yours?' Tom said an uncertain grin on his face.

'Nothing important,' replied Max.

'Are you still poking fun at me over The Man from Atlantis?' the agent enquired. 'It's not so outrageous an idea you know. In my opinion you'd be great in the part.'

Max shook his head good-humouredly.

'I think I'd be a bit too old for it,' he said. 'Physically, I wouldn't have the profile.'

'You could hit the gym in a big way,' said Tom, 'and as for the age factor, they want someone a little older. The concept is that he's a lone survivor, out of his depth in this world, if you'll forgive the pun. A lot of the gags are about how he doesn't fit in. And the script is ready now. They have the final act that was eluding them for so long. We're talking a big budget movie here Max with box office potential written all over it. It's the next logical step for you. Don was going to do it before his accident. And he's the same age as you.'

'He's a year younger actually,' Max corrected.

'Be that as it may, I want you to give it serious consideration,' said Tom. 'It's unfortunate that script problems held it up 'til now. But hey, maybe it was meant to be for you. Think about that Max. Don't reject it out of hand. Think about those shots of you breathing underwater. Swimming faster than a dolphin.'

A nostalgic look shot across his face.

'I remember how excited Don was when he saw the storyboards,' he said. 'He was very pepped up.'

'How is Don?' Max asked, eager to move on. 'I heard he's doing better.'

'He is,' Tom confirmed, 'not as dependent on the wheelchair as he used to be. He'll never make a complete recovery of course. But he's getting stronger all the time. Not quite a miracle, but much better than his family expected. Lee feels it started that day they visited the set in Rome. I only heard about it myself recently. About Don standing up and shouting. Giving you all a shock. His doctors couldn't explain it afterwards – how he managed to do that given the state he was in. Not me though. The question I asked myself was why.'

He paused as if for a theatrical beat.

'You were there,' he said. 'You got any theories about it?'

'No, I don't,' said Max, glancing away to other tables, other hotel guests.

'Do you remember what he said?' Tom asked. 'What it was he shouted.'

Max continued looking sharply around, casing the room.

'No Tom. I can't say I do,' he replied.

David Cousins was back in Cannes for the first time in several years. Outside the Palais, dressed in his tux, he spoke to reporters about future ventures.

'My next project will be a drama called Elya and Ruthie,' he told them. 'Miguel Serrano, who plays Angelo Bertolino in this film, will be heading the cast. It's a story about family problems and self-identity. I hope it will speak to the difficulties many of us face in this present-day world of ours.'

With reference to his latest film, the director paid tribute to all involved, singling out Max in particular.

'He's made his mark with a truly wonderful performance,' he said. 'I want to thank him for that and for his fortitude generally. He arrived to this film at a very tricky moment, had to deal with a smorgasbord of pressures, many of them coming from me. I'm not always the most laid-back of guys as you well know, but I learnt a few things on this occasion. I'm very obliged to Max for that.'

A French journalist asked if the director cared to elaborate.

'Ah now that would be telling,' Cousins said with a faint grin. 'It's strictly between him and me. Not for publication.'

Anthony Chouraqui echoed such praise. He also had news about some upcoming Aggregate productions.

'The next Tyler Pinkerton I'm happy to reveal is moving closer to a start date,' he said. 'Locations this time will include Port Louis, Wyoming, and Algiers. The working title is Riddle of the Portents. As well as that, there's Age of Majority, which my colleague Elizabeth Margules is overseeing, and a biopic about Giuseppe Garibaldi which is being actively developed. Mr. Lorenzo Mastrodicasa, one of the executive producers of Echo, is involved. Miroslav Dobrovsky is currently in talks to make his debut as director. We regard it as a potential companion piece to the first-rate film you're about to see.'

He spotted a white limo pulling up below them, at the base of the Palais steps. David Cousins stopped chatting and watched as well.

Max got out and stood in front of them all. A few thousand people were packed around the famous steps. Excited spectators. Flashing camera bulbs.

A moment of disbelief overcame him.

Am I really here he wondered. Am I really, truly here?

He heard processional music striking up so took a step forward. Then another. And another. He reached the wide area of the staircase, marking the halfway point, quickly. Much too quickly in fact. Turning about, he realised he hadn't waved once yet. And everyone was cheering him. Calling out his name.

'Max! Max!'

Imploring him to look their way. Young and old alike. Little children perched on shoulders. Eager faces. Lively eyes.

Max heard his name again.

He was joined by Cousins and Chouraqui. Toby Devereux, Miguel Serrano and Daniel Joyner appeared too. They put arms around one another for the photographers, for the multitude. A show of team spirit.

Serrano laughed, whispered in Max's ear.

'Not so fast Max,' he said, 'take it at a leisurely pace. Give them a chance to have a good look at you. This is your audience. Soak it up.'

Max followed the advice.

At long last, he gave a wave. They all did.

A few minutes of this and they ambled up to the entrance of the Palais. The others went into the lobby.

Max remained at the top of the Palais steps. For just a few seconds more. For added effect.

A parting flourish.

A wide smile.

Then, he too, disappeared inside.

At the press conference the following morning Max took his place on the stage of the presse salle. Gordon Sawyer, acting as moderator once more, introduced him, along with David Cousins and Miguel Serrano. There was a flock of photographers, reporters and camera crews in attendance. The Aggregate man opened with some good-natured banter.

'A year ago I sat in the Carlton Hotel and told some of you a little-bitty lie,' he began. 'I promised we'd be back here a year later with a movie that would be terrific. A movie that would be wonderful. A movie that would be important. Well, as you can see, we're not in the Carlton this morning; just a little up the street from it.'

A wave of laughter swept the room.

385

Sawyer rattled on in this vein.

'But I'm happy to say everything else I forecast that day has come to pass,' he said. 'The movie which premiered last night received a standing ovation as you know. It was a special honour to be there, one of those unique moments. The early reviews are reflecting this as well. Echoing what I'm saying, pun fully intended.'

This triggered some more mirth.

Sawyer became more business-like, invited questions from the gallery.

A lot of hands shot up.

He picked out a pretty female reporter close to the front.

She introduced herself as Elisabete de Oliveira from the Portugese weekly Expresso.

'My question is for Mr. Pellegrino,' she said. 'Mr. Pellegrino, your performance has been described as highly accomplished and very natural. As if you've been doing this for years. Given your lack of experience at the time of filming, in terms of your long break away from the screen, I was wondering what your chief inspirations for the role were. What enabled your passage back into the world of clapperboards and Steadicams? Do you think you tapped into something that was lying dormant for some time? Or did you have to reinvent yourself as an actor Mr. Pellegrino?'

Max sat forward and began to reply. But there was a problem. The microphone in front of him wasn't working. No one could make out what he was saying.

All at once there was a surge of wigwagging and upraised arms.

'Can't hear you Max!' some of them called out. Fabio Paparazzo, covering the festival again for Il Quarto Stato, was one.

A young-looking sound technician hurried forward to the front of the table. He tinkered with the cabling for a few moments, then popped his head up.

Smiling agreeably, he said, 'that's fixed now Mr. Pellegrino. You can carry on.'

Max blinked into the glare of spotlight and clicking cameras. He started into his response once again. He felt good. He felt sure of himself. He was word-perfect. Sounding the way a star ought to. Which he did. Which he was. Just about.

THE END